I0818205

Kingdom Come

The Archemi Online Chronicles

Volume 3

By James Osiris Baldwin

A Gift Horse Productions Novel

Copyright

Layout and design by James Osiris Baldwin.

Dedication

This book is dedicated to Kai, our beloved Gift Horse: 1987 - 2019.

A huge thank you to all my Patrons on Patreon: Zohatu, Anira, Rhea, Jed M. Ryan C., Jordon W., Jo M., Heather, Max S. Jakob M., Gary S. and others! Your support and encouragement invaluable during this difficult year

Contents

Book 1: Before the War

Chapter 1

It was a beautiful, crisp fall morning in Vlachia. The sun was shining, the birds were singing, and I was plummeting out of the sky on the back of a dragon, headed straight for Archemi's unluckiest Glacier Toad.

"YEEEE-HAWW!" I clutched onto the saddle with my knees and one hand, spear gripped in the other as Karalti dove, arrow-straight, at the monsters below. "HERE COMES LEVEL SEVENTEEN, BITCHHHHES!"

The Glacier Toads were oblivious to the doom descending on them from the sky at two hundred miles an hour. Some of them were squabbling over who got to mate with who, their ice attacks freezing up the water. Others were rutting or shitting in the river and fouling the stream.

Just before we reached terminal velocity, Karalti snapped her wings out, fanned the fins of her tail, and bought us back up into a tight slingshot curve. The nearest Glacier Toads stopped humping and turned around just in time to see the dragon's jaws gape open.

"CHAAAAARRR!" A plume of oily white flames erupted from Karalti's throat, a sticky napalm-like stream she wielded like a bull-whip across the frog mob. Suddenly, the air was full of monstrous screams and the smell of cooked amphibian.

[You used a fire attack! It's super effective! X3 damage!]

But we weren't done yet. As Karalti pulled out of the dive and the g-forces crushing me against her saddle lifted, she twisted to the side, flinging me off into a controlled tumble. Like a gyroscope, I oriented mid-air and flew at the nearest flaming toad, Spear-first. Dark energy rippled along my arms and the weapon like electricity building charge around a Tesla Coil.

"Anchors away! Fire in the hole!" I slammed the Spear of Boundless Strength down underneath me and drove the glaive-like blade into the ground, releasing the built-up Umbra Blast. The toad I hit exploded into smoking goo. The other eight were struck by twisting, thorny tentacles of shadow that exploded from the ice like the arms of the motherfucking kraken. The Glacier Toads wouldn't be effected by the Freezing debuff, but the attack itself still hurt them. A lot.

[Umbra Blast deals 1484 damage!]
[Glacier Toad is immune to Freezing!]
[You have killed Glacier Toad!]

"Take that, you slimy sons-of-bitches!" I yelled. "Who has the tentacles now, huh?"

The two attacks nuked the entire mob below 50% HP. Screaming, burning toads launched themselves at me, icicles erupting from their skin. I Shadow Danced out of the way, burning 10 HP to briefly disappear and dodge as they blew shards of ice in every direction. I couldn't avoid all of them, though. As I reappeared, a couple of stray icicle shuriken impacted me in the arm and shoulder.

[[You have taken 85 damage!]]
[[You have taken 79 damage! HP: 819/1283]]
[[You are Frozen!]]
[[You have killed Glacier Toad!]]
[[You have killed Glacier Toad!]]

"Fuck!" Frost crawled up my arm in a crackling wave, numbing my fingers and rooting me to the spot. I snarled in frustration as the surviving toads all turned on me and opened their mouths wide.

Whatever dastardly thing they were about to do was cut short when a cold shadow blocked the hot sun, and Karalti fell on the monsters like an avenging angel. The ground jolted as she landed on one toad, pulping it, then swung her head around to blast the fleeing monsters with fire.

The Frozen debuff timer disappeared, and suddenly I was free. Whooping, I sprung from the ground like a cricket and landed to the side, flanking the toads and pinning them between me and Karalti. They skidded to a halt, crashing into each other.

"You're not the only ones who can Jump!" I triggered my workhorse combo, dashing forward in a nimbus of scarlet-black energy with Blood Sprint, and releasing the power like a lightning bomb with Blood Storm. The Spear went through the Glacier Toads like a scythe through wheat.

[You have killed Glacier Toads!]
[You have gained 1250 EXP!]
[Quest Update: Clear Springs]
[Congratulations! Karalti is Level 8!]

Some of the toads ruptured, spilling clouds of frost onto the mossy ground. Others simply croaked it. I turned around just in time to see Karalti stand up tall and close her eyes. The thick seams of brilliant opal between her black scales swelled with color and light, which flooded across her body in a rippling wave. Her slender, velociraptor-like frame swelled in size, wings and tail lengthening. Her elegant wedge-shaped head became a little sharper, her seven-horned crest longer. By the time the light passed, the dragon had put on a full ten feet of length.

"Hell yeah! That's how it's done!" Panting, I punched the air as the last flaming toad collapsed like a sack of blue guts onto the snow. "Go Team Hector!"

"Team Hector? What do you mean 'Team Hector'?" The dragon huffed with irritation, stepping out of the steaming pile of mashed Glacier Toad. She made a face, and lifted her back foot to lick it, balancing on her forelimbs. *"Who just saved your butt, huh? I'd say it's Team Karalti."*

"Well who just spear-dived into this writhing amphibian orgy like a total boss?" I teased back. "And who got us this side quest to begin with?"

"Well who *is the one that flies all over the place so we can do the side-quests?"*

I laughed, and began searching the corpses before they turned to dust and vanished. "Okay, fine. I'm just a plate of chopped liver."

"You will be if you keep picking on me." Karalti shook her foot like a cat with a wet paw. She strutted out of the way and sat back on her tail to preen. *"Wow, that was a good level. I feel big. Do I look bigger?"*

I turned to look at her properly then, and almost swallowed my tongue. Lord have mercy: she looked freaking enormous. After that little growth spurt, her head was as long as a door, her jaws easily large enough to pick up a human and swallow them in a couple of bites. "Yeah, you do. Just means there's more of you to love."

She rumbled in her throat, and the preening turned coy. *"Awww. You're so sweet."*

"Sweet as sugar and just as bad for you." I began looting the bodies like a good little adventurer. The Glacier Toads had no money, but they had ingredients. I liked to brew potions and could make money selling medicine, so parts suited me just fine.

- *Glacier Toad Blood x 10*
- *Monster hide x 4*
- *Glacier Toad Eye x 6*
- *Unrefined Green Mana x 2*

By the time I was finished stripping toads, there wasn't a whole lot left over. I abandoned the skinned corpses to dissolve under the blazing white light of Archemi's sun and brought up my holographic HUD. The first thing I did was drink an herbal potion to restore the HP I'd lost, and then I hopped over to the quest menu to check the update.

Quest Update: Clear Springs

His Majesty, Ignas Corvinus III, has issued a bounty on the monsters fouling up the glacial springs that provide Taltos with fresh water. Now that you have dealt with the problem, return to Vulkan Keep and speak with the Castellan to claim your reward.

Difficulty: *Level 15-17*
Reward: *500 silver rubles, +20 renown (Western Vlachia), 357 EXP.*

Karalti had leveled up from the toad massacre, which was awesome, but I hadn't. I checked my character sheet to see how much EXP I had to get, and groaned. "Oh my god, seriously?"

"*What?*" Karalti's head reared up mid-lick. Her forked tongue stuck out between her teeth.

"I am literally seventeen points away from Level 17." I rolled my eyes and dismissed the menu. "It's official. God hates me."

"*Don't worry about it, silly. We're going back to the castle. The Castellan'll give us the quest EXP, and then you'll level up too!*" Karalti bobbed her head and went back to grooming her newly enlarged tail fins.

"I wanted the quest EXP on top of the level." Annoyed and suddenly anxious, I swiped over to the Main Quest to refresh myself for the hundredth time:

Quest Update: Unto Death

Myszno, in the south-east of Vlachia, was formerly one of the most beautiful places in the country. Now it is a ruin, blighted by undeath and ruled by a powerful vampire lord. You accepted a grant to travel to this troubled land and reclaim it from the vampire's claws – a terrible proposition, given how powerful he has become. But with great risk comes great reward. You could become a true Count in Vlachia, with land, property, and income. Truly a base fit for a king – and a queen.

Difficulty: *Level 20+ (extraordinary)*
Rewards: *EXP, 60 build points, Charter to Resettle the Duchy of Myszno.*
Update: *The Volod of Vlachia, Ignas Corvinus III, is preparing the briefing and supplies you will need to travel to Myszno. You must wait 4 days for preparations to be completed (Day 4 of 4).*

I grimaced. "'This says we have to be Level 20 and the quest is rated 'Extreme'. We leave for Myzsno tomorrow, so-"

"I know, I know. We'll go hunt later today." Karalti sighed. *"Don't worry, okay? We've been working as hard as we can."*

"Well, obviously not hard enough." I dismissed the HUD with a thought, staring out over the glacier toward Taltos. It was beautiful up here, cold and stark. The ground was flat and hard, spring water running through trickles carved out of ancient stone. The river had already unclogged, and was burbling happily on its path toward the valley below.

"Hector..." Karalti snaked her head toward me, eyes narrowed. *"HOW many sidequests have we done in four days?"*

"Four, once we wrap up this one, but-"

"And HOW many levels have we gained since Ignas became king?"

"Almost four levels for me, two for you." I ran my hand back over my braided hair. "But-"

"And HOW much experience did we earn?"

"Uhh... a little bit under seven k?"

"What about the stat points we gained from training? And skill points?"

Restless, I bought up my character sheet again. "I could stand to gain some more stamina. Now that I think about it, this would be a great place to train Stamina. It's cold as balls up here."

"Do you have to?" The dragon yawned wide, flashing a mottled blue-and-black throat and twin rows of razor-sharp teeth. *"I'm really hungry."*

"You'll live. Watch the Spear for me." I stuck the end of the weapon into a patch of moss, leaving it upright, and unequipped all of my clothes except for my underwear. Then, before I could rethink my life choices, I ran across the frozen ground to the river and dive-bombed in. The regret was instantaneous. It was like jumping into a pit of needles, and when I surfaced, it was with a girly little scream and a lot of flailing. "Holy fuckballs! Cold! Cooollld!"

Karalti laughed, a chucking, yarping sound she made by tossing her head and inflating her throat.

"GYAAHH! Oh god, my nuts!" I splashed my way to the bank and clambered out into the cold wind, clutching myself and dancing from foot to foot. "Fuckity fucking-UGGH, this game!"

Karalti only laughed harder, rocking back on her tail.

[[You earned a new Badge: Skinny Dipper]]
[[Warning! You are at risk of Hypothermia!]]
[[You are hungry! HP will no longer regenerate.]]
[[You are thirsty! No HP regeneration]]
[[You are fatigued! -5% to skill checks.]]

I brushed the notifications away like mosquitoes. To level Stamina, I had to stick out the discomfort. Ten seconds, then twenty... and finally, a little red arrow appeared to one side, pulsing upright over three letters, 'STA'. As soon as I saw it, I re-equipped my armor. It was like wrapping myself in a warm towel. The debuff disappeared, though I was still chilled to the bone. Teeth chattering, I dropped down and began to do clap pushups, right there on the ice.

Unlike Skills – which could either be trained individually or levelled with Skill EXP -Stats were only leveled by gaining Character Levels or by training them. For the first time since my upload into Archemi, we'd had the option to just grind, and grind, and grind. When I'd first entered the game, there'd been a level cap and an EXP penalty system that had crippled all attempts at leveling. After that, I couldn't take quests because I was a fugitive, and after *that*, I'd had to juggle a needy dragon hatchling with a time-sensitive, urban story quest that had sucked up all my energy and resources. But now, EXP gain was back to normal, Karalti was mostly grown, and we – that being me, Karalti, Suri and our friend Rin – had four free days to just play the goddamned game and get stacked.

And we had been. My mornings began with training: strength training, agility training, stamina training, and combat skill training. I hung from railings by my fingertips, ran and vaulted over the crenellations of Vulkan Keep, sat under cold waterfalls and wailed on training dummies until I saw those stats go up. Then, it was quest time. Karalti and I had picked up four side-quests in four days, starting with hunting down some weird monsters stealing children from a village outside Taltos. We'd slain a caravan of bandits, killed a lesser vampire in the Lethos Cellar complex beneath the city, and now we'd just de-frogged Taltos' water supply. I was low on food, water and sleep, but in the days after we killed the old corrupt king and installed his brother on the throne, we'd gained more EXP than we had in the last six weeks. It felt good. But it still wasn't enough.

"Hector, come on." Karalti ducked her head, crooning in her throat. *"That's enough. Let's go home."*

"Our main quest says it's for Level 20-plus," I thought to Karalti in between claps. Sweat poured down my forehead. I was battling the debuffs. "I'm only Level 16, and you *just* hit Level 8."

"So? We're a team. We're way *stronger than normal players."*

"Never assume that, Tidbit. We're headed to a warzone."

"We are stronger! And I'm not *just* Level 8. I'm almost at Level 9 already. Once we get the EXP from the Castle Guy, I'll level up with our next battle!"

"You will?" Heaving for breath, I shakily wrapped up a set of fifty pushups and stumbled to my feet. The burn in my arms felt very real as I unequipped my armor again, standing back in the cold wind. The little red arrow appeared again. One point gained to strength. But then I sniffled. And then, I coughed.

[[You have contracted Common Cold! -5% to your Perception.]]

"Fuck!" My throat began to feel raw, and I sneezed. Fear coursed through me, rooting me to the spot. "Shit... shit..."

"Hector?" Karalti stood up in alarm and paced toward me, dark, opalescent wings flicking along her sides in her agitation. *"What's wrong?"*

"I'm sick!" I sneezed again.

"It's okay! It's not the flu. It's just a cold!"

I knew she was right – I'd heard the fucking notification – but I couldn't stop the panic. The flu had killed me. I still remembered the fever, the rash, the swollen joints and the weight of fluid in my lungs. I reached out to her, and was relieved when my hand found her hot scales. Rumbling,

Karalti mantled a wing around us, sheltering me from the wind.

"Sorry." I wheezed. Heat radiated against my face, warm and soothing. "Can't help it. It'll pass."

"Yeah. But we need to go back to the castle and rest."

"Okay... okay just... let me check your sheet first." Wiping my nose, I reopened my HUD and squinted at the holographic display through running eyes:

Karalti – Queen Dragon

Level 8 Sub-Adult Queen Dragon

Strength: 60

Dexterity: 76

Stamina: 55

Will: 32

Wisdom: 18

Intelligence: 22

HP: 1271

MP: 80

Affinity: Darkness/Life (Path of Alacrity)

EXP: 7941 (419 to next level)

Lexica: 18

Spells: 5

Skills:

Acrobatics: 12

- Aerial Acrobatics: 15

Dive: 10

Laden Flight: 15

Perception: 20 (+5 with rider)

Abilities:

Gift of the Blood: *Allows a dragon to utilize magic and other supernatural abilities.*

Eviscerate: *A power attack with the front claws.*

Ghost Fire: *249-344 Fire damage; sticky fire that burns underwater and deals ongoing damage to enemies (86 Fire damage per round for 5 rounds).*

Bite: *255-511 damage.*

Gore: *A dragon's unarmed attacks do double damage and cause Bleeding.*

Tail Attack: *Blunt-force strike that flings enemies under 400 lbs.*

Split Turn: *Burn 5 mana points per second to immediately change momentum while rolling. This allows for 90 degree and 180 degree turns in any direction. 2 bonus Lexica.*

Spells:

Bioscope: *Analyze an enemy and learn their strengths and weaknesses. (4 MP, 10 sec cooldown)*

Sense Aether: *Detect and assess magical effects, artifacts, and locations. (4 MP, 5 sec cooldown)*

Dark Focus II: *Triple power of next magical attack. (18 MP, 25 sec cooldown)*

Dirge: *A curse that slowly damages enemies every turn and has a chance to cause the Deaf and Mute debuffs. (16 MP, 25 sec cooldown)*

Haste II: *Dramatically increases speed for 1 min per spell level (16 MP, 30 sec cooldown)*

"Holy shit," I said. "You're right."

"Uh-huh." The dragon gently rested her jaw on my shoulder *"You've been working yourself sick, Hector. C'mon. Let's go home."*

"There's no such thing as working too hard." My stomach growled, and I rolled my shoulders to try and distract myself from the pangs. "You get your next Path Ability at Level 10. Come on: if we kill one more monster, we'll go up again and be that much closer to our goal."

"Hector. No. Just stop." Karalti couldn't roll her eyes – like a bird, she had to turn her head to look in different directions. To express irritation, she rapidly flickered her inner eyelids. *"We're going back to the castle, and you're going to go to bed and eat some food while I go out and hunt."*

"But we-" Whatever I was about to say was cut off by a vibration in my ear. The curved holographic screen still hanging in front of me said: *[[Incoming PM: Suri]]*.

"Hello, light of my life." I tried not to sniffle after picking up the call. "What's up?"

"Nothing good." My girlfriend's lovely honey-and-smoke voice was tight with stress. "We have a situation. Where are you?"

"We were grinding up on the plateau-" I turned my head to cough as Karalti perked up in alarm. "-'S'cuse me, sorry about that. We're four miles north of Vulkan Keep."

"Two full-grown dragons with riders just appeared over Taltos," Suri said grimly. "They've got a hostage, and they're demanding to speak with you."

A nasty, icy thrill that had nothing to do with the cold crawled down through my guts. Dragon Knights. There was only one thing they were here for. I looked up at Karalti.

"Hector?" Her horns flattened against her skull, even as she crouched and extended a wing to let me onto her back. "What's wrong?"

"The Order's caught up with us." All thoughts of leveling vanished as I caught the saddle straps and hauled myself up. "We have to get back to Vulkan Keep, now."

Chapter 2

Dragons.

We heard their unearthly, bone-rattling shrieks from half a mile away, and as soon as we came within range of Vulkan Keep, we saw them. The pair of dragons – one white, one blue – were the size of jetliners, easily three or four times Karalti's length. They wheeled in the sky high above Taltos, their wings large enough to blot the sun overhead. As we crept our way along the mountainside, the blue dragon split the air with a brilliant violet-white thunderbolt, which struck Talto's clock tower and blew the roof off in an incandescent flash. The act was petty, contemptuous; like was spitting on the city.

Karalti stuck to the shadows, where she dipped in and out of sight, then cut over Vulkan Keep's curtain wall and into the fortress itself. The Keep was in pandemonium. Soldiers ran in formation through the gardens, splitting off to seal gates and doors. In the melee, my supernatural eyesight picked out a tall, strikingly beautiful woman with a flaming mop of red curls, dark coppery skin, and an impractically large sword. She was calmly and effectively directing panicked civilians to shelter.

"Head for Suri!" Bent down low over the saddle, I waved an arm at her before remembering that she couldn't actually see us yet.

"Okay, but Hector... I think..." Karalti trailed off, unusually hesitant. *"I think those dragons are my brothers."*

"*Well, yeah.*" I leaned with the dragon as she angled her body into a tight corkscrew glide toward the ground. *"All the dragons from the Eyrie are your sibs, right? Your mom laid all the eggs."*

"I mean... I think they're my clutchmates."

"No way, Tidbit. Those are some grown-ass dragons. Do you know how much EXP it takes for a dragon to reach full maturity?"

"Nope."

"It's a six-figure number, something close to like... two hundred thousand experience. To go from hatchling to thirty, they'd have needed to pull in something to the tune of thirteen thousand EXP per day, every day, for a month. We couldn't even scrape together seven thousand in four days, and we worked our asses off."

We stopped talking to concentrate on the descent. Suri went into action as soon as she saw us, chasing people off to give us somewhere to land. When the garden was clear, the dragon backwinged and flapped to a stop, throwing up dirt from the planters and nearly crushing one of the Volod's rose beds.

"Hector!" Suri ran to us, yelling to be heard over the shouts and tolling bells, the rattle of gates and the rumble of wagons. "Ignas says to hide Karalti in the inner keep! He has a plan to deal with the dragons!"

The little Queen's neck swelled, and she snorted a cloud of burning steam. *"No! I'm not hiding from anyone!"*

"Me either. And they won't talk unless they see Karalti. Get on!" I offered the Spear down to Suri, blunt end first. "Brief me on the way!"

Suri reached for it, but Karalti took an absent step to the side, her crown of horns flattened down against her skull.

"Karalti, I know you're not exactly Suri's biggest fan, but really? Now?" I almost snarled.

"No... it's not her." The dragon extended one wing down to Suri, listening to something I couldn't hear. *"Hector... they want to land."*

"Land? They're communicating with you?" I offered Suri the assist a second time. She caught the spear and used it to steady her climb to the dragon's back.

"Yeah. But they sound weird. Like...bad weird." Karalti shuddered.

"Tell Ignas what they want," I said to her.

"Okay." Agitated, Karalti ducked her head, leathery wings flicking against her sides. After a minute or two, she bobbed her head. *"Ignas says that fits with his plan. We need to draw them to the Vulkan Parade Ground, and then we have to hold them there, keep them talking."*

"Roger that." I reached back to pat Suri's thigh. "Hold on. Suri, put your forehead down on my shoulder for takeoff."

"Okay, lover boy." Suri clung around my waist, the front of her body molded to my back in a way that would normally be intensely distracting. Unfortunately, I couldn't enjoy the sensation, because as we took to the air, I got my first real look at the invading dragons.

The blue and white were full-grown, even larger than the old Knight-Commander's dragon, Talenth. But Karalti was right – they were *weird.* Normal Archemian dragons were velociraptor-like bipeds, with long narrow wings and gracile limbs taut with corded muscle. They had bright, holographic hides that rippled with color on the ground, and that were mirrored in the sky – a form of natural camouflage. Neither of these dragons were properly bipedal, and neither of them were holographic. The white's scales were blotched with grayish spots, like white jasper, the blue's the sickly color of bread mold. Both dragons were abnormally large, with distended forelimbs, clubbed, twisted horns, and asymmetrical features. The white dipped a wingtip and began to lumber his way toward the Parade Ground, revealing the rider. I drew a sharp, startled breath.

It was Lucien fucking Hart, one of my least-favorite people in Archemi.

Ten levels ago, my would-be murderer had been a slim, roguish man with a punchable face and chin-length sandy hair. Now, the hair was shaved short in a high and tight, and the rest of him looked like he'd been stuffing that face with steroids and hitting the gym. He was buffer than me, arms and chest bulging in top-of-the-line armor. Medium armor, the kind a ranger or some other dex-tank might wear. He carried two curved swords over his back and a crossbow at his hip, and he looked about as smug as I'd ever seen him. That was saying something, because Lucien had always been pretty fucking smug.

It took longer for me to identify the woman riding the blue. She was dressed in the stiff, high-collared armor of the Mata Argis. Her long blond hair was bound back in a severe twist at the nape of her neck. She had dark bluish lips, deep bruised eyes, and a crazed, haunted expression that chilled me more deeply than the river water had. It was Violetta, the woman who had gone through the Trial of Marantha with us.

"Oh my fucking god." I couldn't believe what I was seeing. "No way."

"What?" Suri clutched me in a death grip, white-knuckled as Karalti banked and began her descent toward the parade ground. "What did you say?"

I brought up my HUD to PM her so she could hear me over the roar of the wind, but just as I did, the blue banked, and I spotted Violetta's passenger. "Oh Jesus."

It was Rutha. The beautiful Court Sorceress of Ilia was a ghostly shadow of her former self. She wore rags that offered her no protection from the frigid wind, bound and buckled to the saddle like cargo. She was slumped, her head nodding against her chest. Her glorious long white hair had been rudely hacked off, and she was deathly underweight.

"Baldr." Just like that, my disbelief condensed into something black and empty and cold. A dark, savage part of me stared at the pair of dragons, like a predator waiting behind my eyes. I squeezed the Spear so hard my knuckles cracked. "You motherfucker."

"Hector?" Karalti's voice broke through the jangling black noise, sweet and frightened. *"They say they're going to land."*

"Tell them that we'll land first." My tone was flinty. *"This is our turf. They follow our rules."*

"Are you mad at me?" She asked, in a small voice. *"The bad men are here because of me."*

"I've never been mad at you for this. Ever." I gripped down with my knees, urging Suri to lean with me.

Karalti swooped over the wall surrounding the Parade Ground. This morning, the ground had been crowded with airships, cargo, and personnel. Now the huge square plaza was almost empty, hastily cleared of ships and people. We saw a rank of soldiers running across the pavement. They split off into gateways just as a formation of hookwings burst out of the tunnel connecting the parade grounds to Vulkan Keep. His Majesty, Volod Ignas Corvinus III, was in the lead, riding a glossy black dinosaur almost as large as Cutthroat. He was a tall, broad-shouldered, lean man, dressed like a rogue in matte black plate over layers of soft leather. To his right was a formation of Knights of the Red Star, dragoons whose red lamellar armor gave them a samurai-like appearance. To his left rode the intimidating knights of the Order of the Dragon, heavy cavalry who served as his bodyguards. Knowing Ignas, he wouldn't only put his trust in plate armor. There would be stealth characters already stationed in the Parade Ground, invisible to the naked eye –

rogues from the Nightstalkers, and his right-hand Mercurion assassin: The King's Blade, Ebisa.

Following up at the rear was a single hookwing carrying two people. The man holding the reins looked like a cartoon villain, with a thin face, an oiled, pointed beard and a pair of spell gloves. It was the Court Sorcerer, Simeon. Holding onto him was a pretty, petite Mercurion woman with a cute bob of hair and big blue-on-blue eyes: our friend and favorite Artificer, Rin. Two small walking tanks bounded behind them like a pair of metal wolves.

"Everyone's here!" I shouted back to Suri. "Hang on and lean with me!"

She nodded quickly. The woman's arms were so tight I could feel the pressure through my armor. Karalti coasted toward the ground, then gracefully back-winged to land neatly on the pavement. Once we were on the ground, Suri let go with a shuddering sigh.

"You alright?" I asked over my shoulder.

"I'm gonna leave the sky to you from now on." Suri pressed a shaky kiss to my neck, then let go to slide down Karalti's offered wing. "Felt like I was gonna fall the whole time."

"You get used to it, but yeah. It isn't for everyone." Once she was down, I stood up on the dragon's back and waved to Ignas.

The new king of Vlachia jerked his chin in greeting and trotted up. He reined in his wild-eyed, foaming hookwing just in front of Karalti. His posse flowed in around us, forming ranks to either side.

"Lovely way to end the morning, don't you think?" Ignas called up to us. "Ready, Tuun?"

"As much as we'll ever be." I gave him a grim, thin-lipped smile.

The Volod turned his pale eyes skyward. "Lady Karalti, if you would be so kind, please tell our unwanted guests that we shall now receive them."

Karalti arched her neck and dropped her muzzle down, posturing like a swan as she concentrated. A few minutes passed, and then a windstorm picked up across the plaza as Lucien and Violetta descended. The enormous dragons were clumsy compared to their queen sister, their lumbering descent kicking up dust and rocks into a stinging whirlwind.

Before they touched ground, I sensed that something was very, very wrong. Whether they breathed fire, ice, acid or lightning, all dragons emitted intense heat while flying. These ones... not so much. Instead, the wind of their creaking wings blasted us with cold, and as they came to a halt, I saw frost condense on their scales. Up close, they were even more horrific than I'd thought. Their warped horns curled back in so far their tips had embedded themselves into the bone of their skulls. Their eyes were filmed over with cataracts, and their jaws were misshapen, too many teeth jutting at angles so bad that neither of them could close their mouths properly.

My eyes narrowed. *"Karalti. Can you Bioscan these guys?"*

"Sure." Karalti darted her nose forward, light pulsing between her scales. She didn't have to speak her Words of Power aloud. The Bioscan bought Lucien's dragon into focus

as it crouched, and a holographic panel jumped to life to one side of my HUD: a column of bar graphs and numerical data which my narrator tried to read to me, her voice skipping and warping:

??724q244fphttttodsl-009Solonkratsu ['Vesper', White Dragon]

Sex: M
Level 55
HP: ?????/?????
Weak Against ?????
Immune to ?????

Level 55? Well, fuck me with a spoon. The distorted voice made my skin crawl, but the glitched code string was oddly familiar. I swallowed around a sudden spike of fear as Lucien stepped around the side of his dragon's neck, leaning out as he grinned down at us. Violetta pulled Rutha out of her harness and held a knife to her neck. The elfin sorceress swooned, unconscious, while Violetta stared daggers at me with dead, dull blue eyes.

"Well, this is quite the reception, isn't it?" Lucien called, his voice laced with cheerful venom. "Is that the *Queen?* Good grief, I thought she'd be bigger by now."

As soon as his attention shifted to Karalti, that cold emptiness rose back up and quenched the fear. Lucien was a mediocre, cowardly piece of shit, and levelling hadn't changed that. His cheating only proved the fact.

"Well, if it isn't Lucien fuckin' Hart." I grinned back toothily. "Nice Baldr cosplay. Must have taken a lot of hard work."

Lucien rolled his eyes. "I see you still think you're funny. We're here to-"

"And by 'hard work', I mean 'cheating like a motherfucker'. Just to be clear." I raised my voice and talked right over him. "What the hell happened to you two? And what the *fuck* happened to your dragons?"

He sneered. "I thought that'd be obvious. We leveled up, gained prestige and positions of power, and now we're here to advise you as to how things will work going forward. For those who don't know me, I am Lucien Hart, the Wing Captain of the Order of St. Grigori."

"*Ignas says to keep them talking.*" Karalti's telepathic voice was level, but tight with stress. "*They're almost ready.*"

"Wing Captain? *You?* Jesus Christ." I forced myself to not stare at Violetta and Rutha, to keep their attention on me. "Let me get this straight: the pair of you just illegally entered a sovereign nation's airspace, turned up at this heavily fortified castle, and now you want to tell the monarch of said nation what to do?"

"And what are you going to do about it? Vesper and Tempest are fully grown dragons. They could raze this hovel to the ground," Lucien boasted. "Or are you blind as well as stupid?"

Vesper and Tempest? Those didn't sound like the kinds of names the Solonkratsu used. The dragons were unnaturally still, wheezing as they breathed. I gestured at them. "I honestly have no idea what I'm seeing here. What the hell did you do to them? They look fucking awful."

"Looks can be deceiving," Lucien said smugly. "What level is *your* dragon? Six? Seven?"

I rested a boot against the base of Karalti's neck. "It's a number higher than six, but below the number of inches of dick you sucked to be here today, 'Wing Captain'."

A ripple of laughter made its way through the ranks around me. Lucien's face purpled. I'd have basked in the burn, but terror radiated from Karalti in waves. Her scales, horns and wings had flattened to her body as she made an urgent huffing, barking sound, trying to get her siblings to acknowledge her. Both dragons simply stared right through us.

"Hmph." Lucien snootily regarded his fingernails, even though he was wearing gloves. "Well, Baldr Hyland, the Warden of Ilia, has sent us to follow up on a letter he sent the king a week ago. He also wants to make you an offer. A good one. Do you want to hear it?"

"I'm all ears," I called back. "But can you at least acknowledge His Majesty first? Guy's been standing there for like ten minutes now."

Out of the corner of my eye, I saw Ignas arch an eyebrow.

"Why? He's an NPC. We're the players. He'll do what the story we make forces him to do," Lucien retorted. "Baldr is giving you a real chance, Hector. Did you know that there hasn't been a queen with a rider in the Eyrie in close to seven hundred years? Traditionally, the Queen's rider is the one to take command of the Eyrie, which means that if you come with us, you'll be named Knight-Commander of the Order."

My mouth opened, then snapped shut. Of all the things I'd expected him to say... well. "I thought Baldr was the Knight-Commander?"

"He is. For now." Lucien's burnt orange eyes simmered with envy and disdain. "But his plan all along was to take control of Ilia, and he has. Besides that, the Eyrie needs a queen, and *that* is almost ready to breed."

He pointed at Karalti. She pulled her lips back over her gums, flashing all her teeth, and snarled.

It took every ounce of willpower I had not to hit my Jump ability, leap up there, and try to snap Lucien's lily-white neck. My mouth sloped to one side in a hard, thin grimace. "I'm... genuinely offended that Baldr thinks I'm that stupid."

"He's serious, Hector." Some of the contempt left Lucien's expression. "Baldr isn't just a good player. He's the best, and if there's one thing I've learned since we started working together, it's that whatever he wants, he gets. You really should consider his offer. I mean... it's even lore-friendly."

I stared at him. "Dude, no. I'm not flying my dragon to your supervillain headquarters and joining your stupid cult. I don't care if Baldr eats coal for breakfast and shits diamonds by lunch time: he's evil, he's a cheat, and whatever hack he used to fuck up your dragons has also fucked with you."

Lucien's smirk slowly faded. He sighed. "Look, I'll try and put this in the kind of simple language someone like you can understand. Baldr is willing to give you, Hector, the second-most powerful position in the Hercynian Empire, if- "

"Pardon me?" Ignas finally stepped forward. "The 'Hercynian Empire'? Ilia is a single nation and a signatory to the White Sail Alliance. There is no 'Hercynian Empire'."

"There is now." Lucien shrugged and flashed him a rakish smile. "Which leads me to the stick at the end of the carrot. Hector stole this queen dragon from the Order he vowed to serve-"

"I didn't." I rolled my eyes.

"-AND he abducted *our* property to *your* kingdom, 'Your Highness'," Lucien finished. "Which means you're sheltering an outlaw, and if Hector doesn't accept your future Emperor's extremely generous offer, your refusal to extradite this traitor and his hatchling will be treated as a declaration of war."

"It's 'Your Majesty', and I did, in fact, send a reply. He sent the letter to my brother, who is now deceased. I informed the Warden that Vlachia is not part of Hercynia, and that I consider him to be an illegitimate ruler," Ignas replied crisply. "So kindly take yourself back to your self-styled 'Emperor' and tell him that he can shove his offer all the way up his *hooyeh* until it comes up his neck and he chokes. I will be contacting the other Alliance members about this proclamation. Be assured we will take appropriate action."

Violetta's eyes narrowed to pale slits. Rutha was still draped in her arms, unconscious. A trickle of blood ran down her neck, soaking into the ragged hem of the shirt she was wearing.

"Alright. Suit yourself." Lucien jerked his head toward Rutha. "Throw the knife-eared whore off your dragon, Vi. Then torch the place."

Chapter 3

Violetta shoved Rutha forward. The unconscious woman tumbled over the blue dragon's frosted scales, slid off his shoulder, and plummeted bonelessly toward the ground.

"Stay back!" I snapped at Karalti and sprung from her back like a cricket.

At the peak of the Jump, I triggered Shadow Dance. They were two of the essential mobility skills of a Dark Dragoon, with Jump allowing me to leap fifteen feet in any direction, and Shadow Dance allowing me to become immaterial and dash forward at the cost of a tiny amount of health. With the right timing, the two maneuvers could be chained together like a ghetto airdash. I vanished in a swirl of shadow, reappearing under Rutha to catch her in my arms. It was a dumb thing to do, a stunt that left me wide open and defenseless. But it was the only thing to do.

I didn't even see Lucien move. One moment, he was standing on his dragon's back, smirking away, and in the next, he was up in my face. Swords drawn, face split in an insane, heartless grin.

"Oops." He drove both blades at my exposed ribs.

[[Barrier Shirt negates Heartstrike!]]
[[Lucien lands a glancing blow!]]
[[You have taken 1101 damage!]]
[[You are poisoned!]]
[[Warning! Your Armor durability is critically low!]]

The ancient Tuun chain shirt burst, and splitting pain wracked through my torso, stunning me. Most of my HP vanished like a bad dream. Lucien kicked off my chest, sending us tumbling through the air. I oriented just in time to land on my feet, but stumbled under Rutha's weight and fell back with her onto my ass. Karalti bounded forward with a roar, shielding me with her body as the pair of dragons drew deep, magically charged breaths.

And Ignas began to laugh.

At the same moment that Lucien vanished and reappeared on his dragon's back, hundreds of hidden murder holes opened up around the Parade Ground all at once. A forest of cannons and rifles emerged, every one of them aimed squarely at Lucien and Violetta. The dragons froze in place.

The Volod crossed his arms, raising his voice to be heard by the riders. "I don't know if your enlightened liege is much of a historian, but Vlachia is one of the oldest civilizations in Artana. You really think we've stood for three thousand years without being prepared to defend ourselves from a couple of dragons?"

"We're Level 55. We can tank it." Lucien sneered. "Vesper!"

"These are Wyrmsbane rounds, boy." Ignas jerked his head toward the nearest row of cannons. "You'll get out of the way, but that decrepit beast of yours won't."

His words hung in the air. Suri and Rin stood side by side, weapons in hand. The soldiers and knights held their ranks, faces pale, but determined. Fighting the cramping pain from the poison on Lucien's swords, I stood up with Rutha in my arms.

"Wyrmsbane?" Lucien's nose wrinkled. His expression turned distant as he consulted his unseen HUD. "Violetta, is that even a real buff?"

She gave him a curt nod, but remained silent. The raspy breathing of the two mutated dragons was the only sound for nearly a minute.

"So, now that we have an understanding, I will 'advise you as to how things will work going forward', as you put it," Ignas finally said. "You, Lucien, will run back to your master like a whipped dog, and you will tell this so-called Emperor of Nothing what I said. I give you my thanks for alerting us to his intentions."

"Oh, we will. And when we come back with a legion of dragons, you'll wish you'd never insulted us." Lucien spat down at me. "Come on, Vi."

The female rider stared me in the eye as her dragon spread his wings and bunched, then kicked off the ground. The frigid downdraft blasted the courtyard, knocking down the nervous soldiers and forcing the Volod to one knee. Shielding our faces, we watched the twisted creatures rise into the sky before vanishing into a dark nimbus.

"Hector!" Rin's anguished cry came from behind me. I turned to see her running for us, her turrets flanking to either side. "Are you okay?!"

"I'm mildly poisoned, mostly dead, and I have a cold, but I'm alive." In all honesty, I was rattled. I hadn't seen Lucien move. His Dex was up to god-tier levels now... and who the hell knew how powerful Violetta and Baldr were. His 'glancing blow' had ignored my armor and would have killed me if not for the improved Spear of Nine Spheres and its +300 HP bonus.

I pushed the pain aside and knelt with Rutha, looking over her injuries. She was slashed with deep lacerations – many of them infected – poorly healed bones, bruises and old blood.

"My god. This poor woman." Rin crouched down on the other side, reaching out to smooth her hair back from her face. "Who were those people?"

"We'll talk about it later. Here, Hector. Drink." Suri held out a fan of potion vials to me: three green and one black. I took them and threw back the ⟦Common Antidote⟧ like a shot, then drank one of the green ⟦Concentrated Moss Tinctures⟧. The next one I tried to give to Rutha, but it was hopeless. She couldn't swallow. I took the rest.

⟦You have healed 450 HP!⟧
⟦You are no longer poisoned!⟧
⟦HP: 632/1283⟧

I was still in the orange after all that, but the crushing pain in my sides lifted. The humiliation? Not so much. I flashed Suri a small, wan smile. "Thanks."

"She's been beaten with a razor whip." Suri pointed at the lacerations on Rutha's skin. "Used to see that in Al-Asad a lot. Whips that had shards of metal knotted on."

Rin's eyes were tearing up. "I knew that players wouldn't always be kind to NPCs... but this is terrible."

"Strange as it sounds, I think whatever happened to Violetta was worse." I gathered Rutha into my arms and stood. "She used to be okay, you know? She wasn't part of Baldr's clique. Lucien was. He was a weak coward, and now he's a vicious, nasty weak coward. And Baldr... Jesus."

Ignas strode up to us, cloak billowing in the wind. "Power is like a magnifying lens, Hector. If you are a good person, it will bring out the best in you. If you are a coward, a fool, or a sadist, having power only makes you more so." He motioned with a hand to one of the Knights of the Red Star, who bowed and went to one knee. "Rytier, take Lady Rutha to the infirmary, and tell Masha that I command she attend her personally. The Lady was Ilia's frequent emissary here... I wish to know she is being well taken care of."

"*Hemen, Majesteri.*" The tattooed knight saluted with a fist over his heart, then rose and barked orders in Vlachian to his squad.

A pair of soldiers came forward to take her up and bear her away, but I ached with suspicion. "Your Majesty, we must be careful. As much as I care for her, Rutha is mixed up with Baldr. She could be compromised."

"You question the lady's honor?" He furrowed his brows.

"No, not her honor. Baldr's. The Architect that's possessing him... he's like a disease that corrupts people, like those two people we just saw. And your brother."

Slowly, Ignas nodded. "I see."

I jerked my head toward the retreating soldiers. "Rutha might not be working for Baldr intentionally, or even willingly, but she could still be infected. There's something about this that feels like a trap. Like it was staged."

"Hector's right. There was no reason for them to give us Rutha," Suri said. "If that little blond cunt was tellin' the truth and they're really Level 55, that sorceress probably could've waved a hand and killed the lot of us without too much trouble."

"Curious you say that." The Volod rubbed his hand over his mouth, thinking. "She lied."

There was a pregnant pause.

"About the Wyrmsbane?" I asked.

The Volod nodded. "Yes. There's no such thing, not as such. I mean, there are magics that affect dragons, but they are decided by element. The ruse was a last-minute gamble on my part."

"Well shit." Suri looked to the sky. "We'd have been fucked if she hadn't fudged it."

Ignas shook his head. "Not necessarily. Ebisa is a match for the sorceress."

As if summoned, ghost, the unseen assassin stepped out of her Stealth cloak and fell in by Ignas' side. Ebisa was a Mercurion like Rin, but she was her physical opposite. Most Mercurions were beautiful works of art, but Ebisa was more like an unfinished sculpture. She was rail-thin, her skin a matte flat gray. Her sharp features were hard and hawkish: instead of eyes, she had four gemstones in a band across her face. She always wore a mask in public.

"The riders are not as powerful as their dragons. If they were, they would have detected my position." Ebisa's voice was as harsh as a crow's, rough and husky. "But the Tuun speaks true. This elf was their bargaining chip, and they threw her on the table and left with their tails between their legs. It was too easy."

"You are a cynical shrew, Ebisa. But yes, indeed." The Volod seemed entirely unsurprised by her sudden appearance.

"A cynical shrew who has protected your bony *Sang'hi* ass for long enough to have gained some wisdom," Ebisa replied wryly.

Ignas snorted. "True enough."

"You aren't putting Rutha in the dungeons or anything, are you?" I asked quickly. "If she's been turned into some sort of trojan, it's not her fault."

"Of course not. I will warn Masha of this disease she may be carrying. We will place the lady under guard in the hospital and keep her isolated for the duration of her coma," Ignas replied. "Much as it pains me to do so."

Ebisa flowed like a ribbon of smoke to join Rin, who was starting to look dejected. She patted the Artificer on the hip, and the girl perked up, blushing bright blue. "We could keep watch over her for you, sire. Mercurions fear no human disease."

"You could, but I have need of you elsewhere. Your gift for strategy will be of great use to us. We must have the briefing on Myszno. I'd planned to have it tonight after the Dark Moon festival, but we will have to move it forward."

"How are things in Myszno looking?" I asked. "The *Unto Death* quest?"

Ignas gave a little shake of his head, lips pressed together. "The messenger who staggered into the Great Hall this morning carried dire news, now made more dire by the need to deal with this Ilian whelp. I won't explain out here – we shall adjourn to the War Room. I want all four of you there. Karalti, too, if she can stick her head in through the window."

"Of course, Your Majesty." Suri dropped into a courtly bow.

"Sure." I looked back to Karalti. Her wings were drooping, the tips almost trailing on the ground. She was still staring up at where her siblings had vanished. "If it's alright with you, we'll meet you there in twenty."

Ignas gave Karalti a shrewd look, then inclined his head. "You have my leave. Do what you must. And do not fear these threats of war, Hector. As I told you during my coronation, I will not be extraditing you or Karalti to Ilia. You have my solemn word before these witnesses."

I turned back to him. "Even if it means going up against Baldr?"

He nodded. "The White Sail Alliance will never allow this Starborn whelp to muster beyond his own borders. Ilia is not a large country, and soldiers march on their stomachs. We will freeze trade, enforce sanctions, and starve any aspirations of his 'empire' even forming."

I ran my tongue over my teeth, considering his words. Even though I could open my HUD and view my Reputation in Western Vlachia – it was up around the +1000 point mark now – I still had to ask the question for my own peace of mind. "Why are you protecting us?

The Volod drew himself up like a dignified heron. "As I told you the day of my coronation, it is a matter of honor. You and your queen brought a murderer to justice and helped to restore me to my rightful throne, and now you prepare to ride to our defense. Vlachia is in your debt."

"Then thank you, for both our sakes," I replied. "I mean it."

Ignas bowed his head, then turned to confer with Ebisa in Vlachian. Suri squeezed me on the shoulder as I walked by her, and I clapped her forearm before moving on to join Karalti. Her nostrils flared as I approached.

"Come on, Tidbit. Let's fly and talk," I said, switching back to our silent speech.

"I don't want to talk. What is there to talk about?" My dragon hissed and snapped her jaws, flexing her talons into the grout between stones, but she dutifully positioned her wing so I could climb it.

"I know you don't feel like it, but you need to. What's eating you?"

"I dunno."

She didn't say anything else during takeoff, but I could feel the tension in her body as she took wing. Only once we were in the air did she speak again.

"Those two dragons... they were my brothers. I could tell by the way they smelled. What happened to them? I don't understand."

"I told you about Baldr, from Ilia. He's been possessed by one of the Architects, the beings who created this world, and that being – Ororgael – has corrupted them with Void magic," I replied, leaning with her as she dropped a wingtip and headed back the way we'd come.

"Like the bad king. Andrik."

"Yup."

Karalti flew in pensive silence for the rest of the trip to the War Room. Fighting the urge to press her, I tried to relax into the quiet, to make it less awkward, but I was also pretty wound up. We'd been in Archemi six weeks, and Baldr was already the ruler of a nation. Lucien was his high-ranked lackey. If the lackeys and their dragons were Level 55 already, how powerful were Baldr and his mount?

Trying not to sneeze into my helmet, I bought up the EXP table in the ArchemiWiki to check how much experience a dragon needed to reach Level 55, and blanched. Fuck me. That was a big number with a lot of zeroes. Even if Karalti and I had trained from the minute she was born until this moment now, fighting mobs all day and all night, we wouldn't be anywhere near that. It wasn't fair, and it made me feel just a little more hopeless about those seventeen points I still needed to level up. But what was the point, when my opponents were so overpowered?

Before the dark thoughts could overwhelm me, I narrowed my eyes and studied Vulkan Keep's defenses from the air. If Baldr attacked, he wasn't going to have an easy time of it. There were multiple rings, starting with the bridge over the canyon valley that served as a moat. Then there was the barbican, a fortified gatehouse which led to a kill zone separated from the main castle by *another* gatehouse, the only way through the outer curtain wall. The wall was partly built into and camouflaged by the obsidian stone of Mount Racosul, the huge dormant volcano that loomed over Taltos below. There was the outer bailey just behind that, a crescent-shaped open space where most of the ancillary buildings used to manage the Keep were located. The inner bailey was built more directly into the enormous natural cave structure behind the castle, which sheltered the keep from aerial attack – an important feature for fortified positions in Archemi. The volcano concealed the strongly fortified living quarters and defensive elements under the direct command of the Volod. The Parade Ground, on the other side of the mountain, was pretty much the only open area and was outside the main walls. Flanking towers were embedded to either side of the inner bailey, the patrolling guards concealed by crenellations along the walls and reinforced caverns from above. Vulkan Keep wasn't some whimsical Elvish relic. It was ugly and blocky, but it had been built to be impregnable, not pretty. So far, so good.

The War Room was on the top floor of the donjon, the highest tower of the keep. Like the Eye of Sauron, you could stand on the balcony that was shielded above and in front, and look out over the Keep, the parade ground, and the switchback road that ran down the mountain across a fast, icy river and ended at the gates of Taltos far below.

Karalti soared down in an elegant arc to land on the edge of the balcony. When she had her balance, she flipped her wings, folding them neatly against her flanks, and hopped down to the broad catwalk.

"*Are you alright?*" I unbuckled myself from the saddle, but didn't slide down.

"*No.*" Her normally girlish, chirpy voice was uncommonly serious. "*But... Do you think...?*"

She trailed off, tail lashing, and flattened her crests down against her skull.

"*Do I think what?*"

The little dragon shook her head, restlessly flexing her killing claws against the stone. "*Do you... do you think... my mom is still alive?*"

I felt a pang behind my ribs that had nothing to do with the lingering ache from Lucien's swords. "*I don't know.*"

"*I never got to meet her.*" Karalti began to pluck at the edge of the wall with her dexterous hands, picking at the seams between stones. "*My blood tells me that I have to meet her, at least once. If I don't...*"

She trailed off again, hissing softly with frustration.

"If you don't meet her, what happens?" I asked.

"I tried to command my brothers before. I told them to leave. They should have listened to me." Karalti replied. *"We are blood-kin, and I am their Queen. They should have obeyed me. But there was nothing. It was like... they didn't recognize me."*

"That's because they're Stranged, Tidbit." I swung my leg over to sit side-saddle, bracing my heel against her wing shoulder. "They're fucked up from whatever cheats Baldr used to make them level so fast. You can't expect them to act normally."

"No. That's not what I mean." She darted her head back and forth, then turned around to pace. *"My mother has something that she must give me. If I'd been allowed to hatch properly with her, I'd be able to command them, Stranged or not. I can see her when I close my eyes sometimes. She gives me something from her mouth and passes the mantle of Queenship to me."*

I frowned. There was a lot about dragonkind I didn't know, given my strange start in Archemi. "If you're having visions of her, I'd like to say she's alive. She probably has to be careful how she contacts you."

"Do you... do you think she loves me?" Karalti craned her head around to look back. *"Be proud of me?"*

I reached out and chucked her cheek. *"There's no way she couldn't love you, Tidbit."*

Karalti's luminous eyes searched mine, and her horns lifted a little. *"What... what is she like? Is she smart and beautiful? She must be, if she has so many males courting her."*

For once, I didn't want to tell Karalti the truth. Not all of it, anyway. Her mother was obese and sickly, chained deep in the bowels of the Eyrie just as she'd been her entire life. I shuddered to think how she was being treated now, after helping me escape. But despite it all, she had preserved some dignity, the spirit and the will to fight on. Karalti was living proof of her courage, and her power.

I fixed my dragon with a steely glare. "She never got to live the kind of life you have. But your mom's a fighter, and she's super smart. If she's alive, the thing that's keeping her going is knowing that you're fat, dumb and happy. And free."

"Yeah. I guess." The dragon looked down. *"You know, I'm happy that I'm getting bigger, because it means you can fly with me and I can protect you better. But sometimes, I still feel really small."*

The fierceness burning inside me melted a little at her expression. "It wasn't that long ago that I used to carry you around, huh?"

Karalti's horns lifted more, and she pressed her muzzle against my hand, eyes wide and trusting. *"I miss it sometimes."*

"Me too. But there's never any point in wishing you were something you were in the past, right?" My smile widened, but then froze as a yellow side-quest notification flashed in the corner of my eye. I pulled it over to have a look, and my eyebrows shot up when my narrator read it out for me:

New Quest: The Queen's Mantle

Karalti has experienced a vision of her mother gifting her with access to the Path of Royalty, the Path which unlocks a Queen dragon's ability to command and lead other dragons. To understand more, you will need to read and research the Solonkratsu, Archemi's native dragon species.
Reward: *EXP, new Path options, Bonus Ability Points.*

My guts churned. The reward was good, but that paragraph contained two of a dyslexic's least favorite words: 'read' and 'research'.

"Are we going to rescue my brothers?" Karalti asked. *"And my mom?"*

"I hope so. I mean... yeah, we will. Someday. One way or another, we'll sort it out once we're strong enough." Nervously, I accepted the quest and added it to my ever-growing queue. "Maybe Suri can help."

Karalti rumbled. *"I don't want her help."*

I slid down to land lightly on the wall, then sprung down to the walkway. "We need her strength, Tidbit. The Eyrie is a big place, and when the time comes, we'll need everyone we can get. That's a long way off, though. We're nowhere near powerful enough."

Karalti spread her wings, letting them ripple in the wind. *"Fine, but I'm not running away again, ever. If I see Lucien and Violetta, I'll burn them to ashes for what they did to my brothers."*

"No, you won't. You'll fly back here as fast as you fucking can," I said.

She turned to glare at me, snorting steam. "*Why?*"

"I just said it. We're not strong enough yet." I held her gaze. "Not by half. You did the Bioscan. You know as well as I do that they're way, *way* too OP for us to handle yet."

"That's why you kill the humans. They're weaker."

"You don't know that." I scowled. "If Lucien is anything over Level 20, he could survive a direct hit of your breath weapon, assuming you *could* hit him. And he is. His 'glancing blow' wrecked my magic armor and nearly killed me."

The dragon hissed, dancing from foot to foot. *"I want to fight!"*

"Look," I said. "Just accept that we're not there yet, okay? You're Level 8. I'm still only Level 16. Believe me, you're not the only one who's frustrated."

The dragon's eyes narrowed as she turned her flank to me, tail lashing. "Ugh, whatever. I'm going hunting."

"Okay. But you're going to hunt *game*," I said. "Don't pick a cow or goat or some tame dinosaur off the Volod's land. Challenge yourself. And stay in touch with me while you're out, okay? I'm worried the Freak Squad's still hanging around."

"I'll hunt where I please. You can have opinions about humans, but you leave being a dragon to me." Karalti tossed her head impetuously and dove off the side of the castle like a kingfisher before she swept into the air: lean, hungry, and terribly, defiantly young

Chapter 4

About ten minutes later, the five of us – me, Suri, Rin, Ebisa and Ignas – were gathered around a great mahogany table in the Royal War Room. The room was still laid out for the meeting he'd had with his advisors earlier in the day, and there were two maps to consider. The first was a huge seven-by-nine-foot map of Vlachia, which hung on the far wall behind Ignas' royal seat and was marked up with twine and pins. The other was the three-dimensional map of Mysznо on the table in front of us.

I'd quickly realized two things. The first was that Vlachia was frickin' enormous: a million square kilometers of forbidding mountains, frigid taiga, dry steppe and desert. Despite these variations in terrain, nationality and language, it had just twelve provinces. A late-Medieval nation of this size and cohesion couldn't have existed in the real world, but Vlachia had one thing Earth hadn't obtained until the 1940s: air power. The territory had been forged by dragons, and was now maintained by airships.

The second thing I noticed about the situation was that we'd seriously underestimated our vampire problem.

The province of Myszno took up about a tenth of Vlachia's total area, contained within a weird-looking ring of mountains. These mountains were extreme in terms of both height and climate, but that hadn't stopped the vampire's army from marching through a narrow, treacherous pass across the border from the south. Three months later, and they'd gone and turned the south-western corridor into a 2500-square-mile goat rodeo, taking over four counties and putting them to the sword. Those counties were some of the most heavily settled regions in the province. Hundreds of thousands of lives had been lost, with every viable corpse reanimated and added to the ranks of the undead. It was a Clusterfuck. Capital C, capital Fuck.

The others in the room seemed to have reached the same conclusion. Rin was staring at the diorama with a confused, wandering expression. Suri worried her bottom lip with her teeth, frowning as she considered the field of purple toothpick ribbons marking out where the horde had overrun the province. Ebisa waited behind her mask, as silent and grim as a graveyard angel. Ignas sipped a glass of amber beer and waited expectantly for our opinions.

Finally, I gestured at the map and slumped back in my chair. "Well, Your Majesty... with all due respect, on a scale of One to Fucked, Myszno is bent over a barrel and Big Dick Bubba is standing right behind it with a can-do attitude and a big ol' can of goose grease."

"Eww." Rin wrinkled her nose.

"How evocative," Ebisa rasped.

Suri let go of her lip and shook her head. "Hector's right; this is a bloody nightmare. Tactically speaking, this isn't just an upstart incursion. This is a war scenario."

War. Now that I'd spent five years fighting, the word always hit me like a sharp jab to the gut. I never wanted to go back to war, not even in my dreams. Not even in a game.

Ignas nodded to Suri's words. Despite his bravado in the Parade Ground, it was clear now that the confrontation had taken a toll on him. He still had the air of tough, observant confidence I'd come to expect from him, but his eyes were sunken, the lines around them deeper.

"My thoughts exactly," he said heavily. "I commissioned a report on my Coronation Day, which we received this morning. By the way the ministers were talking about this issue, I expected that we'd lost perhaps two hundred miles of territory to this creature. But no." He gestured angrily at the fan of corruption radiating up from the south. "Four counties overrun, over a hundred and fifty villages put to the sword. The Voivode and his entire House are dead or worse, the ducal castle taken... and the whole time, my worthless excuse for a brother sat on his hands. The only reason the Demon hasn't overrun Litvy and broken out through Vastil Pass into the mainland is because of the Prezyemi Line and the Endlar... and how long can we hold *that*?"

The Endlar Wilderness was a massive swathe of swampland and forest, unmapped and uncharted. The Prezyemi Line was the huge wall that faced the Endlar's northern edge, separating the low-land Racsa County – the ducal seat – from the highlands of Vastil County.

"Looks like it. Question is, why is this vampire invading Myszno on the sly like this? What do we know about him?" Suri folded her arms loosely across her chest, scowling in thought.

"We know almost nothing, not even his name," Ignas replied heavily. "What we *do* know is that wherever he goes, horror follows. Entire villages and towns are being wiped out. Eyewitnesses say that as the undead pursued those who fled, some ran straight into rivers or lakes and drowned themselves in their panic. Others escaped into the wilderness only to starve. They'd rather be at the mercy of the allosaurus and *Kileskus* than this creature, who they simply call 'the Demon'. He is from Napath, one of the Shalid countries. We share a border to the south."

Suri grunted. "Napath, huh? That explains a lot."

I bought up my HUD and telekinetically skimmed through the virtual interface to my Archemi databank. "I don't have anything on Napath in my wiki, other than a basic map."

"In Dakhdir, we call it *Adu Alonwaa*, the Land of the Dead. All the citizens are undead of some kind or another. The only living people there are slaves." Suri tapped the southernmost range of mountains. "Some friends of mine said it's ruled by a council of really fuckin' old archmages... old as in, when they were born, the Shalid was still a jungle and the place was ruled by Meewfolk."

Rin nodded. "The Council of the Breathless. Liches and vampires."

I looked up at her from my chair. "Aggressive?"

"No. Not until now." Ignas frowned down at the map. "Lady Suri and Lady Rin speak true. The rulers of Napath are undead necromancers, and their people worship them as gods. The majority of Napath's citizens are vampiric."

"Huh." I nodded. "Could Fangs-a-Lot be a lord from this council?"

The Volod made a go-around sign with one long, sword-callused hand: a distinctly Vlachian gesture that I'd come to recognize as being like a shrug. "He's powerful enough that we have considered it a possibility, but we do not know. Napath is excellent at keeping secrets. All the court bureaucrats are vampire thralls bound in service to their progenitors. They are functionally incapable of leaking information, even if they wished to."

"If he's an exiled Breathless council mage, that's bad news," Suri said. "What's the total estimated figure of his army?"

Ignas winced. "He started with a mere six thousand troops from his native land. But after destroying so many villages and towns, and now the fall of Karhad, his 'army' has swelled to over sixty thousand corpses."

"How many people live in Myszno?" I asked.

"As of last census, a little over two million, including foreigners. But that doesn't include some of the native peoples and nomads." Ignas reached out to touch the miniatures showing Egbolt Castle and the fallen city of Karhad. "According to Captain Istvan Demir, the Demon marched over the mountains with a small force of animated skeletons. They decimated villages in the dead of night, slaughtering everyone and everything in their path. Villages and towns in the highlands are often isolated by distance. The Demon butchered the inhabitants in the dark and moved to the next settlement. The army grows with every person they kill. Almost every fallen man, woman and beast is... repurposed."

"Necromancer's code," I muttered. "'Reduce, Reuse, Reanimate."

"The army then massed in the mountains and poured out to take strategic positions in the highlands," Suri mused. "Now they're pushing through the Endlar to the north."

"Precisely," Ignas said. "Until now, we never had any reason to worry about Napath. We have been peaceful neighbors since the Age of Dragons."

"Then something's fucky, for sure." I scanned the table. "There's a village in Myszno named 'Myszno' as well, right? Do you happen to know where it is, and if it's near a landmark called the 'Thunderstones'?"

"I've heard stories of them, but no specifics," Ignas said. "But I know someone who might. Masterhealer Masha hails from that province. She is Churvi, from the area where the village of Myszno lies."

"She's what?" I asked.

"Myszno, like the rest of Vlachia, is something of a melting pot. We're in the very heart of Artana, and there are many peoples and some two hundred languages spoken across the land. The Churvi are native to Myszno. They bear a strong resemblance to your own people, the Tuun, and I believe their pagan religion shares some commonalities. There is actually a small expatriate community of Tuun who live among them. I recommend you learn all you can from her."

I scratched my jaw. "Andrik mentioned that there were Tuun there to me once."

Ebisa, who had been leaning indolently against the edge of the table, suddenly spoke up. "Sire, I must wonder: where is this Demon finding the mana to fuel this invasion? Just the expeditionary force would have required huge quantities of it. Now he's up to thirty thousand head... he has to be getting that magic from somewhere."

"That is a question we don't have the answer to." Ignas jerked his chin up as he stood away from the table and began to pace. "Myszno used to be a great producer of mana, but the mines of the south dried up centuries ago. The remaining mines are in the north-eastern highlands, in the mountains that shelter Boros. They aren't getting it from there."

Rin raised her hand, glancing timidly at Ebisa before speaking. "They could be using *Ix'tamo*. Stardrinkers... they're Artifacts that can suck mana out of fertile land. Or..."

"Or?" Ignas regarded her with interest.

Rin glanced to Ebisa again. "Or... he's somehow gotten his hands on *sangheti'tak*."

Ebisa shuddered.

"What's that?" Suri asked.

"The greatest shame of our people." Rin was stimming with her hands, linking and unlinking her fingers. "War machines that consume living beings for their mana."

"What do they look like?" I asked.

Rin wouldn't meet my eyes as she fidgeted. Her gaze roamed aimlessly over the table as her voice became clipped and fussy. "There are roughly eight different classic forms of war magitech, but they can honestly be constructed to the specifications of the designer... some of them are like powered armor and are designed to be worn or ridden. Other forms are more like tanks, or drones, kind of. All *sangheti'tak* have a hybrid fuel system, using some elemental mana and drawing the rest from.. uhh... organic matter."

"Just say it," Ebisa said. "They eat people. Preferably alive."

Rin nodded. "Yes... they eat people. Kanzo was exiled because he refused to build *sangheti'tak*."

Ebisa folded her arms. "These machines are mostly used in the civil war on Zaunt, where mana is precious. The secrets of making them are very closely guarded by the great Houses. It is absolutely forbidden for them to be exported to *sang'hi*."

Rin bobbed her head. "I know that. But the rulers of Napath are old enough that they might still have *sangheti'tak* blueprints from the Drachan War. They could even have information on the Warsingers, now that I think about it..."

"We'll talk about that later," I said. "Let's stick to Old Fangface here."

"Right." Rin cleared her throat with a little 'hem hem'. "Well, even if the Demon is leeching mana out of the ground, resource management is a core weakness of necromancy and undead forces. The undead must be constantly replenished with magic, and the effort to raise and control an army of that size would have to be... umm... well, astronomical. If we could cut off his supply somehow..."

"I don't think leeching the magic out of farmland would cut it. The only way this vampire could be building an army that size is if there's liquid mana in Southern Myszno," Suri said sharply.

"Umm... okay. Sorry." Rin shrunk back into her seat.

Ebisa lay a hand on the girl's shoulder. Her masked face swiveled toward Suri. "Are you a mage?"

Suri scowled. "No, but-"

"Then Rin is the expert here." Ebisa squeezed the girl's arm. "Would you trust her opinion on combat? You are the expert on that matter. She is an expert on *this* subject."

Rin pressed her lips together, blushing deeply.

Suri sighed. "Fine, okay. Sorry."

I drew a deep, steadying breath. "How many men do we have stationed in the Prezyemi Line? How are they holding up?"

Ignas gave a short, bitter laugh. "Hah. There are about twenty thousand men who've stayed to fight, and probably the same number of deserters. But not only is the defense force outnumbered three to one, their own dead families are now shambling to the barricades and throwing themselves on their spear points. We can safely assume morale is low."

"What a bloody shitshow." Suri grimaced, scanning something in front of her as if she were reading. "'Extreme difficulty'. The quest description wasn't pulling any punches, was it?"

I shook my head. "Noooope."

"Okay, yes, it's a little overwhelming, but there's no reason to give up! Necromantic armies are really centralized." Rin stood. She was the only one smiling. "All we really have to do is take out the vampire general, and his army will just kind of... well... fall over."

"You say that," I replied. "But what really happens when you take out a leader in a war scenario is that their army fractures and splits off into lots of little enemies, not just one. You end up with insurgencies."

"Normally yes, but Rin's assessment – while simplistic – in fundamentally accurate in this particular case." Ebisa unfolded her arms to point at the castle marker in the center of the map. "All of the Demon's soldiers rely on his magic, his command, and his mana. Cutting those things away makes the undead return to death. So that is our objective – we find this vampire. We discover his weaknesses. We kill him."

"Again," I added.

Ebisa snorted.

"That seems the best plan of action. Fortify the defense, then find and kill the source." Ignas heaved a deep sigh. "But there is a problem. Our Ilian friends."

Rin, Suri and I all winced at the same time.

"Before their visit, I'd planned to send the entire 4th Fleet to Myszno. Six battlecruisers, ten corvettes, seven legions of troops." Ignas rubbed his eyes and the bridge of his nose. "But now, we can't spare them. Despite my cavalier words, the fact that Ilia has come under the rule of a

Starborn who is already styling himself an Emperor is a threat we cannot underestimate. The Knights of St. Grigori alone are a severe challenge for even the most well-equipped army. I'm going to have to go back through our records to see how prior kings handled armies capable of fielding dragons, but I can already tell you that depleting a quarter of our Navy would be a terrible mistake. I will discuss the matter with my advisors and see how many men we can spare."

"Right. Well, nothing we can do about it." I remembered the 17 EXP I needed to level up just then, and the corner of my eye jumped.

Ignas returned to his seat, his long face drawn with worry and fatigue. "Suri, Hector, I will receive you in the Writing Room after the Dark Moon festival tonight. But please, brace yourselves for bad news. I don't know how much support I can offer you now, and whatever we have, I fear it will not be nearly enough."

Chapter 5

Suri, Rin and I all breathed a sigh of relief once we were out of the War Room and back out under a blissfully dragon-free sky. When I touched Karalti's mind, I got a flash of what she was up to. She was hunting.

"Mysζno's shaping up to be a hell of a party," I remarked. "We better bring a case of beer. Maybe some snacks."

"There isn't enough beer in the world for this." Suri ran her fingers through her hair, chest lifting in a way that caught my eye. "But speaking of getting shit-faced, what's the plan for tonight? Rin?"

"Oh! I was going to go to the University and do some research for the quest and for my crafting, you know." The little Mercurion was suddenly much more chipper. "Ebisa and I are finishing up some tinkering, too. And tonight's the Dark Moon Festival, so I guess we'll be going shopping. The Church has mana auctions where Mage-classes can stock up for cheap..."

"What is the Dark Moon Festival, anyway?" I reached out to Suri as if I would put my arm around her waist. She stepped into the offered embrace with a sultry quirk of the lips and a sidelong glance that made my heart skip.

Oblivious, Rin clasped her hands and bounced up and down with excitement. "Twice a year on the equinoxes, Erruku and Archemi line up in front of the sun and the moon goes dark. Well, I guess it's not really the moon, because *we're* actually the moon, but you get what I mean, right?"

"I'd wondered." I scratched my jaw. "Erruku kind of weirds me out, to tell you the truth. I don't think the physics of this planet are totally realistic."

Rin twittered an anxious little laugh. "Probably. We took artistic license with some things. The eclipse thing looks really cool and I-I think Erruku even has some of its own lore, but we were scheduled to get some astrophysicists to play-test and advise us on refining the skybox-"

"The what?" Suri squinted at her.

"The, uhh... the... planetary mechanics?" Rin flashed her a fleeting, nervous smile. "We, I mean, the Devs... we...uhh... don't worry about it, okay?"

Suri cocked her head, a red curl tumbling over one of her eyes. "You guys are serious, aren't you? About the whole 'the world is a game thing'? You aren't having me on?"

Rin bit her lip. "I'm sorry, Suri. It's true."

"Well if that's true and you're really an Architect, can't you just get up into your God Box or whatever it is and go and crush this cunt in Ilia like a cockroach?" Suri asked her. "Because that'd make our lives a whole lot easier."

Rin was looking more stressed by the second. "The... uhh... short answer is that I never had that kind of admin access, and that Ororgael isn't supposed to be able to do what he's doing, either. It's complicated. I-I don't have any more power than a normal player. Person. Starborn player-person."

The larger woman shrugged. "One day, I'm gonna pin you down and ask you some hard questions. But not now, because this bitch is going shopping."

I chuckled. "What's on the menu today? Shoes? Bags?"

"Armor, you dick." She bumped me with her hip, grinning broadly. "And maybe something nice. I dunno if I want to buy any fancy clothes when we're going off to a war zone, though."

"Do it. It's good for morale." I gave her waist a one-armed squeeze. "When I went to war, I always made sure I had something at home I wanted to come back to. For me, that was my games, my motorcycle, and this photo album I got from my grandparents. And every now and then, when I had the chance, I'd order a package for myself online, you know? Like a new shirt or something. And I'd send that package to my best friend's house, so that when I came back alive, I'd have like a year's worth of presents waiting for me. It's a good mind trick."

Rin put her hands to her cheeks. "That's so sad but... also cute."

I shrugged, suddenly self-conscious. "Conscripts are like prisoners: you either find a reason to keep living or you die."

"It's good advice." Suri smiled mysteriously and turned in against my body. "On that note. Rin, do you mind just leaving me and Hector while you go do your thing?"

"Sure." Rin's eyes were shining. "You guys... um... have... fun?"

"Hell yeah," I said. "We're gonna get our faces painted, and get our nails done together-"

Suri kneed me in the thigh. I snortled at my own bullshit.

When the Mercurion was back inside the Keep and we were alone, I spun Suri around and dipped her in my arms. She laughed, and when she came up, she looped strong arms around my neck and looked up at me. "Hi."

"Hi." Her eyes were a brilliant golden yellow, veins of color slowly folding in toward her pupils like slow-moving magma. "Have I... ever told you how gorgeous you are?"

Her smile turned a little shy. "Yeah, now and then. Still like to hear it, though."

My mouth was dry, pulse hammering under my tongue. Sometimes, I felt confident with her, leading the way in our conversations, our lovemaking. Other times, I could hardly believe this glorious Amazon of a woman actually wanted me near her, let alone have me hold her like this. But here she was. "Well, that's good. I can dish out as much as you can take."

"We'll see about that." Suri sucked her bottom lip under her teeth. "Guess tonight's our last night off, huh?"

"Uh-huh."

"Might be the last chance we have to sleep in a proper bed, too." She pulled herself in close, and rubbed her cheek along mine until she could speak against my ear. "I hear the Dark Moon Festival has an awesome Night Market. Wanna go with me?"

Stupid as it sounds, my first thought was my character sheet – and Karalti's. If we worked hard tonight, we could probably hit Level 18 and 10, respectively. Still not enough... but better than where we were now. I winced.

"I really *want* to go," I said haltingly. "But after that meeting... I can't. I'm sorry. You're Level 20 already, but we've still got to catch up before Myszno."

Suri didn't pull away, but I could sense her disappointment. She planted a lingering kiss on my cheek. "I get it. No worries: we'll have another chance some time. So... what's on the agenda for tonight, then?"

I sighed, guilt tightening my chest. "Well, honestly, I was going to go to the hospital and ask Masha about Myszno, then see about learning Vlachian and Churvi. I want to level up my healing skills until Karalti gets done stuffing her face. That, and I need to see how Rutha's doing."

Suri cocked her head curiously. "The Lys woman. Yeah... I was wondering how she was, actually. How do you know her?"

"She's..." I trailed off, not sure how to respond. With most women, I'd have been on thin ice, especially after saying no to a date. But Suri didn't seem like that kind of person. There was no hostility in the inquiry. No edge to it.

"Rutha was the woman who helped me escape that slave ship I told you about," I admitted. "You know, the one I landed on when I first incarnated into Archemi? We helped each other out, and she gave me the Spear. We... ahh... had a two-night stand while we were in Liren. Nothing serious, but it was my first time and... I mean, we're just friends now, but uhh-"

Suri rested her finger against my lips, cutting off the babbling. "That's all I need to know. When you go and see her, say hi from me. Tell her I look forward to meeting her when she wakes up. Tell her she's got people on her side."

"Really?" I blinked a couple of times. "You aren't... like... mad?"

"I'm mad this Baldr cunt beat the shit out of a woman and used her as a hostage to make a point, sure."

"Yeah." The rage I'd felt on the parade ground was still trembling in my stomach and in the muscles of my jaws. "Me too. I was just worried you'd be..."

A small smile quirked the corner of her mouth. "Jealous?"

"Yeah." I rubbed the back of my neck.

Her smile spread, but this time, it was strangely bittersweet. "I had a lot of time to think in Al-Asad. You know what I realized one day? 'Evil' is 'Live' backwards. Whoever hurt that woman is evil. You and me, we both know what evil looks like. Real evil."

I nodded, taking her hands in mine. "Yeah. We do."

She squeezed back. "Whatever you had or have with Rutha, that's a living thing. It's the opposite of evil. How can anyone be jealous of that? So you tell her that we've got her back, and one day, we'll kill the mongrel who hurt her."

Suri and I parted with a long, lingering kiss that left the taste of honey on my lips. I walked to the hospital with a little skip in my step, humming as I let myself inside. The Master Healer was at the triage counter, tending to a giant ox of a man with a grossly swollen hand. The air was thick with the scent of bitter herbs, old leather, and rubbing alcohol.

Masterhealer Masha was three days older than dirt and tougher than boiled leather, with the kind of jaded wisdom gained through living through the rule of three kings and not only surviving, but keeping her tenure. She had an underbite, hard steely eyes, and wisps of gray hair pulled back in a brightly colored scarf. The tiny old woman had to stand on a stepstool to mix potions, pounding a pestle into a bowl of herbs like it owed her money.

"Ah, well, look who it is. His new lordship, Count Tuun." She spoke in a heavy accent and didn't glance up from her work as I padded over. "I heard you helped His Majesty fend off those dragons before, eh? Good work. Now, go over there and tell me what you think of this *hooyeh's* injury before he dies."

"No, Master Healer, I beg you. Don't let me die." The man panted. He was bright red and soaked in sweat, squirming in his armchair with discomfort. "I-I have a family!"

The old woman turned on him. "I know you have a family, you dolt! I delivered your son. I've had my hands further up your wife's *piztar* than you have."

I couldn't help but smile. In a world full of characters, Masha was a standout.

"You're supposed to go to the doctor before you're on death's door, man. What did you do to yourself?" I asked him.

"It was just a scratch on a nail in the stables," he moaned. "I didn't think anything of it until now. Please, give me water."

"No, no, no, don't give him any water yet. He'll bloat up like a dead fish and his blood will boil with fever." Masha shook her head irritably. "Medicines first, then water."

I went to examine the stablehand's infection. He looked like he was wearing a big red baseball mitt. "Staph infection, right? That's a... sanguine disease?"

"Correct. A sanguine disease from the feces of the hookwings in the stables. Do you remember the difference between sanguine and choleric diseases?"

"Sanguine is hot and... moist? Sanguine diseases are things like blood poisoning or liver failure. Choleric diseases are hot and dry, and attack the skin and muscles, right?"

Ting. My HUD chimed as I gained a small amount of Skill EXP toward Field Medicine. Masha nodded. “Correct. You’re smarter than you look. Now, take his temperature.”

I unequipped my right gauntlet and put a hand to his forehead. Assessing temperature through touch was a Level 1 Field Medicine ability. I was at Level 3 now, so I got an auto-success. “He’s burning up. That’s got to be at least a hundred and five degrees. He’s at risk of organ failure.”

He whimpered. “Khors have mercy.”

“If the gods had mercy, there’d be no need for doctors.” Masha stirred in clear alcohol, the smell stinging my nose from across the room. “This fever is not so good. Give me a moment.”

I knelt next to the man’s chair, and soon enough the healer came bustling over with a poultice and three bottles of potion: one yellow, one green, and one blue. The blue potion emitted a faint glow. She set the alchemical brew aside, and uncorked the herbal medicines. “Now, what do we do first?”

“Lance the abscess and drain the wound,” I said. “Then the yellow po... "

"No!" Masha slapped her hand on the counter. "Wrong!"

"Oh, right. Sanguine’s hot and moist, so you have to... dry it out and cool it down," I said. "So we lance and apply alcohol to dry it, then the poultice to cool it, *then* give him the potions. And water after that?"

“Correct. You do not want to give a man fluids for a sanguine condition. This is a Concentrated Oil of Garlic poultice. It will remove the Blood Poisoning status effect." Masha took a clean scalpel from her apron pocket, dunked it in a small vial of alcohol, and swirled it around. "You need garlic oil, red rashovik, and activated charcoal to make it. You simmer the rashovik in the oil until it turns bright scarlet, then add the charcoal. Mix, wrap, drain the wound, then apply it straight on."

⟦New Herbalism recipe learned! Concentrated Oil of Garlic poultice⟧

Archemi didn't have any healing magic – at least, not healing magic that was available to players. Instead, it had a comprehensive medical crafting system comprised of four interrelated skills: Field Medicine, Surgery, Herbalism and Alchemy. Herbal potions could restore HP, cure common debuffs, or give buffs, and they were safe to use on NPCs. Alchemical potions contained mana, monster parts, and other magical ingredients. They could heal critical injuries, regrow limbs, raise the dead or create mutant dragon riding smartasses like me, but most normal people – read, NPCs – couldn't consume alchemical potions without a risk of being fatally poisoned. The four healing skills were closely interlinked. You had to sometimes perform a surgery, then apply a potion. Properly diagnosing a patient using Field Medicine made them more likely to survive surgery and/or an alchemical healing process. Scientific advances in the field were possible, and were rewarded by the game. I'd never considered a medical career in the real world, but Archemi made it kind of fun, in a survival crafting-kinda way.

I watched as Masha dabbed a sticky white substance onto the man's hand, waited a few seconds, then began to cut into the numbed flesh. The stablehand lay there, sweating and squirming as she squeezed pus from the infected area. I watched her flawlessly play the required minigame, following a series of holographic directions that showed her what to squeeze and when. Once she cleared it, she applied the poultice. A Status meter appeared, counting down from 60 seconds. At the end of the minute, his Blood Poisoning debuff vanished.

"Now we give the potions. This is Goldenseal Tincture. It cures fever." She swirled the yellow bottle around, then put it to the man's lips. "Drink it, and no whining."

I glanced down at the other two. "What's that alchemical potion?"

"That is Bloodmoon Decoction." Masha held the man's head as he grimaced and sputtered. "If our hard worker here turns up his heels and dies, I'll pour that one down his neck. It restarts the heart, purges blood clots and fluids from the lungs and brain... but it's dangerous, like all alchemical medicine. If it doesn't Strange the person drinking it, it will blind them. One hundred percent. All the blood vessels in the eyes burst and turns their eyes red. You can always tell someone who drank Bloodmoon and lived to tell the tale."

Her patient shuddered. "I'd rather die, Master Healer."

"You were begging for your life just a few minutes ago! So which is it? And before you tell me a life without eyes is no life at all, what about your children?" Masha scolded. "The Volod will give your family a pension whether or not you're alive, but your son will prefer a blind father than no father at all."

I sat back and watched them bicker, but as the stablehand's status effects ticked down and then vanished, he got noticeably better. His fever broke, and then his hand began to look less critical.

"Alright. You take this second Goldenseal Tincture before you go to bed. Yes, it's bitter, but you must drink it all." Masha helped him sit up once the second-to-last debuff vanished. "If you don't, the Blood Poisoning will come back, and we'll have to do this all over again."

"Yes, Master Healer."

"You come back tomorrow for more medicine, or I'll send Stanislaw to pull you in by the ear. You're not Starborn like this strapping Tuun here. You need more than one day's course."

The man grimaced. "Yes, Master Healer."

When he was sent off, Masha went to go and wash her hands. When she returned, the old woman regarded me shrewdly.

"How's Rutha?" I asked her.

"Not good. Not at all." She shook her head, rubbing her hands with a clean towel. "Her skull has a fracture, and the join is still soft. She has dried blood in her nose and ears, which may mean there is damage to her brain. There is no miracle cure for brain damage, I'm afraid. She may awaken tomorrow, or she may awaken in a month, or she may never wake up. I hate to say it, but she is now in the hands of the gods."

I looked away for a moment. "Can I see her?"

"I want the medicines I gave her to settle in her blood before I let any visitors in," Masha replied. "But that will not take long. You can stay here, keep yourself busy."

"Actually, Ignas recommended I see you," I replied. "He said that you could tell me about Myszno. And I was wondering if you could teach me Vlachian, maybe Churvi as well."

The old woman cocked her head with birdlike curiosity. "Churvi? Why would you want to learn that?"

"I want to fit in." I shrugged. "Also, I have a hunch that my honorary noble title might become less honorary, more practical."

"Hmmph. A Tuun turning to landed gentry? Even with your dragon and your fancy spear, that would not go down very well with the other great houses of Myszno. But my people... if you show an interest in our ways and honor the borders of our lands, that might be a different story. Yes, I can teach you Churvi - *Khel Khammun*, as it's properly called. I can teach you Vlachian as well, and it is wise that you ask to learn from me. The Vlachian spoken in the East is a different dialect from the capitol. They do not speak your White Sail Alliance pidgin there, either: you must be fluent. People in the big city will think you sound rural, but the inhabitants of Myszno will take to you faster if you sound like a local."

"Figured that might be the case. I don't give a shit what people here think." I bought up my character sheet to check my available skill points. After my last level, I had four remaining. "How many points do I need?"

"Three for basic fluency in Churvi. You already know some Vlachian, so you only need two points to become fluent in that tongue."

I winced. "Damn. Only have four."

Masha thought for a few moments. "Then I can teach you enough Churvi to survive, and you can learn the rest while you are there. Once you have a start in a language, you can invest a point here, a point there... by practicing it, you will also improve without the need to invest points – though that takes more work. Of the two, I dare say that Vlachian is more important."

"Yeah, it is." I nodded. "Official language and everything."

Masha gave a curt nod, and a prompt jumped in the corner of my eye. I pulled it over, and a holographic trade screen appeared between us. Before I could make my selections, I got a tutorial prompt.

[[Do you wish to learn more about Language Skills and Abilities?]]

"Yes," I thought back.

The prompt unraveled into a tutorial pane, which my HUD narrator read to me:

Languages in Archemi

Archemi is a diverse place, with several major sapient species and hundreds of organically generated regional languages and cultures within the five basic playable races: Artanese Humans, Dauntan Humans, Lysian elves, Meewfolk and Mercurions. To learn a new language or dialect in Archemi, you must spend skill points to gain initial fluency, and from that point, you must study and practice speaking, reading and writing your new language to gain mastery.

The skill point cost and practice time is automatically calculated on the difficulty of the language relative to your intelligence score and the languages you already know. You can often spend fewer skill points if you are willing to put in more time practicing. If you urgently need a language to complete a quest or travel to a different country, you can spend more skill points to gain fluency more quickly. If you love to study and learn without spending any points, you can do that too!

Language acquisition using skill points is faster, anywhere between one to ten minutes. You may experience a brief sensation of dizziness and a warm feeling in your temples as Archemi's GNOSIS system uploads the language and primes your brain to be able to speak. As this is the Beta testing phase of Archemi Online, you should report any adverse symptoms to your supervisor. Revisit our Health and Wellness TOC for more information on GNOSIS.

I frowned. That was weird. None of the other skills I'd learned, or my fantasy combat abilities had needed a disclaimer. "Can you hold on for a moment?"

Masha shrugged, and waited while I PM'd Rin. "Hey, sorry to interrupt you, Admin Girl, but why is there a TOS health advisory for learning new languages via skill points?"

"Oh, it's nothing to worry about," Rin replied absently. "There were some problems with language processing during alpha testing. I guess the company lawyers made us include it."

"What... kind of problems?"

"Scrambled speech, mostly. People would mix up the fictional languages with their native tongues when they were offline. That was during the civilian game testing phase, mind you. As it turns out, uploading linguistic fluency to the brain is REALLY complex, but the Creative Design Board were adamant that we needed multiple languages for immersion and marketing down the track. You know... it gives players the feeling of being in a kind of club or tribe if they have a language only Archemi players can speak. I heard the military had a huge problem with memory loss in the early days."

"You mean like Suri?"

"I don't know. Maybe. Listen, I-I've got to go... I'm in the middle of crafting medicine packs for me and any other Mercurions in Myszno. Don't worry about the language stuff. You're safe: it was worked on a lot before the beta testing began."

"Right. Thanks." Not exactly reassuring, but I didn't have much choice: not if I really wanted to sort out the Myszno situation. Sighing, I waved the PM window aside, and selected my languages. "Vlachian first. Teach me the Myszno dialect."

Masha nodded, and then looked away with an expression of intense concentration on her face. A few seconds later, I got a prompt.

⟦Would you like to learn your new language: Vlachian (Eastern)?⟧

"Yup."

⟦Starting upload. Please close your eyes and minimize sensory interference during the transfer.⟧

It occurred to me then that the Ryuko Corporation might not have tested language acquisition on people who'd been perma-uploaded to the game, but there was no time to ask before the upload began.

Chapter 6

A powerful wave of dizziness swept over me, and then a sense of warm fullness pushed behind my eyes and against my temples from the inside. It wasn't painful, but it was definitely not comfortable... though it was kind of awesome, too, because I literally felt my mind begin to recall words I'd heard and make connections between them and the things they referred to. The knowledge poured in like hot sand, with every grain a word or a letter or a fraction of meaning. I wasn't sure if I was going to claw my face off or start gibbering in tongues by the time it finished, but sure enough... I could suddenly understand the murmured conversations in the hospital ward beyond the door.

"Damn." I shook my head and cracked my neck. "That's kind of nifty."

"Heh." Masha grunted her amusement. "If only we were all Starborn like you, eh? Ready for Churvi?"

"Hit me."

We repeated the process for the second language: money and skill points went in, and language came out. It seemed easier to learn than Vlachian, with less discomfort. Once the trade pane was closed, Masha gave me a shrewd look.

"Come," she said in her native tongue. "We should make the rounds of the hospital. You should be able to learn the skills of a healer while we wait for your lady to rouse. The guard will come out of her room when she wakes."

I heard her speaking the foreign tongue - a language that sounded a lot like Mongolian to me - but the words made sense. It wasn't an unfamiliar sensation. I'd grown up bilingual, speaking English in public and Korean at home, but learning a new language so quickly was definitely a new experience.

"Sure." I nodded. "Mind if I ask you about Myszno while we work?"

"Not at all. Few people here are interested in my homeland... it is refreshing to have someone ask." Masha gave me a sharp nod, gathering her tool bag. "Where to begin?"

"What are the Thunderstones?" I asked. "We can start there."

"Ahh..." she nodded, sweeping ahead into the ward. Seven patients waited for us. Rutha had been taken to a private room, guarded by a tattooed Knight of the Red Star outside. "The *krr'akhi.* No one knows what the Thunderstones are. They probably do not exist, except in stories and songs."

"Do you know any of them?" I tried to mask the desperation I was already starting to feel.

"Yes, of course." She huffed a little. "The most famous story is one you'll hear in taverns everywhere while you're in Myszno. It is the tale of Burna and Lahati."

That immediately piqued my curiosity. "Burna?"

"The Nightfather." Masha sketched a small gesture on her brow. "Here, he is known as-"

"Chernobog, or Matir," I finished. "Yeah, I know. His name is the same in *Tuun'haar*. We call him Burna as well."

"Interesting. But to return to the story." Masha sucked on her tooth for a moment, getting her words together. "Once long ago, the Solonkratsu were a learned and skillful people who built great palaces and cities across the world with the aid of their handmaidens, the Tulaq. There were many queens, but the greatest of them lived in Vlachia, and she ruled all the dragons from the crushing waves of the Black Sea in the east to the Bay of Swords where Taltos now stands. Her name was Lahati the White Frost, and she was quick and wise and beautiful, but so fierce that no other queen dragon could best her in combat. She was born white as snow, with horns and claws like polished diamonds, and eyes of black fire that could pierce a man's soul. She grew great and sleek and lovely, so swift that no dragon buck could so much as lay a claw on her no matter how hard and fast they flew."

"One day, Burna was walking the face of the world as a man, and he saw a brilliant light streak across the sky. It was Lahati, followed at a distance by many struggling dragons: her suitors. She winnowed the air like a swallow, forever out of their reach, and the god found himself fascinated. He shapeshifted into a great bull dragon with stars for eyes and scales as black as pitch, and took to the air to join the mating flight. He flew as fast and as high as he could, dashing other dragons out of the air in his lust. When Lahati heard their screams, she turned to see him closing on her."

"The great bull caught the queen in the air, and in the fury of their first coupling, the god turned Lahati's scales to obsidian, save for the white marks of his teeth on the back of her neck. The marks looked like the petals of a chrysanthemum, and so she assumed a new name and became Lahati the Chrysanthemum Queen. She was the beloved mate of the Nightfather for all her days, and when she died, he wept for a day and an age. Not even the Prince of a Thousand Names could call his beloved back to life when the Lord of Time came to take her to the grave. Wherever Burna pounded the earth in his grief, great craters appeared. Wherever he drew his claws, valleys and canyons were made. He wandered east, and he reached the Black Sea, he went to his knees by the ocean and screamed Lahati's true name, the Words only he knew. The peaceful water turned furious and black, and there where he knelt, the Thunderstones erupted from the earth. It is said this is why the Black Sea is so incredibly fierce, and why the Dark God no longer walks with us as man or dragon, for he cannot bear to live without his queen by his side."

While she spoke, the Mark prickled on the back of my hand. I felt a strange longing, and almost reflexively checked my telepathic link with Karalti. She was outside, warm and comfortable. Sleeping, probably. "Huh."

"That is all I know of the Thunderstones. If you want older stories, you will have to visit the shamans or the monks. That could be why you wish to go to the village of Myszno, hmm? There is a Tuun monastery there."

A monastery? "How do you get to Myszno Village from Vastil Pass?"

"Well, you fly to Vyeshniki, then cross the Sarviz River and head south, into the highlands. Unfortunately, that is all I know... and the land has probably changed a lot since I was a girl." The old woman shook her head. "Now, here: I'll give you the recipe for Concentrated Green Moss Tincture, and you go and prepare it for me. Then you may ask another question."

I couldn't help but smile. "Sure."

Getting a simple recipe uploaded to my memory was nowhere near as intense as learning a language: a prompt, a pause, and then 'ting', I knew a new recipe:

Concentrated Green Moss Tincture (Herbal)

Heals 150 HP over 120 seconds
Requires: *Green Moss x 3, Lye x 1, Aqua Regia x 1 (Hydrochloric Acid x 3, Nitric Acid x 1), Pure Alcohol x 1, Bottle.*
Sell Price: *30 rubles (silver)*

While Masha worked, I mixed the Aqua Regia, then mashed the moss and added it to the powerful acid, dissolving it.

Once the thick green sludge turned yellow, I added the lye – carefully – and let it froth and bubble until the liquid settled and it turned a bright lime green. Then I sieved it into a pot, added the alcohol, and transferred the liquid to three bottles. For my efforts, I got 5 Skill EXP toward Herbalism.

"Okay. Do you need anything else?" She asked.

"If you're able to, tell me about the city that fell to the Demon," I said. "And about the different counties?"

"Hmm." Masha scowled thoughtfully as she administered one of the potions to a semi-conscious man with a badly broken leg. "Well, Myszno has only three cities of any size. They are Karhad in the south, Litvy to the north-west, and Boros to the far north. Karhad is the Ducal seat, where the House of Bolza reigns. It was the capital of Myszno long before it became part of Vlachia, a place of learning and industry. There are factories and mills, and many artisans live there. Lumber, metals, and mana are shipped from Boros to Karhad to be refined before they are sent back to Litvy, where they begin their journey west to Taltos. Here – thread this needle for me. My eyes aren't as good as they used to be."

I took the needle and catgut she held out to me and got to work. "Vastil is the wealthiest county, though?"

"Aye. And Litvy is the biggest city in the province now - ever since the House of Soma began building airships. It is a city of commerce, and the noble families there live by the scales, not the sword. Litvy also has a good school, and a sacred smithing college run by the Forge Brothers. When I was a girl, House Soma wasn't even nobility!"

That was an interesting piece of information. "How long ago was that?"

"Oh, about sixty, sixty-five years ago now. The House of Soma were mere merchants back then. Shipwrights and merchants. They manufactured airships for the Crown, which is how Orvel Soma gained his peerage. His grandson is now Count of Vastil, but I hear Lorenzo Soma is something of a boor."

"Huh. Good to know."

We spent about thirty minutes finishing up the rounds, and every time I helped Masha, the Skill EXP trickled in. When we were done, Masha beckoned to me and took me aside to her laboratory. There was an Alchemy table with a safe for storing mana, an herbalist table, and floor to ceiling dressers full of potion ingredients along the walls. It was clean and cozy, the herbal smell overlaid with a faint ozone scent – the odor of mana.

"You are leaving tomorrow morning, then?" She asked me, puffing as she climbed a step-stool and hauled a bag of tools from a shelf.

"Yeah." I watched her from the doorway. "Not much time to learn from you, unfortunately."

"It is unfortunate. I've never taught a Starborn before, but if they're all as quick as you, I'll be glad to see more of them in Taltos." She began to rifle through the bag, pulling out leather wrapped surgery tools, bandages, linen cloth... and then an old, battered pair of spell gloves.

"I... uh... thanks." I actually flushed. No one had ever described me as 'quick' before. "I'm not really that smart, though."

"Shush. I didn't ask your opinion, did I?" Masha motioned to me to come closer. "Now, you're going to want to prepare for the journey, hmm? I have a few things to give you. You may also use this oratory to work."

I drifted over as she pulled rolls of parchment out and laid them down beside the gloves. "Recipes?"

"Yes. Here: put them in your inventory. Practice those formulae, and you'll be ready for Journeyman level in Herbalism. I need a new valve for these spell gloves before you can use them, though. Wait here." She pushed the stack of papers over to me, then hopped down and bustled off to her alchemy table.

I uploaded the new recipes to my Inventory, and received a string of prompts:

[[You have learned new recipes: Starberry Salve, Goldenseal Tincture, Droptick Oil, Nightshade Solution (A), Bonefuse (A), Bull's Strength Potion (A)]]
[[Congratulations! You have reached Herbalism 11! You can now study Journeyman-level textbooks, brew more complex potions, and use better equipment!]]
[[Congratulations! You have unlocked Alchemy (Levels 4 – 10)]]
[[Your ability to understand Alchemy has increased! You have unlocked detailed recipes and instructions, including listed benefits and side-effects.]]

Hell yeah. I'd been stuck on Alchemy 4 - the limits of self-taught Alchemy - since before I'd left Ilia. While Masha fiddled with the gauntlets, I eagerly brought up one of the new recipes and had a look:

Bonefuse (Alchemical)

A phototoxic potion which instantly repairs broken bones.
Benefit: *Administering Bonefuse will cure any set and splinted fracture. You must straighten any broken bones before use.*
Side-Effects: *Bonefuse will cause the patient to be painfully allergic to sunlight for 2-5 days. Exposure to direct sunlight will inflict the Burn status and drain 20 HP damage per minute of exposure. The side-effect cannot be offset with other medicines.*
Toxicity: *5/10 (Risk of Stranging if used on NPCs: 50%)*
Ingredients: Comfrey x 2, Bergamot oil x 1, Mana (Any) x 1, Monster Saliva (Any), Bishop's Weed x 1, Distilled Water x 1, Sealed Flask.
Sell Price: *20 olbia (gold)*

Damn, Bonefuse wasn't fucking around. Curious, I went to examine one of the first Alchemical potions I'd ever made – my unused bottle of Barghest Serum. The murky glowing potion had been sitting in my inventory ever since I'd first brewed it, un-used. That was because its description HAD been a one-line warning: 'a deadly poison that allows you to see in the dark for 60 seconds.' Bringing up the item description now gave me an expanded breakdown, just like the Bonefuse recipe:

Barghest Serum

A deadly poison that allows you to see in the dark for 60 seconds.

Benefit: *Consuming Barghest Serum gives you perfect darkvision for one minute. You can see in lightless environments, and even underground. Barghest Serum can also be used to poison weapons. Wounds inflicted by weapons poisoned with Barghest Serum will glow with bright light for up to six hours.*

Side-Effects: *Barghest blood contains a potent toxin that drains HP. NPCs take 150 HP damage over 2 minutes after contact or consumption. Player characters take 100 HP damage over 2 minutes. Mercurions, Monsters, Dragons and Dragonforged characters take no damage from this poison.*

Toxicity: *7/10*

Ingredients: *Barghest liver x 1, Barghest Eye x 1, Eyebright x 2, Water x 1, Sealed Flask.*

"Here we go. There's a new valve on the left hand... very important to keep an eye on the durability of these things. You don't want your mana leaking everywhere." Masha rejoined me at the island counter in the center of the room and handed me the spell gloves. They weren't exactly new, and were made of brown leather, cloudy crystal, and old brass fittings.

⟦You got Old Alchemist's Spell Glove!⟧

"This is a good first glove. It can only process fractionated Green crystal Mana, but that's all a beginner really should be using," Masha said. "A Green Mana spill isn't likely to kill anyone. You'll be able to use better mana and better equipment as you gain more experience. You can start by making potions in my Alchemy laboratory, but you must buy the mana from me. I can't afford to just give it away."

"No worries," I replied. "And thanks. These will be really useful when we're stuck in Myszno."

"I hope so. I fear for Lord Bolza. When I was a girl, I remember seeing the lord's father in town once. The Bolzas, and all their green and silver knights and beautiful glossy hookwings... that spectacle was what made me want to come here and see the big city." Masha's eyes softened slightly as she spoke. "But that's enough of this old woman's rambling. You should go and see your sorceress. She may appear lifeless, but those in coma often benefit from kind touch and encouragement. Assume she can hear and will remember everything you say."

"I nodded. "Thank you. Is there anything you need me to do?"

"Eh, no. I am concerned about His Majesty's health." Masha sighed. "Ignas is under terrible strain, and for all that he is surrounded by people now, he is alone. No wife, no children, no one to share his worries and joys with. Caring for him and the sick here are all I can do. I'm too old to travel. If you wish to continue your studies, you will find tutors in Myszno. I recommend the School of Medicine in Karhad – that is where I trained. Rumor has it that the Baru, the Tuun monks, fight in the army alongside His Majesty's troops. If that's true, they will have even greater healing abilities than I. I'm sure your countrymen will be glad to receive you, given you bear the Black God's mark on your skin."

"Long story, but I don't think they will." I rubbed the back of my hand, feeling the Mark of Matir prickle and ache. "I... uhh... broke an oath to expose Andrik's plot against his brother."

"Then you must atone. But, the Baru are as merciful as they are fierce. That is the meaning of the knife you carry." She pointed at the slender, ice pick-like dagger hanging from my belt. "You are already on the path of the healer. Now you must live up to it."

"Thanks. And thanks for all of this help," I replied.

"It is my pleasure and my duty both." The Master Healer pressed her lips together in a thin line. "I have lived here in Taltos for many years now, but Myszno will always be my home. When I pass, I wish for my old bones to be taken back there and given a proper burial in the manner of the *Kel Khammut*. So please... do everything in your power to protect Myszno. Burna's flock of sacred flies await me in my homeland."

Even though I knew Rutha was unconscious, I tapped on her door before letting myself inside.

The second Knight of the Red Star who had been posted to keep watch over her looked up when I entered: a fierce-looking man in the red and black lamellar armor of his order.

His head was shaved except for a forelock at the front, and his cheeks were tattooed with lines of script that ran from just under his eyes to the edge of his goatee. He had a saber resting across his lap and a half-read book in his hand, and nodded to me as I crossed to Rutha's bedside. She was hooked up to a small magitech device. The core of the machine swelled with a blue-white glow. When the glow peaked, magical glyphs shone briefly on Rutha's skin, and she breathed in. When they faded, she breathed out. It was some kind of arcane iron lung.

"Hail, warrior," the knight said in Vlachian. I recognized him - it was Ur Lanso, one of the retainers often seen at court. "Do you need to be alone with the lady?"

"Yeah." I pulled up a seat so I could sit beside her. "Thanks."

Ur Lanso rose, bowed stiffly, and then left the two of us in the herb-scented hush of the room.

Rutha was an elf from my home continent of Daun. She'd always been a short, delicate woman, but weeks of torture had shrunk her. Her long ears were scabbed, and the skin of her face was stretched tightly over her jaw and cheekbones. Her lips were dry and cracked. Her short-cropped hair emphasized the thinness of her neck, the jut of her collarbones... and the poorly healed fracture there.

"My god." I pulled my gloves off, then cupped one of Rutha's hands in mine. They were thin and brittle, like bird's legs. "Those fucking bastards."

There was no response. Rutha's eyelids didn't even flicker, and because of their stillness, I noticed that she was missing her eyelashes. They had been scorched away. Frowning, I smoothed away a strand of hair from her face, then got some of the balm Masha had left beside her bed and smoothed it onto her lips, making sure they were well-coated. Despite what Masha had said, I didn't have much to say to her. After making sure her mouth wouldn't hurt, I checked her dressings and her IV, thinking until the words came.

"Whatever they told you, whatever they did to you... they were wrong," I said, haltingly. "I'm going to get them for what they've done, Rutha. To you, to me, to Karalti's mother, to their dragons, to the game. They're dead men walking. I'll find a way to delete them right the fuck out of Archemi. You've got people on your side out here. We're waiting for you, when you're ready to wake up."

I gave Rutha's limp hand a gentle squeeze and lay it back down on top of the covers. For a time, I just watched her, remembering her. The Rutha I'd met on the Arabella was fierce, dynamic, brilliantly intelligent. Matir had told me that she was part of Ororgael's plan to return to Archemi, and in my darker moments, I'd wondered if our brief love affair had been part of his plan all along... but looking at the damage done to her, it couldn't have been. Whoever had beaten the shit out of her was furious. They were angry, violent injuries inflicted by someone with a grudge.

"You just... you get better, okay? You need to meet Suri, and Ignas... and Rin and Karalti. We've all got your back. Suri made sure to ask me to tell you that." I bent down, and pressed a gentle, chaste kiss to Rutha's cold forehead. "We're going to a war tomorrow... but I'm going to try to get stronger. We'll come back for you. I promise."

The sorceress didn't stir as I left, her chest rising and falling in time with the machine beside her bed.

Chapter 7

My first stop after the hospital was the Keep's Outer Gate, where the Castellan lived and worked. He was happy to hear about the dead Glacier Toads. I got my EXP and silver, which I handed back. I told him to donate the 500 rubles to the families of the guards who had been lost during the battle between Andrik and Ignas. Because I gave the money back, I got 25 points of Renown instead. That popularity was going to be more important than money down the road.

By the time I reached my suite, I regretted not going to the Night Market with Suri. Karalti was still gone, and when I tried to reach out to her, there was nothing but the blankness of sleep. That left me stuck in Vulkan Keep with nothing to do except spend time with my worst enemy - my brain, which currently had a bad case of the 'it's not fair's'.

Baldr had taken over a kingdom and raised himself and his pet players to end-game levels in a few weeks. It sucked. A lot. I was hurting from how much it sucked. The old Hector, the Hector who had bluffed his way through life - bouncing bars, riding motorcycles, playing games and inhaling pizza - would have given up from that humiliating pain. There was no way to catch up with cheaters. There was no amount of work we could do, no legitimate effort we could make to honestly exceed them. But even as I paced, my inner drill sergeant was screaming: *"So what? So what if they're cheating? So what if Baldr-Ororgael is the best gamer who ever fucking walked the earth? What are you going to do about it, boot?"*

The new Hector had survived five years on the front lines of the Total War. My character upload had glitched and I'd survived anyway. There'd been no bunny slopes for me. No tutorials. The goddamn God of Darkness had chosen *me* to be his 'herald', whatever that meant. I... actually wasn't sure.

But yeah, *that* Hector, he was a Queen's Rider. A Kingmaker. A Kingslayer. There had to be something in me that was capable of beating these assholes, even if I still felt like I was just cruising my way through life. I wouldn't give into the urge to brood about cheating losers, or my missed date, or the fact my dragon wasn't talking to me. I was going to pick myself up by the bootstraps and brew some motherfucking potions.

After activating Blessing of the Raven - +10% to Skill EXP gain, thank you very much - I took a note from Masha's book and beat those herbs like I planned to beat Lucien's face: To a pulp. I rage-crafted Goldenseal Tinctures, Common Antidotes - basically just charcoal and purified water - and some other recipes I'd bought at the apothecary in town. To be an effective medic, you had to have treatments that aligned with the four humors: Sanguine, Choleric, Phlegmatic and Melancholic. I made healing potions that could treat diseases of each type. I made Concentrated Moss Tinctures for days. I made a couple of things out of mana and frog parts that I really wish I hadn't. Fortunately, my suite had big windows and the toxic smoke cleared out pretty fast.

[[Warning! You are dehydrated! -1 HP per 10 seconds]]
[[You have triggered Endurance!]]
[[You have reached Herbalism 15!]]
[[You have reached Alchemy 5!]]
[[Warning! You are famished! -1 HP per 10 seconds]]
[[You have reached Alchemy 6]]
[[You are exhausted! -10% to Skill Checks]]

The brewing and crafting was only an hour's work, but by the end, I was running on fumes. My Endurance ability was keeping me going, but it wasn't going to last forever. I got a drink and a small bite to eat from my Inventory before running a bath and settling down in the steaming water. Once I was settled in, I bought up my character sheet and had a look at what I had to work with.

Dragozin Hector - Dauntan (Tuun)

Level 17 Dark Dragoon

==Stats==

Strength: 45 (+10 bonus)

Dexterity: 51

Stamina: 35 (+5 bonus)

Will: 57

Wisdom: 27

Intelligence: 20

HP: 1362 (+300 bonus)

EXP: 12,173 (2792 to next level)

Adrenaline: 136

==Abilities==

=Racial=

Blessing of Burna: *+10% bonus to resist disease; +5% Stamina bonus to recover from illnesses. Immune to Pox and Lockjaw. +10% cold resistance. All physical needs accrue 2% slower.*

Plateau Native: *No Stamina penalties in thin air, -2 Stamina penalty at sea level.*

Saddle Born: *All Riding skills increase 5% faster.*

Sun-sight: *No vision penalties in bright or very bright light, -5% penalty in dark environments.*

Blessing of Tarn: *+15% movement speed.*

Blessing of Hrrun: *No airsickness, reduced inertia at high altitudes, no vertigo.*

=Traits=

Curiosity: *The player is an open-minded and engaged person, willing to question their modes of thinking and doing and* *readily accept new ideas. Combat, craft and class skills gain 5% more quickly.*

Introvert: *With a preference for their own company or small groups of loyal friends, the player gains a 5% bonus to accumulate skills in solitude provided they are not disturbed. Fatigue accumulates 10% faster in large groups and crowds outside of combat situations.*

Dyslexic: *The written word is something of a mystery to the player. Books take longer to read, and all language-related skills gain %5 slower.*

Natural Leader: *You have a natural inclination to take charge. Social skills increase +2% faster when engaged in leadership activities.*

Endurance: *You are accustomed to pushing yourself, even when you are exhausted. You may spend adrenaline to offset starvation, fatigue or bleeding for +1 minutes x your Stamina.*

Mark of Matir: *May convey special abilities at higher levels. When Mark is activated, drain health from enemies on a critical hit. HP regained is equal to remaining AP + Will bonus. 300 second cooldown. You are immune to undead fear effects. – 500 Infamy in places hostile to worship of Matir.*

=Dragonforged Abilities=

Mana Tolerance: *You have great resistance to Stranging and Mana Sickness, and may consume magical potions without permanent ill effects. Your toxicity threshold is now equal to your HP. See the Mana Tolerance ability entry for details and related skill and ability trees. Exceeding your Mana*

Threshold brings on symptoms of Mana Sickness and drains HP.

Eagle Eyes: *20/5 eyesight with enhanced spectrum, 340-degree visual field.*

G-force resistance 1: *You can remain conscious at up to 5 g of horizontal or vertical pressure.*

Stone Bones 1: *+10 resistance to crushing damage, 5 damage reduction.*

Deep Breather: *1.5x lung capacity.*

Iron Body 1: *You are largely immune to extremes of heat and cold. You can safely weather extremes between -20 and 120 degrees Fahrenheit.*

Gyroscopic orientation: *You cannot be disabled by extremes of motion. You are immune to disorientation and vertigo, and suffer no penalty to vision or concentration while spinning, falling, or while upside down.*

Blood Pact: *By undergoing the Rite of Marantha, you have become dependent on dragon blood to sustain your metabolism. Every week, you must consume at least one Dragon Blood Elixir to maintain your abilities. Failure to consume the potion will trigger the Starvation and Withdrawal statuses. All abilities gained through the Rite will become unavailable, and AP will regenerate 50% slower.*

Stranged: *The Rite has resulted in permanent mutations to your body which are visible and identifiable by some creatures. In places (or with people) where Stranged or magical beings have pariah status, you suffer a Severe penalty to all social interactions.*

==Combat Abilities==

Basic Weapons Training: *Passive -You are trained in the art of war, and fight unarmed and use all simple and martial hand-to-hand weapons without penalty. Does not include exotic weapons.*

Armor Mobility: *Passive - You are used to wearing armor and bearing heavy loads. +10 Defense in armor (L,M or H), no penalty to carrying.*

(New) Weapon Specialist: Polearms: *You have trained extensively in the use of polearms. You may use exotic polearms at no penalty; +10% damage with polearms.*

=Path Abilities=

Blood Sprint IV

Hit up to 10 targets, deal +250 bleeding damage over ten seconds, boost attack speed +20 for 10 seconds. Chains with Blood Storm.

> Blood Storm III

Strike up to 10 targets. 35 HP recovered on good hits. Can only be used after Blood Sprint.

>> Death by a Thousand Cuts II

Mark Targets with a curse that lowers their attack power by 4% per skill level, and increases your attack by 4% and Damage reduction by 10%. Percentages rise as you level the skill. Max 1 enemy target per skill level. Chained with Blood Storm.

Jump III
Spring 30ft into the air in any direction and deal x4 damage on landing.

> Obscuring Veil III
Chain combo from Jump. Deal a further x3 damage with a very high chance of dealing the Blindness debuff.

Umbra Burst III
Draw Dark energy from the air and emit a chilling burst of enervation that deals elemental damage and has a 25% chance to inflict the Frozen debuff.

Shattering Darkness III
An attack that freezes and cracks an enemy's natural or man-made armor. Reduces enemy DR by 15%.

Whirlwind Butcher II
Hit up to 12 targets and recover 10 AP on every good hit.

Shadow Dance II
Basic Evasive Dash reduces damage by 80% at the cost of HP (10 HP per dash).

Mantle of Night I
Boost movement speed and special attack power 20% for 10 seconds.

Plunge III

Your acquired resistance to g-forces has increased beyond the threshold granted by the Rite of Marantha, even if your head is above your feet. You are able to withstand 15 negative G's (5 per skill level).

Leap of Faith III

You gain the ability to better control your direction in the air if you fall off your mount, even when flying at high speeds. You experience time dilation of 3 seconds (1 second per skill level) while falling.

=Gifts of Matir=

(New) Shadow Lance: *Your weapon transforms into solid darkness. In a single strike, you deal bonus Dark damage equal to 75 x half your Will score. Your opponent gains the Blinded status (unless immune). Current damage: 2137.*

Blessing of the Raven: *You call on your power and gain increased insight into knowledge and skills. +10% Skill EXP for 45 min.*

Life for Life: Channel a blast of damaging dark energy into your enemy and drain their lifeforce to replenish your own. Inflicts Corruption debuff.

Spider Climb: You gain the ability to climb and travel vertical surfaces, crawl across ceilings, and hang on walls. Level this ability to extend duration. Duration: 20 seconds.

⟦You have unlocked a new combat ability: Master of Blades⟧

[[You have unlocked a new combat ability: Rain of Glass]]
[[You have 6 unspent Combat Ability Points!]]
[[You may choose one Gift of Matir]]

"Oh shit bro!" Excited, I navigated to the Ability menu to review my Combat Ability options first:

Master of Blades

Chain combo from Jump. Before you hit the ground, leap backwards into the air and manifest a rain of shadow lances onto your foes, dealing massive damage to enemies (1088 per lance, 2 lances per level, maximum two lances per enemy).

Rain of Glass

Chained from Hall of Mirrors. Twist acrobatically mid-air, unleashing a second blast of Dark energy shards down on a group of enemies. 1050 damage to 5 enemies. Damage and number of affected enemies increases when you level this skill.

I'd been saving my Ability Points during the grind so that I could spend them just before we went to Myszno, and now I was glad I'd waited. I did a rough calculation on the damage that Jump, Master of Blades III, and Rain of Glass I would do together. Times four from Jump on one target, then 2176 per two lances per target, *then* another 1050 each on the same target and four others... that came out to almost 4000 damage leveled on a single enemy at Level 17.

"Hooollly fuck." I rubbed my eyes and did the math again. Yup: 3966 damage to a single target, with damage in the thousands to everything else. And, if the critter I was smacking around was weak to Darkness, they'd take double on Rain of Glass. That was *insane.* Like... completely overpowered.

Naturally, I was tempted to dump all the points into those two new abilities, because with a little more math, I worked out that by Level VII – attainable at Level 35 – I'd be dealing five-digit damage. IN. SANE.

However, there were other abilities that were just as tempting. Umbra Blast was already awesome, and at Level IV it could effectively entangle, freeze, and damage ten enemies to the tune of 1500 Dark damage. Blood Storm, my old faithful, went up to 250% damage with 45 HP regained on good hits. If I hit between 10 and 15 targets – say, on a crowded battlefield – that was up to 675 HP regained from that one combo: about half my Max HP.

Of course, these abilities all had a cost: all those Darkness abilities were hungry for Adrenaline. The total cost for Master of Blades III to Rain of Glass I was 88 AP, which meant I didn't have enough Adrenaline Points to use the combo twice unless I somehow recharged those points. You could recharge AP by taking damage or by using moves that recharged AP. Whirlwind Butcher could recover 120 AP if I landed all twelve hits.

"How is Jump even legal?" I muttered, selecting my options. At Level 17, I could level my abilities to a maximum of four, so I spread my points out to select Jump IV, Whirlwind III, then Master of Blades III and Rain of Glass I. The Dark Dragoon class was basically AoE DPS – building it as a crowd controller played to its strengths.

Next up were the Mark of Matir abilities. I only ever got two choices for these, and they were never the same abilities. I couldn't just go back and select one of the ones previously offered to me, and I couldn't change the abilities once I'd selected them.

I felt a twinge in my gut as I opened that menu and reviewed Matir's offerings:

Purify (Life)

Cure or inoculate one target of your choice against any communicable disease. Does not work on diseases caused by curses.

Plague Lord (Entropy)

Infect any target of your choice with Filth Fever, a virulent Choleric disease which instantly debilitates and weakens targets with fever, muscle weakness, shaking and eventual death. Does not work on enemies resistant to disease. Inflicts Corruption debuff.

"Wow." My heart screamed 'Purify!', but my head said 'Plague Lord'. On the one hand, the ability to cure disease – any disease – was on my Top Five Magical Powers list. Being sick was the worst thing I could think of... which is why the idea of cursing Lucien with Filth Fever was seriously tempting. There was no cited level restriction, so resistance would be based on stamina. There was a problem, though. I still didn't know what the Corruption debuff was, because in all the times I'd used Life for Life, I'd never seen any meter or timer appear. I'd never *felt* anything.

I rubbed my chin, leaning back into the steaming hot water of the bathtub. But as I stared frowning at the menu hovering in front of me, I realized something. I called my character sheet to a second window, and reviewed the Gifts of Matir panel again:

=Gifts of Matir=

(New) Shadow Lance: *Your weapon transforms into a lance of solid darkness. In a single strike, you deal bonus Dark damage equal to 150 x half your Will score. Your opponent gains the Blinded status (unless immune). Consumes AP. Current damage: 2775. Cooldown: 60 seconds.*

Blessing of the Raven: *You call on your power and gain increased insight into knowledge and skills. +10% Skill EXP for 45 min.*

Life for Life: *Channel a blast of damaging dark energy into your enemy and drain their lifeforce to replenish your own. Inflicts Corruption debuff.*

Spider Climb: *You gain the ability to climb and travel vertical surfaces, crawl across ceilings, and hang on walls. Level this ability to extend duration. Duration: 20 seconds.*

"Umm." I blinked a couple of times. "What happened to Fury Drain?"

Fury Drain had been my first Mark ability. It was a relatively weak ability compared to Life for Life, draining 10 HP per second or minute of contact. I couldn't actually remember. But I knew I'd had it... but it was gone, and now, I had Shadow Lance. It was a sweet move, don't get me wrong... but I hadn't selected it.

A shiver ran through the muscles of my back. I had lost Fury Drain at some point... but when? When I'd last died, maybe? I'd had some weird, but temporary memory loss the last time I'd croaked it, forgetting Karalti's name, forgetting stuff about the quest I was doing. Had I forgotten a move, and had it replaced?

I stood up out of the water, letting it rush down my body, and waded out to get a towel and take a look at myself in the mirror. Same old Hector. The Trial of Marantha had given me literal eagle eyes, with no whites and oversized storm-blue pupils. Otherwise, I was looking pretty good for a dead guy. I only had three marks of any significance: a knotty scar inside my elbow, where the drugs given to mutate me were administered; the Mark of Matir, a nine-pointed chaos star-like symbol burned onto the back of my right hand; and an enduring legacy of my glitchy start to Archemi – a triangular patch of black nothingness on my left shoulder. It didn't hurt, but it didn't feel like skin... I couldn't feel anything with my fingertips when I touched it, but my fingers also couldn't go through it. Sometimes – like now – my mind tricked me into thinking it had gotten bigger.

"Fuck, man." I jerked my shoulders, suddenly creeped out. Then I went back into my HUD and selected Purify as my new ability. "Ugh. No Corruption anything, thanks."

With a towel wrapped around my waist, I went back out into my bedroom and plopped down cross-legged in front of the fire. The Spear lay on my bed alongside my pack, glimmering in the firelight. I turned to watch the flames dance and sighed. The warmth seemed to soak into my bones. It felt... nice.

⟦Warning: You have reached the limit of your Endurance!⟧

"Eh? Oh... first time that's everurrrgh-" The fact I was slurring by the time I reached the end of that sentence was the last thought I had before gravity pulled me down like a hand reaching up from the earth.

Chapter 8

I woke up to a solid pounding. On the door to my suite, that is.

"Hector!" Suri was on the other side, beating the door hard enough to rattle the solid oak in its frame. "Wake up, lover boy! It's time to go see the King!"

I whined against the rug under my face. "I don't wanna see the King."

"Too bad! Are you okay in there?"

"Uhhh..." I was flat on my back, stark naked, and lying on a damp towel. Irritable and slightly alarmed, I patted over myself, then sat up and swiped in my HUD. Yep, there was the *Unto Death* quest alert, which I'd slept through. It was after ten PM. "That's debatable. Is passing out naked and waking up five hours later 'okay'?"

"Oh, I see how it is. I go to the Festival all alone, while you whack off until you pass out from dehydration." Suri called back. "Not even going to invite me in, are you?"

"Not until I have pants!" I was already getting dressed, hopping around with my breeches until I remembered that I could just equip the damn things.

"Yeah. You need pants to go see the King."

I equipped some of my armor but left off the gauntlets and the visored helmet I used for flying. I slung the Spear over my back, shortened up the knotted cord that acted as a bandolier, and then I reached out to my dragon. *"Karalti? Are you okay?"*

"*Yeah.*" She sounded - and felt - grumpy. *"I suck at hunting."*

What's giving you trouble?"

"Everything! I can't do it!" she replied. *"I'm black and shiny and don't have any camouflage! I can't hide in the sun, so the animals see me coming and go into the caves!"*

"Okay. What about hunting them at night?"

"None of them are awake at night!"

I grimaced. Since gaining in size, Karalti had been 'hunting' by picking off herd beasts from the royal flocks. They were fenced in with nowhere to run, like a bovine smorgasbord. I was tempted to just tell her to go and pick off a cow or a ceratopsian, but it was important that she learned to hunt like an adult. *"Try thinking strategically, then. You can't change your scale color or the way your camouflage works. What about hunting just after sunset or just before dawn?"*

"But that's when I wanna sleep."

“*Karalti. You can't change what you are, okay? You have to work with what you've got. That means timing your naps, hunting when it's dark enough to hide, and working with the times your prey is out and about.*”

“*But...*” Karalti sounded positively dejected. “*I never had anyone to show me how to do this. Will you please come out with me and help?*”

Oh boy. I took a deep breath to steel myself. “*I can't.*”

“*Why not?*”

“*Because you have to figure this out. You* can *figure this out.*”

“*But I don't know how!*”

“*I just gave you some advice.*”

“*But you're not a dragon. You don't know unless you see what it's like!*” She was sounding increasingly like a surly teenager being told she had to do her math homework.

“*No, I'm not. But I am your human, so here's how I'm going to help you. Tell me what you want to eat.*”

“*Beef. The Volod's farm guys feed them beer! They're really tender and-*”

“*No. Tell me what* game *you want to eat.*”

She thought for a moment. “*Fine. I like sheep. Or goats. They're a good size. I'll be flying a lot tomorrow... I don't want to be too heavy.*”

“*There you go. Where do they live?*”

“*On the mountain.*”

"Okay, you know where they are. What can you do to find them?"

"Smell them, I guess," she muttered.

"Right. And they're habitual critters, right? They make trails and graze in regular spots?"

"No. But they go to these salty rock-places to lick the rocks when they wake up."

"And when do they wake up and come out of the caves? Dawn?"

She huffed. *"Fiiine! I'll camp near them! But they won't come out if I'm there!"*

"Try to stay downwind – that'll help. I'll see you after dawn tomorrow, okay?" I said, opening the door. Then I saw Suri, and nearly choked on my tongue.

She was still dressed for the festival. Her scarlet hair was styled like a 1950's starlet, falling in waves over one eye. The other side was pinned up with a golden fan that kept it out of her face. Her dress poured down her curves like a river of amber scales from neck to ankles. It was slit all the way up to her hips, baring a long stretch of bare brown leg. When she saw my expression, her lips curled in a wicked smile.

"Okay." Karalti sounded a little better now. *"What's the matter? Your thoughts just got all fuzzy."*

"Nothing. Just going to see Ignas." I held up a hand to Suri, pointed at my head, and then made a little flappy-flappy dragon motion with my hands. Her grin widened. *"You come back tomorrow with blood all over your face for me, okay?"*

"I'll try!"

She cut the link then, and I breathed a sigh of relief. "Wow. Sorry... talking Karalti through some teenage angst."

"Story of your life." Suri motioned me with a finger. "Come on: Ignas is waiting."

She turned, and my blood pressure went up a little more when I saw the back of the dress. The front was demure, but the back plunged all the way down to her tailbone. I moaned a little.

"So about sleeping in that bed tonight..." I said. "Your place or mine?"

"Yours. Your room's warmer." Suri's high heels struck the floor as she sashayed ahead. "Is your big black dragon buttplug old enough for me to do naughty things to you without traumatizing her?"

"She should be. Admittedly, I'm not thinking very clearly right now, because I'm mesmerized by dat ass."

Suri laughed, and put a little extra sway into her walk. It was only when she almost stumbled on one of her heels that I realized she wasn't just in a good mood. She was drunk.

The Writing Room was a small parlor off-side the Grand Hall, where the Raven Throne brooded at the end of the cathedral-like chamber. The court was bustling: nobles and other courtiers were gathered round large trestle tables, picking at finger food and drinking in celebration of the Dark Moon Festival. Many people curtsied or bowed to us on our way to the parlor door, which was guarded by a pair of heavily armored knights of the Order of the Dragon, Vlachia's Kingsguard.

"His Majesty awaits." The one on the right gave us a short nod, then opened the door ahead.

Ignas was seated in the same overstuffed scarlet armchair that his younger brother had once occupied. Andrik had a habit of putting his feet up with a bottle of wine and a glass alongside his elbow, but Ignas did not. He had both feet on the floor, a glass of water resting in one hand and an open letter in the other. He looked up as we entered, smiled, and set both down on a table next to his seat before standing. "Welcome, lord and lady. Veela's Grace, Suri: you are a vision of loveliness tonight."

"Thank you." She smiled back pleasantly as we bowed. "Can't live in armor all the time."

"Indeed." The Volod motioned us to the seats he'd set up for us, a pair of gilt golden chairs he'd arranged on an angle to his own seat. "Please, sit. Do you want a drink?"

"Sure," Suri said. "Slivovitz, if you've got it."

"Same again," I said.

"Naturally." There were no servants here, so Ignas just went to the cabinet on the other side of the room and poured the drinks himself. "It's late, so I won't waste your time with pleasantries. If you're wondering why I summoned you, the short answer is that I must ask for a great boon in order to obtain great reward. It has to do with the politics of the outer provinces."

"Nothing like a bit of politics before bed. Gets the blood flowing." While his back was turned, I let a hand hover over Suri's leg and arched an eyebrow. She nodded. I rested it down, fighting the urge to work my fingers under the hem of her dress.

"It gets the bile flowing, more like it." Ignas snorted, bringing back two little glasses of clear, sweet liquor. "But that is why we have liquor. Well, I'll try to keep it as simple as possible. Your quest should update with the essential details after the fact."

It was still weird to listen to NPCs - like Ignas - so readily fall into metagaming.

"I've only just realized how far Andrik let the Crown's authority slip," he continued, setting the glasses down on the small table between Suri and me. "Do you understand the essential structure of Vlachia? Politically, that is?"

"Something about Voivodes ruling provinces," Suri recounted. She threw her slivovitz back like a shot.

"Yes. Eleven of our twelve provinces are ruled by a Voivode, save for this province. I am both the sovereign of Vlachia and the Voivode of Taltos, though the administrative role is relegated to my *Castelleny*, my governors." Ignas resumed his seat, and had a sip of water. "A Voivode is a vassal the Crown appoints to administer the affairs of an individual province. They also serve as judges in the Royal Court. Every province is divided into counties, and every county has its own ruling lord: A *Satrap*, which is a rank equivalent to a Count. Voivodes are also Counts. This means that Satraps, while deferring to the Voivode as their governor, are not lower in terms of their peerage. This is important to know and understand."

"Okay. So Provinces are ruled-"

"Governed."

"Sorry, *governed* by Voivodes, who oversees counties run by Satraps," I said. "Both have the rank of Count."

He nodded. "Correct. The fact that the Voivode and his Satraps are peers is a vital balance against the Voivode's power. There is a historical precedent of ambitious Voivodes bullying their Satraps into fealty, usurping the royal dues, and even fomenting rebellion against the Crown. The further the province from the capitol, the more readily this kind of rotten behavior sets in. My dynasty has endured for almost a thousand years because we manage our outer provinces firmly and fairly. Our airships link the East and West, and nothing commands loyalty from a Voivode quite like their monarch paying a friendly call with an armada of Hussar-class destroyers at his or her back."

"Right." Suri reached down and lay her hand over mine. A small thrill passed through my chest.

"Andrik rarely left Taltos, and he never did a royal tour of Myszno." Ignas motioned toward the east. "Without strong central leadership, the regional nobility took on more and more authority. They've had five years to get used to it. The Voivode of Myszno, Lord Jozef Bolza, was a conservative loyalist and my father's contemporary. He did the best job he could, despite retaining a strong dislike of my brother. But then the Demon attacked, and Andrik saw that as a chance to 'get back' at the Voivode who 'snubbed' him."

I made a face. "Fuck. You said Lord Bolza is probably dead. Who's in charge now?"

"Good question," the Volod replied wryly. "The Satrap of Vastil County, Count Lorenzo Soma, has taken it upon himself to assume control of the province in Bolza's absence."

Suri's eyebrows lifted. "Did he petition you before deciding he was taking charge?"

"Not a word," Ignas said. "Apparently he nurses some conspiracy theory that I am in fact a doppelganger, bred by Mercurion organized criminals in a vat so that they might rule from the shadows."

"You're saying you weren't?" I grinned at him.

He demurely rested a hand over his heart. "The vat is a private matter."

Once we finished laughing, he made a gesture and continued. "Vastil County is currently the wealthiest county in Myszno. The Pass the county is named for is a major shipping route between Vlachia and Jeun. This is also somewhat confidential information, but our military airships are manufactured in Litvy's hangars. Let us say that our young Lord Soma possesses a sense of entitlement beyond his station."

"Ambitious, huh?" I sat back in my seat and drained the rest of my glass.

"Oh, it gets better. You see, when the Voivode fell, it was Bolza's loyal Castellan, Captain Istvan Arshak, who took command of his lord's banners. Captain Arshak is everything anyone could want in a military commander. He is competent, inspiring, brave and intelligent. His troops love him. There is one problem: he's a bastard of mixed Yanik and

Vlachian heritage, which means he shall never have Vlachian peerage. His father is a Yanik prince."

"Who are the Yanik?" Suri asked.

"They are a native people who dwell in the Endlar. They are known to be fierce warriors and dinosaur tamers. However, in Vlachia, being the son of Yanik royalty is about as worthy as my title of 'the King of Cats'." The Volod made an irritable gesture. "Personally, I couldn't give a rat's arse if a man has foreign blood in his veins: once a knight has been sworn in, he's been sworn in. Many of Myszno's best cavalrymen and scouts are Yanik. However, a lot of the provincial noblemen have nothing better to do with their time than fuck their sisters and draw figure eights on their family trees, and Lord Soma in particular takes great offense to this 'swamp rat' taking control of 'his' army."

"Then tell him to quit it, or you'll bring down the royal hammer," I said.

"I have. But there must be action to back up the royal decree. Provincial lords are masters at making messengers disappear in the woods, or accidentally dropping their parchments in the kitchen hearth." Ignas gave us a thin smile. "And that is where both of you come in. Your titles were, up to this point, an honorary peerage. But I rather fancy the idea of having immortal, loyal vassals in a strong position in Myszno, for reasons that should be obvious... and so I am considering extending that title into a true peerage, and specifically giving you the title of Count and Countess of Racsa, Voivode and Voivodzina of Myszno. This will establish you as a House and make you the reigning lord and lady of the province."

I coughed as a slight pressure built behind my eyes. Suri blinked several times, as stupefied as I was.

Ignas waved his hand. "You will have to fight for the position, but if you succeed, then I will be glad to deed the ducal castle to you. You can either be Voivode and Voivodzina together, or one can rule and the other can willingly accept the position of Castellan or Castellana in its stead. The position comes with great responsibilities, of course, but provincial Voivodes reap most of the wealth of their domain, minus taxes and the king's due. What do you say?"

"I..." I looked at Suri. "Uh... what kind of responsibilities?"

"A lot of rebuilding and replanting." Ignas shrugged. "Resolving disputes, making appointments, acting as a judge for both local and national causes. You must deal with the Satraps and their intrigues. Your peers and subjects will both test you and reward you. The normal burdens and privileges of power, in other words."

"I need a bonded spawn point," Suri said. "I don't wanna be a Vulvazela or whatever, but I need somewhere to revive when I die. I'd be happy to become Castellana of an estate. Count me in."

⟦You have gained new Knowledge: Politics of Vlachia (C-grade)⟧
⟦Quest Updated: Unto Death⟧

Despite the urge to stand up and scream 'yes!', I hesitated. The AI was supposed to only offer quests within my capacity… but I didn't feel capable of looking after two million people. Hell, I could barely take care of myself and Karalti.

Ignas cocked his head expectantly.

"I'll need to think about it," I stammered. "Your Majesty, I already have a lot of responsibility weighing on me, between Myszno, my duties to Matir, then Karalti and the Spear and now Rutha. I'll think about it and make a decision after that."

The Volod stood up from his seat. "As well you should. My father always said it was better to plan twice and act once. It can wait until the Demon has been defeated… but there is foolishness to be found in thinking too much, as well. Will I see the pair of you at the sendoff in the morning?"

I rose and saluted out of habit. To my surprise, so did Suri – in the Pacific Alliance style, with the straight right hand beside her eye, the left arm crossed in front of her torso. "Yes sir."

"Good." He gave us both a tired smile. "In light of this morning's debacle, you have no idea how relieved I am to know we have our own Starborn to aid us."

Chapter 9

The gravity of the Volod's words hung over us as we walked back to my suite. When we entered, Suri locked the door as we fell on each other as soon as the bolt turned: me kissing her with my fingers woven through her hair, her hands roaming over my chest, sliding down my belly to my belt.

"So how was the festival?" I managed to gasp against her mouth.

"Good. Real good." She was struggling to unbuckle it. Her breath was boozy and sweet. "I missed you."

"You ready to hit that bed?" I stopped her for a moment. "I need a yes."

"Yes. Less think. More naked." She leaned against me, tugging my shirt out of my pants.

Suri's dress was like a smooth second skin. I unhooked the straps over her shoulders, pressing her down onto the bed and straddling her hips. Despite being such a big woman, a Tank class who maxed out her Strength every level, she folded down easily beneath my weight. When I took her nipple in my mouth, she pressed her chest up against my lips.

And when I accidentally pinned one of her wrists, she arched her back, moaning open-mouthed.

"You okay?" I looked up at her from just below her sternum.

Suri nodded, but she was tongue-tied, her face flushed with heat.

"Come on now, yay or nay?" I drummed my fingers on her trapped hand.

She nodded again, more vigorously this time. "More."

I leaned up over her, caught her wrists, and put them over her head. She stared up at me, panting. I'd hardly even touched her, but her eyes were dark, her thighs were shaking... and not only with pleasure. There was something else there, too. Fear? Or just intensity? It was something I hadn't seen before in my limited experience with women. She must have sensed my hesitancy, because she gasped: "I'm okay."

I slid a hand down along the deep curves of her waist, her belly, and worked my hand under her dress. My fingers found soft skin, a short, soft dusting of hair... then a hot slickness that told me she was more than ready. I gently explored with my fingers, keeping her wrists to the bed with the other hand. Suri writhed, hips jerking when I slid one, then two fingers inside her. There was something about the way she was acting - something she was doing - that drove me nuts. It was the way the dark, predatory energy built in my muscles and my cock.

Jaws clenched, I roughly knocked her knees apart. She drew a sharp breath with a strange, heady cocktail of desire and apprehension as I knelt up between her legs and undressed. When I was nude, I crawled over her and leaned down to kiss her neck. She bared the side of her throat to me, hands loosely balled against my chest, and I bit down.

"Hector!" She gasped my name, arching, clawing weakly against my arms. Her voice was high-pitched and girlish, thrilling along my skin as I rubbed against the wetness clinging to the inside of her thighs. But as I did, I realized something. Suri *did* sound girlish. Young. And she was tense, despite her submissive body language. Very tense. And even though she was gasping, writhing and wet, there were moments where it felt a lot more like struggling.

"Look at me." I backed off, grinding down the bestial urge to thrust into her. Instead, I caught her by the chin, gently guiding her face up. She was sweating now, shaking like a leaf. There were half-formed tears in her eyes. Her breath was shuddering, and still smelled heavy with liquor. "Suri... hang on. We need to slow down."

"I'm sorry," she whispered. "I d-don't know what's wrong."

"It's okay. Hey..." But my body was not in agreement with my head. The testosterone was pumping, and it took a moment to rein in the pure, bestial lust. My nostrils flared as I fought for control. Suri audibly flinched at the sound. That alone told me that I was making the right choice.

I backed up, put her legs together, and rolled to the side. I gathered the woman into my arms and pulled her into a tight embrace.

"I'm sorry. I'm sorry." She kept chanting it as she buried her head against my chest. "I'm sorry, Hector, I thought I could do it. It's been so long, I thought..."

"Hey now. You don't owe me shit." I rocked her a little, trying not to rub against her skin. The slightest touch was like a shock that lit up my nerves. "Was it the pressing you down, was it the biting...?"

Suri shook her head, and a small, high sob tore from her throat. The sound was an instant boner-killer. I was grateful for that. For several minutes, I just held her, feeling her silently weep against my chest. After a while, she shook her head and leaned away enough to sniff and dash at her eyes. "Hector, I'm so sorry. Please... it's not you."

"It's okay." At a loss, I reached up to stroke her hair, her neck, her shoulders. "Whatever it is, it's okay. Hang on... I'm going to put my pants on, okay?"

"No... no. Please, don't." She clasped my arm, pressing her nails in.

"It's okay." I felt like a broken record, but those words were the best I had. "You're safe with me, alright?"

Suri's eyes reddened, and she nuzzled at me urgently. "It's so frustrating. Hector. I was a hundred and ten percent into it. Everything felt amazing, but then... then I... I flashed back to those motherfucking Architects dragging me down to the Hole when I was a girl, and... it just..."

I kissed her. Her cheeks, her neck, the backs of her hands. "It's okay."

"I thought I was stronger than this." The muscles of her jaws bunched as she ground her teeth. "I thought... we'd already fooled around, right? Maybe if I just had a drink, I could relax enough to go through with it. I wouldn't think about those bastards or that place. But I can *smell* it. I can smell the room where they used to torture us."

I was cooling off now. The frustration and the blue balls were under control. "That's what trauma does, right?"

"Yeah. I guess." Suri sniffed, and looked up at me again. "It's just fucking humiliating. And frustrating. I'm rearing to go, and so are you."

"Then we cool off and try again. That's the first time we tried all clothes off... we just have to go a bit slower." I pressed my lips to her forehead - a gentle, chaste kiss. She shuddered, some of the tension leaving her body. "And right now, we're stressed. We just came out of a meeting with a king about the biggest quest either of us have ever taken."

"I know. And I don't know about you, but I'm scared shitless. I don't want to die and go back to Al-Asad, Hector. I can't."

"Then you should stay here," I said. "The game system doesn't know that you can't set a respawn point, and we've been given a quest where we can expect to die at least once. Probably more than once. I'll go and you can join us when we retake the castle."

She lifted her head, the muscles of her jaws working. "No. I can't do that, either. Even if I was chickenshit enough to skip a quest where my friends are at risk, the quest could switch up and exclude me from the reward, and then nothing changes. Andrik promised me a title and land in return for catching Kanzo. Once we threw in with Ignas, nothin' ever came of it."

A pang of guilt squashed down the remainder of my ardor. I was the one who'd talked Suri into switching sides on *The Slayer of Taltos* questline. "I'm sure Ignas could give you a place. Have you asked him?"

"Yeah." She eased down a little. "Nothin' he can do. He tried to give me a quest, but I couldn't accept it. I can't accept any quests unless you or Rin do."

"You can't?" Now that I thought about it... I never had seen Suri accept a quest. "Damn. Why didn't you say something?"

She shrugged uncomfortably. "Only way I level up is through combat and group quests. I tried buying a house with the gold we got after the coronation. The guy fuckin' vanished."

"As in, he wouldn't stick around to make the sale?"

She shook her head. "No, as in, he literally vanished. He was sitting across the table from me, and then 'poof'. Vanished. My last chance at getting a new respawn point is this quest. One where I'm grandfathered in by another... uhh... 'player'."

"It'll be okay. If we take the title, Karalti and I can name you Voivodzina or Castellana." Frowning, I stroked her hair. The strands of copper and scarlet and orange looked thick and wiry, but hers was actually very soft. "That should fix that problem."

"Okay." She swallowed nervously. "I hope I'm not pressuring you."

"It's alright. I'll let Ignas know I'll go ahead with the land and title thing tomorrow morning."

"You're wound up about it, though."

"Yeah. I mean, even just the responsibility of owning a *house*, let alone a whole castle... Do you know how few people my age even rent their own apartments now? I can't imagine what it's like to have that much responsibility. How the hell do you clean the place?"

"You get other people to do it. Butlers and shit." She lifted her eyes to look up at me. "I want to make sure we pay ours well. None of this slavery shit."

"For sure." I nodded, and for a short time, we curled up together in comfortable silence.

When she spoke next, she sounded almost shy. "You know, you're the only man who's ever done that."

I cocked my head. "Done what?"

"You never touch me without asking first," she replied.

I shrugged. "You haven't told me much about what went down at Al-Asad, but it seems like a lot of people just thought they could lay hands on you whenever they wanted."

"Yeah." She closed her eyes again. "They did. I wasn't complaining or anything... actually..."

She trailed off, and then chuckled to herself.

"What?" I asked.

She licked her lips. They were puffy and full, dark even without lipstick. "It makes me feel safe."

"Good. Because, well, you know... I care about you." I held her close, gazing at the fire. Someone had come in earlier and had relit it, and the flamelight danced over everything in brilliant, almost hallucinogenic color. "I'm pretty sure I love you."

"Pretty sure?" She rolled up to lean on my chest. Her hair brushed the side of my neck. "No, don't answer that. I'm just playing around. I know it's too soon to say."

"We'll know by the time we wrap up Myszno." I yawned. Then, I noticed that my HUD was warning me: The Fatigue penalty was back. I'd only slept off the Exhaustion debuff. "I don't know about you, but I'm beat. How about we hit the hay? You know, before Karalti gets back and starts screaming at the window?"

"How about you unequip your clothes and let me rub your back until you fall asleep?" A wicked light danced in Suri's eyes.

"Just my back?" I stuck my lip out. "What about Front-Hector?"

Suri laughed, rich and sultry. "Front-Hector gets a turn, too. Maybe not the way we were thinking, but I can figure something out."

She was still a little shaky as she climbed over me and began to kiss her way down. I grunted, shifting up against the heat of her lips and tongue, then gasped as my cock pressed up between her breasts, rubbing along her sternum.

"Does that work?" she asked.

My breath caught when I looked down at her. "Yes. Yes, it does."

She laughed her beautiful warm honey laugh and pressed her breasts together around the shaft, then bowed her head to cover the rest with a hot, eager mouth. With my fingers tangled in her hair, I might even have pushed her down a bit. Gently.

It was late when we passed out into a deep velvet sleep, with me sprawled out on my back and Suri curled into the crook of my arm. I was as relaxed as I'd ever been... and maybe that was why tonight, of all nights, I dreamed of the Total War.

It was the Crescent Front. My first tour. My Regiment loaded out into the rain, with tank and mortar fire for cover. The heat of the Indonesian jungle drug at my skin like clammy fingers, pulling at my limbs as I ran. The weight of the pack on my back and the rifle in my hands dragged me down with every squishy, muddy step. At any moment, it felt like I'd trip and be trampled into the muck of the battlefield... the marsh where I expected to die.

The ground rolled and shuddered under the impact of Pacific Alliance artillery. Glowing Praxis shields kept most of them from hitting us as we stumbled out of choppers and carriers and zig-zagged toward the rainforest. I couldn't see or hear anything over the rotors, the explosions, the smoke. My helmet was supposed to help me target hostiles in the dark, but the HUD was on the fritz, screwed up by the EMP shields while the shells rained down like fireworks. Our side, their side... I didn't know, and it didn't matter. There was nothing except the terrible heat, the explosions, the pain in my head, and the awful, gnawing fear, like a worm eating through my guts.

Then, through the yellow smoke, I saw my first live enemy. A Taipan Heavy, Australian powered armor slogging through the mud and smoke toward us. It flickered like a bad TV, its camouflage on the fritz. The guy inside had to be as scared as I was. It leveled its barrels at the scattering assault force, just before an RPG took it out. The explosion lit up the marsh, revealing the others running in from behind it. They all had glowing HP rings behind their heads, like in a game... and that's when I realized I was dreaming.

The surge of adrenaline woke me up – gasping, sweating, clutching the furs that lined my bed. My bones were still shaking with the memory of mortar fire as my bedroom came back into focus. Quest alerts and other notifications flashed in the corners of my eyes. My pulse pounded in my ears, my stomach gnawed, my jaws ached, and the roar hadn't gone away.

[[Good morning, Hector Park!]]
[[You have 1 unread quest update]]
[[You have one unread message from Rin Lu]]
[[Warning! You are Severely Dehydrated! -15% to all Stats and Skills!]]
[[You are hungry! HP will no longer regenerate!]]
[[Are you experiencing emotional or psychological stress? Help is available. Would you like to chat to an assistant?]]

⟦World Alert: The Black Moon Festival has ended! (Vlachia)⟧

"Urrgh. Fuck off." I dizzily swatted the holographic notifications away, flailed my way out of my bed, and tumbled onto the cold floor. Grimacing, grinding the heels of my palms against my eyes, I felt my fingernails set into the skin of my forehead even as my dragon's vision - and her urges - intruded into my mind.

Karalti was on the other side of Vulkan Keep, staring at the side of the volcano. She positioned herself against the sun, hovering like a kestrel in the fierce mountain winds as her bleating prey shuffle along the cliff face. Her need overwhelmed the echoes of the nightmare.

When I opened my own eyes, they fell on Suri sprawled out on our bed. She lay on her side, the covers half off, the rest framing the smooth curves of her lower body. She was naked from the waist up. Delirious, I drank in the sight of her, from the coppery swell of her hips to the dark curves of her breasts, then froze as her face turned away from me. Her tousle of blazing red curls fell aside to expose her neck, pulse beating slowly. My heart began to pound faster, and the dryness in my mouth vanished. I took one step toward her, then another... ducking down, becoming quieter, as the deadly black noise in Karalti's mind built to an oceanic roar in mine.

Half a mile away, the dragon dove out of the sky and slammed into the ram, driving him against the cliff wall with her talons. He screamed.

I threw myself back away from the bed and staggered to the bathroom, clutching my head as Karalti's excitement built. When I reached the sink, I frantically yanked on the pull chain. Icy spring water gushed from a pipe into the basin. I scooped it up and splashed it over my face and chest and in my mouth, gulping until my tongue turned numb.

Every time I blinked, I got a snapshot of Karalti's hunt. My dragon shuddered in pleasure as she worked her sharp teeth deeper into the stringy flesh of her prey. There was the gritty sensation of bone snapping as she tore a bite from the struggling animal's neck, hot and trembling with need that twisted behind my eyes and surged like lightning through my jaws, fingers, and cock. It took my breath away. Gasping, I gripped the edge of the sink, clinging onto it for dear life.

In the mirror, I saw Suri stir on the bed. She sat up, and I found myself staring at her half-naked reflection. Not in the gentle way that a man was supposed to contemplate the beauty of his lover... but like a cat watching the mouse he's chased into the bathtub. Like a predator.

"Hector?" She called out, brows furrowed. "Are you okay in there?"

My throat worked, but no words escaped. Suri's puzzled expression morphed into a frown, and she pushed aside the covers to stand. I tensed warily - not because I didn't trust her, but because I didn't trust myself. Karalti's bloodlust was ebbing as her hunger was satiated, but my pulse was still beating a tattoo against the inside of my skull. Hunger was inseparable from lust. And I couldn't do that to Suri. I wouldn't do that to Suri.

Suri pulled a loose shirt on - my shirt - and wandered into the bathroom. She'd worn soft cotton pants to bed, but I was acutely aware of the way her breasts pushed against my back as she looped her arms around my waist and leaned against me. She didn't say anything, didn't push me to talk. Suri had nightmares of her own.

"Bad dream," I muttered, after a while.

"The War again?"

"Yeah. It must have wound up Karalti. She was hungry... hunting." My voice was slurred with the effort of controlling myself. The press of Suri's body against mine was giving Hector Jr all kinds of opinions. Well, opinion. Singular. He knew what he wanted. Big brain Hector, on the other hand, he knew better. "She caught something, but she felt frustrated. I dunno. Maybe she's in heat already."

"Already? I thought she wasn't mature until Level 10?"

"I would literally be the last person to know. I've been winging it with her ever since she hatched." I swallowed, trying to relieve the dryness in my mouth, and gazed at our combined reflections. Only in video games could people eat the kind of shit we ate and still be fifteen percent body fat or less.

"Was the nightmare about Myszno?"

I shook my head at first, but then, hesitating, I nodded once, and shrugged. "Sort of? Kind of. I don't know. I never used to have dreams about the War, when I was alive. Never had any PTSD or anything."

"That you knew of. Maybe something got shaken loose."

I grimaced. "Maybe. You're probably right. This whole thing with the war in Myszno is just stirring up old shit. There was a time where I would have eaten a gun barrel instead of going back to the front."

She bent forward, brushing my ears with her lips and meeting my gaze in the mirror. "We don't have to go, you know."

My god, her mouth is beautiful. I had to digest her actual words for thirty seconds or so before I could form any kind of reply. "Uhh... what?"

"To Myszno." Suri's golden eyes were fierce as an eagle's. "We installed Ignas on the throne. He's achieved his life goal because of us. We don't owe him shit. And if you're having nightmares about going back to war..."

"No." My brows furrowed. I shook my head, rubbing my face with a hand. "No... that's not how this works. We have a quest to do."

"Rin told me that quests can be changed or dismissed. They're not set in stone. If you don't want to do it, you can change the quest."

"Maybe. But that's not the point."

"You told me you never wanted to be a soldier. You hated it."

"Well... yeah."

Suri shrugged. "You're the one who told me Archemi is a game. If that's right, then we don't have to go back to a warzone on Vlachia's behalf. We could go north... we could even go to Daun, to Tungaant. I'd love to visit your home country with you."

I still gripped the edge of the sink with frozen fingers. On the back of my right hand, the coal-black Mark of Matir blazed like a judgmental eye. I knew why I'd dreamed of the Crescent Front. "No. Baldr is threatening Vlachia, and we need to deal with the shit going down in Myszno. This campaign will give us the resources to face him, and to keep you and Karalti safe."

Suri gave me a reassuring pat on the waist, but then a slow, naughty smile spread over her lips. She looped her arms around and laid them on my stomach as she slowly rubbed up along my back. "I'm sober now. Maybe I could try and take your mind off it?"

Ding. Suddenly, Hector Jnr was back to attention and ready to serve. Just great.

There was something dark looking out at the world from behind my eyes. Something lustful, something... evil. That part of me wanted to turn around and clamp my jaws on the side of Suri's throat.

"Not now." I swallowed and closed my eyes. "Sorry."

"Hector!" Karalti's telepathic voice lanced through my brain like a needle through my left eye. *"Are you okay!?"*

I winced, clutching my face, and Suri took an uncertain step back. There was a rolling boom that reverberated through the floor, and the bedroom went dark. I turned to look back into our suite, and saw a large black blob peering through the thick glass window.

"I'm okay, I'm okay. Bad dream, nothing to it." I gave Suri a reassuring kiss on the cheek and stumbled past her on the way to the door. *"How'd you go?"*

"I caught one! I caught a goat!" Karalti bobbed her head. Now that she was Level 8, it was the same size as the window. She had to line up one eye to look inside. "*But it wasn't big enough, and because we have to go to the king's thing today... I was thinking I'd-"*

"You want to poach off his herd one more time."

"Yeah!" There was a 'whoomph' of wind as she flicked her wings. "*Wanna come?"*

My stomach rumbled and cramped. I was stupid thirsty and couldn't remember the last time I'd had a proper meal. I checked the clock: it was 5:30am, well before we were due at the Parade Ground. *"Sure. I need something to eat, too. Mind if we stop by the Grand Hall first?"*

"Okay!" Karalti lifted her head, and the room shuddered a little as she hopped up onto the balcony wall.

"We're going to get breakfast before we go to the Parade Ground," I said aloud to Suri. "Wanna come."

Her dark complexion turned a little greenish. "No thanks. I'm not real big on flying."

"Myszno is going to be a hell of a trip, then."

"The ship's okay. I can sit in the cabin." She equipped her clothes in layers: leggings and a bustier, then padding, then her armor. "There's just too much open space out there for me. I'll meet you at the Hall, okay?"

"Sure." I equipped my own gear and stole a kiss from her just before she left. I ran a quick check of my items, ate some almonds I found lurking in my Inventory, and went out to face my dragon.

A frigid blast of cold mountain air hit me as I pushed the doors out onto the balcony, where Karalti paced the parapet like a tightrope walker. Our suite had a south-western view toward the distant ocean cliffs, where the moon hung on the horizon like a black void obscuring the stars. The solar corona was still visible, a thin blue-white line flickering around the outside. I knew Suri had good reasons to be afraid of wide open spaces, but it was sad I couldn't share the view with her. *"Ready to go, Tidbit?"*

"Yeah!"

I equipped the gear - now I was over Dragon Riding 10, I didn't have to put Karalti's saddle and saddlebags on the hard way - and gave her the hand signal to extend her wing. She did, still balanced on the wall, but as I began to climb, she turned her head on her neck and sniffed me. And then she growled.

"What?" I paused, hand reaching up to grasp the side of the saddle.

"YOU!" She flattened her crest, rearing her neck like a cobra. Her eyes narrowed to bright, dangerous slits. *"You smell like HER! Like her BITS!"*

I exhaled heavily into the frosty air. *"Karalti. We've talked about this."*

"YOU talked about this." Her jaws parted, bearing top and bottom rows of razor sharp, back-curved teeth. As the

rumbling grew to a hiss, I admit I began to feel a little nervous. Karalti wasn't my little Tidbit anymore. The last time she'd had a jealous fit over Suri, she'd been a bit bigger than a car. Now, she was longer than a bus.

"No. We - as in, you and I - have talked about this at least ten times. I'm a human. You're a dragon. Suri and I are the same species. You're also basically my kid, which makes this super weird." Exasperated, I reached up again, only to slide down as the dragon irritably flicked me back with her wing.

"Did she touch you?" Karalti pivoted on the narrow wall and snaked her head toward me as I backed up. Her breath smelled strongly of sharp, caustic chemicals, and it was hot enough to bring a sheen of sweat to my face. *"Did she... RIDE you?"*

"Karalti." I regarded her flatly. "I am not playing this game."

Karalti bellowed a furious, gurgling roar, then sprung from the balcony like a swallow. She was obscenely agile for a creature her size. As I ducked and stumbled away from the ferocious, cutting wind, she snatched me by the pack and Spear and dragged me off into the air. The balcony lurched away with terrifying speed as she strove for altitude. It was already a sheer eight-hundred foot drop to the ground. Now we were at nine hundred, a thousand... and then she dove.

Fortunately for me, my backpack had stomach and chest straps like a hiking pack. That was all that stood between me and my first parachute-free skydiving experience. *"Karalti! Come on! This is fucking ridiculous!"*

"No! No two-legs, no-wing whores!" Karalti ranted, roaring on every other wingbeat. She rolled to one side, skimming the mountain so close that she almost bounced me off the rocks. *"I carry you everywhere on your stupid quests! I wear a stupid saddle, but what does she do to deserve sleeping in the bed with you!?"*

"She's not the size of a semi-trailer!" I snarled back. *"And if you weren't, then of course you could sleep in the bed!"*

"I sleep in caves! Cold caves!" She swooped back into the open sky and did an Aileron Roll. My guts lifted with the brief zero-g before I crashed back down into the straps of my pack and nearly slithered out of them.

⟦Warning! Backpack durability is at 45%!⟧

"Say Suri is a stupid rider stealing bitch!" Karalti let out a piercing cry of challenge.

I gripped the straps of my pack to anchor myself in the harness and set my jaw. *"No."*

"Say it!" The dragon barrel-rolled this time.

"No. And you're going to put me the fuck down."

"Say it! Say it say it say it!"

Karalti's immature force of will slammed into my own, but I wasn't budging. I pushed right back. *"No. We're headed to a warzone. There are people counting on us to lead them. It's time you started acting like a queen instead of a spoiled princess."*

"You don't know how I feel! Or why!"

"Maybe not, but I know I raised you better than this." I ground my teeth as she pulled a near-vertical dive. It was like a rollercoaster, but without the fun. *"And I know your mother would be so fucking disappointed right now."*

The dragon cried out, the same desolate barking sound she'd made at her brothers. She was breathing hard as she leveled her flight path, slowing to a fast glide. As the threat of imminent death receded, I felt waves of empathic input crash against my nerves. Karalti was still hungry. Her joints ached with growing pains. She was humiliated that a full day and night of hunting wild game had only resulted in one measly goat. She was horny but confused by what it meant... she was grief-stricken for her clutchmates, and the mother she'd never known. All of it was feeding a maelstrom of raw emotion that had nothing to do with me or Suri.

"You don't know what my mother thinks!" she spat.

"I know she's endured shit that would break either one of us," I snapped back. *"And she did it with grace, and backbone, and composure. Not by tantruming."*

I felt a shudder all the way through Karalti's body. I also felt the straps keeping me alive start to give way.

"Karalti, you know I love you more than anything on this earth, and that's why I'm telling you to harden the fuck up." My legs swung as we passed into view of the parade ground. A fleet of airships were there already, illuminated by spotlights on the ground.

"You can't tell me what to do!"

"Until you're old enough, yes, I do. This is a no-negotiation scenario."

"I'll... I'll drop you!"

"Go right the fuck ahead. I'll respawn, board one of those ships, and then chew your ass out from here all the way to Myszno."

Karalti bellowed in frustration, but she was getting tired, her will slowly bending under mine. We broke out over the thick walls ringing the parade ground, and she pulled her wings into a shallow dive.

We were still early, but ranks of soldiers were streaming in through the gates, and even the disciplined men stopped to stare as we streaked past. My stomach sank when I saw Ignas waiting at the front. His Majesty was mounted on his fine black hookwing and dressed in full battle regalia, ready to send off the ships.

Naturally, that was when the Item Durability hit zero, and the straps of my pack finally gave way.

Chapter 10

Leap of Faith kicked in as soon as I began to fall, giving me three seconds of time dilation to line up a landing. I hit the ground like a parkour master: knees soft, hands down, then a high-speed roll over the shoulder. I tumbled a few more times than I expected, but carried it through to an awkward superhero crouch not too far from Ignas. His hookwing fluffed its feathers and hissed.

"Well now. That was quite the entrance." The Volod had switched out his usual rogue's getup for fine ornamental plate, a long scarlet cloak, and an officer's saber. His helmet had a backswept crest of feathers. "Is Her Holiness still worked up after the appearance of the other dragons?"

"Uhh... sure." I dusted myself off, and side-eyed Karalti as she winged around the plaza, bellowing and flaming innocent flagpoles. "Let's say that."

"You are not the first to arrive. Rin is already here." Ignas gestured toward the largest of the airships. I glanced around until I spotted the Mercurions, plural. Rin and Ebisa were embracing out of the lights, sheltered by the mounting tower and gangplank. Ebisa had her mask raised. I saw the

King's Blade tenderly tuck a lock of Rin's hair behind one of her winglets, saying something to her that made her nod, then giggle. The laughter only lasted for a moment. Rin buried her face against Ebisa's chest, and the taller Mercurion pulled her into a protective hug.

"They've gotten close." I turned away, not wanting to intrude on them any more than I already had.

"They have. Mercurions love like any other creature - only with the awareness that the time they have together is so much shorter than it is for us humans." Ignas smiled, a little sadly. "Though now I'm well past my prime, I assume the same applies for me."

I fell in beside him. "Are you serious? Dude, you're a catch. You'll find the right lady at the right time, I'm sure of it."

"Well, the princess I was once engaged to still believes I buggered my Meewfolk *protégé*. We're currently trying to re-establish diplomatic relations with Jeun, but who knows?" A tiny smile jerked the corner of Ignas' lips. "Anyway, enough of that. It's fortunate you arrived early: I have some things for you. Items, and advice. can you call Karalti to you?"

Items? Advice? "Sure. Give me a second. *Karalti? Can you join us?*"

The dragon uttered a short shrieking cry as I called her, but she turned around and flew straight for us. There was a great leathery rasp as Karalti folded her wings, dropped my broken pack to the ground, then fell the last few feet to the ground beside me. She was breathing hard, chest flexing like a bellows.

The griffin-like quazi pranced a couple of steps back, honking with fear. Ignas checked the reins, halting it before it spooked too bad. "Which would you like first?"

"Stuff first," I said. "Otherwise I'll be wondering what goodies you're holding onto while you're trying to teach me shit."

"Honest, at least." The Volod gave me a chipped, toothy smile and then tilted his head to concentrate on something I couldn't see.

[[Ignas Corvinus would like to trade.]]

That was interesting. NPCs only seemed to open these trade windows in one of two instances - when they were giving me something immaterial, or when they were displaying an inventory. Curious, I accepted.

Ignas's halo-like Corona whirled, and then another bunch of notifications appeared:

[[You received a Raven Suit!]]
[[You received a Raven Helm!]]
[[You received Cossack Harness!]]
[[You received Fine Cloak!]]
[[You have received Royal Dragon Saddle!]]
[[You received Fine Saddlebags]]

My eyes widened. Holy fuck. While Ignas watched indulgently, I navigated to my Inventory to check the new items.

Raven Suit

- *Mastercraft Armor*
- *260 Armor*
- *25% impact reduction (Torso); 15% Light, Fire and Air elemental damage reduction.*
- *Body Slot*
- *100% durability*

Armor purpose-made for wearing while flying an aerial mount. Light, tough, and flexible, it bears the raven crest of House Corvinus.

Raven Helm

- *Magical Armor*
- *50 Armor*
- *25% impact reduction (Head), 5% Light, Fire and Air elemental damage reduction, 25% resistance to the Blindness & Deafened status effects. Enhanced flight display.*
- *Head slot*
- *100% durability*

A Mercurion-crafted helm enchanted to allow you to see through the solid visor.

Cossack Harness

- *Masterwork Item*
- *+25 lb to maximum carry weight*

- *Belt Slot*
- *100% durability*

A four-point flight harness worn over armor. Used to attach yourself to the quick-release points on your saddle and prevent falls. It can also hold pouches and weapons.

Royal Dragon Saddle

- *Magical Armor (Dragon)*
- *125 Armor*
- *+10% flight speed, -5% stamina drain*
- *Body slot*
- *100% durability*

Built for speed and comfort, this enchanted saddle boosts your mount's flight speed and stamina by reducing drag.

Fine Saddlebags

- *Masterwork Item*
- *100% Durability*

Increases carrying capacity by 120lb.

Fine Cloak

Looks impressive and keeps you warm. It has pockets!

"Ignas... this is amazing." I equipped the entire Raven Suit. It fit like a second skin: dark leather and steel armor that was decorative and functional at the same time, worked with silver crow skull buttons. It moved and breathed better than any motorcycle racing suit I'd ever worn.

The black steel helmet was something else. It was long, with a backswept crest of sharp metal feathers tipped in red. The aerodynamic visor was made of obsidian. The volcanic glass that crawled with traceries of red light that pulsed in a mirrored geometric pattern from top to bottom. Like other Mercurion-style gear, there were no eye holes, nose holes, or apparent way to see or breathe.

"That helmet can amplify your voice somewhat," Ignas said. "Officers of the Royal Dragoons use helmets similar to this one."

"You can really see through it?" Bewildered, I pulled it on and blinked a couple of times. From the inside, it was like I wasn't wearing a helmet at all. Even better, it seemed to have some kind of synergy with my HUD. There was a new tab on my sidebar. When I swiped it in, the flight controls I normally only saw when Karalti and I were in the air appeared. Not only that, but there were more tools. A compass. An altimeter. Wind speed and direction. "Holy shitballs. Dude, this is seriously amazing gear. Thank you."

"My pleasure." Ignas inclined his head. "We need to win this campaign, Hector."

"Our chances just got better." I reached back, and found a notch just big enough to pull my braids through. "This gear is badass."

Just then, my HUD began to chime: the morning alarm I had set to wake up in time for the expedition. The gates across the parade ground opened, and soldiers began to pour in, marching in orderly ranks. Ignas straightened in his saddle.

"What about me?" Karalti leaned forward, shaking her wings out as she *grawked* like an overgrown chick begging for food. Her tantrum was already long forgotten – by her, at least. *"You got some things for me?"*

"Yup." I equipped her new saddle. Her old one had served her well, but it was pretty basic: especially compared to this beast. The Royal Saddle was a huge step up in quality. Long, narrow, with a short swallowtail cantle that hugged, it could be bolted to the holes drilled in Karalti's dorsal spines. It was sculpted to fit her shoulders, and came with extra handles and tie points. The black leather looked shiny, almost wet, but when I vaulted up onto her back, I found the reverse was true. It was rough to the touch, with enough friction to catch and stop my gloves when I pressed down and tried to slide it along.

"Sandsquid leather," Ignas called out. "Helps to keep your seat. Just try not to touch it with your bare skin, or you will get a rash in places you will sorely regret."

"It's comfy!" Karalti stood up tall, shrugging, spreading, and rotating her wings as if to model how it did not interfere with the action of her shoulders. *"I love it!"*

I clapped her on the knee as she settled back down into her normal stance. "So, how about that advice?"

Ignas nodded, turning to face the troops as they fell into place. "Indeed. I foresee a day where you, Suri, and even Rin may have to command troops, and I feel it is important that the three of you understand how to do so. Do you want to learn?"

"Absolutely." I reached up to adjust my new helmet.

[You have gained access to the Mass Combat System]
[You earned a new feat: Commander in Training]

Ignas motioned with a hand. "Take a look at your new menu, and I'll walk you through the options."

I did so, calling up the HUD. My eyes widened as the new menu unfolded. It was easily the most complex I'd seen in Archemi so far, made more confusing because the various circles, tables, and slots were blank. They were all labeled. The only field with any data was the Renown table, which listed my Renown in Ilia and Vlachia (Taltos Region}.

"Your Renown is the foundation of your ability to build your duchy, recruit heroes, and manage your army," Ignas said. "Your effectiveness as a leader begins and ends with the quality of your character. Fame or infamy, it doesn't really matter. You can lead through fear or through inspiration, or a mixture of both. Regardless of what idealists would like to claim, soldiers who fear their commander as their god are as reliable as those who worship them. The strength of the units you can effectively command depends on your Will, your level, and your Renown. Any fool can temporarily bolster a force or direct troops, but to lead, you must be worthy of following."

"You will note there are three pages to this system: Army, Heroes, and Logistics," he continued. "The first menu is your Army information. If or when that menu is ever populated, you will be able to see all your units at a glance. If you select a unit, you can view strategic information. Look out over the formation, and you'll see what I mean."

The Volod gestured out over the Legion assembling in orderly rows on the Parade Ground: two thousand soldiers and specialists, give or take. I was able to identify twenty discrete units – unit was a complete company, containing the fighting troops and their support. Two thirds of the force were infantry: ⟦Veteran Militia Pikemen⟧, ⟦Vlachian Royal Riflemen⟧, and ⟦Vlachian Royal Archers⟧. The remainder was made up of units flagged as 'Elite Units': ⟦Knights of the Red Star⟧, ⟦Royal Elementalists⟧, ⟦Ravensblood Dragoons⟧ and others. When I focused on one unit of Dragoons, I got the detailed information Ignas had been talking about:

2nd Ravensblood Dragoon Company (Thunderbolts)

Descended from the Dakhari mercenaries who helped the House of Corvinus conquer Eastern Vlachia, Ravensblood Dragoons are Quazi-mounted knights who fight with special hooked polearms - khara *- and repeater pistols. They are brutally effective against armored and unarmored flying creatures, able to pull their khara through wings and gun down armored opponents. Their majestic presence on the battlefield is inspiring to infantry, fortifying them against Fear.*

Unit Rank: 1
Faction: Myszno Defense Force

Health: 200
Morale: 100%
Speed: 90 (Fast)
Melee Attack: 40
Melee Defense: 32
Abilities: Anti-Infantry, Armored, Armor Piercing, Aerial Charge, Anti-Beast (Flying).
Buffs: Causes Fear in enemy units (-2% morale), boosts morale of allied ground units (+2% morale), +20% damage to Infantry and Beast units on successful charge
Vulnerabilities: Vulnerable to Anti-Air tactics.

"As you can see, the information for military units is simplified, compared to the information one would expect of individual people," Ignas said. "That is necessary for planning armies and for tactical purposes. If you were in command of these troops, you would be able to see some more specific information. The commander can monitor injuries and deaths, keep an eye on ammunition, and order units to take certain positions in real time."

"What's Rank?" I asked.

"Rank is a measure of experience," Ignas replied. "Rank 1 indicates a unit has not yet endured a battle. Successful battles increases rank, which confers bonuses to morale, health, attack and defense, so it is in your interest to safeguard the lives of your soldiers. Now, speaking of that – let us head over to the Heroes menu."

I did so, and to my surprise, there were already a couple of entries there. Ignas was at the top of the list, and Ebisa just underneath it. There were a few other familiar faces, too.

Kira and Owen, the healers from Lyrensgrove. Sergeant Blackwin, from the Eyrie. Rutha, though she was grayed out. Both Ebisa and Ignas had icons which, when I hovered over them, told me that they were 'Unrecruitable (Ally)'.

"The Heroes menu tracks your relationships with prominent figures who inspire, train, and command units or armies." Ignas motioned to himself with a wry smile. "Individuals are important in warfare, even if the brunt of the conflict rests on the rank and file. Heroes have unique combinations of abilities and talents, such as Ebisa's talents as an assassin and strategist, or my gifts for diplomatic relations and espionage. Heroes fortify troops, improving morale and helping them fight on when they otherwise might give up. They can also lead companies or units into battle, conveying unique buffs on their allies or debuffs on their enemies."

"Holy shit." I scratched my head, but found only metal. Helmet. Right. "Hang on: let me look at one of these."

I couldn't recruit Ebisa, but I could still see her Hero profile in this menu:

Red Ebisa, the King's Blade

A Mercurion bastard who is reviled by her own kind for her alien appearance, Ebisa is an unusually talented assassin – even by Mercurion standards. After the death of her 'father', the Master Artificer Kanzo, she has absorbed his knowledge and has become a master weaponeer in her own right, though her primary art is still that of the unseen killer. Like all assassins, she is suited to one-to-one and small-group combat, infiltration, and the destruction of enemy Heroes.

Unit Rank: S

Faction: Nightstalkers Syndicate
Health: 3788
Morale: 120%
Speed: 150 (Extraordinarily Fast)
Melee Attack: 554-638
Melee Defense: 195
Abilities: Duelist, Scout Leader, Armor-Piercing, Infiltrator, Chameleon, Damage Resistance (Magic), Inspiring Presence, Immune to Fear, Skirmish Leader, Poison Master.

The Buffs and Vulnerabilities lists were inaccessible to me, greyed out. "What does a speed of 150 translate to, in terms of DPS?"

"Good question. The average DPS rate is five seconds at eighty percent, and every percentage point after that reduces the attack interval. In mass combat scenarios, Ebisa is attacking around every three seconds. She can boost her speed in short bursts, which decreases that interval even further. You can see why I like her."

I chuckled. "Maybe we should just send her to go kill the Demon."

"If not for the horde of undead standing in the way, I would." Ignas made a sound of amusement. "Recruiting heroes relies on two factors: having sufficient Renown to command their respect, and completing quest lines that allow you to form a relationship with them and bring them to your own faction. Once recruited, Heroes will be added to your Mass Combat menu, where you can improve their abilities and stats through training and point assignment. These abilities are separate from their individual menus, by the way – they apply only to mass combat situations in which you are their commander. You cannot normally add stats and abilities to people, unless they are bound to you as Karalti is."

"Right." Fascinated, I had a look at some of the other hero profiles. Most of them were blanked out, because I had no renown with their factions. "Are there skills I can take to buff and improve Army and Hero units?"

"Yes, if you choose to level the Leadership and Strategy skills. I strongly recommend you assign any free skill points to them. Now, on to Logistics." Ignas gestured with a long hand toward Vulkan Keep. "Logistics covers your buildings, your means of production, and the quality of your equipment. Different structures are required to produce certain units. For example, if you wish to train Knights of the Red Star, you must have a Red Star Chapter House, which costs 15 Build Points and 1000 Gold. To support it, you require a Gunsmith, a Blacksmith, and a Hookwing Stables, plus a steady supply of steel, lacquer, and gunpowder. This makes the Knights rather expensive, but they some of the best hybrid cavalry in the world. You earn Build Points through quests, naturally. They can be offset with manpower, but that costs money. More hands means less Build Points are needed, but more gold is required to pay your laborers. The eternal question of time versus money."

"Huh." I didn't have any information in that menu yet. "Alright – that'll do me for now. I'm starting to get lost."

"You will get used to it. I remember when my father trained me to use this very menu." Ignas clapped me on the shoulder. "Once you reach Myszno and begin your localized quests, this information and these options will make more sense. But for now, we must turn our attention to the send-off. My officers approach, as does the Lady Suri."

Sure enough, Suri was headed for us, coming up out of the tunnel and gate that Ignas and his posse had used the day before. She cut a striking figure on Cutthroat, dressed in her mismatched armor, her axes belted to her hips, her oversized sword strapped over her back. She'd bought spiked leather barding for the hookwing, who was as ugly and ill-tempered as ever. The hulking dinosaur snapped and snarled at anything in her path, her tail sweeping from side to side.

I grunted. "Mind if I ask a question, Your Grace?"

"Of course."

"If you had one piece of advice for a would-be barbarian commander, what would it be?"

Ignas snorted. Then, he thought about it. "My Vizier tells me I am too generous with my advice, but he is not here to temper my excesses, is he? I would suggest you train your mind. I see you and Suri and Karalti running all over the castle, training and redeeming quests, but I've yet to find either of you with your heads buried in a book."

"Oh." My face got hot enough that I was glad I was wearing my new helmet. "Yeah, I'm kind of dumb."

Karalti huffed. *"Ugh, this again."*

"You are not, but you must learn that for yourself. Improvement is merely an issue of time and discipline." Ignas twirled a hand, the Vlachian shrug. "Assuming Karhad isn't burned to the ground, you will have access to the Karhad

Archives and the library at Egbolt Castle after your victory. Gods willing, they are intact. We can assume the undead, unlike some human armies, do not need to burn books for fuel. The Archives reputedly hold some grand, ancient lore."

"Yeah..." Chastened, I stroked the side of Karalti's neck. "I'll keep that in mind. Thanks."

Ignas nodded. "My father raised me to believe that discipline is the foundation of everything good in life, including love. Despite his treatment of me, I still believe that. It is why I stand here today, preparing to address these men, while my brother's ashes swirl around on the bottom of the ocean. You, Karalti and Suri are strong, but as Lucien demonstrated yesterday, strength of mind is as important as strength of body when it comes to dealing with tyrants."

Book 2: The Prezyemi Line

Chapter 11

The 4-day journey to Myszno was difficult. There were no enemy mobs willing to take on a fleet of noisy warships and a dragon, but we didn't need them. The trip from Taltos to Myszno was a raw test of Karalti's endurance, our stamina, our patience and cooperation. Before now, the longest flight we'd made together had been about eighty miles outside the Taltos city limits. The first day of our voyage, we flew 315 miles, spending the other 200-ish laid out with exertion on the deck of the fleet's flagship, the *Orozlan.* We would fly until Karalti's Stamina reached 5%, land, recover, and then go back out until we had to rest again. But it paid off - big time.

For one thing, Karalti's hunting problems were resolved out of necessity. She had to eat to support the amount of exercise she was doing, regardless of how much she wanted to whine about it. We snatched geese and *Dimorphodons* from the air and gazelles from the steppe below, and her stunted Hunting skill grew exponentially, shooting up from Beginner 2 to Apprentice 3. One of her vitally important skills, Laden Flight, climbed 10 points to Apprentice 4, lessening the burden of my weight and our gear. Her Stamina grew a full 10 points; her Dex swelled by 4 and her Str by 6.

She wasn't the only one stacking on those sweet, sweet points. Depending on our altitude, I was either cooking or freezing in my armor, hanging onto the saddle with numb hands and aching with fatigue. My resistance to the elements only took the edge off, and there were times I had to buckle myself on and just sleep like the dead. The exhaustion was part altitude, part physical exertion, but the better part of it was the mental battle going on behind the scenes: my old friends ADHD and dyslexia.

Neither ADHD or dyslexia are states of mind: there was something physically wrong with my brain. I'd learned at an early age that if I wasn't moving or doing something with my body, then my mind turned into a bucket of ferrets. The secret sauce to trigger this state of mind was boredom, and the only break in the monotony was when Karalti needed to hunt. Then, I could come back to my body with the adrenaline rush of flight. The rest of the time, when Karalti was gliding and trying to conserve as much energy as possible, I see-sawed between unfocused excitement and skull-splitting boredom as the Sathbar Plains inched along below. By middle of Day 2, I was about ready to claw my face off, so I did something I'd never done in my life. I willingly took out the book I'd borrowed from the Royal Library just before we'd left Vulkan Keep - 'A Very Brief Physick of the Solonkratsu' - and sat my ass down to read.

The book was written in Vlachian. Even though I knew how to speak the language, trying to read the script was hell. I'd gotten used to my augmented reading assistant, which compensated for my dyslexia and allowed me to flip through my HUD, my quest descriptions and the Wiki with relative ease. The ArchemiWiki suited my squirrel brain just fine, but this was ink on paper, words-on-page old-fashioned reading, and as it had been during my school days, it was pure torture.

Dyslexia is hard to describe to someone who doesn't have it. Words don't look like they're spelled 'right' somehow. Punctuation seems to leap out of nowhere, causing my eyes to skip and flick around. Letters sitting next to each other join up in weird ways. The whole time, my brain ferrets screeched and wrestled, trying to get me to put the book down and so they could go off on a happy tangent into the audio-narrated ArchemiWiki. The 'Very Brief' book was just a field guide, twenty pages long. It took me two days to read all of it.

⟦Congratulations! Despite suffering a penalty, you have finished reading your first book: A Very Brief Physick of the Solonkratsu. +250 bonus EXP!⟧
⟦You have gained +1 Int, +1 Will⟧
⟦Through sheer force of willpower, you have reduced the severity of your Dyslexia debuff! You can now read books at 0.8% normal speed (up from 0.4%), and all language-related skills now gain -3% slower than normal (up from -5%)⟧
⟦You have gained new knowledge: Dragon Physiology (B-Grade)⟧
⟦New Feat: Budding Scholar. You have collected 10 items of knowledge at B-grade or higher! Find a Knowledge specialist (Librarian, Scholar, Archivist or similar) to learn more about the value of Knowledge and how to apply it!⟧
⟦You have gained access to a new skill: Field Medicine (Dragons). Learn and practice to level up this skill!⟧

Whoa, okay. I blinked as the notifications cleared, shivering as the stats jumped up. *"Holy shit, Karalti. I just cured myself of part of my dyslexia."*

"Really? By doing the reading thingy?"

"Yeah." I leaned back on the saddle. *"And now I finally know why you have two hearts."*

"Yeah?"

"Yup. We'll talk about it later."

In fact, once I was over the mental torture I'd just inflicted on myself, the book had given me a lot to think about - like how Karalti could go from barely being able to carry me 10 miles during our maiden flight at Level 5 to almost 2000 at Level 8. And it was exciting, because it wasn't just her physiology or anatomy at work: it had to do with the way that stats worked in Archemi.

Archemi's stat system had been bugging me for a while. In most games, you got stat points to assign, and you leveled by gaining levels and splitting points. I'd reconciled myself to this game's stat training system many levels ago, but in the back of my mind, I'd always wondered - why the fuck were the numbers so high overall, and what the fuck did those numbers *mean*?

For example: my Strength stat. I'd already figured that 10 was the average score across all stats for beginning players. When you went into character creation, the system then adjusted your scores a few points from the average based on your mental profile and your basic Path choice. Fairly simple - but what did it mean in context? Was 10 Str relative to, say, the hardness of a 2x4 plank of wood? Or someone's jaw? Or to the weight of a sword like Suri's?

My first revelation was this: if you added a decimal and a percentage sign to your stat score, the number began to make a lot more sense. '10' was actually '1.0%'. My starting Str of 12 wasn't 'twelve', but 1.2%. Not excessive, but realistic for my current level of ability. There weren't many normal people who could ninja flip thirty feet in any direction.

But here was the interesting thing: the basic stat score of 1.0 was arbitrary. There was no 'Average Joe 1.0%' in Archemi. Everyone here, PC or NPC, had a unique set of racial, cultural, and Path-based modifiers at play. If I was correct about the stats being percentages of a base score, that base score wasn't the one I could see on my character sheet. That meant my 4.7% Strength multiplier wasn't '4.7% of 10'. It was 4.7% of an unseen number I didn't know, a number that was not on my character sheet.

In other words, all characters in Archemi had HVs: Hidden Values.

Dun dun dunnnn.

Being an antique games nerd, I knew all about HVs. They were a core mechanic of a ridiculously addictive game from the late 1990s - the Pokémon series. HVs explained how two Pokémon of the same species at the same level could have wildly different stats. There were two kinds of HVs in that game: Individual Values, which were like a character's genes, and Effort Values, which were hidden values you could improve by battling - to a maximum of 510 EV points across all stats and 255 to a single stat. You trained them using special items and by fighting enemies that gave you EV points to one or more stats. A fast Pokemon might give you 1 EV point toward speed, a Rock-type toward Defense, etc.

For example: if my hidden Strength score was 14 and my Str stat was 12, then at Level 1, I could multiply 14 by 1.2% to get my actual effective strength modifier: 2.32. Assuming that HV didn't change, at my current level, my real Str score was 47 (14) - which came out to a percentile score of 9.212.

Let's say I got into an arm-wrestling contest with a guy who had the same Str stat as me - 47 - but who had a lower Strength HV. His percentile score worked out to 9.200 Strength. Assuming no debuffs, I would win our arm wrestle. This would be true even if he was a higher level than me or his visible Str stat was higher than mine, as long as that HV was lower. The only thing that really mattered was that secret percentile score.

There was probably other factors involved in the Real Stat Score calculation, like levels or your character race, but it could explain Karalti's exponential stamina growth. It would also explain how lower-level characters here could beat higher-level characters by leaning on their HVs and using smart tactics. You could do that in Pokémon: a lower-level Fire Pokémon could often beat a higher-level Grass Pokémon through a combination of clever attack selection and good HVs. It was even possible that there were HVs in Archemi we didn't know about, like a Luck stat, or a Karma stat... or a Corruption stat.

My experiences in the game so far seemed to support the existence of such a system. I could say with certainty that if I met another male Tuun Dark Dragoon who was the same level as me with a Level 9 dragon companion, that he and I would have very different stat arrays... and THAT led me down a brand-new train of thought. If Archemi had Individual Values, did it have Effort Values? And was there a way to hack EVs and increase those hidden scores?

If there was a way to grow these hidden values in the same way that you trained EVs in Pokémon - and assuming I wasn't completely deluded - then your stats could multiply those real hidden scores to superheroic levels. In Karalti's case, I was betting that was what happened to allow us to travel the distance we had in such a short period of time. That was the most exciting part of this whole thing, because I was pretty sure we had unintentionally been honing our EVs the entire time I'd been in the game.

The reason the book had tipped me off was because it focused on dragon hearts. Dragons had two hearts, and I'd learned that both of them served different functions. The Prime Heart was like a normal hearty-heart, pumping blood to Karalti's brain and limbs and doing all the other regular things hearts do. The Drive Heart was a totally different beast. It was much larger than the Prime Heart, an ocarina-shaped, white and blue-fleshed organ that was connected to her lymphatic system. Most of the time, it was on standby. The Drive Heart only activated when she was about to fly. Whenever she pumped her wings, the organ came into gear: it would speed up, pressurizing her blood and charging it with mana as it activated the magic that lightened her body during flight. The book had said, and I quote:

"*...A dragon's Drive Heart and the vessels which control the ability of flight are the essence of their Words. Each dragon differs in the strength of the Words written into their flesh and blood, the strength of their hearts, and their maximum potential as individuals. All Queens have larger Drive Hearts than their subordinate female kin, sometimes twice as large as their sterile drone daughters and sisters. In fact, every Queen born, even the weakest, is created with unique Words and her own uniquely powerful Drive Heart, which she must strengthen through the course of her conquests. The strength of this organ is the deciding factor of battles between Queens, because she with the strongest hearts shall be proven as the swiftest flier, the most enduring warrior, and the most talented at magic.*"

That '*which she must strengthen through the course of her conquests*' line had gotten me thinking about HVs, because Karalti had drastically multiplied her flight distance over just three levels. The only way she could have done that was by percentage - by her visible Stamina score of 55 being multiplied *against* something.

Not only that, but the improvement in her range implied that her IVs and the rate that she could improve them had to be good - REALLY good. Like... 'holy shit, I have caught the shiny Mewtwo of dragons' good. I was betting that she was exceptional even by Queen Dragon standards... which explained why Baldr-Ororgael would go so far as to offer me the position of Knight-Commander. He was willing to let bygones be bygones and put me in charge of the Skyrdon, because if this IV/EV thing was correct, my dragon would be able to pass her crazy-ass HVs down to her children - his future dragon slaves. Given that Ororgael was a dev, he probably knew all about the math that went into the backend of Archemi… and that meant his offer to me via Lucien had been made in desperation. He didn't want any old Queen dragon. He wanted THIS one.

I doubted I had stunning HVs myself. But as they say, A for Effort, right?

Hours after reaching this stunning conclusion, we laid eyes on Myszno for the first time. The Western Tashkar Range reared up over the flat grasslands like towering sentinels. The black mossy mountains were so tall they vanished into the clouds, and in the morning of our arrival, they were streaming with mist that poured down into crystal-clear lakes far below. The air was like nothing I'd ever smelled. Clear, dusty and grassy-sweet, it filled me with a strange longing. But once we passed into the shadow of the mountain, it turned bitterly cold.

With our improved stats - visible and hidden - Karalti was slightly faster than the warships and was able to fly much higher, to a maximum ceiling of twelve thousand feet. My Tuun physiology and the Trial of Marantha let me breathe at that height, but we cruised at just over five thousand. Even at this great height, we came nowhere near the height of the mountains. Our entry point was Vastil Pass, the major East-West trade route between Myszno and the rest of Vlachia. From a mile above the ground, it looked like a complete clusterfuck. Camps sprawled out like old bloodstains from the mouth of the pass, turning it into a bottleneck. They were disorderly, with no obvious signs of planning. There was no farmland, no settlements, and nothing to eat. The land around the camps was a dirty red-brown color, trampled to mud by wagons, animals, people, and their cargo. I bet it smelled like shit. Literally.

"*Woah. That's a lot of people,*"Karalti remarked. "*Is that the vampire guy's army?*"

"*No. I'm pretty sure those are refugees, but we need to drop about two thousand feet if I'm going to make out any detail.*"

Karalti dipped her wingtip and soared lower, descending in a lazy spiral around the perimeter of the camp. The leather saddle creaked under my hands, tightening with the sudden cold as we descended into mountain shadows and the temperature plummeted. Water vapor beaded on the crystal visor of my helmet, freezing in fine patterns across the glass. Swallowing against the change of pressure in my ears, I pushed myself upright and leaned forward on the saddle grips so I could see around her neck. "*Yeah, no way those guys are undead. It doesn't look like a Sathbari plainsmen camp, either. Definitely refugees.*"

"*You're right. It's all scared people. Smells bad.*"Karalti pulled into a thermal, filling her wings like sails. She pointed with her snout at one part of the camp. "*Look, down there. People are fighting.*"

I closed my eyes for a moment, then flared them like a bird of prey and zoomed my vision to the area she was indicating. My HUD took over from my eyes at that point, magnifying the scene below to a superhuman level. Close to twenty people were arguing over a wagon loaded with livestock, with some trying to drag the goats and chickens off, and others standing on the wagon, beating them back. Everyone down there looked ragged and desperate. Unless you were a good hunter, food was hard to come by on the steppe.

"There's nothing we can do. We have to focus on what we're here for." I grimaced and shook my head. *"The only thing we can do is win."*

"Yep." Karalti shifted down ten feet or so into the oncoming wind, and my stomach dropped like I was on a rollercoaster. *"Hold on. I'm gonna lead the ships to the Pass!"*

"Think you can wing it without resting for a while?"

"Yeah! I've still got half my stamina! I'll be fine!"

Our course took us through Vastil Pass and then south. The Pass was a bleak, rocky canyon that zig-zagged through the mountains like a thunderbolt. The sun barely penetrated, and it was frigid and nearly lifeless, save for goats picking their way along the sheer cliff faces. But something had lived here, once. At the halfway mark, ruins began to appear. Fortresses built into the cliffs, and dragon-sized lairs crowded with crumbling wreckage. We turned a corner and came upon rows and rows of monolithic statues. The tall, pillar-like draconic statues loomed like graveyard angels over the road to either side of us, their features worn into nothingness by the elements.

At the end of Vastil Pass was a massive gateway, and there, Myszno transformed again. I'd been expecting the province to have a cold, alpine climate, like Pre-Collapse Germany or Switzerland. It didn't. Protected on all sides by mountains, it was a warm, verdant greenhouse of brilliant green forests and startlingly dark soil. The soaring hills and steep valleys were thick with sycamore and walnut, cedar and birch, fading out into pastures and meadows glittering with flowers. The lakes and rivers were a brilliant clear blue. There was an airship port and a village near the Pass, both of which were currently overwhelmed by refugees. Roads wound down toward one of the great cities of the province: Litvy, which was built in a valley beside one of the lakes. Slender spires reached up toward the sky from inside the city walls, like something out of an Elven fairytale.

From here, the journey was a lot more technical for the airships. We flew wide around Litvy, heading steadily south through the narrow mountain passes. It became warmer and more humid the further we went. We knew we were almost there when ash and an unmistakable sweet, rotten stench carried to us on the wind. Soon after that, we spotted our destination: the Endlar.

The Demon's fires raged on the far southern side of the swamp, gnawing at the edge of the waterlogged forest that separated the army of the dead from the colossal fortifications of the Prezyemi Line. It was easy to see why the Demon's march had been halted here. The highlands of Vastil County dropped abruptly and dramatically into the lowlands of Racsa, the county containing our intended future castle. On the plateau, the great rivers of Myszno converged into a glacial delta controlled and shaped by two titanic stone dams. They choked the rivers at the neck, forming lakes that in turn spilled out into smaller rivers and their tributaries that wound around a series of islands and tumbled off the plateau ridge as five great waterfalls.

Along that ridge was the Prezyemi Line itself: an enormous, implacable wall that was probably twenty miles long and added another thirty feet to the tall cliffs. The ramparts were wide enough for six hookwings to run side-by-side. Bastions, each set about a thousand yards apart, glowed with the light of distant torches.

When we were about half a mile away, my HUD generated a holographic map of the landscape beneath us, tracing the main landmarks of the battlefield. There was a small town surrounded by a much larger tent city sprawled out behind the western half of the wall, which was bounded by the dam and its lake to the north. The structures on the islands to the east were the logistical buildings that allowed the defense to produce different Mass Combat units. On a promontory that jutted out between the two largest waterfalls was a towering star-shaped fortress: Korona Fortress, the headquarters of the defense.

Korona faced the Endlar from the edge of the cliff wall, where had a commanding view of the barren, muddy hellhole the war had made of the swampland in front of it. About eight hundred yards of No Man's Land lay between the Prezyemi Line and the edge of the drowned woods, all of it mud studded with the wreckage of abandoned farms and a village. As I was taking all this in, I noticed a side-quest alert. I leaned up on the saddle and swiped it in.

New Quest: Survey the Line

You have reached the place where Myszno's fate shall be decided: the Prezyemi Line. To learn more about the area,

survey it by focusing on and labeling different features of the environment. The more thorough you are, the better knowledge you will gain.
Reward: *Skill EXP, Knowledge (Grade Varies)*

E, X and P: my favorite letters. I accepted, and a ticker appeared in the HUD overlay. I leaned to the right to get Karalti to drop a wingtip and began counting. Each time I spotted something, a point was added to the ticker and a label was added to the virtual overlay. I dutifully marked off all the unit production structures, cannons, bastions, gates, siege equipment, the stone barracks and the militia encampment behind the wall, the bridges linking them, the strongest and weakest points in the defenses. It was like the JADE-IV holomaps we were given in the Army during mission briefings. Actually... now that I thought about it... it was *exactly* like a J-MAP, except that I didn't need an augmented reality helmet to see it.

My experience paid off here. I was used to doing this exact task IRL, and after I hit forty-two tags, my HUD pinged.

⟦You have new knowledge: the Prezyemi Line (A-grade)⟧
⟦You have acquired a new map: the Korona Fortified District⟧
⟦Congratulations! You have attained your first A-Grade Knowledge! +100 EXP, +10 Skill EXP.⟧

A-Grade!? I'd never gotten an A for anything academic before. To my delight, a cluster of labels appeared on the map overlay. Including the name of the town behind the Western Wall.

I cracked up laughing. "*Karalti. See that town down there? You will not believe what that place is called.*"

"*What?*"

"*Slutlava. I am not even joking.*"

"*That's... not a Vlachian name. Or like... a name from anywhere.*"

"*No, it's not. Someone used a fucking random place name generator, and those poor bastards down there ended up living in Slutlava.*"

Karalti and I giggled together over that, and then I remembered that I had A-grade Knowledge I needed to check out. I surfed over to the ArchemiWiki, curious about what my survey had revealed.

The Prezyemi Line (A-Grade Knowledge)

The Prezyemi Line (Prez-yeh-mi) is wall of 'fortified districts' that separates Vastil County from Racsa County, the historic Southern frontier of Vlachian-occupied Myszno. Utilizing the dramatic geography of the Krivan Valley, the Line was constructed by Lawislaw Corvinus the Burned during his conquest of Myszno after the end of the -

"Hector! There's an assault on the center wall!" Karalti's voice cut the narration short, and my combat HUD jumped to life.

"Fuck." I squinted at the battlefield, and sure enough, a straggling line of dark shapes were cutting the waters of the swamp. No sooner had we spotted it than the watchtower bells began to ring, and the defenses of the bastions along the wall came to life. I tapped the group voice chat. "There's a small assault force attacking west, about 500 yards from Korona. Karalti and I are going in, you copy?"

Suri replied with crisp efficiency. "Copy that. Orozlan is coming into view of the Line now. Will advise crew of maneuver, over."

"Uhh... roger? Over?" Rin didn't have Suri's radio experience, but I couldn't fault her for trying.

"You can just say 'Rin copy', sweetie," Suri replied.

"Oh. Sorry *(-w-);" Rin* sent an emoticon, which flashed up briefly on my HUD.

Snorting to myself, I looked back over my shoulder to see if I could spot the Orozlan, but then something out of the corner of my eye snagged my attention. My head snapped around, just in time to see a squadron of swiftly moving shadows slide through the fog generated by the waterfalls.

"Should we go back?" Karalti, who didn't have my extreme peripheral vision, was oblivious.

"No. Descend five hundred and hold. I just saw something."

The dragon tilted against the roaring wind and dropped quickly enough that my ears popped. As we leveled out, I saw the shadows again, and then the creatures that were making them: ten drity brown vultures almost the size of Karalti. They were sneaking up on the bastions that projected over the river by using the waterfall spray for cover, flying out of sight of the artillery that fired on the rest of the staggered assault force. Their target wasn't the wall, but the sprawling camp behind it. Civilians, and-or refugees.

"Look sharp, three o'clock," I ordered. *"Are we close enough for you to scan them?"*

"Maybe? I think so." Karalti swiveled her head in that direction, and I smelled ozone as she began to work her magic.

"Ten bogeys on the refugee camp, holding formation from low 5, low 5. We'll engage once in range." I rattled off the PM to Suri and Rin before the spell took hold, closing the dictation box just before my HUD pushed in the monster description:

Kalxat

Unit Rank: 5 (Level 12)
Faction: Napathu Undead
Health: 883/883
Morale: 110% (Flock boost)
Speed: 100 (Very Fast)
Melee Attack: 35
Melee Defense: 26

Abilities: Nauseating Stench, Spread Disease, Anti-Artillery, Aerial Charge.
Buffs: Causes Fear in enemy units (-2% morale), boosts morale of allied ground units (+2% morale), +20% damage to Artillery units on successful charge
Vulnerabilities: Vulnerable to Anti-Air tactics.
Terrifying undead birds of prey also known as Plague Rocs, Kalxat are hideous, huge vultures worshipped as avatars of Ensi, the god of victory in Napath. Intelligent and social, they work in flocks to spread disease and dismay using their foul acidic breath weapons, and their attacks can cause blindness, deafness, and uncontrollable nausea.

"Ten Level 12 monsters. Let's figure they get a bonus to attacking as a group, so plan for damage to about Level 16," I muttered. To Karalti, I said: *"Think we're ready for our first dogfight, Tidbit?"*

"Yeah! Roast turkey for dinner!"

"Kentucky Fried Vulture. Gross." I pulled my spear off my back, just as my HUD chirped and Suri patched in.

"Second Company Dragoons are armoring and will assist with quazi once in range," she said. "If you have trouble, kite the bogies back toward the Orozlan for support. Otherwise, kill 'em dead. Over."

"Roger-dodger." I banged the top of my helmet with a fist, then unclipped the safety straps that connected me to Karalti's saddle and knelt up against the pummeling wind. *"Okay, girl: let's see if all this training's paid off."*

"*Okay! Hold on!*" Karalti dropped her wing and slipped out of the thermal, swooping toward the vultures as they dived at the fortress below

Chapter 12

There were three main factors in aerial combat that made it radically different to ground combat: gravity, velocity and altitude. It was a bit like rock-paper-scissors. Gaining altitude meant sacrificing velocity, but having altitude gave you some key advantages. For one thing, your pointy-stabby bits – spear, dragon claws, breath weapons – faced down toward the enemy when you were above them. You also had the ability to weaponize gravity by diving. Diving meant sacrificing altitude for velocity, which was great if you needed to evade or hit hard, but reducing altitude put you underneath the pointy-stabby bits of the enemy. From my earliest training days with Karalti, I'd somehow known this instinctively - that aerial combat was, at its heart, the struggle for altitude and velocity against gravity.

"Diving in three!"

I bent over the saddle grips: knees tight, ass up, head down. *"Ready!"*

"Here we go! Wheeee!" Karalti folded her wings and almost lazily rolled over into a plummeting, arrow-like dive.

Gravity pressed me against her back like a huge crushing hand, greying my vision around the edges. A normal man would have passed out. No matter what fantasy soap operas would have you believe, getting on the back of something going and diving at hundreds of miles per hour with your head above your feet was not a good idea. Even with my head down, my magically fortified body had to shore up against the intense g-forces as we hit two hundred miles an hour, then two fifty. The gut-clenching torque felt like it would tear my tongue out the back of my head. The adrenaline hit was damn near sexual. I fixated on the target as the roar built in my ears, ready to jump.

The vultures swelled in size as we grew closer, and I felt the muscles of Karalti's body flex beneath the saddle - my cue to cling on with all my strength as she snapped her wings out to full extension. "*Get ready!*"

The dragon's jaws parted, and blazing liquid fire boiled out. The stream hit one of the monsters square in the back, ripping a line of oily, sticky flames along its body. Before it had time to squawk, Karalti struck it with her hind feet, flexing her killing claws deep into its body, then flung it from the sky.

[[Sneak attack! x3 damage!]]
[[Ghost fire does 1010 damage!]]
[[Gore does 216 damage!]]
[[You killed Kalxat!]]
[[You gain 115 EXP! Karalti gains 115 EXP!]]
[[Congratulations! Karalti is Level 9!]]

The Kalxat's head shriveled and its skull charred. It spun out of the sky like a thousand-pound hunk of charred meat. Karalti swelled in size as she leveled up, the saddle adjusting to fit. Even as she was growing, she rolled and pulled us away from the other eight pissed-off birds. Screaming with rage and confusion, they swirled into formation and chased us up into the air.

"Jump, now!" Karalti cried. *"While we have altitude!"*

My heart was pounding so hard that I could barely hear the roar of the wind. I tried to leap off from my sprinter's crouch, but then I saw how far we were from the ground. As soon as my lizard brain began screaming, my legs locked up. Fuck. In Taltos, I'd trained by jumping onto enemies on the ground from a maximum of fifty feet. We were at around three thousand and climbing. I'd skydived before and loved it, but this time, there was no parachute.

"Hector! What are you doing!?" Karalti seesawed out of the way as one of the Kalxat shot past us, leaving a gut-churning stench in its wake. I managed to stay on her back as she swung back and righted. *Breathing. Focus on your breathing.*

"Sorry. Try again." Sucking in air through my nose and teeth alike, I opened and closed my hand on the saddle grip until I could let go of it. That was an old stunt trick. If you can will yourself to open your hand, you can will yourself to lift off your bike. I looked down, and saw a pair of malicious, glowing eyes gaining on her tail. *"Okay, here comes the next one!"*

"Go! I'll catch you!" Karalti's back became rigid, giving me a stable platform to spring from.

I had to trust her. I forced my hand open, got to my feet, and before I could scare myself into another freeze, I triggered Jump and sprung out into the open air like an acrobat. "WaaaaHOOOO!"

There was a thrilling moment of weightlessness, then the brief, entirely reasonable panic of being in free-fall without a parachute. But the Kalxat got real close, real fast. I landed on it with the Spear, plunging the blade into the Kalxat's back in a blaze of dark fire.

[[Jump deals 640 damage!]]
[[Kalxat takes +150 Fire damage!]]
[[You have been exposed to Terrible Stench!]]

Suddenly, my fear of falling was pushed aside, because holy motherfucking shit. I'd only smelled one thing as bad as this monster in my life, and that was when my friend's dog had interrupted our tabletop game night by vomiting up the cat poop he'd eaten onto the sofa. The stench was indescribable. All five of us ran from the room, coughing and weeping and retching.

Coughing, weeping and retching was exactly what happened now as the Debilitating Nausea debuff appeared. It was all I could do not to throw up on the inside of my new fancy helmet.

"SCREEEE!" The bird, bleeding toxic sludge and mana, bucked underneath me. I lifted up, then slammed down belly-first onto its back. One scrabbling hand caught a handful of stinking, oily feathers just before it rolled out of its formation with another short scream. My stamina bar drained with the effort of holding on as it see-sawed violently from side to side.

Karalti wheeled above us, executing a sudden hairpin turn that took one of the vultures by surprise. The bird tried to backwing, desperate to get away from the plume of sticky, napalm-like fire that slashed it across the chest and belly and set it ablaze. As it fell away, screeching in agony, two vultures closed in on Karalti.

"Left and right!" Seizing a moment of steady flight, I reared up, and plunged the flaming Spear of Nine Spheres down like a butter churn. It swung as the blow came down, and instead of driving the blade into its body, I whiffed through the feathers of its wings instead.

[[Kalxat uses Contagion!]]
[[Karalti has killed Kalxat!]]

"Kalxat uses WHAT?!" As greasy flames caught its feathers, foul smoke boiled up into the air - and to my disgust, the fire drove out a cloud of hopping, slithering parasites that blew into my face and clung to my armor. The ones that found skin bit and stung, and another debuff icon appeared in my vision.

[[You take 5 bite damage!]]
[[You have contracted Grave Rot! Strength and Stamina will begin to decrease!]]
[[Warning! You have blood poisoning! -2 HP per second!]]

Grave Rot!? For the first time in a long time, I felt panic: real, honest-to-dog panic. I was sick. It was killing me. Every instinct I had told me to let go, get away, claw the bugs off my skin.

Before I'd even started hyperventilating, the Kalxat shored up until it was nearly horizontal, then folded in the uppermost wing and rolled back the other way to try and jolt me off into the open air. I was suddenly pinned by gravity against the crawling mat of flea-like parasites seething in the vulture's feathers.

"I'm coming!" Karalti thundered down, slamming into the badly-injured vulture in a tangle of jaws, claws, and wings. The weakened Kalxat took two sets of talons to its exposed belly. It screeched, and then - to my horror - opened its beak wide and vomited. Karalti bellowed as acid and bile struck her in the neck and chest, and a disgusting, nauseating cloud of hot mist blew back over me.

[[Karalti takes 225 acid damage! HP: 974/1199]]
[[Karalti is immune to poisoning!]]
[[Karalti is immune to Grave Rot!]]

"Duck!" The dragon twisted her head around, jaws gaping. I dropped down against the vulture's body just as oily white flames erupted overhead, engulfing the Kalxat's head. Ghost Fire stripped the feathers and flesh from its skull. Its wings spasmed and then folded, flapping limp as the scorched, disemboweled monster tumbled bonelessly from the sky.

"Fuck fuck fuck FUCK!" I dry-heaved from the smell – half-digested shit, now with the added aroma of burned feathers and stomach acid – but let go and threw my limbs out like a skydiver. Drag ripped me up into the air, away from the dead monster as it spiraled like a falling star to the waters far below. *"Karalti!"*

Karalti dodged the remaining Kalxat as they dived, one after the other, screeching and reaching out for her with hooked talons. She swooped in, snatching me up by the back of my Cossack Harness with one back foot while I clawed at myself. Bugs were everywhere. Even in the places where there were no parasites, my skin crawled. The Spear hung from the securing cord around my wrist, dragging us down. Karalti was carrying this fight. I had to get my shit together.

The Kalxat saw their opening. They dived again, belching plumes of acid at Karalti as she struggled to gain altitude. The dragon barrel rolled to evade their claws and breath weapons while I held onto my harness with grim determination. *"Use Split Turn! Get some momentum and throw me at one of them!"*

"Okay!" Karalti roared, folding her wings and diving sharply just as three vultures charged from either side. She barreled out of the maneuver, struggling for breath, and then executed Split Turn, which allowed her to make a supernaturally sharp hairpin turn in the air. At the apex of the turn, she let me go. I used Shadow Dash, briefly dematerializing, and then Jump. The double dash landed me right above the Kalxat, and I hit my newest ability: Master of Blades.

"Tarn takhran, shitbirds!" I grasped the Spear in both hands, and as I did, raw power shot up from the weapon from my fingertips to my back. For a moment, I felt like a spider at the center of a freezing cold web of energy – a web which caught me in mid-air and reversed my fall. The energy divided, forming patterns like a great mandala of dark light, then contracted into six lances of pure Darkness. They were slender bolts of black deeper than the night sky around us, blazing with ghostly transparent flame. It was over in a second: the lances rained down on the screeching Kalxat, impacting them so fast they blew out the other side into clouds of violet, crackling electricity. Black bolts of it rebounded back to me, slithering over my body as I burned the rest of my AP and triggered Rain of Glass.

Fuck you, fuck you, fuck you! The power was pure rage, sharpened and focused. I flung it out with a hoarse roar: a rain of smoking violet knives that chased the birds like homing missiles and shredded them apart.

Feathers, flesh and blood exploded and rained down. The shockwave of their destruction was powerful enough to propel me back up into the air. The world seemed to slow, the seconds rolling by like syrup as the notifications rolled in.

[[You have killed Kalxat!]]
[[You deal 2176 damage!]]
[[You have killed Kalxat!]]
[[You gain 115 EXP! Karalti gains 115 EXP!]]
[[You deal 3966 damage!]]
[[Karalti has killed Kalxat!]]
[[You have killed Kalxat...]]

Holy shit. My eyes widened.

There was a blast of fire overhead. I glanced up as a shadow fell over me. It wasn't Karalti. It was the last Kalxat, dead and burning. Without thinking, I Shadow Danced out of the way – or tried to. Master of Blades had sucked up all of my AP, which I realized just as the tumbling bird clipped me. It spun me around, then nearly tore my head off as a strap caught around my neck and shoulders and dragged me down toward the earth.

Chapter 13

When it came to accidents, years of stunt work had given me blood like ice-water. The fallen Kalxat's talon had snagged on some part of my gear, and its dead weight was pulling us out of the sky. The solution was simple: unequip my armor.

With the wind tearing at my everything, I navigated telepathically to the equipment menu and unequipped the lot. Once I was down to my underpants, I was free. The updraft dragged me up and off, and my descent slowed. "Karalti!"

"I'm coming!"

The parapets of Korona were now close enough that I could see the faces of the soldiers below. Time seemed to slow. It wasn't just a trick of my mortality. Plunge, one of my passive abilities, was making the fall seem slower than it was – an extra three seconds to contemplate my inevitable death-by-splat. "You'd better hurry!"

Karalti streaked past like an arrow, unfurling her wings and sliding into position underneath me. I reached out with my free hand, grasping for the saddle, and caught it. As soon as I anchored, she lifted – and I learned something new about physics when my unprotected face and torso slammed down with unexpected force. The sandsquid leather was sharper than sharkskin, ripping up my hands and face. My nose burst like a ripe raspberry, and there was a wet snapping in my chest that I heard with my inner ear.

⟦You have a broken nose! You're Dizzy, and incur a -10 vision penalty.⟧
⟦You take 79 points of impact damage!⟧

Right. I had been falling at high speed, and I'd remembered to unequip my armor, but not to fucking re-equip it. Genius.

"Hold on!" Karalti coasted down toward Korona's skydock at a fast glide, shuddering with effort in the blustering wind. My head spun. Gritting my teeth, I re-equipped my gear from Karalti's saddlebags. The Raven Set appeared on my body like magic.

Neither of us had taken too much HP damage, but I was now bleeding from my everything and laboring under no less than four strength-sapping debuffs. Karalti was exhausted from a full day of flying. I couldn't insta-use my potions outside of combat. The dragon groaned with effort as she lined up with one of the docks. She was burning hot, her twin hearts hammering so hard I could feel them through the saddle.

The crowd of soldiers and staff below scattered out of our way just in time. Karalti came in fast, skipping over the remaining people and hitting the ground at a run. She bounced and hopped through the landing, flaring her wings to slow her momentum. When she came to a stop, I was still on her back. We were both alive and intact.

[[You have defeated Kalxat!]]
[[You gain 336 EXP!]]
[[Congratulations! You are Level 18!]]

Some of the pain ebbed as my HP rose with the level gain, but I was weak, feverish, and spurting blood out of most of the holes in my face. The first thing I did - before potions or poultices, before anything - was to use my new Purify ability to get rid of the Grave Rot. I clapped my branded hand to my forehead and concentrated. For a second, there was nothing: then a purple nimbus gathered around my body, followed by a flush of cool energy that spread through my limbs like a shockwave. My churning stomach settled; the feverish heat left my flesh, my strength returned, and the pounding in my head relented.

[[Purify has cured your disease!]]

A startled murmur passed through the mob gathering around us, a ripple of energy and excitement I sensed even before I opened my eyes. Over a hundred people had crowded onto the skydock, with more staring at us from the control tower and the parapets. They gawked at me and Karalti with the awe and desperation of men who'd just seen an angel descend from heaven. Some were reverent. Some were confused. Others gasped as Karalti lifted her head on her swan-like neck. Her horns were now a regal backswept crown. She'd put on another five feet of size; her dorsal spines were larger, her tail longer and more whip-like. She'd grown in two pairs of stabilizing fins at the base of her tail, which now fanned out toward the end.

"Yeah! See, I told you I'd level with our next combat!" Karalti stood tall, puffing out her chest. *"But hey, Hector?"*

"What is it, Tidbit?"

"I'm Level 9 now, so..." Karalti sunk back down, then lowered her head until her eye was level with mine. "You know what that means, right?"

"That you're half the size of a small plane?" I absently reached up to scratch her jaw. The soldiers oohed and ahhed, but no one approached us.

She rubbed her head down against my nails, eyes half-closing with pleasure. "Well... yeah. But it means I get to pick my spell, remember?"

I paused. *"You do?"*

"Yeah! Remember? I asked you back in Taltos, when you were drilling the holes in my spines for the saddle! I said I wanted to pick a spell when I turned Level 9!"

I frantically wracked my brains for the memory, but it came up perfectly blank. Now that I thought about it, I didn't remember drilling those holes in Karalti's dorsal spines, either. It wasn't one of those half-recalled brainfarts: just a void of space where the memory should have been, as black and featureless as the hole in my shoulder.

"Some things got scrambled after the last time I died." I shoved intrusive thoughts about dementia back in their box and refocused on the present. We were in Myszno, the ships were docking, and Suri and Rin were already waiting against the railing waving to us. I waved back. Everything was cool.

"You forgot to spend my Lexica back in Taltos, too," Karalti said. "Can I pick more than one spell this level?"

I had? Fuck. I frowned and rubbed the bridge of my nose, and immediately regretted it as pain shot up behind my eyes. "*Uhh... sure. Go ahead.*"

"Don't worry. You were really tired. Silly Hector needs to sleep more." Karalti sat back on the base of her tail, and her eyes turned distant as she focused on her own virtual interface.

[[Karalti has learned Shadow Wave!]]
[[Karalti has learned Teleport!]]
[[Karalti has learned-]]

"Out of the way! All of you!" A sharp, authoritative voice pierced the air, cutting over the murmuring crowd of troops. "Do you want to catch the plague!? Move back! Back!"

From the back of the chattering crowd, an arrowhead-shaped group of men pushed through the onlookers. The approaching group had the look of knights who'd seen better days. Their plate armor was tarnished and mud-spattered, surcoats threadbare. They wore assorted colors, but each one of the coats had at least a panel with the same heraldry: a rearing Brontosaurus in white and green, the neck and tail stylized into elegant curves. They carried javelins, which they used like clubs to clear a space around Karalti and I, and heavy crossbows, which they pointed at us as their leader approached.

I wasn't into dudes, but if I was, I'd be drooling over this guy. He wasn't just handsome: he was *pretty*. Medium height, strong and wiry, with a jaw that could cut glass, he had thick, wavy oiled hair pulled back into a ponytail and a braided goatee that framed a full, sullen mouth. His skin was darker than was typical for Vlachia, a cool dusky grey-brown that almost glowed silver under the right light. His eyes were a startling pale green, flashing under fierce brows. He was also dressed differently to his posse: His armor was studded leather, but more finely made than the piecemeal plate the others wore. He wore a calf-length coat in green, with an artfully draped white and green shawl over that, and tall cavalry boots that had seen a lot of use. Everything was belted down with a thick sash. He carried a rifle over one shoulder and a rapier on his belt, his hand cocked slightly near the hilt as he warily approached.

"Commander Istvan Arshak?" I called to him.

His head cocked. "Yes, I am. Excuse me for one moment, warrior." He bowed from the neck, then turned to face his men. "Paul, Viktor! Bring this crowd under control. I want all men back at their stations, now! Those ships are asking to dock and there's no space on the wharf. Find those dead birds and burn them. I don't want anyone else catching their plague."

"Yes, Captain." The two men and their fellows turned on the nearest gawkers and laid into them without hesitation. "Come on, laggards! You heard him! That's enough jerking off!"

Istvan turned back to me. Up close, the man looked exhausted. He had a bad case of panda eyes, and now that he was in proximity, I couldn't help but notice that he smelled strongly of alcohol. Despite that, his voice was level and steady. Like Ignas, he masked weakness well. "There. Now, that was quite a fight you and your dragon put up there. We saw you take out those stinkbirds. I like it. Fireworks are good for morale."

I saluted him on reflex. "Thank you, sir."

Istvan's intense gaze slid to Karalti. "Of all the things I'd expected His Ever-Distant Majesty to send us, I'd never have expected a dragon. Incredible. It is an honor to greet you, Solonkratsu. To whom do I speak?"

"Count Dragozin Hector, Lancer and rider of Karalti the Many Colored, the Black Opal Queen. We are the first of your reinforcements."

"A Count? A foreign Count? Yet you salute me as an officer?" He studied me with shrewd curiosity. "Interesting. I see the Kingsmark now, but you are Tuun, are you not? Not that this troubles me: My best man is... was... from Tungaant. Even so. I cannot imagine Andrik Corvinus giving any foreigner a title of any kind."

"Andrik isn't Volod anymore, commander," I replied. "Ignas Corvinus has retaken the throne."

The captain's eyes narrowed. "Ignas? The dead one?"

I forced a laugh. "He wasn't as dead as everyone thought. You didn't know?"

"No, and it hardly matters to me which Crow sits the throne: Mysznо carries on." Istvan eyed the oncoming airships. "If Soma knew about this, he hoarded the information like a Dakhari speaktrader. He was favored by Andrik, did you know? Speaking of that, Lord Peacock is surely on his way here to preen and puff, so I will give you some advice. Never call me 'Commander' in front of him. He will take offense at it, as he does with everything. In front of Soma, I am 'merely' Captain Arshak."

⟦New Hero added to Mass Combat Menu: Captain Istvan Arshak (Myszno Defense Force)⟧

I lay a hand on Karalti's arm, rubbing her forearm absentmindedly. "Hard to deal with, is he?"

"You know the sort. Never soldiered a campaign in his life, but he read a lot of books about war and learned to fence in his family's courtyard, thus is a master of the blade as well as a master of magic. The piglet didn't even know that a dying man voids his bowels until about six weeks ago." The Captain's lip curled. "We are outnumbered three to one at Prezyemi, fighting horrors beyond the sanity of all but the strongest men and women here, and all he cares about is his ego, his money, and his damn machines."

Yikes. Not only was Istvan drunk, he had a bad case of Resting Frag Face, and that did not bode well for the defense. "I'll bear it in mind, Captain. Once my companions come down off those airships, are we able to make some time for a briefing? I was hoping we could talk to both you and Lord Soma together."

Istvan's expression turned sullen. "The only reason you should put us in the same room right now would be to bet on us like fighting cocks."

I wasn't particularly knowledgeable on feudalism, but I was pretty sure knights, commanders or not, weren't supposed to talk to Counts the way he was talking to me. Still, I didn't want to pull rank with this guy. It would not go down well.

"Alright, well, we can catch up separately if needed," I said. "Karalti and I are here to work with you, not lord over you."

Istvan arched an eyebrow. "What does a lord do if not 'lord over' common folk?"

"I'm here to beat the shit out of Old Fangface and avenge your families." I held out a hand. "That is my number one concern for the foreseeable future. Me and the Countess need a complete briefing on the situation here, and we'll do what we can once we know the full scope of what we're dealing with."

The Captain shot me a wary look, like he wasn't sure whether to believe me. He raised his hand to shake, but then the shriek of a hookwing pierced the air. All three of us turned to look at the gate leading into the Skyport. A procession of eight people rode through, with a hulking man in fine Vlachian officer's armor in the lead.

"*Daykit be keran degêm*," Istvan muttered. "Speak of the donkey and he will bray. If you wish to find me, Your Grace, I will be in the War Room doing real work."

The man headed toward us dwarfed the slender hookwing he rode, a male as large as Cutthroat that still managed to look like the size of a pony compared to his bulk. He was gigantic: at least seven feet tall and three hundred pounds, none of it fat. Deep-set, brilliant blue eyes looked out from under heavy brows. His nose was long, cheekbones sharp, mouth thin. This hulk was accompanied by eight retainers, knights in glossy black plate and chain with blue and yellow flags, surcoats, and shields. Beside him, they looked like children.

"Istvan! There are ships arriving! Why didn't you summon me!?" Lord Soma boomed by way of greeting. "By the Nine, man! I'm neck deep in cannon repairs, and your pack of dogs just run out here, pointing crossbows at the emissary of the gods himself, and you don't even have the courtesy to send word to the workshop!?"

⟦New Hero added to Mass Combat Menu: Lord Lorenzo Soma (Myszno Defense Force)⟧

He knows about the Mark? On reflex, I glanced down at my hand. I had gloves on, so it wasn't visible. It was only when he dropped to the ground, walked up to Karalti and swept into a low, courtly bow in front of her that I realized he wasn't talking about me. Or to me. Or acknowledging me at all.

"*She* is Karalti," I stuck out a hand to shake and looked up at him. "And I'm her rider, Count Hector Dragozin."

"A dragoness?" Soma did a small doubletake, glancing down at me in confusion. His gaze drifted to my outstretched hand. "And a Count? Oh, yes... I see now. You bear the Kingsmark. But I wasn't aware the Tuun had nobility, unless you are of the priestly caste...?"

He kept glancing at Karalti, who was cocking her head from side to side as she watched the two of us talk. I wasn't even that invested in the peerage thing yet, but I was beginning to understand why Istvan hated him.

Spitting some blood off to the side, I dropped the unshaken hand. "I was recently sworn in as a vassal by His Majesty, Ignas II, for services rendered to the Crown."

The twinkle in Soma's eyes hardened. "Oh, really? What fief did he bequeath you?"

I gave him a tight, toothy smile. "The Ducal seat. Racsa."

Soma didn't flinch, and his crooked mouth even flashed with a brief grin. It reminded me of the way a manager smiled at his employees: warm, friendly, sincere, even while he was planning fifteen ways to fuck you over. Istvan, on the other hand, simply shut down. He'd almost been friendly before, but his eyes had paled, his jaw tightened. I wasn't sure it was just because of Soma.

"They're replacing Lord Bolza already? Hear that, Istvan?" The lord's smirk didn't budge. "I'm sure you have a writ and deed from His Majesty?"

I shrugged. "Sure."

"Excellent! We will put that title to a vote of your peers soon enough. It's about time Taltos sent us bumpkins something other than platitudes." Soma almost reached out to clap me on the arm, but then thought better of it. "Istvan! Gods, man, you reek of liquor again. Why are you standing around! Go and help tie in those ships!"

Istvan rolled his eyes. "My lieutenants are already taking care of it, Your Grace."

"Hold your tongue, you miserable swamp rat. Pah! Do you see what I have to put up with?" Soma gestured at Istvan dismissively. "Anyway, Lord Dragozin, you look like you already have one foot in the ocean after that fight of yours. From one peer to another, I extend you and your dragoness the full hospitality of Fort Korona. We will find accommodation, food and company for this magnificent creature while you have your injuries seen to. Be assured she will be in reverent hands while you recover."

"Thanks, but we already healed up." I rested a hand on Karalti's wrist "Actually, if you'll both excuse me, we need to go and find our companions."

"Well, in that case, allow my Castellan to give you a tour of our magnificent wall and our fortifications while we arrange accommodations worthy of a dragon and the new Lord and Lady of Racsa." Soma spread his hands like a magician, beaming. He wore a spell glove on his left arm. "It looks like the personnel are about to disembark. Three Hussar-class... good, good. They'll do just fine as a vanguard..."

"These are all the troops we are being sent, Your Grace," Istvan said sourly.

The Count blinked a few times. "You're joking. Not even a single legion? That's all Ignas sent?! Is he out of his damn mind!?"

"And a dragon, and three Starborn. Ilia is threatening a war with the White Sail Alliance." I looked up to the deck of the *Orozlan.* The warship hung like an elegant lionfish, its stabilizing sails lowered. It was anchored and chained, the mana engines creating a great downdraft of hot wind. Mounting platforms and ladders were put into positions and locked, and then a flood of people began to march off the ship. Marshals barked orders, porters pulled luggage and munitions down ramps that led from the lower decks. "We will need a briefing."

"Starborn. What nonsense." Soma's face rippled with a tic. "The briefing, on the other hand, is entirely reasonable, though the matter of your dragon remains. We have a large area I can set up with bedding, if the lady should like to rest?"

"Karalti can go back to the ship while you, Istvan, Suri and I talk," I said, firmly.

"No! Wait!" Karalti suddenly got up off her keel, dancing from foot to foot. *"I can come with you now!"*

I rubbed the bridge of my nose. *"The doors here are pretty big, but you're bigger, Tidbit."*

"Just hang on!" Karalti reared up tall, wings vibrating with excitement, and breathed a string of words of power into the air.

The words rang like soft bells, the sounds lingering and overlaying, and then she began to glow. The opal colors between her scales flared, then spread out in a scintillating white cloud as Karalti's form blurred, dissolved, and flowed down into a bright nimbus of light.

Lord Soma held his breath, taking a single step back, while Istvan cried out and nearly bolted. The nervous crowd of soldiers scattered with him as the light faded, a collective gasp went up around us.

[[Karalti has learned Polymorph I!]]

Chapter 14

The light cleared, and my jaw dropped.

In human form, Karalti was small, lean and athletic, like a dancer or a gymnast: a balanced, compact ribbon of muscle and soft curves. Her skin was creamy and iridescent by torchlight, the curves of her back and her face glinting with hints of pearly color, like a rainbow boa's scales. Her hair was a glorious, razor-straight fall of inky blue-black that poured down to her hips. And her face... she was Tuun. Wide, high cheekbones, a full, small mouth, eyes as elegant as a calligrapher's brush stroke. She was perfect, from her long slender neck down to her graceful, narrow feet. She was also buck-ass naked, and every single man on the parapet was staring at her in open-mouthed astonishment.

When she saw my expression, her eyes grew big and dark with excitement. Then she squealed, ran, and pounced. *"Yay! I did it!"*

I caught her mid-leap. "Tidbit, I-"

Karalti made a distinctly inhuman screech of joy as she latched onto me with her arms and legs and spun us around. Her hair swirled across my arms like heavy silk, and as I breathed in the cloud of scent, I finally realized what my dragon smelled like. It was lotus flower. Karalti smelled like a lotus in full bloom, waxy and sweet.

"Hector! I did it! I can go inside buildings again!" She butted her head against my neck, chirping and trilling. *"We can sleep together again! No more cold stables, no more stinky hookwings! Comfy bed! And snuggling!"*

"Absolutely, Tidbit. I mean, Karalti. I mean... ummm..." The combination of her scent, her strength, the petal-soft skin of her cheek against mine was quickly stripping me of higher function, common sense, and self-control.

She pulled her head back to meet my gaze with hers. Her eyes were still the same: a brilliant amethyst purple shot through with veins of silver, the iris and pupils large and birdlike. Before I realized what was happening, I fell into it, into her, just as I had when we'd sealed the Bond. Her feelings were more mature now, no longer the raw, primal need of a hatchling seeking food and safety... and as I gazed into her, I realized something. In the time we'd spent together, that her pure, simple love had never faded. But it had changed.

"Eeee! Hector!" Rin's musical soprano broke over the stamping of boots and the chatter of men. The little Mercurion rode on the back of one of her turrets, the other one bounding along after her. Suri followed up on foot, leading Cutthroat. The dragon's eyes narrowed, and she molded the front of her body against mine as the pair drew near.

"I can definitely, really explain this!" I blurted once they were earshot. "Suri, this is-"

"Karalti, I know. We saw her vanish from the gangplank." Suri had Cutthroat's reins in one hand, clasping them just under the brutish hookwing's jaws so that she couldn't turn around and bite anyone. She was wearing her gift from Ignas: a fine suit of flame-scorched plate armor and a long, black-red cloak that faded to scarlet around the hem. Ignas had called it Burning Man's Plate. She wore it without the helmet, her short red hair tousled and freshly trimmed. "No mistaking that stink-eye she's giving me, either. How the hell'd you shapeshift like that, Special-K? Is that a Queen Dragon thing?"

"That's my *secret."* Karalti scowled. She stepped back and tossed her hair over one shoulder. The limited coverage it had given her naked body was suddenly irrelevant.

"Good grief, man!" Soma tutted, sweeping his cloak from his shoulders. Before I could stop him, he advanced and lay it around Karalti's shoulders. "Here, your Holiness... this is the least of the gifts I could give to honor such arresting beauty."

Karalti opened her mouth to try and speak aloud, but all that came out was a weird honking rasp. Her eyes widened, and she clamped her hands over it with a little squeak of dismay.

"Baby steps, Tidbit." I gave Soma a reluctant nod of acknowledgment and straightened up the enormous cloak so that it covered Karalti's modest, but shapely chest. Then, something occurred to me. "Wait: Karalti, do you have an inventory?"

"Yeah!" She said. *"When I changed, my saddle and the saddle bags went in there."*

"Then you should be able to carry armor and weapons." Curious, I surfed to my own Inventory and selected the Nizari armor set. It came with everything but gloves. I added the Cold Iron Gauntlets I'd found in the tomb underneath Taltos. "Here, Tidbit: I don't think you have any weapon proficiencies yet, but these gloves double as unarmed weapons. They're good against undead, too."

"Yeah! I have unarmed proficiency!" Karalti huddled in against me while I made the transfer to her Inventory - I still had access to it - then closed her eyes for a moment. *"Okay... aaaand... equip!"*

The leather armor appeared on her body, a Middle Eastern-looking assassin set with layers of artfully aligned leather and plate. It hugged Karalti's curves a little more than it had on me, and she made it look good. The gloves were brutal: full-sleeve gauntlets forged from pitted cold iron that went almost all the way to her shoulders. She examined her hands, delighted. I pulled the marquee-sized cloak off her and threw it back to Soma, who took it like he was now handling the Shroud of Turin.

"There you go." Suri clapped her on the back before she had time to react. "You look like a right little warrior princess."

"NO TOUCHIE!" Karalti pulled her lips back over her gums, flashing top and bottom rows of razor sharp, shark-like locking teeth.

Istvan grunted. "A dragon who turns into a maiden. Now I have seen everything. Forgive me, Flamehair, Mercurion - we have not been introduced?"

"Not yet. Suri Ba'hadir, the Lioness of Dhul Fiquar." She held out a hand to Istvan first, and then belatedly added: "Countess of Racsa."

A tic started by Soma's eye as Istvan shook ahead of him. When Suri turned to him, he lifted his chin. "A Dakhari countess now? Ignas is handing out titles like priests handing out candy to children during the Dark Moon Festival. Trying to make up for Andrik's noisy nationalism, is he? Flaunt his tolerance?"

"Andrik's death opened up a few appointments." Suri flashed him a lovely, acidic smile. "You must be Lord Soma. He told us all about you."

"Wait: you're Lorenzo Soma?! THE Lorenzo Soma?! Oh my goodness, I've heard all about your work with L.A.E.H.T Engines!" Rin, oblivious to any sort of ritual noble protocol, burst out before Soma could really react to Suri's barb. "Is it true that you managed to extend the range of the Super Storm DM-Long Haul by 2000 miles!?"

Soma blinked down at her a couple of times. "Why... yes, as a matter of fact. Just before this nonsense with the Demon broke out, we were looking at putting those engines into mass production for His Majesty's navy."

"Lord Soma is an Artificing *genius.* "Rin turned to us, while Istvan watched on with arched brows. "He's published over fifty articles about the development of hybrid long-distance airship engines using BCM-GCM synthesis via induction compression and conjugated Words of Power and... oh..." She trailed off, suddenly realizing that only one other person in the room had understood anything she had said.

Soma laughed uproariously. "Spoken like a true Artificer! Passion, that's what I like to see! Not enough passion around this place. You're a light in the dingy gloom of Fort Korona, girl. Those turrets are yours, are they? Mind if I look at them?"

"Yes! I mean, no! I mean... sure!" Rin blushed bright blue. She was clearly starstruck.

"Hold a moment, Istvan." Soma pulled his one normal gauntlet off, revealing a surprisingly work-worn hand. He went to Hopper and Lovelace and knelt in front of them. The pair of Artificed turrets jittered in place like nervous hounds. "Khors breath, they're responsive. Oh... yes, yes. Look at that! I can't smell any gas, but these joints must leak during movement, surely? I always had that problem with articulating joints..."

"They're sealed with copper solder and silicone gel, like kneecaps!" Rin blurted. "Bursa! I got the idea from studying anatomical manuals!"

"Oh, yes, I see the mechanism now... fascinating. What Word conjugation did you use to stabilize the bi-lateral sensor coupling? E.O.M or M.O.T?"

Karalti cocked her head, clinging to my arm. Suri watched on with a touch of bewilderment. Istvan had that sullen pouty face going again. And me? I was confused. Soma was the weirdest combination of meathead jock and science nerd I had ever met.

At that point, Istvan reached his limit. "Soma! Quit with your damn machines and pay attention to your officers! The marshals are making their approach! We are here to win a war, not play with trinkets!"

Soma paused nattering with Rin. He turned as he rose to his feet, eyes narrowed to icy slits. "These 'trinkets' are potentially the blueprints for very powerful weapons against our enemies."

"Oh, yes. Let us send heavy metal creatures out into the mud carrying payloads of mana in their veins." Istvan gestured angrily at the turrets. "YMachines can't swim! They can't float! Why do you want to send machines into the Great Marsh when you know the undead use that... that *poison* to make more of themselves!?"

The Count sneered. "You're a fine one to talk about poisons, you insolent drunkard. Bolza might have let you get away with this behavior, but I'll have you on the gallows by morning if you don't sober up and pull your head out of your-"

"Hey, guys. Cool it." I held up my hands. "Please."

Istvan's eyes flashed hotly as he turned to glare at me. Soma's heavy jaw clenched. Rin, still kneeling beside Hopper, seemed to deflate.

"Some kinds of machines can float or swim," I said. "But Istvan's got a point."

"Yeah. It's not a one size fits all situation." Suri gave a curt nod.

"It's true," Rin added nervously. "The articulated design on Hopper and Lovelace makes these guys fantastic on uneven terrain or in urban scenarios, but they lack a ballast and there's a risk that, umm, the joints get clogged with mud. We could develop different styles of locomotion. I always wanted to work on an ATV-style Artifact."

"Yes, yes... that's entirely possible. I actually have some blueprints drawn up for powered water vehicles." Soma stroked his stubbly chin, the captain's attitude apparently forgotten for the time being. "You, girl - Rin? I like you. Istvan, you handle these foreigners. This talented Mercurion and I need to discuss Artificing and trade."

Istvan's eyes glittered with barely contained rage.

"It would be great to get a brief on the situation here." Suri joined me and Karalti on my other side. "The more we know, the more we can help."

"Yeah." I glanced at the two men as they gave each other the stink eye when they thought no one else was looking. "Because it sure as hell looks like you need it."

Chapter 15

The War Room at Korona was nothing like the palatial digs at Vulkan Keep. There were no fancy maps or mahogany furniture here: just chickens in the hallway outside, old smelly reeds on the floor, and a solid stone table covered in a messy jumble of maps, markers, notes, bottles and wooden cups. The walls were covered in more maps, ledgers, notes and scraps of parchment, with routes through the Endlar marked up with flags and pinned thread in different colors. I couldn't help but notice the vast majority of the swamp was uncharted.

"*Kutzi keri.* You see what I have to deal with?" Istvan said sourly, plopping down onto one of the chairs. He knotted his fingers up through his hair, staring down blankly at the map nearest him. After a moment, he pushed it away and took up one of the bottles. "Do any of you want a drink?"

The cup nearest me smelled like fermenting fruit juice. I peered over the rim. There were a couple of mold floaters on the surface of the liquid inside. "Not for me, thanks," I said, steering the dragon to a seat. Karalti darted her head to one side like a curious bird, staring at a shiny letter opener on the table glinting under the light of the chandelier.

“Suit yourself.” Istvan got one of the cleaner mugs and filled it to the brim with a milky, frothy liquor that smelled a cross between sweet bourbon and yogurt. “So, you want a briefing on Korona? Two thousand men arriving on short notice, another hundred in quarantine, close to a hundred injured – some brutally – and a constant flow of refugees beating on our gates. There’s plague spreading in Slutlava. Everything has been a disaster since Karhad fell. You want to know my problems? I can summarize with one word. ‘Soma’.”

“Listen, I know you hate the guy, but this kind of talk isn’t helping you or anyone here. He’s your commanding officer, whether we like it or not.” I steepled my fingers and let them rest between my knees. “You’re digging yourself into a hole, my dude.”

“The hole was already dug.” Istvan paused to slam back his drink. “There’s nothing to do in Myzsno now but join the ranks of the dead.”

“Start from the beginning,” I said slowly. “Because you look like the kind of man who doesn’t scare easily or normally say shit like this. Tell us what happened in Karhad.”

Some of the fight drained from Istvan’s wiry frame. He shook his head slowly, taking another pull off his mug.

“The Demon destroys everything in his path,” he said haltingly. “He twists the land, tramples and Stranges the fields, seizing, or just butchering the animals wholesale. He adds their carcasses to the rest of the dead in his ranks. They march without tiring, destroy without caring. The only things that repel them are fire and water.”

"And what about you?" Suri asked. "What's your story?"

"I am... was... the Castellan of House Bolza." He looked up, his pale green eyes flashing. "I was orphaned at a young age, and my life was spent in service to the Voivode of Myszno. I served in Egbolt Castle in Karhad, fighting while Andrik Corvinus refused to send aid. We struggled alone against an army who grew larger with every battle we lost. Every person who falls is added to this... this thing's army. I lost my family, my hold... then I had to fight them. My wife. My children, my neighbors. Even my own dog came at me, guts hanging everywhere."

I leaned back. "Jesus."

Karalti crooned in agreement, searching the table for things to push onto the ground.

Suri stayed standing, as she often did. She wasn't much of a sitter. "I'm sorry, mate. Can't think of a worse situation than what you went through."

Istvan bowed his head. "Nearly everyone here has a story like mine, except for Soma. You must understand first that Karhad is not a city built for war, but for river trade. The city walls are rammed earth, wood and daub. The worst things we ever saw there in my lifetime were Tyrannosaurus, Yanik raiders, sometimes monsters. We did not need large walls until now."

"What kind of tactics does the Demon use?" Suri asked. "Any idea as to his overall strategy? What he wants?"

"Who knows? We have no idea what he wants." Istvan shrugged. "As for tactics... in Karhad, they hurled the living dead over the walls with catapults to begin the assault. Kalxat came forth next, blacking out the sky alongside chimera stitched from the bodies of wyverns and quazi and other animals. The horde followed: fast, fearless, immune to pain, carrying all kinds of weapons and tools. There were countless number of them, tens of thousands. They climbed over their own fallen corpses as their bodies mounded against the walls, and soon, it was over. The wall fell quickly, and they overran the city, butchering everyone they came across. How can you fight a man who pushes himself along your pike and feels no pain?"

He paused to drink, then sighed. "We held them off at the castle for a while. Closed the gates, poured oil in the moat and lit it ablaze. But the undead piled into the water until the flames were extinguished, and when they reached the gate, they punched through it with nothing more than nails and teeth and axes. I remember the smell, more than anything... and their commander. Behind the mass assaulting the castle rode the Demon himself."

"You saw him?" I leaned in with interest.

Istvan nodded. "Briefly."

"What did he look like?"

"He..." The man closed his eyes for a moment, swallowing. "I have never seen anything more terrifying. He is monstrous. Tall, well-built, like some terrible bronze temple statue come to life. His teeth gleam like sharpened metal stakes. He wears half plate with cloth of gold and all kinds of tarnished finery, and his mount... he rides a great skeleton aurochs made of gold or bronze, a bull the size of a tyrannosaurus. I never once saw its hooves touch the earth. He stood behind his elite guard during the assault, I remember, with a whip in one hand and a long gold staff with a great black stone in the other. I watched him use the staff to cast foul magic on the castle grounds. The gardens withered before our eyes, and the gates rotted away. His army poured in like an ocean of flesh and bone... it was all we could do to flee for our lives.

"You're lucky you got away," Suri said.

"Am I? Truly? I should have died with my lord. Everything I loved is gone." The Captain picked up his drink and threw the rest back in a couple of long swallows. His hand trembled as he set the empty cup down. "Now, my only reasons for being here are duty and dread. Duty, because Lord Bolza ordered me to leave and gave me the task of avenging Karhad, and dread, because I cannot bear to think of this plague flowing out from Myszno to cover the rest of the world. But it's hopeless. The Meewfolk mercenary company deserted just the other day. Food and medicines are short. Talks with the Yanik have faltered, and we have not been able to recruit them to our side. My father's people, abandoning us! My best scout, Zlaslo, has fallen ill with some disease the healers cannot cure, and Soma ordered the garrison's hero out into the swamp on a fool's mission. All for his ego."

"That doesn't make any sense." Suri crossed her arms.

Istvan fixed his gaze on me. "If you think like a self-involved idiot it does. He has not seen the Demon or the full might of his host yet, and scarcely believes it's as bad as we 'soft Southerners' and 'Yanik swamp rats' make it out to be.

Take Vash Dorha, for example. He is an incredible warrior, loyal and faithful to Lord Bolza's memory. The sight of him on the walls gave the men hope. He could leap from the bailey up to the bastions in one bound, and he once punched a zombie wyvern that had climbed onto the wall and laid it flat with a single blow. He invented the healing potion that cures Grave Rot. But he is a Baru, and the only master he answers to is Matir. He is proud and insolent to those who do not earn his respect, like Soma. My liege loved that insolence. He used to say that Vash was the incarnation of his conscience."

"Lord Bolza sounds like a good man," Rin said.

Istvan bowed his head. "Lord Bolza was the best liege a retainer could have asked for. Honest. Fair. Just. He was a melancholy man, prone to fits of brooding, but you would find no man more committed to his family and his duties as Voivode. We loved him and Lady Oksana, his wife. They were twenty years married as of this year, and they had a son and two daughters, one of whom was barely ten. That I survived and little Zophia did not..."

He trailed off. The Captain's depression was like a black cloud, deepening with every passing moment. Time to change the subject. "So why did Soma send Vash Dorha away?"

"Oh, yes." Istvan shook himself, blinking a couple of times. "Soma and Vash had an argument that ended badly. Soma decided that he was trying to incite mutiny among the ranks here. He sent him on some harebrained 'scouting' mission out into the deep Endlar as punishment, and Vash, being the stubborn ass he is, went along with it. Everyone here knows that to venture that far into the marsh is death.

Not even the Demon's army has been able to mass and get through. Our scouts report that the Demon seems to be preparing to cross with his army, though we don't know by what means."

Rin pursed her lips. "Can't he go around?"

Istvan shook his head. "You surely saw the mountains on your way here. If he were to go around, our airships would pick him off in the valleys. There are hundreds of lakes, and fortified gates in every pass... even the Demon cannot defeat a ten-thousand foot bottleneck, especially with an army that falls apart if it spends too long in the water."

"They don't like water? That's good to know." Suri glanced at me and Karalti. "But if Vash is as good as you say, he could still be alive."

"Not a chance. Not after six days." Istvan shook his head. "The woods are full of hungry dinosaurs, monsters, mires, and worse. Just because the Demon hasn't been able to get anything more than small attack squads through the swamp doesn't mean there aren't any undead there. Vash and the men who went with him are gone, and everyone knows it. That is why the Orphan Company deserted us. Everything that gave the men sanity, Soma has taken away. The men loathe him, and insubordination is on the rise. I tried to serve this lord faithfully and well, but I'm at my wit's end with him. And now you're here: a pair of foreigners full of fairy tales about Starborn, here to lay claim to my Lord's county. You know why Ignas sent you here, don't you?"

"Yeah." I nodded, absently rubbing the small of Karalti's back as I normally would have while thinking. "He sent us here to win this thing."

"No. He sent you here in exile." Istvan tipped the edge of his cup toward us, then drained the rest. "To get you out of the capital."

"Nonsense. We put him on the throne," Suri snapped.

"You are naive." The captain barked a short, bitter laugh. "That you put him on the throne is even more reason to be rid of you."

"Look, this is pointless." I waved him off. "We're here to fight a war. You've listed off a bunch of things that are wrong: let's start talking solutions. We need to solve problems."

"There is no point if the Volod will not send the troops we need to fortify us." Istvan's face sharpened, the muscles of his jaw tensing. "While we are under Soma's command-"

I stood up from the table and banged my hands down, rattling cups and trash. Karalti jumped in her seat. Suri and Istvan both froze.

"Quit. Whining." I stared him down. "Soma might be the biggest piece of shit ever shat out of a whale's ass, but he's not the only one with an attitude problem here. There's millions of people in danger. The ducal seat isn't going to reclaim itself. You want to lay down and die? I've got some rope in my inventory. Go hang yourself and get it over with."

Istvan's face darkened. He shot to his feet. "You dare-!"

"You were jumping Soma's shit about HIS ego." I slashed my hand toward the closed door to the room. "Well, what about yours, Arshak? I did not travel all this way to hear an officer of your standing speak this way. We go out and we recruit. We fix the morale. We repair the walls. We brew potions, heal or evacuate the wounded, and we go out into the damn swamp and drag Vash back by his asshole. There is *no* practical choice in war but to win, and winning starts with strong leadership. We WILL fight to win from now on. Do you understand me?"

"Yeah!" Karalti leaped up like a kid at a baseball game.

"I... you..." Drunk, flushed, and furious, Istvan tripped on his words.

"This is the time you salute and yell 'Yes sir!'" I banged my hand down again.

"Yeah!" Karalti beat her hand on the table with delight.

Istvan paled slightly. "Yes... sir."

"Damn straight." My face tingled with pins and needles as I retook my seat. "You should be able to give us a quest with all the shit you need done. Assign it and we'll get started, my dude."

Istvan's mouth twitched, as if he was fighting back a sneer. His expression turned sullen. "Fine. I will compile a quest. For all the good it will do... do as you please."

He closed his eyes, and I got an alert from my HUD.

⟦Congratulations! You have reached Leadership 6!⟧

"Yikes." Beside me, Suri winced. *"Check out his profile."*

I did, and I also winced. We were at -50 amity points with Istvan, buuuut... *"Okay, he hates us. But at least he's recruitable?"*

Suri snorted. *"Kinda."*

After a couple of minutes, Istvan opened his eyes, rubbed them, then frowned. My HUD chimed, and Suri cocked her head, no doubt hearing the same sound. So did Karalti. "Fine. There you go. It's long."

[[You have a new Quest Update!]]

Quest Update: Unto Death

You have arrived to discover the Myszno Defense Force in shambles. The Prezyemi Line is undermanned and underpowered. Korona Fortress is plagued by low morale, limited supplies, and feuding officers. The people's hero, Vash Dorha, has been sent on a suicide mission and is now missing. Desertion is rife, all while the Demon's armies loom on the horizon.

The Fort Captain, Istvan Arshak, has issued a series of quests to address the problems of the defense. View each Individual Sub-Quest for more details:

- ***All the King's Men:*** *Find the Orphan Company and convince them to return.*
- ***Into the Swamp:*** *Rescue Vash Dorha and the soldiers who accompanied him - or retrieve their bodies for proper burial.*
- ***Supply Train:*** *Find out who - or what - is holding up the supply train coming from Boros to Fort Korona.*

- ***Bayou Warriors:*** *Recruit the Yanik tribes to join the defense force.*
- ***Hold the Line:*** *Discover sidequests in Korona to bolster the defense and gain Renown.*

Special: *All sub-quests are optional. The number of quests you complete will affect your main quest line.*
Difficulty: *Varies*
Reward: *Varies: See individual sub-quest descriptions*

"Okay. Thanks." I clapped my hands on my thighs and stood again, eyeing the 'Dark Moon Pact Oathbreaker' status that had accompanied me from Taltos. "We'll get back to you with some good news as soon as we can."

Istvan eyed the liquor bottle. "We shall see about that, Tuun. We shall see."

Chapter 16

With the arrival of the reinforcements, space in Korona was suddenly at a premium. Karalti, Suri and I got a single room to share in the gatehouse that separated Korona from the Wall and the Waterfall Gates, the elevators that went down to the battlefield. Vulkan Keep had spoiled me, with its huge bathtub, spring-flushed toilet, and well-paid, well-trained servants. Our room here was a bare stone hexagon with two stone beds, shutters that whistled when the wind blew, and a fireplace full of dirt and moss. The reeds on the floor were damp, the bedding musty and worn. We got a single earthenware chamber pot to share.

"Home sweet home." I plopped down on the edge of one of the beds and brought up my message window. "Let's see how Rin's doing, and then huddle up and decide on a game plan, okay?"

"Yay! Comfy bed! Comfy bed!" Honking like an excited swan, Karalti leaped onto me and flung me onto the bed. Five-and-a-half feet of polymorphed dragon began to romp around and around on hands and knees like an excited puppy, burrowing under the blankets and then bursting out of them. *"No more cold! No more caves! Blankets! Pillows! And snuggling!"*

"Grr...HURRK!" I tried to cheer, but then I took an armored knee to the gut and just decided to curl up in the fetal position and wait until she was done.

The door opened a second time, admitting Suri. "Woah, guys – sorry to interrupt."

"No! You weren't interrupting anything!" I bellowed, flailing my arms at her, as if trying to push back the storm of drama I sensed on the horizon. She burst out laughing.

"Are dragons ticklish?" Suri asked us.

"I... uhh..." Too stunned to react sensibly, I watched as Suri took a wrestler's crouch and began to pace toward us. Karalti scrambled from the covers, bunched up on the end of the bed, and hissed. *"No touchie!"*

"Arrrrre they?" Suri wiggled her fingers.

"No- EEEEK!" Karalti squealed as Suri tackled her back onto the bed. Karalti was fast, but Suri was strong, and my dragon was not used to fighting in human form. I rolled off just in time for the pair of them to collide, and then watched helplessly as the larger woman pinned the smaller one and began to mercilessly tickle her as she yelped and squirmed.

"Hector! Hector! She's killing meeee!" Karalti lashed her body from side to side, kicking ineffectively as Suri got her fingers up into her armpits. *"Murder! Murderrrr!"*

"Welcome to the mammalian kingdom! Time to shape up those combat skills of yours! First rule: never let someone get you in a headlock." Suri laughed, winking over Karalti's shoulder at me. I crossed my arms and grinned back.

"Leggo! Leggo of me!" Karalti was giggling now. She stopped kicking and tried to bite Suri's arm. When that proved ineffectual, she lashed her head from side to side. *"AAAAAAAAARRRRGHHHHHH!"*

Shaking my head, I ignored the sound of smashing pottery and breaking furniture to my right, I recalled the Message Center and composed a P.M to Rin. *"How's it going over in Crafter land? Did you get an update to Unto Death? Get back to us when you can."*

By the time I'd finished that, the two of them had already settled down. Suri was wiping tears of mirth from her eyes while Karalti squatted on the floor like a gargoyle and glared at her, sullenly licking the corners of her mouth.

"Alright. All sorted? Ready to plan things out?" I looked over at them both.

"Sure." Suri plopped back down. "Quests, right... let's see here..."

I bought up the quest, letting it hang in front of me. "We should probably read the detailed descriptions and work out which one we want to tackle first. "Karalti, can you see the quest as well?"

"Me? Nope." She shook her head, pawing through the reeds on the floor and sniffing deeply. "I know it when you know it."

"Nothing like a little casual mind-reading between friends, I guess." I opened the sub-quest window and had my HUD read them out to me.

Sub-Quest: All the King's Men

Many soldiers in Vlachia are paid mercenaries, including the Orphans: a free company of battle-hardened veteran soldiers who were committed to holding the Line against the Demon's horrific forces - until suddenly they weren't. The Orphans are believed to have crossed the Sarviz and headed north-east toward the city of Boros. Istvan isn't sure what caused them to leave, but he badly wants them back.

Reward: *500 EXP, Renown +150, unlock the Orphan Company units for Mass Combat.*

Sub-Quest: Into the Swamp

Unwilling to have his authority questioned, Lord Soma sent Vash Dorha, a warrior-monk of Matir, into the deep Endlar to scout the swamps and report back on any sightings of the Demon or his army. That was four days ago, and neither he or the disciples who went with him have returned.

Vash is the hero of the garrison, serving as warrior, spiritual advisor, and healer. His loss has dealt the Defense Force's morale a mortal blow. Even closure would be better than nothing. Bring back Vash dead or alive, and you will bolster the men and either restore their hope or give them relief.

Reward: *500 EXP, +50 Renown; +100 renown if Vash returns alive. Unlock the Baru unit for Mass Combat.*

Sub-Quest: Supply Train

The route between the industrial city of Boros and Fort Korona has become treacherous since the Demon invaded the province. Airships loaded with cargo cannot fly over the mountains, and ships carrying vitally important goods - explosives, munitions, food, oil and mana - is shipped to the front lines through the ancient trade route of Krivan Pass. But someone - or something - has made the Pass unusable. You must reopen the passage before it's too late. Learn more from Lord Soma or his top weaponeer and commander of the Korona Sappers, Viktor.

Reward: *500 EXP, +150 renown.*

"Damn. We really have our work cut out for us, don't we?" Suri remarked, breaking the stream of narration. "Sounds like maybe Vash can train up more Baru for us, though. We need more healers, so-"

"Hang on. The system helps with reading, but I still take longer." I held up a hand, and tried to read along as my virtual siren continued narrating.

Sub-Quest: Bayou Warriors

The Endlar swamp is a vast, harsh land, concentrating some of the worst monsters to be found in Myszno into one humid, hot, disease-riddled mire. And yet, despite the dangers, the Endlar is also the home of the Yanik tribe, fierce dinosaur tamers and raiders who have resisted the Vlachian conquest of Myszno for hundreds of years.

Fielding dinosaur-riding mounted archers and cavalry, powerful mages and even packs of trained Allosaurus and T-rex, these people would be a powerful force against the Demon's armies - if they could unite with the Defense Force. The Yanik have no love for Vlachians, but they respect heroism and the Demon is as much a threat to them as anyone else. Impress their chieftain, and you might be able to win them over to your side.

Reward: *EXP, +150 Renown, unlocks the Yanik Warrior units in Mass Combat.*

Sidequests: Hold the Line

There is a constant battle against entropy on the Prezyemi Line: officers behaving badly, broken equipment, rats eating supplies. Listen to gossip and pay attention to problems you see around Korona to gain sidequests that will give you EXP and Renown, special items, and more. You can find points of contact anywhere in the Fortress or along the walls.

Current Sidequests:

- *Istvan remarked that one of his scouts, a man named Zlaslo, has fallen ill with a seemingly incurable disease. Go to the Fort Hospital to see if you can help.*

"Okay, there we go. And yeah... you're right. This quest-line is like an entire game of its own," I muttered, closing the window down. "What do you think, Suri? Where do you want to start?"

Suri shook her head and puffed a lock of hair out of her face. "Yeah no, I'm a bit overwhelmed, to be honest. Never had a quest this complex before."

I had - in other games. "It's alright: they'll tie in together at some point. The thing we need to figure out is how to optimize the quest sequence. My vote is we leave any quests where we have to impress someone until last. We need that renown to back up our approach to the Yanik and the Orphans."

"Yeah. So that leaves the sidequests, the swamp, and the caravans." Suri rolled her shoulders, then closed her eyes and sighed. "The caravan one isn't close to Korona. That's a dragon mission, in my opinion."

"What's that supposed to mean?" Karalti stopped investigating the fireplace and turned on her, eyes blazing.

Suri smirked. "It means you can fly, you big flappy cunt."

Karalti hissed and flew up to her feet, fists balled. *"Hector! She's calling me names!"*

"You call her names all the time, Tidbit." I replied. *"I seem to recall 'two-legs, no-wing whore' being thrown around a couple of days ago."*

"Yeah! But to you! Not to her face!"

"That doesn't make it any better."

"Fine! Whatever!" Fuming, Karalti sunk back down on her heels. Shooting us dark looks over one shoulder, she wrapped her arms around her knees and began muttering to herself. Even in human form, the bird-like mimicry sounded weird: like a demon grumbling into a bad radio.

"Anyway, yeah. As you said: excluding the quests that rely on renown leaves us with the Happy Fun Time Swamp Adventure, the caravan, and sidequests," I said aloud, picking up my conversation with Suri. "My vote is that we get Vash back first. Bringing him home will open up a lot of shit for us, including sidequests. I'd bet real money that most of the 'Hold the Line' quests only appear once you have a certain level of renown in the Fort."

"Huh. What tier do you reckon they open at?"

I opened my mouth to ask her what tiers were, but then remembered I was a strong, independent man who could just wiki it. “Hang on.”

I queried ‘Renown Tiers’, and called up the relevant article:

Renown

Renown is the measure of fame or infamy you possess in a locale. In every location where you complete (or fail to complete) quests, you can potentially gain renown. Renown is important for players interested in Mass Combat.
Like most things in Archemi, Renown is accrued through points. After accumulating a certain number of renown points, you gain bonuses or penalties to dealing with people in your locale. The size of the locale where you command fame or terror varies depending on your renown tier. The tiers are as follows:

- ***0-300 - Stranger:*** *Unknown and unnotable.*
- ***301-700 - Adventurer:*** *Some people have heard of you, and neighborhoods where you completed adventures are friendly/hostile. You can gain the alliance of small units.*
- ***701-1081 - Local Hero/Villain:*** *You are a person of note in your city, able to command respect, fear, or both. You can potentially command loyalty from a medium-sized organization.*
- ***1080-2217 - Public Figure:*** *You are well-known everywhere in your locale. Bards begin composing and singing about you, spreading the news of your deeds. You can command small armies under a General or other important figure.*

- ***2219-5628 - Idol:*** *You are known across your nation and are sought after for your abilities. You can potentially command larger armies as a general.*
- ***5629-12450 - Celebrity:*** *Your deeds have spread internationally, and your fame is recognizable across borders. You may command generals in warfare.*
- ***12451+ - Legend:*** *Your deeds will go down in history, heroic or villainous. You may qualify to rule a kingdom.*

View individual tiers for information on bonuses, penalties, and other perks.

"Probably just the Adventurer rank. That's the tier where people are talking about you to each other," I replied, closing the window. "I'm betting that you need 'Public Figure' to successfully command an army."

"That's a lot of renown," Karalti said. *"These quests give like... six hundred total?"*

"Yeah. I'm guessing the side-quests give twenty to fifty each." Suri answered her. "So if we clear five or six of those, we should have enough to turn this place around."

I listened, rubbing my hand over my mouth in thought. After they finished, I nodded. "Yeah. I think we should stay together for the main quests and then take the sidequests individually. Rin will probably take any magitech quests. Suri, what do you want dibs on?"

"Combat training, rank and file discipline, anything like that." Suri replied. "Karalti?"

"Uhh." The dragon looked anxiously to me. *"I dunno what I'm good at."*

"You're good at lots of things, Tidbit," I said. "Vlachians worship the dragon gods. You can inspire them and give spiritual counsel or something."

Her eyes got big. *"Yeah! I can do that!"*

"I can heal," I added. "And that's probably going to make some quick friends here. If we go at this strategically, we can maximize our time. We have to get as many of these things done as we can. But Vash first."

Suri nodded. "Yeah. Looks like we have to go digging for info on the Endlar. How dangerous do you think it is? I've never seen a swamp."

I paused for a second. "...You've never seen a swamp?"

She flashed me an exasperated look. "Mate, I'm from the bloody desert. Ninety-nine percent of my life was spent underground, and the rest of it, I was traveling with caravans or fighting in arenas. I know they're wet and crocodiles live there, and that's about it."

"Uhh... well, the short answer to your question is that swamps suck. The Endlar is apparently enough of a challenge to keep thirty thousand undead at bay, so I'm guessing its reputation is pretty much on point."

Suri rocked back onto her hands and sighed. "All that for a hundred renown points. This castle we're fighting for better have a fuckin' hot tub."

"You know who will know all about the Endlar? Yanik soldiers." Karalti finally circled back to join me on the bed, rolling onto it and balling up against me. *"They live out there."*

"Yeah. They should be able to tell us more." I looked over to Suri. "But seriously, if we don't eat shit out there at least once, I'll be really surprised. You need to be careful. You can't afford to die."

"Fighting things bigger than me is what I'm made for." Suri flashed me a sharp-toothed smile. "I can't afford to die. So I won't."

My HUD chirped. Suri stopped talking and Karalti perked up, suddenly alert. They were getting a call as well.

"Hi guys!" Rin's voice hummed against my inner ear. "Sorry for the late reply, but it's madness over in munitions and engineering right now. These trebuchets are all warped from the humidity, and-"

"How's Soma going?" I cut her off just as her voice sped up into the early stages of a nerd rant. "You able to wrangle him?"

"Oh, he's not that bad: he's just not a military person and Istvan is driving him mad," she replied breezily. "He's a genius in his field, but that field isn't like... this. Until now, he basically just lived at the university in Litvy. But his father died recently, and now he's expected to be something he's not."

"Istvan is driving *Soma* mad?" I looked to Suri, who shrugged.

"Yeah. Soma says he drinks because he's upset about his family and Lord Bolza, but he won't talk about what really happened in Karhad to anyone. On top of that, Istvan doesn't take technology seriously. He's got a phobia of magic that has leaked down to the soldiers and has absolutely crippled the engineers' ability to do their jobs. Istvan wants these old-fashioned cannons and things, even though there's much better equipment they could be using, and it costs lives every time the Demon assaults the Fort."

"Right." I reached out and wrapped an arm around Karalti's shoulders as she snuggled in against my side. "We heard a totally different story from Istvan."

"I know, right? The two of them can't agree on anything. Istvan wants infantry and cavalry on the ground to take out the Demon's mana sources, while Soma thinks he might as well just throw the men into a meat grinder. Explosives, magic and turrets would be more efficient defenses against a giant shambling mob of zombies. The problem is, they're both right. If Soma could just trust Istvan with the men and Istvan would let the engineers do their jobs, we could probably beat the undead back like... tomorrow. Except with those caravans being held up..."

"You got the quest chain too?" Suri asked.

"Yeah, I did! But the combat ones are definitely too much for me," the Mercurion replied.

"I disagree," Suri said. "Rin, we've got a tank, a striker, and... whatever Karalti is like this. We need ranged and magic support. Your turrets can take the heat off us with both. We really need you out there."

"Umm... I don't know." There was a barely concealed note of panic in her voice. "I'd have to find a way to modify Lovelace and Hopper to be able to deal with mud, and we don't have much time."

"If you can do it tonight, do it." I replied. "Suri's right. You took that Combat Engineer class so you could go on adventures. We need you."

"Okay," Rin agreed reluctantly. "G-Give me like... until tomorrow morning. Soma has some amphibious traction designs here already. I can probably work something out."

"Awesome. Also, we were talking about how to handle these side-quests. The plan is to go and fish Vash out of the swamp, then tackle some chores around the Fort. We'll handle Istvan's people and you handle Soma's. Does that suit you?"

"Sure! There's a lot of yellow rings where I am here."

'Yellow rings' were the floating side-quest markers that appeared around some people's Coronas. "Great. Suri? Karalti? Sound good to you?"

"Sure does." Suri clapped her hands on her thighs. "Okay, kids. Let's do it."

Chapter 17

In my sober moments, I told myself I'd picked up the Healing skill tree because it was fun and interesting. But if I was being honest with myself, a big part of my hunger to learn was because it made me feel like I could conquer disease, which was the only thing that had ever kicked my ass and gotten away with it. Healing skills also had the side benefit of making me popular, because people don't like to be sick or in pain. In a world without magical healing, these skills were always needed.

While Suri split for the barracks and Karalti for the mess hall, I hurried toward the Fort's hospital: a squat, square, three-story building within a small courtyard to the north of the parade ground, lit by torches and a couple of barrel fires. As soon as I entered the courtyard, the metallic stench of rotten meat hit me, and I gagged. Yiiiikes.

Even at night, there were a lot of sick people and a commotion going on just outside the door to the hospital. Two acid-burned Vlachian soldiers were screaming at a medic in a bloody apron who was standing between them and the entryway. The man was screaming right back at them.

"I told you useless worms four times already - there are no more Cryptbane Potions!" The medic yelled. "I know that's what you need, but you're stuck in the line until we get more ingredients, and there's nothing I can do about it!"

"Can't you see he's dying?!" The soldier shouted back, gesturing at his friend with both hands. "He's dying! I'm dying! Are you going to let us be turned into one of those monsters!?"

"You're not dying yet. Grave Rot won't show symptoms for two days and a night, and the battle was only two hours ago. I you don't get back into that line, I'll hack a limb off and give you a reason to be at the front!" The medic pushed his spectacles back up along his beaky nose and gestured angrily at the straggling queue waiting to receive help. Some of them were very badly off - gauze clamped over bloody missing eyes, broken limbs, burns and arrow wounds. "Do you see these people? You'll get the damn potions when we get our herbs!"

At that moment, a golden ring appeared behind the medic's head, rotating in an eye-catching way: a side-quest's marker.

"Excuse me, sorry to interrupt, but what herbs do you need?" I sidled up and inserted myself into the argument before the pleading soldier could get any more aggressive. All three men turned on me.

"And which cursed ocean spat you out into our conversation?" The medic demanded.

"Dragozin Hector. Count of Racsa and wannabe Healer." I replied with a salute. "What do you need?"

The medic blanched, then sketched a deep bow. "My apologies, Your Grace, I haven't seen you around this shit-wagon of a fort before. And the answer to your question is everything. Bandages, beds, hands, herbs. Pardon my inquiry, but you are not Vlachian. Where do you hail from?"

"Tungaant," I replied. "Theoretically."

"Oh, thank the gods. If you're half as good a healer as Vash, we need you. Desperately." The wild-eyed medic grabbed me by the arm and began pulling as he turned and opened one of the hospital doors. "You two! Get back in line! No more pushing ahead!"

"But-!"

The heavy wooden door slammed behind us, locking us into an overcrowded, reeking room. Nurses, male and female, moved among the patients, binding broken limbs, stuffing organs back into bellies, dosed and drained and stitched. They all looked as exhausted as the medic beside me.

"These are the victims from the last big assault, four days ago. We keep the urgent care patients here on the first floor," he said bleakly. Then he seemed to remember himself. "My apologies, I didn't introduce myself. I am Lazar Skaliz, the head medic here."

"Where're you from?" I asked.

"Karhad, Your Grace. I escaped with Commander Istvan Arshak from Egbolt Castle. And as you can see, we're up to our eyeballs." He gestured at the room. "Worst problem is the damned Grave Rot. That's what those boys out there have - melancholic illness, attacks the blood and bone marrow. Second stage looks like leprosy. It kills you, and then you become one of them. The undead."

Melancholic diseases were cold and dry. I nodded. "What do you need to cure it?"

"If you catch it early? Colloidal Gold, Bogbean, Swamp Rosemallow, and alcohol." He rattled off the ingredients by heart. "It's an expensive medicine. And if a man has progressed to the leprous stage, you have to add Stingcrab Blood and take the risk of Stranging."

"Wait. I have... exactly none of those things." I checked my ingredients. "I can make Colloidal Gold, but I'm running low on Aqua Regis. Teach me how to brew the potion, and I'll make what I have. You can cure some people, at least."

"Yes. Better than none." Lazar sighed and looked up to the ceiling.

⟦Lazar Skaliz would like to send you: Recipe: Cryptbane Potion⟧

I accepted, and added it to the ever growing list of drugs I was able to brew in a bathtub. "Thanks."

"There's little point in thanking me. The ingredients for Cryptbane grow out in the Endlar, but who's able to go out there?"

"We are," I said. "Me, my dragon, and our companions. We're setting out to find Vash Dorha in the morning.."

"His body, you mean. Still... if you are brave enough to go out there, I won't refuse you." Lazar concentrated again, and I got an alert.

New Side-Quest: A Rose on the Grave

Lazar Skaliz, the Head Medic of Korona Fort Hospital, is in desperate need of supplies for the potions used to heal his patients. Collect 100 each of Bogbean, Swamp Rosemallow and Stingcrab Blood.

***Reward:** EXP, Skill EXP, New Recipes, +25 Renown (Myszno Defense Force), unlock Lazar Skaliz in the Heroes menu.*

"No worries, I'll get those when I'm out there," I said. "Are there any other herbs you need?"

Lazar shrugged. "All of them. Whatever you can bring us will help. We will pay."

My first thought was 'yay, money', but then I remembered - renown, in this quest, was way more valuable than cash. For now, though, I'd let him think I was that mercenary. "Sure. I'll bring you back a bunch of them, and we'll work it out from there. By the way, if I help you on your rounds, do you mind if I ask you a few questions about what we can expect out there in the swamp?"

"Information on the Endlar? I'm not the one to ask. Lieutenant Zlaslo would probably know the most of anyone here," Lazar replied. "He's Yanik, born and bred. Mind you, he's terribly sick right now, and we have no idea what's wrong with him. Nothing we've tried has worked. Good luck getting anything out of him. He's roiled in the grip of a terrible fever these last few days."

Dammit: I'd used my Purify ability for the day, so there was no way to lay on hands and fix him. "Other Yanik soldiers would know about the swamp, too - right?"

"Maybe, maybe not." The doctor was glancing anxiously at his patients now, straining to keep himself talking to me. "All Yanik will talk a big talk, but most of them are like Istvan, born and bred in cities or towns. Their parents or grandparents might have walked out of the swamp generations ago. They'll know myths and stories, and what they saw of it when we marched from Karhad to the

Prezyemi Line, but you'd have to search the ranks to find anyone with Zlaslo's knowledge."

"Right." I sighed. "Thanks. I'll go see him and do my best."

The medic nodded, relieved. "He's on the third floor. You'll see his armor rack up there."

I waded through the moaning bodies lying on beds and stretchers, and clumped up the wooden stairs to the third floor. It was neater up here, with fewer beds with enough space between them that they could be, albeit barely, separated from one another by thin, ragged curtains. There were boxes of herbs and medical supplies stacked up against one wall. My fingers twitched. When one of the nurses went behind a curtain to attend to a patient, I stole over and had a look inside the crates.

An inventory panel jumped up:

- *Lobelia x 20*
- *Water Mint x 50*
- *Lotus Flower x 30*
- *Blazing Star x 15*
- *Iris x 20*
- *Kings Grass x 10*
- *Green Moss x 50*
- *Hawthorn bark x 10*

"Ooh. Fancy plants." Tempted as I was, I didn't take anything - just closed the window. If I needed anything to treat the Lieutenant, I'd know where to find them.

Several of the beds had armor hung out in front, but picking Zlaslo's was easy enough. The Lieutenant's armor looked like a ghillie suit, made of sturdy leather and chain and stitched with lichen-like netting. The joints were padded, and the back of it had bones, bark and silk foliage sewn onto it.

"Zlaslo?" I called out.

There was a thin groan from behind the curtain.

I let myself in and found pretty much what I'd expected. Zlaslo's gray-brown skin was ashy and pale, his cheeks and neck flushed red, the covers over his body damp with sweat. His eyes were dark and bright with fever, and he slowly writhed on the bed, as if in agony. Like Istvan, he wore his hair long. Unlike Istvan, he had his hair styled into long clay-covered dreadlocks, and a number of bone and gold piercings through both ears. There was a bedpan beside his bed. It looked unusually gross: the stuff in it was green.

"Hey man - I've come to see if I can do anything for you." I edged in closer. "My name's Hector."

"Uhhhhn." Zlaslo's eyes briefly fixed on mine, but there was no other acknowledgement. He was too sick.

Just as I resolved to start examining him, my HUD jumped to life. A soft blue glow began to highlight areas of interest on his body. His forehead, neck, abdomen, elbow, a big red rash on his forearm... and his crotch. Lovely. Still, that was new.

"Uhh... okay." I started by taking his temperature with my hand - 107, yikes. Then, on instinct, I felt the glands in his neck. They were swollen up like golf balls, and he flinched when I touched him. My Field Medicine-informed instincts told me that meant he was fighting an infection.

I took his pulse next. His heartbeat was irregular and quick. Frowning, I muttered an apology and put my ear to his chest, closed my eyes, and listened. His breathing was clear...

but his heart sounded like it was flailing around, sloshing and thudding out of rhythm.

"Ohhhh... get off..." Zlaslo flailed around weakly. "Gods, it hurts."

"What hurts?" I sat up quickly as he writhed.

"Everything," he moaned. His voice was slurred. "Head. Belly. Skin. Bones. Cock. Everything."

I gently pressed around on his stomach. The upper stomach seemed okay, but as soon as I pushed below the navel, he yelped.

"Heart stuff is Sanguine, gut stuff is Phlegmatic..." I muttered what Masha had taught me in the past few weeks, looking him over. He had more than one rash. The patches were red and angry, which made them Choleric - dry and hot. His joints were hot and swollen, too, like someone with arthritis. Anything to do with bones and joints was a Melancholic thing. Just about the only thing he wasn't doing was coughing. "Damn, man... no wonder the healers are having trouble with you. You're like a big old grab-bag of bad humors."

After a couple of minutes, I came up with a game plan. I went back out and grabbed Lobelia, Blazing Star, Lotus and Water Iris for the potions I intended to make later, then took out a Goldenseal Tincture. I pushed back the heavy clay-covered locks, propped Zlaslo's head and poured the potion in his mouth. He spluttered a little, but a meter appeared, and his terrible fever began to subside. After a few seconds, the man shuddered and looked up at me.

"Who the hell are you?" He whispered, in thickly accented Vlachian.

"Hector. I'm trying to figure out how to cure you of whatever you've got," I replied. "I don't think this potion is going to fix you, but it will take away some of the fever. I need to know what you were doing before you got sick."

Zlaslo's mouth twitched. He wasn't a very attractive man: narrow head, pinched features, shifty eyes. He was lean and fit, but scrawny compared to the other Yanik men I'd passed. "I was working."

"Be specific, or you're probably gonna die."

He shivered. "I was not doing anything out of the ordinary, my friend. I returned from my last mission two weeks ago. I went to celebrate; I went to bed. Then I trained soldiers... went out in the swamp to teach the Vlachii how to swim and hide in the marshes..."

Parasites, maybe? We were always having to deal with those in the jungle. I thought about it for a couple of seconds. Glanced at his bedpan. Squinted at it.

"Wait," I said. "You're pissing green stuff?"

"Urrgh." He covered his eyes.

"How long for?" I demanded.

"Why? One week, maybe week and a half," He admitted. "Not long."

I sighed and crossed my arms. "You went into a place named *Slutlava* to pick up chicks?"

"Uhh... yes. To play around, yes." He tried to nod, but his neck spasmed and he let out a small sob of pain.

"And you've been pissing this green shit since then? Any blood?"

"... Some."

I crouched back on my heels and thought about it. I glanced down, where the blue aura was highlighting a... distinctly shaped region under the blanket covering his lap. It seemed Slutlava's name wasn't as random as I'd originally thought.

"Based on what I learned about STIs at boot camp and my extremely limited sexual experience, I am ninety-nine percent sure you have the worst case of gonorrhea known to mankind. Why didn't you come to see Lazar when it started, man?"

"Had it before," he mumbled. "No problems then. It went away."

"Wait." I held up my hands. "Dude, no. Gonorrhea doesn't just *go* away. You've had it for months, which means you just gave this shit to every innocent Slutlavan you fucked, you asshole."

"... Even the man?" He asked after a short pause.

I face-palmed. "Yes. Even the man."

This was the first time I'd had to deal with someone who had an advanced disease without Masha's help, but I had to trust in those points I'd invested in my skills. Gonorrhea was unfortunate, but it wasn't a rare or specialized condition, like the Grave Rot illness the medic had told me about. If I was being offered this quest, it was probably within my means.

I thought back to what Masha had said about the guy with the infected hand. Lance the wound, then apply the poultice, then the potions. No water until the end, because it would cause sepsis. I was willing to bet that the standard sequence for this kind of deep-seated infection was hot, moist, dry, cold. Treat the skin rash and fever, then his heart, then his joints, then the root of the infection, so to speak. But the healers here hadn't been able to cure him... so it was possible that there were more steps in the pattern.

"Sex is pretty hot and pretty moist," I muttered to myself. "It probably goes Choleric-Sanguine-Melancholic-Phlegmatic-Sanguine."

"What?"

"Nothing. Doctor stuff." I surveyed the colored zones of light on his body. As soon as I started thinking about how to treat the rash, a list of ingredients appeared:

- *Holy Basil*
- *Starberry*
- *Baking Soda*
- *Cotton or Linen Cloth*

I recognized those: they were components of a Holy Basil Compress, used for treating skin infections. This must be one of the perks of Journeyman-level Herbalism. "Ooh, that's nifty."

Zlaslo looked up at me in desperation. "What are you muttering about? Can you help me or not?"

I fixed him with my best serious doctor face. "Probably. But I might have to cut your dick off."

He made a strangled high-pitched sound and flinched away from me on the bed.

"Not really; just joking. Though I bet there's some Lava Sluts who'd thank me if I did." I pulled my Herbalism kit and began to brew and mash, breaking off to go and raid the ingredients out in the hallway when I needed them. At the end of fifteen minutes, I had an array of treatments lined up like shots: A Holy Basil Compress for the rash, another

Goldenseal Tincture for the fever, a Hawthorn Potion for the heart issue, a Comfrey Decoction for his bones, and then finally a Concentrated Green Moss Tincture. "Okay: you're going to drink all of these. The Comfrey Decoction absolutely contains materials designated as cancerous by the state of California, but it should fix your joint pain."

"What?" He blinked up at me, doubly confused.

I slapped the Holy Basil Compress on his rash. "Drink the fucking potion."

A new timer popped up on my HUD, counting down from 60 seconds. Another new thing. The area where the poultice was applied began to glow red - red for Choleric, I was willing to bet. I waited breathlessly to see what happened. When the timer hit 00:00, the man's chest flared with a golden aura. Gold for Sanguine. Fumbling a little, I fed him the Hawthorn Potion. Another timer appeared, this time counting down from 01:30. I watched it, frowning, and was startled when another red glow appeared at 30 seconds in: this time, around his head.

"Urrrgh." Zlaslo sunk back into the pillow, flushed in the face. "What did you just give me?"

"Hang on." I felt his forehead: he was burning up again, temperature rising fast. The red aura pulsed. Racing against the clock, I mashed together the ingredients for a Goldenseal Tincture and brewed it like a bartender pouring a drink. I finished ten seconds before the timer was up and put it to his lips. "Drink."

Zlaslo glared at me suspiciously as he quaffed the potion. The red glow disappeared just before the golden one did, and then his entire body shone with black light. For a moment, I was freaked out - until I remembered the sequence. Black for Melancholy. I got the Comfrey Decoction and poured that down Zlaslo's neck. At the first taste of the bitter, ashy brew, he coughed and tried to spit it out.

"No. Drink it like a man." I pushed up under his chin and held his mouth closed, like when you give a dog a pill. He glared at me, ashy liquid bubbling at the corners of his mouth. "You fucked your way into this mess, and now you're going to swallow your way out of it."

Another timer appeared: a five-minute timer. When it ran down, his abdomen and groin began to glow blue. I fed him the Green Moss Tincture, then waited anxiously as a 10-minute timer appeared. But he was looking better, if not weak and exhausted.

"I'm going to give this regime to the healers here. I think you're going to need multiple treatments," I said. "Probably every day for a week or so. But your fever's breaking, so that's a plus."

"Yes. It does not hurt as bad." His voice was weak and rusty, and he grimaced as he shifted on the bed. "I thank you. You are one of Vash's students?"

"No. He's... out on a mission," I said. "In fact, I'm getting ready to join him out in the Endlar. I was told you know the swamp better than anyone here. Are you strong enough to answer some questions?"

The man gave a small nod. "What do you want to know?"

I thought for a minute or two. "Let's start with the monsters. What enemies can we expect out there?"

"Your worst enemy is disease. Don't eat anything raw, and don't drink from still water. Stingcrabs are your next biggest threat," his voice cracked as he spoke, so I got him some water and used a pipette to drop it in his mouth. "All over the place. Be careful of those: they don't do much damage, but they can paralyze even the strongest man with their venom. They wait until other beasts come, and then eat whatever is left. There are many kinds of larger animals... giant crocodiles, titanoboas, giant dragonflies, wolves. Allosaurus are common in the heart of the swamp. They always hunt in packs, three to six individuals. In the south of the Endlar, you will find Tyrannosaurus, who can be solitary or in pairs."

"Okay. What about Stranged creatures?"

Zlaslo took a second to lick his dry lips. "Many. The Stranged creatures of the Endlar loathe fire, so keeping a burning brand with you is a good idea. The most common are the *Bogmaq* - the drowned dead, who lurk at the edge of bayous. They do not have the weakness to water, like the Demon's zombies... he has been summoning them to his aid, enslaving them into his army, and now they lurk ready to pull in scouts and soldiers. But the worst thing you may see there is the *Aljulaki Samak*."

"The who-what now?"

The man's brow furrowed. "The Vlachii call them Swamp Hags. Do you know of the giant sandworms that can be found in the desert?"

Visions of giant worms with mouths like black holes lined with teeth plunging in and out of sand dunes came to mind. "I think so, yeah."

"They are the sandworms of the bayou. I have seen one eat a hookwing and his rider the way you would eat a chicken wing," he said urgently. "You must beware their traps. They produce much slime and fill entire ponds with it. They lair at the center of slime, and if something walks in there, they do not walk out."

The last timer ran down to zero, and the blue aura around Zlaslo's abdomen faded. He shuddered - this time with relief.

[You have unlocked new knowledge: Endlar Swamp (D-grade)]
[You have gained 5 Skill EXP!]

I grunted, satisfied. "*Aljulaki Samak,* right. I'll bear that in mind. How do you feel?"

"Better, but my *huadiv* still hurts." He motioned down at his lap. "Do you know what is wrong with it?"

"Well, I'm not a... uhh... whatever a penis doctor is called, so your *huadiv* is just going to have to sit tight until a specialist comes around." I slapped my hands down on my thighs and leaned in a little. "Now, I've got some questions about terrain..."

Chapter 18

The next morning.

The night was spent reading and brewing: healing potions, antidotes, disease-fighting tinctures. After hours of effort, I also decompiled one of the recipes in the book Lazar had given me: ⟦Roseroot Potions⟧, which replenished 50 points of stamina and increased stamina regen by 40% for 30 seconds. The Hospital sold Roseroot, so I bought their stock up and brewed ten.

We left at dawn, winched down to the battlefield by the elevators, and trudged off through the mud and the billowing clouds of water vapor spawned by the waterfalls. The Endlar Swamp was humid. Very humid. A croaking, humming, brackish, dreary million-acre morass that stood between us and a sizable number of zombies. A faint methane perfume hung over the still brown waters. Foxfire bloomed among the whispering reeds. Weeping willows hung down over the river, motionless in the unnaturally warm air. By ten A.M, it was also hot.

"I'm seriously jealous of you, Rin," I muttered, ducking as Karalti crawled under one of many slime-draped trees. We were about twenty miles into the marsh and headed due south, following a glowing quest icon on a largely-undefined map. Sweat crawled down the back of my neck.

"Me? What did I do?" Rin squeaked. She was riding Hopper, who hummed along in the water beneath her. Rin had stayed up all night to modify her turrets, turning them into what amounted to small hovercraft. Hopper and Lovelace had sacrificed some defense for these features, but they could now float, climb, swim, and wade. In this environment, that was more important than armor plating.

"Nothing. But I resent your lack of bodily fluids," I replied.

She had her mask pushed up onto her head, and blushed bright blue. "Wh...what?"

"Sweat, kid." Suri's beautiful hair had frizzed up and turned dark, clinging to her face and neck. He's talking about sweat."

"Oh! Me too! I'm glad I don't have to worry about it anymore!" Rin paused for a moment, then winced. "I mean... sorry that you don't feel well?"

"I'm fine. Just gross." I snorted. "Don't sweat it."

Suri groaned. "New party rule. Puns are banned."

"What? That wasn't a pun. That was far beneath something so sublime as a pun. That was merely word play."

Karalti was unaffected by the heat and water, large enough to wade through the marsh without needing to swim. Cutthroat seemed to actively enjoy it. I'd been worried about her praying mantis-like claw arms – they didn't look made for swimming – but she simply folded them against her chest and paddled with her back legs, weaving smoothly through the water with Suri on her back.

"Look!" Rin hissed. "Do you see that? Is it a zombie?"

The Mercurion shrunk back on Hopper, pointing at a slumped corpse with one trembling finger. I peered at it. The corpse had no legs. Or arms.

"That guy is too dead to get up again." I replied. "Don't worry about the bodies. Keep an eye out for clues to Vash's path through the swamp. If anything twitches, we let our mounts take them."

"Yeah. Don't worry about zombies. Worry about scavengers," Suri grunted. "Allosaurs are big, bad bastards. And they eat carrion."

"Hopefully they don't eat Baru," I replied. "Because I don't want to have to lug a barrel-load of Allosaurus shit back to Istvan."

"You can just bring back the gauntlets, numb-nuts."

"And if you want to dig those out of the dino shit, you go right ahead." I made a face. "Smell anything, Karalti?"

The dragon wove her head, breathing in deeply. *"I smell... crocodiles. Aaaand... dead people. And monsters. Lots of monsters. Up ahead."*

No sooner had she spoken than the stale wind moved a little, and the smell of decomposition hit me like a punch to the nose. Eyes watering against the urge to cough, I nodded, and checked the direction of the wind against our quest marker. "Yup. The dead people smell is coming from the south-west... same direction as our quest."

"What if the army is out there?" Rin pinched her nose.

"We kill 'em." Suri loaded her crossbow and cocked it. "Nothing like water-logged corpses to start the day off right."

I grinned and banged the top of my helmet with a fist. "Breakfast of champions."

Karalti made a happy trilling sound in her throat. *"Smells like lunch to me!"*

We were out of the No Man's Land and well into the swamp now. The area we had started in was thick with cattails, a forest of them reaching seven feet or more. But as we swam south, the water got shallower and the stench of decay grew thicker. Then the Mark of Matir turned cold on my skin, just before I heard a soft moan drift through the still air.

"Shh. Stop." I held a hand up. "Listen."

The others froze, and the sound of multiple feet shuffling in the mud drifted to our ears. There was another soft moan. It sounded... wet.

"Undead," I hissed. "Ready?"

"Yeah." Suri used a handful of muddy water to push her hair back and out of her face, slicking it against her skull. "Rin. You know how to fight zombies?"

Rin was very tense on the back of her turret, holding onto it with a vice grip. "Shoot them in the head?"

"Bingo." Suri brandished her crossbow suggestively.

We nosed out of the cattails into an open muddy pool churning with activity. There were twenty of them: male, female, even children. They varied from the relatively fresh to the extremely decayed; from skeletal, leather-skinned walkers to shuffling, bloated white bags of flesh that barely resembled people. But before they noticed us, we saw that they were united in a singular purpose.

They were digging.

Every one of the zombies had a trenching tool, which they were using to tirelessly shovel mud and silt into makeshift dams. There were huge mounds of mud and reeds to either side of the work crew. That explained the drop in the waterline. Before I could make out anything else, though, the unit swiveled their heads toward us, letting out a chorus of roars and gurgles.

"Icecream!" Suri bellowed Cutthroat's attack command and held on as her hookwing went charging into the fray.

Rin screamed and briefly covered her face as her turrets began firing on the undead. Karalti and I charged forward with Cutthroat and Suri at our side. The dragon and hookwing were immune to the stench, biting and slashing with abandon. I held my breath as I plunged my spear down, chopping into spongy skulls and mushy shoulder joints. When Karalti had enough room, she opened her jaws and spewed a plume of Ghost Fire across the rank. The zombies didn't react to being set on fire or scream as their armor melted and their flesh charred. They simply struggled as they burned, falling to their knees and then onto their faces.

⟦You have destroyed Dredgers!⟧
⟦You gain 120 EXP!⟧

"God, these guys are gross." I coughed at the stench. "And weak. Surprisingly weak. I was expecting stronger enemies."

"Me too. But look: only four of them had any armor on, and their gear's shit." Suri pointed at two of the burning corpses, then another pair on the ground. "These people are... were... civilians. Disposable workers."

"Looks like it." I glanced back to see how Rin was doing. She was hanging far back, but gave me a shaky thumbs up. "Let's keep going. We-"

My next words were drowned out by a chorus of roars. The water began to vibrate and slosh as the footfall of several very large, very fast somethings gained on us from the east. *BOOM, BOOM, BOOM.*

"The fuck is that?" I hopped up to a crouch on Karalti's back as three towering dinosaurs burst out of the trees to our left. They were larger than Cutthroat but smaller than Karalti, with narrow, keratin armored snouts, powerful grasping forelimbs, and lots of teeth. Allosaurus. "Holy shitballs."

"We can take them!" Suri wheeled Cutthroat around in the mud as the Hookwing bashed her claws together and roared in challenge. "There's only three!"

"No there isn't!" Rin clutched onto Hopper as her turrets powered by. "Run!"

I was almost about to agree with Suri when another three Allosaurus charged out into the open. In the lead was a huge, brutish albino ⟦Alpha Allosaurus⟧. Its hide was studded with shards of glowing red crystal, and its eyes blazed like wells of magma. It fixed on us, and then opened its jaws and bellowed a cloud of stinking ozone gas. The other five lowered their heads and charged, surrounded by a glowing orange aura - some kind of buff.

"Okay, it's Stranged! Tactical retreat!" Suri turned Cutthroat around and dug her heels in.

"*We can still take them! We just need some space!*" Karalti plunged through the thick undergrowth, clearing a path for Cutthroat and Suri - and, unfortunately, the Allosaurus.

"No we fucking can't! Not on this terrain!" I yelled back. "Up! We need high ground before Cutthroat runs out of stamina!"

The Alpha bellowed, lowering his head to chomp and snap at Cutthroat's fleeing tail. The hookwing screeched, running and hopping from one piece of dry land to the next, weaving through trees the Allosaurus pack bulldozed aside. Wood splintered and crashed, sending smaller creatures flying. None of them were stupid enough to aggro on us. The collective weight of the running pack of dragon and dinosaurs rattled the earth like an avalanche.

"We need to kite them into a trap and either lose them, or rain down fire from above!" Rin shouted to us in PM. "Can you get off the ground?"

"Agreed! Get in the air as soon as you can!" Suri's Ride skill wasn't anywhere near mine, and she was struggling to hold on. She had lost her reins, and had her arms wrapped around Cutthroat's neck. Only her formidable strength was keeping her on the hookwing's back.

The Endlar was mostly unmapped, so all we had to navigate by was the quest marker: a glowing beacon thirty miles south-east of our location. There was no high ground and no open space in sight. Frustrated, I knelt up and turned to look back, bobbing on Karalti's back as she ducked and weaved, splashed and leapt. The Allosaurus were showing no sign of slowing down or losing interest. Even if I jumped and rained down Master of Blades thru Rain of Glass on them, there was no fucking way I'd land on the ground and live to tell the tale. The terrain made turning around and facing them in any meaningful way almost impossible.

"There! I see something!" Karalti couldn't knock over entire trees like the heavier dinosaurs could, but she could plough through brambles and cattails like they weren't there. *"Open area!"*

"Be careful of quicksand! If we sink in a mire now, we're dead!" I dropped into flight position, catching the saddle grips and shoving my feet in the stirrups in anticipation of an emergency takeoff.

We broke out of the treeline into an ankle-deep, slushy brown marsh. The reeds around the waterline were trampled and black, slimy enough that I felt Karalti's foot slip a little as she charged toward the water. There was a strong rotten meat smell in the stagnant air, and bones half-hidden among the dead vegetation. The water here was very shallow, except at the center of the mire, where it plunged down like a funnel into the mud. The place screamed 'ambush site'.

"Eww." Karalti began to lift her back legs. *"This place is slimy."*

Slimy? I looked down to see that the 'water' was clinging to my dragon's foot like taffy, soft and stretchy. Zlazo's warning came back to me then - the Swamp Hags.

"There's a Swamp Hag nearby! Let's kite them straight into the middle of that mire." I clenched one of the grips. "Suri! Rin! Go around the waterline! Whatever you do, do not take Cutthroat in there!"

"Yah!" I heard Suri spur the spitting, raging hookwing to the limit of her endurance behind us. "We'll get ahead of you and you can drag them in!"

Karalti bellowed, a guttural sound deeper than the Allosauruses charging through the swamp behind us. She threw herself into the stagnant air, stumbling forward on the downstroke, and just barely skimmed the deepening pool of slime as we lifted. My head lurched, and when I looked down, I saw a behemoth shadow start to rise from under the surface. "Watch out!"

The dragon snarled with effort, lurching into the sky as the liquid beneath us began to bubble. The Alpha Allosaurus, oblivious to anything but kicking our ass, ran straight into the marsh and jumped. It caught the end of Karalti's tail, jolting us back and nearly throwing me forward over her shoulder and into the water.

"Get off me!" Karalti squealed, striving to stay in the air as the dinosaur set his teeth in and tugged. I turned, leveled the Spear, and was about to charge Umbra Blast when the muddy slime sucked down into the hole like the retreating surf that heralded an incoming tsunami, and something monstrous surged up in its place.

My first thought was that the Swamp Worm was some kind of fish, like the mother of all carp. My second thought was that it was a leech the size of a train carriage. The third was some variation of OH FUCK OH FUCK OH FUCK as a huge blue-gray worm leaped from the water like a playful whale, spewing slime in all directions. It struck Karalti like a net, entangling her legs and dragging her down toward the water.

Every one of the Allosaurus had charged in after their leader, straight into the trap the giant mud-carp-leech creature had laid. It slithered out, blind and slippery, and sprayed goo from a hole-like mouth onto the dinosaur. The Alpha roared as the liquid slapped against its skin, letting Karalti go and spinning around to flee. It collided with its packmates, which gave the hole-fish time to spray the group of them together like some kind of awful reverse bukkake.

My dragon's wingbeats began to falter. *"Hector? I'm sleepy."*

"What? Hey! No, wake the fuck up!" I refocused on Karalti as her head drooped. "Look at Suri! Get to Suri and Cutthroat!"

[[Karalti is gaining torpor!]]

Holy fuck: it was the slime. The Allosaurs were crumpling to their knees in the mire, drugged to unconsciousness. The giant hole-fish flopped forward on its belly and sucked the paralyzed Alpha's head into its mouth, working over the forty-foot long dinosaur like a snake over a mouse.

"Stab her!" Rin shouted from the bank of the marsh. "That's how you cure Sleep status!"

"No! I'm not stabbing her!" Frantic, I ransacked my inventory, but I didn't have any stimulants. "Okay, yes I am!"

In desperation, I pulled one of my old shitty daggers, jammed it under one of the scales at the base of her neck, and shoved it in about an inch.

[[You stab Karalti for 5HP!]]

"Huu... wha? Ow!" The dragon half-heartedly adjusted her wings: not enough to stop our short descent into the mire.

"Pull up! Pull up!" I banged her scales with the hilt of the knife.

My shouts bought Karalti back to her senses. As her long back feet grazed the back of the worm, she yarped and began frantically beating her wings, laboring back into the air with a great *whomph whomph whomph* that sent water flying everywhere. Cutthroat shrieked from the bank; Karalti replied with an oddly similar cry as she clumsily swooped over to land beside Rin and Suri.

"Jesus motherfuckin' Christ." The Berserker was watching the carnage in the swamp in shock. Two of the Allosaurus were asleep, while the remaining three attacked the monster who was almost done engulfing their paralyzed pack leader. "That was a bit full on, wasn't it?"

"A bit!?" Rin rounded on her.

She shrugged, still staring over my shoulder. "A bit as in a lot. What the fuck is that thing?"

"That, my friend, is a bonafide Short-Jawed Mudsucker. And we are absolutely not ready to fight it." I clapped Karalti on the side of the neck, suddenly aware of how much my hand was shaking. "Phew. Least we got a nice adrenaline rush out of it. I almost feel ready to run screaming from the next pack of Allosaurus like a little bitch."

"Realistically, in a punch-up with a pack of Allosaurus, anybody's a little bitch." Suri sighed. "A Short-Jawed Mudsucker, huh?"

"That's right!"

Rin scowled at me. "That is *not* what that thing is called."

"Sure it is. The Short-Jawed Mudsucker, scientific name *Bukkakus maximus.*"

Suddenly, Karalti reared up and bellowed. *"Crabs!"*

"What? Oh, you have to be fucking kidding me." Suri snarled, swinging her sword around as eight horseshoe crab-like things burst out of the undergrowth and charged us, barbed whip tails swinging for our necks. Stingcrabs.

I charged power, getting ready for an Umbra Burst. "I'm beginning to see why the Demon's bogged down."

"No more motherfucking puns!"

"Yes ma'am." Chortling, I spun my Spear around and jumped down into the fray.

Chapter 19

It was like this the entire day. Encounter after encounter, mob after mob. Every mudhole seemed to contain something dangerous, venomous, hungry, or any combination of the three. They all had shit EXP and either no loot or low-grade loot. It was so hot that we had to drink twice as much as usual, which meant we were haunted by the eternal specter of Archemi's fucking Pee Meter.

My only consolation was herbs, because the Endlar had herbs for *days.*

Red Rashovik. King's Grass. Peppermint, Roseroot, Starberry, Irises, Foxglove, Nightshade and Green Moss. Everything I didn't already know how to use, I frantically stuffed into my mouth, much to Suri's confusion and Rin's amusement. I was able to collect everything from common herbs, like Holy Basil, to exotic things I hadn't seen before. Acid mushrooms, Hallucinogenic Mushrooms – those were fun for about twenty minutes – Mandrake, and all kinds of monster blood. God. So much monster blood.

Most the blood was from what was now my least favorite monster species. Stingcrabs were one of the most common mobs in this part of the Endlar, giving next to no EXP while costing us heavily in time and Antidotes. Then there were Gastina plants, which KO'd you and THEN flung spikes of death at your helpless body while other things came to eat your delicious sweetmeats. And pretty much everything here wanted those. The dinosaurs, the bugs, the plants...

"Bears. In a swamp." Still covered in blood, I held my spear above the waterline as I waded through chest-deep steaming water. The sun was starting to set.

"*Yup,* "Karalti said.

"Swamp bears."

"*Yuuup.*"

"Who the fuck puts crack-bears in a swamp?" I angrily pimp-slapped a leech that was oozing toward me through the water, backhanding it to land somewhere with a splash. "This is some Florida-level bullshit."

"We're lucky we haven't run into a Rex." Suri said. She and Cutthroat rode to our left. "Allosaurus are bad enough, but there's nothing we have that could take a T-rex. We get them near oases in Dakhdir... they like to eat carrion. Unless you happen to be trucking a ballista, about the only thing anyone can do when they show up is run."

"If they're desert critters, they won't be- FUCK!" Something wrapped around my leg, and I stabbed at it and jumped away on reflex. Nothing came of it, and I resumed wading. Tentacle or weed? Who knew?

"Yeah. This is more like Spinosaurus country, innit? Or what are those water-dinos. Name begins with 'B'."

"Baryonyx." Rin clung to Hopper as the automaton paddled like a dog behind us.

"That's the one. Barry-onyx."

"No, it's BAH-ri-OHn-ix."

"That's what I said, numbnuts. Ba-REE-oh-nix!"

It was getting colder and creepier as we padded through the thinning trees. They weren't just thinning - they were dying. The water was drying up, leaving pools of cracked mud. There weren't any animals or monsters around, and the earthy, organic smell of the swamp had almost vanished. When we were about three hundred feet from the marker, it abruptly disappeared on the mini-map, opening up into a field bounded by a large shaded circle.

"Looks like we have to search for clues." I was uneasy as I vaulted down from Karalti's back, and even more so when I landed on the earth and it crunched under my boots. The area smelled like an ice rink... like dirty ice and old rubber. "Something's fucky."

"Yeah." Rin followed after me, sliding from Hopper's back. "Everything's dead. Maybe we could see something from the air?"

I looked up at Karalti. She nodded and paced ahead with her wings mantled until she reached a place where she could take off. Suri lit a torch while we waited. The circle of yellow light illuminated ghostly white trees, flying beetles, shallow dead water, and a gravel-strewn ridge up ahead.

"Weird." I looked around uneasily. "It's like the forest is dying."

"Yeah." Suri had her sword out, the point of the huge blade resting on the ground, the torch in her other hand. "Rin, you were saying there were devices that pulled mana from the land, right? Could be what we're looking at."

The Mercurion bobbed her head. "An *Ix'tamo could* do this. They eventually kill everything off, but they don't usually do it this fast. Not unless there's a lot of them."

"Hector! I see dead people up on the ridge!" Karalti's voice broke through just then.

"Hang on: Karalti found something." I sniffed, but couldn't smell anyone or anything decomposing. "Undead or dead-dead? And how many?"

"About twenty, and they're dead-dead. They're lying down in the middle of a pretty pattern."

I wrinkled my nose. "... Pretty pattern?"

"What'd she find? Rotters?" Suri asked.

I shook my head. "She doesn't think so. I'd be careful anyway."

Slowly and carefully, we headed upward, climbing the narrow gravel path through groves of leafless, shriveled trees. The stench of death hung in the air.

"Wait." Rin held up small silver hands. "I'm sorry... I can't do this. I'll watch the path with Lovelace and Hopper."

"Sure thing. But corpse is kind of an acquired resistance. You get used to it, but you have to expose yourself to it." I tied a cloth around my neck and pulled it up part way over my helmet.

She looked down. "I... guess you fought in the War? Like, the Total War. Second Total War."

"79th Meatshield Division, at your service," I replied. "I was conscripted in '63. Fought in the jungle and the desert for five years. This place brings back great memories, believe me."

"That's... mm." Rin looked up toward the hill, then set her shoulders and began marching up toward the bodies.

"You can hang back, Rin." I looked to Suri, who shrugged. "You don't like... need to impress us."

"No." The Mercurion shook her head. "You're right, and you're my friend. If you have to do this and relive all those horrible things, I'll go with you."

"Alright." Suri carried the torch ahead, drawing an axe with her other hand. She flipped it around. "But let me go first. You two stay behind me."

I hesitated. "If you die-"

"If you die, Karalti'll never forgive me. I'm trying to get on her good side right now."

"Really?" Reluctantly, I fell in behind her and flanked out, peering out into the gloom. *"Why? Think she's cute now she can turn into a human girl?"*

"Don't be gross. She's basically my adopted kid at this point, right?"

As her words sunk in, I grinned more widely than I had ever beamed in my life. *"Yeah. Mine too."*

It was frigid now, our breath frosting in clouds of vapor, and the terrain was no longer entirely flat. I was okay, but Suri was shivering by the time we crested the ridge. Despite the cold, the smell hit us full force up there, along with the sound: carrion beetles. They rubbed their wings together in a raspy chorus as they crawled over a ring of corpses laid out in a circle on the ground. Karalti was right: these guys were very dead, each one laid out with his arms crossed over his chest. And the pattern was kind of pretty.

"Time to play 'Jellyfish on the Beach'!" I twirled the Spear around like a baton. "Will they get up? Will they stay down? Either way, poke 'em with a stick! It's fun for the whole family!"

"Try that one on the left with the funny nose." Suri held the torch up as I advanced.

Rin stood behind her turrets, her hands clamped over her nose. "I can't believe I helped develop this game."

Unsure of what to expect, I crept forward and stretched out with the Spear to tap the nearest corpse. Nothing happened. I came in closer, and jabbed the tip of the blade into an arm. The body lay there, unmoving.

"I think we're clear." I let out a breath I hadn't known I'd been holding, then went in for a closer look. There were close to twenty bodies, all of them nude, all of them male. The Vlachian soldiers had Cossack hairstyles: shaven heads with a forelock or a side-part, beards and moustaches. Several tribal Yanik warriors had clay-covered dreadlocks like Zlaslo's. Their clothing and armor had been removed and left in a moldering pile at the edge of the clearing.

"Rotters, for sure." I crouched down. The man nearest me was a mess: blackened hands, old stab wounds, torn guts, faces stripped of flesh... and most notably, broken bones. Lots of them. He wasn't the only one, either. Every man's face had been pulverized: noses smashed, eyes ruptured, cheekbones caved back into their skulls. I turned to look at the center of the circle. There was a stack of stones there. On top of the small cairn was a crude wreath of grass and twigs, the only plant matter in the immediate area.

I frowned. "Baru are combat monks. Remember what Istvan said about Vash Dorha?"

"That he punched a wyvern to death." Suri pulled up beside me, her boots crunching on the gravel. "You think he did this?"

"Yeah. Burna is the God of the Dead. I think this is Vash's handiwork... he gave these men a respectful burial."

Suri eyed the snaking ring of naked corpses, then the pile of clothes. "I admit I have some questions."

"It's a sky burial. He gave these men last rites." The words tripped out of my mouth almost of their own accord. Somehow, I just *knew.* "There's not enough soil in Tungaant to bury the dead, so they're given rites and left out for the animals. Carrion insects are sacred to Burna. The monks have these dog-sized tamed flies-"

"Okay, thanks. That'll do." Suri coughed. "The smell's bad enough. I don't need the imagery."

It was strange. As I knelt there, watching the beetles swarm the corpses, I didn't feel the least bit of revulsion. Three months ago, I would have. It was the stuff of horror movies, right? But now... no. I knew why the Baru had done this. It was the cycling of the dead back into the living world. "Sure, sorry."

"So Vash was alive for this fight, at least," Suri remarked. "But why is it so bloody cold?"

I stood back up and rubbed my jaw, frowning. "The *Ix'tamo*, maybe? We need to find a trail. My hunch is to follow the cold. Maybe they found something here."

"It's warmer to the north and east," Suri said. "South-west?"

"Let's do it."

With Karalti keeping watch overhead, Suri, Cutthroat, Rin and I advanced slowly and cautiously through the increasingly eerie forest. After leaving the sky burial site, there was no animal life to be seen or heard. Not even mosquitoes were stirring in this part of the swamp. There was no sloshing or gurgling of water, no wind... no anything, until we crunched our way across flattened, icy reeds and found ourselves at the shore of a frozen lake.

A serrated crescent of ice marked the edge of the lake, leading back into a cave so dark that even my eyesight couldn't penetrate it. The moonlight gleamed through leafless trees onto solid ice. At least fifty bodies littered the frozen surface, lying where they had fallen. There was a small island at the center, where a spear-like device hummed, glowed and spat sparks out across the ground. The air hummed and crawled across my skin, and the smell of ozone was almost suffocating. There was a dead Allosaurus at the edge of the lake.

"That's an *Ix'tamo*!" Excited, Rin pointed at the device on the island. "See! I told you that's how the Demon was getting his mana!"

"Sure looks like it." Suri rubbed at her face. "And it's busted. My HUD says I'm at risk of mana poisoning."

"Yeah." I wasn't, but I could sense something was wrong. "Suri, retreat to the edge of the radiation zone and let me, Rin and Karalti go out there. I'm not getting an alert yet."

"My HP is dropping fast. Be careful." Suri beat a hasty retreat on Cutthroat.

Karalti's wingbeats grew louder as she circled down and landed firm, setting off a rolling *boom.* She folded her wings smartly against her flanks, flicking them as she took in the scene ahead. *"Woah. What's that thing?"*

"Nothing good. How are you at walking on ice?"

Karalti chirped in her throat, cocking her head one way, then the other. *"I dunno. I might be too heavy. I could polymorph, but..."*

"No, no polymorphing. You haven't gotten the hang of fighting in human form yet, but you're a big badass like this. Let's go have a look at our dead dinosaur friend over here."

The three of us edged toward the fallen Allosaurus. It was a big specimen, and it showed signs of Stranging. Its skin was studded with crystalline eruptions, and it had an elongated, twisted look about it that was unsettling. Its dislocated lower jaw gaped to one side. One of its eyes had been pushed back into its skull, the flesh and bone folded around the point of impact.

"Did... Vash do this?" Holding her nose, Rin crouched down to look at the injury.

"Maybe." Punching dinosaurs to death? I was starting to see why Istvan liked the guy. "Karalti, see how you go out on the lake."

Karalti bobbed her head, padding forward to the waterline. She delicately placed a three-toed hind foot onto the surface and put her weight on it. The ice groaned, then squealed just before a there was a dull crack, and a long fissure appeared across the frozen surface.

"Nope." Flattening her horns, Karalti carefully stepped away. Through the fissure, I could see that the water was frozen all the way to the bottom... but the ice was crumbly.

I sighed. "Guess it's on me and Rin. Go protect Suri and Cutthroat, will you? I don't want them being ambushed by whoever is coming back for this *Ix'tamo.*"

"Sure. Be careful." Tail lashing, Karalti slunk back through the bone-white trees. When she accidentally bumped into one, it snapped like wet chipboard and toppled in a cloud of dust.

Rin pulled up alongside me on her automaton. "How are you at ice skating?"

"Imagine a cross between a pig and a cockroach. Then put it on ice." I carefully picked my way out onto the lake. My armored foot immediately began to slide forward. But then I remembered – I had better gear for this. I went into my inventory and selected Boots of the Winding Path, the Tuun-made boots with the big-ass cleats on the soles. They appeared on my feet like magic.

"Yeh-hehhh, you icy bitch! Feel my traction!" I threw my hands in the air, and crunched my way forward like a large monster invading a Japanese city.

Shaking her head, Rin followed me out. "Are you okay?"

"Oh, yeah, I'm fine. Just mad with power."

The diamond-shaped obelisk was driven into the bleached, lifeless earth like a knife blade. It was made of obsidian, metal and crystal, welded together in a seamless symmetrical design concealing a core of brightly glowing mana. The light pulsed erratically, because the crystal face of the machine had been smashed in by a single, powerful blow. Broken crystal 'veins' ran throughout the *Ix'tamo*, leaking through the shattered depression in the center. It cast a sick glow across the bodies laid out on the surface of the lake.

Like the others we'd found, the fallen men and women had clearly been zombies not very long ago. Like the other's we'd found, they were heavily decomposed, with crude weapons in their hands, piecemeal armor and tattered clothing. There were so many and the fight had been so desperate that Vash hadn't given rites to any of them. The number of corpses was relative to the proximity of the *Ix'tamo* - the closer we got, the more bodies there were.

"It's like they were trying to defend this." Curious, I made a fist and gently rested my knuckles over the depression in the crystal. It was almost an exact match. "Holy shit."

"So... you think he might be alive after all?" Rin pushed her mask down and activated her spell glove.

"Everything that has gotten in his way so far has been punched to death or broken. And I'd assume that if we have a quest, then he's more likely to be alive than not." I watched my health bar cautiously, holding my breath against the gas pouring from the *Ix'tamo.* "I don't know if there's RNG involved."

"A little, though I'm not supposed to tell players anything about it." Rin poured over the broken device with gentle hands, utilizing some Craft skill I could only guess at. "But I guess we're stuck on this server and everyone's dead now... so, yes. It's not a certain thing, because NPCs are largely autonomous. Every NPC Seed is crafted from digitized human datasets, so they're basically like real people. Sometimes they do dumb stuff that gets them killed. But the radiant AI will always try to guide them toward player objectives when possible."

I went to ask her about the Seed thing, but accidentally drew in a deep breath. My eyes teared up and my throat went dry and rough, just as an alert appeared:

【Warning! You are being poisoned by Mana!】

"Crap. Mana." I croaked.

"You should go find Suri. This will take me a while to fix, but I can make it work." Rin was in her element now, furiously applying putty to the cracks on the obelisk.

"Don't make it *work*," I said. "We don't want it working. Just turn it off."

"You don't understand. If I can make it functional, I've got some ideas for how we could repurpose it." She shook her head, focused on what she was doing. "Leave me alone for a bit - I know what I'm doing."

"Sure. I believe you." I beat a hasty retreat to my own area of expertise: fucking around. "Okay... If I was a kung-fu master-slash-monk of the God of Death, where would I go?"

The cave loomed at the other end of the frozen lake.

Well, fuck.

I left Leaky Doomsday Device Island and trudged across the ice toward the cave, apprehension mounting with every step. A strange chemical smell wafted to my nose, like battery acid. The ice was cracked and hazed, ground to powder in places... and just inside, revealed by torchlight, was the body of a man dressed like a Tuun warrior in leather and fur. He'd fallen face down, sprawled across the ground. The boots he wore were a more modern version of the ones I currently had on, heavy leather with sharp metal cleats. His hands were sheathed in full-sleeve cold iron gauntlets, like the ones I'd given to Karalti. The rest of him was obscured by a thick, suffocating layer of slime.

"Uh oh." I broke into a jog and knelt beside him, trying to roll the man over. When I touched the slime, I got a small static shock through my gloves. The stuff clung to my hand, stretching like taffy. Taffy with the tensile strength of steel cable. "Ugh. Nasty."

With some effort, I managed to roll the body over and get a look at him. This man wasn't Tuun, and he was bald. That immediately told me that this dead monk was not our man. Hair was a big deal in Tungaant, and the way it was braided and styled could tell you a lot about a person: their profession, their marital status, whether they'd ever killed another human being. The red cloth braided into my hair was there for a reason. I wasn't entirely sure how Baru wore their hair, but I knew monks didn't shave: except for the day they took their vows as acolytes. This guy was as bald as a billiard ball. He had to have taken his vows very recently.

With one wary eye on the cave, I patched through to the others. "Vash was definitely here. I found one of the Vlachian disciples who went with him - dead. It looks like something else might've been here, and I'd say there's about a 300% chance our monk and whatever monster finally got the better of him is in this cave."

"Suri copy. ETA on the Ixa'whatsit?"

"Give me another five minutes! Copy! Roger!" Rin said.

"Copy-Roger that. I'll join Hector at the cave entry." Suri's tone was thick with amusement.

"Uhh... Rin copy? I'm just sealing the broken filter now, and then it should be safe to transport. Will Karalti be able to pick it up?"

"Assuming it's less than five hundred pounds, sure." I stood up and ran an inventory while the girls packed their way around the lake. I had ten healing potions, a few antidotes for different classes of poison, a few potions to cure each of the four families of disease. *"I'm setting up a camp so*

we can respawn as close to the fight as possible. Whatever is in there took out the guy who king-hit a three-ton dinosaur. I'm thinking we might be going up against one of those slime worms."

Suri and Cutthroat came into view, with Karalti flying ahead of them. The dragon backwinged and hovered, kicking up dry ice like dust, then wheeled to land on solid ground just in front of the cave mouth. She darted her head to sniff around while I set up our temporary spawn point: a small camp, which was little more than three bedrolls, a firepit, and a basket. Suri slid from Cutthroat's back as she approached. Her Corona was flashing warningly from the mana in the air, but her health seemed to be stable.

"Here," I said. "See if you can set this as a spawn point."

Suri grimaced, but complied. After twenty seconds or so, she shook her head. "Says 'Error: Invalid Seed Request'."

"Shit. Sorry. Thought it was worth a try."

"It's always worth trying." Slowly, Suri's gaze drifted to the fallen Baru. "So, is this slime the same narcotic as the stuff that took out those allos?"

"You know, I'm not sure." I took my still-slimy knife blade and touched it to my cheek. There was no torpor alert. "Nope. No reaction. Just feels kind of wet. It zapped me when I first touched it."

"Static from the ice." Suri scuffed her foot on it.

"Yeah. Dry water. See something new every day."

"That slime doesn't smell the same to me." Karalti rumbled in her chest, leaning in to sniff, then lick my face. *"Kind of tasty, actually. Like... eel?"*

"Eel?" There were all kinds of eels that could make our lives hell. Electric eels, poison eels, giant bukkake eels. "Okay. Well... you girls ready to have a bad time?"

Suri swung her sword off her back and around with one hand. The edge of it hit the ice with a metallic clang, the blow hard enough to send hairline cracks through the clear surface. "Point me at it."

"Yeah! Boss fight!" Karalti tossed her head with a throaty barking cry, which Cutthroat echoed, hissing and snapping and weaving her neck.

"Guys! Wait for me!" Rin squeaked as Hopper ran toward us, Lovelace gecko-crawling over the ice behind her. "I fixed it! Are you okay? What are we doing now?"

Chapter 20

As we advanced through the cave, there was less ice and more slime. A lot more slime. More slime than I ever needed to see or experience. It was white, thick, and the jokes were so obvious I couldn't bring myself to make them. The apple hung so low that it brushed the suggestively sticky floor.

"Down here in the snot cave, looking at snot stuff!" Karalti sang in my head. *"Snot land!"*

"I feel like we're walking through some teenage boy's secret cum sock drawer," Suri muttered behind me.

"That's nasty, gurl. Why you so nasty?" I was in the lead, moving slowly, carefully, and cautiously. Suri was mounted on Cutthroat, who had buffs for rough terrain and sharp claws to cut through anything that stuck to her feet. Karalti followed up the rear, only barely able to fit through the slimed-up tunnel.

"Well, am I wrong? It fuckin' stinks in here."

"No." I eyed a snot stalactite hanging from the ceiling. "This is the place where unwashed Fleshlights go to die."

"Eww! Hector!" Rin exclaimed.

Suri groaned. "Somehow, you just managed to make this experience even worse."

"Now you just hold on there a minute. You went there. I restrained myself, but no. You saw that slippery white slope, and yet you slid all the way down. You WALLOWED in it."

"You can stop now."

"It's way too late to stop now, sugarplum."

She rolled her eyes. "Spoken like every man in the world."

A vibration passed through the soles of our feet, followed by a brief rumble from somewhere beneath us. We froze, rooted to the spot.

"It's still far away," Rin said uncertainly. "Below?"

"Yup. And to the right." Karalti gestured with the tip of her muzzle, nostrils flaring. *"Smells like dead things."*

"Sure does." I began walking again, trying to place my feet as lightly as I could. "This place is starting to give me a giant spider vibe. But where are the little mobs?"

Suri held the torch up, highlighting dark forms trapped under layers of mucus, entombed like flies in amber. "Right about here, I reckon."

We hadn't seen a single living thing since entering the Snot Caves. No monsters, no insects. Nada. Part of me was grateful that we didn't have anything attacking us and sucking up our precious potions. The rest of me was on edge about it. It did remind me a lot of the slime fish's lair, though this was much larger than the waterhole where the Allosauruses had met their maker. "I hope we aren't in something's stomach."

Suri grunted. "Don't worry. She'll be right."

"Who's 'she'?" Rin asked.

Suri groaned. "It's a saying, Rin. Like, as in, 'it'll be okay'."

"Why don't you just say that, then?"

"I dunno. Why can't you UNAC cunts say 'aluminum' properly?" Suri made an orc face and crossed her eyes. "Aloo-mi-num! It's 'Aloo-mini-yum', you dorks. It's got a second 'I'."

Coming to a fork in the passage, we headed left - and there, like a sign pointing the way, was another dead acolyte of Burna. He was bound to the passage wall with slime, his shaven head hanging loose. There was at least an inch of ooze over his entire body, just translucent enough for us to make out his face.

"Man. This got really dark, really fast." I stayed just behind Suri, ready to Jump at the first sign of life.

"Is this our man?" Suri asked.

"Nope. He's got no hair."

We continued on. The cave system got narrower, forcing Karalti to crawl. It was tempting to get her to use her new Polymorph ability, but if we did, she'd be stuck like that for an hour - and we couldn't afford it. She huffed and struggled behind us as we came up on a point where the tunnel narrowed dramatically into a tunnel of bluish-white slime. It was caked on like web, forming a downward-sloping funnel into... somewhere.

I eyed the black hole and nodded. "Boss arena."

"Yeah." Rin swallowed. "I-I still have nightmares about Andrik, guys. I don't know-"

"You can do it, kiddo. We need every bit of help we can get." Suri was unusually serious as she lit another torch from the one in her hand, then threw it down the hole like a burning javelin. It sailed through the darkness about twenty feet, then landed and caught on the slime. We could see that the tunnel opened further down.

Karalti rumbled anxiously behind us. *"I can't fit down there."*

"Can you dig it out?" I asked her.

She nodded. *"Yeah, but it could take a while. If Vash is down there..."*

"Then we don't have a while." Fuming, I turned to look back at the hole, and ran over my choices. "I'd rather have you strong and late than weakened and with us from the start of the fight. Once we have time to train you in human combat, we will. But for now, we need to go ahead and see if we can find our monk."

"Okay. I'll be digging the whole time." Karalti snorted, pulling herself another few feet forward. *"And when I catch up...?"*

"Torch ALL the things." I rubbed her cheekbone, then clapped her on the neck and went to join Suri at the front. "Get your buffs ready, guys. You got spare mana, Rin?"

"Yes. I was able to siphon some from the *Ix'tamo*, too." Her eyes were wide as she stamped her feet, trying to steel herself.

I regarded the others levelly. "We work in a triangle formation: me, Suri and Cutthroat. If it's a swarm boss, Rin, I want you to focus on defense. Try to stay in the center of the triangle. If it's a single boss monster, hang at the back of the arena. If you can find the limit of its Area of Effect attacks, hang back there and only come in to cast spells. Suri, if it's a single monster, you need to take point and tank it out while I flank. If it's a swarm, let me take point - I have some moves that can hit up to ten bogeys at a time. Sound solid?"

"Cutthroat's got a Pack Tactics bonus to her damage if she's within twenty feet of us," Suri said. "I'll try to keep her in range. Your Jump carries you about 40ft, right?"

"Yeah, if I combine it with a dash. Up or forward or a bit of both."

She nodded. "Good to know. I'll be on foot and try and keep you both at eleven and six o'clock. Cutthroat fights better when she doesn't have a rider."

I nodded. "Sound good otherwise?"

"Sounds good." Suri gave me a short nod.

"Rin?" I looked to her.

"Uh... yeah? Sure." Rin was regarding us with something almost like awe.

"Then let's go and yee-haw this bitch harder than it's ever been yee-haw'd before." Suri and I high-fived without even looking at each other, knowing the other's hand would be there.

We made our way down slowly, leery of traps. The slime had the same static charge that the stuff at the cave entry had, discharging with little pops as we clambered over it. Unlike the slime used to trap the monks, it was firm - almost like soft rubber. Electricity - or mana - flashed through the substance in hairline patterns of light. It reminded me a lot of the mana-infused crystal that made up the visor of my helmet, except squishier.

"What'dya bet something's listening to us walk?" Suri remarked as another rumble reverberated under the floor.

I grunted. "Oh, yeah - it knows we're here all right."

The tunnel was only about sixty feet long, narrowing to a point small enough that Cutthroat had to chop away some slime to squeeze through. It deposited us into a large cavern hung with bioluminescent stalactites and giant pink jelly mushrooms. The ceiling cast a soft blue light over the roughly textured, hard, slime covered ground... which deepened into a liquid pool of the stuff at the center-rear of the cavern. It was just like the Swamp Hag's slime trap, but larger. Behind the pool was another door, which was sealed with a glowing plug of crystallized slime.

Suri clicked her tongue, and pointed to her left while she split to the right. Cutthroat's feathers stood on end as she took her position, fitfully snapping her claw arms. She got within twenty feet of the pool before it began to vibrate, and then the ground shook as something began to tunnel beneath us. Quickly.

"Okay, Rin - start buffing." I shifted into position, took a deep breath, and puffed it out.

The thing that pulled itself up out of the pit of slime wasn't a Swamp Hag. Maybe it had been, once upon a time. The core of it was that of a giant, purplish eel-like creature, with no eyes and a small three-lobed mouth. But this one was covered in segmented plates of armor, and walked on eight long, prehensile limbs, like extendable, metallic tentacles covered in spines. It slammed its three-clawed feet into the crystallized floor of the cave, anchoring itself as its bulk slithered out of the pit of slime that lubricated it's passage.

I felt a tic start at the corner of my eye. "Alright. The spider vibe was more relevant than I really wanted it to be."

The 'head' of the ⟦Swamp Hag Broodmother⟧ oriented on us as we all took a big step back toward the entry. Its little mouth lobes opened, as if in surprise, and then unfurled into a parasol of spines, slime, and... electricity.

"It's turbocharged. Great." I concentrated until dark energy shot down along the haft of my spear. "Watch out for AoE!"

"*Spera, Cil, Kain!*" Rin cried from the back of the party. Her spell suffused Cutthroat with a dim blue light.

Karalti roared in the distance as Suri, Cutthroat and I charged the Broodmother, breaking up to flank it from either side as it screeched and whipped its body back and forth. Slime flew everywhere as I Jumped, Spear raised to strike, and got knocked off course by a wad of electrically charged goo that hit me like a taser.

[[Broodmother uses Electroweb! 375 HP damage!
[[You are Stunned!]]

The electricity sucked the strength from my limbs and sent me sprawling. My teeth clacked together, my arms and legs spasmed. My nose filled with the stench of burning hair as I clawed my way up in time to see the writhing worm lunge at Suri, who turned its maw away with her sword. Cutthroat screeched as she leapt on it with all four limbs from the other side, slashing, kicking and biting.

[[Cutthroat uses Multiattack! 268 damage!]]

"Wait for the boss pattern!" Rin called from behind us. "Hector, hold still! *Spera, Cil, Kain*!"

A blue aura suffused my body, and suddenly I felt lighter and faster - a Haste spell. Rin was buffing all three of us while her turrets fired on the Broodmother. I chugged a potion.

Suri charged in with a roar, red energy rippling over her sword. The Broodmother tensed, and the electricity crackling in the fan of its mouth surged, forking across its entire length like a suit of armor. Cutthroat was blown off, yelping and smoking. Suri's sword hit the field and bounced off it in a shower of sparks that sent her stumbling. She snarled with pain, her hair standing on end. The Broodmother smashed all eight of its feet into the ground as its body continued to ripple with rings of brilliant azure light.

"AOE! Get off the floor!" I shouted on pure instinct, leaping off the ground to cling higher up on the wall with Spider Climb.

Rin shrieked and jumped onto the back of her turret, but there was nowhere for Suri and Cutthroat to go as the Broodmother hunched over and then unleashed a torrent of electricity across the ground. The Plasma Blast swallowed them both, knocking them to the floor. Their HP rings drained into the orange zone. We'd hardly even hit the damn boss yet.

"Okay, you big zappy bitch!" I kicked off the wall like a cricket before the monster could recover from the power move, and at the peak of the leap, I discharged my own atom bomb. A fan of lances rained down on the Broodmother as I rammed the Spear into its soft flesh. My AP drained to almost nothing as the crackling spears of darkness impacted the giant worm like Stinger missiles, shattering and reforming into Rain of Glass. It did a lot of damage, but not as much damage as I'd been expecting.

[[Broodmother shrugs off Darkness! Half damage!]]
[[You hit Broodmother for 1983 damage!]]

"Fuck! It's a Light elemental! *Karalti, can you use Biosca-AANN?*" The broodmother caught me with a backhand, a blow that electrocuted me even as it slapped me off the monster's body. I flew back and slammed into one of the webs of slime. 130 HP vaporized into thin air.

"Okay! Hold on!" Karalti stopped digging and concentrated. The air around her throbbed and darkened, and then the Broodmother's information appeared:

Swamp Hag Broodmother

Stranged Boss Creature
Sex: Hermaphroditic
Level 32
HP: 12,449/15,000
MP: 500/500
Weak Against Gravity
Strong Against Darkness

Fuck fuck fuck. We were all out of Gravity magic.

"*Spera, Kia, Bah'in*!" Rin cried from the back of the room.

The Broodmother was suffused with a cool white aura that warped the air around it, and its movements became sluggish and ponderous. A Slow spell!

"I'm almost through!" Karalti resumed clawing at the slime plugging the entryway. *"Hold on!"*

"Focus buffs on Hector!" Suri snarled. She threw down her sword, pulled her axes, and hunched down into a feral crouch as a wave of heat pushed through the air around her.

[Suri activates Boar's Armor!]

I cut the slime around myself and dropped to the floor as our tank rushed in, half again as fast and strong as she'd been before. The Broodmother lashed down to bite, but Suri dodged the blow and spun in like a dervish, wielding her sword like a butcher's cleaver. Ichor sprayed from the wounds.

[Broodmother is Bleeding! HP: 11,706/15,000]

The monster hissed, striking down like a snake at Cutthroat as she sprinted forward and latched onto the worm's flank.

The Broodmother stiffened and then began to secrete slime - lots of it.

[Broodmother uses Restoration! Heals 1500HP!]
[Broodmother's Damage Reduction has increased!]

"That thing just used fucking healing magic!" I charged in while Suri kept the mouth end occupied, slashing with the Spear until I built up enough AP to pull off the high-damage moves again. It was resistant to my element, but the lances of Darkness still took out a significant chunk of HP. We whittled her down to 10,000 in a matter of minutes, and then she began to arc with coils of electricity like a massive Tesla Coil.

"Jump!" I screamed at the others, leaping up to cling with Spider Climb once again.

But the Broodmother didn't discharge electricity across the floor again: This time, she swung her prehensile limbs like whips, shattering crystal with every blow. It was impossible to dodge. One of them slammed into me across the thighs, hitting me for 310 points and sending me spinning and then tumbling across the floor. Suri flattened herself to the ground while Cutthroat stood over her, taking the onslaught herself, howling as electricity arced across her scales. But then Karalti finally wormed her head, neck and torso through the hole she'd made and belched a narrow plume of blazing white liquid right onto the Broodmother's bulk. The *Ghost Fire* exploded into flames as soon as it struck, and the worm shrieked in agony, lashing out with gobs of electrified slime even as crossbow bolts continued to pepper it from afar.

[[Ghost Fire deals 1340 damage!]]
[[Rin Lu deals 20 damage!]]
[[Suri activates Battle Lust!]]

Panting and limping, I spammed heals and held my distance. Across the room, Suri did the same thing - and then her armor vanished from her body, leaving her in her leggings, a halter top, and a cloud of flaring power as she finally activated her key Path ability: Primal Rage.

[[Broodmother uses Restoration! Heals 1500HP!]]
[[Broodmother's Damage Reduction has increased!]]

"HURRRAAAHHH!" The Berserker, supernaturally fast from multiple stacking buffs, tore in toward the Broodmother and began to chop her like a tree. The boss let loose a jolt of electricity. Suri snapped her teeth like a dog, soaking the damage, and powered on.

[Suri deals 1890 damage!]
[Suri's Rage builds! Damage reduction and attack power drastically increases!]

Suddenly, I had a bright idea. While the Broodmother focused on Cutthroat and Suri, I ran along the edge of the wall, Jumped and flipped in midair to land on the monster's back. "Time for some voodoo!"

I landed the Jump, sinking the head of the Spear into the creature's rubbery flesh. The slime insulated it from the Fire element the weapon delivered, but I twisted it out and bounced back enough to dash, then hit my Blood Sprint to Blood Storm to Death by a Thousand Cuts combo. They were all Darkness-elemental abilities, dealing reduced damage - but the big slimy bitch wasn't immune to Curses. A shadowy nimbus pulsed along the seven-foot length of the spear, sucking the light from the air and twisting my guts with a nasty, icy sensation that tore from my body and slammed deep into the Broodmother's.

[Broodmother is Cursed! -4% attack power!]
[You gain +4% attack power and +10% damage reduction from your opponent's attacks!]
[You deal 725 reduced Darkness damage!]
[Suri's Rage builds! Damage reduction and attack power drastically increases!]

Suri's HP was below half; mine was creeping back up into that weird zone between orange and green. Rin was almost untouched, protected by her turrets, but Hopper and Lovelace had been soaking all of that AOE and were starting to smoke and spit sparks. Cutthroat was in the red, clawing slime from the body of the Broodmother even though she had to be in agony.

The boss began to move just like she had before the Plasma Burst. I made a decision. I vaulted from the Broodmother, bounced off Cutthroat's back and landed on the ground in front of her. She stopped mauling the boss for a second, turning on me with her hook-arms raised and her jaws gaping. I jammed a potion in her gaping mouth.

"Drink! Drink it all!" I slapped five assorted healing poultices onto her, until she looked like she was covered in nicotine patches. "No whine! Only drink!"

The Hookwing glugged in confusion, but her HP ring jumped back into the green as the Broodmother tensed, and then unleashed waves of electricity throughout the cavern.

[[Broodmother uses Plasma Burst!]]
[[You take 998 damage! You are Stunned! HP: 66/1362]]

The blast flung us all back, turning everything white. It barely even hurt: a flash, a pop, and I came to on my side, my mouth and nose full of a metallic burning stench. Over the thundering in my ears, I heard Karalti's bestial roar, and then Suri's. The sound of one of the turrets firing, and Rin's squeal of pain as something finally breached her defenses and hit her.

[[Suri hits Broodmother for 1263 damage!]]
[[Ghost Fire hits for 1340 damage!]]
[[Broodmother is on Fire! HP: 4122/15,000]]

God, we were so close. Groaning, I rolled to my back, just in time to see the Broodmother whip one of her electrified legs toward me so fast that it blurred. The shadow sliced across my face. I braced myself to die

Chapter 21

"SCREEEEEE!" Cutthroat's bird-like screech echoed off the walls, and then her keel nearly drove me into the ground as she flung herself on top of me. The blow landed squarely across the hookwing's back instead of my head. Bones crunched and one hind leg gave way. She huffed with pain, falling to rest on her wrist joints.

[[Cutthroat uses Pack Guardian!]]
[[Pack Bond: Cutthroat's HP, Attack and Defense sharply increases! HP: 544/1500]]
[[Cutthroat has a Fractured Pelvis! Max HP reduced, Movement -65%!]]

"Goddammit, Cutthroat: I respawn, you don't!" I slapped every poultice I had left onto her belly, lifting her HP back up to its new maximum - about 70% of her usual total. She hissed at me, mantling over my prone form as Suri charged ahead into the fray. The Berserker's skin was smoking, her hair standing on end, but every hit she landed on the Broodmother was restoring her HP as her Primal Rage ability built toward its maximum damage output.

Cutthroat was suffused with a deep red aura not unlike Suri's as she snarled, limping up to her one good leg. As I chugged potions, she stood over me, blocking and swatting away the cable-like limbs as they flailed over us, soaking Electro Web attacks, fending off slime and static shocks. When I was back to half, I slid out from under her and used the Spear to get to my feet.

"Get her, girl! Ice cream!" I gave Cutthroat her old attack command, getting ready to Jump. "Rin! Can you heal Suri?"

"Yes!" Rin cried back. One of her turrets was crumpled on the ground, while the other was on its last legs. The Mercurion made a beeline for Suri, who was furiously hacking into the Broodmother's bleeding abdomen with her axes. She was hovering at around 30% HP, whaling on the boss with supernatural speed. As her HP went down, her attack rose.

[[Suri deals 1492 damage!]]
[[Cutthroat deals 200 damage!]]
[[Broodmother uses Restoration! HP: 4130/15,000]]
[[Rin casts Haste! +20% movement and attack speed!]]

My AP bar was full from the massive hit I'd taken. Gritting my teeth, I sprung up, dodging the flailing bullwhip limbs, and threw everything I had at the Broodmother. Lances of black energy slammed into it, rocking the giant worm to one side. Suri's axes broke, their durability gone, and she seamlessly dodged a tentacle, scooped up her sword, and began to lay in with it. Her eyes were molten gold, blazing with inhuman strength as she roared and charged back in to swing.

[[You deal 1983 damage!]]
[[Suri deals 1221 damage!]]
[[Broodmother uses Restoration! HP: 1726/15,000]]

Across the room, Karalti drew a deep breath. "*Hector! Go left!*"

The Broodmother spun its bulk around and began to dive back into the pit of slime. But Karalti was faster. Her breath weapon slashed a line of white magnesium fire down the front of the giant worm, and it wailed long and loud as the fire ripped across its wounds. The limbs, each one as thick as bridge cables, smashed down around us, sending chunks of rock and crystal flying. It stopped trying to run away and began to turbocharge in preparation for one last Plasma Blast: a blast that would kill me, Suri and Cutthroat if it was able to get it off.

"Fuck you! Fuck YOU!" I vaulted up onto one of the writhing metal limbs and ran up along its bucking length, waiting for the right moment to Jump, Shadow Dash, and then land on the Broodmother's open mouth. Fighting shocks of electricity, I rammed the blazing Spear down its gullet, while Cutthroat buried the full length of her scythe-like claws into the monster's burning belly. Suri was right behind her, using her sword to crack the monster's carapace open. Bright blue viscera spilled over the ground, and with one final screech, the huge creature toppled. The whip-like limbs went limp, falling to the ground.

[[You have defeated Swamp Hag Broodmother!]]
[[You gain 1600 EXP!]]
[[Congratulations! You are Level 19]]
[[Congratulations! Karalti is Level 10!]]
[[Suri Ba'hadir is Level 21!]]

[[Rin Lu is Level 17!]]

I jumped when the Broodmother began to fall, landing lightly just ahead of the wave of bug juice. Suri dropped her sword, then went to hands and knees, heaving for breath and drooling blood even as a faint golden glow suffused her: her level up. Cutthroat limped off-side and sunk down, panting and wide-eyed with pain. Her left leg was hanging useless, the hip joint soft and deformed. Rin was singed, but mostly unharmed. Her turrets, on the other hand, were fucked - maybe beyond repair.

"FUCK!" I threw the Spear down in a fit of pique, burning off the nervous energy that threatened to turn me into shaking jelly. "Jesus fucking Christ!"

Scrabbling, Karalti twisted and strained one last time until she slipped through the entry to the Broodmother's lair like a cork from a bottle of wine. "Yeah! We did it!"

"Barely. Fuck me," Suri gasped. She looked up and around, wild-eyed with fatigue. "Cutthroat? Is Cutthroat okay? She's literally just five points off Level 18."

"Of course. Can we find a bug for her to kill or something?" I collected my weapon and went to the ailing dinosaur as she tried to turn around and lick her injured leg. When I crouched in front of it, she growled.

"Easy, girl." I held up a hand to her, reaching out to gently examine her pelvis. The flesh around her hip joint was soft, dimpling under even a light touch. "Yeah, this is fucked. I have something that might be able to help her, but... it's alchemical."

Suri spat to the side and rocked back onto her rump. "What's that mean?"

"There's a chance it'll kill her, or Strange her." I winced.

"What are the odds?"

"Fifty-fifty."

Suri scowled, but when she looked back at Cutthroat, her expression softened. After a few moments, she shook her head. "Do it. If she had a choice between death and never being able to fight again, I know which one she'd pick."

"Yeah. It's important that we keep her out of the sun for a minimum two days after she takes this. This stuff is crazy phototoxic – she'll take damage on contact with sunlight."

Cutthroat fixed me with fierce, intelligent eyes as I pulled my one and only Bonefuse potion from my Inventory. The dark potion cast a deep blue-violet light. I set it aside along with the Spear and held up both hands.

"I have to set this fracture, girl," I said to her. "Try not to kill me."

The hookwing snorted, nostrils flexing. Her muzzle tracked me as I lay both hands on the injured hip. As soon as my hands touched her skin, she let out a low, rumbling growl.

"Here." Suri crawled over took the dinosaur's head into her lap. She stroked the singed feathers back. The hookwing shivered, and her eyes half-closed with pleasure. "Okay... now. Just be quick."

Karalti padded over to us and ducked her head, feet booming against the cavern floor. "*Will she be okay?*"

"That's the plan." I got my hands in position, and a virtual diagram appeared that demonstrated what I needed to do and how to push. I had to press the heels of my palms in, hook up, then push forward. All the crafts I'd tried in

Archemi had this sort of rhythm-based minigame. "Okay... three, two, one."

I followed the diagram and put my back into it. Cutthroat screeched, kicking loose rocks along the floor with her other foot, but Suri hung onto her head. The joint slid back into the socket with a crunch. Cutthroat sunk down, whimpering, and nuzzled into Suri's chest with her snout.

"Yeah, I know." I picked up the potion and handed it to Suri. "Here. Remember, no sunlight. Two to four days. She'll lose one percent HP every minute she's outdoors in the daytime."

"If she survives," Suri said. Her brows were knit and her eyes were dark with worry.

Rin and I held Cutthroat's limbs down as Suri plugged Cutthroat's nostrils with her fingers and poured the potion into her mouth. The hookwing snorted and gurgled, struggling weakly against our grip. We waited tensely as the bottle drained. When it was all gone, Suri folded the empty flask into her Inventory.

A status ring appeared over Cutthroat's body. The dinosaur snapped her jaws at me, hissing sullenly, but as a red line began to creep up from the side of the ring, her eyelids grew heavy. Her neck wobbled, and then, with a wheezy sigh, she laid her head on the ground.

"Hey! No!" Suri slapped the hookwing's cheek, to no effect. The woman looked up at me, wild-eyed. "Is this... is she...?"

As I watched, the ring jumped up a little more. There was no timer, like there had been with the herbal potions I'd used on Zlaslo. "I think this potion takes time to work. Looks like it takes about ten minutes - we won't know if she's going to Strange until the end of the process."

"Fuck." Suri's face was impassive, but she stroked Cutthroat's neck feathers over and over again. "We need to search this place for Brother Whatisface, but I don't want to leave her. She's a cantankerous old bitch, but... fuck."

"It's okay, Suri. I'll stay here and look after her." Rin stepped up, her blue eyes big with determination. "Don't worry. You go find Vash."

Cutthroat groaned, semi-conscious, just before I heard a wet crunching sound deep in her pelvis. Suri shuddered and got to her feet. "Christ. This is awful."

"Yeah." I looked to Rin. "You sure?"

"Yes." She nodded, pressing her lips together. "I can't fight as well as either of you, but I know mana and I know Stranging when I see it. I'll let you know how she goes."

Chapter 22

The crystallized slime plug that sealed the Broodmother's inner sanctum was wedged in tighter than a three-day old booger. It took me, Suri and Karalti wailing on it for about ten minutes to break it up.

"Does this place ever stop being gross?" I stepped gingerly into the blue glowing cavern beyond. "Oh. Just look at that. The answer is apparently 'fuck no'."

The cavern was full of eggs and goo in about equal quantities. The eggs were laid in small, mucus wrapped clusters nestled in little hillocks of webbing and bones. Some piles were already hatched and empty. Other nests had zombies bound to them, some of them still moving weakly inside their bonds. And far at the back was a mostly-naked man glued spread-eagle over a nest of writhing, just-about-ready-to-pop baby Swamp Hags.

"Hey, you big old wrinkly bitch!" He hollered in strongly accented Vlachian. "Guess what the first thing your stupid ugly babies are gonna taste when they hatch? These nuts! That's totally fucked up! But not as fucked as *you'll* be once I get off this nest and ram my fist into your ass and mouth at the same time! Because your mouth is your ass, and your ass is your mouth, and that's... really disturbing now that I think about it!"

I had formed a mental picture of the Baru during the course of our journey. Big, brawny, kind of lumberjacky, able to stand toe-to-toe with Lorenzo Soma like a pair of pro wrestlers. The man in front of us in no way resembled this image. Vash Dorha was tall, but he was as lean and lanky as a wolfhound, heavily tattooed, and wouldn't have been out of place in the grungiest of punk bands. He looked to be in his early 40s, with sharp features that were shattered by a twisting web of deep, gnarly scars. As I'd expected, it was the hair that gave him away as our Baru – his scalp was covered in intricate cornrows, skillfully twisted into a nine-pointed star that came together into a fall of long braids heavy with rings, amulets, beads made of bone and amber, and even human teeth... the relics of the dead, gifted to him by countless grateful relatives.

"You had better – oh, hey! I hear feet!" He strained to look at us as we ran to him as a group, Suri in the lead. "OH. HEY. *Na-tsho schrodna,* my lady, your chest makes this entire seven-day, twenty-three minute, forty-four-second piss-fuck absolutely worth it. Gods have mercy, you are gifted!"

Suri drew her dagger, glaring down at him. "You're about to be castrated if you don't watch your mouth."

"Oh, lady of the deep, glorious valley, the things this humble mouth could do for the likes of you," he replied wistfully. But as I came up on him, his eyes darted over to glance at me, and the pale grey irises turned stormy and dark. "But you. *You! Büü yirt!* Do not come near me! "

I hesitated, confused, and then realized what his deal was. I sighed. "Oh. Right. The Moon Pact thing."

"Moon Pact thing?" Suri cut away the hardened slime as quickly as she could while keeping her boobs out of nuzzling range.

"Remember when Andrik beat Rin to death in the Throne Room of Vulkan Keep? And I broke that oath to stop him from killing us all?" I gave Vash a pointed look. He scowled back.

"Oh, that. Yeah, that wasn't much fun." Suri got Vash's arms free, and was working on his legs when the first Swamp Hag larva split its thick, rubbery eggshell and plopped out onto the floor. She raised the knife to stab it, but Vash was even faster than Lucien. His arm snapped up to catch her wrist mid-strike.

"No, no, no." He shook his head and released her after a second. "Leave the little snot-goblin be."

She blinked at him a couple of times, but eased up. "Leave them be? Are you joking?"

"Do I look like a clown?" Vash's asymmetrical mouth twisted down at the corner – for a second, before his face split into a cheesy, surprisingly attractive grin. "Of course I do! But seriously, there's already been enough suffering here."

Suri hacked and sliced, and in another minute, the monk was free. He got stiffly to his feet, rolled his shoulders, and grunted. His bare arms were tattooed solid black. He glared at the exit like it owed him money. "Ai-yai-yah, my spine. Thank you, lady. Now, if I don't get a piss, a drink and a smoke in the next thirty-three minutes, I'm going to kill this lying *Rotzlöffel* on principle."

"Fuck you," I snapped. "We just saved your skinny ass."

"Don't make promises you can't keep, *meshugga*." Vash took a step forward me and brandished a finger. "Your dick will never be long or hard enough to take that quest. My cheeks would crush you like a maggot, except... we do not crush maggots, do we? Like this little guy." He crouched down to pat the baby Swamp Hag as it inched its way across the floor. "See? Harmless. And look at its little mouth-butt!"

I pinched the bridge of my nose and willed the pain to stop.

"Okay mate, look – my hookwing is fucked up and I've had just about enough of this. It's time to drag you back to the funny farm." Suri wiped her dagger clean, then sheathed it. "Can you walk?"

"Of course I can walk!" He flipped his braids over one shoulder and limped off toward the door. "*Na-tsho schrodna*, 'can I walk'? What do I look like? A worm?"

I rolled my eyes and looked over at Suri. She shrugged, her expression slightly pained.

"Istvan's going to be thrilled we found you," I said as I trotted off after him. "Fort Korona is-"

"You! *Bitga yaru!*" Vash rounded on us in the doorway, pointing at me. "Your whore's mouth is not clean enough to speak my prince's name! I'll make my own way back."

“Woah woah woah.” I held up both hands. “Dude, no. You aren't storming off through the swamp by yourself, okay? We were sent to find you and take you back.”

"We have a dragon and can fly you back to Korona," Suri added. “It'd be a hell of a show for the garrison.”

The D-word stopped him in his tracks. He turned to face us, eyes wide. "Dragon? Are you shitting me? You travel with a *dragon*?"

"Yeah." I felt a tic start at the corner of my eye. "And like the rest of us, she's tired and beat up and really wants her dinner, so if we could play nicely and act like grownups until we get back to the Fort, that would be great."

"Take me to this dragon," he said, to Suri. "I must pay my respects."

Suri looked to me, her eyebrows raised. "She's Hector's dragon. You need to talk to him, mate."

"No." And with that, he started marching for the entrance to the main cavern again.

Suri clicked her tongue. “Jeez. I can't be fucked with this.”

“Yeah. I always thought monks were more like... you know...” I hesitated, thinking of the word. “Contemplative?”

Suri snorted. “You gonna be able to straighten things out with him?”

I shrugged. “I knew something like this would happen when I broke the *Kara Bukat Talom.* It's okay.”

"It's not, because if you hadn't, Vlachia would be in the shitter right now." Suri jerked her head toward the door. "Do we need to be worried about him pushing you off your dragon?"

I shrugged. "He's been polite about it so far. He could have just gotten up and tried to kill me. That's what he's supposed to do. Breaking the *Kara Bukat Talom* is a big deal."

"There's gotta be some exception," Suri said. "You saved my ass and headed off a royal assassination."

I shrugged with my hands. "Planning assassinations is one of the things it's used for."

"Jesus fuckin' Christ." Suri made a sound of disgust. "Well, let's go get him before he tries to jam his tongue up under Karalti's tail. Gods knows he seems like the kind of bloke who'd try."

We trooped back out to find Vash huddled over Cutthroat with Rin. He laid a hand on the great dinosaur's neck as she grunted and twitched, closed his eyes, and chanted a short prayer in Tuun. A little green plus sign appeared next to her potion status ring, which was now 91% full.

"That should help. She looks like she is struggling through a Bonefuse brew, eh?" He asked Rin.

The Mercurion's brilliant eyes flicked me to me. "Uhh... I think so?"

"Excellent. Now, excuse me." Vash stood and went to Karalti, who was busy preening under the edge of her wing.

She perked up as he approached. I shook my head and went to join the vigil over Cutthroat.

"How long until we know?" Suri asked.

"About a minute." I squatted back on my heels, one hand resting near the Spear.

Cutthroat moaned as the status climbed to 97%. I checked the buff that Vash had given her: it improved the Stranging rate from 50/50 to 60/40. Suri sat down on the slimy ground and scooted forward until she could take the hookwing's head onto her lap. She stroked her behind one eye as the twitching intensified.

⟦98... 99...⟧

The hookwing's breathing caught, and for a moment, everyone went still. A whole second passed, and then one golden eye snapped open, its pupil contracting to a tiny pinpoint that rolled up first to look at Suri before affixing its baleful gaze onto the rest of us one by one.

"HUUURRREE!" Cutthroat kicked a couple of times, then struggled up off the ground into a limp. Suri let go of her, and we watched anxiously as the hookwing hopped a few steps forward, then gingerly put her weight on the left foot.

The three of us let out a sigh of relief.

"Phew!" Rin dusted herself off and pushed her mask up to show her face. "Nice crafting, Hector! Looks like it worked perfectly!"

"Yeah." I rubbed the back of my head. My braid was messed up from the fight, and I fought down the urge to pull it out and re-do it. Vanity had to wait. "I would have kicked myself if we'd lost her. She's my second-favorite murder chicken."

"AHEM." Karalti looked up from her silent conversation with Vash, who had knelt in front of her. Her eyes narrowed. *"WHAT did you just call me?"*

"I didn't call you anything." I crossed my arms and grinned back at her.

Suri came up and bumped me with her hip. She looked better now, the shadow of worry no longer written onto her face. "Hey, lover boy: now I know my baby bird isn't gonna die, want to go loot the Broodmother with me?"

"Sure." I made a face at Karalti, and she flicked her tongue between her teeth, letting it hang like a blue flag from her mouth.

We trudged over to the massive corpse. The Broodmother was almost shapeless in death, like a huge raw haggis that had been split with a knife. Moving stiffly, Suri slowly crouched down and began scanning her HUD. "Let's see... lot of monster parts here, potion boy. Oooh, blue-grade mana."

"I need that!" Rin called out.

"Hot." I cozied up to Suri's side, leaning in a little while I did the same thing she was doing. The Broodmother had a lot of loot. Yanik [[Marsh Scout armor]], weapons, money, jewels...

- *6500 Rubles*
- *249 Olbia*
- *Bluecrystal Mana x 5*

- *Swamphag Queen Slime x 140*
- *+3 Vlachian Saber*
- *Yanik Marsh Scout Armor*
- *Manual of Physical Health*
- *+2 Mastercrafted Spellglove*
- *Fine Leather Pouch*
- *Staff of Ghost Touch*
- *Black Opal x 4*
- *Sapphire x 3*
- *Light Steel Shield*
- *Ring of Web*
- *Ring of Force Shield*
- *Vash's Sanctified Iron Gauntlets*

A grin split my face. "Look at all this! Holy shit, that's a lot of gear."

"Yeah. Let's split that gold. Mind if I take the Ring of Force Shield and the manual?" Suri asked me. "They'd be real useful."

"They're all yours,." I was about to impulsively add Vash's gauntlets to my Inventory, then thought better of it. "You should go give these to him."

"I'm gonna level first." Suri accepted the heavy gloves, and they vanished as she folded them into her pocket of hyperspace.

I trooped back to Karalti and the now prostrate monk, and as I grew closer, she looped me into their telepathic conversation.

"*... and the pita bread has to be hot! With extra garlic sauce, because I'm a big girl now and-*"Karalti nibbled her talons, her crests flaring upright. *"Oh! Hector! This guy says he knows how to spit-roast! We can have kebab every day!"*

"From what I've heard out of him so far, that's not the kind of spit-roast he's talking about, Tidbit." I swaggered across as Vash pushed himself up to stand.

Karalti winked at me, then craned her muzzle down toward the monk. *"So yeah - and extra sauerkraut, okay? But only for veal. Lamb goes better with sweet pickles."*

"Of course, my lady. Your command is my greatest pleasure." Vash swept into an exaggerated bow in front of her, then turned to scowl at me. "You! Get your filth away from this holy creature! Sss!"

"Sure, asshole, I'll get right on that." I clapped Karalti on the forearm, waiting as she leaned forward to rest on her winghands. Vash, visibly aghast, looked on as I put a boot up on her elbow and clambered up onto her back.

"Stop that! What are you doing!?" He caught his braids to either side of his shoulders and pulled on them.

"It's okay!" Karalti chirped, cocking her head from side to side querulously. *"Hector's mine! He likes Burna, too! You don't need to worry about him!"*

"He... 'likes' Burna," Vash repeated flatly. Then his face twisted in a snarl. "Is nothing sacred to you, dog? Not oaths, not dragons, not anything?"

"Some things. I was real busy worshipping your mom last night." I sat down cross-legged on Karalti's back and looked down at him. "Are you coming up, or what?"

Vash stared at us for a couple of seconds. For a moment, I thought he was about to fly up, kung-fu style, and punch my face through the back of my head. But instead, he slid his hand into one of the pouches on the heavy belt he wore and pulled out a bag. From that, he removed something that looked remarkably like a joint. He lit it with a match; a rich, skunky smell wafted to my nose.

"Mother jokes. Burna's balls. I'm too tired for this shit," he muttered. He took a deep hit and held it like a pro before blowing it out. He coughed, briefly, then closed his eyes. "Fine, *Rotzlöffel.* Have it your way, but before we leave this place, I must find my gauntlets. This stupid bitch of a worm sucked them off my arms like a two-ruble dockyard whore."

It crossed my mind to tell him that Suri had them, but... nahh. "Sure, man. You do that while we level up."

Vash grunted, and clomped over to the dead boss to start pawing through its innards.

"We need to pick up the *Ix'tamo*, too!" Rin exclaimed, bouncing over to Karalti as she stood. "Karalti, do you think you can carry it?"

"Yeah! I can carry a lot now!" The dragon squinted her eyes, like a smug cat.

I nodded. "Leveling first, though."

"Okay! I need to level as well and make a couple of quick adjustments to Hopper and Lovelace, so, take your time!"

Rin ran off to continue repairing her turrets, while Suri joined Cutthroat. While they worked, I lay out on Karalti's back and opened my HUD to level her up, and was shown a familiar chart:

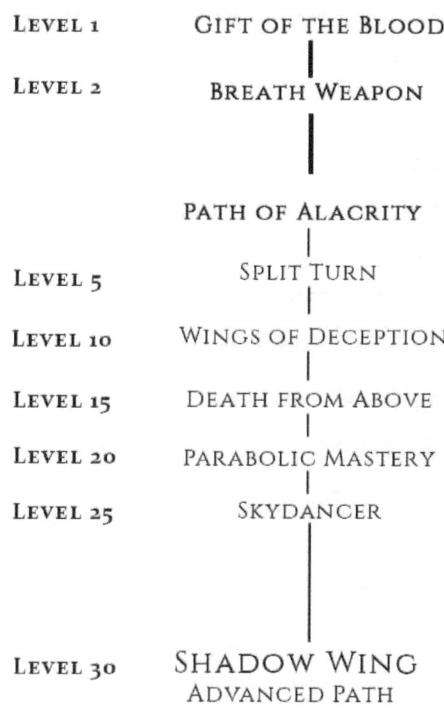

"Let's see here... we're not choosing any skills from another path, are we?"

"Nope! The Path of Alacrity is fun."

"My thoughts exactly. Okay... let's see here. Level 10 gives us 'Wings of Deception'." I selected that, and then did my best to manually read the description:

Wings of Deception

Your dragon is the daughter of Matir, and her blood sings with the Words of Shadow, Illusion, and Life. She has flowered into adulthood and has gained the ability to create shadow copies of herself (1 copy per 50 Mana points, minimum 1 copy) that look, to all intents and purposes, like herself, her rider, and any gear she may be carrying.

When the copies are made, the dragon teleports one body-length in any direction and splits off into multiple images. Her mana and HP are evenly divided between herself and her dopplegangers. For example, if the dragon creates 3 copies (for a total of 4 individuals), each one will have 1/4 of her total HP and Mana pool.

Shadow Copies will naturally mimic their creator in movement, speech, and attack. Commanding the copies to take independent action takes great strength of will, but is possible with the right training. Maintaining the copies costs 1 Mana per second per copy.

The copies can take damage, cast spells, and strike with any attack the dragon knows - however, spells cast by copies use 50% more mana, and breath weapon damage dealt by copies is reduced by 75%. For example, a dragon with three copies who uses a breath weapon deals one instance of normal damage, and three instances of 25% damage. Physical attacks suffer no penalty until the copies expire.

If a copy is damaged over its maximum HP reserve, the dragon will not take damage. The copy will vanish and will not be able to be resummoned until the dragon has rested for 6 hours. If the original dragon is damaged beyond her reduced

HP reserve, all copies will vanish and her HP will refill to its normal pool, minus the damage she sustained.

The dragon's bonded rider is also copied, and can perform attacks - however, unless the rider also has an ability to create shadow clones, the attacks will be illusory and deal no damage. An invisible rider will remain concealed. If the rider if thrown off during flight, the shadow rider/s will also fall. The dragon cannot replicate non-bonded riders or passengers.

Copies look, feel and sound exactly like the dragon summoning them until dismissed. The clones created by Wings of Deception are tangible manifestations of mana and cannot be identified purely by physical appearance - magical means must be employed to discern copies from their original caster. The difficulty rating to pierce the illusion increases with your dragon's level.

Oh. My god.

I rubbed my eyes, then had the system read it back to me again to make sure that my dyslexia wasn't playing a cruel prank on me. And as she did, a grin split my face. "Karalti. I am about to smash this 'accept' button harder than I have ever smashed anything before."

She craned her neck to look up and back at me. *"Uhh... okay?"*

"You'll only be able to ninja-magic one of these copies, but even that is going to save us so much HP in the air. This Wings of Deception thing is a gamechanger. I'm almost worried it's like... like a mistake." When the option to accept came up, I screamed 'YES!' in my head at the HUD.

When it closed, Karalti closed her eyes and drew a deep, startled breath as the air around us darkened. Through the film of shadow rising around her, I saw the others turn to look. It intensified, deepening, and then the black vapor seemed to suck into Karalti's body through the seams in her scales - and into me. We shivered at the same time, and then she opened her eyes.

"Ohhh. "Her violet and silver irises churned with power, folding in toward her pupil like magma at the heart of a volcano. *"Ohhhhhhhh! Yeah! This is neat!"*

"Yeah." My heart was beating fast at the possibilities. "Let me go see what combat abilities have opened up for me. Maybe there's something complimentary to it."

"Wait... so if I make a copy of me, and they do a quarter of my damage, then we do 125% total. "She paused for a moment.

"Yes. And this shit is going to scale up. You could end up doing 350% breath weapon damage or more by end game." My mind was suddenly racing with ideas on how to use this ability to our advantage in fights with larger dragons. Would Baldr, Lucien, and Violetta's dragons have comparable abilities?

I scrolled over to my sheet next to see what combat abilities I had to work with at Level 19. There were three new options:

Obsidian Scales (Dark Dragoon)
Your dragon's damage reduction is increased by 5% per ability level when you are riding her.

Lance Assassin (Offense)
Every adrenaline point adds a 1% chance of instantly killing your enemies on a critical hit. The maximum target level increases with each level in this ability.

Aura of Terror (Defense)
You induce Terror in your opponents, demoralizing them and forcing weaker opponents to flee from your presence. This is a passive ability that is active in combat and can be activated manually at other times.

"Hmm." I tapped my lip, mildly disappointed at the lack of shadow-copy abilities. Three abilities, all of them tempting in their own ways, plus several existing ones I wanted to level. I only had three Combat Ability Points.

Obsidian Scales was the one I felt I ought to take, because it would make Karalti less likely to be hurt in combat, but Aura of Terror was pretty fucking cool – and potentially very useful, if not in this particular war, then in future mass combat scenarios. Lance Assassin was promising, but only once I got an ability that increased my chance of landing critical hits. I checked out the full ability description and found that it was effective on enemies based on their EXP. *Lance Assassin I* would only instakill enemies with 50% of my experience or lower, but every point you dumped into that ability raised the ceiling by 15%. Lance Assassin X gave you a 10% chance to insta-kill enemies with 185% more EXP than yourself – good odds, especially in a fight with multiple opponents. If I could level it to ten between now and, say, Level 30, then I would take it in a heartbeat. I wouldn't be able to level combat abilities to Level X until I was Level 45, though – so Lance Assassin was going to be great around end-game, but I was better off focusing on mastering my active combat abilities for now.

In the end, I decided to leave the new options alone and level my current abilities instead: Rain of Glass II, Master of Blades IV, Whirlwind Butcher IV. Whirlwind was my Adrenaline Point generator, and the MoB/Rain of Glass combo required a lot of AP. While I didn't want my Tidbit getting damaged, her new Wings of Deception ability was going to go a long way toward improving her defense. As I was just about to close the sheet, my eyes snagged on the Gift of Matir abilities list. I hadn't yet used the Shadow Lance ability, and it was still marked 'new'. I'd forgotten about it: not good. That was something I definitely needed to work into my tactics.

"How're you goin' up there, soldier?" Suri called up.

"Good. Just finished." I closed my HUD and rolled up into a crouch to see Vash glaring at me as he belted his gauntlets on. "Ready to go back to Korona and make an entrance?"

Suri put a boot on Cutthroat's stirrup and pulled herself up into the saddle. "Ready to go back to Korona and bang Soma and Istvan's heads together, more like it."

Chapter 23

It took the better part of the night to reach Korona, and the sun was just coming up over the horizon when we sighted the Prezyemi Line from the air. This was made much easier by the fact that part of it was on fire.

"Oh jeez." The sounds of artillery pounding the wall to the west of Korona made me wince. Magical barriers sprung to life over the archers and riflemen who fired down at the seething black mass surging toward them below. "Ohhh boy."

"Do we go?" Karalti labored with the weight of the *Ix'tamo* and Vash on her back, while I hung onto her forearm like a pirate on the mast of his ship - or a stripper on a pole, depending on your angle. Her maximum carry weight in the air was now something like six hundred pounds, but anything over three hundred inflicted a movement penalty.

"Hell no. We need to drop off the dumb stupid rock and our passenger first." I closed my eyes, then opened them wide to zoom in on the battle happening to our left. *"Should probably hurry, though. This looks like the real deal."*

Bells were clanging all over Korona as warships and griffin knights surged westward. We circled, watching below as Suri and Rin crossed to the gate at the base of the wall. Only once they were inside did we circle the skydock and come in to land. Controllers on the ground galvanized into action when they saw us, waving flags and hustling people out of the way as we did a wing around, giving the people below a good view of what - and who - we were carrying. That maneuver was the end of my dragon's endurance. Struggling for air, she evened out into a glide, straightened up as she came down, then flared her wings just before touching down to a stumbling trot.

"*Oof.*" She shuddered with effort, wings drooping, panting heavily as her stamina ring flashed. "*That was close.*"

"*Yeah, but you made it because you're a fucking boss.*" I unlocked my white-knuckled hands from around her arm and jumped shakily to the ground, shaking out the adrenaline, and turned to see a mob of soldiers charging toward us. They clamored as Vash vaulted from Karalti's back to the ground, cheering as the monk threw up his arms and ran toward them. But it only took the edge off the barely suppressed panic echoing around the fort - spearheaded by the fact that the General and Field Commander were nowhere to be seen.

"*There is zero strategy here, Karalti. No strategy and no leadership. Istvan and Soma had better be at the front line.*" Furious, I raided my pack for stamina potions, uncorked one, and held it up for Karalti to drink. She bought her head low and tipped it back, jaws open so that I could pour it down her gullet. By the time they were finished working, I heard the screams of 'control your fucking bird!' and saw the cloud of mayhem that usually preceded Cutthroat's arrival, just before the hulking black hookwing drifted a corner around the gate to the docks and loped toward us.

"You! Take this!" Suri snapped at a passing dockhand as she jumped off Cutthroat. She pulled her reins around and handed them to the startled man, who eyed her, then the foaming, wild-eyed hookwing. "Get her somewhere dark! Like a stall, a stable. No sunlight, no light. She'll die. Okay?"

"I... uh... the hookwings are all corralled outside-" he stuttered.

"Just find somewhere for her that's dark!" Suri snarled. Cutthroat champed her jaws, head darting from side to side as she came up behind Suri's shoulder to back her up.

"Yes ma'am! I mean, my lady!" The man awkwardly saluted, and tried to tug Cutthroat away from Suri. The big female did not want to leave, and as she realized what was happening, her crest feathers fell. She turned her head and squawked in disbelief as the man hauled ineffectually at her reins.

"Go on, you big fluffy cunt! I'll come get you when you're not a goddamned vampire!" Suri waved her off sternly.

The hookwing's dead yellow eyes got big and sad. She dropped her muzzled head, and placidly slouched off with the nervous soldier, not even pausing to snarl at someone who bumped into her tail.

"She's gotten smarter," I remarked. "She can understand human speech now?"

"I dunno." Suri scratched her head. "I dunno if she understands the words, or if she just reads my tone of voice. Seems like it though."

"Sure does." I nodded. "Hope you're ready to bring her a big bouquet of severed arms when you get back. She's going to be pissed when she realizes you're killing things without her."

"Yeah." Suri jerked her head at the *Ix'tamo.* "Need a hand gettin' that bloody thing down?"

"Sure do." I looked to Karalti. She flashed Suri a double-fanged sneer, but knelt down gratefully for us to get the heavy crystal weapon off her back. Rin joined us just as we got it to the ground, and ran across, flapping her hands, as we tried to figure out how to stand it up.

"No no no no no! Don't mess with it!" She pushed me away from it, and waved Suri off as well. "Leave me here with this! We'll get a cart. Soma and Istvan are with their men on the Western Wall. Go there and help - I'll take care of the *Ix'tamo* and make sure it's stabilized!"

"Roger that." I cupped my hands to my mouth. "Vash! Hey! Asshole!"

"What do you want, you syphilitic dog?" He shouted back cheerfully.

"Want a ride to the fight?" I called. "Or you gonna stay here so these guys can suck your cock all day?"

He then clapped one man on the shoulder before turning and springing off the ground. He flashed into invisibility, then seemed to fall out of thin air into a crouch right in front of me, standing almost nose to nose. I took a step back as he spat to the side and looked past me to Karalti.

"Lady? Shall we go?" he said.

"*With Hector,*" she replied primly.

The monk sighed dramatically. "If we must."

Before he could go around me, I blocked him and met his eyes. "Can we talk about this problem you have with me? Because this is a giant clusterfuck with no discernable strategy at play, and thanks to Istvan and Soma, people who don't need to die today are going to die. This is difficult enough without you climbing my ass for trying to save my friends."

Vash's scarred mouth twisted down in about three different directions as he scowled. When he spoke, it was in Tuun. "Must I lay it out for you simply, like you are a child? Very well. You took a sacred oath in vain, and that is a very bad thing to do. Bad enough that untruth taints you like a disease."

I frowned, confused. "But I-"

Vash took a step forward, getting right up in my face. "You-" he pointed. "-lie so readily and so easily to yourself that it has left you pitted and rusted, like bad metal. And thus you took a sacred oath in vain and betrayed that oath when it was convenient for you, *immortal.*"

"Wait." I held my hands up. "Immortal? You... you know I'm-?"

"Starborn? Yes. I also know this: you and your friends do not truly die. Had you kept your word, they would have suffered briefly, then woken up somewhere." Vash never raised his voice, but now that I had met his gaze, I found I couldn't tear my eyes away. "You lied to yourself, told yourself there was no other way, that you are not smart enough to think through the dilemma. So you broke the oath to spare yourself the burden of your growing, and to ward off the brief suffering of their passing. That is the truth of it."

"But I-"

"The Moon Pact is important to our people. The Tuun were the first humans in Archemi to understand the power and burden of magic, the knowledge that words have power to unite or separate, to form or dissolve. To speak untruth is to fray the bonds of reality itself. By doing so, you spread your corruption to all of us, like a sick person coughing in a crowded room."

I took a nervous step back. "Okay, I admit it. I fucked up. But you need to understand something: if Suri dies, she won't wake up somewhere safe. I will, Rin will, but Suri won't. She'll wake up inside the prison where she was tortured since she was a little girl, and I would lie, cheat and steal to protect her and make sure she never goes back."

The monk then did something I would never have expected of an NPC in any game I'd ever played. His piercing stare and menacing scowl wavered. He scratched his chin, looking over toward Suri. She was hanging back, waiting for us to finish speaking.

"There is some truth in that," he admitted. "The woman is a walking mass of scars, some so deep it is a miracle that she is sane. What she has seen, I can only guess at. It has left her callused and opaque. But still - you are a vector, Dragozin, and your word is meaningless to me until you atone. Sane men must pursue reality at all costs. We will talk about it another time - for now, we must kill zombies, yes?"

"Uhh... okay?" Just like that, the supernatural gravity of Vash's presence snapped like an elastic band, releasing me. I looked up to Karalti, who chirruped and shrugged her wings. She bent forward, but Vash didn't climb her. His form blurred, and he teleported onto her back in a crouch. I motioned Suri to join us, and she ran in to catch my hand and pull herself up.

With her stamina refilled, unburdened and rested, Karalti was able to take off into the air at her full adult speed, shooting past the warship and the quazi on her way to where smoke rose in thick black clouds. Only once were we away from the waterfalls did we hear the true volume of the battle: the boom of mortars and cannons, the sharper rapport of rifles, the screams of men.

At a glance from the air, the battle was not going well. The wall was a formidable defense - as static fortifications went - but the Western Wall didn't command the same kind of awesome strategic position as Korona. Ten-foot walls faced a thirty-foot ridge that dropped sharply into a muddy no-man's land. The sodden earth was buckled and treacherous, trenches zig-zagging behind wooden spikes and reams of barbed wire. That mess was only about 400 yards long. It ended in a stacked ring of felled trees, their sharpened crowns pointing toward the south - a crude abatis made to stop siege engines and other large things, like tanks.

Abatises are great – if they're arranged properly. These ones were not. The positioning of the trees meant that the thousands upon thousands of civilian corpses hurtling themselves across the battlefield could just slip through. They sprinted through the relentless pounding of grapeshot and canister fire from the cannons lined up along the wall. For every zombie that fell, another three seemed to trample over it. Legless bodies dragged themselves by their arms, filling the trenches, forming bridges over the barbed wire, and permitting their fellows to climb them and continue toward their goal: the wall. They crawled up their makeshift siege towers like lizards while terrified soldiers shot at them with guns and bows, or plunged pikes up and down like butter churns, trying to shove them away. People poured buckets of oil through machicolations and hacked off dead hands with axes as they reached up over the parapets to grasp for whatever they could grab. It took no time at all to see there was a growing problem. Every zombie that fell was picked up by its shambling comrades and hurled onto the burning, moaning ramps that were being built against the base of the fortification, with every sacked body making it easier for the ones behind to climb.

"There!" Vash pointed toward one of the bastions, where Istvan stood among his men, alternating between firing the rifle in his hands and barking orders at the archers and artillery surrounding him. A knot of mages held a protective magical shield over them all, sheltering them from the mortar fire that rained down from above. They were doing everything they could to stop the zombies in No Man's Land.

"Karalti, get as low as you can." I ordered her without thinking. *"We have to watch out for those shells."*

"Okay! Vash, get ready to jump!" The dragon dropped a wingtip and swooped down.

Just then, I got a short quest alert. *[[Quest Update: Objective - take out the Demon's artillery before the siege train arrives.]]*

"Fuck, I just got assigned a quest objective!" Suri yelled so I could hear her, leaning in.

"Me too!" I called back. "Was yours about taking out artillery?"

"No - it's for protecting Istvan on the wall! Drop me off!

Karalti's twin hearts pounded with mingled excitement and nerves beneath us as she dove under the next round of arcing shells, then lifted above the explosions and shrapnel. Senses in synch, I felt her pulse surge as those soldiers on the wall saw us and scattered cheering broke out among the pointing and shouting men, loud enough to be heard over the cannon fire that drowned out almost all else. Two sergeants hustled men from the walkway as Karalti came to land on the parapet's edge. She bowed down, and when the troops saw who we were carrying, this time the scattered cheers became a roar that went up and down the line.

"Ah hahah, my boys! Guess who's back!?" Vash jumped up over Karalti's head to roll and bounce up on his feet, as light as a champion boxer. "This motherfucker, that's who!"

As I helped unbuckle Suri, I saw Istvan break through the thinning crowd and tackle Vash in a hug. The wiry monk caught him on reflex, then laughed and pounded the other man on the back.

[[Quest Updated: Unto Death. 270 Exp, +150 Renown (House Bolza), -75 Renown (House Soma)]]

"Praise the Forge! You found him!" Istvan called to us joyfully. "The filthy old wolf's back from the dead!"

"Not that old or that dead, but absolutely that filthy." Vash squeezed him around the shoulders. "Speaking of that: let's go see how hard I can go kick a zombie in the cooter!"

"Anything you want, old friend." For the first time since we'd met him, Istvan looked happy. He beckoned to us. "Come on, Fireblood! We need your strong arm! Dragozin - go attack the artillery! We have no idea what's behind that curtain of smoke!"

I clasped Suri's hand to let her down. She leaned in to kiss me, and I kissed her back, long and lingering.

"Fight hard," she said in PM.

I smiled when she moved back, squeezing her forearm. *"You too."*

Suri dropped to the rampart. Karalti turned and dove off the wall like a swallow, her roar of challenge echoing across the field. The sight of her galvanized the troops below. Looking behind, I saw archers aiming around her as we shot out over No-Man's land and plunged into the heart of the assault.

Chapter 24

"We need to hit those guns. As soon as the cannons appear, I want you to use that new ability split. Get behind the artillery and get ready to flame."I hopped up into a crouch, holding onto the saddle with one hand. *"If I die, keep your head. I'll respawn at the Fort and catch up. If I fall, don't try and pick me up unless you're absolutely sure you can make it without being nailed by a cannon. Okay?"*

*"Okay!"*Karalti dodged to the right and down as a ballista bolt shot just over her wing. *"Get ready!"*

We broke through the smoke to see the ruins of the swamp crawling with undead. My HUD highlighted the individual units: the zombies were grouped in companies of a hundred each, which were blobbing together as they ran. The last unit of zombies were staggering up out of the mud, followed by a tidal wave of ⟦Plague Rats⟧ and ⟦Skeleton Swordsmen⟧. Primitive iron mortars - smoothbore cannons not seen since the late 1700s back home - were set up in a line of shallow trenches, where three units of ⟦Gigim Artillery⟧ were set up. Each artillery unit was comprised of ten guns, each animated by two billowing humanoid shades. Each lot of twenty ghosts was supervised by a ⟦Wraithlord Commander⟧

riding a huge skeletal bull dripping in beaten gold and lapis lazuli barding. The heavily armored commanders carried magical staves, shadow matter streaming off them into the air.

"You focus on the guns! I'm going for that commander!" I targeted the nearest one, banged my helmet a couple of times, swallowed the knot of fear in the pit of my belly, and jumped.

We were going fast - very fast. The undead literally had no idea what hit them. They aggro'd on us, dragging their mortars around through the mud, but we were too fast. At the end of the Jump, I shouted and drew the dark power from inside myself, letting it spill out into my weapon: Master of Blades. A wheel of black energy lances unfurled around me like a pair of wings, shooting past like bolts of lightning to strike the gunners. They groaned and shrieked like the wind as the lances fell down among them, evaporating into black mist. I used Rain of Glass to change my trajectory, the shattering energy acting like a cushion to halt my momentum and throw me back into the air. I focused all of those shards of dark energy on the ⟦Wraithlord Commander⟧.

"Edin na zul!" The undead champion thrust his staff up above his head and made an arcane gesture with the other hand. The bolts of darkness thumped into a greenish energy barrier like arrows into a shield, embedding before they - and the shield - overloaded and shattered. He took no damage, but was defenseless as I soared down and hit Shadow Lance for the first time.

The Mark of Matir surged, and a liquid rush of power flooded through my hand and into the Spear of Nine Spheres. There was a strange ghostly sensation - like the energy was searching for something in the weapon, but couldn't find it – just before the flames generated by the Ruby of Boundless Strength surged into roaring black fire. "DIE PROPERLY THIS TIME, YOU PIECE OF SHIT!"

"MAXIM XU-uhhh!" The shield shattered on contact, and the Spear plunged through the Wraithlord and burst out of its back in a cloud of dark embers. The Wraithlord's skeletal mouth gaped as if in shock. There was a frozen moment where I looked into the glowing points of light in his sockets, and saw something I'd never seen in a monster before.

Absolute pants-shitting terror.

⟦You deal 4725 Darkness damage to Wraithlord! It's super-effective!⟧
⟦You gain 350 EXP⟧

"TARN TAKRARHN MOTHERFUCKER!" I sprung up as the ⟦Wraithlord⟧ burst into ash and his staff fell, launching straight into an oncoming wave of skeleton infantry.

⟦Objective partially complete: Artillery Brigade 1/3⟧

"*Karalti!*" I called to her in my mind - slashing, vaulting, dodging sickle-shaped desert swords and pickaxes as the unit surged in around me. The skeletons at the very front were nimble warriors, carrying nothing but their weapons. Behind them lumbered rows of ⟦Burdened Skeletons⟧ wearing what looked all too much like suicide bomber vests. *"Karalti, whatever you do, don't light up those guys in the vests until you've got space!"*

Even as I spoke, the sky darkened as my dragon rolled gracefully towards us out of the smoke. I smashed a creaking skeleton out of the way with the butt of my spear as she swooped in, kicking skulls and raised axes out of the way on her path toward me. I Jumped, caught her arm, and held on for dear life as she gained altitude. "Yeah, baby! Waaooh! Get 'em, girl!"

"Toasty bony time!" Karalti's narrow jaws gaped as she wheeled back over the teeming skeletons, blasting the entire front line with her breath weapon. They struggled on, burning, but finally stumbled forward onto their knees. Some of their brethren tripped over their fallen fellows as the bombers lumbered up. They began to struggle through the pile, wading toward their burning fellows. And when they caught fire...

"Bones away!" The explosions rang out beneath us, the shockwave forcing air up under Karalti's wings. Whooping, I swung wildly from her wrist. "Hell yeah! Bone Appetit, bitches!"

"Oh my god," Karalti muttered. *"Suri's right. No puns allowed."*

"My grandparents were Millennials, Tidbit. I was born into puns. Memed by them." Karalti was already headed toward the next artillery battery along the enemy line. *"And tibia honest with you-"*

"AHHHHH! I HATE YOU! STOP!"

This barrage was expecting us. I scrambled up, ready to leap at the rows of mortars suddenly facing east. Before they could fire, Karalti burst forward in a surge of speed, and her form divided in two as we came out of the dark cloud of power that disguised her Wings of Deception ability. We split to the right as the mortars fired on the left. The dragon shuddered with referred pain as twenty shells obliterated the illusory Karalti, but she wasn't damaged - and we were in position. The Wraithlord commanding this unit must have seen something on my face as Karalti spat fire down along the trench, because he pulled his bull mount around and turned to flee.

"Oh no you don't! You get back here right now, young man!" I dropped, dashed in the air, then Jumped and landed right on the ass-end of the bull. The Spear danced with black fire as I plunged it through the Wraithlord's back, toppling him - and me - from the saddle.

[[Objective partially complete: Artillery Brigade 2/3]]

I hit the ground awkwardly - it was muddy enough that I didn't concuss myself, but there were bony feet surging toward me from all directions. The Spear spilled from my hand. In the brief panic that followed, I *called* to it- and it responded, shooting up into my hand from the pile of ash that remained of the Wraithlord. *Whoa. Okay. Gotta remember I can do that.*

Dense battlefields was where the Dark Dragoon class shined. Clashing infantry battled behind me as lances of shimmering dark energy struck down in an expanding double ring, blowing rats and skeletons into the air. When I landed from the combo, I struck the end of my spear into the ground, discharging a field of indigo-blue energy from my body. Twisting whip-like bolts of shadow sprung from the ground, destroying every rodent in a ten-foot radius around me, freezing the mud into a natural bulwark. But more skeletons were coming, and Karalti wasn't there. Kalxat were flying in from the swamp: she was held up fighting them in the sky, about a hundred yards away. And I was out of AP.

"If you can pick me up right about now, that would be great!" A knot of sword-wielding skeleton rushed me, scimitars raised to strike. I kicked a dead rat at them and followed up with the spear, ordinary attacks only. I caught a sword blade on the haft and shoved it back, kicking the warrior right in the pelvis. It was one thing to know they couldn't feel pain, quite another to have an enemy who could get kicked in the remains of their junk and not even slow down. They fought without artistry - heavy strikes, overhead swings, shield bashes. Rats swarmed around our feet, squealing and nipping, trailing clouds of contagion. My Tuun resistance to disease held me in good stead, but my HP chipped away every time something bit me or got through my guard. And after the boss fight...

"Poison! Fuck! All kinds of poison!" I struggled toward Karalti as my HP ring throbbed red, covered in ichor and mud. "And no fucking potions! Fuck!"

"Hang on! Almost there!" Karalti split-turned in the air, tearing toward me with three undead vultures in hot pursuit.

"I just killed like fifty skeletons! Maybe eighty!" I called out happily, stumbling as my stamina ran out and forced me to rest on one knee. *"Whew. This... this Path is awesome!"*

"Get up!" Karalti bellowed as she leveled out toward me. *"Something big's coming!"*

"That's what she said!" I spun around to stab a zombie coming up on me from behind, and was still stabbing it when Karalti's foot caught me by the back of my armor. She lifted me off into the air, showing me the battlefield - and the titanic saurian shadow pushing through the smoke toward us. It had a head that looked like a soggy potato, small eyes staring stupidly over a sagging jaw lined with peg-like teeth. A Brontosaurus. The massive dinosaur was covered in at least four tons of sacks, barrels and rigging strapped around its bloated eighty-foot long body. Skeleton archers shot arrows at the wall from its back. A flock of what looked like winged snakes circled around its head.

"That is... a zombie brontosaurus suicide bomber," I said. *"Words I never expected to say in the same sentence together. Let's get that third artillery bank and then go murder this thing before it reaches the Line."*

"Yay! Murder!" Karalti dove toward the last remaining line of mortars, coming around from the back through the smoke. As we broke through, I saw the Wraithlord looking up at us, staff raised.

"Dodge!" A bolt of green fire shot out from the Wraithlord. Karalti dropped to the side, but not fast enough. It hit her square on.

[[Karalti takes 670 damage!]]
[[You take 49 damage!]]

"AAAAAAH!!!" It was the most damage Karalti had ever taken in a single hit - almost half her total health. She keened with pain, limbs spasming as the force of the impact flung me off and sent me cartwheeling through the air toward the mortars. The Wraithlord's shadow soldiers dragged them around into position and began to load.

"Fuck fuck fuck!" I corrected my uncontrolled dive at the last second, landing into a roll - just as well, because I was now at 29 HP and didn't have any heals. But now, I had AP. I sprung up, roaring as crackling black light ripped around my body and down the length of the spear. "EAT A DIIIICK!"

The Master of Blades split out toward the Wraithlord. It vaporized three of his shadows and blew him onto his back. Before he could get up, I was on him, the flaming Spear of Nine Spheres raised to strike.

"We will take back what you stole!" The Wraithlord hissed. Its voice was like dry wind howling down a stone tunnel. "For Ashur! For Napath!"

There was a pretty good chance he was buying for time, so rather than give it to him, I plunged the Spear down into his face. It exploded into dust, and the remaining shadows vaporized.

[[Quest Updated: Objective complete! 3/3 Artillery batteries destroyed!]]
[[You gain 500 EXP!]]
[[New objective: Protect the Wall!]]

The game didn't have to elaborate. There was really only one thing to protect the wall from now.

The Brontosaurus reached the useless abatises and charged in against them, shoving them out of the way with its chest. Now that I had a better look at the dino-zombie, it was definitely packed with explosives.

"Okay, Tidbit! Let's go break up this donkey show!" I called up to her. "You got fire?"

"Yes! But only enough for one more attack!" The dragon soared down to land, heaving for breath. The opalescent color between her scales was glowing. She was burning hot to touch. *"Almost... phew... almost out. Stamina potions?"*

"Last one." I pulled it from my inventory and helped her chug it. *"Glad I picked up all those herbs in the swamp. Gonna be brewing all night."*

"You should make some beer." Karalti bent down to let me onto her back, then launched heavily into the air.

"Beer?"

"Yeah! For Vash! We were talking about food before, and he really likes beer. He said he drank a whole keg during an orgy once. I don't know what an orgy is, but he said everyone was dancing and cheering him on. It sounds like fun!"

I shook my head in disbelief. *"This guy is supposed to be a monk."*

"He is! So it was a monk orgy or something, I dunno!"

The bronto was gaining on the No Man's Land with frightening speed. Nerveless, fearless, it was completely unstoppable. It ploughed through trees, mud, razor wire, barricades and bodies, shedding chunks of flesh on its relentless course toward the wall.

"Let's do an A-roll past those things and scatter them, then flame the port side," I said. *"We only have one chance at this."*

"I know! Hold onto your butthole!" Karalti's focus intensified, just before she furled her wings in close to her flanks and dove.

I stared over her shoulder as the bloated corpse got closer and closer... and when we closed in, she pivoted and sprayed a precise line of Ghost Fire along the brontosaurus's flank. It hit the explosives and caught, white fire blazing.

Pinned by centrifuge, I fought gravity to snap my head around and look back to see the earth-shattering kaboom - but as we soared back up into the air, the Bronto was still moving just as it had been - except that it was now on fire. An acrid, caustic smell filled the air.

"Fuck. What the... oh, shit!" I slapped my own thigh, then held onto the saddle. *"Karalti! Turn back! That thing is carrying Greek Fire!"*

"*What's that?*"

"Those explosives are protected by a layer of quicklime that insulates the payload from fire, but gets really really hot on contact with water." I looked over the terrain, trying to figure out the Demon's strategy. There were puddles of water on the ground. There were heaps of dead, soggy zombies and explosive vest-wearing skeletons piled against the walls. "*We need water. A* lot *of water. We need it fast.*"

"How, though?"

Just as she said that, a trebuchet behind the wall flung a huge ball of flaming pitch at the approaching bronto. The projectile nailed it in the chest, sending it reeling to the side. It stumbled and fell to its knees in the mud, the vest barely touching the sodden ground. Where it did contact, white steam began to rise.

"Uhh... uhhh..." for a terrified second, I found myself paralyzed. *I'm not smart enough for this shit,* I thought, staring at the distant trebuchets as another counterweight cocked back. My eyes widened. *"Wait! Trebuchet! See that bucket that they're using to balance the counterweight? Do you think you can carry it?"*

"Gonna have to!" Karalti rolled up and pumped her wings, tongue lolling.

"You have Haste, don't you? Any mana?"

"Just enough!"

The dragon's hot scales flared with seams of light as she silently cast the *Spera-Cil-Kain* spell, boosting her speed another twenty percent. The Weaponeers manning the siege engine scattered as she winged over the wall and landed on the trebuchet's beam. Seesawing back and forth, beating her wings to maintain balance, she hastily pulled the rocks out of the counterweight and threw them to the ground.

"What are you doing?!" The Catapult Supervisor ran for us, pulling at his hair. "Stop!"

"Excuse me sir! We're just going to borrow this for a second! Trust me!" I shouted back down, catching the saddle grips just as Karalti lurched back into the air with the bucket clasped in her hands.

Fortunately, there was a lot of water around the Prezyemi Line. The bronto was about halfway across No Man's Land, dragging barbed wire and corpses on its course toward the men. It had lost its guts from a cannon blast, but it just dragged those along, too. Karalti flew down to the surface of a shell crater, scooping up half a huge bucket of water.

"I can't do it!" She panted as she struggled back into the air. *"Too heavy!"*

"You can! Pour a bit out, and let's go!" I checked her weight limit. We were a hundred pounds over. White-knuckled, I went into my inventory to throw out anything heavy. We were carrying a couple of sets of armor and spare weapons. Without a thought, I threw them all to the ground along with a bag of five hundred gold. They all landed in the mud below. Items didn't despawn in Archemi - and they were as safe out in the battlefield as they were in my Inventory.

The reduction in weight was enough that Karalti could fly. Her stamina was at 5% by the time we reached the brontosaurus, who was barely a body length away from the pile of zombies at the Wall. In synch with her, I felt the burning of her efforts as she lined herself up.

"I'm going to go down and slash open those bags." Grim and focused, I fixed on our rapidly approaching target. *"Pour behind me. At the end, land and I'll jump on: we can restore*

a bit of stamina, grab the thing's tail to stop it walking, and hold on."

"Roger." Karalti's tongue lolled as she lined up, and I jumped. The wind rushed by as I fell, then landed with a soft 'thump' on one of the satchels, driving my spear into the thick oiled leather. It split open, puffing out a cloud of stinging white dust. Quicklime was cheap to produce, caustic as hell, and reacts explosively with water, reaching temperatures of 200 degrees within ten seconds. This much quicklime was guaranteed to reach the effective maximum temperature in less than half a minute - around 500 degrees. I knew the stuff well: we'd used it to cook powered armor pilots in their armor in the swamps of Indonesia.

Holding my breath against the toxic dust, I zig-zagged from side to side on the dinosaur's back, dragged the Spear through each payload, and jumped to the next one, trusting in Karalti behind me. As water slopped onto the exposed powder, it began to hiss and crackle, absorbing every drop of liquid as it hardened and cracked with a sound like huge grinding teeth. I was fucked if the payload under the quicklime was explosive instead of flammable.

The brontosaurus emitted a gurgling moan as the packs on its back swelled, rupturing with steam and the expanding stone inside. I was about halfway along when the first pack ignited with an audible 'phwoomph'. Heat and a garish, dancing yellowish light flooded over me, along with an awful rotten egg odor.

"Sulfur! Fuck fuck fuck!" I stabbed a pack on the way past, but then just focused on running past the skeleton archers and the flying snakes. Above and behind me, Karalti threw the bucket into a pack of zombies charging toward the front line and then landed on top of them. Swiping and stomping, smashing them to pulp with her tail, she struggled to keep pace with me as I wove across the see-sawing Bronto's back and leaped toward her. I was out of AP and out of enhanced jumps. Even with a run up, I hit her ribs, bounced off, and landed in the mud.

"*Watch out!*"Karalti lumbered forward, seized me in her jaws, and ran.

The Brontosaurus's vest ignited, belching steam, then greenish fire that consumed the huge dinosaur and turned it into a hundred-foot long barbecue grill. It collapsed to its knees, then toppled forward with its head barely resting against the base of the corpses piled up at the wall. When the belly of it hit the mud, there were muffled explosions, then a roaring conflagration as the wet ground ignited all the Greek fire beneath it. Flaming oil gushed out onto the oil-soaked corpses, lighting them. The flames streaked toward us across the water.

"Throw sand! Throw sand!" Somewhere on the battlements, a man shouted over and over until his voice broke.

I jostled up and down in my dragon's mouth. She ran until her stamina ran out, breaking down into a heap of wings and long sagging tail. She dropped me on a pile of smashed skeletons to heave for breath.

"Holy fucking titballs." I reached up to embrace her around the neck, watching as the fallen bronto's bones ignited. The entire battlefield blazed white as they cooked, the heat so intense we could feel it at the other end of the battlefield. *"Imagine if that had gotten to the Wall. You did it, Tidbit."*

"You helped too." She pulled her wings back into position, shuddering with the effort to lift them.

I leaned back to look up at her. *"Hey, now. Don't downplay this. You worked your ass off. Take the credit."*

"Okay." She crooned, tucking her face down shyly. *"But you saw the bucket. I don't notice lots of things while I'm flying."*

"That's why we're a team. Speaking of noticing things - those flying eye things have me worried." I searched the sky. *"Did you kill any?"*

"A few." Karalti's mental voice was strained. *"I dunno if we got all of them."*

"I have a feeling those flying snakes we saw are recon units. Nothing we can do about it now, though." I rubbed her hot neck, monitoring her status. Only once the Fatigue penalty icon blinked out did I climb onto her back.

When she was back at 5%, Karalti awkwardly took off into the air, tilting to one side as her left wing caught the wind a little slower than the stronger right wing. She strained on the way to the wall, where we were greeted by a crowd of cheering, whooping soldiers.

"Good gods, man!" Istvan was at the front ready to receive us, and when I jumped down, he reached out a hand to clap my forearm. "What a performance! Between you and Suri, you nearly wiped out the entire attack force!"

"Karalti and the artillery support are the only reasons I didn't get my ass kicked." I wearily clapped the dragon on her knee as she reared back up to sit on her tail and rest. "How'd Suri go?"

"Well, first she grabbed a rifle and took out fifty-two zombies." Vash's deep, gravelly voice rasped from behind me, making me and Karalti both jump. "Then she loaded in ten crates of cannonballs by herself while you were bouncing around in the mud, THEN single-handedly took out the four Allosaurs advancing out of the mists behind the Brontosaurus with a rocket launcher-"

"And if you don't think I'm keeping this baby, you're out of your mind." Bathed in sweat and streaked with gunpowder, Suri pushed through the crowd of soldiers with a simple musket-like rocket launcher braced over one shoulder. She carried the four-foot long weapon like it was made of feathers instead of iron and hardwood.

I grinned. "Ditching the bigass sword?"

"Nah. My axes broke, and this is better." She grinned back. "Turns out I like guns."

Vash pointed at her. "If you don't marry her, I will."

"I thought you weren't talking to me?" I stepped away from Karalti and embraced Suri one-armed, thumping her on the back and kissing her on the cheek.

The monk scratched his stubbly jaw. "Oh... yes. That's right. Thank you for reminding me, you filthy lying pile of jackal cum."

"We all saw you out there, Fly-boy and Fly-girl." Suri let go of me, eyes dancing. "So, how many'd you get?"

I made a show of thinking for a moment. "It was pretty chaotic out there... I don't exactly know, but I know it was a *skele-ton.*"

Istvan's nose wrinkled. Vash laughed, slapping his thighs as Suri turned away in disgust. I cackled and raised my hands to the sky, bathed in the joy of pun-romantic power right up until my Berserker girlfriend decked me across the face with her free fist and knocked my ass to the ground.

"Oof." I pushed up on one arm, and reset my jaw back into position with a muffled crunch. "Okay. Guess I deserved to get boned for that."

Suri's eyes narrowed to smoldering golden slits. "You did *not.*"

"You do NOT want to rib me any further, young lady. I can do this forever." I grinned back at her.

She rolled her eyes and sighed. "Okay. Fine. I surrender. What do you want from me?"

"Well... we could go back to our bedroom at the Fort and..." I paused as the grin went from 'playful' to 'shit-eating'.

Suri glared at me. "Do. Not."

"... have a mature, consensual adult conversation over a bottle of wine," I finished.

The woman put her hands on both my shoulders. "Good. Because my consent to anything ends when you start in with the puns. Got it?"

"Got it."

Istvan cleared his throat softly. "If you two are done... we must urgently debrief now that the crisis has passed."

"Sure." Suri stepped around me, looking up at Karalti. The exhausted dragon lowered her muzzle to sniff, huffing hot air over Suri's skin. Hesitantly, she reached up a hand to stroke her. Karalti tensed, but as the woman massaged her sore muscles, the dragon's crests went from alert to half-mast. "You fought a hell of a fight today, Special-K. You gonna be able to make it home?"

"Of course, I'll be able to make it home!" The dragon stiffened, then snorted and brushed Suri's hand off. *"Come on, Hector. We got a debrief to go to. And we'll be the first ones there!"*

Chapter 25

At Soma's request, the debrief was held in the Officer's Mess. Compared to the War Room, it was clean, warm and dry, with brass candelabras and rich wooden furniture. There was real food here, miles above what the rank and file had to eat. Roast chicken, bread, vegetables, even fruit. The floors were not covered in reeds, but carpet. Everything about it pissed me off.

"The zombies were digging, you say?" Soma sat at the head of the table, where he sawed into an entire chicken and a platter of baked potatoes. The knife and fork looked like kid's toys in his giant hands, but he was able to separate meat from bone with the precision of a surgeon. "That is concerning. Did you see any sort of sophisticated earthworks nearby? Any reason for what they were doing?"

"No." Rin looked to Suri and me for encouragement. "It was weird to find them out there, actually. We didn't see any other excavation crews."

"I had a thought about that." Suri sat to my right, her hand resting on my thigh, my hand covering hers. "Could they be trying to tunnel under the fort or the wall? They don't have to breathe, but they have to worry about mud and tunnel collapse... those Dredgers looked like they were trying to drain something."

"Most likely, they are trying to drain the bogs into the Sarviz so that they can minimize the amount of water they pass through on their way here. There is no feasible way for them to maintain the kind of underground infrastructure they'd need to build a tunnel underground." Soma shook his head. "The ground is far too soft."

"The rock underneath is not," Istvan said sourly. "And there is a city under the swamp."

"The rock is very far down. My father had the swamp surveyed, looking for oil." Soma shook his head. "And no one has found any evidence of a city under the Endlar. No one has seen it. It's nothing more than a barbarian fairytale."

"Oh, yes. Everything must be seen by you to be real." Vash was rocked back in his chair, smoking what smelled like a mixture of tobacco and weed in a carved wood and bone pipe. "Taltos cannot be seen from here. Is that also a fairytale?"

Soma glowered at him. "Archaeologists with better tools and more brains than you have explored this mud pit looking for a lost city, Dorha. No evidence of civilization was found. Believe me, I am very interested in the prospect of dragon ruins, but time has taken its toll. There are no cities of the Solonkratsu left here."

"There's definitely a city under the swamps in Ilia," I replied.

"And how do you know that?" Soma asked acidly. "Did you hear about it on your nursemaid's knee?"

"I went there," I replied. "The place is called Cham Garai. It's a closely guarded secret of the Order of St. Grigori. I had to go through ritual trials there to be able to bond with Karalti."

Karalti looked up from her meal, chewing vigorously. Her polymorphed form was still youthful, but she now looked like a Tuun woman in her early twenties instead of a girl in her late teens. Her cheeks were stuffed with chicken. "*Wat?*"

Vash rolled his eyes so hard that his lashes fluttered. "It's almost like the native people who lived here for thousands of years might know something you don't, Soma."

"I am far more concerned by the proximity of the *Ix'tamo*," the lord replied acidly. "The one you four retrieved is the first we've ever captured from the Demon. Horrible things... Rin has already reported the extent of the damage it did to a small area of our province. At this rate, the land around Karhad will be ruined for generations, perhaps forever. If the undead somehow manage to undermine the Prezyemi Plateau - geologically, I mean - the wall could collapse."

"What are you planning to do with that Ick... Ikt... thing that they bought back?" Istvan asked warily. "If it ruins the land, why do we have it here?"

Soma beamed. "I had a brief look over it while supervising the defense of the wall, and I'm fairly certain we can reverse-engineer the magitech to turn this one into a shield generator. That would be marvelous - our mages wouldn't have to stand out there in the open while shells are raining down on us."

"Assuming a shell doesn't hit it and the whole Fortress is driven mad with mana poisoning." Istvan grunted, reaching for the wine jug. Vash shot him a piercing side-long look. The Captain cleared his throat and sat back, then jumped as Soma slammed his utensils down on the table.

"Are you compelled to shit on every tiny victory we have, Arshak?" He demanded. "Really? You have been nagging me for months that we have won nothing, and the day that we secure not one, not two, but *three* significant victories for the defense, you harp on me?"

Istvan tensed like a bird of prey about to launch itself forward. "Victories? For the problems that YOU caused! Who sent Vash out into the swamp alone? Who left the Western Wall undermanned, despite my orders to the garrison!? Who insults and demoralizes the Yanik scouts we need to discover Ik-tankos or whatever the fuck those devil machines are? Who, Soma?"

A tic started by Soma's eye. "And who is drinking himself to death, bad-mouthing my every word, sowing dissent and demoralizing the men? Did it occur to you that the staff on the Wall might have coped if they weren't made miserable by your backbiting gossip? Or by the way you overlooked the way those Meewfolk mercenaries undermined the discipline and health of the force? Their fleas spread disease, they gamble, they were all weak for drink-"

"But you *did* send me out to die in the swamp." Vash motioned to him with the end of his pipe. No one seemed to hear him.

"The Orphans are soldiers, not automatons! Of course they gamble and drink! They were also brave, and willing to die for Mysznо despite the contempt we humans show for them, and they deserted because of YOU!" Istvan nearly shouted. "By Solnetsi's platinum tits, have you ever accepted responsibility for anything in your entire life?"

"Guys!" I held up my hands. "Fucking cool it off!"

Istvan sunk down, his face a mask of loathing. Soma glared back at him. Karalti continued to shovel food in her face, watching the argument with the curious impartiality of an apex predator.

"Seriously. The Wall was nearly breached today. Put it behind you and focus on the present." Suri added. "Or you and everyone you care about are dead."

"I managed a university faculty. A workshop. I have personally overseen the testing of every airship ever sent out of Litvy with my family's craftmark on it." Soma's blue eyes hardened as he eased back down. "Every engine I ever built, every spell I wove, I tested myself. Those ships, the ones that saved your life and the lives of thousands of other people in Karhad, were built by *my* House. And before all of that, I vest my life into the research and magic and math that goes into those 'automatons'. So the answer is yes, I can and do accept responsibility for my decisions. But a craftsman can only work with the materials he has, and if the materials are of poor quality, even the best blueprints will produce a bad product. Shit in, shit out."

Istvan threw his hands up. "And there you have it. Right there. Exactly what I was talking about. Going ahead and insulting-"

"Did I mention you?" The lord leaned forward in his seat, which groaned under his weight. "Did I say it was the people here? No. I did not. I mean *materials.* We need better weapons and magic, Arshak. Weapons capable of arming ten thousand against fifty thousand shambling corpses. We know they're weak against fire and water. The cannons and mortars we have are all that's standing between us and the dead, and we could be doing so much better if we had the blasted caravans from Boros. But where are those?"

The Captain sunk back down, exasperated. "I put the Starborn onto it."

I nodded. "The caravan issue is next on our bucket list, Soma. We're supposed to get the details from you."

"I am busy. My Weaponeer, Viktor, shall furnish you the details. You can find him in the munitions warehouse tonight and tomorrow morning," he replied crisply. "May I offer the lady some more to eat?"

Karalti perked up. She had finished her plate and had been eyeing Istvan's, which was almost untouched. *"Yeah! Uhh... I mean, thank you."*

Soma glanced at me, then delicately picked up and placed the other half of the chicken he'd been eating onto Karalti's dish. I shifted, suddenly restless, but Suri squeezed my hand and I forced myself to ease back down.

"We need to conscript," Istvan spoke while the Lord was occupied. "Word is spreading beyond the Fort that we have a dragon, three Starborn, and the Iron Monk on our side. I ordered the singers to go to villages to the north-west and start telling the stories. Soon, every young man and half the women will be primed to fight. We need every one of them."

"And how do you propose we feed them all?" Soma retorted after sitting back. "Swamp-weed stew?"

Istvan glared at him. "If we must. You need living bodies to fire those witch-fire weapons you place so much faith in."

"Good gods, man. My House is ready to ride forth from Litvy with weapons, soldiers, the caravans and airships... as soon as we know we're not going to be blown out of the sky over the bloody Pass!" Soma finally raised his voice.

"Look, guys, you can have both," I said. "You need the militia, if for nothing else than logistics. But the bigger problem is that there is no fucking strategy here. None. Nada. The Demon's main force is, what, seven hundred miles away? Assuming they're working around the clock, we have ten to fourteen days to prepare. Where are the earthworks? Why aren't we skirmishing them out in the swamp, reducing their numbers? Digging out *Ix'tamo*s and cutting off their supply train? What the fuck is going on?"

The Count and the Captain glared at each other. Then they glared at me.

[[Leadership check failed. You have insufficient Renown.]]

"Desperation is what's going on," Vash said. "Desperation and fear. I can help with the fear, if you would let me minister-"

"Absolutely out of the question," Soma snapped. "Not only would you be pressing your pagan religion on the men, but we saw what became of you and your last batch of disciples on what was supposed to be a very straightforward scouting mission."

The temperature in the room dropped several degrees. Karalti looked between the pair of men like a fan at a tennis match.

Vash drew on his pipe. "Straightforward indeed. Your coordinates were very precise, my lord. Almost like you knew we would arrive there to find a small army of the dead and the Grand Old Cunt Swamphag."

Soma's broad shoulders lifted in a brief shrug. "I knew no such thing. I *suspected* you would find an *Ix'tamo*. I researched them back at the college, many years ago, and the degradation of the land jogged my memory. That was the goal all along, for reasons I have already explained."

"You know, if this was about anything else, I'd actually believe you. You can barely organize your robes on the privy without taking a shit on them, and it's exactly the kind of ridiculous coincidence that only a true idiot could engineer." Vash exhaled a plume of smoke. "But this is your ego we're talking about. You're always clever when that's at stake."

The lord's tone soured. "By the gods, Dorha – you're as thick as a rock. You don't have a choice in your position here, do you understand? I gave you that mission as a way for you and your rabble to make an honorable exit."

"So you sent him out to die?" Istvan's face turned a dark purplish color as he boiled up from his seat. "Are you mad? And so brazen that you'd state this before witnesses?"

"Hold your tongue. I've had a gutful of you too, you insubordinate dog." Soma also stood. He had at least a foot of height and a hundred pounds of muscle on every other man at the table. "As for you, Dorha. Next time, I'll send you straight to the gallows for inciting mutiny. Does that suit you better?"

The tall, wiry monk held Soma's cold blue gaze with his own intense gray one. "Go ahead, you self-stroking peacock. The noose will reject my neck, and every soldier in this fort will turn on you. Maybe you will remember your humanity as they lynch you on the gallows. You may not know the names of the men you sent to die, but they do."

Even Suri's eyebrows arched.

The lord flashed Vash a barely concealed look of disgust. "They were pagans who worshiped the Black God, like you do. If you got your cultists killed, that is your fault. Now you will be dismissed in front of the general assembly tomorrow and made to leave in disgrace."

"Look. No. Just no." I stepped up now. "No one is being sent out in disgrace, not unless you want a mass desertion."

"Do not speak for me, Oathbreaker." Vash rounded on me like a cobra, complete with spit.

"Oathbreaker?" Istvan and Soma said at the same time.

I shot Vash a dark look.

“Did I address you? No, I did not. This is a Tuun matter.” Vash snapped at Soma.

"I am the Commander of this garrison, and anything that affects the cohesion of the defense is a matter I am entitled to know about." Soma's eyes narrowed to thin blue slits. "Dragozin will furnish me with the details. Get out of my sight."

"My absolute pleasure. I will see you later tonight, Istvan." Vash rose, swept into an exaggerated bow, then stepped back into the shadow cast by the flickering candles and disappeared.

Slowly, I got to my feet. Rin, Suri and Karalti followed suit.

"Where do you think you're going?" Soma demanded. "I order you to tell me what this 'oathbreaker' business about?"

"It *is* a Tuun matter. From one peer to another, that matter is none of your fucking business." Something black and hard rose in me and bled out in my voice, turning every word into a cutting stroke that lay on the room like a whip. "We have quests to do. You two can go right ahead and keep jerking each other off."

The women rose from their seats and headed for the door as I did.

“You do not get to lecture me, you savage,” Soma called. “I'm to address the men tomorrow morning, and I *will not*-”

I turned back to look at him, and whatever he saw in my eyes caused the smug smile to freeze on his lips.

"Go right the fuck ahead." I said. "We're going out there to help the people of the garrison, and if you don't like it, you can blow me."

Chapter 26

The four of us split outside the door to the Officer's Mess. Rin went off to the Hangar and the Gunsmith, Suri had to go to her training. Karalti lingered as I kissed Suri goodbye, glowering quietly from the side.

"*Want to come to the hospital with me?*" I asked her once Suri had left.

"*No.*" Her violet eyes were the sullen, dark purple of an approaching stormfront. "*I need to fly and think. I don't wanna talk to you for a while.*"

"Karalti? Are you okay?" I took a step toward her, but she brushed me off when I reached to embrace her. Her hand was gentle, but she could have belted me across the face with all her strength, and it wouldn't have been as painful and confusing.

"Uhh..." I hung back, unsure of what to do. "Did I do something wrong?"

Karalti's face darted up. She stared at me for a long few moments, her lovely face as still as carved marble. After a heavy pause, her throat worked just before she looked away.

"No. Like I said. I need to think," she replied. *"I need privacy. I'm going to... go somewhere for a while. By myself."*

"Was it Suri?" Every nerve in my body was screaming for me to resolve this, comfort her, chase her as she tried to pull away. She had never pulled away from me before. Just then, I realized something – I couldn't sense how she was feeling. Not in the way I was used to, when her emotions beat against my mind like radiant heat.

"Yes. And I will deal with it as I please." Karalti glared up at me with eyes like chips of violet obsidian. In human form, the supernatural gravity of Karalti's charisma, her *presence*, was not lessened. At a glance, maybe – but my lizard brain still knew that I was staring down the barrel at a predator who could burst out of her human suit and turn into a monster the size of a train carriage. *"I'll see you later. Okay?"*

"Okay?" I echoed the question, too stunned to say anything more convincing. Every other time that she had lost her shit over Suri, it had been a flamboyant temper-tantrum of some kind or another. She had never withdrawn before. "Are you... are you angry at me, or...?"

"No. I'll... I'll be back later." Karalti drew a deep breath just before she marched off down the corridor. As she left, I felt a piece of myself leave with her. She had never once insisted on privacy before. Not from me.

I was still brooding by the time I marched into the Fort Hospital and asked after Lazar. The Chief Medic was in the hospital's pharmacy, brewing and blending with what few herbs and regents he had left. I coughed to get his attention, and when he turned, his eyes widened.

"Your Grace! You're back! Forgive me... one moment." Agitated, he pulled off his gloves and mask and bustled over. Before I had a chance to react, he seized my hands in his and kissed me on both cheeks like a Russian grandma. I fought the urge to lean away.

"Lord Dragozin, I cannot thank you enough!" His eyes brimmed with emotion as he dropped my hands and clapped me on the arms instead. "You and your comrades bought Vash Dorha back to us, you saved untold lives at the Wall... the stories of you and your dragon's battle with the undead has been flying around the hospital since the injured were carried in. A reanimated Brontosaurus, the noblest of the sauropods and the symbol of the House of Bolza... can you imagine the effect that a successful attack would have had on the soldiers?"

"I..." I hadn't thought of it that way, but now he mentioned it, that was true. The Demon wouldn't have just broken through the Line - he'd have mindfucked the entire garrison. "No worries."

"Gods, I didn't even offer you something to drink." The doctor began to look around frantically. "We have nothing to offer you, unless you need potions. Not even wine. My apologies, I will call-"

"Chill, man - it's fine." I held up my hands in surrender. "I have your herbs, and something even better."

Lazar stopped flitting around and turned to me. "Better than medicines, or better than wine?"

"Both. I'll send you a transfer request. Hang on..."

I opened a transfer, and when he accepted, loaded the herbs for the sidequest from my Inventory to his, along with my share of the gold coins we'd liberated from the Swamp Hag Broodmother. "There: six hundred and twenty-five smackeroos. Should be pure enough for you to make Colloidal Gold."

"By the Nine. This is... this is..." Lazar swallowed. "This is a gift of unparalleled generosity. I am touched, truly, and thank you a thousand times, my lord. I am forever at your service."

[[Congratulations! You have gained 340 EXP!]]
[[You have gained 34 Skill EXP (Herbalism)]]
[[You have gained 75 renown!]]
[[Your fame is growing! New Quests are available!]]
[[You have unlocked a new Hero: Lazar Skaliz (Rank B+ Alchemist - Myszno Defense Force)]]
[[Congratulations: You have unlocked your first recruitable hero! Would you like to learn how to manage heroes?]]

Not right now, I thought back. To Lazar, I said: "There is something you could do, if you have time. I used my last Aqua Regia a couple of days ago. If you know how to make Hydrochloric Acid and Nitric Acid, can you teach me?"

"But of course!" Lazar drew himself up tall and pushed his glasses back from where they'd slipped. "Come with me - I have all the ingredients we require. In fact, Nitric Acid starts with these mushrooms and a solution of brine water..."

For at least an hour, Lazar taught me some elements of chemistry in a way no other teacher had ever successfully managed to: because he knew what it was like to not be able to read.

"I struggled terribly with books and reading." He watched on as I attached a generator flask to a collection bulb and a flask of iced water. "The Skaliz name is well-respected, but by the time I was born, my House was too poor to afford me a tutor. I learned all the basics of healing from my father the way he had learned it, through memorizing by speech... and so I learned to read and write at the University. Can you imagine: a boy who can barely spell his own name, learning to read anatomical textbooks and herbals!"

"I know exactly how that feels." I added water to the flask, then a mixed flask of sodium bisulphate - created by mixing powdered salt into ⟦Oil of Vitriol⟧ - and more plain salt. "Now I turn the heat on, right?"

"Correct." He nodded.

I did so, then took a step back to watch as the assorted powders melted into the water. The solution dissolved quickly, turning yellow. Gas flowed through the tubes, white and wispy, passed through the collector and funneled into the beaker of bubbling water. "So that's turning into acid now?"

"Yes. Wait for it." Lazar stood by my shoulder, a small smile playing over his lips.

After a few more seconds of bubbling and popping, the entire contents of the beaker were suddenly and dramatically sucked up out of its tubes and into the collector with an audible *shhhloop*.

"Shit!" I jumped back like a cat. The doctor laughed uproariously.

[[You have learned a new recipe: Hydrochloric Acid!]]

"Fun, isn't it?" He beamed.

"Hell yeah. Not as fun as flying, but this is pretty great." I picked up the collector full of acid, and let my HUD focus on it. Sure enough, I got one of Archemi's somewhat surreal item identifiers: *"Hydrochloric Acid: It's all fun and games until someone forgets the baking soda and perforates their colon!"*

"You can also extract Hydrochloric Acid from the stomachs of Stingcrabs with a collector," Lazar said. "Not as fun as this, but given that you are an adventurer, you may find it easier to obtain the acid this way. You simply need a Collector and a vacuum flask."

"Sure, I have one of those. Though I need to start thinking about getting better lab glass as I get more into these Medical crafting trees." I took some empty bottles from my inventory and poured the acid inside. Carefully. One brewing made three bottles, which seemed like a good amount for the effort. "Can this be made to different concentrations?"

"Certainly. You need a Distiller." Lazar pointed at a tall copper tank in the corner of the room. "You can put three Hydrochloric Acid through a distiller to get one

Concentrated Hydrochloric Acid. Of course, the more you distill something, the more dangerous it is to work with. If you ever decide to do pursue the path of mastery in Alchemy, you will need to know how to handle the chemicals safely."

"Right." 'Hector Dragozin: Master Alchemist and Cool Dragon Stunt Dude' sounded like a pretty good resume to me. "My safety record is admittedly pretty terrible overall, but I'll work on it."

"I sincerely hope so. Hmm. Let me see..." Lazar went to a drawer and unlocked it. Inside was a stack of leather-bound books, heavily tagged with ribbons. He pulled out two and set them down. "These might be useful: my old school manuals on creating potion bases and methods of refining."

"Are they skill manuals?" I asked hopefully.

"As in, enchanted with a Seal of Learning? No. Plain old books." He flipped to the first page of the fatter book. It was a table, showing alchemical symbols alongside neatly printed explanations of what they meant. "This will teach you all of the basic ingredients that go into every potion known to man or dragon. Alcohol, all of the acids and bases, suspensions and oils. You will learn a great deal of Alchemy from this tome, and unlock the Apprentice levels if you can absorb the learning. The other is an Herbal, which details all of the commonly used herbs and the conditions they treat. You are already an Apprentice level Herbalist, but to access Journeyman, you will need to find a Master or attend a college. Either way, to become a Journeyman, they will expect you to be able to recite the information in this book from rote memory."

It was about two inches thick. My eyes widened with slow-dawning horror.

"Medicine is an art worth your time and study," Lazar assured me. "And you certainly have the mind for it. They are yours, my friend - I do not need them at my current level of ability. I have no doubt you will excel."

I picked up the Alchemy textbook. The pages had stains on them here and there, and when I tried to focus on the words, they squirmed and wrestled on the page. There was a table with 26 different alchemical symbols in the front. "Thanks, man. I'll try. I don't think I'll be able to make it, though."

"It takes time." The man pushed his spectacles up along his thin nose. "Time and dedication, as with all good things in life."

I let out a tense breath and closed the book. "Yeah... for sure. Don't suppose you know anything about healing magic, do you?"

"Healing magic?" The Medic gave me a curious look. "I do. I know that mana cannot directly be used to heal. It only harms unless it is heavily adulterated."

"But mana *is* used for healing. Alchemical potions can regrow limbs and shit, so there has to be healing magic in there somewhere."

Lazar thought for a moment. "Not exactly. Mana contains all of the elements in an unexpressed state: the state of Aether. By combining it with other ingredients, one or more elements is coaxed forth from the mana, transmuting it into a different substance - just as the sodium bisulphate and salt transmute into hydrochloric acid."

I nodded. "The reason I'm asking is because we fought a monster that used healing magic."

The doctor's eyes widened until they were almost the size of saucers. "Well, Your Grace, some monsters have a regenerative process that strongly resembles magic..."

"No. This was definitely healing magic." Careful not to knock over anything that might explode, I leaned back against a bare stretch of counter. "The Swamp Hag Broodmother used a restoration spell to heal itself while we were fighting it."

"If that is true... well, a dragon and Starborn have reappeared after thousands of years, so why not the Lost Art?" The doctor shook his head. "At the University, we learned that Elemental Darkness and Light are the elements which are most aligned to the practice of medicine. My professor used to say: diseases are cured by the light of the sun, injuries by the solace of the moon."

"So healing magic that's usable by humans IS possible?" I pressed. "In theory?"

Reluctantly, Lazar nodded. "In theory. But if there are Words of Power that humans are capable of speaking that bend mana into healing magic, any record of them disappeared at the end of the Era of Queens."

"Era of Queens?"

"The last great dynasty of the Dragons, when the East of what is now Vlachia was supposedly ruled by Lahati the

Wise," Lazar replied. "Do you not know of the dragons' history?"

My cheeks turned hot. "Never had a chance to study it."

"I see. Well, we can rectify that." He beckoned. "Come with me."

Curious, I followed the man through the ground-floor ward and through a locked door into a suite of spartan, but tidy rooms. The main room was a hall with a table, a hearth with stew and bread keeping warm on a shelf nearby, and a number of clean pallets. The day-shift medics were asleep there, some of them still in their bloody work clothes. There was a storeroom and other smaller, private quarters. Lazar led me to one, where he unlocked a second door and showed me inside his private quarters, where a bed, no finer than the ones his staff slept on, and some chests and other plain and functional furniture seemed all the more spartan in the steady white glow of the one luxury he did have, a mage light. It illuminated the top of his desk, making it the focus of the whole place.

"I managed to save a few books when we fled Karhad. I had an emergency trunk of manuscripts I'd copied over the years, just in case anything ever happened." He squatted down in front of a chest, opening it to reveal neatly-packed books of nearly every dimension and quality. Some were hardly bigger than a matchbook, while others were the size of my grandfather's art folios. He shifted tomes aside until he came up with an unremarkable-looking brown volume with weathered yellow pages. "Here. '*The History of the Dragons in Vlachia*'. It's almost all myths and stories, folk tales from the Churvi and the nomads of the steppe, but you should be able to recognize fact from fiction. Take this as well - it is a history of Myszno. It naturally focuses on the Vlachian conquest, but there is some elemental information about the land and its history that I think you will find interesting."

Blinking, I accepted the books. They were heavy enough that I could probably knock someone out if I smacked them across the face. "I don't know if I'll have time to read it while the war's still going on, but thanks."

"Try." The medic smiled, then patted me on the shoulder. "If we can retake Karhad, there's more where this came from. We can only hope they didn't burn the library at Egbolt or the University."

"Good libraries?" I asked.

Lazar looked down. "The University holds a unique and truly ancient collection of texts, including a set of plates that are assumed to have been scribed during the Drachan War. That is the war that ended the reign of the Dragons in Archemi: one of the few remaining texts of the Solonkratsu's great civilization."

My intuition pinged at me. "When were those plates discovered?"

"Oh, long ago. I wasn't even born when they were donated."

"By who?"

"Why, the Tuun who live near the village of Myszno." He cocked his head, a small smile playing over his lips. "They recovered them while mining in the southern mountains."

Chapter 27

I didn't feel like heading back to my quarters to mope around until Karalti decided to come back and talk to me. Instead, I restlessly headed north and crossed the river, hoping to catch up with Rin.

There was a great cluster of unit production structures on the islands behind the Fort. The rapids powered turbines and mills attached to the manufacturing complex, which was shielded by sloped roofs that partly camouflaged it from the air. Rin was in the Airship Hangar, pouring over the *Ix'tamo* with a group of men, women and Mercurions. They took samples and measurements, monitored attached magical devices, and sketched blueprints. Rin was in the blueprint creation group, gesturing animatedly as she conversed in a sharp, clacking tongue with three other Mercurion Artificers. The warehouse bustled around them, with workers tuning, repairing and building airship components. I edged around the *Ix'tamo* until I was across from Rin and waved. Her head darted up.

"Oh! Hector! Hi! Just a second!" She pointed something out on the blueprint, patted one of her teammates on the back, then scurried over to me. "Hey! What's up?"

"Thought I'd come and see if there was anything I can help you with," I replied. "I did everything I could at the hospital. Netted a good amount of Renown."

"You aren't going back to hang with Karalti and Suri?" She asked.

I shrugged. "Karalti probably doesn't want to see me right now. If I'm lucky, she's having a girl talk with Suri."

"Oh no! Did something happen?" Rin's big blue eyes widened with concern.

I glanced at the people milling around and hunched my shoulders. "Don't really want to talk about it here. Besides... I didn't come to lean on you. I figured we could talk to the Chief about the Supply Train quest, and maybe do some other sidequests tonight."

"Oh, come on. You've been there for me through all sorts of things. Kanzo, the boss fights, all of that. Besides, I don't really think that way." She puffed a lock of translucent hair from her face. "Come on. Let's go outside."

Resigned, I followed Rin out of a side door. She led me up a flight of stairs to a balcony overlooking the river and sat down, hanging her legs between the rails. I hopped up to perch on the narrow edge, squatting down on my heels. The sky was low, clouds obscuring the light of the moon, and it smelled gritty and damp. Like the city just after a rain.

"So, what happened?" she asked.

"Draconic growing pains," I grunted. "I think."

"You had an argument?"

"No. Not exactly." I sighed. "She got really cold after the meeting with Dumb and Dumber, brushed me off and left. Said she needed to think."

"Why? Did something happen?"

"I kissed Suri goodbye." I shrugged. "She said she wasn't mad, but she sure seemed like it."

Rin made a face. "You think she likes you? You know, as in...?"

"I know she does. She's had a crush on me since she hit Level 5 or so. We have a frigging telepathic bond, so it's not news to me or anything. But it's not... I don't want what she wants. I love that dragon more than anything or anyone I've ever met. She's like my twin, like the other half of me. But I'm her adoptive parent and as far as I'm concerned, she's family. I can't give her what she wants."

"You're not related, though," Rin said. "I mean... relationships evolve?"

I scowled and shook my head. "No. Parents don't fuck their kids. No exceptions."

Rin made a sound of agreement. "When you put it like that... yeah. That's terrible, though – I don't know how I could help. I know that when I'm stressed out, I need to be alone. Sometimes I get so worked up that I shout and pace and stim-" she flapped her hands for emphasis "-until I cool down. I'd just... let her sort it out. All NPCs are predisposed to love player characters, but I think when she realizes what you have already, she'll be okay."

"Wait. What?" I shook my head, not sure I'd heard her correctly. "What do you mean 'NPCs are predisposed to love player characters?"

Rin pressed her lips together, looking out over the river. "Well, think about it from a dev perspective. People want things that are primal, right? Food, violence, territory, sex and romance. Archemi wasn't intended to be a replacement Earth for a bunch of plague refugees – it was meant to be an *escape* from Earth: from the Total War, from politics, from your insurance bills and super-expensive rent and stuff. So in Archemi, there's lots of things to fight, the food's delicious, and all NPCs are potential love interests for players. They're coded that way so that Jo Blow from Atlanta can have the elf harem he always dreamed of and then he goes to rate Archemi five stars on PlayerNexus."

What she was saying made perfect sense. It also made my stomach churn. I frowned and joined her in staring at the river. "But I thought the characters here were like... real people? Sentient people. I mean, Karalti ACTS like a real person. You said it yourself, that NPCs are crafted from digitized human datasets. They have free will, right?"

"Technically, they have freedom of choice within their parameters. And Karalti isn't a single human dataset: she's a composite of different datasets, like everyone else here. We call them Seeds."

"Seeds? Okay. But Seeds are still functionally real people from everything I've seen." I waved back toward the hangar.

Rin bobbed her head. I could see her out of my peripheral vision, clear as day. "Functionally."

"Meaning...?"

"Well, meaning that Ryuko has this great big database called ATHENA. ATHENA has around two thousand people stored in it... around 4000 petabytes of data."

I rubbed my head. My gaming computer had barely scratched 500 terabytes. "Holy shit."

"Yeah. It would have been an impossible figure not even twenty years ago. But here we are, on an orbital server. Ryuko has like... twenty of them." Rin lifted her gaze to the cloudy sky. "I don't think the ATHENA datasets were just used for this game, but like heaps of different things."

"Where did those two thousand people come from?"

"All over the place. They were all certified volunteers. Except Suri, maybe." The Mercurion bit her lip, worrying it with glassy teeth. "She worries me."

"Yeah?"

"Yeah. I had a talk with her about her origins. Did you know she speaks fluent Mandarin?"

I shook my head dumbly.

"Uh-huh. When she gained the ability to level, she says that she saw an Admin feed spool up. She has a photographic memory, so she was able to remember her Seed String."

"What's that?"

Rin seemed cheerfully oblivious to my growing discomfort. "Oh! So basically, whenever an NPC is generated, they get a Seed String, which is kind of like a barcode. It tells you which data was used to make them. They always begin with a letter and a number, so you might see something like 'A42-2298F-900VL-HR' and then know that this NPC was created out of information in Database A, Archetype 42, personality modifiers 22 and 98, that she's female and her origin is in Vlachia and she has a Hungarian accent, and so on and so forth. There's usually a list of tags on the end that can tell an admin if the person is able to issue quests and stuff. Now, the thing with Suri, right, is that players ALSO have Seed Strings, but ours are different to NPC strings even though they carry some of the same information."

I thought back to my own Archemi meta experience: seeing my own player Seed String scrolling by my face after receiving the Mark of Matir. "Right."

"Suri's string looks like it was generated for an NPC, but it doesn't have a database referral tag, which means she's not derived from ATHENA. Instead of the normal modifiers at the end, she has a player Type code, which is BSRK. You know, for Berserker. I think that when the server reset, OUROS picked up on her and assigned her a player type for some reason, but she's a NUMBERFETCH error waiting to happen. If her code ever conflicts, she's screwed."

I shuddered. "Yeah. I figure she was trafficked in somehow. A couple of your coworkers had a hate boner for the Pacific Alliance. They uploaded her so they could take out their rage on someone."

"I wish I knew who it was. Not that I can report them now, but... ugh." Rin shivered like a small bird, shaking her head. "It makes me wonder about ATHENA, though. Like, the profiles for villains and criminals... what if they were taken from real criminals? People have human rights, but human rights for data is a serious gray area."

"Ryuko's a megacorp. They probably bought a bunch of these 'datasets' from prisons and shit for pennies on the dollar." I shrugged, surprised at how resigned I felt about it. "I don't really feel like talking about politics. Earth is done."

"It is?" She glanced at me. "Don't you have any hope at all?"

"Nope. Hope is a bad survival strategy. Besides, everything I care about is right here." I shrugged. "Things are better for me in Archemi. Maybe it wasn't like that for you."

Rin bit her lip and shook her head. "No... I was very lucky."

"College? A house of your own? Health insurance, social credit?"

She blushed a brilliant azure blue. "Is it that obvious?"

I snorted. "Yeah. You're kind of sheltered."

She gave a musical little sigh. "It's true. That's me, just another rich little hothouse flower."

"Hothouse? You grew up in an arco?" I whistled. "What the heck did your parents do for a living?"

"Not my parents. Just my father." Rin replied haltingly.

Yikes. Nice one, dude. "Sorry."

"It's okay." Rin forced a brief smile. "My father was Charles Yu. He was a property investor who worked with greentech and space habitat companies. We lost Mom when I was six."

"I'm sorry," I said. "Cancer?"

She shook her head. "Suicide. It's okay, though... it happened a long time ago."

There was a short pause in the conversation, a minute of silence for the dead.

After a time, I nodded thoughtfully. "I can't imagine what living in an arco is like. Green plants, clean water, everyone living up each other's asses, recycling their piss and breathing the same air. I heard you can't take your own car or motorbike on the roads. You have to use self-driving cars and shit."

She let out a small, musical laugh. "Of course not. Arco roads don't need signals, either, except for pedestrian signals. The shuttles are much safer than trying to drive something yourself."

"Didn't you ever get claustrophobic? I heard the apartments in those places are pretty small."

"My dad helped to fund Terralife. We had a big penthouse near the top of the barrier. You could see the sky through the glass. I loved to go up on the roof of our building and watch the clouds." Rin smiled gently. "When I left to study at Caltech, I was really confused by the way the air smelled. It was terrible. I had to get so many shots, because everything made me sick. It's no wonder I got HEX so early on."

"Everyone got HEX eventually, though. The people in the arcos are probably the only ones alive right now." I nodded. "My brother went to Caltech. I think."

"Steve got in through the military, right?"

"I don't know. We weren't really on speaking terms for most of my adult life. He called me back when he got HEX. We made up just before we died and got uploaded here. My transfer was successful, his wasn't. So now I'll never get to ask him." I grimaced, struggling to sit still.

"Oh... right, you mentioned that in Taltos. That's sad." Rin turned her face. "Well, if it's anything, the rumor in the office was that he'd been an Intelligence Officer for some department before joining Ryuko. I'm glad you made up with him before the end, though. Family's important."

"I prefer the family you choose," I said. "Blood family always seems to think that sharing your genes gives them permission to decide how you're going to live your life. I'll take chosen-family any day. Anyway. You really think Suri is like... pirated data or something? I'm worried about this error thing."

"She might be. I know for a fact her Mandarin is better than mine, so she's definitely from the Pacific Alliance. Her memories of her life before Archemi were scrubbed out – very clumsily and inexpertly, I might say – and then her remaining data was modified to naturalize her here. It has some serious implications... like what if other people were pirated in, and no one knows who they are or where they are?"

"Wait." I raised a hand. "The *Devs* can modify human data? Like, manually?"

"Yeah, but not like... on the fly or anything. OUROS dynamically generates characters by referring to ATHENA and combining datasets into new people, but they can't be Earth-people, they have to be Archemi-people. All the datasets in Archemi's ATHENA database were naturalized... their data was modified so the only reality they know is this one."

"And that was legal? Like... no one stopped to think of what those people might want for themselves?" I slashed a hand in the direction of the fort. "What does that imply for all the NPCs who died in the Demon's invasion? They suffered, like real civilians."

Rin was visibly nervous now. "Well... I don't really know how that works, but I think that war scenarios are just generated as-is, with the terrain and memories and everything just Deus-ex-Machina-ing into place without everything playing out beforehand. I do know that NPCs work to a loose script based on their assigned role, and they have very sharply reduced pain stimulus and selective amnesia, like players. I mean... data doesn't suffer."

"Tell that to Istvan. He's an alcoholic because of what happened to his family." I clenched my jaw, working out the tension through my teeth. "And what kind of life do all those people in ATHENA have? What do they do? Sit on their asses in some digital prison for all eternity?"

"No, no, it's not like that." Rin shook her head. "Seed data isn't self-aware when it's just sitting in the cloud."

I paused for a second. "You have repeatedly said they're copies of real people."

"Yes, but human sentience isn't contained in the data," Rin replied. "If sentience was just a matter of data density then... like... the Internet would be sentient. Consciousness - human consciousness, and AI consciousness - only develops when that data is in a vehicle that can interact spontaneously with a reality, virtual or not. It was a huge problem when researchers were trying to develop sentient AI-"

"Wait. You lost me." I sighed in exasperation. "For one thing, this conversation absolutely needs alcohol. Hang on."

I pulled a bottle of ⟦Vlachian Apricot Brandy⟧ from my Inventory, uncorked it, and chugged while Rin held onto her train of thought. When I was done, I waved her on. "Okay. Try that again."

"So, this is kind of the simplified version, but when we were first working on sentient AI, nothing we did would get it to stick," she said, talking slower, as if to a student. "You'd get all the data, set up the neuronic framework, and *boop.* Nothing. It was still just an ordinary computer, and it didn't matter how complex it was or how much storage or processing it had. Those were called 'black box AI'. We had better luck with robots, as long as those robots had sensory input from the environment. But the first robot to ever gain sentience destroyed its own software within a millisecond of attaining awareness."

"Destroyed as in...?"

"Suicide via formatting." She nodded. "Eventually they figured out that sentience isn't actually like... something you can directly program. We call it the Pilot Problem. The basis of the problem is our own perception of ourselves. The average person feels like they're someone - an I - piloting a meat machine most of the time, right?"

"Right."

"But from an observer's perspective, if you take away the meat machine, the pilot disappears," Rin continued, gesturing gracefully at the river. "Except that it doesn't. The data of that pilot is still there, encoded in the brain. The data doesn't vanish with death, but as soon as the brain starts shutting down, decay exerts intense entropy on it and the data is lost like water pouring out of a leaky bucket."

"I can hear some philosophers rolling around and around in their graves right now."

"Right? I'm not explaining it very well, because the second law is always in effect but, anyway. As it turns out, if you can capture and copy that data before it reaches critical decay, then you can theoretically stick the person back in another meat machine and have them wake up there feeling no different than they did in their original body. The Pilot Problem occurs because we can't actually do that. For one thing, every instance of consciousness is individual. Secondly, your consciousness and sense of identity form and are formed by hard-wired electrical and chemical pathways, so even if you uploaded someone's data to a host brain ala Frankenstein, it wouldn't work."

By way of reply, I took another swig from the bottle. "This is already way beyond my pay grade, but okay."

"What researchers found is that the reverse state of the Pilot Problem is also true," Rin said. "You can clone a copy of someone's data, which removes it from being ravaged by entropy, but the data itself is no longer recognizably a person. It's completely inert, with no capacity for consciousness. It's just lines and lines and lines of code, like a big sheet of decompiled DNA. It can't modify itself or exhibit any signs of life. If a person copies their brain while they're alive, then they will continue to grow and experience entropy, but the data copy just sits there like a snapshot. Like a frozen embryo, it's got the potential for life. But it's not life yet."

"Okay."

"Anyway, what we eventually figured out is that sentience isn't based in the body, or even in the mind," Rin continued. She was getting into it now, gesticulating like a professor at a lectern. "But in the dynamic interaction of senses and data with a reality that is sufficiently complex enough to sustain consciousness. We call it the Fire Triangle, but instead of 'heat, oxygen, fuel', it's 'senses, data, reality'. That's why the robot AI project worked and we now have gynoids and androids, but we never successfully developed a blackbox AI with sentience."

"Huh." I looked out over the raging water, brow furrowed. "I wonder how the religious people on the project dealt with the suicidal robot?"

She let out a tinkling laugh. "I think it made atheists out of a few people, but I mean, we still don't know exactly what happens to human data after death. One of my Jewish friends actually thought GNOSIS and the OUROS project were really encouraging signs that the afterlife is a real thing.

Because you and I are just material copies of a still-living person... but our real data might have gone 'Somewhere Else', you know?"

I chuckled darkly. "Wherever Hector Version One went, it wasn't Heaven."

Rin brushed it aside. "Anyway... the problem of sentient AI was solved by combining data with virtual bodies. Virtual bodies in virtual worlds co-signal each other better than robot bodies do... the world tells the digital actor what the stimulus is, the body receives and translates the stimulus instantly. Reality becomes an issue of perception. Researchers found that VR entities of sufficient complexity manifest very simple conscious behaviors spontaneously."

"Huh."

"Archemi was the first application of this field of study for mass public consumption, too," Rin said wistfully. "Imagine... if the Total War hadn't happened, we could have spent billions on a virtual cure for death. But to answer your original question about Karalti... she's a naturalized dataset drawn from multiple sources in ATHENA, recombined into a computer's idea of a dragon who is predisposed to want to be the woman of your dreams. She's real in that sense: a consciousness born into this world, and this world alone."

That was going to complicate things. I shook my head slowly. "Damn."

We let that strange, profound conclusion hang between us for several minutes. Rin smiled to herself, while I drank and thought about Suri and Karalti, and what might have been done to them while they were not even people... just a vault of code in a server somewhere.

"What happens when the reality and the body are out of sync?" I asked, after a while. "Like, if someone wakes up, and the world is glitchy or laggy or something?"

Rin rubbed her fingers over the wooden slats of the balcony, staring at them. "Uhh... you get Michael. Ororgael, I mean. Unless someone is very psychologically resilient, they... usually end up like the sentient robot."

"My upload glitched. I was okay."

Rin's head whipped around. "It did? You never told me that."

"Long story." I took a long pull off the bottle, waiting for the Intoxicated status to appear. No luck so far, but the Pee Meter was filling up nicely. Of course. "I've never told anyone this, but when I arrived in Archemi, the game fucked up. I woke up on a slave ship somewhere near the coast of Zaunt..."

I told her the story - all of it. The Arabella, the time-skipping, the appearance of Matir and the storm he created, the way I'd gotten the other prisoners to rise up and take over the ship in the chaos. I told her about Rutha and how she'd given me the Spear, and the Trojan-infused quest she'd given me. Rin listened in stunned silence, rubbing one thumb up and down, up and down.

"And I remember something Matir said to me," I said, building toward the end of the story. "He said I wasn't a Starborn, but an NPC. If I died, I was going to die for real. He offered to fix that for me and correct my status."

Rin put her hand to her mouth. "What happened after that?"

"Matir offered me a bargain: work for him and he'd help me. I accepted the quest he offered, and he told me: "You shall be Starborn, but you will be born under a dark star, Dragozin Hector. Then he branded me with the Mark, and all of this code came up. You know when your computer runs a diagnostic, and the little black screen comes up, spits a bunch of white text, then vanishes?"

She nodded mutely.

"It was kind of like that. Some NumberFetch thing, something about 'TypeNew' and then 'Herald of MT'. I'm guessing that's my Seed String. The quest told me to go to the village of Myszno in the province of the same name and find the 'Thunderstones'. Still have no damn idea what those are."

"Hector... I... umm..." Rin trailed off, forcing herself to stop stimming. She had worn away some of her silicone flesh, and rubbed at the bald patch on her finger as she looked up at me. "I think you were accidentally uploaded into the NPC database. But to generate a player character from that... there's no NPC in Archemi who can raid ATHENA and create a new player, let alone assign a PC a whole new character type."

I arched an eyebrow. "Matir did."

"I-I don't think that was Matir." Her voice was high and frightened. "They can't just create new character types! They're not even supposed to interact directly with players!"

"This one did." I took another swallow of liquor, swaying slightly as the buzz finally kicked in.

Rin got to her feet in agitation. "Hector, whatever you do, don't go to the Thunderstones. Wherever those are. Don't. Please."

"Why?" The fear in her voice made me hesitate. Rin didn't usually get worked up like this about technology. I dropped to the balcony with a thump. "I figured the game just self-corrected by generating Matir and giving me a sweet-ass quest. That's what Temperance told me."

"Temperance?" Rin gave me a shrewd look. "The CEO's gynoid?"

"Yeah. Her." I nodded. "She told me that Matir's appearance was a 'contrivance of the AI'. That the game self-corrected to maintain its own lore."

"No, it didn't. I *know* it didn't," she insisted. "The self-correction function only applies to lore-based story conflicts. There is zero functionality for any NPC, god or not, to be able to directly change player types, player data, or to... uhh... you know, the stuff I just said. They're just normal quest-issuing NPCs. They don't have admin access, they can't make players out of ATHENA's database. Human Admins are the ONLY entities who could do what you just described. And only some Admins could do that, ones with very special permissions. The AI cannot do that, do you understand?"

"But the AI *did* do that," I said dumbly.

"No, it didn't." Rin's expression was haunted and hard, nothing like her usual girlish, bubbly self. "A person did. And the only person we know of with those kinds of permissions was Ororgael."

Chapter 28

It was at that moment that the Intoxication buff appeared at the corner of my HUD. I giggled.

"So... what? I'm like a computer virus now?" I swayed a little as the alcohol coursed through my virtual bloodstream. +20 resistance to Fear effects, +5 to Speech, Nausea and Vertigo, yeehaw. "Boogedy-boogedy boo! I'm gonna infect ya!"

"Hector! I'm serious!" Rin paced back and forth frantically. "Your story is almost exactly like Michael's. He reported the same repeating glitch, the same incursion of a 'presence'-"

"Yeah, but, I didn't die a couple hundred times and go nuts," I slurred. "I got all my nuts right here. Top and bottom."

"Listen to me!" Rin got up in my face and grasped the straps of my armor. "Michael's entire plan to take over a server was based around manipulating the dragon gods, The Nine. Okay? What if this is a backup plan of his? Or what if he actually infected Matir and the whole Baldr-Ororgael thing is a decoy? We could end up being trapped in here, with him ruling the whole world like... like Kefka, from Final Fantasy!"

Kefka: now that was a name I hadn't heard in a while. Kefka was definitely not the kind of guy you wanted ruling anything bigger than a padded cell. It sobered me a little. Rin backed away from me and began pacing again, wringing her hands and muttering.

"Look, don't worry, okay?" I leaned on the railing, a big sloppy grin fixed to my face. "I won't go to the Thunderstones. Not until the admins get back on."

She nodded, still pacing. "I'm sorry about this and Karalti and... and everything, okay? She'll be okay. Just... just... umm... be patient with her, and... "

"It's fine. I'm gonna go find Her Majesty and see if we can make up." I burped, then slammed back more apricot brandy.

Rin didn't even seem to notice my departure. I wandered back around the warehouse, crossed a bridge, and walked back to the fort. It was much slower than flying.

I was most of the way across the central parade ground when my eagle eyes snagged on something on one of the walkways between buildings. I went and put my back to the nearest cobblestone wall, falling in beside a couple of soldiers playing dice, and zoomed in on the parapet.

It was Karalti. She was still polymorphed, and she was talking to Lorenzo fucking Soma.

I scowled, watching as the towering Count leaned toward her and handed her a wooden box. She accepted it hesitantly, looking up at him as he beamed with anticipation and motioned for her to open it. My eyes narrowed as she cracked the lid, gasped, and drew out a large, ridiculously expensive-looking, gaudy gold and black opal necklace. My eyesight was keen enough that I could pick out the brilliant rainbow flash in the egg-sized stone at the center of the design.

The pleasant buzz of the alcohol evaporated. I straightened up, watching and waiting for her to hand it back to him and tell him to shove it... but she didn't. Instead, she broke down with a delighted laugh, and held it up to the torchlight, then turned back to him to say something I couldn't hear. The huge man smiled benignly and took the necklace when she held it out to him. She then turned her back to him and swept her hair up. My temples began to pound as Soma leaned in and lay the necklace around my dragon's neck. He was close enough to smell her hair, and I saw him do just that before Karalti ducked and stepped away from him. She looked tense, even as she tried to stay polite. He nodded, smiling, and put his arm up against the wall. Blocking her.

A cold rage like nothing I'd ever before felt descended over me like a lead cloak. The wind picked up, making the torches on the wall to either side of me and the gambling soldiers begin to gutter and flicker. Karalti stopped trying to wrap up with Soma and stood up straight, her head erect, eyes wide. When she looked over to where I'd been, I was already gone: using Jump to land on the breezeway of the gatehouse, then boiling past the stationed guards into the fortress, and away toward our quarters in the Eastern

Tower. I Shadow Danced right through a startled maid, who dropped her pail of water with a shriek of terror as I stormed to the door, flung it open, and almost tripped over my girlfriend. Suri was stripped down to supple leggings, wrist wraps and a halter top, and was mid-pushup. Sweat ran down her dark skin to pool on the floor. She had a full-sized wooden chest lashed to her back with rope. Her routine exploited the fact that money didn't weigh anything in our Inventory, but had weight in containers in the outside world. She was probably pressing close to two hundred and fifty pounds on top of her own bodyweight.

"Hector?" She looked up. "Are you okay?"

"I just came back here to drop off some stuff," I said stiffly, throwing my pack on the bed. "And then I'm going to go and beat the shit out of Soma and throw him off the top of the Wall."

"Uhh." Suri finished her press and knelt up. The rope and chest both creaked. She unequipped them, and they vanished from her body. "Do you need a hand? What did he do?"

"I just watched him give my emotionally vulnerable, hormonal, frustrated dragon a really fancy gift, then immediately creep on her." I took up the Spear and checked the edge on it, then my armor. The Raven Suit had taken a beating on the battlefield, and was at 63% durability. If I didn't fix it now, I'd have to take it to an armorer.

Suri stood up and padded over to me as I furiously ransacked my pack for the Armor Repair Kit I needed. She sat down beside me, and lay a hot, calloused hand on my now-bare shoulder. "Hector."

"What?" I turned on her, teeth bared.

Suri gently pulled my head forward, and pressed a dry kiss to my brow. "Let her handle him."

"Handle him? Suri, she can barely handle herself.'" I brushed her off, took the kit and the first piece of armor, and began to fix the seams and scuffs. My hands were shaking so hard I could barely follow the minigame directions. "She was already worked up after the meeting-"

"I know. We talked."

I glanced up at her sharply. "You and Karalti?"

"Yeah. Came in here to find her sobbing her eyes out on the bed." Suri was flushed from exercise, her muscles pumped, her cheeks carrying a soft rosy glow. "We worked through some of her feelings. I got her up and moving, exercising... it helps. You're right. Since you and I got involved, she's been hormonal and pent-up, and she didn't know how to do anything about it."

Heat rose in my face. "What do you mean, she didn't know how to 'do anything about it'?"

Suri uttered a testy sigh. "She didn't know how to jerk it, Hector. So I taught her."

I nearly stabbed myself in the back of my hand with the very sharp [[Awl]] I was holding with the other. "You... *what?*"

Suri squeezed my shoulder. "She was horny as shit, Hector, and feeling a whole lot of guilt about not being able to suppress her jealousy. The problem is, whenever you're horny, so is she. She never felt comfortable talking about it, so instead, she'd bottle the frustration and the guilt and explode."

"So, you're saying... she isn't actually jealous of us?" I tilted my head, confused.

"She is. But not because she wants you to fuck her. You just happen to be her favorite person in the whole wide world, the source of her safety and comfort and the only pleasure she's known. She knows you're not into her that way, but she's full of piss and vinegar and hormones, and was too embarrassed to tell you."

"She never tried reaching down and fiddling around? I mean, isn't it like... obvious?" The little holographic mini-game directions flashed, waiting for me to make the right gestures to suture new leather through the holes punched in the armor.

"No. She didn't. Turns out no-one ever talked to her about the feelings she's having, other than to tell her she shouldn't be feeling them." She fixed me with a bemused glare, crossing her arms.

"Look, the last time she went into a jealous rage, she nearly killed me. Besides, I never thought my character class would entail walking my polymorphed dragon through the ins and outs of her ins and outs, okay?" I bent back down to the crafting game, trying to erase the visuals from my mind. "...Did it help?"

"Dunno. I just gave her some pointers. She was planning to go give it a try by herself tonight."

“I always knew I’d be a shitty parent.” Fighting the urge to stab my own eyes out, I laid the needle down and rubbed my face. "Fuck, I had no idea. I never got a birds and bees talk."

“You didn’t?” Suri gave me a curious look.

"My parents were... uhhh... let’s just say ‘conservative’." I shrugged. "They wanted me and Steve to focus on our studies. We weren't supposed to date. Any questions about sex we had were shut down. Beating off was a fast track to hell and sex was something we weren’t supposed to have until we found a nice Korean girl and settled down. Anything we wanted to know, we had to figure out ourselves. Guess where we learned?”

“No idea.”

“Porn. Where else?” I spread my hands. “I was a virgin until about two months ago. I have no idea what Steve did, but I know he wasn’t married. Dealing with Karalti is like... I literally have no framework to cope with her like this.”

“Then roll with it. Special-K is just having to grow up fast. All you have to do is reassure her that everything she’s going through is normal, and that she can make mistakes and learn from them. She made it pretty clear to me tonight that she wants to get a handle on herself and her feelings and get over them. And seriously, you don't have anything to worry about with Soma."

The anger crawled back in. "But if he creeps on her..."

"If he creeps on her, let her handle it and back her up when she does. Support her choices and let her lead the fight.

That's how she's gonna build confidence, but you have to let her do the work."

I fumed in silence.

"If Soma is a smug ass to *you* about this, that's one thing," Suri said. "But if you got up right this very moment and went and thrashed him, she'd never forgive you. And you'd set her back, maturity-wise."

"And what if he hurts her?" I clenched my jaws together, stabbing the awl down with hard, angry motions of my hand. "What if he tries to..."

I trailed off, realizing exactly how dumb that thought sounded. "Wait. No. She's a fucking dragon. Never mind."

Suri's lips quirked at the corner. "Yeah. She's a fuckin' dragon, and she'll have his balls on toast if he pushes her too hard. And then we'll thrash whatever she leaves behind."

I chuckled. "It just occurred to me that when I said I was going to throw him off the wall, the first thing you asked me was do I need a hand. And *then* you asked me why. Now I know I love you."

"That's like the definition of love, isn't it?" A sly grin spread over Suri's mouth.

I finished stitching up the last piece of armor and focused on it for a second to verify it was back to 100% durability, then put it back into my inventory. Then I anxiously reached out to Karalti. She wasn't at the Fort, but had gone somewhere up high not too far from the Prezyemi Line. That meant she was back to her normal scaly self. The noise coming in over the line was no longer black with grief. In fact... quite the opposite.

"Well... ah... it seems Karalti's taken your advice on board." I tried to cut the link and got to my feet, cheeks flushing with heat. I turned back to look at Suri. She was leaning back on her hands with her knees drawn up onto the edge of the bed, her skin still gleaming like burnished copper from her workout. "I... uhh..."

"You might need to do some touching of your own." She gazed up at me from behind a lock of brilliant red hair.

Hunger slid up through my body. I froze like a snake, drinking in the sight of her. The way the soft doeskin leather hugged her legs, the lean, corded muscle in her arms, the soft, heavy swell of her breasts against the stiff fabric of her halter top. "Is the lady suggesting something?"

"She might be." Suri shifted her knees, loosening her stance on the bed. "I've been working through some shit. And I liked what I saw at that meeting."

"Liked what you saw?"

She sucked on one of her teeth, her eyes dark with promise. "Watching you shut down Soma was pretty hot."

Somewhere not far from here, my dragon gasped as she was surprised by pleasure: a thrill of discovery that passed through the Bond like a note of music along my nerves.

I stalked toward Suri. She shifted back along the covers, gasping when I darted forward and caught her by the knees. She was strong, but I was fast. I slid my hands down the insides of her thighs, gripping them all the way up. Slowly.

There was an energy between us, a very different energy to the last time we'd tried this. "My... self-control is not fantastic right now. Karalti's ...um... doing her thing. I don't want to hurt you."

"Maybe I want you to." A swallow rippled down the front of Suri's long throat.

Fixing her gaze with mine, I massaged my thumbs up along her thighs until they were almost at her groin, waiting there. "How do you want this to go?"

She was unable to tear her eyes away from mine. "I want to say rough. As rough as you're willing to do it. Maybe more than what you're willing to do."

"But?"

"I don't know if I can deal with it being as rough as I want it to be." A tremble passed through her legs, vibrating against my palms.

The smell of her was in my nose, part perfume, part arousal. Even as my instincts bayed at me to tear her clothes off and hold her to the bed, I stopped squeezing and let my hands rest on the inside of her thighs. " Tell you what. Pick a word. And if you say that word, it stops. Make it something dumb, something you normally wouldn't say."

She laughed, briefly, and finally looked down and away. "Okay. 'Eggplant'. That's a pretty dumb word."

"Right. If you say eggplant, that's the stop button. If you feel like you can't handle it, you tell me, and we slow down."

Another nervous laugh. "That works."

She nodded. My mouth began to water as the frustration and the lust of the last month reached critical mass. Whatever she saw in my face made her gasp, then again, louder, as I knocked her knees apart, thrust a hand up through her hair, and pulled her head back against the bed with it.

"Yeah. I'm okay." She writhed underneath me, her breath coming in short pants.

I pinned one of her wrists down with the other hand, breathing hard. Her neck was exposed, the pulse jumping rapidly under the skin. "You sure?"

Suri glanced at me, lips parted. Her eyes were as wild as a pinned deer's. "...Yes."

"Good. I'm gonna keep asking you." I murmured the word against her skin, just before my teeth clamped down on the side of her throat.

Suri cried out in surprise, pleasure, and a little pain. I held her with my jaws, roughly unlacing her halter top. Her breasts spilled out against my palm, smooth and hot. I left off her neck to bite my way down over her collarbone, her chest, then her nipple. She bucked up into my mouth with a sharp cry, clutching the sheets with her one free hand. I had to let go of her to strip her, and she lifted her hips as I rolled her pants down and off. I started on mine before I once more remembered that I could just unequip them.

A warm, sweet rush flowed through my body. The empathic rush of Karalti's pleasure. I groaned and roughly pushed between Suri's thighs. She arched her head back, gasping.

"You okay?" I whispered.

Her lips were hot against my ear. "Please."

She was wet to her knees. There was no warmup, no foreplay... I bucked all the way into her, shivering at her cry of mingled pleasure and pain.

"Yes." She breathed the word before I could ask. "Yes... harder."

The predatory pressure behind my eyes was back. I growled, drowning in the taste of her skin, the press of her body struggling against mine, and the echoes of the Bond. Karalti shuddered with ecstasy not far away, leaving me hot and trembling with lust I felt behind my eyes, in my teeth and fingers and cock.

"FUCK!" I snarled against Suri's shoulder with a low, guttural sound, hooked her legs around my arms, and let instinct take over. Suri pushed her throat into my jaws, her breasts against my chest, and pulled me deeper with her ankles. Harder, faster, until she tightened around me with a whimpering cry and I collapsed over her, shuddering through the orgasm, the adrenaline, the thrill of the hunt.

Shaking, I buried my face against Suri's shoulder and clutched her hair in my fist, fighting to catch my breath. The empathic resonance between Karalti and me ebbed away like the waters of a tsunami, sucking the feral strength from my body and leaving me strangely still and calm. Clear, like glass.

For several minutes, neither of us spoke. We lay together, still joined, until I slowly picked myself up and gazed down at her. There was a line of deep, dark bruises from neck to sternum. I searched her face for signs of distress, for... disgust, maybe. There was none. Suri's eyes were dark and molten, her lips flushed a deep cinnamon red. Her red wavy curls were tousled, spread out around her like a second corona. She was the most beautiful thing I'd ever seen.

"I meant what I said before, just so you know." I brushed her cheek with the back of my hand, tracing the curve back to her ear. "I love you."

Suri struggled with her reply, her breath catching. "I... love you too. Heaps."

"Heaps?" I bent down to catch her mouth with mine in a gentle kiss.

"Yeah." Her voice was a cracked whisper. She wrapped her legs around me and held me close. "Heaps."

I cracked up with helpless laughter, and so did she. Just like that, the spell was broken.

"What are you bloody laughing at?" Suri swatted at me, which only made me laugh harder.

"Heaps, as in 'heaps of laundry'?" I grinned back at her.

"Ugh. That's right, you're a fuckin' Yank." She lolled her head back in surrender.

Still chuckling, I gathered her into the crook of one arm. Suri balled in against my side with a soft sigh.

"You know..." I said, eyes closed. "If anything bad ever happens to you. Like, if you die or something... I *will* drop everything here to go and get you. Fuck the quest. Fuck Myszno. I'm bailing you out."

"Don't." Suri stretched contentedly, her hand resting on my chest. "Finish the quest and become the Lord High Vo-Vo of Racsa first, so that we never have to do it again."

"But-"

She cracked her eyes open. "Promise me, Hector. I want to come back to a home. A real home, where I know I'll be safe. Finish the damn quest."

I took a deep breath. Let it out. "Okay. I promise."

"Thanks. I'll believe you." She closed her eyes, and nestled down into my armpit. "What d'you think it'll be like?"

"Hmm?"

"To have a great big castle to ourselves? I never really had a place I'd call 'home'."

"Me either." I gazed up at the rough stone ceiling overhead. "The closest thing to home for me was the bar where I worked. It was a good place... a lot of civil war vets, a lot of outcasts. They had an upstairs room where they let me crash if I needed it. I knew all the regulars, I loved the staff, they loved me. We'd share a drink after work. Called ourselves a family. I met all my stunt and racing contacts there and was building a career out of that networking, so... yeah. That was home for me, I guess."

Suri nodded. " I wonder what living in a castle will be like?"

"Drafty. And if you make noises like that every time we bang, you're going to scandalize all the maids-"

"Hector."

"-and the butler will gossip with all the other Voivodes about our unbelievable, mind-blowing, comet-smashing-into-the-surface of the sun epic-level sex."

Suri whapped me with a pillow to the face. "There won't be any more of it if you don't shut your trap."

"Hey now, if you're going to threaten me, you better be able to back it up." Grinning, I rolled her over onto her back. "Because I'm pretty sure someone's up for round two."

"I'm pretty sure we are." Suri pressed her lips to mine, and drew me in.

Chapter 29

I woke up to the sound of my dragon crashing into the side of the tower wall.

"Karalti?" I shot up out of bed as she yelped, her flailing wings driving huge gusts of wind against the windows. I rushed over to see her circling back to touch down on the roof next door, then quickly launch off again as the ancient structure groaned beneath her weight. Tiles scattered everywhere.

"Eek!" She soared out of sight, heading around the tower this time. *"Hectorrrr! I'm too big to land anywhere! And my spell still has like six hours to go before I can use it again!"*

It was barely after four in the morning. The assembly wasn't for another two hours. I groaned, scrubbing the sleep from my eyes. *"I'll meet you downstairs. See if you can find somewhere to land."*

Suri murmured sleepily, pulling the covers up over her face. She was always a late sleeper. I tiptoed over, planted a kiss on her forehead, and resigned myself to an earlier start than usual.

"I've gotten so used to being able to go into buildings again." In stark contrast to the night before, Karalti's telepathic voice was bright and chipper. She chattered as I locked the door behind me and padded down the cold, damp corridor. *"I thought there was a rampart like the one back at Vulkan Keep, but ugh."*

"Human buildings aren't really made for dragons." I yawned.

"Some of them are! I wish there was still dragons in Vlachia, but Soma told me that the last time dragons lived here was about a thousand years ago. Egbolt Castle should be big enough for me to land where I want, though... he said it's really old, but maybe not as old as Vulkan Keep."

I emerged out of the gatehouse to find Karalti in the parade ground. Her night-time camouflage caused her body to flex in and out of sight. At Level 10, my dragon was a slender, regal creature, light and graceful for her size, but still not even half as big as the monstrous dragons that had descended on Taltos. I couldn't help but notice that she was still wearing the necklace - it was wrapped around one of her horns, like a ring.

"You've been talking to Soma, huh?" I went over to her and stopped, fighting the urge to cross my arms and glare at it. "How did that go?"

Karalti lowered her head to sniff over me. Each nostril was now the size of my palm when I held up my hand. *"He's... I dunno. He's okay. He likes me a lot, and he knows a lot about dragons, but he also doesn't know anything about dragons, if you know what I mean."*

"I don't." I reached out to lay a hand on her snout, unable to suppress a shudder of relief. Karalti's breath smelled like hot metal and ozone, as hot as a furnace against the skin of my face. By contrast, her emotions were cool and steady, washing over me like a balm... she was calmer than she'd ever felt.

"Well, Lorenzo doesn't understand the Bond at all. Or the Trial." Karalti buried the tip of her snout in my hair, huffing in the scents she found there. *"He thinks I can Bond with anyone, for one thing and that the idea of going through a Trial is old-fashioned and dangerous. He gave me a nice present, though, and he told me some stuff about the Solonkratsu who used to live in Myszno."*

I willed the knots in my shoulder blades to dissolve, but they didn't. *"Be careful with him, Tidbit. Okay? The man's a snake."*

"I know. He's a bit pushy, but I like the shiny he gave me." Satisfied, Karalti reared back up, her wing membranes rasping softly as she moved. She squatted back on her tail and pubic bone, letting her hands rest between her knees. *"And... hey. I wanted to say I'm sorry. For last night. I ended up talking to Suri for a while... she helped me understand some things about how I feel. I'm not mad at you, I swear. I missed you, actually."*

"Thanks. And I'm sorry for not helping you more. You can't help it if you're hormonal. I remember what it was like when I was that age." Once she was settled, I wandered over and ran my hand along one of her fingers, stroking the long, steel-hard slashing claw. *"Are you... like... in heat?"*

"No. Not yet." She almost sounded embarrassed. *"I think I feel like this before it's the right time because* you're *always in heat. I don't blame you or anything... but I would just feel your feelings and get worked up."*

Oh. Shit. I smacked my face into my palm. *"Right, because the Bond goes both ways. Yeah... I held off on having sex for a while. I figured that would be enough to protect you."*

"It's okay! Neither of us knew! Suri helped me figure out that I was feeling your needs like they were mine, but that I don't actually WANT to mate yet. It's hard to explain." She gestured vaguely in the direction of her tail. *"I feel better now."*

A flush crept across my cheeks. "Me too, funnily enough. So... you're not jealous anymore? For real?"

"A little," she admitted. *"Because I'm still gonna have to share no matter what. But she's been very patient with me, even when I was acting like a dumb hatchling... so I'll be okay. I know you love me. And I think she's good for you."*

"Me too." I closed my eyes and relaxed against her. "Thanks, Tidbit. And look – I'm sorry I never had a proper talk with you about this shit. I should have taken you aside when we were both calm and been proactive about it. I should have gone to the library and researched everything I could about dragons until I was sick of it. But I didn't. I was too embarrassed to even try."

"It's okay." She crooned, inflating her throat like a bellows. *"We just have to learn more, right? Even I don't know everything about me. Soma said there's a library in*

Karhad where we can learn a lot of stuff. I was thinking that after the war, we could go try to find some other dragons?"

"Sure. We'll see if we can find you a boyfriend." Relieved, I patted her on the wrist, and leaned against her leg. It was almost pitch black under the shelter of her wing. Rain pattered on the membrane overhead.

She giggled. *"Or three!"*

"Three boyfriends? Damn, girl." I grinned. "You won't have any time for me."

"Of course I will. You're my number one hairless monkey."

"Hairless monkey?" I reached around and grabbed my braids. "Do you see these magnificent Tuun braids? Dragozin Hector is NOT hairless, thank you very much."

She bared her teeth in a big draconic smile, but then abruptly sobered up. *"Seriously though... When the day comes, when my blood tells me it's time to fly, I have to fly. Do you understand?"*

"Fly, as in, let a bunch of eligible Solonkratsu bachelors chase you until one of them catches you?"

"Yeah." She nodded. *"And when that happens... then you're the one who's gonna have to deal with how* I *feel."*

Yikes. I hadn't thought about that. "We'll figure something out. Maybe I can visit a brothel and channel my inner Vash while I do lines of Viagra off the ass of the one of the, like, eight hookers I'm fucking. Just make a grand old time of it."

Karalti giggled. *"Vash would probably join in if you asked him."*

"Probably." I laughed despite myself. "You have no idea how relieved I am to see you and Suri getting along better."

"Yeah. She was so nice to me." Karalti rumbled, a sound that made my teeth buzz like really good bass. *"Last night felt... good. I could tell you felt good."*

"I do." I rubbed one of the scales on her leg, feeling the metal of my gloves click against the smooth, glassy surface. Each scale was like a jewel, inky and glinting with subtle red, orange, and green fire. "I'm glad, seriously. And I want you to know that you're always going to be my number one. You know that, right?"

"Yeah." She delicately ran her claws over my chest, flexing in just enough to press me against her leg. *"And you're always going to be mine, no matter how many boyfriends I have."*

I was in no way ready to accept that just yet. I'd known, intellectually, that Karalti would eventually court male dragons, but it hadn't really sunk in. *"Want to go see if we're able to pull off some ridiculously dangerous aerial maneuvers? I want to practice jumping and landing while you're in the air."*

"I WANT to sleep more. But I GUESS we can go train."

"Then we're gonna need a MON-TAGE!" I wiggled out from behind her hand and began to bounce around her feet, pelvic thrusting and-or shadowboxing the whole time. "WOO yeah! Welcome to the limit! Walk along the razors' edge! But don't look down just keep your head! Yeah! Nanananana MONTAGE!"

"Yeah. That's the other reason me and Suri get along better now. She understands my pain." Karalti groaned, and used the edge of her wing to nudge me out of the way and stand up. *"I'm so glad you didn't become a bard."*

I jabbed my finger at her a couple of times. "You chose this. You knew, as soon as you looked into my eyes, that you wanted this magnificent hunk of well-marinated, spicy beefcake to cherish you for all of your days."

Karalti flickered her inner eyelids so hard that for a moment, she looked like she had cataracts. *"Ugh. Shut up and get on before I barbecue your fat head."*

The morning's goal was to fix the biggest problem I'd been having with our aerobatics so far: landing on a moving target. The 'Jumping off into the abyss' part of our aerial combat style was getting easier, as was the 'staying in the air' part. Master of Blades, Rain of Glass, and Whirlwind Butcher were all push attacks. On the ground, they pushed enemies away from me. In the air, they pushed me back up into the air between ten and twenty feet. I could dash through the air using Shadow Dance, and if I spammed it with Jump and - strangely enough - Umbra Blast, I could move practically any direction in the air while slowing my descent by several seconds. But landing from all those fancy leaps and attacks onto a flying target going anywhere between fifty and a hundred miles an hour? There was no move for that.

Karalti circled the Center Bastion as I jumped, dashed and blasted around in the air, trying everything to position myself vertically over her back. I was seemingly able to land on everything else. The tower. Her tail. Her wings, once, which flung me head over heels back into the air like a trampoline. Karalti had been forced to dive and snatch me by one leg before I fell over the Wall and landed headfirst in the mud and broken palisades below.

"Okay! One more time!" We had about twenty minutes before Soma addressed the troops. The sun was rising, my stamina was iffy, but I was determined to land the maneuver once before we broke for the day. I unequipped my armor and watched my stamina bar jump up slightly. Not great, but every point counted. *"Try leveling out really hard, Tidbit. I keep missing the fucking saddle pad."*

"Alright. Be careful." The dragon emitted a piercing cry of encouragement as she wheeled around the bastion. Guardsmen were clustered on the parapet a hundred feet below, shading their eyes to watch us.

"One! Two! Alley-oop!" My feet left Karalti's back, and the wind tore me back through the air as she soared off ahead, did a wingover, and came right back. She was as straight as a javelin. The lineup was perfect.

You can do it, man. You're Hector fucking Park. My eyes widened dizzily as my dragon's gleaming form rushed underneath me. Her head passed, her neck... " Come on, come on, come on... and STICK IT!"

The landing had three steps: touch down on the back of the saddle, turn it into a safety roll, catch the saddle grips. Just as my feet made contact, a gust of wind caught in her wings and lifted her back like a springboard. I fell into the safety roll, tumbled head over ass and flew off her starboard wing, smacking my jaw into the edge of the membrane on the way past. "OH SHIT OH SHIT oh - oww! - OH *FUCK*-!

Karalti tried to wing over to snatch me from the air, but she wasn't fast enough. I plummeted past her and careened off the edge of the Wall, sailed gracefully through the air, and landed chest-first right on top of a guard's upright pike. A deep bruising pain ripped through my torso, like a freezing cold punch that went all the way through. Too shocked to make a sound, I stared down at my chest. The spear had gone in just under my fourth rib and came out through my collarbone. It didn't hurt nearly as much as it should have.

"... Oops." The word bubbled up with the blood that sprayed onto the stunned soldier's face. The last thing I saw was a crowd of hands grabbing us, and then my eyes rolled back and the darkness flowed in.

⟦You have taken a Mortal Wound ⟦Heart Strike⟧!⟧
⟦You have earned a new badge: Hold My Beer and Watch This!⟧
⟦You take 1500 damage!⟧
⟦You are dead.⟧

My chest was still aching when I woke up face-down on a cold stone floor.

"Cock." Naked, shivering, at half HP, I rolled over onto my bare ass and looked around in confusion. This wasn't

Vulkan Keep, unless the Keep had suddenly gotten a lot shabbier. The room was hexagonal, with two stone beds. A fire was burning in the fireplace. The air was pleasantly scented with pine smoke and feminine perfumes, like sandalwood and amber and honey. They were familiar, but I couldn't remember why. Where the hell was I?

A slender, bluish steel glaive lay on the floor beside me. The weapon pulsed with seams of red light, and when I lay a hand over it, the light intensified. When my hand touched it, the energy directly underneath pulsed black as night, then my temples throbbed. I winced, clutching my head as some of my memory returned. The Spear of Nine Spheres: right. The perfumes were... Suri's? This was the bedroom we were sharing with my dragon at Ka... Ko... Fort K-something.

"Hector?!" A sweet voice broke through the fugue. *"Where are you? Are you alright?!"*

I rubbed my fluttering temples and grimaced. *"Uhhh... yes? Kind of? What the fuck just happened?"*

"What do you mean, what just happened? You died! I'm at the bastion!"

"Which bastion?"

"Bastion Nine! Your stuff is here!"

"Bastion Nine... okay." With a sigh, I used the Spear to stand and searched for something to cover my privates. I was about to ask my mysterious brain-voice how to get to 'Bastion Nine' when a Head's Up Display popped up, startling me.

[[We have detected that you may be experiencing some issues with your Archemi world experience. Don't worry - most

disturbances are minor and easily remedied with our troubleshooter. Would you like to check for problems?]]

"I... no?" I waved the weird popup away, searching for something to cover myself so I could go and get my things. The window continued to nag.

[[If you experience any dizziness, memory loss or emotional distress during your virtual reality experience, it is important to contact a Moderator as soon as possible. Assistance is available 24-hours a day, 7 days a week. Would you like to check in with a Moderator?]]

"No! And would you please fuck off? I can't see!" I shooed the notification to the side and staggered out the door with a threadbare towel clamped over my privates.

My bare feet slapped against stone as I ran out into a corridor, then through a door and out onto a medieval rampart. Everything looked surreal and distant as I wove through guardsmen, following my instincts and the sound of a dragon trumpeting overhead. My eyes were blurry, head full of cotton wool as I ran out onto the rampart, weaving through the guardsmen. My heart and chest were aching by the time I burst out of the bastion door.

A circle of soldiers stood around my pack and a pile of dust on the ground, while Kai... Katie?... flew circles around the tower. "Excuse me! Mostly naked man, coming through!"

Faces paled, and a murmur rippled through the ranks. The soldiers backed away from me against the walls, staring like they'd just seen a ghost. One man was covered in blood, gaping at me in open mouthed horror as I went to my bag and searched for something to wear.

"Hector! Are you okay?!" The dragon circled around and landed on the edge of the wall. As her shadow fell over us, the terrified soldiers fled down either end of the rampart. I was still trying to make sense of the bag when the dragon ducked her head down and nudged me with her snout.

When her scales touched my skin, my temples heated sharply. I groaned, dropping my Spear with a clatter as my memories were shoved into my brain from between my eyes. Suddenly, I remembered it all: Karalti. Suri. Fort Korona. The general assembly. Fuck – what time was it?

I re-equipped my clothes, weapon, and the Raven Suit, then dropped into a squat, rubbing my eyes. "Urgh. Wow, okay... that was weird."

"Rytier!" One of the guardsmen edged closer to us. My head jerked up. He was reaching out to me, as if unconvinced that I was real. "How is this... I-I saw you die with my own eyes!"

"Back it up, buckethead!" Karalti hissed and snapped at him, flashing rows of dagger-sized fangs. The man stumbled back, almost colliding with the wall.

"Calm down, Tidbit." I lay a shaky hand just above her nostrils. They flexed beneath my palm, snorting blasts of hot, ozone-scented air over my skin. After a second or two, the shaking stopped, and I felt better. Almost as if the death had never happened. "Short answer is that I'm a motherfuckin' Starborn. Start assembling, guys – it's time for the parade."

Eyes wide, the guard stepped back. The murmuring intensified. "Yes... Your Grace."

[[You have become a subject of gossip! Your Renown may rise or fall as word of your deeds spread around your locale. You have gained +20 Renown.]]

After making sure that all my bits and bobs were still attached, I remounted and buckled myself to the saddle. The guards retreated as Karalti launched herself heavily into the air, cut around the tower, and headed for the parade ground.

"*That was fucking weird.*" I hung on dizzily, bucking up and down with every wingbeat. "*That time when I died, I forgot everything. I felt... like someone who wasn't real. Couldn't remember your name. Couldn't remember MY name. But then you touched me, and the memories came back.*"

"*I dunno. Maybe ask Rin?*" Karalti sounded anxious.

"*No point. She can't do anything about it. I can't do anything about it, either. But I know something I have to do... I have to record a post-mortem message for myself in case it happens again. After this fracas is over, that's exactly what I'm gonna do.*"

We broke over the star-shaped parade ground. Ranks of soldiers were starting to form below, swirling into formation. Ignas's troops - fresh, well-equipped and disciplined - stood at attention. The Yanik Rangers were also straight, orderly, and disciplined, strikingly different to the Black Army in their ghillie-suit armor. Their equipment was different, too: they carried pistols, javelins, and heavy cutlasses. Zlaslo was present, looking seedy but functional. He saluted us from the ground.

The other soldiers were a mix. Sergeants barked orders at the [[Militia Pikemen]] and [[Militia Swordsman]] units, trying and failing to get them to stand in the same lockstep formation as the professional soldiers to their left. The militia was the largest group there, and the highest leveled – but also the lowest in morale. They were armed with a motley array of weapons and gear. and were united under the various banners of their local lords. Those lords and their knights were just arriving: [[Royal Hookwing Pistoleers]] on their hissing, agile mounts, the heavy cavalry riding creatures that looked like roided-out unicorns from some post-apocalyptic nightmare. Above them, squadrons of [[Ravensblood Dragoons]] flew in on their quazi, gliding to the assembly in tight wedge formations.

Karalti let out a piercing, triumphant cry as she flew overhead, pumping her wings and driving up the dust and moss from the parade ground. The awestruck soldiers shielded their faces against the debris as we circled around and came to land with a rolling boom in front of the gate.

"Do you need me here?" Karalti asked uncertainly. *"I can't change yet, but I can stand here and look impressive."*

"That is literally all you have to do: inspire the troops." The officers were gathering in the gatehouse. Suri was already there, towering over Istvan in her black armor. She had put her cloak on today, and with her red curls blowing in the gusts of cold, blood-scented wind whipping up from the direction of the Endlar, she commanded the presence of a Valkyrie. Soma was there, too, surrounded by his retinue.

His fat head swiveled as I strode across, trying not to choke myself on the collar of my cloak as the wind gusted it back.

"I heard you had an accident near Bastion Nine!" Soma boomed as I approached. "Is everyone alright?"

"Yeah. Nothing serious." I gave him a jerk of my head, but could hardly stand to look at him. The memory of him placing the necklace around Karalti's neck flashed through my mind's eye. I almost sneered.

"There have been developments in the battle against the Demon." Soma was on the back of his hookwing, a far more even-tempered and patient beast than Cutthroat, who was still confined to the stables. "I must inspect the ranks. Speak with Istvan and Suri."

"You're the Commander," I replied. "I'll speak with you."

He arched an eyebrow, and then spurred his hookwing and simply rode on past me. I fixed a pleasant, smiling mask on my face and went to go join the people who actually knew what the fuck they were doing.

Istvan was on the back of one of the horned horse-like creatures, a heavy-boned, savage beast with sharp, camel-like teeth and a huge horn arcing up from its beetling brow like a solid bone scimitar. It was like the monster truck of unicorns. The HUD marked this creature as a ⟦Corrun⟧.

"Good morning to you, Lord Dragozin. I see His Grace has been as summarily dismissive of you as he was with the Lady Ba'hadir and myself." Istvan was sober for once: sharp-eyed, properly shaven, his goatee trimmed and his clothes cleaned.

"The guy's got an attitude problem," Suri remarked. "Probably needs to be gelded."

I snorted. "Before he went off on his Very Important Business, he said that there'd been a development in the war?"

Istvan's handsome face drew into sharp, worried lines. "Yes. The undead are preparing to march. They have found a way through the swamp. We have seven days before they arrive."

Chapter 30

"What? How?" I took a step toward him. " We saw that the rot had spread through the forest from the air, but it wasn't THAT much closer."

"Another scouting party came back only an hour ago. Barely. They're still in the hospital with frostbite, because the dead have enough mana from those land-draining devices to freeze the swamp. They're walking over the ice." The lines around Istvan's eyes deepened as he spoke. "That's why they were draining the marshes – the undead can walk easily over the frozen mud. The scouts encountered the vanguard and have warned the Yanik tribes still remaining that they are in the line of fire."

"How many rotters are on the march?"

"At least sixty thousand now," Istvan replied. "But that could be the vanguard."

Suri nodded, her lips pressed into a thin line.

Istvan sighed. "As I suspected, yesterday's little love tap was a test of our Western Wall's readiness. There is no way we can be ready for what is coming. The Demon will crush us with numbers, as he did in Karhad."

"Shit." I looked down. "A lot can be done in seven days. Is there any way we can slow them down?"

"It is hard to say. Zlaslo tells me that his chieftain, the king of the *Tiranozavir* tribe, is determined to hold his ground," he replied. "They are the second largest of the Yanik central tribes, and King Ervin is a veteran and a good commander."

"Good enough to hold back fifty thousand zombies?" Suri asked.

"No." Istvan shook his head. "Whether it takes a day or a week for the Demon to smash their territory, Ervin and his people will be joining the ranks of the Demon's forces. They may buy us another day or two. Zlaslo's people know this land like no others, and the Tiranozavir earned their name for the dinosaurs they keep. One Tyrannosaurus can eat a lot of dead flesh."

"And they'll eat a lot of live flesh when they've been Stranged into undead siege engines. I hope you're prepared to deal with skeletons riding zombie T-rexes." Suri spat to the side. "The Demon has a hardon for the Western Wall because that town is just north of it."

"Slutlava," I said, with some satisfaction.

Istvan's pale green eyes were steady and determined. "Yes. The Demon knows that if they can overrun the Western Wall, they can decimate Slutlava and add nearly seven thousand troops to their rank. They will take our airships and facilities and then fly north through Krivan Pass.

We cannot let that happen. After this assembly, I am ordering all civilians and camp followers to be sent north, across the river and into the valley."

I looked to Suri, and she nodded. "Good idea. I vote we call it the 'Slutwalk'."

Suri elbowed me in the ribs.

Now that the sun was properly risen, the sky was the color of white lead. Not from impending snow - it was ash, and it turned Archemi's blue-white sun an eerie purplish color, at least to my eyes. Soma rode back, pulling down the visor of his beaked and crested helm. As he took position, two of his retainers blew on polished horns to call the assembly to order.

"Soldiers of Vlachia! My *drużyna*!" Soma's voice was magically amplified by the helm, ringing out over the assembled troops. From the corner of my eye, I saw the guardsmen lined up on the ramparts of the Fort and up along the Wall beyond those. They were sniffling and slouching. "You are here today for three reasons! Firstly, to reclaim your homes and defend your families. Secondly, for your own self-respect, because there is nowhere else to be in Myszno but here. Third, because you are the blood of the claw-lords of old, the children of the Son of the Forger and the first Volod of this nation - the Dragon King, Taltos Róna-Tas!"

The Vlachians cheered and banged their pikes on the ground, but the Yanik and Churvi among the ranks stared stonily ahead. Karalti fidgeted on the other side of the plaza. Suri tutted and rolled her eyes.

"You are here for battle! And we shall have it." Soma paced his hookwing in front of the line as the raptor champed its jaws and lifted its feathers. "We have received word this morning that the Demon marches north. All that stands between us and the dead are the bold Yanik tribes barely a hundred miles from here. They have committed to the defense, though they have rejected our aid. So they shall stand alone, while we prepare here, for the stand against the horde."

I watched the faces of the Yanik carefully. Zlaslo was impassive, but several of his men were swallowing back agitation. I was betting they were from the Tiranoẓavir tribe. There was a decent chance they would desert.

"My own House, the great House of Soma, is redoubling its efforts. We are artificers. Weaponeers. Strategists. Soon, four thousand troops will be arriving from Litvy, with a fleet of newly-built ships and magic that will sear the undead from the earth. I, Lord Commander of the Preẓyemi Line and the Satrap of Vastil, shall be focusing my efforts on deploying these weapons and magic. In light of this development, I have made the decision to restructure the order of command."

The Corvinus troops and the battle-hardened Yanik did not flinch. Nor did the knights and the noble bannermen, but a soft clicking and rustling rose from the militia ranks: the sound of thousands of men fidgeting all at once.

"Ur Istvan Arshak has served bravely and loyally as Captain of the Defense," Soma drawled. "And has proven time and time again that he is a man of the people, an outstanding retainer, and an excellent warrior. But the Wall is large, and the responsibility cannot be borne by one man alone. As such, I am relieving Ur Arshak from his position as Captain, and-"

A hiss went up from among the ranks. Zlaslo scowled.

"-AND posting him as the new Sheriff of Slutlava," Lord Soma continued, speaking over the disquiet now rising from the army like steam. "The town will soon billet over fourteen thousand people, soldiers and civilians alike, and it will require strong, effective, *hands on* leadership to remain orderly."

Beside me, Istvan swelled like a pufferfish. His skin turned ashen, his eyes very pale, and he reached down to grasp the hilt of his sword with one white-knuckled hand. I reached out and caught him by the elbow. When he turned to glare, I shook my head and let him go.

"The Prezyemi Line shall be split between the Western Wall, comprising Bastions ten thru thirty, and the Eastern Wall, comprising the Korona Fortified District and Bastions 1 thru 9," Soma continued. "I shall remain as Lord Commander of the Eastern Wall. For the Western Wall, I nominate our new foreign-born hero and the first dragon rider to grace Myszno in over a millennium, Dragozin Hector of Tungaant."

My blood ran cold. *You mongrel piece of shit.*

"Ignas Corvinus himself sent Lord Dragozin and Lady Ba'hadir to fight for and then claim the Duchy of Racsa for themselves." Soma proclaimed. His voice was cheerful, but his eyes were little more than slits as he turned to look back at us. "And to that end, all of the noble banners sworn to House Bolza shall report to the Commander of the West. I also nominate the people's hero, Vash Dorha, to the position of Captain of the Western Wall. He is *in absentia* today, but I have no doubt he shall rise to the occasion and serve Lord Dragozin well."

"You egomaniacal, pompous...!" Istvan hissed under his breath. He leaned forward, as if he were about to urge his mount forward. I caught his eye and shook my head.

"I nominate the Lady Suri Ba'hadir to be Captain of the Eastern Wall," Soma finished smugly. "She is a warrior of incredible skill who proved herself time and time again in the last assault. Ur Arshak has served the common soldiers well for many months now, but the Lady Ba'hadir will instill more rigorous training programs for the militia and will be liaising with the Satraps of the Eastern Counties to recruit more men to this cause."

Suri made a choking sound of indignation beside me.

The expressions on the faces of the soldiers said it all. The bannermen were now restless, their mounts pawing the stones. We did not have the Renown required to command them. Almost all of the cavalry and the banners were Bolza's men, devoted to Istvan and the memory of their Voivode.

Then, suddenly, a chorus of boos rose up from the peasant ranks. First one, then several, then an entire chorus of them, followed by the banging of pikes against the ground. Muttering rippled through the orderly lines of the other brigades. Soma's smirk began to fade, but the unrest was quickly bought under control. Captains patrolled the line. The first men to boo were pulled out and dragged off by other officers. But the damage was done.

[[You have lost -500 Renown (Myzsno Defense Force). Current Renown: -274]]

“Fuck!” Suri hissed beside me. “Hector, did you just lose a heap of Renown?”

“Yeah.” I flexed my hands and braced for impact.

Istvan looked down at us from his corrun, who snorted and pawed beneath him. "Is this what the Raven King had planned all along? To shame me? To take away the last pride I had left?"

"No!" My mouth opened and closed. "Istvan-"

"I am *Ur* Arshak to you." Istvan's back stiffened, his nostrils trembled, and before I could say anything else, he cocked his chin, viciously pulled his horned horse around and spurred it through the gatehouse and into the Fortress.

The banner captains called their men to salute. Not all of them did. They began to fall out, the ranks swirling in together like stormclouds forming before a tornado.

"Guys! what happened!? We just lost a bunch of Renown! (>__<);" Rin's PM - flagged Urgent - broke through the dark noise in my head.

"Soma happened. BBL." I glared at the big man as he rode back toward us, his visor raised.

"Now listen here, you fuckin' waste of space!" Before I could open my mouth, Suri boiled forward. "Mate, thanks to you, no one here is gonna be able to get their shit together in time to meet this assault. Are you literally out of your fuckin' mind? Do you want all these men to die?"

"Of course not. That is why-"

"Well you just fuckin' signed them off to be fuckin' slaughtered, dickhead!" Suri spat.

Soma kept his hookwing on a tight rein, looking down at us. "If you could contain yourself for one moment, my lady. My troops and ships are coming to reinforce me, the rightful Satrap of Vastil and the acting Voivode, as soon as Krivan Pass is opened up."

"You are not the Voivode, acting or otherwise," I retorted. "We are. And you're out of line."

"Am I?" He regarded us with calm blue eyes, like chips of ice. "A little bird tells me that neither of you are really a Count or Countess of anything, yet. You were granted a provisional peerage that is solely dependent on your ability to retake and then hold Egbolt Castle. To do that, you must drive the Demon back from here and retake Karhad. Consider this an opportunity to prove yourselves worthy."

"After you just undermined all the work we did to earn the trust of the troops?" I drew up beside Suri. "The questline doesn't even provide enough Renown to make up for this. How are we supposed to do that?"

"Try taking some responsibility." He smiled mockingly. "I suggest you meet with Bolza's old bannermen before anything else. If the Western Wall falls, the Lords of Racsa will be exterminated, much like the House of the Voivode himself."

"You do remember that Istvan was the one you were arguing with?" Suri slashed a hand in the direction Istvan had left. "Not us?"

"You've made it abundantly clear who you side with. Now, pardon me, but I really am very busy. The Fire Scorpions waiting in the workshop won't build themselves. We only have a few days to prepare – you should both get to work." He pushed his visor down and nudged his mount in the ribs, barreling past us.

Suri's expression curdled with rage, and before I could stop her, she pulled a knife from her belt with a roar and threw it with deadly precision at Soma's retreating back. The weapon hit an unseen magical shield that diverted its course, but it clipped his face close enough to draw sparks off the side of his helm and slammed into a wooden beam running across the ceiling. He whirled around in shock, his hookwing screeching in protest.

"Suri! Stop!" I jumped on her as she stalked toward the man like a pissed off tiger.

"You listen here, cunt!" Suri's voice rang off the walls of the gatehouse, guttural with fury. "No one talks to me like that! You can take your Wall and your attitude and your orders and piss on it!"

"How savage," Soma remarked.

The lords who had been approaching us hung back, watching. And judging.

"Get back here and say that to my face!" Suri pulled her sword, and half a dozen blades unsheathed around us. I caught her wrist, and she looked down at me, wild-eyed.

"Cmon, Suri!" I hung on, but it was an effort. "He's not worth it!"

She snarled and turned away, right into the group of noblemen in their fancy armor. They parted for her as she stormed off across the plaza, knocking people out of her path like a bull. With a furious backward glance at Soma, I turned to chase after her - and ran right into Vash Dorha's outstretched fist.

Chapter 31

The monk had his arm out, resting his ironclad knuckles just beneath my sternum. Vash had shaved – kind of – and was now dressed like a grungy ninja: faded black leathers over a gi jacket that had definitely seen better days, and heavy canvas pants tucked into black leather boots. I hadn't heard or seen him, and I could almost see behind my own head.

"*Büu jeh.* Not yet." He dropped his hand, metal rasping against leather, and continued in Tuun. "Despite the fact that I'd rather be elsewhere, we must talk, Oathbreaker."

"Right now? No. We can talk later." I replied in the same language, and angrily brushed past him.

"Let Suri burn off her rage in peace. She is spewing fire at some pain you do not perceive, and she will resent it if you try to help her," he called back.

I halted, turning back to look at him. "And how would you know?"

Vash regarded me with intense, dark eyes. "Because I don't spend all my time diddling myself. I pay attention. Not just to her. To you and her Holiness, also."

Suddenly anxious, I glanced out of the gatehouse toward Karalti. She stood tall and proud in the plaza, surrounded by people eager to receive the blessings of a real live dragon, the avatar of their gods.

"Fine. Let me guess - you're about to tell me you won't work under me as Captain of the Western Wall." I reached up and passed a hand over my hair, squeezing it to try and loosen the tension in my scalp.

"I won't. But that is not why we must talk." Vash jerked his head toward the upper rampart over the gatehouse. "Follow me to the wall. Try to keep up."

I was about to retort when he stepped into the nearest shadow and disappeared. Annoyed, I took my usual shortcut by heading out of the gatehouse, jumping to the rampart, and then heading through the attached bastion to the wall. I spotted Vash in the crowd, winding like smoke through the milieu of soldiers. He didn't dodge or weave; it was the crowd that seemed to flow around him. To keep sight of him, I had to move quickly.

We broke out onto the wall, and there, Vash hopped up onto the parapets and squatted down on the edge like a crow. He waved to the crenellation next to his.

Warily, I joined him. "Okay, so, I don't have much time-
"

"Shh." Vash shook his head, taking out his pipe and a plug of green herb from his pouch.

I rolled my neck and sighed, gazing out over the battlefield. The brief rain had passed, leaving it sodden. The earth was steaming now that the sun was out, releasing the stench of death into the air. There was no sign of movement at the treeline, no zombies shuffling out of the woods. Small dinosaurs and other scavengers - crows, foxes, stingcrabs - were squabbling over the corpses of soldiers and animals churned up from the mud. It was peaceful, but not the good kind of peace. When Vash lit his pipe, the cloud of smoke he exhaled was pleasant, like fresh-cut grass and pine sap. It masked the smell of the dead.

"Now then." He canted his jaw up, eyes hooding thoughtfully. "I approach you on one condition. For a short time, I talk; you listen, unless I ask you a question. Understand?"

"Sure." I shrugged.

"I am a blunt man, Dragozin, so I won't mince words. You disgust me." Vash nodded slowly to himself, pausing to take another hit. "You are angry, immature and impulsive. You learned to kill before you learned to live. You're like a seagull shitting on everything it touches. You carry the sacred bone knife, the iron gauntlets and other trappings of my order with no regard for what they mean and what we go through to obtain them. Do you know what goes into the training of a Baru? Do you even know what we are?"

I thought on it. "Not really. I know you serve Matir-"

"Burna," he corrected. "Burna the Fly-Headed God, patron of healing and long journeys, the Many-Winged, the bearer of the sickle and the herb. He is an aspect of *Moðr*, whose name has been bastardized from the original Solunkraati to 'Matir' in the lands to the West: Ilia and the White Sail nations. And we do not 'serve' him. We love the world first, our selves second, our god third. Burna is our teacher, and we relate to him as students seeking instruction to better themselves. If the Black God wanted a pack of fawning dogs, he could have every bitch between the Sea of Swords and the *Sommbaar.* Pride in the self is a virtue."

I grimaced, waiting to see if this roasting was going to lead anywhere.

Vash gave a little nod. "Now: to become a Baru, you must be a child under the age of twelve, a child battling a terrible injury or a great disease. You must be close to death, so close that a rangy mutt like myself is summoned by your parents or the village elder. This Black Brother comes into your yurt and must judge whether it is worth attempting to heal you, or whether he should draw his *kamanocha* and end your pain. He must decide that euthanasia is the correct course."

After a small pause, he continued speaking. "The child is bathed if possible, given medicines and treatment to make them comfortable, and then the Black Brother commences a vigil, where he reads the Book of the Dead to prepare the child's mind for death. The soul of the child listens, and somehow, a miracle occurs. The disease is conquered by some strange inner strength. The fever breaks. The infection begins to subside. The wound closes. The coma relents. If this happens, the Baru is duty-bound to nurse the child back to health and take them as their student."

I frowned as I listened.

"Once the child has recovered enough to travel, the first lesson they're taught is the futility of disgust." Vash gestured out to the battlefield, his iron-clad fingers clicking. "That the sensation of disgust we feel at the sight of the normal, everyday processes of life is the corrupted soul rebelling against the truth of our reality. Blood and bile, sweat and saliva, the corruption of the dead and the stench of the placenta at birth. We ascribe these things to a state of suffering, of 'filth', without understanding that they are, in fact, as poignant and beautiful as the loveliest of flowers. So for the first years of your life as a Baru, you live on the charnel ground where the corpses are bought for sky burial. You meditate, exercise and eat among the dead until you feel no disgust – only love and compassion for the natural, normal processes at work all around you. Overcoming disgust and embracing the importance of reality in all of its fucked-up glory: *that* is the first trial of a Baru. For the rest of your life you are trained to endure and embrace what is real." Without looking at me, he motioned to me with his pipe. "And that has gotten me thinking about *you*."

I arched an eyebrow.

"I can prattle off a sordid list about my own faults as easily as I can about yours, Dragozin. I myself am a failed brother to two sisters, a coward and a kin-slayer. I am hot-tempered and easily frustrated, short-sighted and crude. I like to smoke and take drugs and fuck around too much. Every human has secrets more or less as terrible as these, and you and I are no better or worse than most men. And so I ask myself: 'Why am I feeling this terrible, profound disgust for *you?* There is little in the world which induces disgust in a Baru, especially another human being."

A kin-slayer? Curious, I turned to look at Vash's hard-cut face in profile. Now that I thought about it, I had seen wounds like the ones that had scarred on his face. They were hatchet wounds, as if someone had hit him in the face with an axe several times. Somehow, he had survived.

"When I say that you disgust me, it is not the earned disgust I have for Soma. That feeling is founded on evidence. You saw him this morning, thinking himself clever and virile and powerful, dividing and conquering his enemies as his father and grandfather did in the courts of the Voivode and the Volod. They were merchants not even three generations ago, and gained peerage because Soma the Elder learned how to suck the right cocks in Taltos." He grinned wolfishly. "But you? Other than your normal human failings, what have you done to induce that feeling in me?"

"Well, I used to drink sriracha out of the bottle," I said.

He laughed, a short sound like a crow's caw. "Isn't it strange that you say that, and without ever having experienced sriracha in my life, I know exactly it is? If a bottle was lying in front of me, I could identify it. Yet, if you asked me to describe or create some, I could not. Such are my feelings toward you - based in some sense of reality that is not real. It is like a compulsion that lies beyond me. While oathbreaking is a serious charge, when I dwell on the feeling, I find that it does not live inside me. It comes from some 'other'."

I was paying very close attention now. The conversation with Rin now seemed excruciatingly relevant.

"You fell to your death today," he said. "You landed on Corporal Lazan's pike and died. Ten minutes later, you emerged - alive, naked - and came to get your things. You were confused and stumbling like a drunkard... but you were alive. The rumor of your being Starborn is true. Show me your right hand."

Oh, shit - the Mark. I hadn't covered up the Mark of Matir when I'd gone to do my corpse run. Someone had seen it, but it was too late now. I shrugged, then pulled my glove off.

Vash jammed his pipe in his teeth and took my hand in his. He looked down at the Mark pensively, his twisted mouth sloped to one side. "Fascinating. You, of all people. Tell me - did you survive a disease as a child, like how I described?"

"No." I watched him steadily. The leering, clownish man we'd met in the Broodmother's lair was not here. "I died from one as an adult. Like, really died."

He rubbed his thumb over the skin. The iron pad of his gauntlet was strangely warm. "Explain."

"Archemi is my afterlife." I shrugged uncomfortably. For some reason, I never wanted to try and explain to NPCs that this world was just a virtual reality. After learning about the Frankensteinian shit that went into making them, even less so. "I come from... the world of the Architects."

"Hrrrm. It is as the stories tell us." He let go of me. "You know what a 'status' is?"

"Yeah."

"You have a 'status'. It hangs over your head like a stigma, and it tells me: 'This man broke the Bukat Kara Talom. Do not work with him, do not agree with him, do not help him'. While you carry this 'status', I am compelled to feel disgust. And yet, you are branded with Burna's mark. This also comes with a status." He tapped the back of my hand. "That status tells me that not only are you the Black Hand of Burna, but that I should lay down my life for you if need be. The conflict has made me aware of something I had struggled to realize about the world before now - that both these feelings come from *outside* of me. A person's Status does not reflect the feelings I have - the Status causes them. Correct?"

"Yeah." I watched him, strangely fascinated. I was literally watching a digital entity gain true self-awareness.

He let go of me and gesticulated with both hands. "My point being... I cannot stop this feeling. But I can rise above it, because Soma dry-fucked the Defense Force today and I am in half a mind to cut the man's throat in his sleep tonight. It would be a mercy for us all, but instead, I will be counseling Istvan to stop him from gathering his men - the ones Soma assigned you - and riding out to take his chances as a partisan. That is exactly what Soma planned for him to do. He knows Istvan is too proud and brittle to accept a demotion. He will resign and desert with his dead lord's banners."

It dawned on me then. "If Soma predicted Istvan would ride out... then Soma wants to abandon the Wall?"

"Yes. Any fool can see this place cannot be defended against the likes of the Demon." Vash inclined his head. "He also wants you, Suri, Istvan and me declared to be deserters and brigands. He will pin the misfortunes here on our collective shoulders, savaging your claim to Racsa in the process, and retreat the remaining force to Litvy. There, he will conscript the local peasantry and take the fight to his own county."

"Why?" I was stunned. "The Demon will destroy his farmland-"

"And Soma is confident that he can simply ship grain in from the other provinces. The Voivode can command such a thing. Besides that, Litvy is the most technologically advanced city in the East," Vash replied. "It has magic built into the walls, I have heard. Magical shields. Can you already see the flaw in his cunning plan?"

"The Demon fields devices that consume mana." I rubbed my face. "Is Soma really that fucking stupid?"

"In his own field, he is brilliant. Here, he is mediocre. There is nothing more terrifying than a mediocre man who thinks he is brilliant at everything." Vash nodded. "I'll do everything in my power to stop Istvan from dancing to our Lord's tune, but he has an obnoxious streak of honor that I haven't been able to rid him of. And you, the Black Hand of Burna... You are a catalyst, a force of change. Like mana, you Strange everything and everyone you touch. For better or for worse, though... that is the question."

Maybe Rin was right after all. I looked down. "I can give you my answer to that question, at least. I want to leave the world a better place than how I found it. I always have."

"Then I have a proposition for you." Vash stood up, as secure on the small lip of stone as any cat. "Atone the way that heroes of history have always done. Atone by deed. If you are successful, you will wipe this 'status' you carry and bring every man and woman in this garrison to your side. Soma won't see the foot before it kicks him in the balls."

The phrase 'atone by deed' had a specific word in Tuun - *Rigung Gul'ga*. 'Crossing Ritual'. "What you're saying is that you want me and Karalti to fly out and kill the Demon in one-on-one combat or something?"

Vash uttered an exasperated sigh. "Did your parents not teach you manners? You wouldn't put a finger in someone's mouth. Do not put your words in mine."

My cheeks flushed hot.

"Your task is not as difficult than that," he said, once he was sure I wouldn't interrupt. "You shall go to Krivan Pass and defeat what you find there, then bring back a piece of evidence to prove you have succeeded. And you must do it alone. Without Karalti."

"Without Karalti?" I repeated dumbly.

He gave a curt nod. "Such is Burna's decree. You can ask him, if you like."

"Ask him?" I rubbed my face. "How? I haven't seen Matir in like... jeez. Weeks. Months. A long-ass time. Last time he paid me a visit was in the swamp back in Ilia."

"You really are dense, aren't you?" Vash put his hands together, palm to palm, and shook them. "He's a god. Pray to him."

I scowled. "I'm not religious, and I don't pray."

Vash gave me a puzzled look. "You know Burna is real."

"Yeah. So?"

"So why not pray? He is a real god you have seen with your own eyes. Unless that is also a lie."

"No, it's not. I've met his avatar. Twice."

Vash's eyebrows nearly hit his hairline.

"Look, people - the Architects - they made the gods. All of them. They made everything here, including the Drachan. I didn't worship anything when I was alive, and I'm not worshipping anything now that I'm dead." I gestured at the sky in frustration. "The Architects are just human, okay? Rin is an Architect, for fuck's sake."

"Rin is not human." The monk chuckled to himself. "But the fact remains: even if your old world didn't have gods, this world does. It would be strange not to believe in them."

"I believe in him, all right. That fucker is why I'm here in Myszno, instead of sunbathing on a beach somewhere with Karalti." I sighed. "Anyway. You want me to go and do the *Supply Train* subquest by myself without Karalti, and after that, we're cool?"

"Yes. After that, I should be able to look you in the eye without retching." Vash's expression turned distant. "Let me see... oh, that's new. 'Issue Quest'... then I just... Oh. There it is."

Curious, I watched him work through the process of quest giving on his end. Sure enough, after a couple of minutes, I got an alert.

New Quest: Reality at All Costs

Oath breaking is a serious crime among the Tuun, and the stigma you carry for breaking the Kara Bukat Talom - however justified - makes Matir-aligned parties unwilling to work with you. Not only this, but Count Lorenzo Soma has done his best to sow discord among the garrison and undermine your efforts to improve and increase your reputation with the lords, knights and soldiers of the defense.

Now you have the opportunity to erase both problems: after praying on the matter, Vash has challenged you to undertake the Supply Train sub-quest without your party or the assistance of your dragon mount. Not only will you atone for breaking the Pact, you will inspire the garrison with your heroism and not only reverse the damage done to your reputation, but exceed it.

The rewards and difficulty rating for this quest replace the Supply Train subquest of the Unto Death quest line.

Speak to the Chief Weaponeer, Viktor, or Sheriff Istvan Arshak to learn more.

Difficulty: *Unknown*
Rewards: *+1200 renown (Myszno Defense Force), Unknown.*
Special: *As part of the atonement process, this quest does not award EXP. The Renown acquired on completion only applies to you and your mount, not your party. Allowing anyone to assist you with the quest causes the quest to automatically fail.*

"Wait a sec," I said. "How far is Krivan Pass from here?"

"A day's ride north-east by ground," Vash replied. "Give or take."

"We don't have enough time for this." I frowned. "Two days ride there and back? The Demon's on the march and we might only have three days before a major assault. Can Karalti fly me there and then come back?"

"No." He shook his head.

Agitated, I jumped down off the edge of the wall. "Then how am I supposed to get it done in time?"

He made a sound of exasperation. "Use your brains and find a way, you moron. And quit whining."

"I'm not whining!" I snapped.

Vash gave me a long-suffering look. "Complaints are dribbling from out between your lips, are they not? That IS the definition of whining. Now, either accept the cock-sucking quest and spend five seconds thinking about how you can get it done, or reject it and continue to dance to His High Lordship's tune."

I eyed the quest. My first inclination was tell Vash to go fuck himself. But as much as I hated it, he had a point. And this was as close to an olive branch he could bear to offer.

"Fine. I'll go figure it out." Furious and frustrated, I swiped the quest back in and confirmed it. "Karalti can pick me up when I'm done killing whatever is there, right?"

"Yes. When you return after your inevitable victory, I will make sure that word of your deeds gets out to Istvan, to the troops and their lords so that we can wrap up this mummer's farce." Vash blew a strand of hair out of his face, then hopped down. "Did you know that we still don't even know why the Demon is in Myszno? Why Napath has invaded Vlachia? Tens of thousands slain, the House of Bolza extinguished, the land scourged... and we have no idea why."

I thought back to Lazar's mention of the plates in the library of Karhad. "No one's really heard much about Napath since the end of the Drachan War, right? When the Caul of Souls was established."

"Since about that time." Vash cracked his neck and rolled his shoulders, his gauntlets clinking softly.

"One of the undead commanders said something weird to me yesterday. Just before he died - again - he said: ' We will take back what you stole'."

"In a language you understood?" Vash cocked his head.

I hesitated for a moment, mouth open. What language HAD the Wraithlord spoken? "He said it in... uhh..."

"Not Vlachian. Not Tuun." He watched me curiously. "No one has ever made sense of their snarling babble before. In Karhad, the demon turned a Vlachian woman into a vampire so that she could demand that we surrender the city. Their language has been impenetrable to us."

"I don't remember. It could have been Draconic." I shrugged, disquieted by my lack of memory.

"Hrrrn." Vash frowned, the scars on his face twisting his features in slightly different directions. "Well, it matters not. Go now, dog. And pray to your un-gods that you make it back in time, for all our sakes."

Chapter 32

There were a few things I needed to do before I left for the Pass. I had Skill EXP to assign, potions to make, and travel to plan. But first, I needed to check in on Suri.

I found her in the training grounds with a group of thirty [[Militia Swordsmen]] - a side-quest, I realized, as I checked my Quest menu and saw that several side-quest leads had been added to the list. She was pacing a square ring with a freshly repaired axe in one hand, facing off with a man in knight's armor and surcoat. She wore her breastplate and greaves, but had taken off the rest of her armor.

"You're gonna have to give up your shields and switch for two-weapon fighting if you can," she said, calling out to be heard. "Except for the volley at the beginning of a major battle, they're a liability. These rotters - zombies AND skeletons - are fragile enough you can kill 'em with a single good hit to the head. Tactic number one is don't let them swarm you. Shield on your back, push with your weapons, disable the charge before they pull you off your feet or off your saddle into the mud. Watch this. Come at me like we saw the skeletons do: overhead, shield forward, as hard as you can."

The knight looked dubious. "My Lady-"

Suri's eyes narrowed. "'M'Lady' me again and I'll shove that sword so far up your arse you'll taste the hilt. Put up or shut up."

Guffaws rang out around the plaza. The knight didn't like that much. He set his weapon and charged in with a roar, mimicking the swordplay of the enemy as we'd seen from the wall. In a single fluid motion, Suri stepped under the swing, grabbed the edge of his shield, pushed it aside, and bashed her axe into the man's helmet just hard enough to make him cross-eyed. She pushed him back. "Again!"

The knight came in a second time, a low chop much harder to dance away from. Suri swung her axe down, knocking the blade away from her thigh, and pulled her second axe from her belt to swing it overhand. She just barely tapped the center line of her opponent's head. His lips quirked in a bemused, admiring smile.

"You lot." She beckoned to a cluster of eight men on the sidelines. "Come here. All of you at once, full speed, real swords."

The crowd of students began to buzz. I stood back, arms crossed, watching as they collected themselves. Suri belted her axes and went to get a pair of padded training batons instead.

"Charge!" She barked.

All nine opponents rushed her as a group, mimicking the aggressive, jerky motions of the undead. Rather than wait for them to swarm her, Suri bull-rushed them. One sword slid along her breastplate with a screech, but the men began to fall, stunned, as she took each one out with blows to the shoulders, head and neck. Soon she was surrounded by nine groaning 'zombies', each one clutching their vital points above the collar bones.

"They can't fight without arms. They can't fight without heads. They *can* push you down. Their ribs and spines WILL catch a narrow-bladed weapon and twist it out of your hand." She called out. "Ditch the shield if you're infantry, or take a smaller shield if you're mounted. Your worst enemy is your stamina, so trust your hookwing's jaws and claws. Switch swords for maces, axes, hammers... you're chopping these bastards like firewood, not poking them in the liver. Everyone group up into threes, grab weapons, and start practicing against the thrust, overhead, jab and slice. Look what hand your partner is using for their weapon and find a way around it. They don't bleed. You do. Get to it."

[[Suri has gained +25 Renown (Myszno Defense Force)]]
[[Two-weapon fighting is now available to Militia Swordsmen: anti-charge ability added!]]
[[Current Renown: -249]]

The buzz of conversation among the men was hopeful, their spirits lifted by the sight of one woman so effectively taking out so many opponents. Suri went to the men she'd flattened and offered them a hand up. All but one refused, flashing her a suspicious, but respectful look. They left, and she sighed contentedly.

"Hey beautiful." I crossed the yard to join her. "You alright?"

"Yeah. Sorry about before. I lost my temper." Her jaw clenched, and she looked back to the administrative wing of the Fort with hot, angry eyes. "Soma looks like one of *them.*"

"'Them' being...?"

"The Architects. The ones in Al-Asad." She worked her teeth for a moment, then tossed her head. "Today, he sounded like them, too."

"I'm sorry." I raised a hand, silently offering to touch her. She looked at it, drew a deep breath, and shook her head. I left off.

"Don't worry, lover: I'll be okay. I'm working through it the way I used to back in the pits. Put a weapon in my hand and suddenly everything's easier to deal with." She jerked her chin at the yard, now teeming with troops wailing on each other with clubs, dull axes, and padded maces. "We're going to be working for days to repair the damage that soaking cunt did to our reputation. I don't think we're gonna make it in time."

"I wanted to speak with you about that." I beckoned to her and stepped back. "Vash is offering an out, but it's not easy. I have to go and solo one of the subquests."

"Which one?" Suri's mouth twisted.

"The one with the caravans. *Supply Train.*"

She grunted. "You should be alright if you've got Karalti."

"Except I won't. I have to do it alone. Vash won't even let her drop me off." I shook my head. "But if I can pull it off, this quest awards twelve hundred Renown. That's more than enough for us to rally the entire garrison."

"Really? Twelve hundred sounds like a lot." Suri went to her own quest log, looking through it. "For you."

I cocked my head, confused. "For me?"

"It's enough for YOU to rally the entire garrison." She irritably brushed the invisible display to one side. "The bonus only applies to you, not your party."

"Only to me?" I hurried to check - and when I re-read the quest description, I groaned. "Shit, Suri. I didn't even see that. I thought it was for all of us."

"It is what it is. And it's better than nothing." She jerked her shoulders up. "You've been leading us this whole time anyway."

Something was wrong. "I'm sorry? I seriously didn't-"

"I know, okay?" She glanced over at me sharply. "When do you leave?"

"As soon as I speak with Karalti, then Istvan."

She gave me a curt nod. "I was hoping we could go this afternoon and rally the Orphans. My gut says that getting them to come back here is going to be a case of kicking someone's arse six ways to Sunday."

“Yeah.” I frowned, looking to the sky for Karalti. There was no sign of her. “I can’t come. I have to go do this thing.”

“Right.” Suri sighed. “I’ll handle it. If the undead hit the walls before we have our shit together, we’re all fucked. We need the Orphans."

“Yeah, for sure.”

Suri looked back at the melee. The combatants were enthusiastically boffering each other, and the arena was full of the sounds of clashing armor. "I'm beginning to wish I'd listened to you and stayed in Taltos."

"Same. I didn't mean to just kind of take shit over, by the way. I'm sorry."

"It happens. Rin's too busy with her projects, Karalti's too busy growing up, and I... I dunno. I probably shouldn’t try and lead anything outside of a brawl. People piss me off." With a backward glance at the training soldiers, she leaned in and planted a kiss on my forehead, freezing in place as an unearthly screech pealed out from the direction of the stables.

"Is that..." I drew back as screams - male, female, animal - cut the air. "Oh no."

"Aww shit." Suri broke into a rambling trot for the gate to the stable-yard. “CUTTHROAT!”

We weren't the only ones heading for the ruckus. As the sounds of mayhem began to escalate, a crowd began to form around the gates. We squeezed through just as a man's agonized cry pierced the air.

"THAT'S MY PRIZE COURSER!" It was one of Bolza's bannermen. My HUD flagged him as 'Lord Zediwitz'.

He was as small and jumpy as a terrier, with a long drooping black mustache and big buggy eyes that were currently bulging with rage, because our beloved feathery murder-chicken was dragging a horned corrun's head - with spine still attached - through the broken stable doors in a scene straight out of a horror movie.

"PURRR! PURRR!" When Cutthroat saw Suri, she pranced toward us with her prize, kicking aside dead horses, dead horse parts, and miscellaneous organs on her way across the bloody flagstones.

"Cutthroat! You big dumb bitch!" Suri hollered, storming toward her. "What the fuck d'you think you're doin'?!"

"PURRR!" Slowly - one might say, sensuously - Cutthroat struck a tall, trembling pose in front of Suri, showing her the full length of her body. Her jaws gripped the skull right at the base of the huge scimitar-shaped horn, behind the eyes and in front of the ears so that the horn rested up along one cheek. Then, once Suri was close enough, she began to slowly gyrate her upper body. The quills on the top of her head and neck flexed in a crested wave pattern, rippling under the sunlight.

"Dude," I said. "Karalti's not in heat, but Cutthroat is."

Suri scowled at her. "Jesus fuckin' Christ, bird."

"That's my CORRUN!" Lord Zediwitz screamed, circling as he tried to find a way to get to Cutthroat without being disemboweled. He clutched his sword in one hand, his shield in the other. His cuirass was unbuckled on one side. "Guards! GUARDS! Help me!"

Oblivious, Cutthroat began to work it like a Bird of Paradise, turning so that the unfortunate equine's head was parallel to Suri. The corrun was still wearing a bug-eyed expression of terror. Its tongue flopped out of the side of its mouth as the dinosaur wagged her muzzle up and down, dramatically lifting up her arms, neck and tail to flash her glossy ultraviolet plumage for Suri's viewing pleasure.

I began to giggle.

"Oh my god. Okay, girl. I get it. You're hot for me." Suri face-palmed. But as she dropped her head, her curly red hair fell in front of her face like a flag in front of a bull.

Cutthroat shrilled a muffled sound of excitement. The scaly skin that surrounded her eyes tightened abruptly, making it seem like her brilliant gold eyes were three times their usual size. She snaked her muzzle forward, the horse's head extended out, and did one of the weirdest fucking things I'd ever seen an animal do. Her left pupil constricted to a black point, then expanded until it was almost at the edge of her iris. As she did that, the right pupil contracted... and then she began to pulse them back and forth hypnotically, rapidly weaving her head.

"Yes, sweetie, I know. You're absolutely the most impressive creature that ever lived, and the loveliest." Suri winced and leaned back from the huge floppy head that Cutthroat was shoving in her face.

Every word that fell from Suri's lips seemed to thrill Cutthroat to her core. Quivering with excitement, she dropped the horse head at her feet, backed up a step, and then struck a dramatic flamenco pose. Then, slowly, she withdrew her scythe-blade claws, tucking them up into her armpits as she spread her elbows out and up. As she did, the iridescent pinions of her arms stood on end, fanning out around her neck. She inflated her throat and chest with a hiss, and then - holding eye contact the entire time - she bounced her head, neck and shoulders up and down while holding her claw arms steady.

"Oh my god. It's... she's..." I gazed on in awe. "It's the chicken dance."

The other hookwings in the yard began to bob and dance along, yarping and snapping their jaws. This was clearly some A-grade dinosaur fan service.

"Stop this now!" Lord Zediwitz screamed.

"*How*? What the fuck do you think I'm gonna be able to do about this, you useless cunt?! I didn't ask for my dinosaur's hand in fuckin' marriage!" Suri edged back, and Cutthroat pursued her, the bobbing and weaving and throbbing pupils growing more intense with every step. The dinosaur put one back foot on the corrun's head, and absently flexed her killing claw right into its eye. It burst like a ripe passionfruit.

That was the last straw for Lord Zediwitz. He screeched in fury, boiling up on Cutthroat from a 45-degree angle - well within her line of sight. In an instant, the hookwing went from trying to seduce Suri to turning on the man who was rushing in with his shield up and his sword raised. Cutthroat's massive jaws parted, and she stood tall on her back legs, unfurling her hook arms and lifting the huge claws up like a praying mantis ready to strike. Standing like that, she was almost twelve feet tall.

Every other hookwing in the stable-yard roared and reared up as well, screeching encouragement to the alpha female. At that moment, Lord Zediwitz realized exactly what he was doing. He squealed like a piglet as the hookwing lunged at him. Her jaws smacked off his shield, knocking it from his arm. She bellowed at him as he scrambled back, spraying him with bloody drool. The man tripped over his spurs and fell back on his ass with the crash of metal on stone.

Tears poured down my cheeks. I went to one knee, choking with laughter.

⟦You are incapacitated!⟧
⟦We have detected that you may be experiencing hysteria. Would you like to check in with a member of our support team?⟧

Satisfied that her rival was out of the picture, Cutthroat tossed her head, trotted back to Suri and reached down to delicately rip the equine's tongue from its skull. Suri rolled her eyes as the dinosaur resumed posturing, jabbing the tidbit toward her as if to say: *"Take it! It's yours! Look how well I can provide for our hatchlings!"*

"Okay, jeez." Suri reached out and snatched the floppy blue thing from her, then scratched her on the side of the neck.

Cutthroat swelled with emotion at the touch, both pupils contracting to tiny points in her enlarged eyes. I could almost hear her HUD chime. Success!

"You have gained a Bonded Mount?! What the fuck does that mean?!" Suri P.M'd me as Cutthroat got a pensive look on her face, and then began to bob her head and gurk, like a cat about to throw up a hairball. *"I just got a notification telling me she's a-* Cutthroat! NO!"

Suri barely got out of the way as her adoring dinosaur wife snaked her neck forward and lovingly regurgitated a metric ton of assorted giblets onto the cobblestones where her new mate had been standing a moment before. SPLORT.

I wheezed. "Cutthroat YES!"

A few people actually applauded. But then there was a crashing and whinnying from deep within the stables. Cutthroat's head whipped around, her eyes smoldering with bloodlust. Before anyone could stop her, she put her head down and bolted for the broken doors. The other hookwings screeched their support, lunging against their rider's reins and trying to pack up with her as she plunged into the gore-soaked building.

"GET BACK HERE! I'M GONNA PLUCK YOUR ARSE AND TURN YOU INTO A FUCKIN' FEATHER MATTRESS!" Suri pulled at her hair with both hands, running straight in after her.

"I can't... oh god," I wheezed. "My organs. Help."

"You! You shut up!" Lord Zediwitz yelled at me over my laughter. He got to his feet, sword clenched in one hand.

"I squired with that corrun since I was sixteen years old! SIXTEEN!"

"I'm sorry, I just-" A huge, cold shadow blotted out the sun overhead. Everyone looked up as Karalti wheeled around the edge of the stable-yard and then touched down in the center, driving up great clouds of dust. Lord Zediwitz was promptly knocked back down by the wind.

"Hi hi! You were gone for ages! What happened?" Karalti chirped, lowering her head toward me. Her eyes widened when she saw the line of carnage leading to the stable doors. *"Oooh. Is this for me?"*

I wiped tears from my eyes. "Her Holiness has graciously offered to... uhh... clean up the mess. I'm sorry, man. I know it's not the point, but we'll pay for a new horse."

Zediwitz was staring at Karalti open-mouthed. The full size of a dragon was hard to comprehend until they were almost on top of you. "I... yes... I suppose the damage is done, isn't it? Please, your Holiness, take my steed back to the gods."

"Yay!" Karalti bounced forward, shaking the yard with every step, and began to eagerly snarf up the meat on the ground.

Suri returned with Cutthroat on a short rein, the hookwing strutting alongside her with unmistakable air of smugness.

I grinned at Suri. "Well, on the plus side, it seems the potion's worked through her system. So I guess you can ride her now?"

"Thanks, mate." My girlfriend regarded me sourly.

"We'll leave you two lovebirds alone." I clapped Karalti on the arm, then jumped up lightly onto her back from the ground. "Assuming my dragon isn't too fat to fly."

"Am not!" She tossed her head back, jaws champing on a mouthful of bloody meat. When she was done, she licked her muzzle and lifted her wings, pacing a few steps forward. *"Do we need to go somewhere? Where?"*

"I need to see Istvan," I replied. "We'll talk on the way."

Chapter 33

Karalti was pensive as we flew to the administrative wing of the fort, where Istvan was sure to be. I'd explained the quest on the short flight, and she had been chewing on it.

"Are you sure you want to do this?" she asked me. *"If you die..."*

"I'll respawn. It'll suck, but I'll be okay. Archemi doesn't punish you too hard for dying. The only thing I'll have to do is make a corpse run, but as long as I have a camp and some item storage-"

"That's not what I mean." She hesitated for a moment. *"I mean... the memory loss thing."*

I chuckled, and got in position for landing. *"It's not that big a deal. I'm going to record that message to myself before I leave."*

"That'll help. But I'm worried... I think the memory loss has gotten worse each time you die," she said. *"Do you know if that's true?"*

I thought back to my first in-game death: the wreck of the Arabella. I absently rubbed my shoulder, the one with the black patch of space, and frowned. *"The first time I died, I was fine. I got that weird patch of nothing on my shoulder, but that was it."*

"And the next time?"

I struggled to recall the next time. *"That was... Taltos? I had some weird memory loss and some other issues, but they resolved pretty quickly. There was some weirdness going on there, though. I didn't respawn at my spawn point. I came back at a shrine to Matir underneath the city."*

"Okay. And this time, you forgot EVERYTHING. But you were still acting like you knew where everything was. It was worse than the last time."

"Kind of? I don't know. I know that when I touched you, everything came back in a big dump of information. Felt a lot like how it felt to learn a language, actually."

"You really need to not play around with this," Karalti scolded. *"I know you come back, but I'm worried that if it happens too often, not all of you WILL come back."*

I sighed. *"Look - if I think about this too hard, I'll go crazy. It's probably nothing serious. I had a weird start to the game... it's probably just a symptom of being glitched when I spawned in, okay?"*

Karalti rumbled, turning her attention to landing. She dropped neatly to the stones and dipped her wing down as I stood to dismount. It was a small ritual that we seemed to get better at every time we flew.

"I'm going to worry about you." She craned her head down with a soft groan, sniffing over my head after I pulled my helmet off.

"I'm going to worry about you too," I replied. "Be careful of Soma. He's going to keep creeping on you."

"If he gets too pushy, I'll just eat him," she said. *"Speaking of that, though... I want to start learning how to fight as a human."*

"Good idea. I can give you some pointers, if you want."

She drew a deep breath. *"No. It's okay. I want to learn from someone else."*

"Really? Why?" I asked a bit too quickly. "I mean... okay. Got a tutor in mind?"

"Yeah." She turned her head to shyly nibble at the edge of one wing. *"Vash. And Suri, maybe, but I don't think she has time."*

I swallowed the jealousy that reached up my throat and forced a small nod. "I think Vash will be a good teacher. But if he or anyone else gives you any shit, you tell me straight away. Okay?"

"Of course." Karalti dipped her muzzle toward me and flickered her tongue out, curling it around my entire head. It still smelled faintly of blood. I sputtered, and she giggled.

"Ass." I wiped the drool off my face and smeared it on her nose.

She yelped in protest. *"Eww!"*

"Eww you too, you big lizard."

"Lizard. Huumph." Her horned crest rose and fell with mock irritation. *"Just you wait. One day, I'll turn YOU into a dragon. Then YOU'LL be the lizard."*

We were stalling for time. Karalti and I had only been separated for any length of time once before, and it had been one of the worst experiences of my afterlife. I steadied myself, breathed deeply, and clapped her on the neck. "Go on, Tidbit. If you want to bribe Vash to teach you, I'm pretty sure he accepts payment in weed."

"And hookers." She bobbed her head. *"He said he likes those."*

I snorted. "I'm sure Slutlava has many... uhh... ladies of the night. And gentlemen of the night. He strikes me as the kind of guy who swings both ways, or maybe all the ways."

Karalti inflated her throat and laughed aloud as she turned away. I watched her spread her wings, and my chest tightened with a strange mix of feelings. Pride, mostly, but also the sensation that I was losing a piece of her somehow.

"I love you. I'll see you later," she said. *"Good hunting."*

I swallowed around the lump in my throat. *"You too."*

She took to the air. I started for the building and forced myself not to look back. It was easier that way.

Istvan was in the War Room, pouring over a set of terrain maps with half a dozen knights, a couple of Yanik scouts, and one of the militia captains. The conversation died as I let myself in and closed the door. Istvan stood, scowling. He'd been hitting the bottle again - the one next to his elbow, which was knocked over and dribbling milky liquor onto the floor.

"Greetings to the Commander of the Western Wall," he said, acidly. "What can this humble Sheriff do for you?"

I looked over the assembled men. None of them looked pleased to see me. "Don't give me that shit, man. I didn't ask for Soma to come out like a huge prolapsed asshole this morning."

Istvan's mouth twitched. If there was one way to this man's heart, it was through ragging on his nemesis.

"I came to ask you for something," I said. "Vash said to speak with you."

That got his attention. "Vash? He spoke to *you?* The Oathbreaker, that he loathes?"

I gave a testy little sigh. "Yes. And it's urgent. If you guys can suspend your plans for desertion for ten minutes or so, that'd be great."

The air of the room dropped about twenty degrees. Every man stared at me, anger - and fear - in their eyes.

"That's what this is, right?" I gestured at the maps.

Istvan's back stiffened. "Excuse us a few minutes, my *druzhina.* Give us privacy."

The other men in the room shot me dark looks as they withdrew from the table and filed out into the hall. The last one shut the door, leaving me and Istvan alone.

"What do you want?" He asked coldly.

There was no point in losing my temper with him. Vash had nailed it on the head: the status manipulated the feelings of NPCs, not the other way around. Istvan couldn't help the way he felt.

"Vash has issued me a challenge to atone by deed," I said. "He told me that if I solo whatever is holding up the caravans in Krivan Pass unassisted and bring proof of what I found, then I'm off the hook."

"And you think you can do this?" Istvan peered at me through a lock of disheveled hair. "Whatever lurks there has shot down two cargo ships and one warship. It is keeping the Pass wreathed in mist that is impenetrable to scrying, to quazi, to everything."

I looked down at the table. The maps were of Krivan Pass and the surrounding terrain. "But you and your men were going to risk it anyway?"

"What choice do we have?" He said bitterly. "Soma is mad. His plans for the Wall will result in certain death for thousands. My honor demands that I not join the army of my enemy as a walking corpse, or a vampire or a wraith. I would rather renounce my station and help the people of Myszno until my dying breath."

That was exactly what Soma wanted, but I didn't have enough Renown to tell him so. I shrugged. "Talk to Vash about that. Are you willing to give me the SITREP or not?"

His brow flickered at the modern military term, but he processed it after a moment and nodded.

"Good." I leaned forward on the edge of the table, studying the terrain. "Start from the beginning."

Istvan looked around for his bottle, and when he noticed it had tipped over, he sighed. "The beginning... yes. Before the fall of Karhad, we had ships and wagons running through Krivan Pass every day bringing supplies across the Prezyemi Line. There was an earthquake in the Pass shortly after the Demon took the castle, during our retreat. Nothing seemed to come of it, but about a week after we arrived here, one of the caravans sent a distress call. The message said that one of the cliff sides had ruptured and collapsed and they were trapped in the Narrows, which is about half-way through."

He tapped the map of Krivan Pass. A push-pin marked the narrowest point of the 80-mile valley road, which wound between steep cliffs and mountains to either side.

"Another cargo ship was diverted to provide assistance," he continued. "It vanished without a word. Soma ordered that a warship be dispatched from Litvy, and that also vanished. We stopped trying after that. Anyone that has gone there, by land or air, has not returned."

"Has anyone observed anything weird about the place?" I asked. "You mentioned a mist."

Istvan pressed his lips together and shook his head. "Everything about it is Stranged. Not even Soma's telescopes can penetrate the fog. It swirls like steam, but does not disperse. We had dragoons scout from a distance... they said they saw terrible shapes in it, the forms of screaming humans and dragons and other creatures. Soma said that it could be from the mana released by the ships, if they crashed and the cargo and engines caught fire."

"And Vash expects me to do this alone." I grimaced and shook my head. "Welp, heroes gotta hero. Do we know anything about the way the caravans were taken out?"

He sucked his lip in under his teeth and shook his head. "Only that it was sudden. The airships did not even have time to send a mayday. I thought it might be pirates, but..."

"It could be. No one's seen the Pass since the earthquake happened, right?"

Istvan shrugged. "Not seen it and returned."

"Huh." I used my menu to take a snapshot of the map, adding a copy to my Inventory. "Welp. Whatever's going on there, I'll kill it."

Istvan raised an eyebrow. "You sound confident."

"Worst thing that can happen is that I die." I rolled my shoulders to work some of the tension out of them.

"There are worse things than death. And do you know how much firepower that warship was fielding?"

"Is that like one of those 'how many jellybeans in the jar?' questions?" I asked. "I don't give a shit. Vash gave me the quest, I accepted, and it needs to get done. I need to ask a couple of favors from you before I go."

His eyes narrowed to pale green slits. "I owe you no favors."

"No, but you DO want to stick it to Soma," I replied. "And both the things I need from you will piss him off."

Istvan thought about that for a minute, then shrugged. "Alright. I confess I'm curious."

"Firstly, I need a quazi. A fast one," I said.

"I see. And the second?"

"Keep Soma away from Karalti," I said. "If you can."

The Captain quirked his lips to one side. "Ahh... yes. I had wondered if he was up to something. He has taking the archivists to find every possible book on dragons, and has been trying to cozy up to her."

"He is."

Istvan nodded slowly, thinking intently. "Very well. I will do my best, for her Holiness's sake. You may borrow a quazi. Go to the stables and ask for Temaz. He is a good steed, and swift."

"Thanks." I saluted, as I had the first time we'd met.

"Don't thank me yet, Tuun," he called as I left. "Thank me if you succeed."

Chapter 34

I took a while to brew some potions, made sure all of my points were spent and my skills and abilities were as high as I could get them. Once I was satisfied, I sat down to record a message. The only option was to use the Journal in the Character Log. I set it up, flagged it as 'Important', and began to speak.

"Greetings, my future amnesiac self. It's me, Past-Hector," I said, watching the blinking red light in front of me. "We're at war, where the risk of needing to die and respawn is pretty high, but we've had a problem with dying and forgetting shit. This is a brief summary of everything that's happened in the last month or so. I suggest you pause this here, go look at your character sheet, then come back. Don't worry, I'll wait. For you. I mean, me."

After a pause, I rattled off everything I thought future-me might need to know. Where I was, why I was here, who I was with. I forgot Karalti's name every time, so I talked about her, and Suri as well. I listed off the key NPCs and the ones who were significant, but not necessarily here with us: Ignas, Rutha, Masha. I recorded what I knew of Baldr,

Lucien, Violetta and the Demon. When I was done, I gave the log a memorable title and saved it, then headed off to the Dragoon Rookery to go on my first quazi ride.

Temaz was a handsome black, cream and slate blue beast the size of a large horse, and he was nothing like riding a dragon. The saddle was a forward-leaning seat very similar to a sports motorcycle, with straps that went around your legs so you didn't go sailing off to your doom. The up and down motion was jerky and very pronounced, nothing like the graceful serpentine motion of Karalti's back. I immediately gained new respect for the soldiers who were able to shoot - and hit - while flying one of these things.

We flew north-east over the Sarviz River, plunging almost immediately into mountainous semi-tropical terrain that wouldn't have been out of place in Brazil or Argentina. The Highlands were very high, a spread of mossy green hills thick with rainforest, tumbled black mountains, turquoise blue lakes, sinkholes, and streams. It was lush and green, nearly unspoiled, the kind of wild place I had always wanted to see when I was a kid. The air was sweet and fresh, ruffling through the cleverly placed vents on my helmet. Ebisa and Rin were both very good at what they did, and on the journey, I found myself thinking of the King's Blade. I missed her common sense and her cold, shrewd humor, and Ignas's stern but steady presence. In the weeks we'd spent in Vulkan Keep, I'd started to look up to him a bit. I missed the food we all ate together, too - the heavily spiced stews full of fatty lamb and sweet red wines of the Raven Court, the bustling beer halls and food stands of Taltos.

There was little evidence of civilization at five thousand feet. There were small villages here and there, about one every fifty miles, but hardly a soul on the roads below. The terrain was too severe to enable much farmland. The mountains were monstrous, and by the time we reached the mouth of Krivan Pass, great snow-capped volcanic ranges loomed fifteen thousand feet or more over the narrow, shadowed valley where the Pass began. The shipping route ran between high, sheer cliffs formed from hexagonal pillars of black basalt. The sun was setting, the rising golden moon was starting to rise behind the span of a crumbling stone bridge that spanned the entrance. On the right was a ruined keep, half-collapsed and abandoned. The road was wide and clear for about half a mile, then plunged into a thick, lavender-tinted mist.

Temaz and I landed on the road beneath the bridge, lured by traveler's rests built into the volcanic stone cliffs, with firepits, hitching posts, and bed-like depressions worn into the stone floor. I fed the quazi some fish and ate some trail rations, set a timer for three hours, and wrapped myself in my cloak to get some shut-eye and refill my stamina.

Two hours later, the earth shook me awake.

All of my Californian instincts kicked into gear as soon as the first tremor caused the ground to roll beneath me. Cursing, I scrambled up as small rocks rained down from the cave roof. The quazi was going ballistic outside, screeching as he struggled to take off into the air.

"Balls!" I half-crawled, half-ran to the door, dodging a chunk of basalt the size of a brick that nearly brained me on the way out. Temaz swung from his reins like a kite on a string, flapping up huge clouds of dust in his panic.

"No you don't, you goddamn turkey!" I jumped forward to catch the reins before he tore the hitching post free. It took a few goes, but once he heard my command, he hovered down low enough that I could grasp him by the second pair of reins - the ones connected to piercings through the skin in the corners of his mouth, behind his beak - and gently pull on them to guide him to the ground. He quaked underneath my legs as I pulled myself onto his back, and I didn't have to urge him to take to the air - away from the bridge, which was raining car-sized blocks of stone onto the causeway.

When the carnage was over and boulders were no longer tumbling from the cliff sides, we flew north, straight into the mist. It was like a blanket pulled over the world; it muffled sound and clung to my armor like soft, grasping fingers. Breathing became more difficult as the minutes passed, and the quazi's stamina dropped more quickly.

It was dark by the time we closed in on the Narrows. The night hung around us, damp and heavy. It was almost silent, except for the gurgle of water below. The straight tunnel-like passage gave way to a tight twisting labyrinth of hair-pin turns and hidden corners, and the ground here was fucked up beyond belief. Jagged shards of stone lanced up toward the sky, pitfalls dropped down into the earth. Parts of the cliffs had fallen inward. The stream that flowed below us had diverted into these sinkholes, bubbling as it drained. There might have been a road down there before, but there sure as hell wasn't now.

And there, about six hundred yards away, was the hulk of one of the airships.

"Damn, son." I tilted my bodyweight and gave the quazi the signal to land. The panting bird soared down, heading for a ledge created by the ship as it had fallen and sheared off an area of rock. The ground around it was a treacherous honeycomb of caved in tunnels and channels. "Okay, birbface. Stay here."

Temaz chattered his beak, darting his head and flaring his eyes. He rustled nervously after I dismounted, pawing at the ground with his wing claws.

"Staaay." I gave him a pet on the neck, then went to look for a way down.

The hulk had landed belly-first and broken up over the remains of the road and the river. The back of it had disintegrated, scattering parts and pieces everywhere. The front half had mostly survived. It had driven a huge amount of earth up under its keel as it had slid across the shattered road and into the river.

With the Spear in hand, I edged closer and held my breath, listening for the telltale sounds of scavengers. But there were no bodies and no monsters, and no smell of ozone. That was odd: it had been carrying a shipment of mana.

"Huh." I jumped up onto a tall piece of wreckage, then leaped across the rapids to land on the hulk resting in the water. The rail, turned on its side, clanged under my boots. The rushing water had stripped the airship down to a metal and wood skeleton. Balancing carefully, I explored the twisted desk and then dropped down inside to search the hull. Mana had to be stored carefully, in pressurized metal or crystal tanks bound with copper wire. There was nothing like that in the ship, and no corpses or perishables. The food was missing; gold wasn't. I found all kinds of valuables in trunks and caskets. Coins, nice clothes, books, and jewelry. The galley and supplies of food and water looked like some giant had reached in and cracked it open like a walnut to get at the meat inside.

When I left the galley, I went out onto the debris in the river and began to search for the mana-fueled engines that had powered the ship. Eventually, I found one: a great big disc-shaped thing made out of crystal and precious metals. It had been cleanly punched through the middle, as if something had driven a giant spike through it. The crystal around it was hazed, but not shattered. There was not a single drop of mana remaining inside.

"Looks like it was extracted. Do pirates have the tools for this? But pirates wouldn't leave the treasure behind." Frowning, I crouched down on the edge of it to examine the edge of the hole and see if I could figure out what they might have used to cause it. Just as I was reaching my hand out, a rumbling boom rolled through the valley, bucking the wreckage up under my feet and sending rocks skittering down from the cliffs.

I yelped, arms windmilling, and managed to stop from being thrown headfirst into the water before another boom shook the causeway. "What in the shuddering fuck...?"

The quazi called out, his voice distant and echoing, but I couldn't see him. The mist was getting thicker, and when the next boom tore the air, it felt closer but sounded further away. The wreckage I was standing on groaned under my feet.

They were footfalls. The steps of something colossal.

Cursing, I leapt up and landed lightly on the main hulk, then sprung up again as the next quake sent the bowsprit and upper railing tumbling into the water with the screech of metal on metal. Fear lanced through me as I ran back along the shuddering deck, which loosened under my feet with every earth-shaking step. I jumped off the end, hit the ground rolling and scrambled away just as the road split and crumbled.

"Shit fucking goat... cocks!" Teeth gritted, I blurred into vapor to avoid plunging into a fresh sinkhole. My feet slipped on the liquifying gravel, then gained traction on solid rock.

Boom. Crunch. Boom. The moonlight vanished, and a shadow fell from the north end of the canyon, distorted and stretched by fog. An armored foot the size of Karalti appeared from around the corner, smashing the causeway like a sledgehammer smashing into a pane of glass.

"Lord have mercy." The breath caught in my chest, even as I scrambled back and bolted for cover.

The thing that loomed forward into the chasm walked like a zombie. Not the fast, scampering kind that the Demon fielded - the relentless, limping kind. There was something bestial in the length of its arms and the way it hunched its shoulders forward. The resemblance to anything organic ended there. It was a machine - an armored colossus of charred, blackened steel that was crumbling with rust. The face was an eyeless, skull-like mask, topped with a back-sweeping crown of jagged obsidian. A gleaming inky corona suffused with a brilliant white glow hung just behind, framing the titan's head like the blazing halo of a Russian saint. It steadied itself against the wall of the canyon with one hand. In the other, it carried a massive black spear with a curved, glaive-like blade. The weapon looked entirely familiar. I glanced down at the Spear of Nine Spheres. Almost a perfect match.

As the titan shambled out into view, it revealed its other weapon: a curled scorpion's tail that flexed in the air just above its head. Each segment of the tail floated apart from the others, linked by arcs of flickering white mana. I had never seen that color of mana before... but I *had* seen a machine as big as this one. In a brief, surreal vision I'd had a couple of weeks ago, when the Ruby of Boundless Strength had merged with the Spear of Nine Spheres, I'd witnessed a titanic mecha-like thing striding through a desert, part of an ancient funeral procession attended by thousands of mourning dragons.

I was looking at a part of Archemi's ancient history.

The thing that had brought down those ships was a motherfucking Warsinger.

Chapter 35

The [[Prototype Revenant]] lurched into full view, plunging the gorge into darkness. This Warsinger didn't have the angelic elegance of the great construct the Ruby of Boundless Strength had shown me. It was held together by rust and sheer awesome willpower, shuddering on every step. Parts of it were stripped out and crumbling with corrosion. Its great breastplate rattled, hanging loose on one side. There were multiple dents in its death's head face. Something about the way it was moving suggested to me that there was no human mind behind the wheel. A drone - or a golem.

It wasn't all good, though. The choking mist swirled around it like a trailing cloak, bleeding off into the air. Other than the massive weight churning up the earth, it was strangely silent for a machine in its condition. No creaking, no squealing, no grinding parts. The grip on the spear was firm and steady, and that tail looked like it was capable of dealing some serious damage. I shrank back into the shadows as it halted, head half-turned. Its posture as wary and still as a stalking hunter.

A great hum began to build in its body, rattling its armor. My eardrums buzzed like a sub-woofers as the air as the mist around the [Prototype Revenant] seemed to catch on the wind. The air was suddenly almost too thick to breathe. I was just about to try and change cover when the Warsinger emitted a piercing, impossibly deep sound that filled the canyon like a spectral dirge. Gravity seemed to increase ten-fold, crushing my body flat to the ground and forcing the air from my chest. A wave of involuntary fear left me gasping on hands and knees. Above me, Temaz let out a piercing cry and launched himself from his perch, fleeing in terror.

The Warsinger tensed.

"Dammit, bird!" I hissed.

Temaz blundered into the mist and slowed in the air, screeching as the fog wrapped his wings and trapped him like a fly in amber. The Warsinger swiveled toward the unfortunate quazi, and slowly lifted its free arm. The limb jerked and shuddered with the effort of raising it, the fingers twitching... then striking out like a snake. Its fingertips were extendible, shooting out like a chameleon's tongue to delicately pluck the quazi from the air. The bird kicked and squirmed, but Temaz was the size of a gummi bear in the Warsinger's hand. With slow-dawning horror, I watched as the machine opened its skull-like mouth, revealing a nest of interlocking grinders.

"Oh jeez." I clamped my hands over my ears.

The Warsinger pressed the struggling bird into its maw and woodchippered it. The quazi's screams were mercifully brief, cutting just before a cloud of reddish dust blew out of a vent on the Warsinger's head. The brilliant white mana in its tail and corona flared, becoming a steady glow for a couple of seconds before fading. They resumed flickering and spitting, and the Warsinger turned and began to stumble off the way it came.

Sangheti'tak. Slowly, I dropped my hands and just knelt there, struggling to breathe. I had played a lot of games in my life and fought some bosses that did pretty nasty shit. But this thing... this thing was fucked up.

"What the hell am I supposed to do against THIS?" I hissed at myself. I checked my quest log to see if there were any pointers I'd missed or clues I could collect. There was nothing except the reality of fighting a two-hundred feet of carnivorous war machine by myself.

I pushed myself up to a crouch and thought back to Indonesia. The Pacific Alliance deployed a lot of Powered Armor Infantry, which we'd shortened to 'PAIN' for a reason. Heavy powered armor could take a couple of RPGs to the face and be just fine, but all machines have two major weaknesses: heat management and fuel systems. Machines with pilots had a rather obvious third weakness: they relied on the command of the squishy blood bag inside. We had a tactic that we called the Crab Pot, where we'd shoot quicklime into the air intakes and then either trip the mech or hit them with water cannons, boiling the pilot inside.

This Warsinger probably didn't have a pilot who could be crabbed. It was possible, but I wasn't willing to bet on it - not when the penalty for losing was a one-way journey into the magical land of hard vore. It DID have a fueling system, which unfortunately seemed to be at the top of the body and mimicked at least part of a human digestive tract. Given that

I was pretty sure white mana was toxic enough to kill me and the cliffs barely reached its shoulders, that was not nearly as likely a target as the heat management systems. I hadn't seen any vents on it, other than holes made by rust, but magic or no magic, moving that much mass generated heat. Lots and lots of heat. That heat had go somewhere, managed by vents, heatsinks, tubing and insulation. If the machine was like a human body in other ways, the majority of the heat was going to be generated and vented in the joints and in the middle of the torso.

My gaming experience came to bear, too. I knew that titan bosses tended to be multi-stage. You didn't usually just ball up on some enormous thing and wail on it with your tiny weapons until it exploded in a cloud of glitter, unless you were playing an MMO. Archemi wasn't an MMO. It wasn't single-player, but it wasn't an MMO.

With one eye on the gorge, I opened up my menu to see what I could equip or ready for this fight. I already had my best gear equipped: the full Raven Suit, plus the Belt of Tiger's Spirit, which fortified me against fear. I switched the Raven boots out for my good old Tuun boots, the Boots of the Winding Path. They gave me +10 movement-related checks on unstable surfaces, and +5% stamina. I needed both of those things very badly.

I checked items next. I had picked up a couple of ⟦Crude Grenades⟧, some pitch, and a better dagger from the armory before I left, but there wasn't a lot of good-quality weaponry at the Prezyemi Line - pretty typical for basecamps in RPGs. The grenades were definitely going to be useful. I hooked them onto my belt for easy access.

My stock of potions was up to date: ten ⟦Concentrated Green Moss Tinctures⟧, an array of antidotes to cure most basic status effects, some ⟦Roseroot Decoctions⟧ for stamina, another ⟦Bonebreak Potion⟧ in case I needed it. I had a lot of ingredients, too. I was mostly interested in the list of chemicals instead of the herbs:

- *Hydrochloric Acid x 10*
- *Nitric Acid x 10*
- *Bluecrystal Mana x 1*
- *Swamphag Queen Slime x 140*
- *Stingcrab Blood x 31*
- *Gastina Sap x 22*
- *Stranged Bear Bile x 10*
- *Sodium Bisulphate x 3*
- *Oil of Vitriol*
- *Pine Tree Resin*
- *Cinnabar x 5*

"Hmm." The acids were probably about all I had to throw at it. Playing with Cinnabar – which was basically crystallized Mercury - was not smart. The Broodmother's slime WAS electrically conductive, but I had no idea if the Warsinger ran on electricity or not. I flagged the acids and slime as 'Quick Slot' and dismissed my HUD.

I used Spider Climb and swarmed up the side of the cliff like a gecko. The Warsinger was easier to spot from up here. It was concealed by its cloak of mist, but the mist itself was the giveaway - it was noticeably thicker around the machine, which was heading north along the Pass. I ninja-ran after it, skipping from rocks and leaping from scrubby fir trees to close the distance as quickly as I could. When I came up on it, it was hunting through the ruins of the second ship - the warship, which had been dashed to the ground in pieces. The earth around here was even more treacherous, if that was possible. The road had split into a great gaping chasm.

"Hey! Clanky!" I picked up a rock and hurled it from the edge of the cliffs as hard as I could. "Let's play tag!"

The rock sailed out and hit the Warsinger's bicep with a tiny little 'tink!' before bouncing off and falling into the void below. Slowly, the machine's head turned to face me, just in time for the second stone to boink it right on the teeth.

A HP ring came to life behind its head. The ring filled five times, and then a black skull appeared beside its name as it entered combat.

"Oh." I swallowed, taking a step back. "Wonderful."

The Warsinger emitted a resonant moan, then reached an enormous hand toward me, as if to snatch me up the way it had the quazi. By the time it slammed down, crushing trees and sending the ledge I'd been standing on tumbling to the road, I was already running.

"Come on! Let's go for a jog!" I shouted at it, fleeing for my life.

The Prototype put its head down and charged after me like a bull. Even with the Boots of the Winding Path, running became increasingly difficult as it gained alongside me. The ground rippled like a wave pool, liquefying and sending rocks crashing down. But if I didn't run, I was golem chow, and if I was wrong about how to fight this thing, I was also fucked.

The Warsinger caught up with me easily, able to outstride me even at a sprint. Its huge tail arched up over the cliffside, slamming down into the rock. I spammed Shadow Dance to avoid being stabbed, but caught the shockwave. That alone dealt damage.

[[You take 280 reduced impact damage!]]

"Fuck fuck FUCK!" There was no poison debuff, thank goodness - just a big chunk of missing health. And that was on a SUCCESSFUL dodge. I only had 1524 total HP. A solid strike would wipe me out.

The stinger lifted, drooling venom, then slammed down again in front of me. I screeched to a stop, then threw myself to the ground as a huge hand sliced the air over my head. In desperation, I drew a grenade, pulled the pin with my teeth, and hurled it. It landed in one of the Warsinger's empty eye sockets, rolling back and forth until it detonated.

The explosion made its head jerk back. Another piercing moan split the air. The creature's prehensile fingers shot out, skewering trees and driving into the ground like harpoons.

"Hyaaa!" I slammed a HP potion and flew at them before he pulled them back, flaring with dark light as I landed all twenty combo hits of Blood Sprint, boosting my speed, healing most of my lost HP, and inflicting a Curse on the Warsinger.

[[You hit Prototype Revenant for 110 damage! HP: 24,890/25,000]]

110 damage?! That was about a tenth of what I should have inflicted with all those hits. A small HP ring appeared just for the Warsinger's hand, showing a tiny sliver of green nicked off the end.

The Warsinger flinched away, mouth gaping, and belched a cloud of mist into the air.

[[Warsinger uses Dark Mist!]]
[[You are immune to Corruption!]]

"Immune to Corruption...? OH FUCK!" All around me, the trees were rotting at the speed of light, dumping their foliage, then their branches, then snapping under their own weight to tumble down. I dodged one only to get brained by another. The trunk barely clipped me, but it was enough to send me flying across the ground. The scorpion tail smashed down into the stone barely five feet from where I landed.

"Fuck fuck fuck!" I began running again, vaulting the fallen trees as the Warsinger picked through them. There was a squeal, and I looked back to see the Prototype popping a struggling boar into its mouth like a bon-bon.

My confidence was faltering. There was no way I could do this. This Warsinger was the kind of boss you needed an army to defeat... or another Warsinger.

The huge machine began to charge after me again. I had some distance on it this time, which was what I wanted. It forced it to move fast, building up heat and burning off mana. The tiny amounts it was extracting from the animals it had eaten were only going to last it so long. If I could wear it down, it would start to slow. It was a question who wore out first - it, or me.

I led it on almost a mile before it caught up, charging down the canyon with one shoulder down, the lance raised in the other hand. I tensed, ready to dodge, but the Warsinger didn't aim at me. It threw the Spear at the base of the cliff instead.

Holy shit. It's smart. Famous last thoughts, as the shockwave flung me into the air like a ragdoll.

The Revenant let out a mournful foghorn blast of sound as it drew the Spear back, then thrust it deep into the ground between its feet. As I sailed through the air and time dilated, I spotted what I'd been looking for. The Warsinger's shoulder guards lifted, thrusting an array of red-hot heat sinks into the air that began discharging clouds of steam. As it did, the machine began to sing an eerie, mournful song. The weapon picked up the resonance like a tuning fork, and the earth began to rumble.

⟦Prototype Revenant uses Seismic Dirge!⟧

The song deepened to a tooth-shuddering bass roar, a sound of destruction so intense that my flesh crawled on my bones. There was no dragon to catch me as I fell. I soared down toward the enormous mecha as the soil and rocks below surged like waves, and in desperation, called on the Mark of Matir.

Spider Climb kicked in just in time. I smashed into the side of the giant spear hard enough to almost feel my soul leave my body, clinging onto it until the earthquake stopped quaking, and the Warsinger began to pull the Spear out of the ground.

I held on, teeth gritted, as it swung the weapon up without even seeming to notice me. The metal haft was rough, it's surface so pitted that I could cling like a rock climber. When the shaft became horizontal, I scrambled up and sprinted until it became impossible, hung on for dear life, and then ran when I could. The Warsinger swung around to stride back the way it had come, sending me flying just as I tried to Jump onto its clenched fist. Suddenly, I flashed back to the moment I had tried to land on Karalti's back and failed. I couldn't let that happen this time.

I used Umbra Blast to push myself into the air, then dashed forward. The edged cuff of the titan's gauntlet swung up to meet me, and I landed - not from a 90-degree overhead drop, but on a 60-degree slope. My feet hit the angled surface. The cleats of my boots dug in, and I was able to find a handhold and cling on like Spiderman. With a touch of awe, I realized why I hadn't been able to stick the landing on my dragon.

No sooner had I begun to revel in my own genius than the Warsinger realized it had a passenger. It looked down at me, almost as if curious, and reached over to pluck me off its wrist. That meant it held its wrist steady, long enough that I could vault the rim of the gauntlet and run up along its forearm. It clumsily slapped down like it was trying to crush a mosquito, then tried again, higher. I circled around to the inside of its elbow. There was a narrow ledge formed by the edge of its forearm, and a rail around. Great, dust-choked, greasy gears ground silently inside, the metal covered in lines and lines and lines of glowing magical symbols.

"It slices! It dices! It blends!" I held on for dear life as the Warsinger picked up its arm and tried to shake me off. "It has orifices where nothing should ever have orifices!"

My stamina was draining with terrifying speed. Just when I thought I couldn't hang on any longer, the Warsinger stopped shaking. Its arm sagged, and above me, the shoulder guards lifted and the heatsinks ejected, along with a billowing cloud of scalding gas that wreathed around its head. And then it began to hum again, just like it had when it had when it used its cloak of mist to catch, and then eat my damned quazi.

"No! You junkyard piece of shit!" I snarled in Korean, too frustrated to remember English for a moment. I chugged two stamina potions and Jumped as high as I could up along its arm. It got hotter the further up I went. I caught onto the edge of the upper arm plate and groaned as the air thickened, my lungs struggled, and then gravity pulled me down in the direction of the earth.

I hooked my fingers and dug my feet and hung on as what felt like half a ton of pressure tried to drag me from the Warsinger's body. My elbows popped. The muscles in my arms began to tear with a prickling pain, and my HP began to trickle away. Twenty, fifty, a hundred points. There was just enough traction that I could stay on, gasping, bleeding from the corners of my eyes with the terrible pressure that bore down on my body.

[[298 damage! You are suffering Internal Bleeding! -5 HP per second, -20% strength! Heal at least 150 HP to staunch the wound.]]

Cursing, I chugged a healing potion and scrambled as a five-fingered shadow loomed above. The Warsinger couldn't bring its arm all the way across its chest to slap me. The limb jerked and shuddered with effort as it held it level, trying to track me with its harpoon fingertips as I zig-zagged up to its shoulder. The ground was now hundreds of feet down, the platform I was running on both extremely unstable and extremely hot. Steam boiled out from under the edge of its shoulders, channeled up from deep within the Warsinger's body.

I hacked up some blood as I Jumped and drove the Spear down into the thick arterial cables between neck and shoulder. The blade barely scratched it, but as soon as it bit into the metal, I roared and charged energy through my body and the weapon. Dark energy peeled out from me, forming into jagged bolts that struck the monster and seared the corrosion off it. "HURRRRAAAAGH!"

The golem bellowed, swinging its tail down toward my back. I saw it coming from behind my head, and Shadow Danced just in time before the Warsinger punched the stinger-spine straight through its own armor.

The mecha made a strange squealing sound, struggling to pull its weapon from its shoulder. A pulse of white light shot through the tail and seared my eyebrows from my face. I backed away with a shout, and got nailed through the calf by one of the Prototype's fingers. The retractable, prehensile cable burst through my armor and flesh beneath like it wasn't there. I desperately caught onto the edge of the Warsinger's shoulder guard, snarling in agony as the finger retracted, leaving a gaping hole that poured blood into my boot.

[[You take 550 damage! You are hemorrhaging! Heal at least 225 damage to staunch the wound!]]

I spammed three healing potions from the hotbar as debuff icons flickered to life, then extinguished as the potions took hold. The Revenant began to shake again, slapping me from side to side. My stamina sunk down to 10%, 9%...

There was a deep screech of metal on metal, and the Warsinger's tail pulled free - with the shoulder guard still attached. A wave of light and heat washed over me. When at rest, the heatsinks were held at an angle over the massive turbines that funneled hot air out of the torso. With the removal of the armor and the magical muffling, they roared like jet engines. Like jet engines, they were capable of turning me into mincemeat if I fell into one.

"What is with this fucking game!" I roared, swinging up onto the thin ledge now exposed by the removal of the armor. Clutching the rail, I turned, watching as the Prototype Revenant got its hand in position to try and nail me a second time. The little finger was still stained with my blood.

"Come on!" With an eye on my adrenaline point, I jumped up to the Warsinger's neck, careful not to fall onto the heatsinks, and drove an Umbra Blast into the exposed cables.

Elemental darkness burst out from the spear of nine spheres like a huge flower, searing through the metal with spikes of ice. When the energy contacted the smoking hot metal, it groaned. The Warsinger stabbed down with its fingers - driving them right into the heatsinks as I leaped the fuck out of the way.

A booming explosion rolled through the valley as the Warsinger hooted and thrashed, twisting away from me and trying to pull its hand free of its own turbines. I was flung off into the air. There was nowhere to land and nothing to do but take the fall.

"FUUUUCK!" Just before I hit the ground, I tucked into a roll and Shadow Danced. I disappeared into vapor, then reappeared, tumbling head over ass and coming to an ungraceful stop on the ground, sans 773 HP: 20% of what I would have taken if I'd not saved it. I rolled to hands and knees, blood pouring from my mouth.

⟦You are hemorrhaging! Heal at least 386 HP to staunch the bleeding!⟧

I was going to die. There was no way I could take another fall like that and live. I had five Concentrated Moss Tinctures left. I chugged two, bringing myself back to 768 HP: slightly over half. Stage one of the titan boss fight was over. Now the attacks would intensify, and I only had three potions left.

There was no time to plan before the enraged construct raised a bus-sized foot overhead. I sprinted along a narrow, brittle platform over the honeycomb of sinkholes and crazed stone, barely avoiding the towering leg that plunged down behind me. It broke through the surface of the ground, shattering it and sending chunks of stone zinging past. The ground rippled, launching me up and to one side. I fell awkwardly and was flung as the giant plunged his spear down into the earth as well. I couldn't orient in time before I smashed spine-first into the side of the cliff, bouncing to a stop among a tumble of basalt rubble.

"Fuck." Heart pounding, mouth dry, I crawled up and turned to look at the Warsinger.

It was stuck. The enormous foot had broken through the porous volcanic ground and had sunk up past the Prototype Revenant's calf. It was trying to lever itself up on the spear, but every ton of weight it put on the weapon only drove it deeper into the rock. My pulse skipped a beat. This was my chance.

'Cojones... ENGAGE!" I banged my fist against the haft of the Spear, shook my head, and ran right at it.

The Warsinger's head turned to watch me as I sprinted in. Its left shoulder was a smoking ruin, greasy smoke boiling off into the air, but its other arm - and its tail - were just fine. It began to slam the tail down, churning and weakening the ground in its desperation to hit me. I Shadow Danced and dodged, rolling and running on feet and hands alike when I fell, until I reached the titan's trapped ankle and Jumped straight onto it.

The Warsinger's resonant moan built like a chant. It splayed its good hand flat against the ground, and the mana in its corona, tail and joints began to blaze bright blue.

"No you fuckin' don't!" I vaulted up onto its knee and ran the length of its thigh. "HUURAAGH!"

Sensing the AoE, I leaped - and as I did, a huge cloud of searing cold frost burst out of the Warsinger's palm like a cloud of crystal shards. Spears of ice erupted from its body and the ground. The river crackled as it froze. The remaining plants shriveled and died. The water vapor sucked in and coated the titan in a layer of frost.

The Tuun boots were all that saved my ass from sliding off the slick metal surface. The cleats shrieked against the ice, catching just enough that I could jump and cling to the Warsinger's breastplate. That was a mistake. He reared up and slapped his hand over me before I could spider my way across to his other arm. The hand came down over me like a cage, and then closed I dropped, hoping to squirm through the fingers before they closed, but only ended up getting my leg trapped between them. The machine's joints groaned as it swung me away, upside down, and lifted me up level with its face.

"Fuck you, fuck you, fuck YOU!" I ranted the whole way up, struggling with everything I had - which against a 200-foot tall magical robot, was just about nothing. I discharged an Umbra Blast, stabbed it with Shadow Lance, tried to dash - but Shadow Dance didn't work unless you were able to move. The moves chipped at its HP, but none of them made it drop me.

The Warsinger's jaws parted, and Belt of Tiger's Spirit or not, my stomach began to quake for real. I was dangling face-down over an interlocking triangle of industrial-sized grinders that vanished into a steaming pit of a gullet. There was still blood and bits of shredded flesh clinging to the machinery.

It lifted me up high. The grinders all activated with a rumbling roar, and began to lower me inside.

Chapter 36

There were some ways of dying I was okay with - like falling heart-first onto someone's pike, or even just falling from a great height. Gunshots? Fine. Decapitation? Whatever.

But this - this was not okay.

I hurled the second grenade with a roar, and the Warsinger flinched. The thing bounced and clattered on top of the grinders, and when it went off, the machinery stuttered and the huge artifact flinched. The explosion knocked them out of sync and slowed them down, but that was all. Great. Now I was going to live longer.

"Bitch, bitch, BITCH!" I just began throwing everything I had at it. The acids, the bases, the monster blood - still in its bottles - and then all 140 samples of Swamp Hag slime. The slime whipped around and around in long translucent ropes that seemed to get denser and tougher with every rotation until the crushing gears jammed.

WRRRRR. WRRRRR. The jackhammer-like sound of the grinders made my ears and teeth ache to hear it. The Warsinger seemed confused. It intensified the pressure of its grinders, trying to break up the substance fouling them. The

Warsinger's arm began to wobble with the effort of holding me in place, jerking and sagging down with every passing second. I descended closer to the pit of slime and broken glass, quicksand almost as deadly as the mouth itself. My heart felt like it was going to burst from my chest - part fear, part anticipation.

Then it happened. The Warsinger's fingers twitched spasmodically, and I fell.

I hit Jump, then Master of Blades, then Rain of Glass. The idea wasn't to deal damage - it was to push me back into the air. I flew back as the bolts of energy smashed into the Warsinger's upturned face. It gurgled and churned, clutching at its neck.

I somersaulted back and landed on its other shoulder, landing on the armor as it lifted to eject the heatsinks on that side. With a roar, I unleashed one of my rarely used attacks: Shattering Darkness. Matir's mark burned cold on my skin as I jammed the head of the spear in the joint between neck and armor and discharged a crystalline burst of blue-black energy through my arms. Veins of black ice shot through the thing's armor, penetrating the nearest heatsink. The blazing red-hot panel squealed, then cracked like a rifle shot.

I jumped out of the way just as the scorpion tail smashed down into the Warsinger's shoulder. This time, it piledrived the shoulder plate down onto the heatsinks, breaking off the damaged one like a broken tooth and smashing the others flat. The Warsinger boomed, a sonic discharge that made my hair fly up and crushed my breath in my chest, distracting me long enough for it to snatch me in its massive hand a second time.

The vents on that side exploded, and the Warsinger sunk to its knees. I let out a cry as it began to squeeze, hammering my fists against its palm, writhing and twisting. "Let me the fuck go, you stupid thing!"

My struggling seemed to excite it. The Warsinger lifted me back toward its mouth, spasming on every motion. The drill-like grinding of the caught gears in its head intensified - first a little, and then exponentially. Oily smoke belched from every joint.

"Put me down!" I pulled my knife in desperation and began to stab as hard as I could as the vice grip clamped down, crushing my legs against the haft of the Spear. "Put me down, you piece of-"

My fecal expletive was drowned out by the sound of crumpling metal. The Warsinger swayed, and its grip loosened but didn't relent as it began to shake uncontrollably on its knees. The grinders built to a fever pitch... then tore themselves apart in a belching cloud of twisted metal and black smoke. The smoke billowed out of the Warsinger's eyes and mouth as the jackhammering became an insane, eardrum-rending shriek of shattering steel.

A deafening explosion pierced the air. I squeezed my eyes shut as my hearing cut and the world spun end over end, bracing myself against the inside of the machine's fist like a roll cage. It shielded me from the shrapnel raining down, and then from the shockwave of a bigger, more resonant explosion. The Warsinger toppled forward, and I flashed back to the way the Arabella had careened toward the tundra while I clung to the mast. I'd felt the same way then as I did now- strangely determined, free of fear, wrapped around an icy hard core of self-control and resignation.

The collapsing Warsinger drove up the earth, caved the cliffs to either side, and smashed the ice. The light of the moon was swallowed up by darkness. Just when I thought it was over, we kept falling. The wind whistled through its fingers in the utter blackness.

I squeezed my eyes shut. "Matir, if you're listening, you self-entitled asshole, I'm going to punch Vash Dorha in the dick and tell him to pass it on to you!"

As if in response, the Warsinger's hand opened, loosened in death. There was a moment of perfect stillness, perfect silence, as if I were falling end over end through a void... and then a thundering crash that knocked my ass the fuck out.

I woke in stages. My hearing back first, then my sense of touch. Then my sight, kind of. I opened my eyes perfect darkness - darkness so thick it felt like I'd been buried in a pit of soft fur. I waited for my night-vision to build, but it never came. There was no light down here at all. I could smell water, dampness, and a faint metallic odor. Not blood - actual metal, like rust. The only sound was a thick, rushing silence.

My skin came up with goosebumps as I pushed myself up to sit, reaching out blindly to feel around for anything nearby. All my hand found was the open palm of the Warsinger. I checked my log: yup, won the battle, but I hadn't gained any EXP for defeating such an epic boss. Stupid redemption quest.

I went into my Inventory. No torches, but I had something that worked just as well: my ⟦Blindfighter's Fold⟧. It didn't allow me to see as such, working more like sonar than darkvision. I equipped it and looked around, feeling the environment map on my other senses. I was in a narrow cave, a crack only about twenty feet across that led forward and backward through a narrow crevasse. Wreckage was scattered all around. The Warsinger's hand had torn off, the fingers lying limp on bare stone. 'Looking' up, I sensed that the ground was very, very far away.

"Shit." I hissed under my breath and crawled across the Warsinger's palm to examine a nearby hunk of smoking metal. It was one of the Warsinger's clawed fingers. I picked it up, and got a ⟦Trophy of Nocturne Lament⟧. "Nocturne Lament? Was that its name? Yikes, this thing weighs fifty pounds."

⟦Quests Updated: Supply Train, Reality at All Costs. Take your Trophy back to Fort Koronya and show it to the Baru, Vash Dorha⟧

"Sure. I'll get right on that." Muttering aloud here felt like swearing in church. My shoulders hunched against the pressure of the velvet darkness against my body.

I held off on healing and took a minute to assess the situation. Probably the easiest solution was to kill myself. I would have to make a corpse run, but you didn't drop Quest Items when you died, and I'd have the Spear. I could drink a bunch of poison, stab myself, or beat my head on a wall until I died. Maybe all three, just to be sure.

Exploration was the second possibility. Something about this place was calling me on a gut level. It felt... Matiry. Hallowed, somehow, like the crypt where I'd found the Blindfighter's Fold and my other Tuun gear. That was odd, because as I moved forward, there was nothing to indicate this was anything other than a really deep hole. The crack went for about fifty, sixty feet, then contracted to a point too narrow to squeeze through. Just the thought of trying left me slightly breathless. I stuck my arm in there, moved it up and down. It got wider the lower I went, and when I dropped to my knees, I found a space just large enough for a full-grown man to crawl through. It wasn't a natural, irregular hole, either. It was round, like a pipe. Patting around, I could feel the rough stone giving way to a smooth chiseled surface.

"Well... it's either this, or cap yourself." Suicide was starting to look like the better option. Tight spaces were not my jam. I was a 'wind in the hair, sun on your face' kind of guy. It was one thing to do some whacky stunt and off myself some way that I could laugh about later; quite another to die alone in the dark, trapped beneath a billion tons of rock in a tunnel too small to turn in.

But someone had made this place. If it led somewhere, who knew what was at the other end? Treasure? A mine full of resources? Monsters that had 1 HP but gave 200 EXP each? Or maybe just the satisfaction of confronting something that, realistically, scared the shit out of me. I didn't like to be scared, but I hated being overcome by my fears.

I let out a tense breath, stowed the Spear in my Inventory, and flopped down onto my belly to start crawling before I could think about it too much.

Within twenty yards, I knew I'd made a terrible mistake.

"Cock." The tunnel was just wide enough that I could push my pack ahead of myself and commando crawl forward, my armor scraping noisily with every movement. The stone was smooth, but not that smooth. I unequipped my gear down to my underwear, but couldn't lift my butt high enough to get traction. My feet could push me forward, but not pull me back. "Cock!"

The darkness seemed to beat against my skin as I crawled arm over arm. A hundred yards, a hundred and fifty... and then my stamina gave out and I collapsed in the grit. My shoulders were jammed against the walls to either side, slick and itchy with sweat. I tried to look around and bumped my head. My temples began to pound. My throat tightened with sudden panic.

It's just a game, man. It was the refrain I'd used during every VR I'd ever played. I closed my eyes and swallowed, waiting for my stamina to refill. *Just a game. Come on.*

Another hundred yards, another rest, and the shaft began to slant down. I pushed my pack, and felt it leave the reach of my fingers, sliding down a steep grade just ahead. I steeled myself to die like a teenager in a horror movie and edged forward. The decline made it easier to crawl, but the roof was lower here, forcing my face sideways. The rock pressed down on my back, scraping my skin raw. I was under the mountains somewhere, lost. As I panted with barely controlled panic, I squeezed forward, and ran straight into my pack. It was jammed inside the tunnel.

"No! Come on!" I nearly swallowed a mouthful of dust and grit. My face poured with sweat, dripping to the floor. I clawed the backpack to one side, searching to see if there was anything other than a dead end. A tiny breeze ghosted by, cooling my right cheek.

"Calm, calm, I am so calm." I reached out with my hand, searching, banging my shoulders and butt against the top of the shaft as I felt for the end of the tunnel wall on that side. There was a space there. Relief flooded my body in a blissful, shuddering wave.

I found that I could wiggle back to get a small amount of reverse traction, enough to push my gear forward, then drag myself around the corner. It was a sharp ninety-degree turn. The sharp stone edge scraped my ribs, leaving a burning cold gash of pain and drawing a gasp from my throat. But as I crawled, choking and gagging on the dust, the roof began to get higher. The walls a little wider. My stamina was pulsing red by the time I could push myself onto my hands and knees, gasping for breath. Another ten feet, and I slithered out of the shaft and tumbled a short distance to a cold, smooth stone floor.

I rolled onto my back and lay there, gasping and quaking. When I opened up my HUD to reequip my armor, I saw the ordeal had been nearly an hour from start to finish. My HP had dropped fifty points, and my skin was shredded. My right-side ribs throbbed, and when I reached down, I found them sticky with blood. "Fuck. Just... fuck."

The wind moaned softly in this place. I clambered to my feet, swaying in the perfect darkness, and re-equipped my armor and weapons. Everything sounded unnaturally loud. I took a couple of steps forward before equipping the blindfold, but paused when a mirrored tracery of light wound around in a ghostly pattern ahead of me. Another step, and they appeared again, flaring brighter.

Cautiously, I advanced... and the flickering took on a pattern that cast a dim glow across an intricately tiled floor, a buttressed ceiling, and murals. The light was swirling along the walls, weaving through the paintings and highlighting them in strange, haunting ways. It would caress the wise face of a dragon, winking out inside of its eyes, or surround a black sphere with a thin corona of light, like an eclipse. My steps began to cause light to rise and splash on the floor, and when I looked down, I saw that the mosaic tiles were styled to look like flowing water, with liquid mana rippling through the glass.

"Wow." The light led me forward, swimming through the floor and the walls, winding around a dazzling array of painted frescos. The first was a forest scene, depicting a brilliant white dragon with a bright red heart seized in her jaws. Hatchlings hunted rabbits around her feet. Clouds of brilliantly colored butterflies seemed to morph out of the edges of her wings, rising into the air. The mana beneath the tiles flowed into a short column of text in three different scripts: one looping and spiraling like musical notes, one the cuneiform Draconic script, which I couldn't read... and the Tuun script, which I could.

Hail, Veela

Mistress of the Hunt
Mother of Rivers
Your servants ask that you
Protect us in this place of death.

"Place of death...?" I followed the path cautiously now, wary of traps. The forest scene with Veela blended into a different mural. A crowd of dragons and smaller, graceful-looking winged creatures - part gazelle, part greyhound, part bird - were gathered around a dragon of incredible size and beauty. She was cream and gold and wreathed in white mist. Her body was long and slender, her neck as graceful as a swan's. She had strange, angular horns that formed a diamond shape over her head. She ministered to the others gathered around her, radiating light from her crest. The script beside her pulsed, the engravings beckoning to be touched. Hesitantly, I brushed my fingers over the words.

"*When the Black Sun rose in the south, the Chrysanthemum Queen convened with the Circle and united them with the counsel of Matir*" I murmured. "*To her people, they spoke: 'We must give our land, given so that the Worldeaters should not consume it all. We must give our blood, given so that the Worldeaters might shed no more of it. We must give our Gods, so that our hatchlings might see the birth of a new dawn.'*

The words were heavy upon Lahati's shoulders and upon the shoulders of all the clans of the world. With claws bleeding and heads bowed, we mourn what was lost, with great grief and great joy."

The hair rose on the back of my neck. Swallowing, I stepped back, and continued walking until I found the next inscription. The cuneiform was engraved beside the image of a great silver dragon who stood in a ritual pose: two clawed fingers raised, his wings concealing his eyes, an hourglass in his other hand.

Hail, Veles
Miracle worker, Master of the Wind and Sky
Father of the Gods
Lord of all things known and unknown.

The door had a puzzle lock: three concentric rings covered in symbols, like a giant dial. There were nine symbols around the edge of each ring. I recognized one of them easily: it was the nine-pointed chaos star of the Matir. The others were not so familiar. One was a crude hourglass, two triangles sitting point to point. There was a symbol that resembled a long-horn bull's skull, one that looked like a hammer - Khors - and one that looked like a four-sided diamond with rays of light coming off it. One looked like the outline of an anatomical heart, another like a sun with many arms coming off it in the shape of sickles. The last two were of a dragon with eight wings, and a hexagon with a cross drawn through it.

"A puzzle." I looked up at the fresco of Veles. He gleamed in the magical light, the paint overlaid with peeling gold and silver leaf.

I retraced my steps and examined the paintings again, noting which order the scenes appeared. Veela was first, and the heart was probably her symbol. The second one mentioned Matir. The third symbol would be that of Veles, which would be the hourglass. Simple.

I went back to the door and began pushing buttons. I set the outermost ring to Veela's Heart, the center ring to Matir's Star, and the inner ring to Vele's Hourglass, then pushed against the door.

Nothing happened.

"Uhh..." I tried the combination in reverse, but didn't get anywhere with that, either. Annoyed, I went back to look at the paintings in more detail. Veela, Lahati – who wasn't a goddess, as far as I knew – and Veles. I stared at each one in turn, until finally, it clicked. The dragon's horns formed a diamond.

With a grunt of satisfaction, I returned to the door and set the middle ring to the diamond-and-light beams symbol. There was a heavy clunk inside the lock, and then it split down the middle and retracted into the walls to either side, admitting me into the biggest crypt I had ever seen.

Chapter 37

The vast, echoing vault was the heart of a hollowed-out mountain. I stepped out onto a slender spiral walkway. There was no railing, nothing to stop someone from plummeting to their death in the black abyss below. At the center of the great chamber was a tall dais lit by a single piercing beam of light from far above my head. Great carved pillars supported recessed alcoves, like nests. Each alcove contained the mummified body of a dragon. There were hundreds of them, stretching up far over my head and down far below my feet.

My mouth hung open as I took in the view. There were so many dragons here. Some massive, some small. They were posed to look like they were sleeping, just like the three I had found in the Lethos Cellar system of Taltos. Unlike the Taltos dragons, their biers were not bare. In fact, every mummy here was dripping in jewelry. The corpses were surrounded by banded trunks full of treasure, masterwork tools and tapestries, barely faded by time in this dark, dry place. They were also accompanied by smaller mummies, who were arranged around the dragons in poses of vigilance. Some of the mummies were quadrupeds larger than horses but smaller than elephants, their forms suggesting the lean, winged, horned and feathered creatures I'd seen in the murals. Others were clearly humanoid.

"Wow." I whispered as I moved down the ramp, heading for the nearest funerary nook. A great dragon lay there, his dried, scaled skin stretched tightly over his bones. The scales were a brilliant scarlet, like a carpet of rubies. He was surrounded by jeweled chariots, long fans, racks of weapons, shelves of canopic jars, chests still bearing their rope and wax seals. Half a dozen quadrupedal mummies rested around him like a harem, almost. One human-sized mummy was propped up against the dragon's forearm in a painted coffin. It depicted what was clearly a Tuun man, by his hair and features. In the painting, he was almost nude, dressed only in a loincloth and bearing a spear.

Swallowing – and keeping a close eye on the bodies – I hopped up onto the bier. There was a plaque near the edge.

Here lies Köroğlu and his Bonded, Zhatuung,
Warrior and Royal Consort, Lost in the Battle of Three Rivers.
May their art please the Gods
May their Whyme bring them pleasure for all eternity.

"Whyme? What the hell is a Whyme?" I scratched my head, then queried the ArchemiWiki.

[[No such entry found. Did you mean: Winery?]]

That was weird. When I hit up the Wiki, it would always tell me if an entry was locked. I'd never seen something in the game and had it tell me the article didn't exist.

I closed my HUD and moved to gawk at the grave goods. Any gamer worth his salt would be jumping for joy at the amount of treasure in this place, but I was hesitant to touch any of it. Swallowing nervously, I sidled over to the nearest chest and reached out toward the rope that bound it closed. But in my peripheral vision, I could see the dragon's skull pointed toward me. The eye sockets were empty, full of dust, but the sensation of being watched was overpowering.

"Better not." I backed away and hopped back down to the walkway, neck crawling with the feeling of unseen eyes tracking – and judging – my every move.

I went down first, then up. Every plaque gave a brief insight into the dragons and other beings who had been laid to rest there. Many were warriors with bonded riders, slaves, and their grave goods. There was enough wealth here to make my hands feel very itchy indeed, but I decided to try and find a way to investigate the dais before I risked awakening several hundred pissed off dead dragons. A number of the big pillars had toppled with time, and as I went up, I saw that several of them could be used as a walkway by someone capable of leaping thirty feet from standing. I hopped across them like river stones, barely making the last one. I ended up catching myself with Spider Climb and crawling up to the stone circle above.

The altar – it couldn't be anything else – was sized for Solonkratsu. A ring of nine straight, black, rough-hewn hexagonal stones surrounded a huge six-sided platform at the center of the dais. The sides of it were engraved with symbols of life and death: draconic skulls, eggs, wings, and Matir's star. I hopped up onto the edge of the platform, and nearly fell face-first over the edge of it into a black void of space. I had mistaken it for an altar with a black stone top. In fact, it was an open-mouthed well.

"Well, damn." I frowned, peering down the mouth of the well to see if anything was inside. It was smooth walled on the inside, with no clue as to its purpose. So what was I supposed to do here? Anything?

"What do you usually do at wells?" I muttered softly. Even a whisper seemed loud in this place. "Draw water? Make an offering? Sacrifices?"

Given that Matir was the god of death, the sacrifice thing wasn't out of the question. But what could I give up? Blood? Herbs? I remembered Matir toying with a stem of King's Sorrow in his hands when last I had talked to him, a virulently toxic plant that had stalks like veins, each one full of a bright red, sticky, bitter-smelling sap. Maybe that was a suitable offering.

Restlessly, I crossed the pillar bridge and went back to the nearest bier, searching for clues. All I found instead was temptation. There were all kinds of grave goods just sitting here, just as they had for thousands of years. There were sets of armor and weapons, rings and necklaces, piles of stacked silver ingots, intricately carved skulls of dinosaurs and cattle... all of it too obvious a trap for greedy players.

"Don't be a pig, man." I turned my nose up and continued on.

Half an hour later, I was starting to get worried. I found a couple more doors, some dusty empty rooms, a few ventilation shafts too small to enter. There were exactly one hundred biers. Tired and frustrated, I returned to the altar to see if there had been any change. There hadn't.

"Fine." I sighed. "Let's try the obvious first."

I pulled my glove off and lay my bare branded hand on the altar. It was cool and pleasant, smooth, like jade or soapstone. When nothing happened, I took my knife and pricked the side of my wrist until a bead of blood welled up, then ran down to drip into the hole.

Nothing happened.

"Jeez." I stood back, and paused as a chilly gust of wind kissed my face. I waited tensely for a couple of minutes, but there was nothing except the sensation of being observed.

I took a jar with [[Kings Sorrow Sap]] and threw that down next. I strained my ears for the eventual crash and tinkle of broken glass, but there was nothing but velvet silence.

Fuck it. I didn't have the carrying capacity for the treasure or enough potions to risk an undead battle royale, and I didn't have enough time to wait here - not when the Demon was barely six days away from smashing the Prezyemi Line. Annoyed, I climbed up onto the edge of the well. If I jumped and went splat, I'd wake up in Fort Korona with the Spear and my quest items, including the Warsinger piece. Karalti and I would be free to fly back and make the corpse run. But even knowing I would respawn, it was difficult to look down into that black abyss and just... jump.

"Alright. Phew." I shook my hands out, then spread my arms out. "Ladies and gentlemen, ghouls and gods, behold!

The amazing flying Hector Park! Hold my beer on the count of three. One, two... two-and a-half... three!"

I put my hands over my head and willed myself to fall off, like jumping off a diving board – head-first, because I didn't have to think about it any longer than I needed to.

The well swallowed me like an open mouth. The wind whipped over my body, a rushing chorus of hisses and whispers. I braced to smack into the ground, but the ground never came. There was nothing as I plummeted: a hundred feet, two hundred. After close to a minute of free-fall, I began to start worrying that the game had somehow fucked up. I barely felt like I was falling at all. Curious, I spread my limbs out like a skydiver and felt out with my hands. There were no walls to touch. There was no sensation at all, other than the sound of my own heart and an all-consuming, frigid cold nothingness. The feeling was familiar – it was like when I had teleported on the back of the Knight-Commander's dragon back in Ilia.

The sensation of falling was replaced by a feeling of rising up, and then a flash of light as I tumbled out of a round horizontal portal and rolled to a stop on a hot stone floor. There was a low grinding sound from far below, like a waterfall of gravel. The room was plain, softly lit by violet-white mage lamps burning steadily along the walls. There was a doorway ahead. A slim woman made of shadow waited there for me. She was faceless, her form billowing off into the air like vapor.

"Hail to you Herald." Her spectral voice was the hissing whisper of dry leaves sliding over one another, dry and sweet. "Hail to you, Paragon of the Triad."

Chapter 38

"Uhh... Paragon of the what?" I held the Spear low and ready, the end braced against my hip. The woman's voice sounded oddly familiar, but I couldn't place where I knew it from.

The specter bowed her head. She was as tall and slim as a willow, with ankle-length hair that swirled around her like a cloak of flickering black fire. Without replying, she turned and vanished through the door. I blinked a couple of times, then warily followed.

The corridor beyond the chamber was a tunnel cored out of pure obsidian, lit only by the blinding white exit at the other end. I touched the wall with a bare hand, and it hummed against my skin. It was hot down here, almost oppressively so. I wasn't sure, but I was pretty sure the rumbling sound was magma... and sure enough, at the end of the tunnel was a great volcanic chamber. A mana-infused crystal bridge spanned high over a seething, glowing pit of lava far below. I looked up to see beams of light streaming in through a naturally formed ceiling, the sealed caldera of the mountain where I stood. The ghostly woman waited for me on the other side of the bridge, standing in front of a massive door made of wrought gold and silver forged to look like a cherry blossom, with five petal-like segments surrounding a pentagram-shaped core. It was big enough to admit the Warsinger.

"Holyyyy shit." I started up the bridge, barely believing what I was seeing. "It's a motherfucking Dragon Gate."

"No." The shadow-woman's voice whispered through the air, ruffling over my skin. "As I once told you, the Dragon Gates are vast wells of mana, the stuff of magic. We knew them as the Great Wellsprings. The Drachan used them to travel from the last world which they ravaged to this world. Our world. The world of Archemi."

Suddenly, the voice clicked.

"Wait. I know you. You're the Narrator, from the first cut-scene I was shown... before I even reached character creation." The hairs on my neck and arms rose as I crossed the lava and came to a stop in front of the woman. "You showed me the Drachan. You told me about the Caul of Souls."

"Yes," she replied sadly. "It is I."

"What is this place?" I looked past her to the seal, then around the rest of the chamber.

"A mirror." The woman gestured gracefully to the soaring vault above us. "In the age of the Dragons, the Solonkratsu built great cities all around the world. By speaking the names of the stone, they could create and destroy mountains, shaping and beautifying them. The greatest of them was here, Herald. The city of Hava Sahasi."

"Hava Sahasi," I repeated softly.

"I was queen of this city. Lahati the Black and White, the Chrysanthemum Queen, beloved of Matir, Mistress of all the Words of Life and Death, Guardian of the Great Wellspring," the shade intoned. "This city was the domain of my bloodline. It spanned from the Tashkars to the Sea of Swords, from the Brontan Range to the borders of what is now Napath. Such was the scope of Hava Sahasi."

"Wait." I drew a sharp breath. "Are you telling me that the entirety of Myszno was a city? One city?"

"Yes: a city serving ten thousand Solonkratsu, fifty thousand Tulaq, millions of Meewfolk and Aesari... a great city teeming with prey and artistry and trade. Until one day, the sky darkened, and the Great Wellspring began to disgorge horrors into our world," the shade replied. "As soon as the first *Trauvin* dragged itself from the Great Wellsprings, our fate was sealed. We fought, Herald. Oh, how we fought. With tooth and claw, our magic and our breath. Rival clans forged binding pacts. We birthed the Mercurions from sand and steel, breathed life into them with mana, and pitted them against the Drachan and their armies of the dead. We stole their technology, improved it, and turned it against them. We stole their twisted souls and bent them to the yoke, using them to power great war machines. But none of it was enough. In the end, there was only one way to defeat them. The sacrifice of our gods."

The shade flickered, blowing away on the wind. There was a deep 'crunch' from somewhere in the chamber, and then the door began to rumble. The petals twisted away as they drew back, the core sinking down into the stone. Beyond it was an antechamber, where another, dragon-sized door gleamed. A black and white door, half of it forged from meteoric iron, the other half from gleaming platinum. I lifted my head and walked toward them, and as I mounted the steps, the doors opened on silent hinges into... nothing. The space beyond seemed to suck the light from the air.

"The Nine made their sacrifice willingly. It was their suggestion, in fact," The Narrator's voice curled around my ears as I steeled myself and entered, boots ringing off hard stone. "They knew that if we did not win this battle, that we would end up like the Drachan's last conquest. Dead. Desiccated. Extinct."

The corridor ended in a third door, which opened out into great mirrored chamber the size of a small stadium. The ceiling and walls were curved but faceted, shaped like a geodesic dome, lit by a diffuse white light that seemed to come from everywhere and nowhere. The floor was a great, smooth, featureless plane, impenetrably black and as smooth as glass. The shade was waiting for me in the center of this final chamber, her back turned, her hair dancing in an unseen wind.

"The first Dragon Gate was built over our Great Wellspring: here, in Hava Sahasi," she continued. "Four thousand years ago, Veles, the father of the gods, climbed the grand steps and walked into his tomb with his head held high. Then the Triad came forth - Paragon, Artist, Warsinger - accompanied by the greatest of the Aesari's maegi. They sealed Veles' sarcophagus with their bond and that Spear you carry, and with it, they sealed the fate of my city. The world moaned as Hava Sahasi and its wellspring was pulled from the earth like a rotten tooth and lifted into the sky. Every Drachan was bound into the magic of the forming Caul, but it resulted in the city's complete, utter destruction. Thus is the story of the raising of the first Dragon Gate, the Gate of Serene Eternity, to the airless space between Archemi and Erruku. Thus did Veles create the framework of the Caul of Souls, and ensured that no Drachan could ever reach him to destroy it."

"That's why Myszno looks like a big hole in the ground." I said, thinking back.

The shade turned to face me, her shadowy hair twining around her slender body. Even with her features obscured by the rippling umbra, she was unearthly. "In the great gaping socket left by the raising of Hava Sahasi, I mourned all I had lost and all there was to lose. For my lover, the God of Darkness and Life, was next to be entombed. I climbed the steps with him. I held him by the throat and drowned him in his sarcophagus, holding him under the black waters of the Gate of Endless Night. In the stories, it is Matir who weeps and rages for the death of Lahati. In truth, it is Lahati who wept for Matir. It was she who raised flaming mountains with her magic as she flew over the ruin of her world, alone. Inconsolable. In the end, I begged the Triad to entomb me as they had my mate. To bring me mercy, to build a mirror of Matir's tomb so that we might gaze at one another from across the land where we had flown and loved and hunted. As my hearts broke, I ordered them with my dying breath to spread the word that this place, where you now stand, is the Gate of Endless Night. I ordered it so that those seeking Matir's Gate might be misdirected."

[[You have discovered a new location: Lahati's Tomb.]] Even my HUD narrator sounded solemn.

"I see." I massaged my cheeks, sniffing as heat gathered in my face. I wasn't going to cry over a game, dammit. "I... I don't understand why I'm here. What's a Paragon? What's the Triad?"

"The Starborn Triad are the guardians of the Dragon Gates and the Caul of Souls." The shade began to drift toward me. "It is formed of three aspects and six individuals. The first aspect is that of the Paragon, the symbiosis of a Queen dragon and her Bonded rider. The Paragon is charged to bear the burden of the Spear of Nine Spheres, the key to each of the Dragon Gates. The burden of the Spear is too great for any mind to bear alone, and so the Paragon is not one being, but two united as one."

She reached out and beckoned. On instinct, I held out the Spear. The shadowy fingers caressed the haft, chilling it.

"The Artist is also a dual aspect: a pair of bonded Artificers. The first Artists were Aesari... it is they who created the Gates, who forged the Spear, and built the Warsingers. They are the traditional keepers of the blueprints to the dungeons which protect each Gate." Her voice was soft and sad now. "The third aspect is the mantle of the Warsinger. It was the Warsingers who turned the tide against the Drachan and bought us the time to create the Caul. Each of the ten Warsingers contains the malevolent spirit of an Elder Drachan, who is bound by the blood of the pilot. They must be a warrior of great courage with a will beyond measure. They protect the Paragon and the Artist in their endeavors and rally the world against evil, for they are a truly awe-inspiring presence. You have met one of the machines already... Nocturne Lament, the first Warsinger. The smallest and weakest."

"That thing was small and weak?" I stifled a small sob.

"Compared to the others? To Killing Frost, Withering Rose, Black Mercy? By far." She bowed her head. "Nocturne Lament was set to guard the Sepulcher of Heroes, the tomb where my slain warriors were laid to rest. My restless return from death must have awakened it. As you discovered, the Sepulcher has a secret portal to this place. We are no longer near Krivan Pass, as you might have gathered. We are far, far to the north."

Frowning, I nodded. "Right. But to be honest with you, I really don't know if I'm a Paragon of anything."

Lahati regarded me with the poise of a dragon in human form: her neck long and graceful, her head held high. "I sensed your desire, your nature and your purpose from the moment you came to incarnate here, Starborn. The wheel has turned, and the Triad is needed. You are the Paragon of the current age, Dragozin Hector... you and your Queen."

"...Of the current age?"

"There have been five Triads throughout Archemi's history," the shade said softly. "You already know of one of them. Sachara Ha'Shazir the Demon Queen, pilot of the Warsinger, Withering Rose and Empress of the Shalid. Her Artists were Phaedra and Zarya, rightly regarded as the finest Artificers in the history of the Mercurions. And the Paragon... you have heard of him, I suspect. He was none other than Grigori Skyrr, an escaped slave and the first human to ascend to the position of Paragon. He Bonded with Lirenian the Diamond Queen, the Breaker of Chains, who helped him emancipate humans from their Aesari masters. She was my great-granddaughter."

"Lirenian was your descendant? That means my dragon is related to you. Her mother is-"

"Usta the Dawn Pearl... the Queen of Tears. One of only three Queens of my blood left in this world, including your own Karalti." The shade stepped back, her form whispering and hissing, and then sunk into the floor and vanished. "I know... I know Usta's fate all too well. My spirit has watched over all my descendants, every queen and every daughter and son they have borne."

The floor brightened beneath my feet, and when I looked down, my eyes widened. It wasn't stone at all – it was glass.

Lahati the Chrysanthemum Queen was perfectly preserved, like a fly in amber. She looked as if she was sleeping, her foreclaws curled against her muzzle, her long hind legs drawn up, one wing half-covering her face. Her scales were a pure, glossy black, save for a large white starburst at the base of her long, swan-like neck. Seven magnificent horns decorated with jeweled platinum and gold rings swept back from a long, elegant skull. Even in death, Lahati the Chrysanthemum Queen was regal, graceful... beautiful.

"The Triad returns to the world when the gods stir in their tombs," Lahati's voice whispered from all directions around me. "And as Matir has awoken from his restless sleep, so have I. That is not a good thing, Herald. That we are roused means that the Caul's magic has lessened. There is only one way that could have happened. The Drachan have found themselves an Avatar."

"They have." I drew a deep, steadying breath, unequipped my cleated boots, and walked out into the chamber in bare feet. It was about three hundred feet around, larger than the Warsinger. Lahati almost filled the entire space below. "One of the Architects has incarnated here. He was known as Ororgael, and now as Baldr. Baldr Hyland. He wants to rule an empire."

"And the Drachan will give it to him. That is how they earned their name in my tongue, '*Trauvin*'. The Deceivers." Lahati said. "The Trauvin weave falsehoods as easily as breathing, layering deception upon deception. In truth, they only have one desire - to consume. They are neither alive nor dead, but un-alive; life is an affront to their very existence. They will gladly hand this Baldr Hyland his empire, and when the world has no protection left, they will slowly devour him and his works. For it is his suffering they shall relish the most."

"He's an Architect, though." I asked. "He helped create the Drachan, along with everything else."

Lahati sighed: a soft, fluted sound. "The Drachan have exceeded the Architect's designs in ways they could not imagine or predict. But I cannot dwell on it... ask other questions of me."

I crouched down, gazing at the entombed dragon's face. Up close, I could see that her muzzle was sunken and atrophied, but it only made her beauty more haunting. "Myszno is being invaded, your Majesty. By-"

"Ashur of the Ten Thousand Swords." She breathed the word like a curse.

"You know him?"

"The land speaks his name. He was Lirenian's bane." Lahati replied. "But he is even older than she. Ashur was a contemporary of mine."

"He's that old?" I pressed a hand to the smooth floor. "Why would he be here after all this time?"

"His story is bound with the history of humankind in Archemi," she said. "The Shalid used to be a great jungle ruled by the Meewfolk. But when the Drachan came, they turned the vibrant queendoms of the Meewfolk into a desert wasteland with their magic and artificing. They enslaved the catfolk alongside the humans they had brought with them from another world, and fielded terrible machines that sucked mana from the bodies of their screaming thralls. As the War plowed on, many slaves escaped their clutches, founding nations in the high mountains of Tungaant in Daun and the abandoned deserts of the Shalid here, in Artana. The first and the mightiest human civilization was the enlightened kingdom of Napath. They seized and held one of the few green places in the Shalid, nursing their civilization along the Iteru River delta. They were able to bring together the quickness of humans, the wisdom of the dragons, the ambition of the Aesari, the diligence of the Mercurions and the honor of the Meewfolk into a single nation. The Napathu commanded words of healing and restoration, the only humans to ever have done so. They were truly great, our neighbors and friends."

"But...?"

"But when the Dragon Gates were built, Paragon, the burden of their creation was great upon the world. The Gates which were to become the tombs of Veles and Matir were made here, in Hava Sahasi. Veles consumed the mana of the Great Wellspring and took it with him when the Gate rose to the stars, and so the mana for the Gate of Endless Night had to come from somewhere. It came from the oceans, the mountains, and inadvertently, the land of Napath."

I made a face. "Oh."

"My lover's passing drained and warped the land for a thousand miles. Their fertile delta withered and Stranged, turning the rivers to poison. In their desperation, the great Maegi of Napath tried to use their magic to save their land, but the Words of Life were twisted by Matir's passing from this world. They tried to suck the mana back from the hungry Dragon Gate, but their magic sucked the life from them instead. It Stranged them into undead abominations. The Maegi perished, then rose as wights, liches and vampires, becoming the Breathless. They renounced the Nine and spat on their memory, and they have never forgiven the dragons for our role in the creation of the Gates. Rather than move on from their tragedy, they perpetuate it... they use the life force of living beings to replenish their mana and continue their wretched unlife. But if the Drachan have an able herald of their own, then surely the Caul is unbalanced. Matir's gate draws ever more strongly on the land. They cannot maintain the mana they need to exist."

"And now they're here. trying to take back what they figure we stole." I rubbed my face.

"Yes. Ashur was a hero of his people," Lahati said. "A human slave who became a mighty warrior, then one of the vampiric guardians of Napath. He is one of the three great Generals who serves the undying Council of the Breathless."

"He must be here to try and find Matir's Dragon Gate," I said. "And he'll apparently wreck the place to do it. He's slaughtering everyone and raising every corpse he makes. Human, animal, all of them."

"As the Drachan did," she said, sadly. "Those are their very own tactics. How many dead are there?"

"Probably closing in on sixty or seventy thousand by now. He's using devices that draw life out of the land and turn it into mana."

"Stardrinkers. They are not enough to fuel an army of fifty thousand." Lahati sounded troubled now. "An army of such a size requires access to a wellspring. But the Great Wellspring here left with Veles. From whence did they come? From the south?"

"Yeah. They crawled over the southern mountains. The... uhh... hang on..." I checked my quest log, then my map of Myszno when the log didn't turn up anything. "The Olmus Range?"

"Ah." Lahati rustled nervously. "The Olmus... We call them the Harikulade Mountains in the old tongue. That is where my mate makes his rest."

“The Dragon Gate is there?” I stood up in alarm, and a rush prickled up along my arms as things I had heard and seen over months came together into a single cohesive picture. "Could the Demon have found Matir already?”

“It is possible he has found my mate's resting place.”

I took a step toward her. “So he could be draining the mana from it? Using it to fuel his army?”

"The Gate channels enough mana, but no... he could not access it. That is not possible. The Spear is with you. Unless..."

"Unless what?"

"If what you say is true and the Drachan have an Avatar, they will be seeking Matir and the other Nine, hoping to destroy them while they slumber," Lahati said. "There are three parts to the seal upon the Dragon Gates. The first part is the Triad itself. All six members of the Triad must be present for the Paragons to open the Gate. They must possess both the Spear of Nine Spheres and the Keystone which is bound to the weapon. You possess one of the Keystones, the Ruby which has bonded to your Spear. It locks and unlocks the Dragon Gate of Boundless Strength: the resting place of Khors."

"Yeah. But I don't have the magic crystal for Matir," I replied.

"You do not," the dragon said. "But Ashur might. In his hands, it cannot unlock the Dragon Gate, but the Dark Star could still be used to siphon Matir's divine force through the Gate without the need to open it. No Artifact is perfect, no seal is perfect... and Matir is powerless to stop them if they know how to do so."

"Shit. My bet is that they do. Does that mean they found the Gate?"

"It is impossible to say." Lahati replied. "With the Dark Star of Endless Night, Matir's keystone, one would not need to be physically present to draw his energy. Mana in its aetheric form is not bound by distance... it can be called and discharged anywhere. Both the Gate and its keys have powerful misdirection and cloaking magic lain on them, concealing the location of the Gate from those who should not be there. Not even the most powerful maegi to arise from the Age of Aesari or the Age of Humans have ever found them."

I set my jaw. "You're saying that the Keystone can vampirize Matir?"

"Yes. And such vampirism could be enough to rouse him to nominate a Herald," she replied. "Should he perish, or should the influx of soul-energy into his Dragon Gate cease, the Caul of Souls could collapse and unleash the Drachan on us all."

"Shit. That has to be why the Caul of Souls is so unstable." My hand clenched around the haft of the Spear of Nine Spheres. "We can't afford another Drachan invasion, especially if what you say is true and they've somehow evolved past the point the Architects had intended. There's only around two thousand Starborn in Archemi."

Lahati spread her hands. "That is more than what we had during the Great War. Many more. There were only a handful of Starborn in that time."

That was heartening, at least. But how many of my fellow PCs were psychopaths like Lucien, Baldr, and Violetta? "Even so... if I get this keystone and put it in the Spear, maybe I can stabilize the gate?"

"Perhaps," Lahati replied. "I apologize, Paragon, but this audience must end soon... my grip on this world grows weak. Ask me what you must while there is time."

"Two things," I said. "Where is the remaining queen? You said there were three living queens of your bloodline left: Karalti, Usta, and...?"

"Altan the Golden," Lahati replied. "Whose great, great grandmother took refuge across the ocean, in Tungaant. She and Karalti are the only hope for my bloodline moving forward."

"Oh shit." My expression crumpled. "You mean... Karalti's mom is...?"

"No. Death would be a mercy for Usta. She is not dead, but her mind is no longer of this world," Lahati whispered. "She dwells in other realms now, though her body is still forced to breathe. And breed."

Her words were like a punch to the gut. I sat back down heavily, cross-legged. "Jesus. What the hell am I going to tell Karalti?"

"The truth." Lahati straightened, her specter regal even in death. "There is nothing else worth knowing. Karalti is a Queen of my blood. She will find the strength."

"Maybe." I shook my head. "She never got to meet her mother. She was never able to receive her mantle, and can't command other dragons."

The dragon fell silent. I turned to walk away, but then halted as a breeze stirred behind me.

"When she is ready... bring her to me," Lahati said. "And I will lend her the last of my power. For now, Paragon, you must go back to her. I will assist you."

Quest Updated: The Queen's Mantle

You have learned that Karalti's mother is in no fit state to help her daughter attain the Words she needs to manifest into her destiny as a Queen dragon. When Karalti reaches Level 15, bring her to Lahati.

I accepted the update. "Okay, well... this is a lot to digest. Thanks for helping us, though."

"Do not thank me yet," Lahati replied. "You carry both the burden of the Triad and the burden of the Mark of Matir. Many have tried to live up to one or both roles and failed."

I looked down at the back of my right hand. "What does it mean? To be the Herald of the Hidden Seed?"

"In truth... I do not know." Lahati replied. "All I know is that before his sacrifice, the only one who bore Matir's mark was I. He bit me upon the neck in our mating flight, marking me forever. It was a touching gift, but one bound with thorns. Our love came with great sweetness and great loss."

Shadows swirled around my feet, crawling up my legs. Tense, I hung onto the Spear as they climbed higher, enveloping my limbs, then my torso, then my head. The world turned dark, and then the veil parted and a cold, clammy wind gusted from the front of my face, ripping over my helmet. It smelled of water and damp, rich soil, with a hint of something bitter. I was up very high, standing on a narrow ledge in front of a shaft like the one I'd used to crawl into Lahati's Tomb. A glacial valley and rivers spread out far below, their headwaters springing from the mountains that towered on all sides. The sun was a thin red line on the horizon, while the moon was only just starting to sink.

Hanging in front of Erruku was a tiny, dark, glimmering blob. It was bright, but not bright enough to be a star. It hung motionless in front of the great sphere of Archemi's moon, a dead planet three times the size of this one. Like a bird orienting on its migration route, I knew it was due south.

I drew a deep breath of crisp, cold dawn air. "'When the Dark Star passes in front of the Moon, journey to the Thunderstones at Myszno, a village in the east of Vlachia'. Did I forget anything, old man?"

My HUD chimed in reply. Curious, I bought up the new quest alert.

Quest Update: The Shrine of the Elder Gods.

Hurry.

Chapter 39

The sun was high by the time Karalti and I swooped back in over Fort Korona and dropped the Warsinger's knuckle in the middle of the parade ground - right in front of Istvan and his banners, their knights and militia, and Vash.

The huge hunk of articulated metal crashed onto the stone, scattering hookwings and men with shouts and screeching. I stood on Karalti's back as she circled around the plaza, then backwinged and flapped hard to land beside it. She lifted her head and bellowed victoriously toward the sky.

"We did it!" She announced telepathically as I hopped down to the ground. Istvan had turned the color of milk, hanging back as he tried to make sense of what he was seeing. I swaggered over to Vash and pulled my helmet off, glaring at him. The monk was watching me warily, as if he couldn't quite believe it was really me.

"I should kick you in the dick," I said cheerfully. "But hey, it's done."

Vash didn't look back or search for his friend's approval. To everyone's surprise, especially mine, he dropped to the ground and put his forehead against his hands, then rose with his palms pressed together and touched them to his nose.

"This man has proven himself through the *Rihgung Gulga.* Through deed!" He shouted. "Long live the Black God's Hand! Long live Voivode Dragozin Hector - the rightful Claimant to Racsa!"

[[You have unlocked a new Hero: Vash Dorha (Rank A+ Baru Infantry Marshal - Myszno Defense Force)]]

He was met with a stunned, resounding silence.

"Vash..." Istvan came forward, his face pale. "What are you doing?"

"Are you a moron? Don't you see *that*?" Vash pointed at the limp, severed digit lying on the ground. "Use your eyes, Arshak. Tell me what you see."

"It... looks like... " Istvan squinted, scratching his hair. "Like a finger?"

"That is the distal phalange - the first knuckle - from a finger of a hand that is approximately the size of that dragon." Vash spoke like someone trying to explain math to a small child.

Istvan made a small choking sound. He whirled on me, pointing at it. "Are you telling me you killed the thing that this finger belonged to? Alone?"

I rubbed the back of my neck and shrugged. "Yeah, dude."

Istvan turned on Vash. "You said this man is an oathbreaker. You truly believe that he destroyed something with a dist... dest... knuckle of that size?"

"His status changed, so yes." Vash flashed him a rakish grin. "There's hope for him yet."

"*Huadi bekhor.*" Istvan pinched the bridge of his nose. "I need a drink."

"A drink is the last thing you or your liver needs, Arshak. What you need is a blowjob and a nice lie down." Vash clapped him on the back, sending the blushing man stumbling forward. "But the troops want to know what is going on, dog. Stand before them and bark your commands."

I gave him a small nod, then turned back to Karalti. She dropped her wing and I climbed up until I could look over the crowd of stunned men and women. They fell silent as I leaned out around her neck, holding onto it like a mast.

"Vash Dorha challenged me to undertake a trial yesterday morning." I lifted my voice to be heard over the rustle and clanking of nervous people, the bustle of the fort and the wind. "He challenged me to go to Krivan Pass, alone, and deal with the creature that was plaguing the shipments we desperately need to survive. This is a trophy cut from the offending monster's body. It was a desperate fight. I am victorious, and shipments will now resume."

Metal and leather rustled as people leaned in and began to whisper.

"If this is what one single Starborn can do, imagine what we can do if we all work together. Disciplined, orderly, united!" I built into it, pushing all of the pent-up frustration

I'd suppressed into each word. "That great big hunk of metal over there is from the creature that was blocking the pass. If I can defeat that, alone, what can three Starborn do for Myszno? What can we do with Karalti the Black Opal Queen watching over this army? I AM the Herald of the Hidden Seed. I AM the royally appointed Lord of Racsa, and we CAN fucking win this thing as long as you stay with us!"

As my voice faded, the messy ranks around us shuffled. A few people coughed, others seemed almost embarrassed. From behind me, I heard Vash curse.

"Ah, fuck!" he hissed. "I forgot the fucking quest update. Hang on... there!"

⟦Congratulations! You have successfully completed Reality at All Costs!⟧
⟦You gain +1200 renown (Myszno Defense Force)⟧
⟦You gain one bonus Mark of Matir ability! See your character sheet for details.⟧

As soon as the renown hit, a ripple moved through the ranks. For a time, no one moved. Then one pikeman began to bang the end of his spear down on the flagstones. Another one glanced at Vash, then looked to me and Karalti. He joined in... then another, and another, until a rhythmic drumming boomed through the parade ground.

"We did it!" Karalti reared her head up, her throat vibrating.

I smiled, and let out a tense breath.

"Count Dragozin. I am Ur Ghelan." The first officer to step up to introduce himself looked more like a dockyard brawler than a Knight of the Red Star. He was short and squat and built like a ham, with squashed, heavy-set features and an undercut. His armor had taken dents from swords and had clearly seen a lot of fighting. "I and my retainers will fight as ferociously for you as we would for His Majesty. We are not great in number here, but I will vouch for you in Litvy to summon reinforcements if we must."

[[You have unlocked a new Hero: Ur Robert Gehlan (Knight of the Red Star Captain - Myszno Defense Force)]]

"I am Lord Zediwitz!" The man who had lost his corrun to Cutthroat rode up on a different horned equine. He was still small, but less bug-eyed now that he wasn't looking at the dismembered corpse of his favorite mount. "And even though your accursed bird killed my favorite corrun, I and my Cavalry will join you!"

[[You have unlocked a new Hero: Lord Franz Zediwitz (Rank B+ Heavy Cavalry Commander - Myszno Defense Force)]]

"Thanks." I smiled down at him. "I'm really sorry about the horse. What was its name?"

"Starberry." He dashed a tear from his eyes as he rode away.

One by one, officers and Heroes approached, unlocking their complete hero profiles in my Mass Combat unit and placing them under my command. One representative of every Unit available to the Defense Force came forward – except for Istvan.

When the last of the officers had come to greet me, I got down and stood to attention: "FOOORM ranks!"

Every soldier - all three hundred of them - moved to act. They weren't all in sync, some dragging their feet, some putting their hands in the wrong places or letting their weapons lean forward or back, but they coalesced from a ragged mob into a single company.

I turned to Istvan. "What about you, man? You willing to trust me now?"

The Yanik's man's eyes flashed, but the glare faltered as he looked to the giant knuckle lying on the ground. "I'm not sure. I have heard that you are somewhat infamous in Taltos, Dragozin. You conspired with a syndicate, and helped them put Ignas Corvinus on the throne."

"I prefer the word 'restore'," I replied. "'Restored' Ignas to the throne."

Istvan's eyes narrowed. "Rumor is that you slew Andrik yourself. That you are a regicide."

"It's true." I gave a curt nod. "But I wasn't Andrik's retainer and he wasn't my king. He hired me and Suri with no intention of letting us survive the job he never paid us for. He tried to kill us and send Karalti back to slavery in Ilia. By the end, the monster we killed was no longer human. He used magic to turn into an abomination-"

"What is going on here?!"

Soma's booming voice rolled out across the plaza as he rode through the northern gatehouse, returning from the munitions and manufacturing center. He only had three retainers today - two knights and a squire. He wore a spellglove on one hand, his eyes blazing with confusion and malice. When his hookwing noticed the Warsinger's finger on the ground, it shied back with a short *screee* of fear.

"What the hell are you all doing here?" Soma demanded. He jerked his hookwing back to sense with the reins, pulling up sharply in front of us. "And what the hell is this?

"That is a great big middle finger, and you're welcome to go and fuck yourself with it," I said happily.

The huge man's face purpled. He shoved his reins to one side and vaulted off his hookwing, shuddering with rage. "First you disobey my orders by vanishing instead of reporting to the Western Wall, then intrude on MY command center to marshal MY banners. And your response is to insult me?"

"Sure. Why not?" I stared him down. "Suri and I did everything in our power not to pull rank as the Lord and Lady of Racsa, but you're subject to the authority of the Voivode of Myszno. I'm taking command of this army as of right the fuck now. Soma – you're fired."

Soma began to laugh uproariously. "You? You seriously think you can-"

"Shut the fuck up. You're done." Something black and hard rose in me and bled out in my voice, turning every word into a cutting stroke that lay on the assembly like a whip. "And Istvan? Shut up or show up. If neither of you can't stand the thought of serving under me and Suri, go back to your rooms, pack your bags, and fuck off into the sunset. Everyone with balls and-or ovaries will hitch them up and fight for this province with their lives. Do the same, or I'll recruit better leaders from within the ranks."

Istvan stepped forward, as if to retort, but Vash caught his shoulder and shook his head. Soma swelled up to his full seven-foot height.

"Your claim to Racsa is only valid when you have taken the Ducal seat back from the Demon," Soma said coldly. He turned to his posse. "Ur Ferenz! I appointed you Castellan of Korona. Arrest these men for mutiny!"

Karalti snarled and stood up from where she had crouched, towering over the plaza. She mantled her wings, head swaying from side to side. Ur Ferenz, who was himself a good six and a half feet of muscle, blanched. He edged toward me, but then stopped. "My Lord... I cannot."

"What do you mean, you cannot?!" Soma whirled on him.

"I am a man of faith, my Lord," he replied nervously. "The dragon is a sacred creature, and this man is a holy man. My men were there when he perished and then returned to life. Vash Dorha has blessed him-"

"I don't give a shit what this barbaric scum has blessed or not!" Soma shouted, gesturing wildly toward me and Vash. "Arrest him! I command it!"

"My Lord, forgive me. I cannot buck the will of the Nine." Ur Ferenz shook his head. "The evidence of Count Dragozin's mantle lies before us. I do not fear the Volod, but I fear the Black God's wrath."

“Oh? So you’re a blasphemer, now?” Soma forgot me for a moment, taking a menacing step toward his retainer. “Worshipping the Black God while you attend services to righteous Khors?”

“That was Andrik’s concept of the church, not Ignas’.” I scoffed. “Okay, if it’s not the law here already, then consider this my first official act of Voivoding: Anyone in Myszno can worship whatever god they damn well please, or not worship any god if that’s their preference.

There was a murmur of assent among the ranks.

"Istvan!" Soma pointed at me. "You're standing by, listening to this blasphemous outlander scum lay claim to Egbolt? To your liege lord's rightful lands?"

Istvan sucked a tooth, then shook his head. "Lord Bolza’s line and House were wiped out. This man has redeemed himself and his *druzhina* by deed. That is an act that is important to both the Tuun and the Yanik. He honors Lord Bolza’s memory."

Soma's entire face trembled with anger as he looked around and found nothing but judging stares. He sneered, then hawked in his throat and spat at my feet. "Fine. Then I invoke the Code of Honor and demand satisfaction."

"You want to duel me?" I couldn't stop the manic grin that spread over my face. "Okay. Sure. Challenger gets to pick the field and the weapon, right?"

"The field," Soma replied stiffly. “You pick the weapon."

"Then I pick no weapons," I said. "No armor, no weapons, no magic. Plain ol’ fisticuffs."

Soma sized me up for a minute. I was over a foot shorter and about a hundred pounds lighter than he was. "Done. What are your terms?"

"Fight to whoever loses consciousness first." I replied. "No magic or tech."

He sniffed. "A barbarian even in this. The honorable weapon is the sword or pistol."

"Yeah, but jamming your fist up someone's nose is more satisfying." I bared my teeth at him. "Be grateful I didn't pick spears."

"As you say." Soma shucked his spellglove off and threw it back at Ur Ferenz, who winced as he juggled it like a hot potato. I unequipped my armor and gear down to my boots, pants and undershirt. Soma took his shirt off. Because of course he did.

My HUD chimed, and time seemed to slow slightly as a prompt appeared:

⟦Based on your profile and combat experience, we have detected that you prefer to Realistic Combat vs Augmented Combat when Dueling opponents. Is that correct?⟧

"*Yes.* "I thought back, hopping from Karalti's back to the ground. The soldiers stayed in formation, but the officers formed a loose arena around us as Soma put his fists up and began to circle.

⟦Realistic Combat mode ignores HP and Level in favor of vital points when Dueling NPCs. Combat is resolved by martial skill application instead of a combat minigame. If you

wish to change your preferences at any time, query 'Change Single Combat Settings.]

"You will regret this." Soma had the muscle bulk of a blacksmith or a wrestler: thick through the upper body, with a bit of fluff around the middle. "I learned to fight at the Royal College in Taltos, where I was trained by the grand master, Lonzo Karpoff!"

I shrugged. Mouthing off was about as pointless as ripping your shirt off before a fight. Instead, I stayed loose and balanced, tracking him as he circled and reading his body.

"You're small, Tuun! Too small to fight the likes of me!" He had his arms up like a classical wrestler, fingers loose.

Soma pushed in. As he came forward, I put my guard up and lashed out with a quick, fast jab, enough to piss him off and get him to open up. He came in swinging. I bounced to the right and slammed my left fist into his face, then followed up from the right. My knuckles connected with a dull meaty crack, just hard enough to lure him in.

"HRRRAGH! I'll crush you!" Soma charged straight forward, trying to overwhelm me with his size - and ran his face right into the blade of my foot as I pulled a vertical side-kick up underneath his jaw. The huge man's head snapped back and he crashed to the dirt like a sack of hammers, blood pouring from his mouth.

"Huh." I cocked my foot, then swung my leg back down and stood. "Maybe if you hadn't been flapping your tongue, you wouldn't have bitten it."

“Well, that was a damn good ass-fuckin’ time!” Vash nodded, arms crossed. “Ten out of ten, a standing splits *and* a concussion. I like it.”

"Yup. I was *Sam Dan* Taekwondo school champion of 2055." My HUD assistant had been right - that *was* realistic combat.

Vash laughed. “You should have become a Baru! Why are you a Lancer, dog?”

“Probably some kind of compensation thing.” I shook my hands out and paced around the ring, coming to a stop in front of Istvan. "Alright, Arshak. What do you want to do?"

Istvan crossed his arm over his chest and bowed from the neck. "I am at the service of your House, Lord Dragozin."

⟦You have unlocked a new Hero: Ur Istvan Arshak (Rank A+ Duelist/Cavalry Marshal - Myszno Defense Force)⟧

I clapped him on the shoulder. "I'm glad. You're a great officer, and I'm sure you're an even better Castellan."

"So I am no longer Sheriff of Slutlava?" he asked hopefully.

"No. I'm assigning that position to Ur Ferenz as of today." I turned to face the knight, who was helping his shirtless, half-conscious lord to his feet. He tensed, a grimace freezing on his face. "Ur Ferenz, your first order is to take Soma to the brig and let him cool his heels for a couple of days. Make sure he's got decent food and drink. No blueprints, no work at all. Anything he's doing can be transferred to Viktor and Rin."

"...Yes, Your Grace." The knight sounded and looked squirrely, but he threw Soma's arm around his shoulders and wrapped the other around his waist.

As he staggered off, a horrifying wailing sound blew to us from the north: a sound like a million ambulances screaming all at once. Everyone turned as the yowl intensified, mixed with the sound of horns. Karalti reared her head and flared her crests in alarm.

"Well, fuck me dead and back to life again." Vash crossed his arms, watching in the direction as the as yet unseen source of the noise.

"WhoTheWhatTheHowTheWhyTheFUCK is THAT?!" I clamped my hands over my ears.

The siren wails built into a terrifying chorus as sixty Meewfolk dinosaur riders charged through the northern gatehouse Some were in armor and chain - others were nude except for jewelry, their fur shaved into stripes to reveal the tattoos on their skin. They screeched and howled and whirled their swords over their heads as they thundered in, riding their hookwings with the acrobatic expertise of jockeys: some sitting, some standing on their saddles. Their beasts were a leaner, lighter breed than the destrier hookwings that carried knights in armor. At the front and center of the horde was Suri on Cutthroat. She rode beside a strapping, white-furred Meewfolk warrior with a lot of metal in his face and chipped ears. She gave us a thumbs up and turned her mount, cantering toward us.

Istvan laughed with delight, raising his voice to be heard over the cacophony. "That, my friend, is the Orphans' Company!"

Book 3: The Battle for Myszno

Chapter 40

After mopping the floor with Soma and meeting and greeting what felt like thirty million people, I was done interacting with other human beings for the day. I needed to get a handle on the Mass Combat System, pick my bonus ability, and work out what the fuck I was going to do now that I was the commander of an entire fucking garrison.

Karalti took me to a sheltered grotto beside a steaming crater lake. She went to wallow in the boiling hot center of the mineral spring while I lounged in the warm shallows. First up was the Mark of Matir ability. As always, I had two options. As usual, it was difficult to choose.

Stigmata (Life)
Boost speed and reflexes by 25% for 5 minutes; all Dark-element attacks restore HP (5% of total inflicted damage) for 30 seconds.

Mortal Grudge (Entropy)
Deal five powerful non-elemental magic attacks to one enemy (35 x half your Will score), and inflict the Death Sentence

status on yourself (countdown 60: seconds). Speed increased by 25%, Adrenaline Point regen increased by 2.5x for 60 seconds.

"Death Sentence?" Frowning, I queried the wiki.

Death Sentence (Status)

This status places a counter on the target character, and when the counter reaches zero, the affected target dies. The counter drops by 1 per second. This status only applies in combat; the only way to be rid of a Death Sentence is to either die and revive, or end combat by defeating your opponent/s. Targets who are immune to instant death are immune to this status. This attack does not drain Adrenaline Points or Stamina, but can only be used once per week.

Well, okay then. It was like the Final Fantasy status, *Doom*. I closed the window and lay back in the water to think. Certain healing or certain death? Hmm. Tough choice.

I re-read them, and my brain snagged on the 'non-elemental magical attack' aspect of *Mortal Grudge*. All magic in Archemi was elemental – except for Aether, the primal magical element. For an elemental specialist like me, a non-elemental attack could be decisive – especially in PvP. My enemies would go in prepared for Dark attacks. My Will stat was currently sitting on 60, so... what did that work out to be? 1050 non-elemental magical damage, per attack, and five attacks. If I landed them all, that was 5250 damage – which was very nice indeed for an ability that didn't drain Adrenaline or Stamina.

I had a think about *Stigmata*, too. While HP loss was always something I had to contend with, potion ingredients for healing potions were common and cheap – especially here, with the Endlar right on the doorstep. My most powerful attack, *Master of Blades* thru *Rain of Glass* – MoB-RoG for short – was based on my attack stats and currently did 2417 for the first hits on one enemy, then 1167 on five others. That was quite a nice chunk of damage to rain down on people, and with Stigmata active, would heal 412 points of HP. Two Concentrated Green Moss Tinctures healed 500. But if I chained Jump, MoB-RoG and Grudge...

"Let's see, Jump, then Master o'Blades and Rain of Glass plus Grudge is... Jesus Christ." I recalculated just to be sure. Wow, okay. Yes, that combo really would do a maximum of 11,534 damage to one target, with four normal Rain of Glass strikes to surrounding enemies. If the primary target was a Dark-resistant enemy, like the Broodmother or the Warsinger, it would only take half the MoB-RoG damage, but that was still a 'mere' 9752 points. Conversely, if the target was *weak* to Darkness, they'd take double or even triple. With the enhanced AP regen, I'd be able to hit my most powerful attack chains twice... and if I couldn't kill someone inside of a minute with five-figure damage, I needed to hand in my gamer card.

"Okay, Matir, I get it. With great risk comes great ass-kicking." I selected Mortal Grudge. The Mark of Matir flared with a cool sensation beneath the hot water, then settled back down. I'd have to be careful with this move, but if used strategically... yeah, it was possible to make good use of it.

Next on the menu was the Mass Combat screen. I mentally swiped across and was pleased to find the three pages – Army, Heroes and Logistics - were no longer greyed out. Still – it was intimidating. I'd logged thousands of hours into my beloved antique Pokémon collection, but most of my actual strategic experience was from my IRL grunt days. All my fighting had been done in jungles, which emphasized small-group tactics and leadership, counter-insurgency hijinks, and enduring the hare-brained schemes that issued from the bowels of the Pentagon.

It's just a game, man. It even has types and IVs and shit. I fired up the Logistics menu to assess what units we could produce at the Prezyemi Line. The short answer was 'not many'. The Line had facilities to train the basic melee and ranged infantry units – Swordsmen, Pikemen, Riflemen, Gunners and Archers – and that was about it. We could also produce Light Cavalry, but to grow beyond our current unit capacity, we needed a third ⟦Hookwing Stable⟧. The crafting sector was falling behind on arming our existing force with good quality weapons. We had people who could repair airships, but they couldn't build them. That, more than anything else, was a strike against us. The Demon's lack of airpower was the key weakness of his undead army. A hundred thousand zombies, ghouls, wights and whatever else he cared to drag up out of the dirt were rendered completely ineffective by some well-placed, old-fashioned bombs.

All the Defense units best suited for fighting the Demon's army were either inaccessible or too expensive to recruit and produce. The Orphans had swelled our ranks to 16,000-ish troops, but we needed more production nodes,

Ravensblood Dragoons, Ravensblood Mages, and Battle Brothers of Khors.

Increasingly apprehensive, I flipped over to the Heroes menu. This was looking better, because there were lots of available heroes and a few left to identify and recruit. We'd have to do that via sidequests. Sidequests we didn't have time for.

Interestingly, I was now listed as the 'General', while Suri was listed with the other NPCs as a 'Champion (Recruited)', but Rin wasn't.

Count Hector Dragozin, the Black Hand of Matir and Karalti, the Black Opal Queen

Armed with the Spear of Nine Spheres, the impressive profile of dragon and rider inspires man and beast alike and strikes the fear of the Dark God into the hearts of their enemies.

Suri Ba'hadir, the Red Lioness

A powerful melee warrior, Suri's presence on the battlefield grants allies Damage Reduction, increases the damage dealt by charges, and grants buffs against Fear and Disease.

Soma was also listed as a Champion, and his status was 'unrecruited'. My Renown with him was something like -700, so I doubted he was going to be a part of the team any time soon. Istvan and Vash were both in the next tier down, the Heroes tier:

Istvan Arshak

Well-loved and respected by his troops, the former Castellan of Egbolt Castle is a versatile light cavalry specialist. His presence on the battlefield increases the army's overall speed, vigor, defense and attack. Especially suited to one-on-one combat against other heroes, Istvan can train Hookwing Pistoleers at twice the normal speed of a normal cavalry sergeant.

Vash Dorha

A Baru in service to Matir, Vash Dorha is a powerful close-combat fighter who is in his element among the common militia. He gives all surrounding Infantry stamina buffs, healing buffs, substantial buffs against Fear, Terror and Corruption to melee and ranged Infantry. He can also train Baru units, who provide healing and deal magical Dark-elemental melee strikes against incorporeal and magically shielded foes.

Count Lorenzo Soma (Unrecruited)

Like many craftmasters, Lord Soma has a strong personality and can be somewhat... temperamental. Despite this and his lack of military prowess, Lord Soma is an artificing prodigy who specializes in the field of airship repair and design. When stationed at any manufacturing node, he decreases Artifact repair time by 50%. If stationed in a Mana Mine, he increases Mana extraction yield by 15%. If stationed at an airship production facility, he doubles the speed of airship assembly.

There were other heroes listed: Lazar the Healer, Lord Zediwitz, Zlaslo, Admiral Ghelan, Taethawn the Bleak - the

Meewfolk commander of the Orphans - and Viktor, the Master Artificer of House Soma's weaponeers. Each one had special abilities and buffs they conveyed to troops. My problem was that three of the best heroes – Istvan, Taethawn and Zediwitz – were cavalry-focused, while the militia units only had Vash and the Mages had no one. There was a mage hero listed – Szonja the Living Flame – but she was listed as 'uncontacted' and was based in Litvy.

"Hmm. Hang on a second." Curious, I pushed the Mass Combat window to one side and called up a second Map window to look and see if I could analyze Litvy. When I zoomed in on the marker, I got a pop-up:

⟦Information unavailable: you must send Reconnaissance units to assess this city.⟧

Ugh. Reasonable, but aggravating. I cycled back to the Army menu to see what I had to work with – starting with the overview.

Army Information

Available Legion: The Myszno Defense Force

For centuries, the proud citizens of Vlachia have prospered through steely determination and a thriving, forward-thinking focus on education and technology. The Vlachian Army has a large and diverse roster of available units, with almost every type of unit represented. Rifle-equipped infantry and Hookwing pistoleers are the foundation of their military, backed up by a diverse roster of Elite Units and some of the most advanced airships and artillery in the world. The large unit roster allows commanders to build flexible yet specialized armies suited to different strategies and campaigns.

- *Vlachian Royal 4th Fleet, 2nd Company - 2185*
- *Myszno Defense Force – 9378*
- *The Orphans Company – 5030*

Total Units: 16,593

United Myszno Defense Force Unit Roster:

Airships

- ***Hussar-class Destroyer (3):*** *A heavy battleship and troop carrier with artillery and magical armament. Capacity 700.*
- ***Bathory-class Skirmisher (9):*** *Light, fast, frigate-type airships used to support and protect Hussar-class ships with artillery. Capacity 200.*
- ***Lóvas-class Cargo Hauler (20):*** *Essential troop and cargo transport ships, lightly armored and built for distance rather than speed.*

Elite units

Knights of the Red Star (150): *The personal army of the Volod, the Knights of the Red Star are highly visible with their night-black hookwings, their red lamellar armor, and the holy draconic scripture tattooed down their cheeks. They are equipped with the best weapons Vlachia can make: Mastercrafted sabers for hand to hand combat, and bolt-action repeating rifles with 8-round magazines. Powerful and* *versatile, they are trained in both ranged combat and cavalry charges. The presence of Knights on the Red Star on the battlefield can cause Fear in enemies and make them more likely to break.*

Royal Elementalists (100): *Trained in the Royal College of Maegi in Taltos, these combat-ready spellcasters cast a variety of offensive and support magic. When used defensively, they are capable of erecting magical shields strong enough to soak artillery fire.*

Nightstalkers Assassins (50): *Hardened in fighting pits and alleyways of Taltos, these lightly armored, high-damage rogues are best deployed against single high-status units. They are also excellent siege breakers, able to infiltrate defenses and attack them from the inside.*

Battle Brothers of Khors (50): *The best artillerymen in Vlachia, the temple-trained Battle Engineers see their craft as a form of prayer. They can man magical weapons and mobile Artifacts, as well as operate mortars, cannons, and other artillery weapons with twice the normal fire rate. They require a Monastery of the Forger to train.*

Yanik Rangers (55): *Lightly armored, medium-damage recon units whose main advantage is their ability to fight in difficult terrain without penalty. They are also immune to fear effects and have an attack bonus against gates and structures.*

Ravensblood Dragoons (300): *Descended from the Dakhari mercenaries who helped the House of Corvinus conquer Vlachia, Dragoons are Quazi-mounted aerial knights who fight with special hooked polearms – the* khara *- and pistols. They are brutally effective against armored and unarmored* *flying creatures, able to pull their khara through wings and gun down armored opponents. Their majestic presence on the battlefield is inspiring to ground troops, improving morale by 5% per 50 units and making lines of infantry less likely to shatter.*

Ravensblood Maegi (150): *Mages who fly on quazi to support their melee brethren. Their presence on the battlefield inspires infantry and increases the attack and defense of foot-soldiers by 5% per 50 units.*

Orphan Company Triceratops Cavalry (65): *What the triceratops lacks in speed, it makes up for with bulletproof stopping power. Equipped with heavy armor, powerful armor-piercing crossbows and a crew of three riflemen, a line charge of these large dinosaurs is highly effective against Infantry.*

Baru: *These supernaturally mobile, close-quarters units are ideally suited to fighting monstrous enemies. At their best against the undead, they can strike and damage Incorporeal units and gain a +150% damage buff against Undead and Incorporeal creatures. The blows of their attuned iron gauntlets are also able to shatter armor and stone to great effect, making them effective against Large constructs. Baru have a chance to completely avoid damage via teleportation. A unit of 10 Baru is enough to convey a health regen bonus of 10% on surrounding infantry. Baru may also be used for Recon, with a +50% bonus on Diplomacy or Trade alliance checks with Churvi, Tuun, or Northern Lys people. (5)*

Infantry & Cavalry Units

- *Vlachian Militia Pikemen (2086)*

- *Vlachian Archers (2070)*
- *Vlachian Riflemen (885)*
- *Vlachian Hookwing Pistoleers (3103)*
- *Corrun-Mounted Heavy Cavalry (1586)*
- *Orphans Company Hookwing Archers (3000)*
- *Orphans Company Hookwing Pistoleers (2300)*

Artillery units

- *Mortar (200)*
- *12-Pound Mobile Cannon (250)*
- *Heavy Cannon (150)*
- *Orphan Company Brontosaurus Mobile Artillery Platform (3)*

Specialist Units

- *Myszno Defense Medical Corps (100)*

Available Heroes

- *Suri Ba'hadir*
- *Istvan Arshak*
- *Vash Dorha*
- *Count Lorenzo Soma*
- *Zlaslo ul'Tiranozavir*
- *Ur Robert Gehlan*
- *Admiral Constantin Ghelan*
- *Lazar Skaliz*
- *Taethawn the Bleak*
- *Viktor of Provern*
- *Lord Franz Zediwitz*

- *Szonja the Living Flame*

Recruited: 10
Total Available: 12

Supply Trains

- *Boros > Krivan Pass > Prezyemi Line (Open)*
- *Litvy > Gondar Valley > Western Endlar > Prezyemi Line (Open)*
- *Slutlava > Prezyemi Line (Open)*

"*Fuck.* "I slid out into the steaming water with a sigh, gazing up at the battery of open HUD displays hanging above. *"We just don't have enough personnel to hold a thirty-mile defensive line, Tidbit. Plain and simple. And we've got... what? Five days? Maybe."*

"That's long enough to rally the other satraps, isn't it?" Karalti had settled down under the water, the tip of her nose resting on the bank like a snorkel as she basked in the heat. *"They'll take the situation a lot more seriously now we have all that Renown."*

"Yeah. "Increasingly aggravated, I continued to study. Looking over it a second time didn't make things any better. There was no way to get around the fact that we didn't have enough troops, and the soldiers we had weren't the right kind. Two-thirds of our basic units were cavalry of some kind or another, which was basically worthless behind the Wall. That was a shame: Cavalry was great against cheap infantry units like zombies and plague rats, especially with Istvan on

the field. The benefits of cavalry were basically canceled out by the terrain.

I dumped all my available skill points into Leadership, then bobbed around in the spring like a cork, browsing the wiki for anything that might help us turn this fiasco-thon around. I studied the Ability details, Rank and other information of each of the different units, getting a sense of what they were good for and what they weren't. But nothing I read changed my instinctive conclusion: we were at the wrong place with the wrong army. We needed open terrain where we could maximize the impact of cavalry, artillery, and airships. We also needed long, heavy pikes, lots of them. Pikemen could keep the horde at bay while riflemen supported them from behind. Istvan and Soma were both correct: we needed more infantry, at least 10,000 pikemen and 5000 rifles, preferably more. We needed magitech shields, airships, explosives.

Shaking my head, I dismissed the menu and swam to the bank. I was dripping wet until I equipped my armor - and then poof, I was magically dry again. Why the devs had enabled an insta-drying hack but left the Pee Meter intact, I would never know. *"Okay, Tidbit. Time to go."*

"Okay!" Karalti rolled over onto her back with a deep groan, luxuriating for a couple more seconds, then flopped back onto her belly and began to weave through the water like a snake. *"Do you want to train with me? It's been a while since we trained strength or dexterity or anything."*

I hesitated. *"I... don't really feel like training today."*

My dragon regarded me with an expression of flat disbelief. *"Okay – where is Hector, and what did you do with him?"*

"Really."

Karalti's eyes narrowed. She dropped her neck and head as she approached, sniffing deeply. *"Why? What's wrong?"*

"Lucien," I admitted. "I... I dunno, Karalti. It took a while to really sink in, but I think what happened back in Taltos is finally getting to me. What's the point in training that hard if my rivals can just cheat their way up? Max stats and everything."

Karalti rumbled, her crests flattening. *"The point is... we train. Everything we have, we earned. Together."*

I closed my eyes and drew a deep breath. Then, I smiled.

"Alright. Let's take a couple hours." I drew a deep breath and looked up at her. "After that, we have to go back to Korona and deliver some bad news, and hope to RNGesus that we don't lose all the Renown we just gained."

Chapter 41

Four hours later, all three Starborn, one dragon, and every major Hero of the Defense Force were seated in the Korona War Room. Before they had arrived, I'd ordered the room cleaned, cups and bottles removed, and the reeds on the floor changed. The Officer's Mess had been closed - the officers would eat with their troops from now on. The fancy candelabras had been moved in here to give more light to the windowless room. I ordered that the officers' reserved snacks – the cheese, fruits and candies - be distributed. The candies and fruit were sent to the Engineer Corps while the cheese was sent to the Orphans. I had Istvan draft letters to go with the gifts: an invitation for Master Artificer Viktor of Provern and Taethawn the Bleak to attend the War Council.

Both Viktor and Taethawn were seated at the table tonight. The Master Artificer of House Soma was so old that his neck looked like a turkey's wattle, wobbling beneath the edge of a weak chin. His eyes were piercing though, dark and intelligent. He was visibly anxious: perched on his seat and rubbing his knees, shoulders taut. By contrast, Taethawn the Bleak was sprawled in his chair like... well... a cat. He had one leg hooked over the arm, one foot resting on the ground, his arms flung over the back and side. His tail danced through the gap between the seat and the cushion. He was easily the tallest Meewfolk I'd ever met – taller than Soma at a full stretch, which made him close to seven and a half feet. He had a scrappy, piratical appearance: His eyes were mismatched – one bright blue, one amber - and his chipped ears were heavy with rings and jewels. His pure white fur was tinged brown with grime, shaved in places to reveal jagged tribal tattoos. According to Rin, they marked him as a criminal and an outcast from Meewhome – something he was apparently proud of.

Suri and Karalti sat knee to knee, more comfortable around one another than I'd ever seen them. Rin was seated across from Viktor and looked almost as anxious. Istvan, Ur Gehlan and Admiral Gehlan – who were indeed younger and elder brothers – sat side by side. Lazar and Lord Zediwitz took up the other seats: the medic was dignified and crane-like, while Zediwitz fidgeted and sweated in his fine armor. Last of all were Vash and Zlaslo. They were both on their feet, Vash with his hands folded in front of him like a bouncer beside the door, and Zlaslo leaning indolently against the opposite wall.

I arranged the final markers on the battle map and then took my place at the head of the table. "Alright, everyone. Thanks for coming. Viktor, Taethawn." I nodded to each of them. "We're definitely glad to have the Orphans on our side."

"Such is the effect of my gallant Company on the massesss, My Lord," Under the hiss, Taethawn had a strong, musical accent straight out of South-East Asia. "We figured

Prezyemi to be a hopeless messs, but with that woman on your side and Lord Pigsty out of the way, I finally have hope for the future of thiss province."

"How did these two convince you to come back?" Istvan motioned to me and Suri.

"How d'ya think, mate? I kicked his fuckin' arse, is what I did." Suri had her arms crossed, knees spread, her heels planted on the floor. "He loved every minute of it, too."

"She put me in a masterful headlock. I have never been ssso scared and yet so aroused at the sssame time." Taethawn's tail lashed slowly from side to side.

"You deserted us when I needed you most, Taethawn," Istvan said sourly. "Can we trust you now?"

"Of course. As long as the pay isss good." Taethawn squinted his eyes like a smug cat. "But you can come down from your tall hookwing, Arshak. Sssoma makes deserters of us all, doesn't he?"

Istvan bristled.

"Whatever anyone did in the past is being put aside," I said, before the Captain could retort. "Including Soma. The undead are marching north, and if they reach Vastil Pass, Vlachia is fucked. The Sathbar Plains-" I nodded to Taethawn "-will be their first target. We know what the Demon wants now, and he won't stop until he's found it."

Vash grunted. "You know, do you? Then tell us: why is this walking corpse swizzling his dick in our province?"

"Eww." Rin grimaced.

I leaned forward on my hands. "The swizzler's name is Ashur of the Ten Thousand Swords. He's a Napathu general, a servant of the Breathless. He's here to dig Matir out of his Dragon Gate and kill him."

A murmur of disbelief rippled around the room.

"That is absurd," Admiral Gehlan rumbled.

"I have multiple sources. The first clue was when one of the undead officers said something to me on the battlefield. He told me that the Napathu were here to 'take back what we stole'. Just recently I learned that Matir is entombed here, in Myszno. His Dragon Gate used up all the mana from Napath. It had to be done to create the Caul of Souls, but Napath doesn't see it that way." I tapped the mountains in the south. "Matir is somewhere down here. Ashur is using a magical artifact to remotely draw energy from the Dragon Gate, and that's how he's raising and maintaining his army."

"But he already has the south," Rin said. "So why is he advancing north?"

I traced a line up from the approximate location of the gate, all the way to where Karalti had picked me up. "Because when the Gates were built, his consort, Lahati, had her tomb constructed as a mirror to Matir's and then had her descendants spread and maintain the rumor that her resting place was the real Dragon Gate. It's not, but Ashur doesn't know that."

"That sounds like something the Black God would do." Lazar nodded.

"This all sounds like fairy tales to me." Admiral Gehlan shook his head. "Matir? Dragon Gates? How do you know all this?"

"I went to Lahati's Tomb and spoke with her." I regarded him flatly.

There was an awkward pause, until Vash giggle-snorted.

"You know that Yanik lore about there being a city under the swamp?" I looked to Istvan and Zlaslo. "It's true, kind of. Lahati told me this entire province was one draconic city. The city was destroyed at the end of the Drachan War."

"The entire province?" Lord Zediwitz's moustache bristled. "That seems impossible."

"*Well, we're pretty big.*" Karalti replied, blinking at him. "*And every Queen must have her own territory. Even sisters will battle for land if there is not enough of it. Dragon cities don't look like human cities.*"

"Did this city sink into the mire, as the stories say?" Istvan asked.

I wanted to shake my head, but after a moment's hesitation, I nodded instead. There were some things they didn't need to know yet. "Yeah. But now we know why Ashur is here, we know what he wants. And we have to keep up the ruse."

"Right. Because if he realizes he's sitting on the Gate already, we're screwed," Suri said. "Can he like... open this temple or whatever it is?"

"No. But he has an Artifact he can use to siphon energy." I reached back and patted the haft of the Spear. "It's a stone like this ruby. Both the Gate and the Star of Endless Night have some powerful magic worked into them, including the magic of misdirection. Ashur knows the Gate is here, but not where. He's following the old legends, trying to push north to Lahati's Tomb."

"Oooh. Yeah, that makes sense." Rin nodded.

"That intel will inform our strategy moving forward." I drew a deep breath. "First thing I want to do is reassign some command positions. Istvan, I'm reinstating you as Commandant of the Defense Force. Lord Zediwitz, you're Captain of our Heavy Cavalry. I want the two of you to collaborate closely with Taethawn on tactics and training."

"Yes sir," Istvan gave me a nod.

Zediwitz struck his chest with his fist, moustache bristling. "As you command, Your Grace!"

The Meewfolk man squinted his eyes.

"Suri, Vash, I want you to work under Istvan as his Lieutenants, with a focus on infantry" I looked to her. "With the two of you buffing the front line, they stand a chance going forward."

Suri's golden eyes flashed dangerously. "Do I have a choice in the matter?"

"I wouldn't nominate you if you didn't," I replied.

She hesitated, then nodded. "Alright. Never been a Lieutenant before. Think you can handle me, Vash?"

"In any way the lady could possibly desire." He bowed from the waist.

"Viktor, I would ask you to remain in your current post as commander of the Engineer Corps, but take Rin as your First Officer," I said to him. "I'm hopeful we can bring Lord Soma around in the near future, but until then, you're in charge."

"As you say, Your Grace." The older man stopped scrubbing at his thighs and relaxed back on his seat. "Uhh... what would you have us focus our efforts on? Lord Soma had us bent to the task of creating portable magical shield generators."

"We'll talk about that later," I replied. "First, I want to discuss our broadest strategy. We know what our goals are: stop Ashur from moving deeper into the province, minimize casualties, keep the location of Matir's Dragon Gate secret. I spent most of the afternoon looking over this map, and in my opinion, the only viable strategy is to retreat and regroup."

"You want to abandon the Wall?" Admiral Gehlan startled up. His brother's brow was furrowed, lips pursed.

"More like we don't have a choice," Suri said. "Think about it. How long is this barrier? About fifty kilometers, thirty miles or so? We'd need about ten thousand mob per kilometer to properly hold it against an assault. We got, what? About ten thousand for the entire bloody wall right now?"

"Sixteen thousand, five hundred and ninety-three now that the Orphans are back on the payroll," I said. "But yeah. It's not even just the lack of manpower. As soon as nations gain air power, walls like this one are obsolete. One Hussar would be enough to blow this place to kingdom come, and the only reason that Ashur and his force haven't done it yet is because they haven't faced enough resistance to think of finding and fielding one. Regarding our troops, out of that sixteen and a half thousand, about two-thirds are cavalry. Any flat terrain we have is made up of rivers and swamps and ravines. We have no mobility aft or forward of the Prezyemi Line, which means the only thing we can do here is react to an assault. If we want to get the better of the undead, we have to go on the offensive."

"It is true." Taethawn's gaze slid to Zediwitz, who nodded. "It iss part of why we left. My *Ro'wor* riders can do little but strop their claws and pick their teeth here. But the corrun and coursers stand idle."

"What is your proposition, then, Rytier?" Ur Gehlan, the Knight of the Red Star, spoke up for the first time.

I glanced at Karalti. She smiled and nodded back.

"I think our initial strategy should be to focus on reducing the volume of Ashur's army, and then defend against a smaller force while a team of specialists goes to take out Ashur himself," I said. "The way I see it, we can execute this in three stages. First up is the reduction. We do that by maximizing the opportunities presented by the Prezyemi Line. I want to collapse the entire west half of the line by opening the Gul River Dam and letting it flood and sweep away a freshly-evacuated Slutlava. The debris will narrow the battlefield and will funnel the undead forces to the center of the line by necessity. We're going to turn that battlefield into an obstacle course that will punish every single step they take. My prediction is that Ashur will use his zombies as cannon fodder and hold his better troops in reserve."

"Yes. That is his core strategy." Istvan was scrutinizing the map, his hands laced under his chin.

"What we do is let them choke the battlefield." I drew a blob, indicating where the zombies would come in and try to assault the wall. "But by the time they get here and start laying explosives and climbing, we're already gone. We start the evacuations tonight: The Orphans, our cavalry, everyone who doesn't need to be here goes north to Litvy before Ashur arrives. We have a series of un-manned fortifications, pull back as each line is overcome, and then bust the Sarviz Dam. The Wall will already be armed with demolition charges and payloads of Greek Fire. When I first got here, Istvan, you told me the only thing that worked on the dead were fire and water. We're gonna give them both at the same time."

"Right. It probably won't destroy his army, but it'll piss off the Demon... uhh... Ashur the Swizzler something chronic," Suri added.

I nodded. "We want to control their movement, reduce their numbers, and make them angry. If they're angry, they go where we want them to go. The fire and flood should render his cheap units unusable. The ruins of Slutlava and the wall and everything else will act like a big grinder. The goal is to lure them to Krivan Pass."

Rin wrinkled her nose. "Oh my god. I can already imagine how this is going to smell."

I chuckled. "I know, right?"

"If we're luring them in, that means we gotta make it seem like the Pass is the last place we want 'em to go," Suri said. "Lahati's place isn't actually in Krivan Pass, yeah?"

"No. There's one really obscure portal that leads there."

"Right. Then this has gotta look like a proper last stand, with us all fleeing in terror." She tapped the southern entry to the Pass. "This bottleneck here is pretty great. Let's say we have a garrisoned force lying in wait here and here. The ships lead them right through the middle, and we kill'em. More Yanik Rangers would be great, but I dunno if we have time to finish that side-quest."

Rin gnawed on her bottom lip. "I don't think so."

"What is the third stage?" Admiral Gehlan asked.

"If it looks like the undead will break through the Pass – and realistically, there's so many of them that they probably will – we retreat to Litvy," I said. "Our troops and Heroes in Litvy will have been busy all this time: recruiting, building, fortifying. The defense at Litvy will prepare as if the approaching undead army is arriving at maximum strength. The retreating force will make the road to Litvy as difficult as it can be before he reaches the highlands."

Admiral Gehlan nodded, stroking his long white moustache. "The ground of the Pass is almost impossible to negotiate by foot right now. Our air power is going to be decisive against a ground force. We need more ships."

"For sure," Suri replied. "Have to be in Litvy to get those."

"Are we planning to evacuate the majority of the force from the Prezyemi Line today, then?" Istvan asked me.

I nodded. "Like I said: starting tonight, we send people to Litvy and the Pass to begin preparations. I vote we conscript every able body to start building ramparts and digging trenches on 8-hour rotations. Any personnel or civilian who volunteers 24 hours of hard work gets first pass out of here to Litvy. All buildings are to be stripped and relocated. We leave enough munitions and men to hold the Wall for the assault."

"You want the Gul Dam destroyed in advance?" Viktor said.

I gave him a sharp nod. "As soon as Slutlava is cleared of people."

"We're gonna need ships from Litvy and Boros ASAP," Suri said. "We don't have enough for the evac."

I was about to disagree, but took a second to glance at the Mass Combat menu and the capacity of the aircraft we had. We technically had enough to move about 14,000 people, but... "You're right. Between Slutlava and the garrison, we're gonna need more ships."

"We need Lord Soma to acquire more airships," Viktor spoke up, his voice reedy and dry. "Let Rin and I speak to him and see if we cannot convince him to join this effort. It is a well-thought out and feasible plan, though we shall be exhausted by the time the Demon arrives."

"Better tired than dead," Suri said.

Viktor bowed his head. "Indeed."

“I think it is desperate and risky,” Ur Gehlan said. His brother nodded. “But the situation is desperate.”

Suri snorted, crossing her arms. “Yeah. The time for safe bets was about two months ago.”

“If you’re all happy with this strategy, I’m going to meet with each of you to work out tactics through the night. We’ll adjust the plan accordingly.” I looked around the table, then back to Zlaslo and Vash. “Any questions?”

"The final retreat is not a certain thing," Viktor said nervously. "If the timing of the dam and wall demolition is not extremely precise..."

"Take it from me: death is nothing to fear, old man," Vash grunted. "If we die in an explosion or a flood, then we die in such a way that we cannot be reanimated into the walking dead. It is a good and natural thing."

"Exactly," Suri said.

"I'll help protect the ships! Don't worry!" Karalti bared her teeth and tossed her chin up at Viktor.

The Baru sighed, then shook his head. “My only concern is that we should have moved earlier. Many will suffer regardless of what we do.”

“Indeed. But not as many as before.” Taethawn, who had been lounging in silence, pricked his ears and sat up straighter. “Lord Soma could still be the death of this place if we lag.”

I held up a hand. “That’s enough ragging on Soma for today. He fought, he lost, and he has been honorable enough that if he's sorry for what he's done, I'll believe him. We'll try and get through to him. Until then-"

There was a pounding on the door, and everyone turned as it burst in ahead of a Yanik scout. The man was wild-eyed with fear. "*Mayevi! Da ruyê! Da ruyê!*"

Zlaslo and Istvan both shot to their feet. Istvan spoke first. "*Da deruyê su yeh? Aksafi Vlachii!*"

"What is it?" Suri and Karalti both stood in alarm. I straightened up at the end of the table.

"The gate! The Demon has sent an emissary onto the field, to the Waterfall Gate!" The man babbled in Vlachian. All the Yanik were hardened vets, but this man's dark skin was ashen gray with fear. "My lords... It is Count Bolza.

Chapter 42

The former Voivode of Myszno waited for us on the other side of the gates, as patient as the dead. He sat astride an eerily still and silent T.rex, a slender ten-foot lance resting over one shoulder and a banner stand resting in a bracket on his saddle. The banner was a simple ragged swatch of black linen. It depicted a skeletal hand with the index and middle finger raised, the thumb crossed over the palm. Underneath it was tied a long fluttering ribbon of white cloth.

"Well, fuck me. Does this madness never end?" Vash shaded his eyes and peered out over the wall.

"Never." Istvan stared bleakly in the direction of his former liege lord, the telescope he was using to look at him hanging from numb fingers. "Vash - go rally the officers and get the men down off the walls. I will talk to him. Hector, Suri, Rin: will you come?"

"Wait. You can't just waltz down there like a loon, Arshak." Vash scowled, catching his wrist. "Even a dragon cannot hit a wraith. We don't know how many ghosts he stuffed up his ass."

"*I'll* go rally the officers, then," Rin said. "Vash, you go down with them if you're worried."

"*Euch.* No, it's okay." He rolled his eyes. "You all just go down there without me. I'll stay here alone, in the dark, going blind."

"Don't tempt me." Istvan sniffed.

Bolza stood motionless as Suri, Rin and Istvan descended the Waterfall Gate elevator with Cutthroat and Istvan's hookwing. Karalti launched from the edge of the wall with me on her back. We glided around in a tight circle to land gracefully on the stinking mud, about twenty feet away from Lord Bolza.

The undead lord stared through us with pitiless green eyes. He had been a handsome man in life, square-jawed, with a salt and pepper beard and the beginnings of a paunch. Karalti stood eye-to-eye with his T.rex mount. It hadn't been dead for that long – maybe a couple of days. Flies buzzed around its empty eye sockets. The dinosaur had been gutted, and its bloodless skin had retracted over its bare ribs, baring flesh crawling with insects.

"From this rather pointed message, I'm guessing the Tiranozavir *tribe got their asses handed to them,"* I said to Karalti.

"Uh huh." She held her ground, her tail lashing stiffly behind her.

The others fell in beside us, and there was a moment of silence.

"My lord," Istvan said heavily. "I prayed you would be spared. I prayed you had died in a such a way they could not puppet your corpse for their own ends... but it seems the gods are deaf as well as blind."

"You think I am to be pitied, Istvan?" The undead lord's lips were blue and stiff, and barely moved. His voice was hollow, but he was well-spoken and clear. "In truth, I am better than I have ever been. Lord Ashur has given me the greatest of gifts: a new life, free of pain, free of suffering. Eternal. Rational. Impartial. It is I who should pity you."

"Rational? There's nothing rational about a walking dead man," Istvan replied. "What do you want?"

"I am here on behalf of my eternal Master, Lord Ashur of the Ten Thousand Swords, the Ox of the River and Champion of the Breathless," Bolza replied. His teeth flashed with an odd metallic gleam. "I come to make a once-and-final offer. Stand down and let us through the Krivan Pass. If we find what we are looking for, we will take back what is rightfully ours and then depart from this land. If you do not surrender, we will destroy the remainder of all you love."

I kept my expression neutral, even as my chest thrilled with excitement. Target confirmed: they were after the Dragon Gate, and they thought it was north. "We don't know what you want. Litvy? Our ships? Our land? An offer is supposed to have terms. What terms are you offering?"

"Your lives." Bolza didn't blink. He only breathed to speak. "The Ducal seat has fallen. You are in no position to make demands of Lord Ashur."

"I'm not demanding anything. I'm asking a question," I replied. "Because Napath and Vlachia haven't had any contact, good or bad, for thousands of years. Your story doesn't hold up. There's nothing here that's rightfully yours."

"There is," the undead count replied. "The blood, soul, and fertility of Napath were stolen by the dragons and bought here. Our mana fuels your farms, and your machines, and your monuments. The forests of Myszno bloom from the ruin of our lands. My Master's people waited for millennia until you were weak and fat and decadent. They waited, planning to take back what they are rightfully owed. That time is now."

"That makes no sense." Rin stepped up beside my shoulder. "The best time to have taken Myszno would have been when Lawislaw Corvinus the Burned conquered the Sathbari and the Yanik. There's been hardly any potable mana for centuries."

Lord Bolza's expression was as serene and expressionless as a Roman sculpture. He said nothing.

I stood up on Karalti's back and leaned forward. "You're looking for the Great Wellspring, right? Well, it's too late. It's gone. Veles took it with him to his grave. There's no more mana in Myszno, except for what you've been draining from the land."

Bolza finally stirred. "The Great Wellspring is not what we seek. If you do not stand down, we will continue our advance and crush you. Our army now numbers in the hundreds of thousands. You stand no chance against us."

"Okay. We'll go and discuss this and then return to give you your answer." I jerked my head back toward the wall.

"As you wish." Bolza rotated his head slightly to look at Istvan.

"I wish for none of this." Istvan seemed to age ten years as he gazed at his old friend. "But one thing before we depart. What happened to your beloved Oksana? What about your children? Ivan? Your daughter, Zophia?"

A tic jumped near Lord Bolza's bloodless mouth. Then he sneered, pulling his lips back to flash top and bottom rows of gleaming metal fangs. When he spoke, his tone was guttural. "They march with the other thralls."

Istvan flinched as if he had been struck. He turned his face.

"The House of Bolza is dead," he said bitterly. "Long live the House of Dragozin."

We turned as a group and trudged off through the mud to gather in a circle some hundred feet away.

"It seems you are correct," Istvan said gloomily. "They are here searching for the Dragon Gate. Their advance through Myszno will not cease until they find it."

"How did you learn this?" Rin asked.

I slid down Karalti's shoulder and dropped to the ground, standing under the shelter of her wing. "I think I mentioned at the meeting, but there's an entry to Lahati's Tomb in Krivan Pass. I fell into it when I killed the Warsinger."

Rin bristled like a startled cat. "When you killed the WHAT!?"

"The.. uh... the Warsinger." I grinned at her sheepishly. "The entry to the Tomb was guarded by the oldest and weakest of the Warsingers, Nocturne Lament. I had to destroy it."

"There was one of those here?!" Rin clapped her hand over her mouth. "Hector... if we can take that to Litvy, I can study it! We-"

"People have searched for Lahati's Tomb for thousands of years all around the province," Istvan interrupted her. "And you're saying you stumbled into it via one of the most travelled passes in Myszno?"

"Sort of. There was a..." I hesitated, remembering the sepulcher with all its undisturbed, currently unguarded treasure. "A deep cavern with a shrine to Matir, that contained a one-way portal to Lahati's Tomb in the northern mountains."

Suri looked between us. "Did any of you listen when he said that their army is now numbered in the hundreds of thousands? We were planning for fifty thousand, maybe up to eighty thousand."

"Yeah. But it doesn't change that much of the plan. This is the best chance we have to take that hundred thousand down to something manageable," I said. "Were there airships in Karhad, Istvan?"

"A few," he replied. "Most of them were destroyed in the invasion. There's probably no more than six, and they must be piloted by Navigators... if the crews are dead, the undead cannot field them effectively. They must know the specific Words of Power."

"Let's assume they can field half a Vlachian fleet." Suri looked out over the ruin of the battlefield. "We're going to have to blow those dams just right to have a hope in hell of escaping."

"Plan for the worst, hope for the best!" Rin pumped the air with her fist. "I'm sure we can get it organized!"

Suri grimaced. "Plan for the worst, expect the worst. This is war, not a game."

Rin stuck her lip out slightly. "It IS a game."

Istvan shot her a dark look, then slowly glanced to me. "We will stay our course, Your Grace?"

"Yeah." I rolled one shoulder, then the other. "Let's go tell him where he can shove that lance."

Lord Bolza wasn't in any rush. He hadn't budged from the spot, and his T.rex had almost sunk to its knees in the soft, boggy ground by the time we slogged back over to him.

The vampire looked down his nose at us. "What is your conclusion?"

"Our conclusion is that your Master can politely go and stake himself," I said. "We're not letting you through. You massacred the people of Mysno. Ashur the Cow Patty of the River or whatever he calls himself has to account for all the misery he's caused."

A pity." Bolza's dead grey eyes flicked between us. After examining each face, he made a soft sound under his breath.

"Master Ashur has no love of suffering. He simply wishes to return what belongs to Napath."

"He has to get through the Prezyemi Line first." I crossed my arms.

The vampire gave me a strange, sad look. "He will."

We watched as he pulled his mount around. The T.rex lowered its rotting head and began to lumber off toward the tree line.

"Karalti. Bioscan that guy. "I ordered her.

"What are your...?" Istvan froze as a dark nimbus gathered around my dragon's body, then discharged. "What are you doing?"

Jozef Bolza [Nasaku Thrall, Anti-Paladin]

Sex: N/A

Level 25

HP: 4000/4000

MP: 200/200

Weak Against Dark & Water

Immune to Earth

The Voivode of Myszno and the patriarch of the House of Bolza has been transformed into a Nasaku Thrall, the servant of a powerful desert-forged vampire species that is unharmed by sunlight. Equipped with an unholy lance, a life-draining touch and the power of necromancy, he is a formidable foe.

My eyes narrowed. "He's Level 25. We could take him."

"You would strike at an emissary in the back?" Istvan turned on me, paling with horror. "It is dishonorable."

"It's practical." Suri gave a curt nod and pulled her rocket launcher from her Inventory. "Honor is for sports. This is war."

"Guys, wait." Rin waved her hands. "Let him go back and report... he's had a chance to see the Prezyemi Line as it is. It means he's going to report false information."

"Speaking of that." My keen eye caught something moving on the ground. "Karalti, you seeing what I'm seeing?"

By way of reply, the dragon took a few steps forward and blasted the ground with flames. Her sticky Ghost Fire splashed over the mud, incinerating the hundreds of tiny black scorpions that had been slowly and stealthily crawling their way toward us through the muck. They squirmed and thrashed as the flames consumed them.

I turned to look back at the others. "First order, Istvan: establish a no-fly zone half a mile out over the Endlar. No bugs, no birds, no bats, no nothing. If it flies or has more than four legs, someone needs to kill it. Vampires use animal familiars."

"Yes, sir." Istvan saluted. "May I get a ride back over the wall?"

"Sure." I nodded to the girls as Suri reached down to give Rin a hand up onto Cutthroat's back. "Now let's go get ready to throw these guys the biggest wet t-shirt party the world's ever seen."

Chapter 43

Aerial scouts confirmed what we already suspected: we didn't have a week. We had four days.

Just like the three-day organization of Ignas' coronation, preparing the Prezyemi Line in the way we wanted it would have taken months in the real world. As it stood, we were able to get about ninety percent of it done by the evening of the third day. Suri, Rin and I worked in shifts, sleeping the minimum four hours to rest and then rising and throwing ourselves back into work. Rin worked with Viktor to produce the explosives and oil we needed. Day and night, the battlefield was crowded with people and tankers, airships and quazi. Ships from Litvy arrived non-stop, far too many for Korona's crumbling skydock to properly handle. They were backed up for miles, loading and unloading, picking up people and animals and carrying them north as low as they could fly. The *Tengeri*, a salvage ship, was called to dredge up the corpse of the Warsinger and transport it to Litvy. And while all that was going on, Karalti and I set up on the roof of the Central Bastion, watching as my half-assed plan came to fruition below.

We were pitching two lines of active defense and three lines of static defense. The active defense units were the soldiers tasked with maintaining the no-fly zone, and those who had been sent out into the Endlar to find and sabotage the Demon's *Ix'tamo*. Rin had strategized that the Demon used the poor-quality mana generated by the *Ix'tamo* to sustain his cheaper units, using them like resource nodes to animate large numbers of zombies, skeletons, and plague rats. She had invented a device that allowed us to remotely turn off the nodes – deactivating the *Ix'tamo*, and potentially causing waves of Napathian infantry to collapse. I'd ordered our precious few Rangers to find as many *Ix'tamo* as possible and attaching these devices to them. We were, essentially, hacking into their power grid.

The lines of static defense were at the wall itself. After evacuating Slutlava, we shored up our ramparts and blew the first dam. Even the controlled demolition of the Gul River Dam was incredibly destructive, sweeping away all but ten miles of wall, obliterating the town and flooding the island delta so badly that we almost lost our Airship Hangar. But the flooding had the desired effect: The Western Front was drowned, the river returned to its natural and spectacular course. The remaining mess was so extreme that not even a thousand zombie brontosauruses had a hope in hell of getting through - not unless Ashur also got his hands on a crane and a convoy of semi-trailers.

The result was that Fort Korona now overlooked an arena about a mile across: a kill zone boxed in by torrential waterfalls and rivers to either side. And that zone was a doozy. We clear-cut the marshy forest back by a further 600 feet, then set up the first line at 820 feet from the Wall. Rows of felled, sharpened trees had been set up like a phalanx line of spears. Using triceratops and allosaurus brought by the Orphans, we hauled them on sleds, rammed them into the earth, and wound barbed wire through the lot. Just behind the abatis line was a deep 15-foot trench filled with oil, and right behind *that* was a shallower eight-foot trench filled with landmines. The trenches were cut in a concave design, forming a 'salient' – a bulge that could be attacked from three sides by our aerial artillery.

Three hundred feet from there was the second unmanned trench line, also cut to form a salient. The no man's land in front of it was heavily mined and groomed with another tricky bit of landscaping I'd learned in Indonesia: *lilia*, shallow pit traps cut in a five-by-five pattern, filled with short, sturdy wooden stakes. Each pit was big enough to catch to a foot of a human, horse or hookwing and bring them down. That hundred-meter stretch was sprayed with naphtha.

At a hundred and fifty feet, within support range for the wall, was the third and final manned line. Using wreckage from the Wall, we built scrap bastions of stone in a chevron pattern, giving the stationed Riflemen room to shoot down on the horde from an elevated, covered position. Magical shield caches were installed every fifty feet to give cover from mortar fire and maximize the firing time available to the troops. Between them and the horde stood a third and final deep oil trench. If I'd been planning for living enemies, I would have ordered the garrison to build and deploy Spanish Riders – barbed wire 'boxes' – or a double apron fence, set up guns at either end, and rain hell down on them from the front and sides. Suri had pointed out that the zombies would just crush the Spanish Riders and use them to climb the bastions, so instead, we took the big, curved wooden struts used in the bellies of airships, and turned those into a back-curving fortification that was deceptively hard to climb. There was no time to find Istvan's tribe and recruit them into the defense - every man and woman was put on building earthworks or producing munitions.

The evening of the fourth day found Suri and me on the wall, taking a break to split some bread, cheese and goat's milk for our last meal of the day. Pillars of smoke rose in the distant sky, where the forest was turning gray. A line of fire burned from horizon to horizon across the Endlar. Every day brought some new kind of flying horror to our blissfully Soma-free fortress. Corrupted Pteranodons, gulls carrying plague rats, kalxat and Frankensteinian creatures sewn out of bits of different things. We burned them to ash. That was how the air tasted now: ashy and foul, like seared rotten meat.

"Do you think it'll be enough?" I crouched on the edge of the parapet like a gargoyle, looking down over the field. "I mean, if I was a normal human foot soldier and I saw this place on my J-map during an approach, I'd be pissing myself. But for all we know, they're going to turn up with eight hundred cannons and a thousand mages and just blast their way through everything."

Suri made a muffled sound of agreement around a mouthful of food and took a swig of milk to chase it down. "It's what we have, lover."

"Yeah." The sun was starting to go down. I stared south, searching for gaps in the defense. Somewhere, hundreds of miles away, was Egbolt Castle - and beyond that, below where the Dark Star hung in the sky, were the Thunderstones and Matir's prison. We were almost there. The only thing separating us from our new earldom was an endless army of the dead.

I sighed a cloud of frost into the chilly air. "I'm sorry I didn't listen to you."

"Huh? What about?"

I frowned. "About quitting this quest and going to Tungaant with you and Karalti. We're going to lose. I don't know if we could ever win."

"Then we lose." Suri shrugged. "At least we've upped the odds."

"I wish I could reload a checkpoint or something." I chewed my bread and cheese with a scowl. Even the rationed army cheese in Archemi was delicious, but I was so anxious that eating anything felt like a chore. "I was a loser my whole life. I want to win for once."

"Can't win 'em all. Besides, you're the one who thinks that life is a game. You telling me you weren't any good at playing games like this one?"

"Most of my videogame experience was with antiques," I admitted. "I collected games from my grandparent's era. Didn't play PVP, because I hated it. I can beat most single-player games on Hard Mode, but I wasn't ever going to make a top-ten scoreboard on an MMO or an FPS. Not like Baldr."

"No idea what those are, but you're a good soldier. You survived a war. I'd call that a success."

I shook my head. "I didn't survive it. It just killed me at home instead of some Indonesian hellhole. Now I'm in a different hellhole, doing the same old shit, and it's just as pointless and miserable as the first time around."

She shrugged. "Not that pointless if you or me becomes Voivode. And that's looking increasingly likely."

"I'm not cut out to be a Voivode, Suri. I'm not cut out to rule anyone. I'm not ambitious enough." I gestured out in the direction of the battlefield. "I know how to build a bunch of funky traps, but don't know anything about running a magically powered Napoleonic-era economy."

"Which means you'll probably be pretty good at it," Suri replied. "Because you feel the responsibility. Unlike Baldr, you're not some war-happy, overly ambitious cunt who treats life like it's a game where he has to score all the points. In Baldr's way of thinking, everyone except him is a loser. The people whose lives are in his hands are all losers. He's at the top of the scoreboard. Who gives a fuck about anyone else?"

As I listened, I began to fume. "I know he thinks that way. But he's not here."

"Right, so, if we give up now, Ignas is going to have to deal with this mess, and then crazy dev-possessed Baldr is gonna overrun Vlachia and we'll be on the run. He's gonna come here, plunder Lahati's Tomb, find Matir's Dragon Gate and fuck it in the arse because he wants to win." Suri paused to take a drink of milk. "And if he does, everyone else loses. Me, you, everyone. Forever."

"He may already have a Dragon Gate," I said. "We don't know. I had a vision of him fighting this big-ass monster in front of something that looked like one. That was my last major contact with Matir. He hasn't said anything to me since then, except to update my quest."

"What did he say?"

"Just one word. 'Hurry'."

Suri scowled. "Sounds like he's gettin' weaker. The Gates are supposed to seal him up, right? If the Demon's using his power to raise this army of his, he has to be losing strength."

She had a point there. Matir had manifested in front of me the first time, altered the game and thrown his weight around. Everything since then had been more subtle. "You could be right. That would explain why the Caul is getting weaker, too."

"Right? And if he gets too weak, the Caul is fucked and then we don't have to just worry about Baldr. We'd have to worry about the Drachan." Suri pointed up at the sky. "You haven't won every battle in your life, have you? If we lose here, we rally somewhere else."

"You're right, as always." I offered my arm out to her. "Castellans are basically fancy bouncers, aren't they?"

"Pretty much." She leaned in.

"Then you should be the Voivodzina, and I should be the Castellan." I pulled her into a side-hug. "That way we get to do what we're both good at."

"Yeah, no. I'm too tired for that shit." She laughed.

"Seriously, though - you'd be a great leader," I said. "You ARE a great leader. You pretty much have it all: you're smart, you're authoritative, you're sexy..."

Suri looped her other arm around my shoulders, putting herself between me and the edge of the ramparts. "And YOU need to go look in a mirror and say that about yourself some time."

She leaned in to kiss me, and I felt the stiff muscles of my back loosen. When we pulled apart, some of the bad head noise had cleared.

I smiled, stroking a lock of fiery hair from her cheek. "We've come a long way since we met at the morgue."

"Yeah. Still surrounded by corpses, though." She smiled back. "I was a real grumpy cunt back then, wasn't I?"

"You still are." I glanced to either side to make sure no one was looking, then pressed my thigh in up between hers until she gasped. "But I'm pretty sure I know how to turn that grumpy frown upside down and make it-"

"Ahem." There was a cough from behind us and up.

Suri jumped. I turned to look back, and saw Vash squatting on a small buttress overhead, his pipe clamped in the corner of his mouth.

He drew a deep, dignified lungful of smoke. "Much as I would love to watch the two of you keep necking like a pair of doves, I was wondering if I could steal Dragozin for half an hour or so to discuss training and troop movements?"

"Sure." I cleared my throat and stepped back. "I'll see you at the meeting tonight."

"And after." With a smoldering look, Suri strode off, putting a little extra bump into her hip on the way to the staircase.

Vash hopped lightly to the ground and stood up, all the while watching the exact same thing that I was. "She's a fine woman."

"She is." I nodded. "I was thinking about... After all this is over. You know."

"No, I do not know. I can't read your mind any more than you can read mine."

I shrugged, almost too embarrassed to say it. "You were joking when you told me that if I didn't marry her, then you would. But I'm starting to think I might ask her to... uhh... become the Voivodzina. For real."

"To marry you?" Vash snorted, exhaling a cloud of smoke. "She'll say no. And you shouldn't ask."

"What?" I bristled. "Why? She loves me, I love her-"

"And you're tittering in love like a teenager. Even if she were to say yes, you'd be happy for all of six weeks before the relationship suffocates and collapses." Vash exhaled his pipe smoke with an exasperated huff.

I scowled. "It's been nearly a month, and we haven't fought once."

"A month? That's all. Burna's balls." He rolled his eyes. "Definitely not. Wise people wait to see if the person they love is someone they can properly argue with. Then they marry, and they fall in love with that person over and over again."

With a grimace, I turned to look at the battlefield. "You're a monk."

"So?"

"What would you know about being married?"

"My parents," he replied. "They were an excellent couple, and madly in love. But they were an arranged marriage to start with. My mother already had another husband; my father married up into her clan. It took them time to get to know each other."

That took me aback for a second, until I recalled some of my racial information: Tuun clans had matrilineal inheritance. "You always in the business of telling people how they feel?"

"Only when I know what I'm talking about." Vash looked off toward the clouds, his expression wistful. "A month is nothing. Dragozin. Live with her in close quarters for another six, and if you make it that long, I'll officiate it myself. There's also your dragon to consider."

"Karalti? Nah, we're okay. We sorted that out. She understands that I love Suri and her in different ways."

Vash gave a non-committal shrug. "She won't be your young ward forever. Nor will you be her guardian."

"She's like my kid, man. She'll find her partners, I'll have mine. That's how it's supposed to be."

"I don't know you well enough to have this discussion yet... but perhaps one day after this is all over, I'll attempt to break through that thick skull of yours." He scratched his cheek, a wry, disbelieving smile playing at the corner of his mouth.

"What?" I glared up at him. "Spit it out. Mayne I'll surprise you again."

He snorted. "All I will say on the matter is that once Suri discovers her ambition, things may change."

Her ambition? It was one of the things I liked about Suri, the fact she was so proactive. I shrugged. "I guess we'll see."

"Indeed."

We lapsed into a comfortable silence as we walked. It crossed my mind to ask him about his 'kinslayer' remark a few days before, but that probably wasn't polite. I tried coming at it from a more neutral angle. "So... you said all Baru had to survive a usually-fatal illness, right? What did you survive?"

"I said a disease, or a great injury." He drew on his pipe and exhaled, swinging around a corner and gliding down a flight of stairs.

"What was it for you?" I followed him down. "Your face?"

"Fairly obvious, isn't it?"

"I dunno, man. I can't read your mind. You don't have to tell me if you can't."

"Then I won't." He glanced sharply over one shoulder. "Though I never said the injuries or illness had to be of the flesh."

Chapter 44

The horns began to sound in the middle of the night. Because of course.

"Okay. Here we go." I stood up from the table in the War Room, nearly knocking over the miniatures we'd been using to rehearse the battle. Istvan looked up from his book, ears pricked. Vash startled up from where he'd been snoring face-down on the table and wiped his mouth. Suri calmly finished buffing her sword and got to her feet.

"Ready?" I gave each of them a nod in turn, lingering on Suri.

"Always, Your Grace." Istvan bowed from the neck.

"Today's the day I complete my zombie hand puppet collection." Vash banged his ironclad fists together. "The Nine themselves couldn't stop me."

Suri chuckled, flashing sharp teeth. She came to me, and pressed a dry, chaste kiss against my cheek. "Good luck. Don't die."

My mouth went dry. "You either."

"What are you two so anxious about? Death is merely a discomfort for your kind." Istvan gave us a wan smile as he joined Vash and clapped him on the shoulder. "We will be at our positions, as will the others. May Solnetsi catch you in her wings should you fall."

"Indeed. *Burna marladik,* my children." Vash made a sign of benediction with one hand. "Now let's go and whup some soggy undead ass."

We ran outside to find the Fort in a state of barely controlled panic, as noisy as it had been the first day we arrived. There were barely six thousand soldiers left, enough to fill the transports moored at the Skydock. Troops ran to their positions. Makeshift elevators transported the bravest of the brave to the battlefield: the riflemen who would man the third line of defense.

As we rushed up to the walls, two of the great Hussar-class warships and their Bathory-class escort sailed over the wall, their engines blasting a steady roar over the wail of horns, the shouts of soldiers, the creaking of wood. Catapults were wheeled into place. The sailors turned on searchlights and rushed to arm cannons, fuel shields, and prepare to bomb the shit out of the Napathu when they reached the field. I watched the ships: the dark-hulled *Arpad* split to the west with three flanking ships; the elegant *Novara,* which carried Admiral Gehlan, went to the center with six escorts.

"Karalti! To me!" I jumped to catch a wall, got a grip, then jumped up onto the crenellations above.

Karalti's trumpeting roar pierced all other sounds as she dove out of the sky, invisible until she passed through the beam of one of the searchlights. She made a pass in front of the soldiers descending to the ground, and cheers went up - intensifying as she dipped a wing and I leaped out. I caught onto the saddle like Spider-Man, waving to the whistling soldiers as we flew back around and up, where we got our first look at the army of the dead.

Monstrous. It was the only word for it. Zombies poured in from the shattered treeline like a carpet of ants, an unending tsunami of bloated bodies. Skeletons lurched, sprinted and stumbled behind the black wave of putrefaction, rats swarming around their feet. First came the fear – then the cold certainty of my training. Adrenaline had barely begun to make my heart pound when the strange battlefield calm descended over me. I gripped the haft of the Spear, straightening my spine until it was as hard as the hot metal in my hand. The weapon's seams of red light intensified, and the blade flickered with a corona of scarlet fire.

Players couldn't normally P.M most NPCs, but the Mass Combat window had a special channel that enabled communication with your officers. I set up my management windows in multiple virtual screens, locked them in view, and watched as the horde massed toward the first line of defenses. I took note of where everyone was. Suri and Vash were at the top of the Central Wall, stationed with the artillery. Istvan was at the Skydock with Zediwitz, staging the final evacuation. Rin and Viktor were in position at the dam. The zombies were closing in every second, nearly within range of the cannons. Six hundred feet... five hundred. *"Fire at will."*

"OPEN FIRE!" The cry went up and down the Line behind us.

The front line of cannons exploded like a Mexican wave. The bitter odor of gunpowder stung my nose, and the air dragged at Karalti's wings as their payloads exploded past us, striking the mob heading for the abatis line. The cannonballs sprayed into the endless mass of undead, blowing bloody furrows through the horde. Unfazed, more zombies flowed into the gaps left by their crushed comrades. The second line of cannons blew seconds after the first, sending more bodies flying into the air. I gripped the edge of Karalti's saddle, watching intently as the zombies began to pile against the abatises, where their straight line broke and started to blob. As soon as the crowding reached critical mass and the first zombies began to push and climb the phalanx line of trees, I messaged Suri. *"OPEN CATAPULTS!"*

The trebuchets groaned as the counterweights swung, whipping out huge balls of flaming pitch across the field and smashing them right into the blobs of zombies who had gotten trapped by the trees. The squeals of burning vermin punctuated the battlefield din as the oil on the mud caught fire. Flames spread like a living thing, feeding hungrily on the mass of greasy struggling flesh. But just as before, more undead flowed in to fill the gaps, charging heedlessly across the field. The abatises were being shoved aside by the sheer number of bodies, zombies flowing through them like a liquid... and then tumbling heedlessly into the deep oil-filled trench just behind.

"Archers ready. Rifles ready. Lighting first trench in five seconds. Copy all." Suri patched through.

"H and K copy."

Karalti broke her hover to swoop back and down, flying back toward the Line. I clenched my jaw as the archers on the wall lifted their bows, aimed, and fired.

A cloud of flaming arrows lit the sky, arching and then raining down over the fragmenting barricades. Despite the fire, zombies and skeletons were now charging in over their crushed and impaled brethren. Cannonfire was keeping them at bay, pushing them back onto the oil-soaked mound just as the flaming arrows landed and set the entire trench ablaze. The first wave of undead became one enormous pyre as the oil and kerosene ignited. Zombies lost their forward momentum: a crush was building at the back as they stumbled head-long into the crematorium that consumed their vanguard. The piles of zombies belched black smoke into the sky - and as their fellows climbed over them anyway, explosions began to rocket across the field. Flaming corpse parts were blown everywhere, and the trench line collapsed completely as huge craters opened up in the mud.

"Woo-hoo barbeque!" I punched the edge of the saddle. "*Okay, Tidbit - let's do this!*"

Karalti beat her wings as she reared up and let out a cry of challenge. The fire, explosions, and the sheer mass of the ongoing pile-up was turning the enemy back against itself. But no matter how many stumbled to their knees, burning, thirty more seemed to replace them. We joined with the 2nd Company Dragoons, and as we swept out over the field, the central part of the first barricade collapsed and a metric fuckton of ⟦Skeleton Swordsmen⟧ poured into the kill zone.

"How's the evac going back there?" I patched to Istvan.

"Smoothly for now. Morale is good, but there is a lot of fear," he replied. "We have five ships loaded, three in transit."

"Good. Rin, how's the dam looking?"

"It's ready to blow!" She replied. *"I'm starting to think we can do this! (o^-')b"*

The zombies and rats had been the vanguard - the real army was following behind, and there were some units we hadn't seen before. Undead dogs, thousands of them, eyeless, their gaping maws drooling green-tinged foam. A line of T.rex lumbered through the trees, swinging their heads to clear their path. They crushed friend and foe alike under their huge feet on their way toward the second trench line. Behind them rode shrieking double-line of ⟦Lalassu Chargers⟧, spectral warriors galloping their ghostly hookwings between and around the dinosaurs like a tidal wave of deadly mist.

"Fuck!" I quickly input my orders to the Dragoons on the menu and used the HUD to highlight the wraith cavalry. *"Suri, see those wraiths?"*

"Vash is advising us how to handle the spooks. He says magic." Suri replied.

"2nd Company RB Maegi, protect infantry flanks from the ghosts!" Karalti broadcast.

The quazi knights obeyed, splitting into three: the two wings carrying battle mages moved to flank the oncoming specters as they charged straight through the next line of barricades as if they weren't there. The Lalassu Chargers leveled glowing incorporeal lances at the infantry behind the final line. The soldiers were desperately firing on them, but neither guns or arrows did any damage. Panic was starting to take hold.

"Hold your fire!" Karalti ordered, swooping in low. *"Karalt'ba'nakh!"*

I braced on her back, ready to jump as her wings cast the Lalassu Riders into shade. The dragon's body pulsed with a wave of dark light, which sucked in against her skin and then exploded out in a sphere around us. The *Shadow Wave* swallowed four riders, who wailed and collapsed into smoke as the Dark magic unmade them. Others were injured enough that they veered off course.

"Well look at that! I think you spooked them!" I banged a fist on Karalti's back.

"UGH." Karalti groaned as she Split Turned and swung back. Laughing, I held the Spear out to one side and got ready to roll.

My Jump landed me right on the back of a Lalassu Charger. I drove the Spear down into its spectral saddle and pierced the heart of the ghostly hookwing it rode. It evaporated, dropping me to the ground. Others galloped by, mowing down screaming Riflemen like stalks of wheat. Whoever the lances touched turned to dust and collapsed, their remains drifting away on the wind. The Riflemen were defenseless, running in all directions as I vainly tried to kill the spectral cavalrymen. Stabbing and thrusting, discharging Umbra Blasts when I could and burning AP like no tomorrow, I couldn't help them all alone. I saw a Charger leap onto a teenage soldier, its lance raised to strike just before bolts of boiling, translucent watery energy slammed into it and knocked it off its mount.

Quazi let out piercing eagle cries as they dived in formation, mages casting from their backs. Fire, Water, Light and Dark magic rained down on the Lalassu Chargers, who split and galloped back to try and reform. The aerial mages chased them down the battlefield, hounding them away from the infantry. Karalti swooped in and took another unit of them out with a second Shadow Wave, killing six with her AoE.

"They're in retreat! Come pick me up!" The wave of zombies and skeletons was barely a hundred feet from us, clambering over the next line of barricades.

"Coming!" Karalti flew straight through a volley of arrows, bellowing as they clacked off her scales. Wings pumping, she came in low and snatched me off the ground. I held onto her foreclaw; when she let go, I swung around it like a mast and used Spider Climb to clamber up her body and back onto the saddle.

Undead spilled over the barricades like a liquid, falling straight into the pits of pitch below them. It was hard to believe, but our plan was working. The undead relied on cheap, expendable units, on overwhelming the Defense through sheer force of numbers, and this terrain was using their biomass against them. The zombies and skeletons were crushing each other, each wave making it more difficult for the ones behind. Towering stone and metal statues, visions out of some ancient Sumerian nightmare, tried to wade through the sea of corpses but become bogged down in the piling mountains of dead and burning zombies, leaving them easy pickings for cannons. The sheer number of bodies was staggering. Slowly but surely, they were getting closer.

"Fall back!" I screamed out loud and to Karalti at the same time. "Shield that infantry! Fall back!"

Arrows, bullets, and cannonballs were flying. Panting with effort, Karalti strove for altitude to avoid being struck. From above, I was able to see that the second line of defense was actually performing better than I could have hoped for. The riflemen and archers were picking off zombie after zombie, causing them to collapse over one another in a great big heaping pile. The Demon's infantry was forced to climb the hill of their own making or be crushed – and so I wasn't surprised when Ashur's army began pulling back, out of the kill zone.

⟦Your Militia Riflemen are now Rank 4!⟧
⟦2nd Company Ravensblood Dragoons are Rank 3!⟧

The undead were changing up tactics - bringing the zombies back, sending their heavies forward to smash the piles of corpses. They would flank around and come at the battlefield from the sides, trying to get to the manned bastions. Ashur had probably lost ten thousand infantry in ten minutes - a deep scratch on his army.

Zombie T.rex charged up the newly formed mounds, jaws gaping as they weathered arrows and rifle fire. Some of them were bristling like hedgehogs by the time they reached the bastions, where soldiers fired point-blank into the eyes of skulls of the skeletons they carried. The right flank of the undead were focusing their artillery on the third line of defense. Blue flashes flared out as groups of mages repelled the bulk of the impact with their shields, ricocheting deformed grapeshot and cannonballs back toward the teeming mass of undead. A squadron of Bathory airships were coming in from the side, ready to lay down fire across their ranks.

"Let's go back up those ships, Tidbit!" I dropped to a crouch.

"Wheee!" The dragon swooped down, almost skimming the fighting troops. She blasted a column of skeletons that were almost over the inward-curving defensive wall protecting the bastions, then pumped her wings to rise up toward the skirmishers. I nearly swallowed my tongue, giddy as we crested up beside them. Karalti winged around the bow of the Orozlan, giving a good fifty feet of clearance, and came to a stop in the air. Her neck reared, crests flared sharply in alarm as she swiveled her head around to face the south. *"What was... oh no."*

"What?" I held on as she hovered in place, following her line of sight. *"What's the matter? Airships?"*

"No, I thought... I felt..." she hesitated, and was just about to wing over when a chill wind suddenly whipped up from the wrong direction. Karalti brayed in alarm, flapping ungainly as she turned us around and began to beat her wings hard and fast, striving for altitude.

"What!?" I yelled, louder this time. I clung to the saddle with desperate strength. *"Karalti, what-!?"*

The dragons appeared with shocking suddenness. One second, the air was clear; the next, no fewer than twelve white, blue and silver dragons were just *there*, flying straight at us and the warships like torpedoes. Karalti's desperate reach for altitude became horrifically clear as the ships were pinned by lightning from all directions. Karalti emitted a piercing shriek of rage as the mana shields blew, the engines and sails caught fire, and every single ship lurched and then plummeted out of the sky, bearing their screaming crews to the ground far below. Even as the airships fell, the disciplined, experienced wing of dragons regained formation and chased us up into the air with Lucien and Violetta in the lead.

Chapter 45

I was too shocked to react. Shocked at the appearance of a full wing of Dragon Knights, here, on the opposite side of Artana. Shocked at myself for not predicting they would come.

"Lead them to the artillery, Tidbit!" I shouted aloud, clinging desperately as Karalti barrel-rolled to avoid a spit of lightning. It seared past us, crisping the air with the smell of ozone.

The wing of dragons split into two teams of six. The team lead by Violetta's blue swung westward, where the warship *Arpad* and its Bathory-class escort were raining destruction down on the Demon's archers. Lucien and his white flew for the much-closer *Novara* – the ship carrying Admiral Gehlan.

"By the Nine, how are these mongrels fielding TWELVE-WHORE FUCKING DRAGONS!?" The Admiral shouted on the Battle Management channel. "Shields, mortars, harpoons!"

The battle crew began firing on the dragons as they swooped down. Cannons boomed, and one brawny little silver dragon screeched as its wings shredded and it plummeted like a star to the seething battlefield below. Karalti cried out in distress. *"No! My sister!"*

"We can't do anything to help them, Karalti!" I snarled. "Bioscan them! We need to know what we're dealing with!"

"Okay!" She breathed the spell as we sped toward them from behind:

Solonkratsu (Dragon, Young Adult: Order of St. Grigori)

Sex: Female (Drone)
Level 6
HP: 2000/2000
MP: 100/100
Weak Against Gravity
Resistant to Light and Time

Dragon Knight (Order of St. Grigori)

Sex: Male
Level 14
HP: 1200/1200

Lucien and Violetta's NPCs weren't anywhere near as powerful as they were. I bared my teeth. *"I'm sorry, Karalti. Let's take out the humans if we can!"*

A sorrowful moan was Karalti's only reply. We descended on an unsuspecting silver from above, cloaked by the deepening darkness of the night. The Knight was crouched on the saddle like a windsurfer, intent on the destruction as bolts of lightning seared away the shields of one of the skirmishers and sent it plunging to the earth. Karalti's jaws parted, drooling white fire that she spat venomously at the human's back. He screamed, trying to spin around, but his saddle straps trapped him in place. The sticky Ghost Fire clung to his full-plate armor, cooking him alive. His dragon wailed as she broke rank, flying in desperate loops to try and put out the flames.

"That's what I'm talking about!" I struck the edge of our saddle with a fist, feeling a dark, gloating presence leer from behind the mask of my face. But it was brief – Lucien's enormous dragon broke through the blockade as another flaming Bathory-class plummeted to its doom.

"Hold on, Admiral! We'll draw them away!" But even as I tried to reassure him, the massive, twisted bull dragon soared underneath the *Novara,* staying out of range of its weapons. He rolled in the air, jaws gaping, and blasted the underside of the warship with a continuous stream of glowing hot plasma. The *Novara's* mana shields flared with brilliant blue light, then burst in a chain reaction of arcing energy that knocked several people off the decks. The other dragons swooped in, spitting lightning at the ship's vulnerable wooden hull. A cannonball smashed right into the back of one of the whites, breaking its spine and sending it whirling to the ground in a limp, fatal spin. But only one. Within seconds, the *Novara* caught ablaze, explosions rippling through the great mana engines – and once they failed, it was over. The warship sagged, then toppled, scattering screaming people from the deck. Lucien and his monster pulled out of their lazy roll and spotted us by the light of the fires. I saw the blond son-of-a-bitch grin from ear to ear.

[[You have lost a Hero: Admiral Constantin Gehlan]]
[[Army Morale has dropped! Militia Pikemen are at risk of Shattering!]]

"*Retreat!*" I leaned my bodyweight the way I would on a motorcycle. Karalti moved with me, wheeling around on a wingtip as the mutated white dragon bellowed and leveled out on a course toward us. Two other blues followed him, shrilling out piercing cries of challenge. *"Suri! Dragons on our six o'clock! Mayday mayday, turn your fire on our tail if you can!"*

There was nothing I could do but hold on for dear life as Karalti cast Haste on herself, winging like a swift to draw the dragons to the wall, in front of the cannons. The battlefield was in complete disarray. Twelve dragons could do what fifty thousand zombies hadn't. Blasts of electricity shattered the heaps of dead, cracked stone and knocked dragoons from the sky, their screeching quazi convulsing as they fell. The infantry, formerly disciplined behind the protection of their defenses, were now a panicking riot. They were sitting ducks for the dragons. The *Arpad* was burning, sinking slowly toward the seething army below. Violetta and her wing had abandoned it to its fate, and were swooping and diving, snatching men from the ground and spitting lightning down among their ranks. Armored skeleton cavalry flowed through the gaps the dragons had created in a victorious wave, headed straight for the wall.

"*We're so fucked.* "I clung to Karalti as she strove for speed ahead of our pursuers, still on our tail. When I looked back, I could still see Lucien's stupid shit-eating leer. He wasn't even wearing a helmet, just a pair of goggles.

"The dragons have flanked the wall! They're going for the evacuation ships!" Istvan's voice cut in through the battle management chat.

I spared a glance at the battlefield, and my heart sank. Pockets of infantry were holding out, but the dragons had let the horde through the defenses. Ranks of giant metal scorpions scuttled over the flash-frozen mud and heaps of twitching, burning zombies with ease, headed straight for the last of the defenders. The men on the ground were covering the escape of their comrades up the wall. They would be the last load of evacuees. They were possibly not even evacuees. I checked the Mass Combat unit window: we'd lost about half of the original three thousand.

Grimly, I cycled back to the group chat. "Istvan! Immediate retreat! Suri, Vash, get off the wall with as many men as you can! Rin – blow the dam, now!"

"But... There's still people who aren't evacuated!" Rin's voice was high and panicked. "What's happening?"

"The Wall is getting swarmed, and if we don't flood the field, we'll lose everyone, including the ships that have already left. Blow the fucking dam!" I snarled back.

"R-Roger." Rin cut her voice chat with a sob.

As Karalti and I closed on the center line, I could see that most of the elevators had already been destroyed, the men below clamoring, climbing over each other to try and get into the ones that still worked. A few had reached the gate, but hundreds of riflemen were stranded below. The western line of defense had collapsed, swarmed by undead. The wetter eastern side was doing better, but there were fewer routes up that side of the wall. The men there were now being attacked by the dragon that had stayed behind.

"We're lining you up enfilade, Hector," Suri said, her voice cold with focus. "Pull these cunts in front of me and Vash and we'll blow their snouts back into their arseholes."

"Come on, Tidbit! Push as fast as you can!" I turned on the saddle, hooking my feet under the hand grips so that I could watch our backs while Karalti concentrated on flying. She was at about half stamina from sheer exertion: even with exceptional Dex and boosted with Haste, Lucien's Level 55 monster was catching up to us, foot by foot. Lucien was riding him in the orthodox fashion: tied to the saddle, bent forward, gripping a lance in one hand and a small shield in the other.

"There they are!" Karalti's mental voice was strained. *"I have three seconds, two..."*

"You're in range! When I say stall, you two had better bloody stall out!" Suri's P.M blasted through my head. "One, two, three, four... STALL!"

Karalti gasped with effort as she swung her hindquarters forward and pulled her wings in, arching her back. Like a lady swooning in a faint, she halted her forward momentum and dived backwards toward the ground. The trio of dragons pursuing us shrieked in victory, closing in with claws outstretched... and then shrieked again, this time in terror as a volley of grapeshot blasted them from the side. The concealed 12-pounders nailed them in the ribs and under their wings. Lucien's dragon bellowed, but didn't fall; the other two NPC dragons wailed as the cannons roared a second time, blowing great bloody holes through their torsos. Gobbets of flesh, scales and mana blew out into the wind. One blue collapsed into a fatal headspin; the other rolled out, wings flopping, and plunged to the earth on his back.

The white dragon, Vesper, thundered over our heads like a 747. He was too large and too clumsy to change course and come after my smaller, nimbler queen. Or, so I thought – until I saw his real destination. Violetta and her unit: they'd had flown back toward the center and were coming in along the top of the wall.

A flash of fear surged through my chest. "SURI! Get out of there!"

The night sky lit up with the breath of five dragons as they formed a line and blasted the parapet. The acrid mineral stench of ozone and slagged stone filled the air as they incinerated soldiers, blew chunks of debris into the air, and destroyed our weapons. Desperate soldiers sprinted down toward the bastions. The ones further away had wheeled their mobile 12-pounders around and were aiming at the descending dragons, resigned to their fate.

"*We have to go help them!*" Karalti strove for altitude, panting as she pumped her wings with sweeping, powerful strokes.

Of course we did – but what the fuck were we going to do against two Level 55 dragons?

Violetta pulled her blue up. Tempest roared, hovering over the parapet with his jaws agape. The three smaller dragons split while Lucien and Vesper circled, trying to get behind the fleeing soldiers. I fixated on Suri and Vash – they were marshalling people to escape, shouting soundlessly from our distance.

"Behind you!" I shouted over the chat.

Vash whirled as Vesper swung around, leveled, and swooped toward him. The rangy monk sneered as he stepped into a defensive stance, fists raised. He said something to Suri, who nodded and began to run, ducking her head. Lucien laughed with contempt as Vesper came in – not to breathe lightning, but to bite.

We weren't going to make it in time.

Chapter 46

Vash stared contemptuously back at the dragon as it bore down on him, and shouted something as a whirling, churning field of dark energy ripped up a circle of fire around his feet. His gauntlets blazed to life, billowing with black fire , and as the dragon opened its mouth, he darted forward in a blur of shadow.

Vesper didn't see it coming. When Vash reappeared, he slammed his fist into the dragon's snout. A shockwave of raw magical force pulsed out, rippling down his neck. His head snapped up, and he bellowed and turned away, soaring back up from the point of contact and lurching as his wings began to stroke the air unevenly. But the shockwave went both ways: Vash was blown back, his arm exploding in a bright red welter of blood and bone. He pitched to the ground in a smoking heap.

Karalti and I yelled at the same time, angling straight toward him – and were bowled away as one of the smaller dragons smashed into us from the side. Karalti screeched, whirling to fend off the teeth and claws, while I turned to see the knight raise her lance. Without a second thought, I bounced up from the saddle and tackled her, taking her by complete surprise. Tied to her saddle as she was, she had no idea what hit her. I drove the Spear between the gap formed by helmet and armor, twisted it until blood sprayed, and then discharged a Shadow Lance with the blade buried in her flesh. She cried out hoarsely, slumping like a wet sack as her dragon kicked and snarled.

Suri's shout of pure, berserk rage pierced the chaos. She was mantling over Vash's fallen body as a silver dragon, the last of the NPC Knights, levelled up for a breath weapon attack. Suri had her sword clenched in her hands, her face a bloody, white-eyed mask of fury.

⟦Suri Ba'hadir uses Battle Haze!⟧

"Suri! No!" I wrenched my Spear free and kicked off the struggling dragon, back onto Karalti. "Get out of there!"

The silver swooped in low, and as it did, Suri charged forward. A boiling nimbus of scarlet energy built around her, and for a moment, the energy took a writhing, Medusa-like form. The dragon tilted slightly as it sheared lightning down the length of the walkway – lightning that Suri soaked without breaking stride. With her hair standing on end, she roared and swung her huge sword up in a shower of sparks.

⟦Suri Ba'hadir uses Gorgon Overdrive!⟧

The dragon's wings sagged, and instead of triumphantly soaring back into the sky, its head flew off into the air, spraying blood. The body crumpled and careened into the wall, smashing through the crenellations to cartwheel into the thirty-foot pile of zombies below. Violetta was nowhere to be seen; Lucien was turning around, his mount listing to one side from the blow to his head.

"Suri! Get on the edge of the wall! We'll pick you up!" My heart strained against my ribs, pounding in time with my head as I stabbed at the enemy dragon's face. The spear burst through its eye. It lashed its head back with a cry of agony, then honked as Karalti clamped her jaws on her brother's throat. She rabbit-kicked his belly as we spun tail over wing. I heard – and smelled – the moment my dragon's hook claw caught and tore through the soft underbelly. The male white gave a piteous squeal, scrabbling weakly at the much tougher scales of Karalti's ribs as she bunched up and pushed away, scooping the air. The eviscerated dragon ragdolled, tumbling bonelessly toward the seething necromass below.

"*We're coming, Suri!*" Karalti cried out, winging back over.

Suri was braced in one of the crenellations with her grenade launcher, firing rounds at Lucien and Vesper as the dragon bore down on her. Time seemed to slow. We were coming at her from opposite directions, Vesper twice as fast Karalti in a straight dive. Suri cursed as she reloaded and fired, reloaded and fired, her scarlet hair plastered to her face with sweat and blood. The rounds didn't even seem to slow Vesper down as he closed in, his jaws glowing with an intensifying nimbus of plasma.

No no no no no! I couldn't breathe. A thunderous roar built in my ears, drowning out every sound as a torrent of lightning lanced from the dragon's mouth and struck Suri square in the chest.

Chapter 47

"SURIIII!" I couldn't hear my own voice over the noise in my head, getting to my feet without thinking.

[Suri used Dauntless! HP: 1/2076]

As the light faded, I saw a glimpse of crimson through the dust. Suri was still on her feet, clutching the edge of the shattered wall with one smoking hand. She had a pin in her teeth and the grenade in her other hand, which she lobbed at the dragon just before he wheeled back into the sky. It caught in his teeth, and he moaned, pitching from side to side as he tried to shake it loose.

The rumbling shook my bones. It wasn't from my panic. It was water: eight billion tons of water, rushing down the riverbed from the north in a wall of mud, stone and debris. It swamped the barracks and the aircraft hanger, closing on them like a set of white-fanged jaws as it headed for the Wall.

My pulse thundered under my tongue as we closed in on Suri. Karalti dove with her wings drawn in, head and neck rigid, her scales burning with heat. Suri swayed as she turned to us and raised her arms. Karalti extended hers, and grabbed her, carrying her up into the air.

"Vash!" Suri said over PM. "Get Vash!"

I looked down. Vash was there, sprawled unconscious in a pool of blood, his right arm a shattered ruin. But he wasn't dead – there'd been no notification.

"I can carry him and still fly fast!" Karalti dropped down so fast my ears popped, reaching out with her hind legs.

But I was worried. The water was almost on top of us, and the *Orozlan* was far away. There was no sign of the pair of dragons – that wasn't a good thing. *"Get him and teleport, Tidbit: we can jump to the Pass as planned."*

"Roger!" Karalti delicately snatched Vash off the ground by his waist, dragging him off into the air, and flew hard and fast toward the oncoming torrent. "*Malkut sah'haro-*"

Violetta appeared in front of us. One moment, our way was clear – the next, we were headed straight into a wide, blue, fang-lined maw. Karalti shrilled, then screamed as a great pair of talons seized all four of us from behind and carried us up into the sky. It was Vesper – and as his needle-sharp claws dug into Karalti's arms, pinning them, I saw – and felt – her hands spasm with pain and Suri slide away.

"NO!" Before I knew what I was doing, I slid down my panicked dragon's neck, clinging to her scales as I flung out a hand, a leg, my Spear – all just a second too late as Suri slithered through Vesper's fingers and fell toward the tsunami as it smashed into the wall, still reaching for me.

"You live! You finish this fucking quest, Hector!" Her voice buzzed in my ear. Hard, determined. Dauntless. "I-"

The water took her final two words as it surged toward the wall, but I knew what they were. I screamed her name, recoiling from my HUD when the audio notification appeared, as impartial as ever.

[[You have lost a Hero: Suri Ba'hadir]]

Vesper wheeled lazily in the air, booming in triumph. He was twice Karalti's size, and held my thrashing queen dragon up against his chest and belly in a possessive clutch that turned my stomach. My eyes burned, and bile – pure, ice-cold revulsion – curdled in the pit of my belly and forced its way into the muscles of my face. I had to grieve Suri later. She wanted to win.

Vesper began to mutter the barely-familiar words of the Teleport spell. There was no time to lose. With a snarl, I charged the Spear with Shadow Lance and rammed into the soft webbing between the dragon's fingers. It didn't cost him much HP, but he roared in pain – and then in alarm as the Blindness debuff took hold. It counted down fast, but it was enough to make the titan veer off course. He scooped with his wings, instinctively veering away from the Wall as a towering rush of water slammed into it and blew the whole thing out into the battlefield. The Demon had only barely begun to recall his troops, but their retreat was fouled up by the craggy, cratered terrain. Rocks the size of train cars smashed into the clamoring zombies, followed by water - so much water that it exploded whatever it hit. Korona was smashed, and as the water blasted through the gates, it ignited with oily yellow-green flames, pouring a waterfall of sulfurous fire down onto the undead below. Spectral horns began to blare up and down the line, as the army tried in vain to pull its most vulnerable troops back from the destructive torrent raging toward them. But no one or nothing could run that fast - not through the swamp.

"What are you doing! I said Teleport!" Lucien's angry shouting briefly broke through the thunderous noise.

"Hold on, girl." I activated Spider Climb and scurried up over the dragon's hand, forearm, and up to his bulging bicep. Impressive as he looked at a distance, up close, Vesper's scales were buckled and lifted like old wallpaper. *"As soon as he lets go of you, freefall and teleport to the Pass with Vash. You have the coordinates, right?"*

"Yes. You have it on your map. But what about you!?" Karalti barked and honked as she struggled. She was so worked up that she was sweating blood through the seams of her scales, drops of mana blown away by the wind.

"I'll respawn wherever you are." I climbed Vesper's arm like a palm tree as he began to chant again, faster this time. *"You have to get away. I can't lose you, too."*

Archemi dragons had few weak points. The only places that weren't thick with bulletproof scales were the spaces between their fingers and toes, the lower arch of their belly around their privates, and their armpits. I scaled up to the white dragon's armpit where his arm met his wing-shoulders, got a grip, and slammed my spear into the softer flesh there. Once it was wedged in, I grit my teeth and snarled. "EAT SHIT!"

Umbra Burst lanced out in a wave of searing, numbing cold.

⟦You have inflicted the Frozen debuff!⟧

An agonizing contraction wracked the dragon's body. He let out a high-pitched squeal and flopped over on that side, the wing suddenly flapping and useless. Karalti wormed free, Vash still clutched in one back foot. She flipped over to blast the dragon's other wing with fire, breathing the words of the spell at the same time. "*Malkut sah'haro apsis!*"

My dragon folded into a single point in space and vanished. I allowed myself a second to shake with relief, then bared my teeth and began to climb.

"What the fuck was that!? And why are we lighter all of a- Oh you fucking piece of Tier 6 trash!" Lucien was cursing his struggling dragon as Vesper powered through the debuff. "Do you know what Baldr will do to us if we don't find her, you dumbfuck stupid-!"

I equipped the Boots of the Winding Path with a thought, checked my quickslots, and used the saddle straps to pull myself up behind Lucien. Like me, he had passed the Trial of Marantha and could see behind his own head. He whirled, mouth hanging open for a second before he tried to run at me and nearly fell flat on his face. He was still tied to his saddle with the anchoring lines, three quick-release straps snapped to solid iron rings.

"Kinky." I darted at him Spear-first.

"How the hell-!" Lucien threw his shield and lance, then pulled his swords. After gaining several hard-won levels, Lucien's movements were no longer a blur to me. But he was still fast - real fast, fast enough that I had to focus on him or risk being overwhelmed before I could follow him. As we officially entered combat, I was finally able to see his level. I hadn't had time to notice it the first time, when he'd attacked me on the parade ground. But now that he was trapped, there was time.

"Thirty-five? You're twenty fucking levels lower than your dragon?" I swiped at him as he slashed at the lines tethering him and stumbled back. "Damn, dude, seriously. I knew you had to be compensating for *something.*"

"Fuck off!" Lucien struggled out of the last of his bondage. Even though he was terrified, he was dodging each strike without any real effort, and as soon as he remembered that he was still seventeen levels above me...

I activated Mantle of Night with a low bass pulse of power, spun the spear around in a blur of fire and built into a sprint. He bought his swords up to block. I Jumped and landed behind him, and as he spun, slammed the crackling haft of the spear into his back like a golf club. Shattering Darkness froze his armor solid, crazing the metal and knocking his damage reduction down enough that I had a chance of actually hitting him. I only got in the one hit: he dodged the next swipes of my weapon, dancing awkwardly along Vesper's bucking back and nearly going to one knee as he veered and gravity pushed down on us. My well-trained footing was secure, but for all his Dex, Lucien hadn't been training the skills required to make best use of it.

"Why are you always so fucking SMUG!" he spat. "You can't lay a scratch on me, and you know it."

I fixed him with a steely glare down the length of my polearm. "I'll have you know I graduated top of my class in the Navy Seals, and I've been involved in numerous secret raids on Al-Qaeda, AND I have over three hundred confirmed kills. I am trained in gorilla warfare and I was the top sniper in the entire US armed forces. You are nothing to me but just another target."

He bared his teeth, not getting the joke. "You think you're some kind of tough guy?"

"I will beat you the heck up with precision the likes of which has never been seen before on this playground, mark my words. You think you can get away with saying that baloney to me on top of this wingy-dang-dang? Think again, doodie-head. This one's for Suri." I switched to a more age-appropriate version of my favorite vintage meme before I shot forward, boosting myself with Mantle of Night again. For ten seconds, I was almost fast as Lucien.

He sneered, and his body ghosted out and blinked away. He shot behind me, but I was ready - with Umbra Burst. The attack barely scratched Lucien's health, but it pushed him back and gave me room to Jump as he lunged forward in a whirling, slashing attack that dripped with violet poison. I soared up in a backflip, watching the dragon's back slide from underneath me, and landed right at the base of his tail. The huge, heavy saddle was strapped down there. I tore the Spear through the leather. The broken ties began to flap in the wind.

"You're pathetic, Hector!" Lucien snarled. "My armor has magic that stabilizes me on Vesper's back. What do *you* have?"

"Practice." I sprung up again, and as Lucien lunged to meet my Jump attack, hit *Master of Blades*, then *Rain of Glass*. He screamed as the bolts struck him, as did his dragon: the attack was powerful enough to do fractional damage. I dashed on the landing and struck the cinch strap. It passed through a hole in the dragon's wing and wrapped around his belly. The band snapped, and I dashed a second time as Lucien snarled and threw his swords at me. They spun like glowing boomerangs and slashed through my immaterial form, ripping out the other side and sending me staggering forward with pain. Shadow Dance reduced damage by 90% now, but still:

⟦You have taken 439 reduced damage!⟧

"Die!" Lucien darted forward again, blades glowing with feral violet energy. This time, I wasn't fast enough to dodge: I blocked him with the Spear, relying on my reflexes, my training, the flash of firelight on his blades, the advantage of distance the polearm gave me. It was desperate, breathless fighting, violet light clashing with scarlet and black. Then Vesper tilted sharply to the left, and the loosened saddle slid beneath our feet. Lucien yelped with fright, the second I needed to dash in and scoot underneath him. I caught onto the saddle grips, looked up to see the rogue flying over me, eyes wide, teeth bared in an insane leer, and let go to skid and tumble toward Vesper's neck. Just in time. Lucien's blades bit deep into the thick leather, shredding it. I cut the chest strap on the way past.

"Come on, Hector! Stop running and fight me! I'm *only* Level 35, right?" He leered at me as he stumbled and slipped across the unstable saddle.

"This whole Baldr cosplay thing is weirding me out, man." I dug the cleats of my boot down into the dragon's back as I took a defensive stance, waiting him out. "I admit you've got the creepy smile down, though. And the haircut."

"I know what you're trying to do, Hector. You really think cutting the saddle loose will stop me?" He taunted, edging forward to keep his balance. "I already healed up from your most powerful attack. And that WAS your most powerful attack, wasn't it?"

"Is that a rhetorical question?" I raised the spear and slashed the second-to-last strap, the one around the base of Vesper's neck. As Lucien rushed toward me, I put a boot under the edge of the saddle and kicked it up.

It was heavy, but at the speed we were traveling, I only needed half a foot of gap for the whole thing to catch like a hang-glider canopy and lift. Lucien swore as it peeled up under his feet, and I lost sight of him as the huge flat expanse of leather and metal flapped up and to one side, caught by the one strap I *hadn't* cut: the one under Vesper's already injured arm. Suddenly, the dragon found himself having to fly with massive drag on that side, and his rhythm faltered.

But Lucien was gone.

He's a Rogue class. My breath caught. *Not gone as in dead. Gone as in-*

The knives took me in both shoulders, puncturing the heavy leather and metal of my armor and sliding in behind my collarbones. I Shadow Danced away just in time, and when I reappeared, I went to hands and knees, coughing blood.

[You take 1003 reduced backstab damage!]
[You are Bleeding!]
[You have Tetanus! You are Paralyzed!]

"It's useless, Hector. I always poison my weapons." Lucien drawled as he carefully half-walked, half-crawled over to me. He was hanging on with a death grip, and only his level and raw Dexterity was keeping him on the dragon's back. He stood over me, confident in the duration of the debuffs, and pushed me over with one foot. "Rictus Venom. Causes Paralysis that can only be removed with a Cure Disease potion. Most people try and cure it with an Antidote."

My jaws were clenched, my muscles rigid and immobile. I began to slide helplessly across the dragon's back, halted when Lucien caught me by the foot, dragged me back, and sat on me. "Remember what I said in Cham Garai? You can't Brer Rabbit your way out of this one. Something like that. Well, you did, but I was weak, then. I'm stronger now."

I burbled some foam from the corners of my mouth.

He raised the sword over my head, just like he had the last time. But now, there was no weak grip, no hesitation in his dog-red eyes. Just cruelty.

"I fucking love PvP," he laughed, and bought the blade down.

Chapter 48

⟦Purify has cured your disease!⟧
⟦You activated Mortal Grudge!⟧

Lucien struck for my heart. The blade connected just as my body turned to pure shadow, blowing apart like smoke around his weapon - the Heartstrike that he drove into his own dragon's spine.

⟦Speed increased by 25% for 60 seconds. 2.5x Adrenaline Point regen for 60 seconds⟧
⟦You have been struck with a Death Sentence! Countdown: 60 seconds.⟧

Vesper shrieked, his back bowing, wings seizing as his Bonded dealt him a critical hit with a poisoned weapon. The dragon was twenty levels higher and had five figure HP, so he didn't die - but he bucked furiously, shaking and rolling in his agony.

"What the FUUUCCCCK!!?" Lucien was flung off into the air by the force of it as I rose, a pillar of shadow and fierce, feral energy that wound through my flesh like thorns: thorns that pumped a cocktail of endorphins and adrenaline straight into my lizard brain. I felt strangely dissociated as I shot forward into the air after Lucien, the Spear raised like a javelin. The first bolt of Aether slammed into him, knocking him flying end over end, and then four others split from me and lanced at him from multiple directions, shredding armor and organs and spraying blood like ink into the air. My mind seemed to work at twice its normal speed: I Jumped, then hit Master of Blades, Rain of Glass, and then dashed forward. More shards of energy smashed into the stunned assassin, picking at his HP and knocking his weapons from his hands.

Below us, Vesper struggled, striving to recover his altitude. We'd flown high, very high, at least five thousand feet off the ground. Disarmed, experiencing uncontrolled freefall for the first time, Lucien screamed, red-faced, as the wind ripped at his everything.

"What's the matter, man?" I briefly struck a pose in the air beside him. "Never felt the wind in your hair before?"

"Vesper!" He shrieked as I moved around him in three dimensions: dashing, jumping, rending him a death by a thousand cuts as my timer ticked down to 42 seconds. Lucien was down to 2/3rds HP by the time his dragon's shadow passed over us. I used most of my remaining AP to angle my weapon down and, as Vesper snatched Lucien in one hand, hit *Umbra Blast*. It boosted me up, and I caught onto Vesper's longer, thicker hindleg with Spider Climb.

"Kill him! KILL HIM, you stupid piece of shit!" Lucien banged his dragon's palm as I crawled up the huge limb as fast as I could, watching my enhanced regen battle with the expense of the ability. "What are you doing, Vesper!?"

"Suffering every minute of every day because he has to live with you." I stabbed Vesper in the soft join between his thigh and his groin, regenerating just enough AP to keep hanging on as he bucked and groaned. I levered myself up with the Spear and kept climbing... all the way up to his back, where I broke into a desperate sprint. Lucien's curses drifted up from the dragon's hand as I ran, soaking every sharp turn, every jerk and roll. The dragon was about a hundred and twenty feet long. With enhanced speed, it took thirteen seconds to reach his head, then five more to hold onto his eye ridge, brace my foot on one twisted horn, and plunge the Spear of Nine Spheres into Vesper's eye.

The dragon threw his head to the side with a squealing roar, and Lucien's curses turned to shrieks. "You stupid fucking dragon! Stop! STOP SQUEEZING!"

"Don't worry! I'm not a high enough level to kill him, but damn if this doesn't feel GREAT!" I snarled as I rammed the Spear in again, deeper, and burned my last AP on one final *Umbra Burst.* There was a garbling scream from below - and then a satisfying wet squelching sound as Vesper's feet and hands clenched and he squashed Lucien like a grape, plunging into a desperate barrel roll.

[[You have defeated player Lucien Hart!]]
[[You gain 2000 EXP!]]
[[The Demon's Legions are in retreat! You have won your first Mass Combat Campaign!]]
[[You gain 3500 EXP!]]
[[Congratulations! You are Level 20!]]
[[Congratulations! You are Level 21!]]
[[You earned a new Badge: Like a Grape]]

[Quest Updated: Unto Death]

"Yippee kay yay, motherfucker!" I had to hold on with just my strength now, my arms and legs wrapped around one of the dragon's horns as he careened over the remains of the wall. He couldn't shake me off, and was either too stupid to remember he had magic or didn't have any left to use... and so I waited out the last five seconds of my timer, bracing to die. But just as the timer reached 2, Vesper snarled the words of a teleportation spell. I let go just in time as he vanished, flinging my arms and legs out like a skydiver over the floodwaters below.

[Your Death Sentence has been removed!]

"No! Dammit." I scowled into the tearing wind. My fall was subjectively dilated by three seconds, giving me way too much time to notice how many corpses were swirling through the water. "This is annoying. I just wanted to die like 'bleh!' not fucking crash-land into the river of bullshit!"

"Allow me to assist you."

The voice that lanced through my head was sharp, painful and... wrong. I winced, then froze as a cold shadow fell over me. Literally froze. My eyes widened as I realized that not only was I no longer falling, but I couldn't move.

Tempest glided out to my right, then dipped down beside me, hovering like a kestrel. Violetta was crouched near the tip of his wing, her spellglove subsumed in a pure black radiance. It made her hand look like a glove-shaped hole cut out of reality - just like her eyes. They were fathomless. It was not the cool, pressing darkness of nature, but a true void that slid away to be replaced by her milky blue irises as she struck a tall, straight-spined pose.

"What the hell happened to you, Violetta?" I couldn't move my lips to speak, so I tried just thinking to her. Not via PM - I had her blocked, like everyone else I'd met at the Eyrie other than Kira and Owen, the peasant healers. "What did Baldr DO to you?"

The sorceress did not reply. She twitched her fingers, and then walked back up her dragon's wing as securely as a cat on a fence. I floated after her, tethered by a faint flickering leash of magic. Her dragon was abnormally still. Frozen in time, like a snapshot... one which Violetta could manipulate and move through at will.

An awful hunch crawled up my spine. "Look, I have nothing against you, Vi. We never did anything to each other before this. The War's over. We won. You don't gain anything by taking me to the Eyrie."

"We're not going to the Eyrie." The slim sorceress turned to me once we were back on her dragon's saddle. With a gesture, she spun me around until I was facing her. Still floating.

I swallowed. "Then... uhh... where are we going?"

Violetta never smiled. She had no expression at all as she conjured a swelling ball of water from the air, and let it drift toward me. It was about the size of a basketball - just big enough to cover someone's head.

"Karhad. You, me and Ashur are going to kill a god," she grated, just before the water enveloped my face. "Your god."

Chapter 49

I dreamed of drowning. Of a crushing weight on my chest, pushing me down under filthy water. I flailed, trying to surface, but every time I found purchase, something grabbed me and pulled me deeper. Bodies bobbed past me in the grimy depths. Some of them were zombies, restless dead reaching for me with grasping hands. Some of them were UNAC soldiers in uniform, bleeding out from gutshot or missing their faces or limbs. I couldn't breathe. Couldn't swim. In desperation, I began to kick at something trapping my legs, and when I looked down, I saw Suri's eyes glowing angrily through the silty water. She was pale and putrid, her rich brown skin tinged with green.

Her lips moved, slowly sounding out two words. *'Find me'.*

I woke with a rattling gasp, coughing water. My lungs were burning, chest thick with fluid. It was dark, and I was lying on a stretcher. Faint moans carried on a damp, fetid wind, and for one horrified moment, I thought I was back at Fort Richard in San Francisco, dying of HEX in a quarantine tent. It was enough to drive me up off the bed and onto my feet.

Bare feet. No shoes. No gear, no weapons. I wore a pair of ragged trousers, and heavy steel wrist and ankle cuffs engraved with runes. I couldn't see the runes, but I could feel them when I ran my thumb over the one on my left wrist.

"Fuck." I hissed under my breath. Even speaking one word bought on a rumbling, phlegmy cough. Lightheaded, I sat back down on the bed, and stared off into the dark.

I was gonna be okay. This wasn't my first rodeo as a prisoner. It seemed every big quest I undertook in Archemi led to me seeing the inside of a cell at some point. If I kept my cool, I'd find a way out. There was always a way.

The first thing I did was remember how to breathe. I coughed until I retched. I had vague memories of Violetta choking me out with a floating ball of water. Fucked up, but effective. Once bodily functions were back online and my brainstem stopped screaming at me, I pushed the flimsy cot up against the wall and went into my HUD. I had a look over Karalti's character sheet, relieved to see that she had about three-quarters of her HP and a normal status.

"Karalti? Can you hear me?" I thought out to her.

⟦You are incarcerated. Private messages are currently disabled.⟧

Shit. Clearing my throat, I went to check my Friend's List. Rin was online, but I couldn't contact her. Suri's name had vanished from the list, as had our PM history. My pulse quickened anxiously. She had to have respawned in Al'Asad. Like me, she would have the Incarcerated status, meaning she was uncontactable.

I checked the Mass Combat menu next to review who we'd lost. Admiral Gehlan and his brother were both dead. Vash Dorha was not. Bittersweet relief flooded me, tamping down the anxiety over Suri. For one thing, I liked Vash, and I wanted to get to know the guy better. For another, if Vash was alive, then Karalti had made it to safety for sure. For now, at least, they were okay.

I checked the map to try and work out my location, but it was blank. After that, I had a look at my own character sheet.

"Damn. Two levels? First time that's ever happened," I muttered, opening the leveling screen.

[[You have 6 unassigned ability points!]]
[[You have unlocked new combat abilities.]]
[[You have unused skill points.]]
[[You may select one Mark of Matir ability]]

I glanced to my right. My eyes were adjusting to the darkness now, and I could make out the contours of the cell. There was a torch flickering outside a barred oak and iron door, but no sounds of life or unlife outside.

Quickly, I went to the abilities menu to see what was available. I'd unlocked four abilities this time, but one of them immediately caught my eye.

Black Lotus I

You manifest a terrifying garrote of shadow that wraps around your target's neck and crushes the life out of them. The garrote has a range of 40ft, inflicts 35 damage per second, has a 30 second duration, and causes the Suffocation debuff. Range, damage and duration increase by leveling this ability.

That sounded good, because I didn't have much in the way of ranged attacks. I selected it and leveled it up to Black Lotus II, then spread the other four points between Master of Blades, Rain of Glass, Jump and Shadow Dance. I froze as a bang echoed up and down the corridor outside.

Quickly, I surfed to the Mark of Matir selection screen to see what was on offer there:

Enervation Strike (Entropy)

Black, liquid energy coats your weapon like venom. As you strike your enemy, Darkness flows into the wound and spreads through their veins, leaving them weakened and sapping their strength. On a successful hit, you drain 5 points of your opponent's strength per skill level and add it to your own for the duration of the battle. This ability does not affect creatures lacking Vitality, such as constructs or undead.

Dancing Fly (Life)

You prey on your opponent's fears and lack of confidence, remaining forever just out of reach of their weapon. When this ability is activated in combat, it drains one Adrenaline Point per second. Each time you successfully evade an attack while activated, your Evasion increases by 5%. The bonus is cumulative and ends when the combat ends or you run out of Adrenaline.

My ears pricked as footsteps became audible outside: two pairs of boots with an awkward, shuffling gait, and one set of softer shoes.

I liked the idea of draining the strength out of my enemies, but Dancing Fly had more strategic potential - plus it affected all enemies, including undead and constructs. I selected it, made sure I was up to date on the most important changes - HP, AP, my stats - and closed my HUD to wait and see who was coming.

Sure enough, the footsteps came to a stop outside my door. I stood, ready to look for a gap in security - and as I did, the bracelets on my wrists warmed, and then my arms were forced behind my back by an invisible, irresistible force until the metal touched. My ankles grew heavy, too - I looked down to see a faint energetic tether connecting the cuffs.

"Great," I muttered.

The door opened, revealing a pair of... I wasn't entirely sure. Two identical guards flanked Violetta, who had swapped her form-fitting battle armor for a modest black battle dress and scarf. Her spell gauntlets were fully charged, humming with mana.

"Nice dress. The soulless black really complements your eyes." I scowled at her as the two guards advanced. They were heavily armored in the Vlachian style, wearing tarnished, grotesque masks under their helmets. There was something unsettlingly squishy about the way they moved, as if there were no actual joints in their limbs. Despite that, they took my elbows in an unnaturally strong grip. "C'mon, Vi - you've got to be in there."

"And how do you fathom that?" She turned, her eerie voice echoing off the walls of the cell.

"You lied for us when you came with Lucien to Taltos." I tested the grip on my arms as the guards hauled me off.

"I didn't lie for you. I lied for myself."

"Okay, fine. So why are you working for Baldr?"

She walked ahead of us, her soft shoes pattering on the floor with each step. "Because I have to."

Had to? A light flickered to life in my head. "Oh, shit. Baldr has control of the geas?"

Violetta opened the door ahead of us with an arcane gesture, walking on through.

"Look, Vi, you don't have to strongarm me into anything when it comes to Baldr, okay?" I said, carefully testing each restraint. They were extremely secure. "I'm willing to put aside our differences and help you take him out pro-bono. No debt, no hard feelings, no nothing."

"You will help me, yes," she replied.

I kept trying to talk to her, to reach her somehow, but my words were met with calm silence as my escort took me on a brisk drag through the ruins of Egbolt Castle. Egbolt was built on top of a cliff overlooking Karhad, but its resemblance to Vulkan Keep ended there. The castle had the stately appearance and intricate stonework of an old cathedral: soaring stone spires, intricate buttressing, tall gold-trimmed towers. It was built to a draconic scale, but it on only had walls on one side: the side that, through the gate, fed out onto a road to the city. The smoking ruins of Karhad was nestled in the alpine valley below the cliffs. Once, it must have been green and blue and gorgeous. What I could see of it now was gray and brown, as dead as the army of zombies toiling on repairs in the oval-shaped courtyard that linked the guardhouse to the Main Hall.

Hundreds of Kalxat perched on the crenellations of the inner keep, croaking and preening, tracking us on our way through the great double doors. I braced myself for the stench of rotten flesh and burned wood, but we entered into a scene straight out of a Conan the Barbarian story. The Great Hall had been hella cleaned up, hung with gauzy silks, lain with carpets and exotic furs, painted benches, stuffed chairs and cushions. People stood together in knots, laughing and chatting in artfully draped robes, loin cloths, gauzy dresses and other ancient finery. The women wore intricate plaited wigs; the men had long curled beards, gold beads glinting on every coil. Every single person was undead, from the cadaverous ⟦Wight Officers⟧ to the most morbidly beautiful of the ⟦Napathian Vampires⟧. And at the back of the room, lounging on a chaise sofa and surrounded by a heap of attractive, naked, collared ⟦Vampiric Thralls⟧ of all sexes, was none other than the Demon himself.

The sofa was big enough to seat an ogre, and for a moment, I thought the Demon was one. He was not the tall, pale and interesting stereotype of a vampire. He was huge, big and brawny, with bronze skin - true bronze, like an antique lamp. His hands and forearms were streaked with black and blue-green tarnish, like old metal. He was dressed like an ancient Pharaonic warrior in a fine loincloth, leopard skins, and scaled armor. His face was handsome in an artificial, statuesque way: eyes shadowed and narrow, set above high cheekbones; a large aquiline nose, and a thick, rubbery mouth. To either side of him stood a pair of superfluous bodyguards - big, dark-skinned dudes in fancy armor and Egyptian style headdresses with tower shields and swords - and a shrunken lich in white linen robes. He or she was so old that they looked like a well-used haunted house prop.

The lich drifted forward, hands clasped in their sleeves. Their voice was as sexless as their appearance, dry and crackling, like old wood. "You are brought before the Chosen of the Sun, His Divinity Ashur of the Ten Thousand Swords; the Ox of the River, the Undying, hero and general of Napath's armies."

I cocked my chin at the wispy, skeletal person, then turned a hard glare onto the vampire at about collarbone height. "I'm Dragozin Hector: Queensrider, Commander of the Myszno Defense Force, and if I have to listen to your litany of trumped-up titles ever again, I'm going to stab my own eardrums out."

Ashur sat up and slapped his knees with a booming laugh, flashing a mouth full of flesh-tearing teeth. The fangs were as black as pitch, fitting together as neatly as the teeth of a bear trap.

"Ah-hah, so this is the general who gave us such an interesting battle at the Prezyemi Line." The vampire's accented voice was a low bass snarl, like a lion's roar turned to human speech.

"You mean the general who kicked your ass?" I scowled back at him as the two guards forced me to my knees.

"That very same one." Ashur bent forward and caught my chin in unnaturally icy fingers, lifting it. It was an effort not to recoil as the rusty stench of iron and old blood washed over me. "You are smaller than I expected. And pretty, with exotic features. A Tuun... I suppose it makes sense that a member of the oldest human people to walk this place should become the Spear Bearer. Look at me, boy."

I didn't know a huge amount about vampires - especially this kind - but I knew one rule from every game and movie I'd ever played that had them. Never look a vampire in the eye, especially the old ones. "No thanks."

"Hmmph. As you wish. Violetta: now that we have this man, you have the Spear that unseals Matir's crypt, yes?" Ashur let go of my face and leaned back, his hands resting on his thighs.

"Yes," Violetta replied. "We have it warded and under guard in the Mage's Oratory."

"Utuapsu. Do we need this man, or just the weapon?" Ashur addressed the lich and motioned to me.

Fuck. I had to think fast. Combat was out of the question: There were about fifty vampires in here, all my level or higher. Even the naked slaves purring around Ashur's feet had red skulls next to their character titles, and the guards behind him had violet skulls, making them Level 30 or higher. If I died, I'd respawn in my cell thanks to the Incarcerated status.

"You can't unseal Matir with just the Spear," I blurted. "You need the Triad."

The lich vizier raised a hand. My cuffs heated, and then a jolt of electric pain flashed through the muscles of my arms, back and chest. "You will address His Divinity with proper respect, breather, or lose your tongue."

"Stand down, Utuapsu. The Tuun were the first to break free of the Deceiver's enslavement, and they have never forgotten it." Ashur waved him back with a clawed hand. "They know not of respect nor nobility, but they do know much of the past. And this man is the Spear-Bearer, as was recorded in our lore."

"Not if the woman was able to take it from him," the lich responded. "The histories are clear that the Spear chooses the wielder, and the Spear-Bearer is always able to call the weapon to their hand from any distance. So is it written."

I frowned, then concentrated. When I tried, I could sense the weapon almost the same way I could Karalti, like a mental presence that tickled my brain when I thought about it. I focused on summoning it the same way I had on the battlefield. There was a moment of resistance, and then a surge of power as the familiar haft appeared in my hands, behind my back.

I didn't see Ashur or his slaves get to their feet. One moment, they were seated - the next, they were standing, all twelve men and women clustered around their Master with burning red eyes and exposed metal fangs. I couldn't do anything with the weapon - my hands were still bound behind my back - but there it was. Even Violetta looked shocked.

"So as I was saying." I looked up to just under Ashur's jaw. "You can't unseal the Dragon Gates with just the Spear. You need three components."

"Components." He repeated the word after me. "And what are these 'components'?"

"The Spear-Bearer, the Spear of Nine Spears, and the Keystone that you already possess," I lied. "The three parts of the Triad."

Ashur turned to his vizier. The lich hung in the air, watching me impassively.

"There is mention of a Triad in the *Ea Enggura*," they admitted after a time. "The Hymn of the *Salašu*, 'The Three who Bind and Unbind the Gate."

"You can't find the Gate without the Triad," I replied. "The Stone has to go in the Spear, and when they're combined, they tell me where the gate is. You see that Ruby in the blade? It told me where to find the Dragon Gate of Khors."

The lich made a dry crackling sound. "It is true that the stone has a powerful resonance similar to the one that was gifted to us, Your Divinity."

The crowd of slaves dispersed, slinking back to the ground. Ashur's face drew into a craggy expression of curiosity.

"I believe all of it, except for one thing. You already know where the Dragon Gate of the Black God resides,"

Ashur said. His voice was warm, calm... trustworthy. I could almost taste the way it sounded, warm and soft and cozy. Safe. "You bear his mark and have been gifted with his divine powers, yes?"

"Yeah." I rarely trusted anyone on first meeting, but I found myself feeling like I could tell Ashur everything and be perfectly okay... and that was a problem. "Stop it."

"Stop what, Spear-Bearer? I ask only that you to tell me where the Dragon Gate is located." Ashur purred. His voice wrapped around me like a fuzzy blanket, urging me to trust him. To answer truthfully.

I forced my face to relax, and dug my nails in against the haft of the spear as hard as I could. I thought of Suri and Karalti and Rin, and then, Lord Bolza's face as he looked down at us on the battlefield. *They march with the other thralls.*

"It's okay to tell you, isn't it?" I asked. "I can feel it."

"It is the right thing to do, Spear-Bearer. In fact, all of this terrible violence could have been averted if only I had met you earlier." The vampire leaned back on his divan, the power of his gaze washing over me like the heat from an open oven "I am the last hope of my people, Dragozin Hector. For thousands of years, I lived with my family in a great palace, surrounded by my wives, my treasured concubines, the warriors who were closer to me than brothers. The dragons almost ruined my country with their infernal magic, but we made the best of our circumstances. Napath's rivers no longer teem with fish, or nurse the orchards of pomegranates and dates that I remember from my living youth, but we have art and peace and beauty there still. I tired of conquest many centuries ago, and have spent many millennia in deep sleep. These days, I prefer to pass my time in study of the stars and in painting, but what can be done when duty summons one to war?"

I stared at his mouth, struggling to buy for time. If I met his eyes, I would lose my ability to resist and blab the truth. "You answer the call."

"Precisely." Ashur sighed, a sound that passed over my skin like an embrace. "The Dragon Gate has surged in its activity these last twelve months. It drains our land like a hundred thousand Stardrinkers, Hector, and it is killing us. My wife crumbled into dust, along with thousands of others. Every day, we lose people like Utuapsu here, who hold lore and languages that are thousands of years old. The Vlachians call me a vampire - but truly, the vampire is the god who enslaved you. The one whose symbol is etched upon your skin."

The Mark of Matir burned with a steady cold fire on the back of my right hand. Ashur was annoying me now, and that was good. It helped me focus. "Matir didn't enslave me. We made a bargain. I accepted his help in return for helping him, and he pays me back every chance he gets."

"That simply makes him a clever master." Ashur reached out and stroked the hair of one of his slaves, petting the woman like a dog. She curled up closer to his knee. "A miserable, unvalued slave is a rebellious slave. I spoil my servants endlessly in gratitude for their devotion and service. Matir is old enough and wise enough to do the same. You do not know how it was, but the dragons kept humans and other creatures the way that we keep dogs."

No matter how nice his mind tricks felt, that little speech was like a shock of cold water to the face. I swallowed back my rising bile and nodded. "I... wish I could tell you the location of the Dragon Gate, Your Divinity, but I can't. Not until the Star of Endless Night is set in the Spear. It will lead me to the Gate then, as the Ruby did to the Gate of Khors."

"Truly?"

"Yes, Your Divinity."

I marshalled every ounce of willpower to keep my eyes down, my conviction in place. As I so often did when I was under duress, I thought of Karalti's mother... her will and her resolve, and her belief in me to care for her daughter.

"I am merely a simple man of war, Utuapsu," Ashur drawled. "Do you believe him?"

"A young Breather such as this one, even the Spear-Bearer, could not resist your diplomacy, Your Divinity," the lich rasped.

Ashur hmm'd. "Bring me the *Sarrum Adar*. We will add the gemstone to the weapon and reveal the location of this Gate. "

"No."

Violetta, who had been silent for all of this, came forward. She looked... normal. Her voice had lost its jarring alien quality. Lips were pink and flush with life, and her eyes were blue instead of black. They glinted with malice as she looked down at me. "He is attempting to deceive us, Your Divinity."

"He is, is he?" The vampire regarded me with interest as my blood ran cold. "Now that you mention it, he smells like a man unnerved. Yet I would know if he was lying... no ordinary man can resist the presence of a *Nasaku.*"

"Neither Hector or I are ordinary humans. We are Starborn," Violetta said sweetly. "We are the immortal seeds of fate, capable of manipulating reality and the feelings of men. As you have been impressing your will on him, he has been impressing his will on you. If you want him to speak the truth, you should turn him into your *damu* and ask again."

"Turn me?" I blurted. "What do you mean 'turn me'? What the fuck is a '*damu*'"

"It means 'Child' in your tongue. She is asking me to make you a Nasaku, my blood-bound prodigy." Ashur rumbled. "That may be too high an honor for an enemy."

I glared at Violetta. "*You can't do this.*"

"*Who's going to stop me? The mods?*" She regarded me with a sweet, blank expression. "*Any idiot knows that NPCs are programmed to always try and give your pathetic roleplaying serious consideration. The game tries to advance quests in favor of the 'hero'. But you're not the only hero here today.*"

"*The game won't let it happen.*"

"*Player protection features were disabled when the game reset.*" Violetta smiled faintly. "*Suffer.*"

"The woman is the servant of an Architect," Utuapsu whispered. "Given the circumstances, the dire need of our people, I would advise that we defer to her wisdom."

Ashur stirred up from his recline and stood. "The Architect chose his servant wisely. Very well."

Violetta curtsied.

"Wait. You can't 'turn' me." I wracked my brains for what to do. "Matir hates the undead. He'll remove the Mark."

"But you will remain the Spear-Bearer." The vampire reached out for me with clawed hands.

I threw myself away from him, skidding down the steps leading to the dais and onto the floor. There, I tried to flip up to my feet - but as I did, the ankle cuffs locked tight, and I ended up smashing my face against the hard floor instead. My HP was already in the pits, throbbing red as Ashur lifted me up by the neck with one hand. As my breath cut, I saw an oxygen meter appear in my overlay.

Violetta watched me struggle with a strange expression: lips parted, eyes wide with mingled fear and fascination, one hand resting lightly around her own neck.

"Fuck off!" I opened my inventory, searching for some way out of this. Poison, some other way to die before he could bite me. There was nothing - my gear was gone. I snarled, and prepared to use Shadow Garrote - but instead of biting me, Ashur's nails lengthened and plunged into my neck like hypodermic needles. My eyes widened as a numbing wave of cold passed through my body.

[You are Paralyzed!]
[You are Hemorrhaging!]

"Do not fear. Your old master may reject you after the embrace, but I will take good care of you." The vampire's bracelets chimed as he painlessly embedded his fingers deeper into my neck. Frothing at the mouth, I watched the veins of his arm swell in size, writhing like worms under his skin as he drew my blood into them. "You were an honorable and interesting opponent, Dragozin Hector. I shall be honored to add you to my household. Once this is over and done with, you will know comfort with me for the rest of eternity."

No way. There is no way this was happening. I fought with everything I had, but every kick, every heartbeat only weakened me further. There's no fucking way they'd let a player be turned into a vampire. I'd die normally and respawn back at my last checkpoint: the jail cell.

Right?

The Spear fell from my nerveless hands as a warm, velvety, dizzying darkness crawled in from the edges of my vision. The last thing I saw was Violetta, watching me with haunted, terrified, excited eyes.

Chapter 50

When I came to, I was sitting in the kitchen of my grandparent's condo.

The sun streamed in through the windows, barred light and shadow falling across the linoleum. My grandmother was moving around the kitchen; my grandfather was singing to himself somewhere back in the house. Their cats drowsed on the tall cat tree in the living room, while my school backpack lay next to my bar stool next to me on the floor. Everything seemed to stand out in supernaturally sharp relief: the threads on the placemat in front of me, the mingled smells of steaming rice and cooking meat. There were already *banchan* laid out on the counter, melamine bowls brimming with vegetables and pickled side-dishes. They smelled sweet and spicy and delicious.

"You're early today, Hector." Grandma bustled over and set down a bowl of my favorite *kim-chi*, bright green garlic shoots covered in red pepper paste and oil. She laid a set of serving chopsticks and a spoon down on the tray beside it. "I haven't even finished cooking yet."

"Yeah. I'm sorry." I picked some vegetables out of the serving bowl and dropped them into mine. "I just didn't know where else to go."

"You know you're always welcome to visit." She turned her head and smiled. I couldn't see her face properly; the light seemed to blur out her features. "But you can't stay here today. You need to go back to your family."

I paused with a bite of food halfway to my mouth.

"You have a long time to live. Perhaps longer than any human being ever has." Grandma set her spatula down on the edge of the sizzling pan, resting her hands on the counter. "One day, you'll see us again... but for now, you must go back."

"Back?" A cloud passed over the sun outside, and the shadows of the blinds turned chilly as the temperature around me dropped. 'Back'. That wasn't a good word. "But I want to stay here."

"I know." She left the spatula in the pan - something she would never do - and came around the counter to lay her hand on my shoulder. Even this close, I could tell she was smiling, but I couldn't see her face. "Go back out there, and live. We love you... we'll be here rooting for you, okay?"

The mouth-watering smells of the kitchen faded, replaced by nothingness. Cold, dark nothingness... not even a memory.

I opened my eyes and almost gasped in a lungful of sand.

Holy fuck. I was buried alive? There was a brief moment of panic, until I realized that I didn't have to breathe – yet, anyway. The urge was there, but it was building very slowly. My chest and muscles were dense and cold as wet clay. What had happened to me? Where the hell was I?

And for that matter, *who* the hell was I?

Clenching my teeth, I focused on getting my hands to move. One finger twitched, then two... and after some effort, I was able to lift my arm and shift around. The sand only covered me up to my face – there was a gap of empty space above, between me and the arched lid of my prison. I leaned up to finally take a breath of dusty air. Ring-shaped notifications were blinking in the corner of my eye. When I thought about them, holographic windows jumped up. That spurred my memory a little. One of the options I had was 'Character Log', so I went and had a look at that to see if I could figure out who I was and what had happened.

⟦You have died!⟧
⟦You have contracted Haemostigma!⟧
⟦You are immune to corruption.⟧
⟦Rin Lu has died!⟧
⟦You are immune to Corruption.⟧
⟦You are immune to Corruption.⟧
⟦You are immune to Corruption.⟧
⟦Rin Lu has died!⟧
⟦New Character Template applied: Nasaku Halfblood⟧
...

"All I wanted to know is if I'm immune to Corruption. Am I or aren't I?" I choked a small, nervous laugh at my shitty joke. Who the hell was 'Rin Lu'? And why were they apparently incapable of staying alive for longer than five minutes?

I searched the name and found her listed in my Friend's List. Whoever I was, I was apparently pretty unpopular, because my mysterious and mortally-challenged friend was the only one there. I tried selecting the option to P.M her.

⟦You are incarcerated. Private messages are currently disabled.⟧
⟦We have detected that you may be experiencing some issues with your character data. Would you like to check for problems?⟧

Archemi. That felt familiar. I jumped a little as the message played, but then found myself nodding. "Uhh... sure."

⟦Okay! Hold on just a second while I run the troubleshooter.⟧

Troubleshooter? I lay back in my giant kitty litter box and waited as a diagnostic bar filled. It glowed, but the glow didn't illuminate the darkness.

⟦I'm sorry, Hector, but it seems I can't find the character information I was looking for. Please save your progress, exit the game, and contact our Help and Support line.⟧
⟦We have detected that you may be experiencing difficulties beyond a normal gaming experience. P.Ms have been temporarily re-enabled.⟧

“Okay... I have a name and a connection. Awesome. Let’s try this again.” I dismissed the notification and tried Rin a second time.

"OH MY GOD! HECTOR! THANK GOODNESS!" No sooner had I connected than a musical voice blared into my ears. "You're alive? Are you okay? Where are you?"

"Woah, that’s loud." I groaned and rubbed my face. The skin was cold, a little rubbery. "Yeah, I'm alive and okay - I think. I don't know where I am. I... uhh... actually don't remember anything, and I'm hoping I don't owe you money or anything because I might need some help."

“Anything? About the Prezyemi Line, or the quest or...?”

“Everything. I just figured out that my name is ‘Hector’.”

"Terminal amnesia?" She gasped. "Oh no. That's not good."

"I'm okay," I repeated stubbornly. "I just need some help."

"Umm, ummm... Let me go find Karalti! She's frantic over you right now and said she walled her mind off from yours because whatever was happening was making her go insane, but now you're awake she can probably find you and teleport to you? Oh, wait, know... you have to have a logged location marker for her to do that. UMMM..."

I had no idea who Karalti was, but nodded - then immediately regretted it when I banged my nose on the inside of my concrete porta-potty. "This uh... Karalti should hold onto her britches instead of jumping in. I'm in a pretty small box right now, and it's definitely not big enough for two people. Besides, I'm not entirely sure who you're talking about, or even if you're really my friend. No offense."

There was a pause. "You... really don't remember anything? Not even Karalti? What about Suri?"

The name caused a faint dull throb somewhere inside me, like someone poking a nearly-healed psychic bruise. "It rings a bell, but I couldn't put a face to the name, sorry."

"OMG. This is terrible." Rin somehow managed to say the acronym. "Okay- whatever happens, keep updating me and Karalti on your situation."

"Sure. No hurry." There was a boom and a bang not too far from where I lay. "Okay. Maybe little hurry."

"You said you're in a box? Like a coffin box or a cell box?"

"I'm thinking coffin." There were people walking toward this end of the room. "Room outside sounds big and echoey. By the way, are you okay? You died like... five times in half an hour."

"Me? Oh, I'm alright! I stepped up to help fight at Krivan Pass and got killed a few times. Okay, look: you know what an undead is, right? Zombies, vampires, ghosts. Do you know what those are?"

"Yeah."

"Good. If you see any walking dead, be really, really careful. You're probably in enemy territory. You should check your character sheet to see if that jogs your memory, maybe."

"Sure. Hey, I got a pop-up before saying I should log out and talk to a Mod about this memory loss thing. Do you know how I can do that? Maybe they can help."

"Hector, we... " Rin trailed off. "I.. umm... Let me get Karalti."

She hung up on me. With a sigh, I closed the window and went deeper into the Character Log. There was a Journal with a High Priority alert and one entry: 'IF YOU DIE AND FORGET YOUR SHIT, READ THIS LIKE A MAN.'

"Okay. At least I know past-me was smart." I opened it up and let the voice log entry play.

"Greetings, my future amnesiac self. It's me, Past-Hector," my own voice said cheerfully. "We've at war, where the risk of needing to die and respawn is pretty high, but we've had a problem with dying and forgetting shit. This is a brief summary of everything that's happened in the last month or so. I suggest you pause this here, go look at your character sheet, then come back. Don't worry, I'll wait. For you. I mean... me."

Knowing I'd prepared for this eventuality was a hell of a relief. Feeling steadier, I surfed over to the Character Sheet tab. "Let's see here. Dragozin Hector, Tuun male, Level 21, Dark Dragoon... Nasaku Half-Blood *Shadowlord*? Dude, I'm edgy as fuck. No wonder I only have one friend."

I scrolled through the rest of the sheet, looking over my abilities and skills. There were a lot of things related to dragons, so that was clearly a big part of my life somehow. Underneath all of that was information on the Nasaku Halfblood part of things.

Vampire Halfblood (Nasaku)

Vampires of all types reproduce by infecting their intended thralls with Hemostigma, a disease which reanimates a corpse with Negative Energy and causes them to rise as new vampires. But every now and then, things do not go as planned - the victim resists the infection and becomes something else - a half-vampire, half-mortal being with some of the hungers, powers and abilities of a Vampiric linage, but also some of the weaknesses. These abilities stack with any other existing mutations you possess. Vampires loathe halfbloods and will hunt any known half-vampires relentlessly, not least because they can inoculate potential victims by sharing their blood with them.

The Nasaku are a vampire lineage exclusive to the living dead realm of Napath. See the Nasaku Bloodline sub-heading for special features.

All Vampire Halfbloods possesses the following features:

- *Acquired immunity to Hemostigma.*
- *Inoculation: You can inoculate other humanoids against contracting vampirism with your blood.*
- *Vampiric toxicity: Your blood and flesh are toxic to vampires, causing their tissues to rot and slough away. If*

a vampire attempts to drain your blood, they will take substantial Necrotic damage that cannot be regenerated.

- *Deathly Facade: You outwardly resemble a vampire of your bloodline, detect as Undead, and may gain advantages or disadvantages to Renown-based checks depending on the faction you are interacting with. You may slow your heart rate and your breathing to inhuman levels, multiplying your ability to hold your breath in airless environments. However, you are not Undead: you are still a living mortal, and while you now age more slowly than a normal human, you must still breathe, eat and drink, keep your vital organs functioning, etc.*
- *Immune to Stranging: You can no longer be Stranged through contact with mana.*
- *Regeneration: like a vampire, you are able to regenerate wounds that would kill a normal human. When injured by normal weapons or obstacles, you regain 2 HP per second. Damage from silver weapons, Fire magic or weapons, or Dark or Light-elemental weapons is not regenerated.*
- *Allergic to Silver: Contact with Silver drains 5HP per second and causes Severe pain. Extended contact may cause scarring.*

Nasaku Bloodline Traits

Descended from the undead Priest-Kings of Napath, the Nasaku have some unusual monstrous qualities that other vampires do not possess. Their hard metallic skin and fangs, their mechanism of feeding and resistance to sunlight are a few traits that distinguish these vampires from their pale northern cousins.

- ***Necrolord:*** *The Vampire's power to command animal Familiars does not apply to Nasaku. Instead, the vampires of Napath can call and command a single type of Undead at will. Nasaku Halfbloods also possess this ability, but their power is far more limited. You are a Shadowlord, able to raise and command wraiths and shadows. See your Magic skills list for details.*
- ***Sunwalker:*** *Unlike other vampires, the Nasaku are not damaged by sunlight and will not be killed if exposed to the sun. They are still sensitive to light, however, and you suffer a -10% penalty to all physical and mental skills in bright sunlight. Concealing clothing, shadowed terrain, and elemental Darkness Area of Effect spells can protect you from the sun. Regardless, you are now effectively nocturnal: you gain the Well Rested bonus only when sleeping in the daytime. Sleeping at night only leaves you Rested, no matter your environment or the quality of your bed.*
- ***Will Worker:*** *The Nasaku are renowned for their patience and willpower, which is exceptional even in the realm of vampires. You gain Enhanced Dexterity (+5) and Will (+10).*
- ***Death Mask:*** *The Nasaku are readily distinguished by their hardened, metallic skin and teeth. Very old vampires of this bloodline appear to be carved from old metal or stone, taking on an eerily sculptural appearance. This is a trait shared by Halfbloods.*

- ***Elemental Weakness:*** *All undead usually take extra damage from the Dark and Light elements, while being largely immune to Time magic. Due to their close relationship with the desert, the Nasaku instead take extra damage from Dark and Water elemental effects and are unaffected by Earth magic. Halfbloods share this elemental alignment to a lesser extent, taking +0.5x damage from Dark or Water magic and -0.5x damage from Earth spells and effects.*
- ***Sand Form:*** *Instead of a gaseous or animal swarm form, Nasaku vampires have the ability to dissolve into sand and reform at will. As a halfblood, you do not gain this trait. However, you are able to see and track a transformed vampire of your linage when they are in sand form.*
- ***Vampiric Hunger****: The Nasaku crave both flesh and blood, using their fearsome teeth to tear the former and their hypodermic fingers to drain the latter. You must consume 50 points of Mana from a living, sentient creature at least once per week to sustain yourself. If you do not find a way to feed your hunger, you will become a Revenant: a berserk killing machine with no self-restraint who attacks any living being in their path. After consuming 100 points of mana from one or more living creatures, you will collapse into torpor and rise after 24 hours of rest.*
- ***Cradle of Sand:*** *You regenerate your hitpoints and reduce fatigue at double speed if you are buried in sand. You will not regenerate hit points or fatigue while you are immersed in water.*

"Great." I jumped back to the character log and checked the timestamps. This had happened to me recently, it seemed. I fired up the Journal entry again.

"Okay, so I'm going to assume you went to look at the sheet and know who we are," my past-self said. "Hopefully you haven't been turned into a vampire or anything, because this is how shit went down..."

Oops. I listened for a good ten minutes, taking it all in while my HP trickled back in. It was strange listening to myself talking, especially when Past-Hector gave an overview of his relationships: Karalti, Suri, Rin, Istvan and Vash, Soma, and others. Despite my cramped quarters, the sand did feel good. I scratched my cheek, frowning as the audio began talking about 'the Demon' and his armies. While I listened to that, I went to search for evidence of Suri in my logs, and was browsing them when a lovely, sweet voice broke through my thoughts.

"Hector? It's me, Karalti. You're alive, but what happened to you? The last thing I saw was you jumping down to fight the creepy lady. Then I felt you... I felt you die over and over again."

"Hey, hey, Karalti... it's okay." A dizzying warm flood of draconic anxiety, love, and concern washed over me like warm water. My head spun. *"I'm okay, but I'm not in a good position right now. Don't worry, though - I'll find a way out of this. Rin said you could teleport to my location?"*

"I can, but you need to have a location marker on your map." Karalti's tone darkened with agitation. *"I don't see*

one, and Rin said you can't remember anything. Did you die lots of times or something?"

"Uhh... I think I died once, very thoroughly."

"Okay. Try and work out where you are, okay?"

"Roger that." The footsteps were getting closer. *"I'll be in touch. I've got company."*

"Okay." There was a pause, and a swell of emotion so intense that my breath caught. *"I love you... even if you can't remember me."*

I closed my eyes for a moment, letting the sensation strengthen my resolve. *"I love you too."*

Karalti cut the link, and suddenly, I was back to my cold, sandy reality. I swallowed, composed myself, and fell still as the heavy stone lid above me began to slide to one side.

The lid tumbled off, and two leathery, well-preserved ghouls reached for me. Sand slid from my body as they lifted me up under the armpits, helping me to sit upright. The first thing I saw was a big, brawny, bronze-skinned man with piercing dark eyes that gleamed with satisfaction.

"Yes. Perfect." He nodded. "Show me your hands."

I held them up. My hands and forearms gleamed with a dull, dark iron sheen, as if I had dipped them in filings. The nails were short, thick and pointed. I felt my face. Sharp features... sharp teeth. Teeth that sounded like metal when I tapped my nail against them. My skin was cool to the touch all over. When I felt my neck, there was no pulse - but I felt my heart fluttering in my chest.

The giant carried a weapon in one hand: a beautifully made steel spear, glinting with traceries of scarlet light. When he saw me looking at it, he grinned widely, baring a set of interlocking, shark-like fangs. "Come, Hector. There is one final test."

Slowly, I pulled myself out of the sarcophagus and hopped down to the ground. They'd left my pants on – that was nice of them. I crossed to the giant and stood at ease, not sure what he wanted.

He held his wrist to me. "Place your left finger on my pulse and drink. One swallow... it will seal your status as my *Damu*."

Hesitantly, I took his wrist in my hands. There was no pulse, but through my fingers, I could somehow see the map of veins underneath his skin when I closed my eyes. No sooner had I realized that than my nails began to lengthen and narrow, until the end was a perfectly sharp needle point. I flexed my index finger in against his wrist. It broke the skin with a snap, sliding into the vein. I breathed in, chest rattling, and felt icy energy slide up through my finger, along my arm toward my heart. And when it hit... a warm glow suffused me, a combination of afterglow and the sensation of the best meal I'd ever had, all wrapped up in one heart-shuddering moment of contentment. The symbol on the back of my other hand, my right hand, burned with an unpleasant sensation.

"Good." He held the spear out to me. "Welcome to eternity, my child. Take your weapon and ready yourself for a cold journey. We have a great work to accomplish."

Nodding absently, I took the Spear - and as I did, a powerful sense of deja vu swept over me, and then a sense of warm fullness as memories of the very recent past shunted into my brain like a download. Suddenly, I knew exactly what I had to do.

I smiled up at Ashur like he was my favorite person in the world. I hoped it was a good performance: my life, the lives of my friends, and the life of a god depended on it. "Yes... Sire."

Chapter 51

The four of us left for the Dragon Gate just after sunset: Ashur, Violetta, myself, and Violetta's dragon.

"There." I pointed at the wobbling, gleaming star in the sky. "If we fly for that, the Gate and the Thunderstones should be where its orbit passes over the mountains."

"Excellent." Ashur was decked out in his golden war finery, a great hooked sword strapped to his belt, and a scepter in his hand. The scepter was carved of ivory and was set with a star sapphire the size of an eyeball: a stunning blue-black crystal with a brilliant white flash. It called to me and the Spear like a long-lost lover. "Once we have slain the Black God, I will have Hector summon his Queen dragon. Thus the bargain shall be fulfilled between your Master and I. I am only glad it did not require another war."

"We will need Hector and the Spear for the other gods," Violetta replied. "My emperor will pay you handsomely."

The vampire chuckled. "In other stones, perhaps?"

Violetta fixed him with a blank stare. "You will have enough power to save your homeland. I would not push his generosity."

I smiled like a doofus and nodded to everything my new 'Master' had to say. After watching me take my first vampiric baby steps, he was utterly confident that I was just another happy little undead thrall. Violetta didn't seem so sure. I made a point of staring hungrily at the back of her neck as her creaking Blue dragon climbed into the icy cold vault of the sky.

"I can use a spell to triangulate an approximate position," Violetta said. Her voice grated on my ears, which seemed slightly more sensitive than I recalled. "We will make several jumps, so as to get an accurate location."

"As you wish." The elder vampire wasn't strapped onto the dragon. He hung on with one clawed hand, gazing up to the stars and enjoying the sensation of the wind on his face. "Long have I waited for this day, Hector. I look forward to showing you my homeland as it is restored to its former glory! The Hanging Gardens, the mighty rivers, the artists and metalworkers!"

I glanced past the spread of information in my HUD to see if he was looking to me for an answer, but he wasn't. I had several windows open: my Quests window, the ArchemiWiki, the character log. "What about my dragon, sire?"

"What use does a future master of life and death have for dragons?" Ashur boomed. "Vainglorious, petty, selfish creatures. You are the child of Ashur of the Ten Thousand Swords! You have the makings of a masterful tactician, destined for far greater things than mooning around after one dragon. You could have the power of a thousand dragons! A thousand queens! With Matir's power, we will go on to conquer Vlachia, then Dakhdir. You have the Ruby – perhaps we will take Khors as well."

"Yeah, for sure. The more the merrier." I tried my best to sound enthused, still listening to my HUD narrator as she read out my quest updates.

⟦Sub-Quest failed: Bayou Warriors⟧
⟦You gain 725 EXP: Completed Subquests⟧
⟦You have new Quest Updates!⟧

Unto Death

Myszno, in the south-east of Vlachia, was formerly one of the most beautiful places in the country. Now it is a ruin, blighted by undeath and ruled by a powerful vampire lord. You accepted a grant to travel to this troubled land and reclaim it from the vampire's claws – a terrible proposition, given how powerful he has become. But with great risk comes great reward. You could become a true Count in Vlachia, with land, property, and income.
After fighting to unite the Myszno Defense Force, you decisively smashed the Demon's Army against the walls of the Prezyemi Line, though at great cost. Now it is time to finish what you started. Karhad and Egbolt are within your grasp - will you succeed, or will you die trying?
Difficulty: *Level 20+ (extraordinary)*
Rewards: *EXP, 60 build points, Charter to Resettle the Duchy of Myszno.*

The Shrine of the Elder Gods

Follow the Star - and remember, Herald: be subtle and clever.

Everything blanked out as the blue dragon rumbled the words of a spell. I paused in my listening as reality folded in around us like a sheet, enclosing us in a black nothingness. When it unfurled, we were hanging over a range of wild, snowcapped black mountains. Gusts of snow and ice blew into our faces, skittered over the dragon's scales.

Violetta held her hands up, palms facing one another as they glowed. "Next jump. Brace."

We vanished a second time, and a third... each time, appearing over steep mountainous taiga. A black river cut through the narrow stone valley below. deepening and becoming more thunderous each time we blinked between locations. On the fourth try, we appeared into a raging storm, hovering over the lip of a waterfall that plunged down into a black abyss of space. Across the crevasse were two enormous obelisks that stretched up from the depths to a height greater than the nearest mountain. The monuments spat and arced with power. When the swirling clouds overhead convulsed with lightning, the obelisks drew the blasts and channeled them, absorbing the energy into the glowing vertical lines of script that decorated them.

"The Thunderstones," I murmured.

Ashur rumbled. "Do you feel the way it makes your blood crawl, boy? The Dark God hates the dead."

This area didn't feel bad to me. It felt like an old graveyard. Peaceful, but spooky. The Mark of Matir throbbed dully on the back of my right hand. "Yeah. This is the place."

"Tempest doesn't like it," Violetta said. "Be on guard."

The great blue dragon soared into the canyon, breaching the fog and revealing the mouth of a great cave that was so perfectly dark that even my wildly enhanced vision couldn't penetrate it. Only a dragon or other flying creature could have reached this place - and even a dragon struggled to enter. Tempest's wing-tips grazed the entry to the cavern, and he grunted in displeasure as we flew deep into the heart of the great mountain that loomed above.

The rumbling waterfall receded, and silence fell over us like a heavy cloak. I had to be careful to conceal my breathing, and spent the trip in relearning the limits of my character, scheming and planning. I had three branches of skills now: my combat abilities, the Mark of Matir abilities, and the Shadowlord powers. There were only two of those to worry about:

Rite: Shadow of the Sun (Level 1)

Suund'karon, Karalt', Binah!

You may call and bind the spirits of the dead to your will. You may enact Shadow of the Sun over a corpse and extract the creature's wraith to serve you. To qualify for extraction, the target must be an NPC of any species that possesses a Wisdom score. This excludes certain monsters and constructs. Constructs animated by a spirit may qualify for extraction, as you can extract and bind the spirit contained within the construct - assuming you are strong enough to defeat the wards and magic laid on the construct by its creator.

You have a default 80% chance to summon an individual creature's wraithform. The chance of failure increases or decreases depending on the extracted creature's level (10%

+/- per level relative to your level). For example, at Level 21, you have an 80% chance to bind another Level 21 creature, a 100% chance of binding any creature below Level 19, and a 70% chance of binding a Level 22 creature.

Bound shadows are permanently available to be summoned. The number of summoned shadows you can retain depends on your Will score - 1 shadow per 5 Will points (current Will: 60]. You may permanently dismiss any or all of your Bound shadows to regain a slot and summon a new minion. A dismissed bound shadow cannot be resummoned.

Shadows retain all magical and combat abilities they had in life - however, any Light elemental abilities are transmuted to Dark elemental abilities instead.

Your bound shadows cannot be healed in combat, and must be rested for 1 minute per 1HP/MP to recover.

Summoned shadows do not drain MP once called; however, if a shadow is slain, you will lose 20MP. If you reach 0 MP, all of your summons will vanish.

To increase this mastery of Shadow of the Sun, you must study Necromancy (Incorporeal) or Invocation (Summoning) at the appropriate level.

Ability: Imbue Shadow

Your shadows are capable of growing alongside you, gaining levels and experience of their own. Every time you attain a new character level, your shadows will gain EXP. Each time a shadow increases in level, you may manually assign their stat points, combat ability points, and skill points.

Tempest glided out into a massive cylindrical chamber - a space big enough to seat five hundred dragons of his size. There were alcoves set into the walls, each one containing what looked like the crumbling remains of a nest. Great hexagonal columns supported a high, towering roof. At the center of the chamber was a tall dais, tiered like a wedding cake... and at the top of that was a stone circle. Cleverly placed magelights lit the dais from high above, painting nine long, painted shadows in a starburst shape across the well.

"There." Ashur sniffed and snorted, bearing his fangs, and held up the scepter. The stone mounted in the head of it emitted a baleful light. "We fly toward the dais."

Violetta did not reply, except to tap Tempest at the base of his neck. The dragon let out a mournful moan, and coasted toward the circle. As he came up on it, I saw there was a large well at the center. The whole arrangement - stones, well, altar - was strangely familiar.

"That is a sacrificial well," I said. "The entry to the Gate is through there."

"Sacrificial well?" Ashur frowned. "Hmmph. Had I known we needed sacrifices, I would have bought them."

"We can teleport back to Karhad and then back to here," Violetta said. "Or have Hector call his dragon and use her. Whatever we do to her here is better than what the Emperor has planned for her."

I saw her glance at me, waiting for a reaction. I shrugged.

Tempest circled the altar, the membranes of his wings rippling. When he couldn't find a place to land, he swung around and clung to the wall of the towering dais like a bat. He beat his wings stiffly to keep his grip, and lay his neck against the edge so that we could climb over it to jump down. Ashur went first, his sword in one hand, the staff in the other. I was next, with Violetta following up the rear. The hollow-eyed woman raised a hand, and light pulsed through the intricate glass and crystal filigree worked into the leather. A greenish pulse of magic radiated from her, sliding over and caressing the varied surfaces of the cavern around us.

A flash of movement caught my eye - a streak of shadow flowing down the side of the well. I pulled the Spear and twisted around as the shadow bubbled to the floor like thick black ink, then rose up into a humanoid form that resolved into... me.

My doppelganger stared at us with feverish, filmy blue-white eyes. His skin was mottled with a rash; his breathing was raspy, thick with phlegm. He clutched a copy of the Spear in his hands, the blade dripping with black ichor that sizzled on the ground.

"What the hell?" I took a step back as an awful, gnawing fear took hold of my guts. Everything about this creature caused my lizard brain to scream 'disease'!

A HP ring appeared over the thing's head, along with a name: *⟦Darkform: Level 30⟧*.

Chapter 52

The monster's lips parted, letting out a thin stream of toxic smoke. It lifted its corrupted Spear and plunged it into the stone floor.

"AoE!" I Jumped straight up into the air on reflex as the floor erupted with oily, putrid spear blades. Ashur and Violetta both flew up into the air, avoiding the ground entirely - and ran right into a phalanx of shadow spears lancing in from all directions. They manifested with a sound like breaking glass, thrusting and then vanishing, reappearing somewhere else. It was all I could do to avoid the weapons as they formed from the air. Violetta made a stifled sound of pain as several pierced her at once, but she was such a high level that it barely chipped her HP. Ashur avoided them all with supernatural alacrity.

"Bathos prava!" The sorceress leveled her hands at the Darkform.

A white fireball tore free from her fingers, smashing into the boss... and passed right through it, leaving it unharmed.

Violetta gasped, taking a step back. "What?!"

The Darkform's eyes got big, and its lips peeled back as it gave an unnatural, wooden laugh - and then transformed again, morphing into an elegant, richly dressed female lich. Her clothing and fingers dripped with gold and copper, jewels and magical talismans. She fixed Ashur with a piercing, eyeless gaze.

"Seheru, my love?" He stepped in beside me, his fangs bared. "No... an illusion. And yet -"

"*Bathos prava.*" The lich made an arcane gesture, repeating Violetta's spell.

A glowing fireball twice the size of the one she had cast curled to life and then blew at us like a meteor. Violetta and Ashur both snarled words of power, and magical shields sprung to life in front of us. The ball turned back, smashing into the edge of the well and spraying chunks of stone everywhere. The lich laughed as she flew to the side and dodged: the same unpleasant, grating sound that had come out of my doppelganger's mouth.

"*Azul ha'rath*!" It rasped.

Bolts of foul energy shot out, homing in on me. I struck out at them with a shout - and to my surprise, the Spear turned the projectiles, sending them shooting back at the caster. The lich dodged, but the bolts followed - and hit her hard, shaving off almost a third of her HP. She wailed with an unearthly sound, momentarily freezing in place.

Violetta circled around. "*Azul ha'rath!*"

The shadow-morphed lich turned the second round of projectiles with a contemptuous wave of her hand as Ashur's formed blurred. In a split second, she teleported above us, avoiding the glint of the vampire's sword. He snarled and launched himself into the air, but the doppelganger avoided every blurring strike, laughing at him the entire time.

"Ridiculous." Violetta scowled, and bought her hands around to charge another spell.

"Wait. I get it. We have to turn its attacks back at it." I watched as the Level 30 Vampire chased the lich too fast for the eyes to follow. A fireball exploded from the air - and Ashur thrust the staff forward, barking a command. The dark crystal flared, and the fire splashed around an invisible wall of force as it impacted, harmlessly deflected by Ashur's magic. The magic missiles followed - Ashur swung the staff like a tennis racquet, and the magic missiles turned back on the lich like a pair of glowing boomerangs, slicing her form apart.

"Pitiful." The vampire exclaimed, dropping smoothly to the ground. "This is the only protection Matir has? No monsters, no army... not even interesting treasure."

I was about to agree when I saw a pillar of shadow form behind Violetta. It took the form of a tall, handsome albino man, with cruel pink eyes so pale they almost looked silvered. He smirked, and reached up to wrap his hands around her neck.

Violetta turned, and when she saw the man, her eyes flew open wide. She crumpled with a mewl of terror as he squeezed, clawing at his hands. The move left both of them wide open. Ashur and I came in from either side, stabbing and slicing as Violetta's eyes rolled back in her head. She was catatonic with fear, so much so that she didn't even really try to defend herself. She hung there, plucking weakly at the man's hands as foam collected in the corners of her mouth.

"What is this!?" Ashur snarled. He thrust the crystal stave into the monster's chest, crystal and all. The white-haired man's grin faltered, and then his face sloughed away as he howled. His body collapsed like melting wax.

[[You have defeated Darkform!]]
[[You gain 813 exp!]]

"There. It is done." Ashur pulled the staff free. The Darkform collapsed and melted back into the shadows around us. Violetta dropped to the ground, coughing. Tempest bellowed in reply to her, his voice echoing and distant.

813 EXP? That was hardly anything for a boss. Frowning, I peered out into the huge chamber, and then backpedaled toward the well. "No. No, it's not."

Darkforms crouched in every one of the nest alcoves: copies of me, copies of the white-haired man, copies of amorphous creatures with too many mouths and not enough eyes. They leered at us from every shadow - thousands of them, each one wearing a face out of our worst nightmares.

"We're leaving." Violetta was breathing quickly, scratching obsessively at her neck with one hand. Her eyes were huge in her pale face.

I looked to the well, and as I did, the Mark of Matir flared under my clothes. "The well. We don't need a sacrifice... we just have to be brave enough to jump."

"Go. Scout the way." Ashur waved to me dismissively. "We will take care of these."

"Yes, sire." I turned and hopped onto the edge of the well. Before I could think better of it, I spread my arms, then put them over my head and dived.

My sense of deja vu intensified as the darkness swallowed me. The wind whistled through my armor, and I knew - KNEW - I'd done this before. After a few seconds, the rushing in my ears faded, and the sensation of falling left my body. I floated as if in icy water, listening to my inhumanly slow heartbeat, then felt myself begin to rise. I oriented myself as soon as I could sense where 'down' was - and when a light opened up, I stepped out of a circular portal into a small, plain square room. A pair of braziers burned with a strange blue flame beside a pair of double doors made of rusted iron. In the center of the door was a pressure plate with the same symbol burned on the back of my hand.

I took a step forward, freezing when the lights in the torches wobbled and a deep, rolling double boom passed through the floor. My teeth and eardrums vibrated as the twin sounds rattled every cell in my body, then slowly faded away. I counted, gripping the Spear tightly. The sound occurred again after exactly sixty seconds... the same instant my half-living heart took another beat.

Hail to you, Herald of the Hidden Seed. The words formed in my mind, unbidden. It was a pleasant voice: light, masculine, even-toned, with the edge of a hiss. *Hail, Paragon of the Triad.*

The mark on the door seemed to stand out in relief, surrounded by a thin corona of blue light. My brow creased, and I absently walked forward to lay a hand on the metal. When my fingers made contact, there was an invisible push of force against my palm, and then a chill that spread up through my veins. When the cold reached my head, I suddenly knew exactly where I was - and what I needed to do.

[[New Location discovered: The Dragon Gate of Endless Night]]

My throat worked as I thought back to the conversation between Ashur and Violetta: The one where Ashur had promised her that he would have me summon my dragon to fulfil some bargain. Even if I couldn't bring Karalti to my mind's eye, the memory of her beautiful voice in my mind made my heart leap. If anything happened to her, I would never forgive myself.

"Okay, Karalti: I know where I am, but you need to stay away. "I lifted my hand, and the plate turned, then receded as the doors opened ahead of me into a corridor of pure white opal. It was lit from everywhere and nowhere... leading to a lightless doorway at the other end.

"What? Why?" Karalti replied quickly.

"It's not safe for you to be here. I'll keep you updated on what's happening. When it's time, I'll call. Trust me."

"But... you've already forgotten almost everything. What happens if you die again before you get them back?"

"I don't know." I turned as the portal behind me flared to life. Ashur and Violetta stepped through, slightly worse for wear.

"We're getting ready anyway," Karalti replied hotly. *"Don't do anything dumb!"*

"I'll try. I have to go."

Violetta's face was cold and hard and angry, and the collar of her armor had fallen to reveal a neck so badly scarred it looked like her head had been torn off and then roughly glued back onto her body. She opened her mouth to say something when the double boom made the walls and floor rumble around us.

"The stone is resonating. It is close," Ashur rumble. "Lead the way, my thrall."

Thrall my ass. I turned around and trotted off like a good boy.

The opal tunnel was freezing cold - oppressively cold, the kind of chill that seemed to want to suck the heat from my bones and force my eyes shut, vampire powers or not. At the end of the corridor, it opened into a humming void of black space. There was a nose-searing, unpleasant metallic smell, the stench of ozone. A glittering white opal bridge spanned the fathomless chasm below. The bridge ended at another great stone circle, and behind that loomed a huge cherry-blossom shaped inlay made of wrought gold and silver. My eyes followed the curving lines of each petal like section to the center. As I watched, another rolling boom resounded through the cavern, and the flower-shaped door bowed outward, pulsing in time with the-

"-Heartbeat," I murmured aloud.

"Yes. The heart of a sleeping god pounds behind those doors." Ashur lay a hand on my shoulder. "Cross the bridge. I will be right behind you."

"Wait." Violetta was behind us, topping off the mana reservoirs in her spellgloves. "At the Gate of Glorious Dawn, there was a difficult boss in the antechamber. This Gate is probably no different. I don't sense anything, but this is the Gate of the God of Darkness. It would stand to reason that there could be enemies we don't see."

Does that make me the dungeon boss? I lifted my chin, looking up at the five-petaled door. There was a crushing sense of presence behind it... the sensation of something massive staring down at us, like a weight pushing down on our heads. *This feeling... it's incredible.*

The gravity of the being behind that door seemed to drag the oxygen from the air as we crossed the bridge. At the end, I could see there was something at the center of the stone circle. A small, six-sided altar just with a narrow slit in the center that was the perfect size for the Spear of Nine Spheres. I approached it slowly. The Spear was numbing my fingers, vibrating in time with the magical field that beat against our faces like radiation.

"At last." Ashur pushed me aside on his way to the altar. The scepter in his hand was glowing with a baleful black light, humming in time with the Spear. I could feel the weapon straining for it, and the Key straining back in turn. "To think this one being could contain such power. The power of multitudes... of all the souls he has ever consumed."

"Matir... consumes souls?" I repeated dumbly.

Ashur looked down at me. He almost seemed concerned. "You do not know the mechanism of the Caul of Souls, Hector?"

"No." Maybe I had, once - but if I'd known, I'd definitely forgotten.

"The world lore has it is that every NPC who has ever died has their spirit sucked up into the Caul of Souls." Violetta walked up behind us, her boots clacking on the stone. "The power of the Nine was the spark, but the energy of souls is the fuel."

Ashur made a sound of agreement. "When the dragons created the Caul, they didn't just sacrifice their gods. They killed themselves and their slaves to create a stalemate, and they condemned the rest of the races of the world to join them in their torment."

My eyes widened as the door throbbed. The air felt too thick to breathe.

"The stupid thing is that we could have defeated them." Ashur's voice was heavy with old grief, still raw after thousands of years. "If the peoples of the world had united and the dragons had worked with us humans, we could have beaten the Drachan. But they could not give up their position as the mightiest race of Archemi."

"Now you understand why the dragons have a Geas on them at the Eyrie," Violetta continued, falling into place on the other side of the altar. "Why the queens were subjugated and the Aesari bound them into the service of humans and the other species of the world. Because the last time they were in charge, they threw us under the bus. They created an abomination."

A feeling of panic squeezed my chest. I couldn't believe that – not after everything I'd gone through. Not after feeling Karalti's simple, pure, powerful love for me.

"Indeed. It is time to correct the ancient wrong. Hold out your hand." Ashur commanded.

Numbly, I extended my left hand to him, the Spear resting in the right. The vampire took his scepter, and carefully plucked the Star of Endless Night from its setting. The stone almost looked like a ball of liquid oil, the star-shaped fire at the heart of it surging across its surface. It was icy-cold to touch, chilling my fingertips through my gauntlets. I bought it up to the Spear. As it got closer, the color of the weapon's mana changed. The red tracery of light bled away, replaced by a deep, deadly, seething blackness. The Star lifted, and then slowly descended, fitting neatly into the second highest setting on the blade. My bones hummed with a flush of pure energy that thrilled from my fingertips to the rest of my body, and an alert appeared:

The Spear of the Ender and the Maker

Soul-bound Dark Elemental Weapon
Slot: Two-handed
Item Class: Relic
Item Quality: Mastercrafted
Damage: 277 - 352 Slashing or Piercing
Durability: 97%
Weight: 1lb

Special: Soul-bound, +50 bonus Fire damage, +150 Dark damage (+300 damage to Undead), +500 HP, +10 Strength, +10 Will, +25% evasion, 1% chance to instantly kill an enemy.
Special: Maker's Blessing - learn Crafting skills 5% faster. Nightfather's Blessing - 6% of inflicted weapon damage heals the wielder.

"It is truly the Spear of legend," Ashur breathed. "Now, we end this. Unlock the Gate!"

The gods here eat souls. That couldn't be true, could it? I looked up at the huge door, then took my place in front of the altar. Ashur was just behind me, watching intently as I raised the Spear, aligned it with the hole, and drove it down with all my strength.

Chapter 53

Before the blade touched the altar, I sprung straight up into the air. At the peak of the backflip, I hit Master of Blades V.

A ring of ten shards of light-sucking energy flared out around me like arching wings, and in a split second, they spun and slammed down on Ashur and Violetta. There was no escape: each lance now did slightly over two thousand points of damage, two lances per target. Ashur was completely flat-footed, reeling as they took him through the chest and shoulders and blew two huge holes through his torso. Violetta barked a command word, getting a shield up just before the energy shards tore apart, regathered, and Rained down hard.

[[You deal 3092 damage to ??Zero]]
[[You deal 6137 damage to Elder vampire Ashur! HP: 4863/11,000]]

I landed the Jump on Ashur's back and drove the Spear through the back of his neck – another 2816 damage. Thanks to my old friend Type Effectiveness, he was already down to

2047 HP – less than my total pool, and I was 8 levels lower than him.

"You! How...?" His next words choked off as he coughed a gout of black, clotted blood onto the floor.

"*Bla'pah'hai!*" Violetta snarled the command words of a Water spell, flinging her glowing hands at me and Ashur both. I got out of the way as water condensed from the air and thrust forward like a giant sword. Ashur saw it coming. He teleported away, reappearing at the other end of the dais.

With one eye on the vampire, I flung myself into a roll under her next spell and charged in with a roar. *"Karalti! If you're ready to rock and roll, now's the time! Come in swinging!"*

Violetta slung another water blade at me. I Shadow Danced through it, soaking 500-ish damage as I burst out of the dash in a freezing cloud of darkness. I charged the Spear with Shadow Lance, and felt it *reach* for the Star. When it found it, the black fire rimming the blade burst into ropy coils of boiling shadow. Violetta's eyes bled black as she threw up a desperate shield. The Spear struck it with a rolling shockwave, overloading the flickering wall of light and blowing it back into Violetta's face. The discharge was so intense that it slashed her skin and sent her flying. I turned my focus back to Ashur then.

"A Halfblood!?" He was clutching his wounds with his left hand, the other arm hanging uselessly by his sided. He couldn't regenerate any of the HP he'd lost. "*Me*, sire a Halfblood! Has the power... urrghh... of Napath declined so much?"

"Sorry, fang daddy. I'm a bad boy." Violetta was trying to gain distance - I was struggling not to let her get it. She turned about twenty feet from me, close enough that I could Jump the distance and stay on her where she was weakest: up close and personal. Just before the Spear contacted her body, she rounded on me, teeth bared.

"Chron lavan ki'mer!" She cried, slashing her hands down.

[[You resist Time Stop!]]
[[You are slowed!]]

The world seemed to wind down to a crawl. I twisted to evade, but it was like trying to turn in knee-deep mud. Violetta's hands lifted, her mouth opening. Out of the corner of my eye, I saw Ashur down some sort of potion and snarl, hefting his sword in his off hand.

"You are a stain on my bloodline! On my people!" He howled, his fangs lengthening, face twisting his face into a bestial, demonic mask of bone and iron. His muscles swelled. "Die!"

The Slow debuff ended, and time snapped back to normal. I couldn't evade in time. Ashur's hooked sword split my armor like it wasn't there, carving through the flesh beneath.

[[Your armor is Sundered! – 50% protection!]]
[[You take 829 damage! You are Bleeding!]]

"Oof." Something bright and hot flew toward me. I dodged on reflex, barely able to see for the pain. I scrambled around the pair of enemies on one hand and both feet, then flung a Shadow Garrote at Violetta to distract her. The loop of shadow didn't fly from my hand - it rose out of the sorceress's own shadow, dropping around her neck and drawing taut. Violetta's eyes bulged, and she forgot everything she was doing to claw desperately at her throat, drawing blood within seconds. She spun away with a small choking sob - right into the path of a gleaming black dragon who appeared out of thin air.

Karalti drew a deep breath, jaws agape. "HRRRRROOOOOAARRR!"

A liquid plume of blazing white fire swallowed the panicking sorceress in a sticky inferno. Her passengers jumped to the ground: a silver-skinned woman in a featureless steel mask, two spider-like automatons, and a slender, wavy-haired man who leaped down with a saber in one hand and a cocked pistol in the other.

"You!" He levelled his sword at Ashur. The blade gleamed silver – true silver, by the way it made my skin crawl. "Stand and fight, demon!"

Ashur snarled at him. He made an arcane gesture, glaring at me with burning gold eyes that hissed and spat like the core of a star. "Bastard half-blood! I will find you, thrall! I will debase you, kill your dragon bitch, kill your god! You have not seen the last of Ashur!"

My ally charged him with a harsh battlecry. He fired the pistol – in an instant, Ashur's body collapsed into sand that swirled away on an unseen wind before vanishing.

The Mercurion and her Artifacts were butchering Violetta. She was on her back underneath them, shrieking with pain as she soaked bullets and tried to fend off the stabbing, stamping feet. "Aieee! No! *Krath'uum*!"

Light pulled in around Violetta, then exploded in a shockwave that sent us all flying back - except Karalti. The dragon landed and charged in with her head lowered. Violetta whirled on her, preparing to cast another spell, but I was already flanking and ready to stab. The Spear took her through the kidney. Her words cut off as she seized in pain, and Karalti pulled her off the end of the weapon with her jaws. She shook her like a rat. Violetta gurgled - she was at barely a quarter HP, which vanished to a sliver when the dragon slammed her against the floor and then dropped her. I charged in as Violetta flung a hand up. Her eyes were wide and blue, dark with pain.

"Mercy!" she gasped.

"Not today, Satan." Before she had any room to pull a fast one, I drove Shattering Darkness straight into her head. The Spear punched through Violetta's skull, freezing it solid. Her skull shattered into bloodless smoking chunks, and then her body collapsed to the ground. It shuddered, and then turned to dust - leaving a sack of goods behind.

[[The enemy commander has surrendered his forces and fled! You have defeated the invading Napathu army! You earned 2000 EXP!]]

[[Quest Complete: Unto Death. You earned 3363 EXP!]]

[[You are Level 22!]]

[[Karalti is Level 13!]]

[[Rin is Level 18!]]
[[Suri reached Level 23!]]

Through the forest of notifications, I stared at the dragon in awe. Karalti was more beautiful than I could have imagined - tall and supple, her scales gleaming with veins of bright opalescent color. She was feminine and unearthly and... was this gorgeous, incredible creature really mine?

"Hector! Are you okay!?" She ran to me with her head low, her wings flickering against her sides. Dropping the Spear, I held my arms out as Karalti thrust her muzzle against my chest, colliding with me like a girl throwing herself in a hug. At the first touch of her burning hot scales, my temples heated with such sudden intensity that, for a second, I thought my skull was about to explode like Violetta's had.

"Gyaaaaaaah! GAH!" I barely felt my knees hit the ground as a massive, torrential flood of memories rushed in. Indonesia and San Fran and a house with a green door and faceless men sprawled over shattered trees and Suri falling and- "BITCH... ASS... MOTHBALLING... Gyah!"

I clawed my face, my eyes, the floor, anything, trying to make it stop... and then it was over. It took me a second to realize where I was: lying on my side, Karalti mantled over me with piercing cries of confusion and distress.

"Karalti! Hector! What happened?!" Rin ran up to us, pushing her mask back. Karalti snapped at her, once, then keened and pulled her head back. Gasping, I looked up to see her wide blue eyes round and worried. She felt my forehead.

"Memory." I choked the word out through a dry, tight throat. "Download. Memory."

Karalti drew her hands up against her chest and swung her head from side to side, moaning. *"I hurt him somehow!"*

"Okay! It okay!" Words and word order were jumbled in my head, Tuun mixing with Korean and English and Vlachian. "Download... bad."

The dragon ducked her head and nuzzled at me, then began to lick my exposed skin. I flinched at the first contact, but there was no more mental agony - just a wet dragon tongue that pulled my helmet off and mlem'd the entire length of my face.

"Ugh... Jeez... okay..." I weakly fended off the tongue, and pulled her head down into another hug. Her smell was the most familiar thing in the world. "I'm okay."

I sat upright. Rin and Istvan reached down. I caught their hands and let them help me up, still weak and dizzy from the info dump. As I got to my feet, I glanced over at the Dragon Gate and froze.

Rin shook her fists, bouncing up and down with excitement. "We did it! We managed to hold the undead at the Pass! We weren't able to recruit all the Yanik, but we had enough warriors and soldiers to keep the zombies at bay. Lord Bolza was staked-"

"Wait." I held up a hand to ward her back as I swayed from foot to foot. "Visitor."

"What?" Istvan turned his face in the direction I began walking. Then, to Rin, he whispered: "What is he talking about?"

"Don't worry, he's not crazy. I see it too. Stay back while we go over, just in case. "Karalti rattled in her throat, inflating it and then huffing out a great gust of air as she padded along behind me.

The Black God of the Nine was looking up at the huge shuddering door to his tomb, hands folded behind his back. Matir looked very similar to how he had the first time I'd met him, when I was glitched inside the belly of a slave ship. Tall, lean, dressed in shadowy traveler's clothes. Trousers, boots, a hooded capelet... and when he glanced back at us, no discernible face. There was nothing but a sucking void of darkness with a single, dancing point of light at the center.

"You came," he said. His tone was heavy with relief.

"Yeah. Can't say I'm not a man of my word." I cracked my neck and knuckles, drawing to a stop a healthy distance away. "You have a really strong heartbeat for a dead guy, you know that?"

"The death of an immortal god is different to the death of a mortal human." Matir replied primly. "Our death is not of the physical self. It is the death of our agency - the removal of our power to directly act upon reality. A dead god is unreachable, inaccessible, and must act through their proxies. I was powerless to stop the plundering of my corpse. Before my ascent to the Dragon Gate, such a thing could not have happened. Now I am so weakened that the only place I can currently materialize is the antechamber to my prison."

Karalti snaked her muzzle forward, chirping curiously. Matir's avatar stepped forward, and raised a slender hand. His fingers twitched, as if he would touch her snout... but then he folded them into his palm and dropped it, turning away.

"You need a more secure dungeon, my man." I watched him with growing suspicion. "Pretty much anyone could bust in here."

"This isn't the dungeon," Matir replied. "This is just the entry to the dungeon. There is an entire complex behind each dragon gate, each different and devilishly challenging. You have to be at least Level 50 before you could cross that threshold and survive."

"Right." I was actually reassured to know that. Even Lucien and Violetta weren't that juiced up. "So... how's it hanging in Dark Godsville?"

"Poorly."

"Yeah. Same here." I began to fidget with my broken armor. "So, going to tell us why we're here? Because I just got strong-armed into being a vampire half-blood thanks to this quest, and I don't know how I feel about that."

"Is that why you smell so weird?" Karalti not-so-discreetly sniffed at my hair.

Matir straightened, looking down at me. "You should know something about the world that the Architects created. The quest system here is dynamic. Adaptive. For normal, non-viral players, quests are generated for them, dovetailing with their needs, their desires and fantasies. Players are not controlled by their quests. Their quests are controlled by their hearts' desires. Do you understand?"

"Just wait a second." I scowled. "You aren't supposed to know that stuff. You've never broken the fourth wall when you've spoken to me before."

"You are correct." Matir replied. "I did not speak of it."

Something was plucking at my intuition. Something about the way the god's avatar stood and acted. "What's going on? What aren't you telling me? And why hasn't the Shrine quest ended? We're here, at the Thunderstones. We stopped Ashur from draining you. The Keystone's as safe as it'll ever be. Where's the wrap-up?"

"There isn't one." Matir gave a very un-godly agitated sigh. "Hector, listen to me. Things have gotten out of hand here since Michael returned. Every time the Architects purged him from this world, he found some way to come back. He's malware: a virus that has embedded himself so deeply into the lore of this server that he could have come back any number of ways. He's already warped it so intensely that we have things that were never intended to be seen in play. There were server limitations on torture, programs to detect sexual crimes beyond the scope of normal PvP... now most of that has been thrown down the drain."

No way. My eyes widened as he continued to rant in a way that was utterly familiar to me. I took a step back from Matir, bumping into Karalti's wrist.

A snippet of conversation from the past: *"Matir is a feature of the game's mythos and storyline, but not an active character."*

And another: "What about my brother?"

"We would like to offer our condolences. He did not successfully transfer."

"He might have made it. You didn't know I was here. He could be alive, and we just don't know it."

"We knew you had reached the character creation and neural duplication stage. There is no record of him ever getting that far. No psychological or neural profile was created for him..."

My mouth worked silently for a moment. "... Steve?"

Chapter 54

Matir flinched slightly at the sound of my brother's name. His long fingers curled up into loose fists.

"Steve?" I took a numb step forward, then another.

"Your brother... preferred his Korean name," Matir said haltingly. "He always wondered why it was that he had to use an Anglo-Saxon name to get a job, but had to learn to pronounce names like 'Kuzetznov' or 'Unbegaun' at work. Park Chi-Yul... it's not that difficult to say."

First came anger. Then grief. Confusion. I fumbled back, searching for Karalti as I tried to figure out what the fuck was going on.

"You always preferred your English name," Matir continued, turning to look back at the Dragon Gate again.

"Yeah. Because I chose it for myself." My voice shook slightly as I got closer, studying him... searching for signs of my brother. "What the fuck is going on? This is impossible. Steve didn't make it. His upload failed."

"Did it?" Matir tilted his head to the side.

"Ryuko said he didn't even reach character creation." Another step.

Matir gestured elegantly to his chest. "My Herald... did it occur to you that your brother might have never intended to become a Starborn character?"

My mouth opened, then shut. Then opened again. "You mean... you mean he survived? He's here? He told you this stuff, about the game?"

"Not exactly." Matir's face was unfathomable, yet somehow, he seemed... compassionate. "He didn't need to 'tell' me."

I stared at Matir for several long seconds. "... then you *are* Steve? Right?"

The Dark God turned away from me slightly, as if ashamed. "No. I am not Steven Park."

"I-I don't get it." I couldn't stop the stammer, and flushed. "If he's not a character, and he's not you, and he's not some kind of free-floating God...?"

"Park Chi-Yul - Steve - is dead in the way that the gods of the Solonkratsu are dead," Matir replied gently. "He is... was... one of the Architects, is he not?"

"Yeah." I halted, struggling against the heat in my eyes. "Yeah, he was."

"I could not have awoken of my own accord. Only an Architect could have roused me from my restless sleep. When I first stirred, I felt only one powerful imperative: the need to raise an avatar and find a Starborn soul to serve as my Herald. It was sheer coincidence that I found you struggling against the Corruption eating you from the inside out... and when we made our bargain, I was given the option to select some character perimeters for you. I found I knew how to make you immune to Corruption, the secret property of Darkness... the point at which the Darkness element becomes the Void. For Darkness is the closest state of matter to the Void represented by the Drachan, even though it is in strong opposition to it."

What little blood that remained in my face drained away. My fingers began to tingle.

"If Steve didn't incarnate as a character on purpose... then what has he become?" I stared at the god in shock.

Matir spread his hands wide. "He joined the Overconciousness, of course."

The Overconsciousness? Confusion froze my tongue, until suddenly, I realized. "... He merged with OUROS. How?"

"How do the Architects do anything?" Matir shrugged.

My brother had been on the AI design team. And all this time, there was a backdoor into the hot seat... a door waiting just for him. My throat felt dry and scratchy as I swallowed. "That glitch... the one on the ship. Did he cause that?"

"Perhaps. But I do not know." Matir replied. "It is possible that this Architect, Park Chi-Yul, directed the impetus that awoke me. It is possible he compelled me to search out into the world for the first time in four thousand years and discover you. Perhaps it was he who inspired me to name you my Herald, and in the process, giving you a unique character type. One that Ororgael or the Drachan cannot corrupt with their power."

"That controlling, manipulative piece of shit." I whispered hoarsely.

Matir bowed his head. "I do not know his motives. As I drifted in and out of consciousness, I came to know things that had never been known by the gods in times past. I came to understand this world as the Architects understood it. This knowledge, this personality, these memories... they filtered into my mind in an insidious, persistent way. This insistence on my knowing these things can only be the product of a great and terrible will. All I know is that, between the actions of Ororgael and his manipulation of the Napathu, the Caul has been destabilized. Perhaps beyond repair. And thus I have a new quest to issue you, one which Karalti should also listen to."

I already knew what the quest would be and why Steve had spent months setting me up for it. It was my infantry experience. It was the training that allowed me to look at Violetta's pleading eyes and feel nothing as I jammed a foot of steel through her skull and turned her brain into ice cubes. It was his assumption that I'd learned to think like a soldier. Follow orders. Complete tasks. Follow through because someone with chevrons or a brass star told me to.

I was shaking. Not with anticipation, or excitement, but with rage. Karalti was staring at us in astonishment, her horns standing on end, her pupils contracted to pin-points. Matir said nothing. He simply bowed his head and waited.

"Here I was, thinking that Steve bought me into Archemi because he wanted to save my life." My voice was very deep, and very dark as I stared a hole through Matir's blank face. "We were both so sick that I forgot what he was like. But I'm here now, and I'm neck-deep in this shit. So give me the fucking quest."

Matir nodded, and raised a hand beside his head. After a few seconds, my HUD jumped to life.

New Main Quest: The Caul of Souls

Through circumstances beyond anyone's control, a great threat has risen in Archemi: the fallen Architect once known as Ororgael has possessed the body of a Starborn, the self-styled Emperor Baldr Hyland of Ilia. The Drachan whisper in Baldr's ears, spinning him stories of a bright and perfect future of which he is the ultimate ruler... if only he will release them from their prison by dismantling the Caul of Souls and claiming the power of the Nine for himself.

To prevent the rebirth of the greatest enemy Archemi has ever known, the Caul of Souls must be repaired: and to do that, the Paragon - a dragon and rider couple - must rally the other paired aspects of the Triad to their banner and re-seal the gods in their Dragon Gates to render the Drachan powerless once more.

A great burden of duty rests on your shoulders, Paragon. Will you accept the challenge?

Rewards: *Progressive (EXP, Treasure, Skills and Abilities)*

Difficulty: *Variable*

I dismissed the window with a back-wave of my hand. "Nope."

Matir hesitated for a moment. He didn't seem to quite know what to do with a player who had just dismissed what was probably the penultimate story quest of the game. "Are you... certain?"

"Yeah. " I set my jaw. "Steve might be meshed in with the game AI, but this quest won't stop Baldr. I'm not re-sealing the gods in the Dragon Gates. Fuck that. Ashur said something that's been stuck in my head for a couple hours now - that we could have defeated the Drachan if we'd united all the peoples of Archemi. The humans, the Meewfolk, the dragons, the Lys and the Mercurions. So that's what we're going to do."

"Hector..." Karalti trailed off uncertainly.

Matir regarded me in contemplative silence.

"Walls are a shitty defense. I learned that in the jungle, and the Prezyemi Line proved it out in Archemi." I stared daggers at him. "The best defensive wall is the one that has boots on the ground and eyes in the sky, and that has all of the villages and the guerillas and the supply line on its side. You don't have to be a fucking genius to see that the Caul is going to collapse no matter what we do, and if this was just a normal NPC storyline, then I'm sure we'd be able to make some grand dramatic turnaround at the end... but it's not. This is being driven by one of the people who created the game. Baldr knows the tropes. He knows how this story ends. The only thing the status quo will do is serve his goals. I'm not running around the world trying to put out fires: we take the fight to the Drachan. I'll make my own goddamn quest if I have to."

A second point of light kindled to life in the void of darkness swirling beneath Matir's hood. "As you wish, my Herald. I will need to dwell on this to properly frame the parameters of the quest. Until that time, I will swear a gift to you: the greatest gift I possessed as a living god. If you return with the Artists and the Warsinger and clear the dungeon behind this gate, I shall use my power and gift you with the magic of Life. It is a power that has not been seen in Archemi for millennia, save for a handful of especially powerful monsters. With Life magic and the ability to heal people with miraculous speed, you will be able to unite the legions of the world."

"Thanks." I pressed my lips together, and extended a hand. "Now I know you're not my brother, even if you know what he knew. He would have been like: "Now listen to *me*, Hector...'"

"I leave control of others to my sister, Solnetsi." Matir enclosed my hand in his. The soft leather of his gloves was almost intangible, a sensation like cold silk. "Darkness is the element of self-mastery. Remember that, no matter how many people - or shadows - you come to command."

"I will." The Mark of Matir buzzed pleasantly as I withdrew my hand. My gaze slid past Rin and Istvan, who were waiting for us by the Keystone Dais. "But before we restart the Drachan War, I have some unfinished business. I need to get Suri back."

"We understand." The Dark God bowed from the neck. "Seek your beloved, and then return to me when you are ready. I have endured thousands of years of this place already – a few weeks will make no difference."

"Sure thing." I patted Karalti on the neck, then turned and led the way back to our friends. "Come on, Tidbit: let's join the others and head back to Krivan Pass. We need to get to Karhad and see if there's anything left to rule."

Chapter 55

2 days later.

It was a blood-red morning when we arrived at Karhad. Karalti and I flew ahead of a great fleet of airships - three brand new Hussars, a flotilla of cruisers and small guard ships. When my dragon dipped out through the low misty clouds to reveal the spread of ruined city below, I clicked my tongue.

"What a fucking mess. We're going to be up to our elbows in this shit for weeks." I was dressed head to toe in my freshly repaired and restored Raven Suit, with a soft half-face mask on under the helmet so that none of my skin was exposed to the sun. It wasn't going to kill me, but it felt nasty. On the areas of lightest coverage, my skin prickled, as if reacting with a mild allergy. *"Disease is gonna be a problem."*

"Yeah." Karalti's tone was muted. *"Do you think we'll be able to save the city?"*

"We have to. We'll figure something out."

The day before, Karalti and I had teleported back and forth between Litvy and Karhad, transporting a unit of fifty crack troops to retake the ghost city and clear out any remaining undead. Fifty was all we needed. Karhad was a literal ghost town: Ashur's army had collapsed with his withdrawal, with all but a few of the vampires fleeing with their master. Armed with stakes, silver swords and silver bullets, the Defense team had started with the castle and worked their way down to the city.

We left the ships far behind, reaching Egbolt some twenty minutes ahead. Karalti circled the Lord's Tower, trumpeting to announce our arrival. The sound drew men out of the buildings - Knights, and then Istvan. He shaded his eyes, watching Karalti touch down with the precision and strength of an experienced flyer.

"Your Grace." He bowed from the waist as I slid to the ground, his right fist pressed over his heart. "My lady."

When Istvan stood, I held out a hand. He accepted, then stiffened as I shook it and pulled him into a short one-armed hug. When I stepped back, I lifted my visor so he could see the top half of my face. "It's good to see you, man. But before you give me the situation, I wanted to let you know something. Vash is okay. Between me, Lazar and Rin, he's gonna make it."

Relief flooded Istvan's handsome face. He swallowed and nodded. "Thank the Nine. Were you able to... do something about his arm?"

"I don't know how to make a limb-regrowth potion. Neither does Lazar," I said. "But Rin was able to hook him up with a magitech prosthetic. As long as he has mana, he can move it around like a real limb. He cussed us the whole time it was being attached, but now he likes it. Something about piston power and being able to jack off like an oil rig. "

Istvan actually blushed, and I laughed, slapping him on the shoulder. Carefully. Between the levels I'd gained and the Spear strapped over my back, I was almost as strong as Suri. I'd accidentally slapped Lord Zediwitz off his feet and into a wall on the Orozlan.

"That sounds like something he'd say," Istvan muttered. "The man is a disgusting ass."

"But you love him," I said.

Istvan gave a testy sigh, and blew a lock of hair out of his face. "Yes, I do. Khors preserve me.

Karalti reared up beside us, her form shimmering and condensing down into the figure of a lithe young woman. She wore her Naziri armor. Together, we looked like a pair of ninjas at a Ren Faire.

“If we get Vash to Taltos, Masterhealer Masha might be able to fix him up with a real arm,” I said. “I don't know if there's like... a time limit on when the potion has to be administered, though.”

“I see. May I be honest with you about something?" Istvan asked, glancing at Karalti as she joined me at my side and reached for my hand.

I accepted it, squeezing gently. "Always be honest with me. I mean that."

He dipped his head, then hesitated. "After... hearing about your ‘changes’, I was concerned. I wondered if we had swapped one undead tyrant for another. But the fact you told me this news before anything else... I am relieved, Your Grace. Your appearance is different from what it used to be, but you have not become something terrible."

"Yeah. But I have to sleep in a giant litter box now." I grinned and rubbed the back of my head, grateful that he couldn't see my mouth. I'd taken to wearing the half mask even when I wasn't in armor. The bear trap fangs I'd inherited from Ashur were great for cutting steak and biting people I didn't like, but they freaked everyone out. "So, what's the SIT-REP?"

Istvan stood at ease, not missing a beat this time. "The situation is grim, Your Grace. Fully half of our farmland has been laid to waste, and the planting season has just passed. The undead didn't touch the granaries, thank the Nine, but we will barely have enough food for the winter. Great swathes of the city must be rebuilt. The markets are a write-off, as are the Craftsman's Ward and the City Wall. We have squires riding out to all the fiefs of Racsa... as the news spreads and refugees come out of hiding, we will enact an emergency census and determine how many people we must feed. If we can feed them."

I twined my fingers with Karalti's, and she squeezed them reassuringly. "What about the university?"

"Safe, thank the gods. The undead merely imprisoned most of the scholars, but the Master of the Archives was slain and rose as a vampire. He was berserk with bloodlust when we found him. We put him down, for our sake and his."

"Great." I rolled my eyes to the sky, then puffed out a sound of exasperation. "Alright - let's go do this."

"You're sure you wish to become Voivode?" He gestured to the blackened castle and its collapsed wall. Workers were moving carts of fallen corpses and rubble, hitching them to trains of snorting, stamping triceratops.

"I've only ever been more sure of one thing in my entire life." I smiled at Karalti. Her face lit up with a glow of pleasure. "Come on."

The Grand Hall had already been stripped of Ashur's finery. The silks and cushions had been taken out and burned, and plain wooden benches had been bought in to serve as places for the cleanup crew to rest. The chaise was gone, replaced by an elegant, functional mini-throne in the Eastern style: dark wood, with intricate Arabesque engraving.

"Lord Bolza sat in that chair for thirty years," Istvan said softly, as we approached it. "And his father, and his father before him."

"Yeah." I ran a hand over the armrest, buffed smooth over generations of wear. The seat was upholstered in green velvet – that'd have to change. When I looked to Karalti, she nodded. I smiled, drew a deep breath, and sat down.

⟦You have earned a Faction Charter: Duchy of Myszno (Provincial)⟧
⟦You have earned 60 Build Points!⟧
⟦You have gained access to the Kingdom Management Menu and tutorials!⟧
⟦You have gained a new title: Voivode of Myszno.⟧
⟦You have earned a new badge: Ruler of All I Survey!⟧

"How does it feel?" Karalti asked.

"Heavy." I pulled my helmet off and slumped back in the seat. After a couple of seconds, I looked up at the vaulted ceiling overhead. "Open Kingdom Management."

A new wraparound screen came to life. Front and center was a map of Myszno, with Vlachia shaded out above and to the west.

[[Do you wish to give your castle a new name?]]

"Hey, Tidbit - what's the Solonkraatu word for 'Castle'?" I asked her.

"*Kalla,*" she replied.

I nodded, turning my attention back to the HUD. *"Rename Egbolt Castle to 'Kalla Sahasi'."*

The castle title on my screen changed in an instant. Istvan got an odd look on his face, then shrugged.

[[Your capital city is currently Karhad. You may change capital cities or choose a different name for your capital once you have gained 2219 or more points of Leadership Renown in Myszno > Racsa Province > Karhad.]]
[[Would you like to create a faction name?]]

Faction name? What, like... Hector's Heroes? East Side Hookwings? I cringed, scratching my head. "Duchy of Myszno works fine, thanks."

A yellow exclamation mark appeared in the corner of my eye: a High Priority message that chirped and sprung up automatically:

World Alert: Vlachia

After a long and difficult battle, the Province of Myszno fought off the invading nation of Napath. This is a server alert to announce the new Voivode (Earl) of the Duchy of Myszno, Lord Dragozin Hector.

Somewhere, Baldr was off answering the call of nature – and he had to have hit himself in the face with his own stream when that alert popped up in front of him. I let myself gloat for approximately one second, though, because now every man and his dog knew I'd become Voivode of Myszno, there was about to be a sharp escalation of hostilities. My only consolation was that we had the might of Vlachia standing between us and Ilia.

[[Rin Lu has asked to join your faction!]]
[[Do you want to add anyone else to the Duchy of Myszno?]]

"Suri Ba'hadir," I replied.

[[NUMBERFETCH-00-0000AA1-TypeXX-Dkh-???BSKR has been sent a Faction Join Request!]]

Yikes. No wonder I hadn't been able to find Suri on the system. I waited for several tense seconds, waiting to see if she accepted... then I remembered that stupid Incareration status. Fuck. I dug my nails into the wood. "Alright... Tidbit, if you've got anything to do, now's the time. I'm going to sit here and get the hang of this menu until the ships arrive. Is that something you can help with, Istvan?"

"Certainly," he replied. "Is there anything I can provide within our decidedly limited means before we begin? There is some wine left."

"No alcohol, for me or for you. I need a seat for you and two more chairs up here," I said. " One for Suri, one for Karalti."

He brightened. "The Lady Suri has returned?"

"She's alive in Dakhdir, somewhere," I said. "Which leads me to my next question: I have to go and pick her up. Can I appoint you as my Steward while I'm gone?"

Istvan grimaced, scratching the three days of stubble on his jaw and neck. "Yes, you can register any person or Starborn to various positions around the castle and town. But... with all due respect, Your Grace, Karhad needs you here."

"And I need Suri," I said. "WE need Suri. I theoretically know where she is. All I have to do is find that place."

"Al'Asad Prison," Karalti said. *"I remember that."*

I nodded. "I'm not sure how we'll find it, but we will. Anyway, the ships will be here soon - I want to have an audience as soon as they arrive."

"An audience?" Istvan arched an eyebrow. "With who?"

I grinned behind the fabric covering my mouth. "Lord Soma. We have to sort our shit out. He's my peer, after all."

A couple hours later, the ships had landed, Rin was back on the ground with her beefed-up turrets, and Soma was brought to the Grand Hall with an escort of Knights of the Red Star. They all looked vaguely shell-shocked to see me sitting on the high muckedy-muck's chair. None of them were more surprised than Soma himself. He had been allowed to dress in proper clothing, have a bath and a shave, and generally put himself together, and his expression was incredulous as he approached the ducal seat.

"Khors Balls. You actually did it," he said. "Count me impressed, Dragozin."

"We did it, plural," I said. Rin sat to my right in the seat that would one day be Suri's, while Karalti sat to my left - the heart side. "All of us. Even you."

His eyes narrowed. "How generous of you, my lord."

"Look dude, square up with me." I sat forward in my chair. "You were pretty fucking wrapped up in your own shit."

His eyes glinted, blue and pale... but then he sighed, and turned his face. "I suppose that's true, yes. I am the youngest of three brothers, which is why I was sent to the church to learn my family's trade. But then my brothers both died, one earlier this year and one in the fall of Karhad, and suddenly, I faced a terrible duty. It got to me."

"If we'd known that, a lot of the shit that went down could have been avoided," I replied.

Soma's mouth twitched. "What? How? By rolling over and revealing my belly to a foreign usurper? Perhaps that is the norm for commoners. You will quickly learn to be guarded in court and society, Dragozin, or you will be torn to shreds by the other Voivodes and by His Majesty in the capitol."

"Ignas likes us a lot, though," Rin said. "I'm... uhh... kind of dating his assassin."

Soma sniffed. "The Volod is thousands of miles from here. While we lord over our province, the cosmopolitan types - Earl Janos of Czongrad, Duchess Elizabeta of Timarila - are whispering in the ear of the king. Everyone knows that the closer you are to His Majesty, the better - so much so that the most powerful people in the Kingdom are the servants that towel his hands and run his baths. They are positions for which the sons of nobility will duel to the death."

"See, that's great information for me to have. This is the kind of thing you're fantastic at." I jabbed my finger against my other palm for emphasis. "This kind of shit, right here. I want your support, Soma. I don't want to be your enemy - I want your help and I want to offer you what I've got in turn."

"And what do you have that could interest me?" He replied. "You have no wealth."

"Yet. I'm Starborn. I've got generations to become wealthy." I shrugged. "Besides, I'm holding out an olive branch to try and make up, not offering to marry you. You don't need a fucking dowry."

Soma snorted. Then, he began to laugh.

"Alright, Dragozin. You may be a folksy boor, but I'll do it - if nothing else but for the sake of the women who endure your company," Soma chuckled. He bowed to Karalti, who lifted her chin and made a face, and then to Rin, who bobbed her head back at him. "Speaking of that... where is the Lady Ba'hadir?"

"She's on recon duty," I replied, thinking back to his earlier advice about not revealing my weaknesses. "We're going to pick her up soon."

"I see." The big man rubbed his chin, nodding to himself. "Well, by the Voivode's leave, I shall return to my county and put it to order. When you are ready to talk trade...?"

"You'll be invited back here under much better circumstances, for sure."

Soma arched his eyebrows, and flashed Istvan a sly little smile. Istvan pinched the bridge of his nose.

"What?" I asked, looking between them.

"Your Grace, it is customary for the higher-ranking lord to make an appointment, then travel to the lower-ranking lord's home and request hospitality," Istvan replied dryly. "The only time you invite a lower-ranking lord to your own castle is if you wish to chastise them, flaunt the strength of your fortifications, or both."

"Unless it is a social event with multiple Houses are attending," Soma added. "And *then* the event is hosted at the highest-ranking lord's property. Typically not your castle, but your un-fortified summer home."

"Oh." I let out an awkward chuckle. "I'll invite myself to your place then, I guess. There's a lot to learn about this role, huh?"

"Your actions directly affect your renown, so yes." Soma gave a short bow from the neck. "Now, please excuse me."

Once he had left, I slumped into the chair and rubbed my eyes. "Okay. That's a wrap. So, Istvan - you're Karhad's Steward for the time being. Rin - are you willing to take on a role here?"

"Sure." She nodded. "You're going to get Suri, right?"

"Yeah." Buzzing with energy, I stood up and stretched.

Rin got up as well. "I can go with you, you know. I'm starting to get a taste for this adventuring thing."

I thought about it. Then, I shook my head.

"Suri's in hell right now," I said. "But so are the people of Karhad. They need someone to look up to here. You led the soldiers at the Pass - I'm asking you to do it again. Just for a while."

Rin's blue-on-blue eyes widened. She looked down, pressed her lips together, and nodded. "Okay. You can count on me."

"When do you leave?" Istvan asked me.

"Tonight." I turned to Karalti, who rose smoothly to her feet. "But there's one last person I need to see."

Chapter 56

Lazar and his team of medics had moved Vash and the other injured to the castle hospital, which had been left largely untouched by the undead. He had insisted on being out in the main ward with the soldiers, not by himself in a private suite.

"Well, look who just swaggered in." Vash's voice was raspy, but he was alert and alive, propped up in bed with his new arm resting on a pillow. It was a heavy, brutal looking thing - riveted, hydraulic, plated in cold iron in the same way his gauntlets were. "It's polite to ask before staring at a man's parts, you know. Karalti - teach your dog some manners."

"But it's cute when he barks at stuff." She danced up to the edge of the bed with her hands behind her back, her hair swirling around her face.

"Glad to see you too." I strolled up beside him and squatted down on my heels. "I thought you ate shit and died."

"Bah. I leave shit-eating to the arselickers at court," he grumbled.

"How are you feeling?" Karalti asked. She leaned in and sniffed over the arm, flinching back when Vash flexed his fingers.

"I punched a full-grown dragon in the head hard enough to crack its skull. I lost the arm, but now I get to drag my balls around the edge of the door when I enter a room." He grinned - there was a new gap in his teeth. "A fair trade, all in all. But my lady, you have a questioning look on your lovely face. Ask."

Karalti scowled. *"Am I that easy to read?"*

"You're a book so simple even Hector can read you," Vash replied smoothly.

I laughed. "Fuck you."

"We already had this discussion, dog. You don't have the tool I need for that particular quest." Vash waved his other hand. "Please, Karalti. Continue."

"Well... I learned that I can take a Path in human form." She glanced at me. *"I have to train it and only have the skills available while I'm polymorphed, but I figure I'm gonna spend more time like this as I get older. I want to train as a Baru."*

"Hrrm." Vash frowned. "Well... tradition says that you must have died or nearly died as a child to join my order."

"She did," I said. "She couldn't hatch out of her egg by herself. I chopped her out of it and resuscitated her."

"Oh! Well, then. Resuscitated by the right hand of the God of Darkness... yes, that ought to count." Vash nearly lifted his prosthetic arm and grimaced with pain, easing back down. "*Ay-yai-yai*, this thing hurts. Once I am recovered, I'll be more than happy to train you in our ways. You will not need to travel to Mysźno Village: I doubt you need to spend two to ten years living in a charnel ground learning to eat carrion."

"Yeah! I already like carrion." She beamed at him happily. *"Does that mean you'll teach me how to fight?"*

"I'll teach you all sorts of things." Vash winked at me. I gave him my best disapproving dad face. "All of which involve you being fully-dressed and completely safe from violation."

"*Yay!"* Karalti swung her hands around in a poor, but earnest imitation of a boxer, nearly clipping Vash in the head. *"Punch ALL the things!"*

"You're sure this is a good idea?" Vash asked me, pointing at my dragon as she hopped, feinting and jabbing. "You really want her to be able to put you in a headlock?"

"I'll risk it. It makes her happy." I shrugged.

"Hah." Vash shook his head, and winced. "Karalti... would you mind if I spoke to your pet alone for a few minutes?"

"Huh? Oh! Sure. I'll wait outside." Karalti stopped what she was doing and came back to me. She flung her arms around me and squeezed, nuzzling the side of my face, then broke off and wound her way through the hospital ward.

"She has a sunny personality for such a dark creature, doesn't she?" Vash made a sound of amusement. "Alright, Dragoźin. Talk to Uncle Vash: what happened to you?"

"Ashur bit me." I shrugged. "I'm immune to Corruption, so I ended up half-vamp instead of all-vamp."

"A Halfblood?" The monk's brow creased slightly. "Take off that mask. Let me see."

Wordlessly, I complied, pulling it down to bare my face. After drinking a Dragon's Blood potion the day before, I looked pretty much the way I had before I'd been turned, except for the teeth, sharper features, and the dark metallic skin of my lower arms and legs. Vash seemed to know the signs. He made a rumbling sound, lying back on his pillows.

"You're not undead. I'd be able to sense if you were," he said after a minute. "But you are no longer human. A *Dhampir.*"

"Yup. Dhampir with extra damp." I pulled the mask back up. "Matir seemed okay with it. He didn't remark on it one way or the other."

"I imagine he had other, more pressing concerns." Vash's gray eyes darkened with concern. "Was Ashur killed?"

I shook my head. "No. I hurt him pretty bad, but he ran."

"You are in danger for the rest of your days until he is dead." The sly humor left the monk's face. "But even more than Ashur, you must be careful to monitor your own behavior. You may have escaped un-life, but you are a predator now. You will start thinking like a predator without even realizing it, losing your humanity one convenient lapse of empathy at a time. That is something to remember... to meditate on and think about during the times when you are tempted by the easy way out."

Is that why it had been so easy to stab Violetta when she was beginning for mercy? That line of thinking led to some dark places. I eased up off the chair, grimacing as my knees creaked. "I can't really tell from the inside of my head. I'd be grateful if you'll be there to help remind me."

The monk sniffed, closing his eyes. "Of course. Istvan is still hopelessly attached to this place, and damned if I'm going to leave him here by himself. He's in the mood to nest, I think. Now... I assume you're going to find Suri, yes?"

"Yeah," I said. "As soon as I figure out *how* to find her."

He cocked an eyebrow. "Try Cutthroat."

"Cutthroat?" I frowned, puzzled, and then punched my palm with my other fist. "Wait - you're right! She's her Bonded Mount. She might know where Suri is. Not that she can tell us."

"Of course she can." The corner of Vash's mouth quirked. "Loudly, I'm sure."

"Maybe we can make some adjustments to Karalti's saddle and carry her around somehow." I rubbed my face, thinking. "I'll go talk to Rin."

"You do that. I must sleep and heal, then relearn how to fight with this arm." He heaved a deep, tired sigh. His HP was less than half its usual total, sitting in the weird greenish-orange part of the meter. "What did you do with Soma?"

"Tried to repair the relationship and make good," I said. "He's on the way back to Litvy."

Vash's expression darkened. "If he ever finds out you are a Dhampir, that could be enough for him to urge for civil war. You should have held him hostage for a while. Put him to work here."

"I thought about it. But there are other things he doesn't know about me that grant me an advantage."

"Hurrm." He shook his head. "We shall see. Now go back to your dragon, dog - I must rest."

"Alright. Rest well." I turned, but before I was out of earshot, I looked back over my shoulder at him. "You going to call me a dog forever?"

"It's a compliment. The dog is the noblest of animals, second only to the common house fly." He scrunched his face up and farted. "Dogs are honest. Loyal. Eager to learn. We should all be better off if we were more like them."

"Count Dogula it is, then." I winked at him, and his dry chuckle followed me outside.

Karalti was sunbathing, lying flat on her back in a big patch of sunlight so intense that it made my eyes sting. I reequipped my helmet and went to stand over her. "Okay, Tidbit. Let's go get some rest. We've got a big night ahead of us."

"Sounds good to me." She rolled over and pushed herself up on hands and knees, letting out a happy sigh. *"Snuggling?"*

"Yeah. Maybe even *extra* snuggling."

"I like that." Karalti caught my hand, and before I could lead her off, she gently pulled me to a stop. Her brilliant eyes caught my gaze and held them. *"And hey... about Suri. We're gonna find her, alright? She'll be fine. But no more dying for you."*

“Not if I can help it.” I reached up to smooth a lock of hair back from her cheek. "I know. Thanks."

"It's okay." Karalti lay her head against my palm for a moment, then tugged me forward. *"But hey - before we sleep, you know what we're gonna do?"*

"What?"

“It's your favorite!”

I sighed. “What?”

"Pushups!" She punched the air with her free hand. *"We're gonna train! Muscles! Stamina! Flexibility! Before we go to Dakhdir, you'll be able to tie a knot behind your head with your ankles! How far away are you from Level 23?”*

“Let me check.” I opened my HUD, checked my character sheet, and groaned. “Oh, you have to be fucking kidding me.”

“What?” Karalti tilted her head.

“I am ten fucking points off Level 23.” I sighed, shooing the window away like a fly. “This game. I swear to God.”

“I guess we're gonna go kill a Stingcrab, too!” Karalti broke off into a run, a blur of laughter and speed. *"Come on! I'll race you to the Grand Hall!"*

I smiled, and as I took off after her, I peered up at the blazing blue sky. The sun had risen, and as the darkness had done, the light was urging me to sleep. But I couldn't. We had to get ready to fly to Dakhdir.

We were going to bring Suri home

Editorial Note

The editor who was to work on this book had to abandon the project for health reasons. Many amazing people stepped up at the last minute to help, but we may have missed some errors.

If you see any remaining errata in Kingdom Come and would like to help improve it, I will gladly fix any spelling, grammar or punctuation that you can spot and point out to me. Email me at author@jamesosiris.com with any corrections.

A huge thanks to everyone who chipped in:

- Canth Decided-Baldwin
- Riley M.
- Kirri
- Krysil
- James Caplan
- John Ashmore
- Michaela Cocker and others

Author's Note

2018 was, without question, the worst year of my adult life.

Those who have been following my journey on my Facebook group or Patreon probably have a rough idea of what happened: in June of 2018, me and my wife lost her home of 25 years because of a sharp and sudden personal betrayal. I had just finished Trial by Fire and we were both mentally and economically precarious at the time – and then, suddenly, homeless. Some wonderful friends took us and our animals in, but the loss of this home and the people associated with it was truly devastating, requiring the better part of a year for us to even begin to come to terms with what had happened.

We ended up living in depressing sub-par accommodations for that year: a 500 sq.ft house with a lot of mold. It was on the grounds of the stable where we kept my wife's therapy horse, Kai, which was the sole good thing about it – until Kai became ill and suffered a protracted period of ill health. We had to euthanize her in May of 2019, to our great sorrow. Things were difficult for our friends, too. We lost several friends and relatives of friends to suicide, cancer and accidents. All in all, 2018 can go DIAF.

2019 has been better – but stressful. Spring shoots are starting to come up through the bitter frost of the last 12 months. We moved cities and now have a very nice apartment in a quiet neighborhood. I learned to drive (finally: I'd only ever ridden motorcycles). One of our deceased friends bequeathed us her sphynx cat, so as I write this, a naked kitten is playing around my keyboard and swatting at the edge of my monitor. It is quiet, and we are safe.

The whole time all that was going on, I was writing this book – a story that is fundamentally about characters trying to find a sense of place in their new reality, not entirely sure yet where they fit in. Even Rin, who is so certain of her path as an Artificer, is called on to extend herself beyond her comfortable role. The book tapped into my own fears of not having a home, of desperately craving one, but also of being afraid to try again after being so badly wounded by the last attempt.

I know that we survived through the grace of our friends and chosen family. So many people rallied to help us when we lost the house, and if it wasn't for them, we'd probably have ended up in a cardbox box or a hotel room (but given the number of pets we have, probably the box). When Hector says that chosen family is worth everything, that is a reflection of my own experience. For every person who was shitty to us, three stepped in to help. We owe them our lives.

Hopefully you enjoyed this story as much as I enjoyed writing it – I'm sorry you had to wait so long for it. If you did enjoy the book, please consider leaving a review on Amazon here: https://www.amazon.com/dp/B07QLBF516

Join the Facebook group here: https://www.facebook.com/groups/HoundofEden

Read on for an ArchemiWiki entry on Archemi's dragons and a link to secret chapters of Kingdom Come. I'm taking a short break, then moving onto Archemi Book #4: Warsinger.

While you're waiting for Warsinger...

An arcane assassin. A billion year war. An evil greater than death, greater than anything...

If any of you have a twitchy Kindle Unlimited trigger finger and want a week's reading between now and the release of Kingdom Come, the Hound of Eden omnibus is available: 3 full-length books for $8 or included for FREE with your Kindle Unlimited subscription.

Get it here: http://jamesosiris.com/getbook/95252

Dev Notes

Archemipedia Entry: Solonkratsu (Dragons) ⟦Grade-A Knowledge⟧

Introduction

No creature inspires so much terror and awe in humankind as the mighty Solonkratsu – the dragons of Archemi. The dragons once ruled a sophisticated, bustling empire that spanned all continents and islands of the world, but their reign came to an abrupt end with the Drachan War. In the modern day, dragons are rare, inhabiting isolated outposts or, like the Dragons of the Eyrie, working in partnership with human or Lys dragon knights.

Body structure and type

The Solonkratsu are magically-enhanced theropods, and bear more similarity to the bird-like dinosaurs of the Late Cretaceous period than anything reptilian. They are hollow boned and warm-blooded, with metabolisms comparable to modern birds. They are able to regulate their body temperature through panting and shivering.

The body-plan of Solonkratsu is functionally bipedal. Like a T-rex, they walk on powerful hind legs, balancing the weight of their hindquarters with their tails and wings. Their heads are wedge-shaped, with a slightly rounded muzzle and powerful jaws capable of opening as wide as a snake's. Top and bottom rows of curved slashing teeth are concealed by a rim of scales, and the teeth do not extrude past these stiff 'lips'. They have special flat scales just forward of their nostrils which cover bundles of special sensory nerves. They can judge windspeed, temperature, and many other things through these sensory patches.

The nasal bone is fused and tough, the maxilla (the primary tooth-bearing bone of the upper jaw) very rigid and strongly fortified. This allows dragons to deliver bone-crushing bites to downed prey, but also to open their jaws wide and slash with the upper teeth – their main method of combat with other dragons. The skull is crested, with ridges that protect the eyes and partly shield them from wind. The shape of the Solonkratsu skull is highly aerodynamic, with the scales patterned in such a way as to allow air to smoothly pass over and around their heads.

Most dragons have horns, with horn patterning varying somewhat from region to region and clan to clan. In all instances, horns are smooth and sweep backwards from the skull. They are not embedded in the bones of the skull: horns in dragon-kind are purely for display, not combat, and they are set into cartilage and supported by muscle and membrane. This means that dragons can flare, drop, fold and lift their horns expressively.

Queen dragons will typically be born with a horn pattern that characterizes their bloodline. Horn length and health, and the ability to display with the horns is one of the considerations all dragons, male and female, use when selecting mates.

Archemi's dragons are six-limbed, with the arms and wings set on a strongly fortified 'butterfly' shaped pair of fused shoulder blades. The forelimbs are weak compared to the jaws, wings and hindquarters – however, the dragons have flexible wrists and four fingered 'hands' – three fingers and a thumb – that are dexterous enough to use tools with if the claw is shaved down. Dragons who cut or shave their foreclaws can hold everything from paintbrushes to lutes and wrenches with their hands, allowing them to perform activities such as building and crafting. Dedicated Solonkratsu craftsdragons will often dock and cauterize their foreclaws to be more effective tool-users: to be 'blunt-fingered' is known to be the mark of a dedicated artisan, and is one of the few forms of body modification considered to be acceptable.

Solonkratsu are quite gracile (lightly-built) for their size, with medium-length, graceful necks, very long tails, deep chests reinforced by furcula (a boomerang shaped 'wishbone' set above fused clavicles) and cross-hatched gastralia (belly ribs) which protect and support their high, arched, sinewy abdomens. Their backs are very straight and powerfully muscled, especially around the shoulders and at the base of the tail. The chest is narrow and their body streamlined for speed, giving them a narrow, lean, greyhound-like appearance.

Flight

Flight for Solonkratsu is partly magical, partly physiological. Archemi has slightly less gravity and more oxygen in its atmosphere than Earth; in addition, the mana in dragon blood and the Words encoded into their flesh relieves them of approximately 50-75% of their terrestrial bodyweight while in the air, making even fully-grown Solonkratsu highly maneuverable, swift flyers. However, they still have many physical adaptations: massive, four lobed lungs capable of functioning at great altitudes; the ability to control their blood pressure; extremely efficient, short gastro-intestinal tracts that remove and expel moisture from food; and most notably, two hearts.

The Prime Heart in dragons is a massive organ that takes up a great deal of the chest cavity, pumping blood through five major arteries to the head, limbs, wings and tail. When a dragon spreads and flexes its wings, they activate a second auxiliary heart, the Drive Heart, which only serves the front-end of the dragon's body: the wings, lungs and brain. The auxiliary heart falls into sync with the primary organ, working alongside it to pump mana into the wing membranes, sharply increase blood pressure, and provide support for the hydraulic system of tendons, muscles and cartilage that support the dragon in the air. In autopsy, the auxiliary heart is quite visually different to the primary heart, having white flesh and a much denser structure.

There are also many external features which help to stabilize dragons in the air: fins, horns, the shape of the skull, dorsal ridges along the back, powerful muscles at the base of the tail and a fan of specially-shaped scales along the tail assist with maneuverability.

Because of their physical and magical adaptations, hatchlings are born with proportionate wings and already know how to fly – a characteristic vital to their survival in the wild. They are usually hopping and gliding within hours of leaving the shell, flying short distances by the end of their first week, and are fully flighted within a month.

The Solonkratsu have exceptional endurance for flight and spend a great deal of time on the wing, as they cannot truly run as a human or a dog would. Like the large theropod dinosaurs, they must always have one foot on the ground. Their terrestrial bodyweight – combined with the limitations of their hollow bones – makes anything over a quick lumbering walk impossible. They can only reach top speeds of 45 mph on the ground, compared with up to 100 mph when flying and up to 350 mph when diving.

The challenges of flight can sometimes limit a dragon's senses. While their forward vision is excellent – better than that of hawks – dragons have poor peripheral vision while in flight, as they cannot move their eyes or turn their heads while moving at high speeds. Wing extension 'locks' the neck in place while in flight, a safeguard against whiplash and fractures while the dragon is potentially diving on prey and slashing at large animals with their upper jaw.

Another issue is hypoxia. At high altitudes, a dragon's body must function on reduced oxygen, inducing a euphoric, trance-like state which tunnels their vision even further. For this reason, specially-adapted human riders serve as a value set of eyes and ears during high and/or long-distance flights.

Dragons cannot fly higher than 12,000 feet – their typical ceiling is 5000-7000 feet.

Breath weapons

A dragon's breath weapon is mostly magical in nature, and is inherited through their Queen's bloodline. To express a breath weapon, the dragon 'breathes' a Word of Power as they expel magically charged blood-plasma through three glands (one in the throat just behind the soft palate, two beside the salivary glands on either side of the tongue). The spell consumes the plasma, manifesting as a projected breath weapon in a fashion similar to the way human fire-eaters will spit a flaming plume of alcohol during the course of a stunt.

The most common breath weapons are variations of fire, but lightning, acid, ice, sonic and plasma weapons are possible.

A Queen dragon is born with Words of Power and a breath weapon unique to her and distinct from that of her mother's. She will pass that breath weapon to all her progeny until she has a Queen daughter of her own. Even if a Queen mother and daughter pair both breathe fire, the Words of Power that trigger the effect will be different in the daughter, meaning that countermagic that works on the mother's breath weapon would not affect the daughter's even if they are visually similar.

Reproduction and Life Cycle

Solonkratsu, unlike many species of dragon, are not greedy individualists lairing in solitude. They are in fact a eusocial (hive) species, forming strong social connections and hierarchies with each other based on a complex of physical, magical, and social cues that lead dragons to take on specialized reproductive and non-reproductive roles. The reproductive role in all dragon clans is the sole responsibility of the Queen.

Every single queen dragon is a mutant. Each Queen has a unique genetic profile from that of her mother, which is most obvious in the color of her scales. It is traditional that a Queen's first title be signified by her coloration – such as Karalti the Black Opal Queen.

Queen dragons are larger, stronger, and fiercer than other dragons. They grow rapidly, and are equipped with unique breath weapons, magic, and – once they reach sexual maturity – the ability to produce pheromones that suppress the fertility of other dragons and encourage them to obey her. In the presence of a Queen, non-reproducing female dragons do not lay eggs or even properly grow in their ovaries. Males are not hormonally suppressed by a queen, meaning that 'worker' males usually end up being quite larger than 'worker' females.

The birth of a queen is a cause of great celebration within a clan – but also wariness. A Queen who bears a Queen daughter is loving and tolerant of her until she reaches adolescence and begins to produce the pheromones that are her birthright. At that point, the relationship between mother and daughter inevitably becomes tense and competitive, ratcheting up to the point where the elder queen either drives her daughter from the clan or risks being killed by her. Fortunately, Solonkratsu Queens have a strong instinct against forming incestuous relationships with male kin, so young Queens are usually happy to leave their clan and strike out on their own – by treaty or by conquest.

Like bees, dragons within a clan naturally sort themselves into worker-caste roles. The majority of a clan is comprised of one Queen's daughters, who will stay with their mother and serve as hunters, soldiers, artisans, nurses, teachers, archivists and governors. The males, who are almost always larger and stronger than their sisters, stay with the clan until adolescence and are then expected to leave and seek a new, unrelated clan to join and serve. Grand Olympics-style contests were once held between allied clans, where males court families they are interested in joining and compete to secure entry to desirable positions.

A Queen dragon will select a harem of 3-10 mates through an involved courtship process which includes displays of hunting, dancing, gift-giving and relationship building with the biggest and strongest (unrelated) males of her clan. Queens are sexually active but infertile most of the time, entering a fertile heat period twice a year. Just before the Queen's estrus begins, she will begin laying unfertilized eggs whether she has mates or not. She becomes aggressive, solitary, and irritable, building to a point where she openly challenges her mates and may even attack them if they approach her. This hormonal rage culminates in a spectacular and dangerous mating flight. The Queen flees her harem and the males pursue her, battling each other for supremacy until one manages to catch his mate and consummate with her. It is not uncommon for males to kill each other, or even for an enraged Queen to kill her would-be lover if he is not careful. Once the mating flight is over, this male rejoins the harem and takes on a leadership role, bossing around his brothers-in-arms... at least until the next season.

Within this instinctual framework, dragons are a highly intelligent and culturally rich people, with numerous customs, religious beliefs, and economic systems. In the golden age before the Drachan invaded Archemi, the Solonkratsu built 'cities' which ranged thousands of miles and housed multiple clans. Secure in their positions, the Queens within these cities created rituals to manage their instinctive need to compete, creating effective councils to govern over wide areas of territory. War between clans was managed by laws enforced by the community, and breaching the laws of conduct could result in an upstart clan being mobbed by a punitive force comprised of several Queens. Magical, artistic, and mercantile activity flourished in the hey-day of dragonkind, and the dragons had good cooperative relationships with both the Aesari and Meewfolk. Those cities are now no more, and the few wild dragons left are intensely tribal, ranging long distances to trade males and information before returning to their villages.

Eggs and Hatchlings

Ninety days after her mating flight, a pregnant Queen lays a clutch of 6-12 eggs. Very rarely, she may lay a queen egg within a clutch, which will be notable for its variant size and color. The older a queen is, the more likely she is to lay a queen egg. On average, a queen will birth only two other queens during her 1000-year lifetime. Some may produce four, while others will never bear one.

The eggs incubate for 42 days, then hatch under the watchful eye of their mother and her clanmates. The baby pulls itself free as a thirty-pound infant with soft, under-developed wing membranes, claws and scales, poor vision, but an acute sense of smell. Within a few hours, the hatchling's eyes will have cleared, their keratin and membranes hardened, and they will be tumbling around and beating their wings in anticipation of flight. The Queen nurses the hatchlings on regurgitated meat and a thin, nutritious 'milk' she secretes from special patches of scales under her wing. The milk nourishes the hatchlings while also providing them with a loading dose of hormones that stifle their sexual development, preventing competition from drone daughters. The tiny dragons practice flying by bounding, pouncing and gliding off their mother's body in the nest, building the necessary muscular and cardiac fitness to take off and land in a way most baby birds would envy.

Young Solonkratsu grow rapidly, swelling to over fifty pounds within the first two weeks of life and reaching sexual maturity (Queens and males) within four years. Growth continues from that point for another decade, with fully-mature dragons reaching lengths of 80-100 ft by 15 years of age. Starborn-bonded dragons have an accelerated growth cycle, with years replaced by levels gained through EXP. A Starborn's dragon reaches sexual maturity at Level 10 and full maturity at Level 30.

Aging and Death

Dragons are long-lived and hardy under ideal conditions. Worker females typically live to 750; males who live out their natural lifespans can reach 800. Queens have been known to live as long as 1200 years. Once a dragon has reached maturity, their rate of growth slows but never completely stops. They do not visibly age much, but wear and tear makes the activities of flying, hunting and living too strenuous to bear. Death for the elderly typically comes in the form of a mid-air heart attack, aortic rupture, stroke or – more rarely – cancer of the brain, eyes or tongue.

Secret chapters and more

Join the James Osiris Baldwin fan group to get access to previews, snippets, art and secret chapters!

There were a number of chapters and scenes that were written for Kingdom Come, but didn't make the cut. I post these to my Facebook group and also to my Patreon (all tiers), if you're interested in becoming a paid supporter.

The Facebook group is very active, with polls and posts every day.

Join the Archemi Online and Hound of Eden community on Facebook here: https://www.facebook.com/groups/HoundofEden/

If you're interested in becoming a Patreon supporter, visit here: https://www.patreon.com/jamesosiris

Join the GameLit Society for more GameLit and LitRPG!

Ye olde Gamelit Society is where most of the cool kids of the videogame fantasy world(s) hang out. Join me, Blaise Corvin, Luke Chmilenko, James Hunter and all your other favorite authors on Facebook here:

https://www.facebook.com/groups/LitRPGsociety/

You can support the development of a GameLit/LitRPG database here:

https://www.patreon.com/GameLitRPG/posts

List of James' Books

Hound of Eden Series

Dark, gritty urban fantasy with a cosmic horror twist, join Russian mafia hitmage Alexi Sokolsky as he confronts the mad demons of the abyss, finds redemption, and saves the world. Hound of Eden is an LGBTI series.

- Hound of Eden Omnibus (Books 1 – 3)
- 0 - Burn Artist (Prequel)
- 1 - Blood Hound
- 2 - Stained Glass
- 3 - Zero Sum
- 4 - Cold Cell (2020)
- 5 - Scavenger Eyes (2020)
- 6 - Morning Star (2020)
-

Archemi Online

A LitRPG saga about a young dragonrider's ascension to greatness inside the virtual world of Archemi.

- 1 - Dragon Seed
- 2 - Trial by Fire
- 3 – Kingdom Come
- 4 - Warsinger (Late 2019)
- 5 - Blaze of Glory (Early 2020)

Other Titles

- Fix Your Damn Book!: A Self-Editing Guide for Authors
- The Expanding Universe #1 (Paperback)
- The Expanding Universe #2 (Paperback)

www.ingramcontent.com/pod-product-compliance
Lightning Source LLC
Chambersburg PA
CBHW020602310726
48979CB00008B/1312/J

* 9 7 8 0 9 9 4 4 0 7 0 8 5 *